LEGACY

EPISODE I: The Search For Love

A novel by

ROBERT MAXXIM

HARDBACK: 978-1-948556-13-2
PAPERBACK: 978-1-948556-12-5
EBOOK: 978-1-948556-14-9

Acknowledgments

Artistic renditions:
Buzz Erlinger-Ford, saint Lucia; 99designs.com/users/916115
Rodrigo Aldebaran Diaz, Mexico; www.roaldimage.com.mx

Book Website
www.RGaetan.com (color pictures, information updates, links, discussions)

Ordering Information:

For orders and inquiries, please contact:
1-888-375-9818
www.toplinkpublishing.com
bookorder@toplinkpublishing.com

Printed in the United States of America

Dedication

I dedicate this narrative to the true inspiration behind its contents: my gentle, loving, higher brethren of Light, my eternal friends, whose sole mission in life is to nourish their hearts with God's love, and no selfish blemish will ever be found in them. They are the epitome of beauty and the everlasting articulate torch of universal inter-dimensional understanding of life. My search for love starts with them.

Words stemming from their graceful, joyous lips heal the heart of fear and relieve the soul's plight from desire's noxious smears. In their presence, let the heart not be saddened at the sight of love, for our future lies in higher realms; all we need is love's purpose, not mundane notions at the helm. Their existence is a perpetual ode of fondness for the Infinite Creative Consciousness, radiant beacons of peace, vast fountains of higher cognizance.

Without their loving presence in my life, their constant encouragement, and the sweet call to honesty from my beautiful starry sapphire, my teacher and my one, I could have never conceived this book or experienced what it's like to love His Majesty. Therefore, I take no credit for this book's substance. No leader or teacher am I, no spiritual channel or master—far from it. I'm only a humble student of Truth.

Follow the Infinite with all your heart and might, not I.

Contents

Illustrations

Preface

What would you do if you witnessed real events that took place in ages long ago, on distant lands and foreign worlds far beyond ours—eccentric, formidable events that diverge extensively from common-day views? What if one such event was an awe-inspiring, personal experience with elevated realms of reality; higher dimensions of existence where God's love and truth gleam constantly from joy-filled beings, and all living things are composed of the essence of celestial light itself?

This multi-episode narrative was inspired by such remarkable events, revealed in the form of visions that began the evening of July 13, 1973. I devoted the last forty years trying to refute them, but did not succeed; rather, I confirmed them. This book is a novel based on such corroboration.

At first, these revelations materialized as dream state visits to higher realms on Venus, Mars, Saturn, and worlds far beyond our system. But three years later, I unexpectedly experienced several conscious past-life flashbacks that date far, far back into the annals of time. These revelations continue to this day, revealing countless sojourns and lessons that I deem invaluable in my life.

I was fifteen at the time these experiences began, a young Cuban migrant devoted to become a world renowned concert pianist. Quite honestly, I was unschooled in the sciences, and definitely oblivious of such topics as re-embodiment or psychic revelation. Being immature in such matters, I never expected to have these experiences and did not fully decipher their meaning until years later. Eventually, facts came together, culminating in this book.

For many years, as I slipped into bed for the night, I silently pleaded God for hours with all my heart until passing into sleep. I begged to know Him, and yearned to someday meet my beloved one, the heavenly princess and sole companion of my heart, to whom I dedicate this book and soul. Tears poured in my nightly appeals, even more so during the day as I relived evening pleads.

I realized I did not know God at all, and the thought of it frightened me sorely. The Architect of my soul and what my life needed most was the greatest of mysteries, and that did not settle well with me. I scoured the planet for answers, leaving no stone unturned, but nothing satisfied a growing crevice in my bosom. Being so distant from Him, and unable to find my one, brought terrifying omens to my inapt life, battered by fears and numbing desire. Hence, Father and my beloved one lived only in my dreams with enduring hope, and my heart as an ardent wish. But all that was about to change drastically in ways I never expected, as my search for love was about to begin.

On that memorable Friday evening, I witnessed several extra-terrestrial craft dart the skies above my Whittier, California, home. Outright excited at the prospect of seeing something of cosmic magnitudes, I raced down a set of concrete steps to the street below with a three-inch telescope, hoping to get a better look at these objects. But after a few minutes, I suddenly grew tired and felt compelled to go back into the house. As I trudged up the steps, I started to feel unusually heavy. By the time I reached the doorway, I was barely conscious and collapsed at the entrance.

The next thing I recall is inexplicably lying in bed on my left side, eyes fixed on a bedside clock questioning just how I got there. Moreover, I wore uncomfortable pajamas I never donned, my clothes were neatly hung in the closet, and the telescope was folded away by the door—a tall order for someone not known for neatness. Exactly five seconds before 10:00 p.m., I abruptly fell asleep as if suddenly sedated.

Darkness briefly prevailed in my mind's calm eye until a lighted tunnel swiftly unfolded like the iris of a camera. I travelled hastily through this lighted tunnel and merged with a flash of light that dwelled at its end. The very next moment, I found myself standing inside a rectangular room with two large bay windows overlooking nature outside. I did not know where I was—other than very, very far away from home—and no clue just how I got there.

I was alone, far removed from the windows and next to a stairway leading to a lower level. Everything was quiet, and darkness kept me from seeing what was in the level below, as if I was not to go there. Wondering where I was, an unfamiliar, yet sweet female voice I could not place said suddenly, "You will be returned within two hours; you are on Venus."

What transpired next, which seemed as long as one hundred years, I leave to the story. To make a longer account shorter, I was given a tour of Venus by the higher beings inhabiting this wondrous realm, and received a lifetime education in science and life's universal principles. Its people always smiled, rejoicing from uncontainable love, for they are in love with each other and with Him. They know no selfishness and are therefore fear free. Venus was such an exquisitely beautiful world that no words can fully describe it. Its air carried a delightful scent that was both natural and spiritual; the story will further speak of its countless wonders.

Five seconds before midnight, precisely two hours later as promised, I awoke. My eyes bolted open and I was shocked to find myself back on this world, picking up my old physical life where I left off, a life I no longer felt was real or desirable by any means.

After living for so long in these heavenly, spiritual realms, returning to Earth was a colossal "bummer." The amazing celestial wonders I observed on Venus, its vast, breathtaking landscapes, my new friends, their tenets, and the astonishing precepts I learned were all precipitously replaced by a drab, dark room hosted by an equally dark world. I had pretty much forgotten my earthly life with all its cares and concerns, transformed into a new person accustomed to a different way of life on a world millions of miles away.

I suddenly sprung up from bed barely connecting with the present only to find, at the foot of my bed, the semi-transparent image of the same beings I met on that far distant world, smiling gently and hinting that I should never forget them. After ten seconds, they slowly faded away, and I passed out again. This time, I reemerged in one of Saturn's moons, Titan.

Though it was night time, Saturn's glowing disk illumined the gentle landscape before me as if by twilight. I stood some two kilometers from small smooth hills to my left. Soft clouds quickly raced above them, masking heaven's majestic jewels. No trees were visible, but prairie-like incandescent crystalline flora covered the silent landscape.

Close by, a tall man asked me into a strange glowing building to his side that looked like a small cylindrical booth. This building was no more than three meters tall by one in width. But inside, its dimensions were absolutely enormous, hosting a conference of sort. You will learn more about Titan in the pages to follow.

In the coming days, I visited the underground cities of Mars as well as numerous magnificent worlds far beyond the confines of our system. By that time, I felt like an alien living in a backward world, without purpose or plan, dominated by a selfish being I did not yet recognize or understand—until my soul awakened much later in life.

The following morning, just days after getting my driver's license, I wandered aimlessly into the Whittier public library. I had never visited a library before, much less cognizant of the fact they actually had books one could take home for a while. But I was not there on a mission, looking for a special tome, or doing research on any particular subject—far from it. In fact, while I truly did not know why I was there, I was there nevertheless.

I strode silently into the vast, still library, dazed by its impressive dimensions and innumerable range of books, unsure where to go or what to do. Slowly, I involuntarily turned south and headed like a mindless zombie alongside check-out and information desks. I went past the card catalogues and proceeded down a central aisle until I entered a dark section of the library.

Since there was no one else in the area, I surmised the material in this specific section held all but trivial significance to most library patrons, reason perhaps for its profound seclusion. But I could not elect any other place to be at or voluntarily move my body.

About twenty paces from the end of the aisle, I stopped suddenly and stared forward in rapt, senseless intent. Then unexpectedly, my right arm raised itself and my hand started tapping on a certain book, seemingly on its own volition.

Three taps later and still somewhat out of it, my eyes finally focused, my consciousness roused, but my hand was still tapping on this one book. I realized this was rather abnormal behavior, but my arm stubbornly kept tapping on the book, and it did so until I decided to take the book into my hands. Then, the tapping stopped. The book was titled *Inside The Space Ships* by George Adamski.

What I found in this book validated what I saw in my "altered state." My heart was filled with boundless faith, energy, and vitality enough to last an eternity. It was then that my search for love deepened, and my heart fervently surrendered to the Eternal.

As the years crawled slowly by in morbid, sequestered solitude, I wondered what to do with the knowledge I gathered from so many visions, so I innocently decided to tell others about them. It would have been best had I not, for when I did, I was quickly rejected and profoundly ridiculed. Still, I resorted to specialty channels such as the air force, universities, and space contractors like Martin Marietta, offering to provide them with scientific information. Prior public humiliation clearly foretold what I could expect. Thereby, Adamski's book became the only friend I had in a hostile world, keeping numerous secrets within.

Alone, and sorely dejected by everyone I shared my experiences with, I spent day and night drawing Adamski's ships, writing about the spiritual kingdoms I visited, and verifying scientific concepts learned during such sojourns. In the end, since I had no one to share them with, I destroyed most of it. In spite of the grave sadness I secretly held within, powerful memories of heaven's kingdoms lived on in my heart, keeping thriving hopes of someday returning to the stars in constant blossom.

My heart continued to seek my beloved friends, called Brothers, with compelling yearning; it was all I cared about. But since no one showed any interest in my visions, I became totally fed up with this world and longed to flee to Mars in the worst way. There, I was certain my starry sapphire waited for me. But little did I know the real reasons why I felt that way. Hence, I drew exacting space craft technical plans and began to procure components necessary to build it. But then, an incident came along that suddenly arrested my plans, for in my beguiling innocence, I thought I had found the Brothers—on Earth, of all places.

In the years to come, I discovered the Unarius Educational Foundation in El Cajon, California, and promptly paid them a visit. While I sat undisturbed in its beautiful lobby reviewing a book by Dr. Ernest L. Norman, *The Infinite Concept*, the book suddenly slipped from my hands, I dropped over the table before me as if dead, my eyes closed, and a dreadful space battle around Mars played itself in my mind. I saw and felt myself in that battle, an experience as real as it can possibly get.

It was then that, for the first time in my life, I believed in reincarnation and understood my plight—yes, I had lived before, and I had been there, on Mars. I then understood why I wanted to return to my home world, and seek my one. Soon after, my dark legacy slowly revealed itself, and I learned why I was interned on Earth.

Thousands of past-life images revealed themselves over time; many are documented as testimonials in the foundation's extensive library. Some were based on factual visions of past events and I fully stand behind them; you will read of them in this narrative. Others, on the other hand, I wrongfully conjured up, moved by an irresistible yearning to gain rank among Unariun students. Recalling past lives became an elaborate effort to merit pardon for prior baseless errors without really trying.

I painfully wasted four years literally deceiving myself and abusing wondrous spiritual teachings. In those troubling days, I overdosed on self-inflicted scorn and admitted to countless past deeds that were just not true. Seemed like the ghastlier I fabricated the past, the more I was esteemed—an addictive domain I gravely overlooked and shamefully regret. My wayward conduct went unchecked, so I thought, believing I had my leaders fooled. Truth was, it was I who suffered from truth deficiency.

I endured four painful years of self-imposed slavery until a sixth sense finally broke through stubborn anxiety, and I learned long-overdue lessons; trust no man to be god, search for Love and not salvation, and long to serve God but not for your own sake.

The wondrous teachings brought forth by Dr. Ernest L. Norman, the Unarius founder, were gradually eclipsed by other interests that surfaced following his transition. Accepting this fact, and rededicating myself to his original works, I realized it was time to leave the Unarius Center, for it was no longer the pure science Dr. Norman conceived. No sooner, the visions for this book deluged my mind and could not write them down fast enough.

Today, a group of students devote themselves strictly to Dr. Norman's original writings [1]. I praise their initiative to seek love and truth, not invent false past lives and hype spaceship landings that will not happen. A celestial brotherhood spans and guides all worlds in this galaxy—together, not divided. The Brothers would never disunite the galaxy by forming isolated space federations detached from the galactic fold, as some propose. We are brothers—we are one, not a clique.

A million years ago, several lost souls did just that—isolated certain planets into a federation supposedly to help them evolve. The results are detailed in this book, our detestable legacy. I should know. I was partly responsible for that colossal selfish blunder. And we mean to repeat history? Are landing enthusiasts reliving their hand in that massive blunder?

Let this testimony be clear warning to the inexperienced and gullible. Always test the spirit, mainly your own, for you may be gravely deceived. Learn from my mistakes, and do not push yourself to know the past. Rather, know your feelings, an act more important than knowing your past, one that will lead you to such past. Search in peace, not fear or haste. Trust the Brothers in every way. They will enlighten you with truth, love, and knowledge of who you are, when the time is right.

I felt inwardly impressed to compile all visions and their graceful lessons into story form, conveying a vital, yet simple message to everyone on Earth from the heart of His Majesty: do not fear Him. Be patient; haste will deliver you into the hands of your lower self. Do nothing under stress, do everything overwhelmed by love, let your higher self always be near. Lead not mundane life as if it's the normal thing to do; step above it. Always question your desires, for they are vain insecurities born from memories that will not rest. Remember, anger and desire are nothing more than fear suppressants.

I sincerely wish this book helps the reader understand what that critical message means. May it inspire you to live according to God's ways, and foster a deeper understanding of our dark and complex legacy, a past that enslaves us to adore error and scoff at genuine love. May it convey the importance of telling the lower self and higher essences apart, a feud described in the pages of this book. Such is the search for Love.

One might rightfully ask: why did it take me so long to publish these visionary incidents? The answer is rather simple: I was not ready to humbly serve the Infinite for the same reason mentioned above; I could not tell the self and the Brothers apart.

The years following that memorable July eve brought endless birthing turmoil, at times beyond my ability to withstand. My heart leaned critically to mundane appeal, beguiled by desires I failed to understand and promptly hid from myself. I betrayed God and the Brothers many times, heeding not their call but rather passions and fears of a tangible world, and a conceded heart.

I thought to be someone of great importance, but all the while lived a monumental lie, for I was just a lowly learner without Light. I was an offense to truth, an eyesore to humility, a total disgrace as a messenger. My noblest intentions and aspirations were nothing more than obsessive desires, driven by the darkest error stems. My heart was selfish, devious, living in shameful pretense of piety, for the ignorant being inside laughed at the face of love, acting kindly only for self-benefit. I was absolutely no good to Father like that.

I was devastated to learn this and strongly opposed giving life a chance, preferring to die than face truth and inner pain. But deep inside, I felt the Brothers do not condemn, and pains were simply resistance to truth. So then, where was the sense of choosing death over the Infinite? And so, I stumbled back on my feet and forged ahead time and time again, rendering pride a forgotten nuisance—rekindling my search for Love.

Let me introduce you to the higher Brothers of Light, the true teachers and leaders of our hearts. Love them and Father with all your might, and then some. Trust them. Let them show you, as they showed me, the darkness that blinds mind and heart; without their higher love and wisdom, I can achieve nothing noble.

Today, most conventional beliefs do not exemplify a comprehensive understanding of the science of life or a veritable view of higher realms of expression. Yes, there's more—infinitely more—to learn. Be open to the possibility that life is just the beginning of infinity, not the end. The reasons why this is so await your pleasant discovery, and what a surprise these shall be. Search for higher love and truths, not salvation, for he that tries to save his life will lose it, but he that sacrifices it for God will gain it [2].

As you read the pages of this book, come to know and adopt the great love that abounds in the cosmos. Discover the grave sins that thrive in our hearts through my testimony, and know that higher Brothers are with you in thought, always ready to bounce you back on the winning side.

I cannot thank Father enough for the unexpected honor granted this truth-challenged student to step onto higher spiritual grounds, to be stirred by God's endless wonders, to become aware of my heavenly sapphires, and to have this humbling opportunity to share of so many priceless virtues with my brethren of Earth, more so, the honor to carry Him in my heart. It is a privilege of such immense magnitude that this heart of carnal substance will never conceive.

I highly encourage the reader to be strong in Father and be of good courage because commitment to Love, not a person, is the ultimate highway to heaven and tolerance is the essence that will keep you on that road. Be patient. Do not obey your negative self but rather deny it. Be as the sons of God, the free and selfless, who beg that you join them in loving embrace—soon.

The Infinite is all you will ever need. Let the brotherhood share His essence with you and my words inspire its safe-keeping. Deny yourself;

hear the calm rhythm of God's works. Feel His love pour through emotive eyes—true love, beautiful beyond description, clean, potent. His essence will drive the heart to live in love with creation, and not the negative self—such is the test of spirit.

My life for Him, His glory be in us. Fall deeply in love with Him with all the fury and potency of the heart, more so than any other thing under or above the heavens. Let life become a memorial to His great faithfulness. Wait on His love and cherish it with all your heart, soul, strength, and might. Let there be no other thought of the mind, or search in life, but Him.

---

[1] Unarians United, "UnariansUnited.com."

[2] R. W. J. Morford, "Luke 9:24," in *The One New Man Bible*, Travelers Rest, SC: True Potential Publishing, Inc., 2011.

Chapter 1: *Still Firmaments*

Dearly beloved father and brother, love eternal be unto thee. Two eventful Masar [3] years have come to pass since our fateful departure from primeval lands of bondage. On that jubilant day, His Majesty's glorious light returned to its rightful resting place below your brow, and the windows of your soul beheld life through different, untainted eyes worthy of celestial wonder after such long, trying sojourn.

Rejoice, for the imperishable doors of ancient legacy have closed forever and mankind's heavenly dreams are finally a reality, visions that shall never fade or darken. Malevolent burdens shall never again arrest the Master of the Heavens from our sights, and truth shall forever kindle cosmic hearts with divine love as it was meant to be. Therefore, "Be strong! Be of good courage [1]! Be strong in Father and in the power of His strength. You must continually be clothed with the full armor of His Highness to enable you to stand against the strategies of the enemy [2]."

No fleeting chronicle will ever give our embarrassing legacy adequate rendering, for our plight against verity is quite lengthy and gravely contrary to Father's ways. I therefore beg that this humble narrative unfasten the virtuous doors of every heart that hears them and stirs the timeless breath of life that only His Majesty can provide.

The lush emerald cradle we once called home no longer shines its glorious beacon amid the great void, arrested by tacit, morbid peace. It is a wounded world, now in forlorn precedent, surrounded by still darkened firmaments that beckon not a single conscious soul to its lonesome bosom. Heavenly luminaries, perched silently in an airless expanse far off, can only witness wondering cinders seeking respite among heaps of senseless aspirations and sacrifices committed through the ages. Still, such ancient lit wonders softly shed radiant tears over fallow domains tainted by once humiliating passions that only an errant humanity could inspire.

Behold man's selfish hopes and pursuits, resting bemoaned among Saras's [3] distressed dust, incapable of enduring Infinite Majesty's will. Only spoils from our defiant avarice linger amid predestined worldly ashes, slowly consumed by an invisible stellar judge that discerns no forbearance for mankind's ignorance. Endless faith placed on doomed ideologies, human beliefs, immortal kings, and inspiringly monumental idols built to trump creation; none lasted the test of time. They are all found spread across what's left of an ill-fated world, reduced to meaningless embers. So what good is our intellectual prowess in the end, compared to Father's eternal, ever-mounting glory, "for His loving kindness endures forever [4]."

The wordless elocution of an injured world warned us with ample vigor that we knew not how to live, but even the most learned among us ignored its counsel and looked the other way. With loving patience, our old world feebly ascertained humanity's mastery over self-demise while we gorged on sin, even though death neared. Now, alone in the frigid currents of space, relentless human chaos no longer exerts sins upon Saras's newly fashioned yet dismayed shell—a mature world tired of bearing fruits to belligerent, possessive beings long in contempt of truth.

In those days of perished reason, judgment slowly came upon the world shrouded in utter anonymity to those whose barren thoughts strived edgily to betray His Majesty. Meanwhile, the age of imperishable verdict drew steadily closer from afar, pouring its abstemious chalice upon gullible souls suffering severely drunk from its vile heave.

People became as children, playing pretend games and recklessly living to death without a care. Dissolute amusement and false doctrines, inspired by reprobate minds, corrupted young souls away from truth and love. With no Father left in the will of the people, their hearts failed and no God could be found in them. In the end, mankind endured a wretched, sinful life beguiled by mundane, secular gloom. It was the only life they chose to know, submitting to assurances offered by profitable iniquity and wrongful beliefs far from spiritual reality.

Wholly disconnected from Father, humanity carried on with forged lives without a care pretending all was well, unaware that behind every thought stood sinister beasts fostering ungodly conduct. The enemy's will to extinguish the breath of life was relentless, the evil arsenal at its disposal seemingly boundless. It fought fiercely against anyone siding with His Majesty, keeping the spiritually infirm in check by unleashing untold fears and disease upon them. Influenced by countless imaginary yearnings and baffling ignorance, mankind became lost in a world swelling with complacent darkness, slowly diminishing in intelligent life force.

Deceit, threats, and frivolous goals led us to abandon His Majesty's hand and turn to ourselves for answers, right where darkness wanted us to dwell. We lost the way of truth and replaced reason with guile, under the direct influence of belligerent ideologies. We hailed man's feats in awe, but deplored God's presence even for a meager hour. We stopped loving God and chose to impersonate other lost souls' mannerisms instead. We took joy in materialism but revoked divine behavior. All the while, prudent masters and brilliant leaders we believed to be. Renegade initiates of truth were we, stricken by aberrant, malignant hearts subject to personal fearful motives.

Why cherish a life teeming with deceit, moved by dread rather than peace, ruled by blind existentialism and the limited wisdom of freewill bearing subjective heuristic truth? How can humanity persist behind intellectual penal bars without endearing beyond, convinced that physical reality is all-inclusive?

We fail the moment we look away from Father and unwisely rely on personal aptitude to unravel life's mysteries. If actualization and experience are limiting proclivities leading us to partially seize duly ignored reality, then where is the fountain of realism assuring life's integrity and fulfilling universal quest?

Love, truth, faith, ideas, insight—these are not physical but spiritual manifestations, evidence of things unseen [5] that are born not from existential matter but rather the universal Architect that made matter existential. Hence, to know truth and accept faith, the Architect must be part of your life. That's where the brotherhood comes in, inspiring truth to those who would listen.

Love and truth are creation's true exclusive leaders since we are subject to them, not man's assertive nature or innovative intellect, for no world order conceived by man endures, much less leads to ultimate reality. Hence, do not follow blindly after promises and putative ideals conceived by sinful men, for you will surely perish profoundly deceived. Instead, "seek first the kingdom of God and His righteousness [6]." By letting the brotherhood be your guide, you will know the deceiver in you. Let honesty and love leave no personal desires hidden, so you may tell deceit and Him apart.

Realize that reverent love is the sum of compliance with life's divine role. From the simplest atom to the majesty of starlight, creation displays its glorious forms in an unmatched cosmic pageant with flawless artistry and integrity. Life is virtuous and reverent, inspired by righteous thought, holy behavior, and spiritual discipline. Uphold reverence first and foremost in all that is of spirit, for mockery corrupts creation, but respect builds love.

Understand that living beings are wondrous creations, bearing life vessels created by and belonging to His Majesty. The vessel is God's uniform and an instrument to inspiringly exhibit His endless loving attributes. Do not defile it by expressing selfish, vulgar needs or achievements through it, or give of it without infinite guidance.

We need not impress others with our works or possessions, for these things are a small subset of that which is already rightfully God's. Instead, travel through life filled by Infinite Father's abundant gifts of holy expression. Ask for and desire nothing, except His Majesty, for only he knows what you need and His blessings are bountiful. In His heart there is no want; in yours, all is need. Beware of wrongful hunger for the mundane, for it is a sign of departure from Him and an act of desperate necessity, like that of a child lost from his mother.

Give and teach not, unless you are first asked and Father approves of it. Your infantile, wicked spirit corrupts absolutely, and the curious usurp truth without regard, but His truth endures faithfully forever. Therefore, consult Father on every thought and action you must take. Let His will predominate in your daily life, for he knows better. Do not let go of His reliable hand or stop loving Him, for His is the only voice you should ever trust. Never love anything more than Father, for he is love itself. Love of man, rather than Father, destroys life; for man is sinful, sin is error, error is conceit, conceit is desire, desire is fear, and fear is lack of truth. His truth is the key to the universe.

Father's love, and my eternal companion, did I seek for endless ages, but how often did ignorance and lack of faith detour me? I could not live with celestial dreams so big that my heart could not contain them or express divine passions in such a vulgar world as ours—so I thought. My silent thoughts betrayed me to think my one did not exist, that I would never be forgiven or be freed from my evil self, that my dreams were not real, that God did not love me, that I did not truly love Him or my beautiful one, that any hopes of leading an inspiring divine life beyond ours were best arrested, considering my wretched state of sin; well, I was wrong.

I came to know the Infinite and my beloved one the moment I ceased to believe it could not be. My eternal companion now lives in my heart, her hand always in mine, sharing glorious loving wonders from His cosmic gardens. She is the most wondrous, radiant light and softest divine melody to enliven my soul. She is the heavenly majesty and crowning magnificence of my life, who I searched throughout the heavens eons for and I'm desperately in love with.

No corporeal warmth or softness will ever eclipse my one's heavenly heart and kind spirit. In her thoughts, Father's love is manifested. From her lips, His songs of life bring me peace and purpose. In Father, through her, my life is made whole "and loving kindness will pursue me all the days of my life, and I will dwell in the house of Father forever [7]."

Do not lose hope; do not fear that your wicked life cannot be salvaged. Depart from your inner wrongful advisor but never let go of His hope or faith. His wait is your test of love and an opportunity to give "I" up for Him.

May the Infinite always be with you, and memory of this legacy be well guarded by your side for eternity. Walk through life with grace, endowed with spiritual elegance. Rejoice in His peaceful offerings and rest your soul upon the brotherhood, for we are one: *oh-joi*! Welcome to heaven, my brother, where love for His Majesty and one another transcends all desire.

To His Magnificence be all glory, for our wisdom, deeds of truth, and manners of righteousness are absolutely not ours by any means but His. To His Majesty belongs the origin of truth, kindness, and the essence of love—the cornerstone of creation. He is the architect of love and the eternal voice that whispers epics of life, Lord of gentleness and epitome of perfection, joy of living and rhythm of the cosmos. My life for Him, His glory be in us, forever.

"His loving kindness is great toward us: and the truth of Father is forever [8]. Father is my rock and my fortress and my deliverer; my God, my rock in whom I shall trust; my shield, the horn of my salvation, and my high tower [9]." Father is my love.

---

[1] R. W. J. Morford, "Deuteronomy 31:7," in *The One New Man Bible*, Travelers Rest, SC: True Potential Publishing Co., 2011.

[2] R. W. J. Morford, "Ephesians 6: 10–11," in *The One New Man Bible*, Travelers Rest, SC: True Potential Publishing Co., 2011.

[3] G. H. Williamson and A. C. Bailey, "Saras, Masar," in *The Saucers Speak*, Meta Physical Research Group, 1989.

[4] R. W. J. Morford, "1 Chronicles 16:34," in *The One New Man Bible*, Travelers Rest, SC: True Potential Publishing Co., 2011.

[5] R. W. J. Morford, "Hebrews 11:1," in *The One New Man Bible*, Travelers Rest, SC: True Potential Publishing Co., 2011.

[6] R. W. J. Morford, "Matthew 6:33," in *The One New Man Bible*, Travelers Rest, SC: True Potential Publishing Co., 2011.

[7] R. W. J. Morford, "Psalm 23:6," in *The One New Man Bible*, Travelers Rest, SC: True Potential Publishing Co., 2011.

[8] R. W. J. Morford, "Psalm 117:2," in *The One New Man Bible*, Travelers Rest, SC: True Potential Publishing Co., 2011.

[9] R. W. J. Morford, "Psalm 18:2," in *The One New Man Bible*, Travelers Rest, SC: True Potential Publishing Co., 2011.

Chapter 2: *Memories Know No Rest*

The real reasons we embody on this hostile world remain a mystery to most. Some staunchly believe that you live only once, and this is the only world where you may do so. Others devote their lives to pursue eccentric creationist and scientific beliefs subject to debatable authorship, construal, and purpose.

While there is no one right way or belief over another, an inescapable fact remains cleverly veiled from humanity's reach, partway to control mundane existence: life is pluralistic, meaning it's universal, convergent, recurrent, experientially collective, and associatively restrictive. In other words, we embody on this particular world simply because we fail to put certain recurring memories to rest, opt to deceive rather than love individuals we grimly associate them with, and live consumed by fear of dying.

We share a common grotesque legacy that will not respect heaven's benign cadence or the natural way things should be. It is that loveless legacy, not creation, that makes life what it is upon this penal planet, reserved for the spiritually infirm, where we meet periodically to put ancient memories to rest—though at times we fail to do so, and regenerate rather than nullify the past. Oblivious to this fact, I freely repeated memories and disrespected heaven's cadence life after life without concern, and this life was no exception.

Nearly four decades lapsed since the dawn of tolerant polity last touched our hearts, so long in fact that not a soul knew for sure what olden days were like, except by way of illicit fables about a world buried deep beneath the same pestilent rubble that christened its dreary fate.

Amazing stories of those days still lingered, but few cared to hear them. It was said that, in those times, lofty mountains made of metal and glass towered proudly above the land, defying nature's unwavering destiny to reclaim that which is rightfully worldly. Within their lavish foyers, ambitious overlords wielded untold authority over pleasure, and arduously held nature captive for unmerited ransom. Ravenous merchants rose upon the land to suitably supplement their opulent masters by cunningly instituting common standards of living that turned mankind into slaves of fortune.

The wealthy held personal indulgence and power in much greater esteem than human love or sympathy; the most struggled to survive amid mundane conventions quite distant from God's essence. Rampant leisure was the norm, wasting vast resources on rather trivial quests that spoiled both mind and body. The world toiled in stark poverty rendering the few ever richer, but the time neared when exploitation would suddenly desist and social insecurity meet its fate. Eventually, man's reluctance to confront sin and lead a virtuous life triggered a massive holocaust that destroyed mankind's hyped achievements in the blink of an eye.

Thus, it was that, on the morning of that memorable September day, the end of opulent avarice finally manifested its long-ordained calling. Out of thick wintry skies, gods of death soared their way into the heart of Manhattan from disguised cargo ships far off at sea, depriving millions of verve. Moments later, the same sweltering onslaught devastated other cities along the North American coastline, thus silencing the mightiest nation on Earth and casting the entire world into everlasting darkness.

Beguiled children festively witnessed bright rising pillars of doom from afar, unaware their deeds destroyed innocent lives, not the principles they sought to silence. But such invasive ignorance promptly begged it had not been so, for it merely served to awaken a sleeping colossal leviathan moved by irrepressible odium most grueling to bear.

It took vengeance but a few moments to burst free from latent bindings and hastily fix its baleful sights on distant homelands with unmatched fury and absolute supremacy, much like starved beasts suddenly unhindered to feast. That same afternoon, hundreds of tormenting furnaces swiftly traversed the skies beneath the face of the deep and plummeted upon millions of startled souls that never knew their plight in such ungainly sea of rancorous wrath.

At the end of that tragic day, entire nations and their proud achievements were no more. Human ashes blanketed earthly soils while winds spread their still voices to morbid neighbors fearing the same fate. In the heavens above, stars lost their usual luster against the deep cloak of night, and celestial radiance faded warily away into bleak obscurity. In their place, dazzling auroras covered the skies, charming mystified observers around the world. But what seemed like splendid works of nature to many in reality brought dread to those in the know. Hours later, unexpected tragedy struck.

Gradually, sunlight surged upon morning horizons like a giant scrolling veil, dispensing lethal radiation that sorely burned anyone braving its rays for days. The planet consistently warmed, and fires ravaged arable lands, soon flooded by rapidly melting ice sheets. Eventually, Earth's axis tilted aimlessly about, and unparalleled disasters humbled every nation, sparking a massive global refugee crisis.

Unable to feed their people, nations turned on each other to survive. States vanquished neighbors in rapid succession, and ambitious dictators hastily came and went. But these were trivial woes compared to what followed: the spliced wars. Seemingly overnight, countless ogre creatures called beasts invaded every corner of the world, destroying everything in their path and reducing Earth's population to two billion. Some speculated they were space invaders, others mutants. Time passed before the world realized these monsters were spliced humans, originating from the ambiguous Amarna Alliance headquartered somewhere in the Sahara.

The year was 2058. Eight years into the war, I found myself in the Calanshio Sand Sea hunting Amarna down. Becoming a marine was the last thing I looked forward to, but pressure from the compulsory service and a moment of weakness was all it took to forever serve the will of warlords. I once aspired to reach the level of Brahman and respected the great truth that "just as certain as death comes to the born, birth is also certain for the dead [1]." Now, I pray from the *Gitopanishad* with one hand as the other kills people I never knew.

Our unit combed the desert for weeks until reaching an abandoned airfield near Bu Attifel. After we established camp, it didn't take long for eyelids to reflect mental reveries in hapless reenactments. But in a life-forsaken place like this, that was easier said than done.

Strong winds minced down scorching desert sands in abrupt bursts, imposing tiny grits that nastily found their way into unsuspecting maws. In the old landing strip terminal, heat relief seemed far from attainable in spite of climate controls built into our cobalt-laced exo-suits. Sunlight seeped through fluttering canvas furrows draped over broken windows, breaking up slumber into fleeting catnaps difficult to mind. Fowl stench invaded senses struggling to ignore it, with stagnant settlement worse than an elephant's bin. Privacy was such rare luxury that both genders thought little of it anymore. Still, a tired brow could not endure the torturous jaunt and slept oblivious to nature until midday.

Shades of past events littered the sands, tarnishing away under the blazing Sun. Digging them up seemed a rare yet esteemed prospect to overcome otherwise painful monotony. Bored marines scoured the desert like bogus treasure hunters, taking prideful ownership of whatever oddity they unearthed. Not far from camp, they stumbled upon an old rusty vehicle, mostly buried, and decided to dig it up in spite of the searing heat. I had no time to take part in that operation, but something about this old contraption captivated my thoughts to the verge of passion. Thus, I kept a willing close eye on progress, hoping to see it finally exhumed.

It was early that afternoon when a grunt hastily left the dig site and ran my way, politely interrupting a logistics discussion with Benghazi MPP brass. "Sergeant, sir, there's something you have to see" he said excitedly.

"What is it, jarhead?" I said, resolved not to get dragged into senseless sand prospecting. "This better be important."

"It's about that vehicle we found, sir. You have to come see it."

"It's not worth our while, Private," I said, rather dry. "That's just a relic from another time and has no appreciable military value. Will that be all?"

"We don't know that, sir. Seems like something brutally drilled and tore it apart. Other than fuel fire, there are no projectile casings, fulgurite, or evidence of plasma discharge in the vicinity; but we did notice this," he said, showing me a large piece of weathered bent metal cleanly pierced through by some unknown force likened to a stamping press.

"Whatever hit this vehicle," he added, "left no chemical residue behind and drilled four-centimeter holes like this one all over it, even right through the engine. We don't know anything that can inflict this kind of damage, seriously thinking that new Amarna weapon we heard so much about is what did it."

I had mixed feelings about visiting the dig site. But if Amarna had indeed tested a new weapon on this vehicle, it was our duty to investigate. So I dismissed my staff, stepped into the glaring sun, and walked west of the old tarmac to the site, passing several sweaty souvenir hunters along the way.

The vehicle, or what was left of it, was pounded with sufficient force to slant its frame diagonally, apparently from the sky on the driver's side. Most holes pierced completely through to the other side, injecting bored-out metal slugs deep into the sand. Other large remains flung far and wide, seemingly ripped off the frame like paper scrap, though there were no signs of explosion.

Upon closer inspection, bored holes showed clear evidence of aging, indicating they were inflicted well before Amarna's time. Though comforting to know, that still did not lessen my wistful concerns any. Rather, it proposed an unexplained phenomenon meaning to resolve. Hence, I deliberately lingered about to see what was in the cabin, slowly being exhumed.

Not long after, standing silently by with nothing else to do but wait things out in the scorching sun, a strange sense of weariness forced me to withdraw from the crowd and seek solitude a short distance away, but this helped little.

I felt increasingly heavy and of uncertain footing, oppressed by obscure feelings that drifted my sentient awareness far from reality and unto a restless daze. As I was unsettled by revelations artfully more authentic than cognizance advised, my withdrawn gaze sensed unnerving events I could not decrypt—yet lived. Though my eyes liberally sealed shut in insentient submission, the barren desert still unfolded before my mind's eye in full golden glory. But it was an inciting canvas, deceivingly born from a time other than the present, for it was a memory that knew no rest.

And then, something completely unexpected happened. A mental story emerged from suppressed subliminal chasms, rapping fatefully at my mind's gates like a fleeting dream longing to complete. It was a persistent tale of a long lost life, endowed with sweeping passions for the plight of restive memories, granting these a chance to stir ancient lifeless shadows back to life. So it was that a past memory came alive by witnessing in the present.

*****

In the far-distant haze, the ghostly outline of a light-colored truck rapidly journeyed south along the Sand Sea's remote wavy contours, partly concealed by endless sand mounds stretching far into land's end. Some distance behind, smaller vehicles followed in brash pursuit, speeding down the desert as fast as wheels would take them. Inside the truck, a sweat-filled countenance anxiously implored the gods for protection, aware its hold on life might cease any moment at the hands of a sinister few. He was a cavalier thief that pilfered, into his interim fold, Earth's greatest secrets from none other than the evil of ages bowing to recover them at any and all cost.

His fears enticed a trail of vengeance for chasing vehicles to follow, slowly closing in with irrevocable demise in mind. Before them, open plains offered few adequate shelters or the means to melt tracks away from evil's keen sights. With nowhere to hide, it was just a matter of time before the halls of Naraka reassessed rebuke and determined where this thief would live and die next. In due course, bullets decisively found their mark, and the truck's wounded engine sputtered to a halt. Its pierced wheels dug deep into the sand, and soldiers hastily surrounded the smoke-burdened vehicle weapons drawn.

The driver promptly hid a set of documents beside him below the seat but stayed inside the cabin unsure what would transpire next. From there, he yelled angrily, "What's the meaning of this?" but got no response.

"I'm on a secret mission, sanctioned by Marshall Graziani, and you're violating the chain of command," he added, but met silence once more.

Stillness was swiftly revoked by the hasty arrival of a black convertible. A ghastly figure, dressed in a black Nazi SS uniform, leisurely turned a squeaky door handle, stepped out of the vehicle, calmly wiped extensive sweat from his brow, and stood safely behind the truck. He wore a relevant smirk across the jaw and stared forth with glassy blue eyes, hands gripped behind his back.

"Guten tag, mein Freund Giuliani," he said, clicking boots together. "You're headed the wrong way; the British are down there. We must protect Mussolini's elite officers, no?"

"I have orders from Marshall Graziani to report immediately to Egypt and deliver critical documents in support of Operation E," Giuliani said.

"Ah yes, of course," the officer said sarcastically. "Operation E is very important. I should have known. Everything nowadays is Operation E, and I keep forgetting Italians are most clever and liberal. But changing the subject, maybe you can explain why this Ministero della Difesa certificate says you died in the Balkans months ago. Don't you find that rather disturbing?"

"Sir, obviously, if I'm here, that certificate must be wrong," Giuliani said.

"You're absolutely right," the officer replied calmly. "The ministry deals with so many deceased soldiers that mistakes do happen—on occasion. So then, tell me how you acquired highly classified Flugscheiben documents" he said, raising his voice. "Who authorized you access into the facility, and why is a petro truck waiting for you at Al Jaghbub?"

"I only take orders from the marshall," Giuliani said. "With all due respect, I'm not at liberty to provide any information regarding my mission, sir."

"You're a most disciplined soldier, my respects; but no one can access those documents without the Führer's approval, and you're not authorized," the officer said calmly. "Why don't we return to Gialo, contact Graziani, and put this matter to rest? Do you have a problem with that, Tenente?"

Giuliani, at a loss for words, remained silent. Then, with firm tone and irrepressible anger, the officer shouted back in English, "I'm done wasting my time! Your real name is John Richards, an American maggot working for British intelligence! Mike, your next-door neighbor, is a devout follower of the Führer. He recently told us all about your mission here, even sent us a picture of you and Heather to prove it. What do you have to say to that, maggot?"

Silent at first, John replied, "Io non parlo inglese."

"How do you know I'm speaking English?" said the officer, raising his voice confidently. "You choose. Confirm who you really are, or I'll put your wife and little girl on a lead diet. What will it be, maggot?"

John's face sunk forward stunned by betrayal, aware he was doomed to perish. Meanwhile, the officer became ever more sarcastic. "All right, you Nazi jerk," John replied suddenly with despicable sharpness, hoping his next move would ensure his family's safety, "I'll cooperate, but don't hurt my family."

"Ah, you see," said the officer in a slow sedative tone, "that wasn't so hard. I admire courage in a man, so hard to find in a Yank. But there's something very important you need to know; it's about your wife. You see, she's having an affair with your friend, Mike. I'm terribly sorry to bring this up at this time, but I thought you would want to know this right away, no?"

At the sound of these words, anguish helplessly draped upon John's face where fear and endurance once held prominence. Pain and odium subdued upward rolling eyes stressing revenge, soiled by ravaging thoughts he would never mature. "Think of it, what can a woman do with her man gone all these years behind enemy lincs?" he said casually. "I hear it's an intimate affair, and Lilly is now with her rightful 'papa.' Ah, did I hint that you're not Lilly's father? John, there must be something you believe that's actually true! How can one live deceived for so long?" he said, laughing heartily.

The flame of life gradually extinguished from John's gaze, and fierceness surged in a cesspool of daring fortitude devoid of concern, possessed by another being simmering with vengeance. Emotional hot tears mixed vaguely with consuming sweat, swelling fervently with rage where a wounded heart would give it all to vanquish the baseless evil imposed.

"Think about it. What better way to get a divorce than to turn your husband into the party and have him conveniently and professionally disposed of?" he said, gasping from excess laughter. "Don't you get it? You're nothing. No one wants you! You're just a maggot, crawling in disgrace all over the world like some vulgar disease! But I'll be merciful and give you a choice; come work for the Führer and his enlightened Order or die here as a nobody."

"You can only force me but never convince me!" John replied, defiant.

"I like that in a man! So be it, maggot, I'll see you around—in Valhalla!" he said, quickly putting some distance between himself and the truck.

Aware of imminent consequences spelling agonizing interrogation and possibly even execution, John reached impulsively for his side arm, but soldiers flung weapons forward and readied to fire. "Halt!" yelled the officer hastily. "Gentlemen, don't act unwisely! After all, we are professionals, and bullets do cost money. There's another way to resolve this most unusual and unfortunate situation. But first, I'll ask you one last time; are you sure you won't join us? We could use your, shall I say, ancient talents."

"I will never join your Order," John replied firmly.

"What a shame. If you only knew what you're missing. So long, maggot." The officer turned northward, and proudly waved arms over his head several times. A soft mysterious hum, almost musical, suddenly pervaded the desert from places unknown, growing in intensity as if it neared. In moments, a rounded shadow gradually concealed astonished spectators from the sun as a saucer shaped metallic object calmly glided above them. Iron-cross imprints on its sides left no doubt of its origins, and large 80 mm KSK ray guns on its lower hull spelled dread wherever they pointed.

Soldiers gazed upward in awe, marveled at technology they trusted would quickly swing the war in their favor. John, on the other hand, knew what this weapon could do and that it was meant for him. Dread besought his angry demeanor, staring frozen at the heavens perhaps for the last time.

With fulsome step, the officer smiled at Germany's newest technological wonder: the Haunebu I anti-gravity disc. "Let me introduce you to my new friend, the crowning glory of Third Reich ingenuity, the wonder machine that will conquer the world for Germany. I think this is a perfect occasion to see what it can do. Shall we put it to the test, maggot?"

With a quick hand sign, punishing blasts from the disc's guns thundered loudly across the desert, and tongues of smoke raised high into the air, leaving deep craters behind for the truck to submerge into. The vehicle crumbled under intense phaser muscle, bending feebly like a dry leaf. Fuel lines burst and ignited, but expired quickly in the shifting wind and sand.

John, confined within the cabin with no means of escape, struggled to evade the gun's menacing course, but there was nowhere to run. Flying shrapnel flung deep into his body and life immediately left his brow. His hands dropped feebly by the side devoid of verve and his soul swiftly ventured off to imperceptible domains beyond physical reality. The disc then turned north and quickly vanished into the far horizon whence it came.

"What a magnificent machine this is, don't you agree?" said the officer, carelessly approaching the demolished truck with a proud, haughty stride.

"Four more years and we'll have hundreds of these things. We'll be unstoppable, marching unchallenged through air, land, and sea. Your mightiest weapons will be no match against ours. America will be reduced to powder, and its armies will pave the streets of Berlin, upon which our elite forces will parade victorious. We will build a new world, ruled by our enlightened alpha."

Side arm in hand, he reached into what remained of the cabin shouting "Bang!" cynically. Beneath a gravely gashed seat, he discovered a Hauneburg Gerat manual containing several gravity-defying disc designs. Recovered documents in hand, the officer smirked in relief and walked away. But his jolly gaze progressively turned solemn, pondering a sudden fleeting, disturbing thought: what if John was actually telling the truth?

Mussolini formally asked Germany to grant his scientists access to disc technology, but Hitler declined his request for the time being. In haste, he may have arranged to obtain secret Wunderwaffe materials by less than virtuous means, involving Brits in this thorny affair as relevant cover. The idea was not that far-fetched. Based on Allied espionage incidents surging in the Sahara, the thought had considerable merit.

Graziani was dug in at Sidi Barrani with an enormous contingent, though inflicting Brits negligible spoil seemingly on purpose. John, a Brit agent, was delivering sensitive Flugscheiben documents not to Britain, but Graziani, in the middle of a war, the least secure time to do so. Things just didn't add up, unless both sides were collaborating to steal disc technology. Perhaps, Operation E was nothing more than a clever sham to deter suspicions of an Italo-British accord—apparently enemies on one hand but covertly cooperating on the other.

With Germany's greatest secrets exposed and war against the Allies looming on the horizon, the Sahara no longer offered reliable haven and the disc program had to be promptly relocated to some remote location conveniently far from human existence. New Swabia seemed like the ideal place, but building and maintaining basic facilities there required substantial resources. Transferring large numbers of labor personnel and supplies while keeping the entire operation secret was in itself an imposing undertaking, let alone sustaining the effort in such adverse environment.

Solutions were few, but a vicious idea to smuggle people of certain ethnic origins out of Europe and Asia undetected gradually evolved, one that would cost millions, already targeted by the regime, their lives. The plan was rather grisly: select the best, exterminate the rest, and keep Allies busy fighting while new facilities were constructed totally unnoticed. Pleased with the idea, the officer resolved to convince the Führer to proceed immediately, and thus one of the vilest holocausts the world has ever known gained political sympathy.

Taking a square object from a pocket, the officer reached into the tattered cabin and placed it in John's hand, saying, "Auf wiedersehen, maggot! By the way, don't believe a word I said about Heather," he said, leaving John to the mercy of consuming sands, and a memory in his hands that knew no rest.

* * * * *

A fretful yet vague voice suddenly emerged from the furthest recesses of my mind and gradually deepened its hold on consciousness by calling my rank repeatedly, but I chose to ignore it. Soon after, a nagging pat upon my exo-suit finally lured my reluctant attention, hastily ending the vision.

Briskly coming back to my senses, I found my IO, Greg Sullivan, worried stiff about my unrelenting haze. We first met a few years back when our units regrouped in what remained of Rome. He turned out to be the only individual I could safely discuss banned subjects like re-embodiment and history with, though he was a former pastor. I called him 'dog jerky' out of respect because he was an American and, as he said, dogs over there ate cooked meals just like people. Lucky mammals, anywhere else they'd be what's for dinner.

His intel gouge revealed a massive beast column, the largest ever tracked, heading our way. It didn't take a genius to realize Amarna expected company soon and would try breaking up advancing flanks by night. He was a most clever fellow never to be underestimated. One never knew what novel gas traps he would deploy, reason we always wore MOPPs [2].

"Will you look at that?" yelled a jolly grunt from the dig site suddenly, disrupting Greg's chilling report. "Sarge, there's someone dead in here, what's left of him."

News of a corpse came as no surprise, and there was absolutely no doubt in my mind who it was. Seized by irresistible sentiment, I excused myself rather hastily and approached the dig site unsure what I would discover, followed by Greg. In the cabin, skeletal remains leaned inert against a thrashed door, wearing a badly weathered uniform identical to the one I envisaged. Nostalgia then conquered the moment, suddenly realizing that this man, John Richards, was me years prior.

Pushing grunts slightly out of the way and reaching impulsively through the broken driver's door, my hands frantically sifted through cabin sands, earning rash slap from fellow marines looking on. "What you hoping to find in there, Sarge, cheap old smokes?" said one of the men sarcastically.

"Something I left behind a hundred years ago, jarhead," I replied to absolutely baffled comrades. Moments later, I sensed bony hands and, within them, a flat square object. Somewhat faded, it showed a black and white picture of the same man I saw in my vision holding hands with a young lively lady I presumed was Heather. Everyone gathered around to get a better look at it, though unaware of the foregoing significance it held.

"How did you know there was a picture in there?" said Ravyn, the group's bully, trying to show sincere interest in the subject when, in fact, nothing was furthest from the truth. He was an impulsive, turbid South African gone Brit, the type that delights depriving others of amity but can never be in the wrong. We had witnessed his masterful skills at making other's lives awful glum before, and his inquiry was a sure sign he was up to something past its best. Guess some past-life manners never change.

"If civil affairs allowed it," I said, "I'd advise giving re-embodiment due thought."

"Nah! That stuff's bent as a nine bob note," he said cynically, seeking group consensus. "That re-body thing is just dodgy duff, the kind of stuff you read about in khazi walls until you get shagged, and I'm not the only one that feels that way, right mates? I'd rather spend time thinking how I'm going to enjoy what life I have left, not how to die. Don't you chums agree?"

"You can't deny truth when re-body evidence glares you in the face," said a grunt. "Sarge's incident just now is a perfect example of what I mean."

"What evidence are you talking about? You mean that old picture? Come on, that's not evidence! For all I know—and I'm not saying this is the case—someone could have planted that picture in there when you guys weren't looking," he said, earning swift discord from fellow grunts.

"Ravyn," said a female grunt, "if you keep brewing doubt like this, truth will pass you by and you won't recognize it. In the end, it will be your loss."

"Don't be a mug, princess. Your puny brains can never hope to go up against the brightest minds in civil affairs. Those guys spent years studying the subject, testing theories, and interviewing people. In the end, what did they find? Not a bloody thing, bakvissie."

"And you believe them? You have to be joking."

"Of course I do. CA ranked this weird soul thing as a hoax, and with good reason. If they say we get just the one chance, that's good enough for me. Besides, what's the sense of coming back to hell, only to die again, ha? You tell me. I wouldn't do that lass again."

"If the soul isn't in the flesh, why did CA waste time looking for it there," I said, "unless, they intentionally didn't want it found? Besides, CA never fully revealed their sources, so that makes you question motive. Bear in mind the law is a political instrument designed to unite the world's majority against Amarna. It isn't truth but a compromise."

"Well lads, then fine, I'll be sensible. If you can prove that I'm coming back again, then I'll believe," he said scornfully. "I'll even change my will and leave everything to myself. How's that for a change of heart?"

"Might as well sit cozy tight by river-side and wait for a log to get ya downstream, schmuckatelli, because damn CA covered up subject matter to quell civil protests long ago," Greg said, to my surprise.

"They had every right to. Findings were considered final, so case closed."

"Arrogant, atheist bastards!" shouted Greg. "They claim to practice evidence-based understandin and critical thinkin, but it's all just stinkin prejudice to discredit Christian faith. Them coon swipers don't know a thing about the Bible, or care to either, but sure like insultin it."

"Well, well, look who decided to hum a tune. It's the ex-padre throwing the book around," Ravyn said, confronting Greg who kept calm.

"You got a problem with that, doofus?" Greg replied daringly.

"Still trying to take the biscuit, I see. What can I say, tin head? I'm glad someone had the balls to do away with past failures like religion and put you pulpit bunnies out of a job. War and suffering—that's all you brought us. Don't get narked, but whatever it took to get rid of you religious hordes, I'm fine with it. So good-bye, faith, and hello, reason."

"Looks like baby fink here, along with his brilliant secular pen pushers, didn't bother to read the *Encyclopedia of Wars* [3] where it says that only 7 percent of wars had religious overtones. So I wonder why books like the Bible, the Quran, and others were outlawed back in twenty eight without motive. I find only one explanation, pet squeak: competition."

"Is that a fact, your holiness?" said Ravyn, pushing Greg forcibly.

"You want some, chicken-snappin dweeb?" Greg said, pushing Ravyn to the ground and standing over him, arm weapon pointed at his face. "I got everythin ya needs right here, so just give me a reason. Four billion dead, mostly women, including my wife and daughter, triggered by atheists like your dad. So why are ya a marine? Don't ya like the world your daddy made for ya? Religion ain't the problem, but rather, a lack of it!"

"Grunts, stand down!" I said, backing Greg away. "Think with your head, not your butt. Leaders, not people, start wars. Since leaders are not religious, neither are wars."

"Don't you know the Bible's rigged?" Ravyn said, getting up rather upset.

"Improved is more like it," Greg replied.

"Bull. Its books quote content from older books, proving they are not originals. Even Moses is referred to in second person. How about Benjaminite Hebrews with Greek names and thousands of discrepancies in every book?"

"Ravyn, Greg, stand down and desist—now!" I said.

"And another thing, butt swab," Greg said, "next time ya wanna start somethin, flux or get off the pot," he said, dodging a quick swing, then pushing Ravyn away briskly, both rolling each other blows on the ground like twitchy badgers stuck in a tight trash hull. Ravyn got his suit's front upper plate bashed up in the broil—a permanent marker that would come back to haunt him later on.

"That's enough, dimwits," I yelled, setting them apart after grappling long enough. "Quit pig roping and save it for Amarna. You fobbies want a fight? I promise you'll get some tonight. The largest chug column on record is headed up this way, and it won't be a beauty pageant; these creeps are after your six. No unit's faced these many chugs before and survived, and we have no back up. I won't let you down; there will be casualties. If you don't want to end up in a bag, you know the drill: quit lollygagging goat screws, and act like marines! I won't have provoking fanny wipes in my unit. Do I make myself clear?"

"Sir, yes, sir!" replied troops.

"Spear tip moves in five hours, huddle in four. Let's give Amarna a real colonic experience, not an excuse to put you under!"

"Oorah!"

"Check your gear. Pack all the ammo you can hump—plasma bloopers, zaps, pelt cutters, pineapples—any and all widow makers you can carry until you can barely walk. You may not get a chance to rearm tonight. We came to get some chugs; here's your chance to get hundreds. Now, get busy."

I headed back to camp, but I wasn't alone. Few grunts paced along, wanting to genuinely learn more about re-embodiment; how refreshing that was. "Who's the slim guy in the picture, is that your pops?" said a grunt.

"You're looking at him," I said leisurely, storing the picture in a pocket.

"Don't get me wrong, Sarge, but that's a really hard gaggle to swallow. How you figure that?"

"If this re-body thing is real, what makes you think you're him?" asked a female grunt, mystified by my answer. "The odds of finding yourself again, especially out here in hell's corner, must be in the trillions. Seems like too much coincidence to me," she said.

"Memories reveal themselves to those who listen in a language composed entirely of feelings," I replied. "These lead you to places and people you've met before," I replied.

"What happened to him . . . you, rather?"

"He got clipped smuggling German secrets a hundred years ago."

"You know what lit him up? The shape that vehicle is in, you don't see standard ammo or beasts doing that."

"Back then, Germany had weapons that make B19Rs look like a toy."

"No wonder CA keeps history under wraps," Greg said. "Who knows where it all went?"

"Germans stashed it somewhere in Antarctica under a canopy of secrecy, genocide, and war to mislay its whereabouts, much like our own times when you think of it. Maybe this war is another sham to cover something else up."

"I won't have to worry about that much longer. I got my six compulsory years in, and I'm goin home to get my old pulpit back. Let leaders fight their own wars."

"You won't re-up?"

"Nope."

"I thought you were a lifer. What's up with that?"

"Not for them secular half-brain bandits runnin the world to death for the past forty years, stuffin bales of made-up beliefs down our throats!"

"Didn't religious pride play a role in getting us where we are" she said.

"No one had the right to force people to comply with mutual ways of thinking, then and now," I said. "Truth needs not force to be right, and wisdom is one's measure of truth. Thus lessons, not force, is the way to truth."

"Speaking of wrong spirit, Ravyn is right," Greg said. "No one knows for sure who or when biblical books were written. But I value it cause its teachings are inspired and utterly priceless. Besides, what else is there?"

"May I suggest, eastern writings?" I said with a smirk.

"Only the meek will inherit the earth [4], but don't push your luck."

"That's really profound, dog jerky. Since you're on a roll, why don't you link up with SAT-OPS and get me updated chug trends."

"Good cookie coming right up, sir," Greg said, jokingly saluting.

Back at the terminal, I spared few moments to ponder on fate's mysterious labors, sheltered by ambiguous events mutely hidden from the heart's deepest prodigious longings. Like a crude compass, my restless past gazed down upon fate's hazy view finder for answers, only to render feeble before infinity's vast causeway, for destiny is not written by one's actions alone, but rather all manner of creation in God's vast expanse.

After losing my wife Mona to Amarna's death machine, I renounced the ways of spirit and embraced vengeful habits. How I missed her—unwilling to let her go, though powerless to bring her back. Consumed by her loss, I blamed myself for it, forgetting that destiny is a book written into by many scribes. I wished I could relive that ill-fated day and cheat the outcome; only then would I rest—what an unfeasible thought that was. Rest and just be—that's all I could do—for the outcome had many other authors besides me.

Mona and I were visiting family in Arcot when terror gripped an otherwise tranquil city. Human clamors suddenly emerged from the vicinity of the Palar River, stalked by loud growls and thunderous ground stomping. At first, we thought jungle beasts had entered the city, but waves of frightened people had another story to tell. Looming behind them, giant creatures concealed by clouds of dust briskly coursed through the city, crushing buildings along the way and tossing objects through the air like weightless darts.

Terrified by impending menace, I felt it wasn't a good idea to stay indoors and urged everyone to abandon the house. We took to the streets, already thickened by waves of desperate souls dashing south for their lives. Not far behind, several monsters followed in hot pursuit, effortlessly leveling buildings and throwing large objects on fleeing masses to hinder our escape.

In the ensuing chaos, Mona and I became abruptly separated, and she instantly vanished into the trampling mob. I screamed aloud for her, pushed forward by hordes, but couldn't discern her delicate voice among such dense human throngs emotionally shouting for similar reasons as I. Rather than move on, I forcibly pushed people aside with fraught anger trying to find her, however futile. When least expected, everything went dark and quiet, only to awaken in an outdoors medic tent sorely wounded.

It took weeks for the body to heal, but the soul roamed infirm to date. As soon as I got back on my feet, I scoured the globe looking for Mona, but my eyes never met her grace again. I mourned her for months in the agony of my soul, with no marked grave to honor or family to comfort. Everyone I once knew and cared about was gone, hidden inside any one of hundreds of dark earthly mass graves rising tall like morose ritualistic mounds throughout the land. Yet I was still alive, and I could not help but ask myself why.

My spirit's weak fabric swiftly broke down and I traded the sanctity of spiritual life for one of blatant savagery, giving in to vengeful delights, all too willing to have me as a client—a decision I surely made in previous lives, for memories know no rest.

I trained with indescribable passion day and night, rain or cold, twice as everyone else. I was tirelessly driven by despicable inner anger others dreaded; for the beast within had awakened, discovering welcoming gesture in my ravaging soul. I feared no one and hated everyone, willfully shutting down my heart to life as if I deserved it. I welcomed war ahead of schedule, pouring ancient odium upon terrified victims that soon discovered my solemn obstinacy. Before long, I led others under my command to deprive combatants of life, serving my darkened dreams as if I were a god.

After eight years giving into blind rage and beating myself harshly, nothing I did ever brought her back. Rather, my hatred only served to further me from love. Not from Mona but someone else, my true one, the true jewel of my life and song of my dreams. The eternal essence of my soul I had lost to the annals of time, such that I no longer knew she existed.

I looked upon Heather's image overcome by sorrow, for here was another casualty of rebirth amnesia. How forbidding, I thought, is to love someone, for death quietly comes along and unjustly revokes a loyalty blessed to endure the bonds of time, vows obliviously replaced in the next life with someone else. I will re-embody again; but when I do, Mona and Heather I will not recognize, for we live in a world bent on subsisting blind to restless memories. I will therefore be at the mercy of destiny's journal, written into by so many.

Amarna's air force didn't allot me much time to reflect upon such matters, bombing our position thrice that afternoon with bioelectrical pathogens designed to shut down and get us off our suits, followed by pesky paralyzing neurotoxins; nothing a good plasma blast couldn't fix. No other unit on the wire was fired upon, implying we either held tactical leverage or Amarna wanted to take us alive. That evening, we would find out the real reason.

As the sun neared the horizon, our CO, First Sergeant Johannes Gantz, sat alone, admiring reddish skyline hues. Bright blue eyes commanded highest discipline, often interrupted by waving gray hairs that consistently failed to inspire its master. A morbid gaze complemented clasped hands, resting forcibly on his legs. His sunburnt face gently leaned forward, not in prayer but inner torment, concealing profound anguish.

He stared at family pictures hanging from his tags with wistful demeanor, knowing I subtly sought his attention. But as usual, he didn't make visual contact. Rather, he asked briskly, "What is it, Sergeant?"

"Ready to cross the wire and get some, sir," I said aggressively.

"I know," he replied grudgingly, never taking eyes off his tags as if silently begging for notice.

I remained glued in place by sheer curiosity, excusing my presence to the fact I had not yet been dismissed. Boldly, I asked, "Sir, if you don't mind my asking, is that family?"

Surprised by my question, he raised his head as if something connected within. With a brief aloof smile, he asked if I had a wife. Stiffly, I replied I did, at one time. Nodding back with tight lips in agreement, he said, "Who does anymore? I wonder if I could have done more to protect mine. When chugs attacked Hamburg shelters, my wife was working there, unconcerned for her safety. I was in Bulgaria fighting Amarna's cloned armies and never thought she was in danger. To this day, I don't know where she is or how she died. Fritz, my youngest son—I don't know where he ended up either."

"This is Fritz," he said, showing me his picture. "Fine kid, a marine Private. Loved science, never did anything dreadful except chew pencils. He vanished along with millions during the reaping. One night, he and several friends went to a marine ball, but none made it back."

Amarna's twisted mind aimed to eradicate females and turn youth into monstrous beasts to feed his wicked crusade. I figured Fritz was exposed to one of Amarna's nerve agents, perhaps by ingestion, later activated by inaudible waves. Those affected felt an irresistible urge to travel into alliance territory, where they were incorporated into Amarna's war machine.

"He's out there somewhere, cursed to trek these sands by night like some evil ghost, depriving souls of their right to live," he said with certainty, making strong motion to bring our conversation to an end. "I won't let him go like that. That will be all, Sergeant. You're dismissed."

I saluted and turned about, but he suddenly stood up and called me back, "Sarge, I want you to do something for me," he asked with mystifying trust, warily guarding deep sentiments unsuitable for his rank. "If I don't make it, find my son, take him to Benghazi Ops, and notify his older brother Frederick in Hamburg—if he's still alive."

Reasoning with a mentally controlled beast, in my opinion, was out of the question, much less recognize Fritz had he turned into one. It took chutzpah to stand in front of a bewildered creature, hypnotized to take you under, and ask its name—utter suicide. Not to mention, one of them things took Mona from me. My scheme was rather simple: put it down, then ask questions.

"That's a tall order, sir," I replied. "Considering what these things did, I'm not inclined to risk my life, or that of fellow marines, to save a chug."

"I know, Sarge. My wife is also gone; my son is one of them. What more can you hate? The safety of marines is a priority, but think about who's inside those bodies; they are hostages, not combatants. Our orders are to save imprisoned civilians before ourselves, and that's just what these things are. And if I find a way to save Fritz, then we'll have a way to save many others. But if it comes to putting him under, then so be it."

"I understand, sir."

"Tell him it's time to go home . . . or we'll bust his chops for going AWOL," he replied confidently, giving me a quick tap on the back.

"One more thing," he added. "I keep a DNA homing device in my right pocket. It will flash when you get within twenty meters from Fritz, assuming there's enough unique genetic code left in him. Consider what he's been through and knows."

He left me to my thoughts, well aware that many misgivings haunted me, but not for long. It was time to push the spear tip further into alliance territory, certain to meet doomsday creations along the way.

That evening, we journeyed south along Amarna's projected eastern flank to acquire and contain alliance targets. The Moon, radiant and unruffled by petty Earth grumblings, journeyed through the sky, casting somber shadows on sands. Western skies glowed with colors of war, bearing gloomy lights that nimbly illumined the horizon for some time before vanishing. Faint roars permeated the dry desert air while traces of explosive chemicals descended upon the palette with distasteful appeal. We called it 'the taste of death.'

We pushed the wire about twenty five klicks south when Greg, monitoring for Amarna targets, stopped abruptly atop a large flat summit and said, "First Sergeant, thought I saw somethin about a klick due southwest, as if somethin really big got up, then dunked fast. There's nothin out there now."

"Did you make out what it was?" Johannes said.

"That's a negative, it was just a quick blip, somethin shaped like a really big potater. Whatever it was, it had to be bigger than a human and rather hot."

"Chugs, they're here," said Johannes resolutely with zealous confidence. "All right, we found what we were looking for. Get your gear out, check, recheck. Take as much out of the MAV as you can haul. I want a 3-60 defense perimeter decked with twenty pelt rippers. Everyone else, fall in behind them, launch gerbils, and hit flanks in front of our perimeter line. Set infrared sensors to max, weapons to kill, and fire only on my order. Fire-power has right of way, beasts don't. Now, move it!"

In spite of constant exposure to adversity and fear over the years, latent reluctance to harvest aggression's consequences impulsively roused, and death's reality coursed through our minds unopposed. Our hearts hit bottom for a moment, driven by dreadful ambiguity and a spirit averse to deprive itself of vive. Meanwhile, an eerie sense loomed amid the formless, murky eve as if we were being watched, so ominously that our sights helplessly perceived illusory moving shadows in darkness's compelling maze.

Sands were littered with fresh beast tracks leading to the summit's rim as if pointing the way to certain demise. In the sand trough just ahead, three beasts paced carelessly about, highlighted by glowing green eyes. They were sitting targets, our forces could easily overwhelm them, but something just didn't add up. How could they not know we were there?

Johannes, a cunning warrior, wasn't buying it either. "Decoys, it's a trap. We're not going down there," he said, hinting through hand signals we regroup on the south side of the rim and maintain high ground.

"Maybe that's what Amarna wants us to infer," I said.

"I'm not taking us down there. Everyone, back up real quiet."

As we backed away, a grunt tripped over something and fell down hard, making a pronounced metallic thump certain to alert beasts. But for some odd reason, they didn't rush us. Rather, they continued to pace senselessly as if nothing happened, hoping to draw our attention down there. Area scans showed no active heat signatures, but that eerie sense of being watched would not go away, prompting imaginative sounds and fearsome shadows to swell amid somber dunes.

Curious grunts hastily sifted sands looking for tripping objects and came across a thin pipe protruding out of the ground. Helmet sensors showed mild air rise, then fall back regularly from it. Knowing what this meant, one of the men repeatedly gasped unable to deny sheer panic, screaming, "Chugs!"

Fellow grunts tried to silence him, but he stepped forth and fired several rounds at the sand before being restrained. Blood and skin gushed up like a spouting geyser, ushered by loud echoing growls. And then, impulsive numbing silence dreadfully conquered the night with inaudible sorcery, just as deceptive as the calm before the storm.

Weapons on hand and ready to dispense death, we gazed tensely at our immediate surroundings unsettled by familiar suit servo sounds and rattling combat ordinance. The desert's mute whisper lingered mysteriously, its covert substance we could not hearken; grave menace we felt, looming secretly from life's distant margins. Something was undeniably lurking out there, hidden from view by gloomy veil, agley agents from life's mortal horizons, cloaked by eve's reticent realms.

Without warning, a brief plasma barrage suddenly struck our unit, forcing us to spread out and burrow into the sand for safety the best we could. Bright white-violet plasma rained harshly upon protective sand burrows, turning these into fulgurite upon contact. But then, just as mysteriously as it appeared, it hastily vanished, booming thunderous bellows across the desert until silence reigned again.

"Anyone hit?" Johannes said.

"No casualties or injuries to report," Greg said.

"I need something to shoot at," I said hastily. "You get no Purple Heart for being pinned down."

"Greg, scan and find them wenches," Johannes said.

"I got something," Greg said abruptly, "half a klick south, ten o'clock, top of that there tall sand dune."

"Can you ID that damn wench?"

"Well, I'll be a leanin possum. It's a mongrel."

"Friendly fire, out here? 2/7's five klicks from here," I added.

"Nope . . . it's Ravyn."

"How the hell did he get way out there?" Johannes said.

"And when," I said.

"Probably that last turn five klicks back," Greg said.

"Kojo, you were supposed to watch his six!" I added.

"I never saw him slip, sir," Kojo replied.

"He mapped our route to this spot. So . . ." Greg said.

"He knew just when to bail. Damn ratfink set us up. Ravyn, what the hell are you doing?" I said over the radio.

"Sanjeev," Ravyn replied, "you're surrounded and right where we want you. If you want to live, do exactly as I say, and no one will get hurt. So stay put and accept my superior's invitation."

"This is treason! Surrender now or suffer the outcome!"

"Not going to happen. And if you want to know what's out there, go ahead, make a move, but don't say I didn't warn you."

"We don't know what we're dealing with," Johannes said privately. "There could be a thousand chugs hidden from scans."

"Who cares?" I said. "When in doubt, empty your magazine. We can take on whatever they throw at us. You hear that, Ravyn?"

"Don't count on it," Ravyn replied. "Tonight, you'll meet foes a bit out of your league. Don't fight them unless you really believe in re-embodiment."

"That won't stop us from trying!" I shouted, but Ravyn did not reply.

Deafening growls suddenly echoed through the dark wasteland like malignant phantasms, summoned by vile powers haunting the living. "You hear that? That's your welcome wagon. Don't try anything stupid; you have no idea what you're up against."

"Ravyn, you're going down ahead of Amarna. Mark my words!"

"I'd love to chin wag, but my job here is done and Amarna is waiting. I leave you in good company but only if you behave. If you move or fight, you're as good as dead. Cheerio for now, I'll see you at the citadel," he replied, vanishing from our scopes.

"Not in this life," I replied, getting up, aiming zaps in Ravyn's heading and firing a half-dozen shells in spite of Johannes's advice. Loud explosions razed the remote steep sand dune flat. But when dust settled, Ravyn was nowhere to be found. Rather, off in the distance, a small jet aircraft hastily vanished to the southwest, presumably with Ravyn in it.

Moments later, countless luminescent green eyes surged across the desert as far as the eye could grasp, spreading their glows deep unto night's dismal darkness like a vast plush carpet set ablaze by green evil lanterns. Beasts in the trough swiftly jumped over the rim while others rose from concealment a short distance away, placing their fierce green eyes upon us.

Anxiety briefly set in at the sight of these imposing creatures programmed to put us under. Their meter-long hands and wide jaws could easily gnaw metal constructs apart. Their formidable strength could crush an aircraft with ease, and thick hide shielded them from standard ordinance, requiring multiple flares to penetrate it.

Crouching on all four, beasts readied to overrun our position, and a prompt decision was at hand; but Johannes placed me in charge of the unit, walked off tautly reviewing a strange device in private, and repeatedly called for Fritz. Without another thought, we opened fire, and rushing beasts dropped limp just before reaching our lines. No sooner, dunes came alive with wave upon wave of advancing emerald eyes as far as scanners could discern.

Ghostly shadows headed straight for our defense lines like a writhing swarm of army ants seething hastily over the sand. Swelling deafening roars marked their wave-style approach, looming ever closer in a concealing cloud of dust. Their thunderous numbers set off considerable sand slides on nearby steep dunes forcing our forward flanks to cluster back from the dune's edge.

With no time to lose, front lines opened fire on beast flanks, doubtful any of us would make it out alive. The gruff sound of pelters echoed continually across the desert, gushing out bright consuming plasma flares. Forward combatants rapidly fell in vast numbers briefly obstructing rear advance, but beasts pushed onward regardless, coming ever closer to our position.

Zaps accrued heavy rear formation casualties and blinded beast clusters struggling to move forward. Still, beasts kept surging in the distance, charging past fallen comrades and pushing the wire closer to our ranks such that we barely kept the upper hand in spite of salient precision momentum.

Aggressive shouts of war emerged over a field of callous corporeal defilement, duly testing any being's fidelity to valor. Our resolve boiled with striking courage, stirred by inherited synthetic motives designed by a sinister few—meant to silence any inkling of treason. In the heat of that trying moment, we bowed to a worldly god testing our sworn tenacity to overcome adversity and likewise merit honor.

Unexpectedly, beasts stopped on queue about fifty meters from our position, forming a circular verge around us. We were surrounded by hundreds of these five-meter-tall creatures under Amarna's control, but they did not attack. Surely, Amarna was up to something.

"Sanjeev," Johannes said, surprisingly coming forward.

"Grunts rearmed and good to dance some more," I replied.

"Chugs by the thousands, mass frontal wave attacks, no air support. It can only mean one thing: a gather and recruit raid."

"Reason we got bugged rather than bombed earlier this afternoon."

"Still, why us? Sarge, hold present positions and prepare for hand-to-hand combat. Chugs will leap from five meters out, so ensure rear support is ready to engage them and also deal with the mess that will make. Also, shoot zaps at front lines, not the rear. Their numbers cluster tighter as they near, so losses will be greater. We want obstacles slowing down their advance, not urging them forward. That will make it easier to pelt them."

Helos suddenly arrived on the scene from the south, flooding the ground with bright searchlights. "Drop your weapons and surrender immediately," said a highly accented voice from a loudspeaker. "Amarna promises you will not be harmed. He wants to talk to someone among you. If you don't, we'll let beasts overrun your small unit." We wondered who Amarna meant to talk to, but there was no time to think. Beasts slowly advanced toward us, and calls to surrender continued, forcing a hasty decision.

Each beast locked sights with one of us, assuring fearfully a willing executioner in waiting for the pending engagement. We reloaded, raised guard, and waited impulsively for orders. However, neither side committed to engage.

Johannes's cryptic DNA gadget suddenly blinked, and he marveled, joyfully reviewing beasts nearby. "Fritz," he yelled merrily several times. But with all the noise about, we thought he said "blitz," so we opened fire; and the deadly encounter begun, to Johannes's detriment.

The cold still night came alive with weapons fire reaching far and near. Aircraft were quickly brought down, but beasts proved much harder to acquire due to their incredible agility at close range. Pelter flares thundered piercingly across the sands like fiery knives, wounding hostiles straight through. Rear support showered the desert with flesh-scorching zaps. But our best efforts seemed futile, holding stern before enduring waves of roaring adversaries forging closer to our ranks.

Combat intensified near our front lines, close enough for soaring claret fluids to veil our visors and bodily fragments strike exo-suits, some massive enough to impose serious injuries and partially weaken defense lines. We rotated those injured to the rear and held the line while beasts struggled to rack up spoil by any means possible before meeting their fated lot.

Then suddenly, front lines yelled "Incoming!" as leapers hurled their massive forms against our perimeter, crushed several gunners in their path, and gravely compromised defenses. Dozens of beasts trampled over ruptured defense ranks and poured hastily through gaping holes on our eastern flank while others leaped over remaining pelters trying to overrun rear support. They mashed anything in their path, and brisk hand swipes sent men flying through the air to certain demise, mostly disfigured. But they proved gawky and conflictive, giving us the edge.

Once inside our perimeter, beasts seemed confused, as if desperately searching for something, but at the same time sorely distracted from active engagement. Rear units had no problem mopping them back and reinforcing the line until the last beast fell and stillness finally reigned supreme.

Sooner than expected, living forms conceived by gods of war piled feebly across foreign soils deprived of the breath of life. The stench of cindered, rotting flesh permeated the air, overshadowing somber remains in a manmade killing field that stretched far into moonlit horizons. Six fallen grunts and thousands of beasts laid still, lives sacrificed for vague human ideals.

We strolled about the sands in celebratory gala acting overly motarded, totally oblivious to lingering menace. It was a victory to be proud of, yielding record beast kills and still walking away for the most part alive. Conversely, this seemed like one of Amarna's worst coordinated offensives. Everything about it was an outright blunder, oddly. Amarna rarely messed up, especially this bad, though we didn't mind it. For the moment, we confidently tended survivors in the field, reveling our rare triumph undaunted.

Johannes turned up missing at first, but we eventually found him near the line, covered head to toe with hefty beast remnants. As we helped dig him out, an unusually large beast, originally from the trough I took for dead, silently grabbed me tight and silently rose up. Fellow grunts quickly aimed weapons on the beast, yelling and threatening it to put me down, but it wouldn't.

"If you fire, I will crush him," said the beast in a raspy, intimidating voice as marines surrounded and kept weapons on it, though unsure what to do.

"Don't listen to it. Shoot us both," I said.

"Can't obey that order, Sarge," said a grunt.

"That's not your concern, Julio," I said. "Don't compromise the mission. Get it over with! Do it!"

"Hey, cupcake, how ya want yur chops done, medium or rare?" Greg said, limping from a leg and firing at its legs to keep it from running off. "Got ya'll mad, don't I? That's it, chum, point them butt-ugly BCGs this way. I got all ya need and don't want ya doin without. Tell ya how this works, sweetie; put guy in bunny suit down, and we'll all get along."

"I got what I came for," said the bleeding beast, squeezing me tighter until I yelled, "This is not your fight, so back off!"

"You better do as he says, LC," replied a grunt.

"Chavdar, in the ring, it's best to give than to receive [5]. If ya don't give now, you'll never get Sarge," Greg said.

Suddenly, Johannes partly freed himself and yelled, "Hey, scheiße kopf, where do you think you're going?" The beast looked full tilt at Johannes just as he fired a sustained blast at its head, taking a toll on flesh and blood. Startled, the creature stepped back disoriented and released me. But surprisingly, it didn't die. Instead, it moaned briefly before plummeting to the ground dazed.

"There ya go," Greg said. "What goes up can come down."

"I want six whoopers containing and shielding that zero, fire on my word!" Johannes said. "This chug isn't going anywhere. Everyone else, tend the wounded, reload, and set up 3-60 watch. Move it! Are you all right, Sanjeev?"

"Calcium's a bit low, otherwise fine," I said, regaining offensive position.

"What are we doin with this chum?" Greg added.

"Putting it on layaway for intel extraction," Johannes said.

"We're what? That's insane. Only Amarna can get through to them things. Anyone else trying that ends up dead."

"We have an opportunity to gather intel. You a problem with that?"

"It can also be a death trap," I said.

"What this chug knows can help us win the war and save thousands of lives, maybe even your own. Someone get over to the MAV and bring me some electric straps to tie it down with. Snap to it!"

Suddenly, Johannes's mysterious DNA device blinked again. Surprised, he immediately panned the desert, looking for a matching source. But whenever the device pointed at the dazed beast, signal strength increased. He marveled anew and readily digressed from duty's immediate matters, slowly moving toward the beast wholly undaunted in night's cloaking darkness.

"Sir, chug is not restrained!" I said, concerned about his safety.

"I'm aware of that," he quickly replied. "Keep men back. I'm approaching bogey alone."

"What about those straps?"

"I don't need them. Just watch my six."

"First Sergeant, your objective is highly irregular and risky . . ."

"I know what I'm doing, Sarge, so back off."

"Sir!"

"That's an order, Sergeant!"

In spite of my warnings, Johannes approached the beast confident and unafraid, so close his suit resonated in unison with the creature's deep breaths. Its massive heart slowly pounded aloud as a menacing reminder of sheer burly power, pulsing Johannes's hand resting upon it. We kept weapons fixed on the creature, aware it could unexpectedly wake up and fatally injure Johannes who stood vulnerably close to it.

The beast cast its drained emerald eyes upon Johannes and moaned feebly. In return, Johannes opened his visor, fixed his eyes upon the creature, and gently caressed its dark purplish hide. "What have they done to you?" he said tenderly, but the beast didn't respond. "Do you recognize me? I'm here to rescue you. Come on, Fritz, snap out of it."

Johannes's sudden passive stance with such dangerous adversary and his peculiar shift in mission objective took us completely by surprise. Previously galvanized by victorious, epic combat, we were impulsively angered by his handling of the situation, surging emotive quarreling among us.

"Sir, bogey is hot and remains an active threat," I said hastily. "We can't let our guard down, much less contain or debrief this thing."

"You think a single chug is much of a threat against two dozen marines?" Johannes said. "You sound ate up, so let the dog out."

"With all due respect, I seriously question whether First Sergeant's passive actions and the risks these implicate are in line with mission objectives."

"Concern noted. That will be all! Speak up, Fritz, or I'll bust your chops," he said frustrated, failing to get the beast to respond.

Gradually, urged by Johannes, the beast raised its large head slightly and lent a few short growls, struggling to regain its sense of reason. Its big glowing eyes leisurely panned the area looking for something, shouting an indistinct name in a deep raspy voice. Unable to locate what it was looking for, it pounded the sand and growled fiercely, locked sights with Johannes, and swung its arms aggressively—but missed.

"I don't like the looks of this," Greg said. "You're too close to bogey. Pull back. We got your zero."

"Cap it, LC. I don't need your opinion," Johannes said, anxiously trying to get through to Fritz but to no avail.

"Talking to it is mere goat ropin. You're just pissing it off more, and someone's gonna get whacked if we don't torch it."

"Rip it before it reactivates!" I replied quickly.

"Delay that order!" screamed Johannes, dodging repeated beast blows.

"Negative, First Sergeant!" I yelled boldly. "Bogey won't respond to verbal exchange. It's hard to kill and a threat to this unit!"

"Are you refusing to follow a direct order, Sergeant?" asked Johannes angrily, trying to stay just out of the beast's range.

"Call it what you will! Your personal crusade places marine lives into a Charlie Foxtrot, and your behavior demands a 1-38!"

"You're out of line, marine! Do your job, and I'll do mine!" Johannes replied hastily with authority.

"You're critically compromised by a family situation, prejudice to good order, and unresponsive during hostile conflict! I find you derelict in the performance of duty and question your ability to lead these marines!"

"You just got page 11! Another word, and I'll have you court-martialed!" he said irately. Meanwhile, the beast swung its large powerful arms tirelessly at Johannes and writhed frenziedly to stand up but stumbled back to the sand every time unable to regain definite footing.

"I stand my ground! We are RECON, not pet search and rescue!"

"I have orders to control a chug, and someone I know is my best chance for success! So shut your blow-hole or be subject to restraint!"

"I know nothing about that order!"

"That's not my problem!"

"I relieve you of command on grounds of endangerment and dereliction!"

"And you're under arrest! LC, disarm and restrain Sarge!"

"With all due respect, no can do, sir," Greg said, calmly standing down.

"You want to be charged with insubordination?" Johannes said angrily.

"We all agree. You've been compromised, and that thing must die."

"Not on my watch! Who said this is a damned democracy?"

Unexpectedly, the beast leaped to its feet without warning, quickly swung its right arm, and connected with Johannes, gashing off the front section of his exo-suit. The blow hurled him far on his back unconscious, gravely cleaving his torso and face from which life's waters streamed forth without regard.

Without a moment to lose, we fired at the beast's legs to stall its thrust and gathered about Johannes who remained impassive on the ground. Dozens of plasma blasts lit up the beast like a flare in the night until it buckled to the sand, stricken by multiple wounds. But surprisingly, its injuries swiftly healed.

"Sarge, ya see that?" Greg said.

"It's still alive and just healed itself," said a grunt, rather dismayed.

"Sanjeev," the beast said suddenly, "witness my latest creation and the new indestructible adversary you will face going forward. It will also adapt to pelting. So go ahead, pelt it; it will only make it stronger."

"What do you want?" I said.

"Let this beast bring you to me. If you don't, I'll set it lose on your puny marines, including you!"

"What do you want from me?"

"No questions. Are you coming?"

I had a tough decision to make and no time to stop and think. In that desperate moment, Johannes's orders and Amarna's threats persisted loudly. Any way I looked at it, evading Amarna's grasp seemed impossible. But just then, I noticed two lobes pulsing in the beast's neck, the only place we had not hit yet, and had an idea.

"All right, I'll come willingly. Just don't hurt my men," I said.

"Arrangement accepted," replied the beast, "for now."

"Sanjeev, ya crazy bastard!" Greg said. "Gotta pelter right here!"

"You heard him; it will just make it stronger."

"That's a crock of coon latte! Don't trust him!"

"I know what I'm doing. This feels right."

"That's what chief thought!"

"I can't ignore Amarna's warning. You want a million pelter-resistant critters to deal with?"

"Why does it have to be ya? Who knows what they wanna do to ya?"

"That's not important. Report our situation and keep the fight going. I'm making you corporal and placing you in charge of the unit. Call up Doc at 2/7, have him come take care of the chief."

"I'm getting tired of waiting!" said the beast, pacing slowly toward me.

"Just hold on! Corporal, never give up the fight," I said, saluting and giving him a particular hand sign. Meanwhile, the beast came up close and lowered itself to the ground.

Greg returned the salute, nodded in agreement, and said, "I understand completely. We'll see you around, jarhead."

"Get on his back, and don't try anything foolish," said Amarna through the beast. "I'll be watching your every move."

"This better work," I said to Greg, pacing slowly to the beast's right side, eyes glued on its throbbing neck. Likewise, the beast's piercing emerald eyes watched my every move, never blinking.

Then swiftly, my suit locked onto the beast's right lobe and fired a sustained blast. Instantly, the beast yelled long in agony; lobes sparked brightly to a halt, and the creature surrendered its head to the sand as if dead with eyes barely open—turn of events everyone praised in relief.

"When in doubt, the head's always the weakest link," Greg said, stepping my way. "Since no one uses it anymore, they'll soon evolve out of the gene pool. How's the chief?"

"Hurt bad. Radio still jammed?"

"Nope, it's hot."

"Julio, call up 2/7, get Doc off his rubber bitch, double snap! The rest of you, tend the wounded and reinforce our perimeter. There could be more of them out there! How are the wounded?"

"Med kit's makin its rounds. They'll fight another day."

"How many?"

"Six dead. Chief's getting weaker. Other than stop leak, can't do a thing until Doc gets here."

"Might be too late by then."

"Leave me behind," Johannes said barely conscious. "Doc's no use."

"You have to hang on for Fritz," I said.

Taking my right arm, he entered a code into my suit's control pad and lit up chevron E-7, surprising me. "Get through to him, Gunny."

Unexpectedly, the beast regained consciousness and partly opened its eyes, earning our immediate attention. Taking a deep breath, it feebly moaned, "Oh, mein Kopf" and stumbled slowly to its knees, wrath subsided.

"Fritz," Johannes whispered softly, struggling to stay conscious.

The mighty beast froze when it heard the name and looked at Johannes as if it knew him. Its large fingers slowly reached for his dog tags, stared at Fritz's picture, and gently raised Johannes unto its long arms, wailing desperately. I didn't know what to think until it said *vater* in a low chilling voice. Then I knew, this creature was really Fritz. He stared my way unsure what to do, but destiny swiftly seized Johannes away to realms where we had no sway.

Johannes slightly opened his eyes and said, "I knew I'd find you. You need bigger clothes." Fritz chuckled sobbingly as Johannes held on to life as long as possible. "Gunny, get him to MPP. Fritz, we need intel. Use device, find—"

Johannes silently placed his sights yonder and exhaled, fastened the windows of his soul to rest, and leaned motionless upon Fritz's arms who bellowed anxiously for someone to help; but there was nothing we could do to infringe upon life's gates.

"This was Amarna's doing, not yours," I said. "We'll get him. It's just a matter of time. Meanwhile, we must get you off the track for debriefing."

"How will people react when they see me?" he said. "If I don't scare them to death at first, hatred will eventually consume them. I'll never be trusted or accepted; that's what I look forward to."

"Amarna didn't give you much of a choice, except death. We're offering you a chance at MPP to get back to normal and help end this war."

"I remember everything I did under Amarna's control, things I can't get off my mind. I killed tens of thousands, leveled towns from Cairo to Moscow, destroyed staple resources that starved millions. You don't know what it's like to live with those memories."

"Yes, I do. I lost my wife, family, and soul, all because of one man's twisted apocalyptic fantasies. You think you have daunting memories? Try mine or these marines here."

"Do me a favor. Fire a sustained blast at my neck until both implants burst. It's the only way this madness will end."

"Was that some kind of joke, eight ball?" I said loudly, staring at him with burning eyes as he lowered his head shamefully. "Answer me, you turd wrangling, overgrown dimwit!"

"I can't accept protection after what I did. What if Amarna reactivates me?" he replied dimply.

"Now listen here, you spoiled, swine-tail kissing coward," I said fiercely, boldly stepping up to him like a drill sergeant, bashing his head with my arm weapon, and placing a micro-transmitter into his head. Meanwhile, fellow marines gathered about to see what was going on.

"That's the vilest insult I've heard coming from someone claiming to be a marine because we never throw in the towel! That hideous head of yours been jammed up your keister aerating all that rarefied air for too long. So pull it out of that filthy, decomposing blowhole and get real, you moron! Come to attention and get your heinie up, cry baby! Have you no respect for rank?" I yelled, but he wavered slowly up.

"You're no marine but the worst festering, deformed, five-meter pile of crap I've had the pleasure of personally smelling! And for your lack of bravery, you deserve the best colonic impalement imaginable! I've never seen a marine dishonorably break down and wail like some wounded girly road-kill or wriggle like a broken hearted sweetheart, not until today! Who was the CS genius that signed you up into my dearly beloved world corps? I'd like to pump steel up his stopped-up moosh also!

"Your intel can save millions of marine lives. But no, you'd rather betray and watch these brave marines drop dead instead of Amarna, don't you?"

"That's not what I meant, sir," replied Fritz fretfully.

"Shut your flute, carper! Where's your sense of sacrifice?" I said, peering intensely into his large stressed eyes. "Don't flash distress signals with your drawers like some frail damsel squealing for rescue. You insult these brave men and women that gave it all to save your oversized butt."

"I understand, sir," Fritz said halfheartedly.

"That's 'sir, yes, sir' to you, Fritzo. Loud, not like a pet squeak mating call!"

"Sir, yes, sir!" he replied mildly.

"Did any of you guys hear that pin drop?"

"Sir, no, sir!" replied gathered marines.

"Your kisser constipated, sweet cakes? I didn't ask for a whisper, princess!"

"Sir, no, sir!" he replied with a roar that made the ground quiver.

"Marines specialize in ass kicking, and if you haven't noticed, our industry is doing great these days! We don't know the meaning of fear or surrender. Rather, fear runs from us like a bat out of hell! Even the devil trembles when he sees us overrun his perimeter and outflank, outgun, outwit, outrun, and outright fold his top brass demons just by looking at them! A marine is the deadliest weapon on Earth, but I question if you're really one!"

"I am, gunny, sir!" replied Fritz emotionally.

"Then prove it! Death is stronger than fear, but these marines are stronger than death because, tonight, they bravely overcame it! I won't let some wimpy liver stand in hallowed presence and contaminate valor incarnate! What would your father say if he found out, after the epic sacrifice he just made, that you're nothing but a yellow wussy? He overcame fear and death, so tell me how you'll do better. For your sake, I suggest you do!"

Fritz didn't answer right away. Instead, he boiled in silent anger before his father, reflecting deep credit on his shameful conduct and blatant disregard for Articles one and two. "His sacrifice won't be for nothing!" Turning to a smoldering aircraft, he pulled a flashing box from it, crushed it, and hurled it far into the night with a roar. "I'm Private Fritz Gantz, a world marine, and I will make my father proud!"

Fritz stood by his father, and said, "Gunny, sir, I've been ordered to MPP, but I can't leave the wire. You need me here, not sheltered in some military compound. If you think you're winning the war, think again; Amarna deceived you into believing you are. He has countless offensive deterrents no one has a clue about, all quite deadly. I know where he is and what these secret weapons are. Think twice about attacking the citadel because you're walking into a trap," he replied, earning my immediate attention.

"We beat everything Amarna's thrown at us. What don't we know?"

"Anyone approaching the citadel won't know what hit them."

"Some kind of new weapon?"

"More than that. Amarna has a secret base in Antarctica at coordinates 72°01' S, 26°04' E. There, he keeps his final solution." At the mention of Antarctica, the previous vision dawned with unique clarity. I felt compelled to share it with Fritz, but ultimately guarded its secrecy for good reason. If Fritz got probed, that knowledge would not be compromised.

"What's in that base?"

"Your worst nightmare. Amarna has craft that defy gravity, become invisible, and are nuclear resistant. He plans to unleash these craft once federation forces close in on the citadel—that is, if you make it past their cathode disintegrator array. Scan the area for iridium, and you'll pick them up. Don't attack the citadel until you destroy that base and the array. If you can't, then all is lost."

"What do you have in mind, Private?" I asked.

Any scoop on Amarna's operation was crucial to the war effort, but I was not prepared for what he offered next: insert and sabotage Amarna's C3 facilities, liberate fellow beasts, and prompt revolt. It was a dicey plan, but if he pulled it off, there was no telling the damage it would bring Amarna's citadel. But risk is what makes us marines, most upsetting when there's none.

Before leaving, Fritz placed Amarna's complex five klicks northeast of Rabyanah along the mountain's midwestern slopes, in an alcove five hundred meters wide by 1.5 kilometers long. The citadel was a kilometer underground, with escape routes within fifteen klicks. He cautioned me to be vigilant; what

Amarna wanted, he got, despite cost. His eyes were all over the desert, and nothing escaped his grasp.

Placing an empty exo-suit on his back to fool alliance monitors, he saluted his father and dashed away until lost to dark southern horizons, leaving behind a field of gloomy remains for sands to conceal.

"Ya beat up that corn bread pretty darn good," Greg said. "Ya sure lettin him go was such a good idear?"

"We have all the intel we need. Fritz is now a plug. All we have to do is track his movements."

"How ya figure doin that?"

"He doesn't know, but I implanted a probe into his head when I whacked him. We'll know where he's at and what he hears; pick him up on TP065."

"TP065 and . . . there he be. That dawg's doin eighty klicks. Got audio, video, and power windows. Smart move! Ya believe all he said, especially about Antarctica?"

"Already knew about it."

"Let me guess, that reborn thing."

"Keep your eyes and ears on Fritz. Stream audio video live to OPS."

My report on current citadel sabotage operations and information on the Antarctic base were received by HQ OPS with great excitement. Regrettably, my orders were to regroup our unit with the 2/7 "war dogs," then return to Gialo and transfer to Fox Company intel to help with curtain closure logistics.

We collected blood and skin samples left behind by Fritz for analysis. Hopefully, it would provide a means to counter Amarna's latest adaptive creations. The tracking device placed Fritz deep underground two klicks north of the citadel, and his movements helped map Amarna's subterranean world.

Right at o-dark-thirty, the war dogs showed up at our hooch, and Doc got to stitch people up. Three days later, I resupplied and started the long eighty klick trek back to Gialo in our old MAV, alone by choice, with only plausible ghosts to keep me company. Halfway up there, the MAV broke down, and I wondered through scorching Cyrenaica plains for about two days until I finally reached the southern Gialo palm fields.

When I entered the city, its sandy streets were strangely deserted, and unsettling stillness prevailed. People apparently fled hastily, leaving prized possessions behind and food served on the table. But in the center of town, signs of sizable struggle lingered, sorely reminding me of the Arcot massacre.

Fox Company's command complex was demolished. Lifeless combatants rested side by side amid smoldering vehicles. Leveled structures blocked passage ways and warded guests away. Just north, hundreds of civilians rested on the ground sorely burnt after vainly running for cover, probably victims of that new cathode weapon Fritz mentioned.

The alliance seemed determined to force the federation from the region, but it came at a hefty cost. Amarna committed hundreds of aircraft and beasts to the front line, even though the strategy placed enormous strain on thinning resources. Why he took such risks while suffering from supply shortages made absolutely no sense unless he was plowing open an escape route to the gulf.

Beast tracks led into a manmade pond to the north and vanished into it, leading me to believe the pond held a hidden alliance access tunnel. The shallow pond didn't seem all that uncommon, but Benghazi had me keep an eye on it nevertheless while reinforcements arrived—troops that never came.

To be on the safe side, I dumped as many heavy vehicles into the pond as would fit, hoping weight would foil attempts to use it. A nearby home served as base of operations, where I patiently waited for combat action. I packed the house and other fallback positions with heavy ordinance, setting up explosive traps around the pond and at key defensive flanks. But little did I know that someone kept a watchful eye on my every move.

Three uneventful days passed by. But on that final eve, something big loomed in the direction of Amarna's citadel, often emphasized by distant bright red flashes and blue aurora-like emanations—the signature of anti-matter ordinance. At about 0300 hours, powerful flares suddenly lit up southern skies like daylight. As flares dimmed, far-off red hues boldly stained the heavens, revealing morbid tales of adamant demise. And then, everything went dead quiet. Only dim red glows lingered, slowly billowing eastward.

An hour later, a jubilant OPS broadcast issued a stand-down address to all field officers; Amarna committed suicide, and his forces surrendered to world marines. Incredible as it seemed, this bloody ten-year conflict was finally over!

A new beginning was in store for a world torn by hedonistic odium currents, a rebirth kindled after wondering so dangerously close to extinction's abyss. But would history in time repeat itself? The scent of dreadful tears persists upon our ruthless nature like an unkind flower plagued by misgivings from past restless actions, simply because we know not ourselves. Man's worst enemy is not his past but his insensible fear and desire of it. Unless these respite as lessons, peace is unachievable, and memories will steer the present.

I spent two more days in Gialo doing nothing but think endless yarns about this long war and Fritz's whereabouts. He improvised like a true marine and set out to boldly conquer death in the face of danger. I had an oath to keep and had to find him, but little did I know he was closer than I thought.

I finally received orders to pack up and head north, so I picked up a working MAV from our old complex and prepared to leave first thing the next day. But during the night, mysterious burbling sounds got my attention. Water hastily drained from the pond and its bed nudged slightly, making objects above it tremble with twisting clatter, but weight kept it from rising.

Were alliance survivors planning to escape through Gialo? More troubling, was Amarna among them? Benghazi took my report as a prank and largely ignored it. Meanwhile, the pond continued to vainly discard whatever kept it down.

Zaps in hand, I anxiously came to the edge of the pond and stood ready to neutralize whomever was trying to crop up from it, unaware I was being watched. As the tunnel continued to push unsuccessfully upward, steel rods emerged from the sands, emitting a mild hissing sound. Without a helmet, I was quickly overcome by drowsiness and lost consciousness trying to retreat.

* * * * *

When I came to, I rested near the pond host to uncertain company. Footsteps from someone unknown hauntingly approached from behind, pleading I promptly break silence.

"You're headed the wrong way, maggot; the federation is up there," expressed a familiar accented voice I could not immediately place. "We must protect the Order's elite prospects, yes?"

Oblivious of the individual's identity, I turned slightly and to my indignant surprise, it was him: Amarna. Without hesitation, my right arm quickly swung his way and fired, but no blast came out; someone had drained my weapon.

"Looking for me?" Amarna said, wearing an exultant smile garlanded by a red-grayish uniform and uncontrollable sweat. He was a tall muscular man in his forties with blond curly hair and distant stares impressing callous dread on the living. Cold stanch blue eyes commanded utmost desire on a moment's notice and strictest discipline from his subordinates. His face described a man living for inexorable pride regardless of cost. In his presence there was no compromise, only blind servitude daring not confront his stanch will.

"Gunny Sanjeev Patel from Madras, India," he said casually. "I've been meaning to talk to you for quite some time, but you're a hard man to snag. One thing is certain: you won't be joining those pathetic marines anytime soon. You now belong to the Order."

As Amarna flaunted his intellect, I only imagined the new shady fate about to grip the world and what little I could do to prevent it from my humble vantage point. What else could this self-deluded soul think up next to destroy the living? I was about to find out.

Amarna partly stepped aside, and someone in a federation suit approached his side. I immediately recognized damage on the suit's front plate and knew who it was: Ravyn.

"Did you miss me?" he said, handing Amarna a control box of sort, but I remained quiet. "Look, lad, in a few days, your brain will get flushed, cyphered, and we'll both then be on the same team. You won't thank me enough for it."

As Ravyn walked away, Amarna activated the box and verbally ordered Fritz to step forth. Not far from us, a beast answered the call and approached in robotic motion. His stare solitary, breath trivial, he was a pitiful sight to behold. "Join me in bidding this marine goodbye," he said, playfully flouting pleads to spare his life. Fritz's neck briefly expanded, his eyes closed, head lowered, and body plummeted slowly to the ground where he rested motionless with no breath to give him life.

"This . . . thing sparked rebellion and destroyed my command center before I could shut him down. But I'm not defeated, far from it! Your futile plans merely caused a minor setback. Not to worry, I have other terrifying options at my disposal and I do intend to use them."

He smiled looking for support, but I refused to lend his twisted sentiments the pleasure. Noting my censure, he added derisively; "Only elite intellects like me have souls. Everyone else, like Fritz, is just flesh, driven by environmental animal instincts. So I put them to good use like domesticated animals; it's no different. All it takes is deception, some flesh, splicing, and cloning to create an invincible army. So who needs women anymore?"

Amarna leaned against a palm tree laughing at first senselessly, but soon billowed at some bizarre revelation. "It's so easy! I did all this with just a simple odorless gas that adheres to the nervous system like a virus and inducts my every command. It's the latest in communication, and it's completely biodegradable. Isn't that utterly ingenious?"

Speaking of communication, I suddenly had an idea: my helmet. If I could only activate the radio without getting caught, then Benghazi would confirm Amarna's escape. I slowly sat up, reached for my helmet nearby, discreetly activated the switch, and positioned it so the cam had a clear view of Amarna; I only hoped it wasn't disabled while I slept.

"I must admit you're an absolutely brilliant intellect," I said, subtly leaning over the helmet. He took extremely kind to my words, thanked me, and slightly brought down his guard. "You cheated death once more and here we are, in northern Gialo. The big question is: where will you go now?"

Oblivious of my dealings, Amarna replied completely unconcerned, "The war is far from over, and all is proceeding according to plan." As he touched other buttons, several gravity-defying craft rose out of the sands and made ready for takeoff. "These craft will ensure a swift undetectable get away to a backup command center in Cyprus stocked with millions of cloned dinosaur embryos. My future army looms, deadlier than anything ever encountered, and you will play a vital role in that future."

"Why do you insist in destroying innocent lives? What good can possibly come from it?"

"You should ask yourself that question because you were once one of us. You seem surprised; don't be. In previous lives, you were an expert in, shall we say, eliminating really big problems, bigger than this war even. You have unique talents, and that's why you're coming with us."

"Give me a good reason why I should trust you," I replied, though not questioning a deep feeling of guilt from his previous past reading.

"Ah, denial, the first sign of admission. No matter, you will know who you really are, or were, soon enough. As for me, my job is to depopulate billions of useless feeders, breed global unity through chaos, and deliver you to the Order. We designed this war over a century ago with global unification and scientific maturity in mind. The first three world wars were staging trials. The second inspired the development of final solution technologies. The third rid the world of history, religion, and ethics, paving the way for the Order's new tenets and cosmic conquest agenda.

"You are destined to become a prominent federation space minister, a beta that will promote the Order's agenda in the world senate and make the government subservient to us. It's all been arranged. If you don't, I have ways to persuade your compliance. Now that the world is united, the time has come for the Illuminati to take its rightful place among the stars."

"Your Order is responsible for murdering billions needlessly . . ."

"You didn't care back then for the lives of trillions! So why bother now with a few billion?" interrupted Amarna, though I still didn't want to believe him. "You fit right in with us. Where else can someone like you end up? You were the destroyer, a death specialist second to none, and you'll be so again.

"We are the only leadership worthy of ruling the world, the epitome of evolutionary perfection and rightful heirs of all things. We start wars, control emotions, economies, political agenda, crime, even fashions and music. Fear and desire are our best allies, and everyone's got some. That consistency makes our job rather easy. No one knows who we are, much less where and when, but feel the effects."

"We've been enslaved by monsters," I said stunned.

"A monster is technically an illusory creature, a powerless thing that thrives briefly in the minds of dreamers and then vanishes into whatever nothing it came from. The Order is not some brief dream; we're quite real and here to stay. The real monster is you. We once bred you to be a fearsome destroyer, and you can't aspire to anything else, maggot!"

The word "maggot" suddenly got my attention, mentioned many times by the German officer in my vision. "Maggot," I said, thinking things through.

"That's what people are, crawling in disgrace all over this world like some vulgar disease. Just say it bothers you and I'll arrange to see you—in Valhalla."

His response confirmed my deepest fears; Amarna was the re-embodied German officer. Matter of fact, I was still the same individual giving his secrets away and contributing to his fearsome inner fiend. With the past undeniably reenacting before us, I realized that arguing with him only fanned our negative past. Thus, I kept quiet, and didn't reply.

With assured, determined poise, Amarna pointed his arm weapon my way and said, "You're most wise. Arguing with me is futile. The time has finally come when you must pledge your solemn allegiance to the Order or pay the price for insolence! Make your choice—now."

"I will never join the Order," I fearlessly replied. "This pond, north of Gialo, suits me just fine for a place of rest. You may fire when ready."

Amarna, unprepared for my response, hesitated for a moment unsure what to do. His lips tightened, and raging menace overcame his being, yelling madly with bemused stare. His nose constrained inducing stifled heavy breathing. Teeth gnawed fiercely in absolute wrath exposing indomitable reprisal meant to exhume terror.

"You," he quivered irritably, though quickly deploying an attitude of sarcasm and silent wrath, "you will join the Order, but you will also be mine! You are special because you stand where others give up; that's why you've earned my admiration."

Placing hands on my shoulder, he caressed my face with repulsive intent. "Indian men are strong, refined, perfect; it's a shame we didn't meet sooner."

"Don't touch me," I said, moving sideways to evade his touch.

"We'll see about that," replied Amarna, ordering his men to remove my exo-suit and throw it, along with my helmet, into the pond. He took off his heavy coat, proudly demonstrating bare muscular chest and arms while sweat and odors poured profusely from his body.

"The desert is hot, isn't it?" he said, gazing upon me like a starved predator ready to pounce on game with malicious intent. "It's about to get even hotter," he said, arrogantly bragging his physique.

"I lived the life of Emperor Nero," he said, moving daringly close to me without scruple. "I admire that man, so candid and yet so . . . distinguished."

Putting his forehead against mine, he said, "You are my long-lost Petronius Arbiter, my judge of elegance and voluptuary inspiration, endowed with reckless frankness and pure dissolute wonders. Excel in sensual appetites as he once did by my side, for we belong together."

"Whatever little I know about Arbiter makes me sick to my stomach."

"Your life is in my hands!" he said with great assurance at first. But then he softened, seductively touching me as I backed away. "I am twenty times the woman you had, so don't resist me. The entire world and all its wonders can be yours. Together, we will take over the world and rule it to a glorious future. We can become an example to the rest of the galaxy and conquer it, conquer the universe. This I offer you, if you would only care for me."

"And if I refuse?"

"You can't refuse me," he replied sharply. "No one can!"

Amarna's breathing strengthened, his desires determined to climax. His face sparkled with personal uncontainable yearning for pleasure, bringing terror to my soul. "You are mine, maggot. Don't delay the inevitable," he said desperately. "Release yourself to me with that candor men are known for."

"That will never happen!"

"Of course it will," he replied, striking my face with outright malignant forthrightness. "It's already happening, can't you tell? You can't debate with me. It would be futile, for I am a superior being to your kind."

He slapped me several more times and proceeded to tightly caress my face. "Be with me the nice way, or rot to the earth maggot you are."

"You can only force me, but never convince me!" I said defiant, yet consumed by utter dread.

"I like that in a man!" Amarna quickly jumped on me growling like a cat, kissing my left cheek with insatiable, trembling desperation. His passionate despair for lust mounted and breathing quickened, giving himself into perverted, imaginative pleasures.

"You will be mine, Petronius. I must have you. It's my destiny. Feel my body. It will be beside you for a lifetime." His eyes shone with unshaken conviction, mine with terror. His heart trusted the veracity of secret possessive desires, fatally surrendered to subliminal fantasies. He was merely a deceived sensual slave of his own making, altered by indulgent unrecognized addiction. Nature's veritable instincts had left this man, now ruled by contrived deceptive delusions seeking to be served from memories that know no rest.

Amarna's strength was formidable, rendering me helpless on the ground without much effort. He braced my terror-laden face still with one hand, sadistically nearing his complacent countenance to mine. His fingers clamped my cheeks, forcefully opening the lips such that only a mild whimper exhaled. His warm breath was upon mine closer than comfort allowed. Like a cat playing with its meal, he taunted my ability to escape his clasp and sarcastically joked about it. There seemed no hope for deliverance. My soul agonized amid certain bodily defilement, witnessed by willingly mocking officers.

Suddenly and without warning, massive blasts roared near our position, jolting Amarna from me. Gialo came under surprise artillery attack seemingly from all directions, but its source remained a mystery. Powerful plasma blasts rained down arbitrarily, setting aircraft and supplies ablaze. Beasts and soldiers swung helplessly through the air, imputed by potent flares and lethal shrapnel. Bright fireballs emerged from blown alliance depots, spreading across the oasis without regard. The air burned with an intense scent of asphyxiating ozone, and airborne sand blinded any fighting spirit's will.

Amarna shuddered, unsure what to do. His forces, sorely confused, sought safety within oasis confines, but there was no place to hide. Death was upon us, delivered by an invisible foe whose presence could only be felt. Unable to gather intelligence or regroup, Amarna's forces could only brace for chance under an unstoppable heavy barrage, bringing upon them imminent demise.

Wingless craft, similar in design to Amarna's discs, materialized out of thin air, dashing rapidly about and surrounding badly confused alliance forces. These were remarkable craft, marvelous to behold, and swift as ancient Vimanas. An invisible shield surrounding the craft repelled incoming fire and served as a weapon, turning matter into powerful ionized plasma bursts.

Amarna, caught totally by surprise and caged by federation forces, came to an abrupt decision and headed back to the tunnel, holding me at gunpoint. But as we reached it, a craft hovering nearby opened fire and destroyed it. He ran desperately about without heading or reason, dodging plasma fire and exploding ordinance only to find advancing marine flanks closing in on every front. Surrounded and with no means of escape, he quivered anxiously and cried out, "Verräter, Verschwörer, Maden" to imaginary individuals about him, assessing the reality of defeat in disbelief.

Regaining authoritative poise, he stood proudly before imminent destiny, holding his head regally and anxiously smiling with triumphant gleam without reason, except by Order protocol. "You're now with the Order," he said, "the most powerful intellectual society in the world. Be proud. Fail them, and you will die, now and in future lives!"

Cobalt suits stepped through fiery curtains and approached from all directions, arms raised ready to fire in perfect marching cadence. Marines suddenly stopped, dropped in tandem to their right knees with a loud "oorah" cry, and aimed weapons our way. Green lasers spotted our bodies, but Amarna did not back down. Instead, he yelled, "Abbas alpha, recolitus beta. Ego usus quis vos volo!"

His call went unanswered, so he tried again, "Abbas alpha, es vos illic?"

Lonesome silence lingered amid cracking fires, but Amarna was undeterred. "Father alpha, operation Fox Run is a success, and Mercury is ready to deliver the package. What you're looking for is in my hands!"

"Amarna," said a marine, "drop your weapon and raise your hands—now!"

"No, tin man," he replied. "You all back off, or Sanjeev dies!"

"Don't be a fool," I said to him. "You're dealing with federation marines. They won't let you go. If I die, you will die also."

"You don't know the power of the Order," Amarna said confidently. "They are millions strong, and anyone can be an agent. We watch over each other and always have a plan. Today, the world shall bow to our superior minds, daunted by an intelligence far from mortal grasp. They're out there—I know it—and they've come for us. Watch for a sign, beta Sanjeev. That's where we must go."

"Did you ever think you might be expendable?" I said.

"The Order never abandons their kind. The Order is family, performance, perfection. Watch for feet pointing the way."

Amarna panned marines close by, ignoring calls to surrender. But as he looked to his left, two grunts joined the line from the right and tapped their feet. Exo-suit damage gave away the identity of one of them: Ravyn. Between us, the sand churned slightly, and I surmised it was another alliance escape burrow. If so, I had to think fast before Amarna saw it and escaped.

Hastily, I caught a grunt's attention, pointed to Amarna's feet with my eyes and foot, and nodded. He acknowledged my proposed diversion and waited to fire on my signal. I anxiously gathered strength and counted silently.

On three, I closed my eyes to avoid flying sand and spun to a side. Simultaneously, the grunt fired a blast near Amarna's feet. Not expecting this action and focused entirely on escape, he immediately jolted as a cloud of sand flew into his eyes and briefly loosened his grip, long enough for me to jump into action.

I fiercely swung at Amarna's ribs and jaw several times, causing him to grumble from agonizing pain and bend to my mercy. Fellow grunts urged me on, but Ravyn, seeing Amarna lose control, immediately stood up and readied to fire. Anticipating Ravyn's reaction, I placed Amarna in Ravyn's zero to shield myself and continued striking him until he offered no further resistance. Swiftly taking Amarna's feeble right arm, I turned and fired a sustained blast at Ravyn, instantly consuming him.

Amarna, though in pain, would not give up and ineffectively fought back until he tired and rendered his left arm free. I placed it hand up over my shoulder, and said, "This is for Mona" and forced the elbow back as far as it would go, producing a brief shattering sound.

Amarna instantly yelled in agony taking few steps back, though never losing sight of me. Marines instantly rushed to apprehend him, but he quickly recovered and aimed his arm weapon at me up close. Everyone froze in place, waiting to see what Amarna would do; but he just stood there staring at me, sobbing like a child overcome by chattered dreams.

"Maggot, traitor, you're not going anywhere if I don't command it," he screamed, his eyes mixed with tears and sand. "Tell me why, Arbiter. What does it take for you to love me willingly? Don't you know what I mean to you?"

Weakened by bashing, I easily pushed his right arm away. "This is for Johannes, Fritz, and six dead marines," I said, kicking his right knee inward, breaking it with a quick sharp cracking clatter. He fell to the ground in earnest anguish, crying and rolling desperately on the sand like a frantic child after belting. Meanwhile, marines surrounded Amarna and advised him to concede.

"Why deceive me, Arbiter?" he said in agony. "I love you, can't you tell?"

"Your love is polluted by twisted material abominations," I said, as marines restrained him, though he continued yelling out orders to nonexistent officers. "Lost to yourself and without godly intelligence, you engaged in unbeneficial, horrible works meant to destroy, not foster, humanity."

I turned my attention away from Amarna for a moment and went looking for the churning spot, but I lost track of it. Without appreciable identifying marks, every sand parcel looked no different than the other. After searching in vain, I gave up looking for it. As for the tapping grunt at large, they all looked alike as well, though I soon suspected everyone to no avail.

"Gunny, sir," said a corporal with a peculiar American accent, hiding his identity behind a helmet, "Amarna is neutralized and under marine control. Welcome back." I thanked the grunt, though I was in for a surprise when he said, "Do I get that good cookie now, lifer?" he said, pointing to my undies and ordering a fellow woofer to bring my exo-suit over."

"Can't be, dog jerky!" I said, giving him a hug. "Last I knew, you were limping. And here you are, trying to live forever. When will you give that up?"

"Doc patched me up with some of that—what's it called—emmo-tolerant somethin splicin whatever, and I feel good as new. It's really hard to die nowadays, thanks to Amarna when you think of it; it's his technology. And this thing about fightin nude, I hope it never turns into an article."

"What's with these discs. Where did they come from?"

"Don't know, but ain't they great? They get ya there in no time and no travel sickness. So fast I can go get Granny's toilet water and be back in time for lunch! Well, gunny, this is it. What I really mean to say is—goodbye."

"So this is it for you then?"

"Yep, this is it. I bought me and my ex a place in Tennessee few years back in a small town called Big Ivy, just down river. Nice place and folks. Coons are pets, beavers contracters, and overalls mandatory. And the corn bread, it's to die for. Not to mention, them southern belles sure know how'ta put one or two in ya. They'll be needin a preacher out there someday, and I wanna sign up for the part. I hope future Sullivan generations keep that legacy goin. Why don't ya swing on by and stay with me and my surviving boy? We can talk about re-embodiment, and I can make a convert out of ya yet."

"Just remember, as certain as death comes to the born . . ."

"Yep, I know. Birth is also certain for the dead. I'll think about it. Well, see ya'round, gunny. Been a pleasure servin with ya."

"Same here. I'll be there," I said grasping his arm. "Count on it, dog jerky."

"Watch it, Maharaja. I get all mushy at times like this."

"It's never the wrong time for that. That's what we're really made out of, but we foolishly hide it. Return with honor, get your pulpit back, and change the world. But never forget what we've been through, so it never repeats again." After a strong arm shake, he was off to help with mop-up operations and I remained still as one of these magnificent craft landed nearby.

From it, the marine in charge emerged, saluted, and thanked me for a job well done. I found it hard to explain why I was in the buff and stressed apologies, but she replied, "You improvised and overcame, whatever gets the job done. Your quick thinking finally got Amarna apprehended," making brief account of it.

"You got my message."

"And we tracked Fritz moving north toward Gialo an hour before the citadel was destroyed. Your helmet video confirmed our suspicions."

"New aircraft," I asked, suiting up. She explained that American scientists achieved levity a hundred years prior in response to growing alien craft sightings and lingering threats from Nazi disc programs but kept it a tightly guarded secret. These ships proved their worth in the last days of the war, successfully destroying Amarna's hangars, the citadel, and thwarting his last escape attempt. But no one counted on the fact that the alliance had an even larger hangar on the moon, cleverly hidden by complex ridged flanks on Copernicus.

As the Antarctic battle dawned to a close, federation forces were unexpectedly attacked by a new foe, descending fiercely over southern polar skies from the lunar outpost. Unbeknown to the world, secret titans spread across the heavens stirring death—like wingless firebirds seeking vengeance. Warned of their approach, federation ships quickly surrounded the lunar fleet and took the fight to the moon. Overcome by superior numbers and tactics, alliance forces surrendered and the lunar base was promptly impounded.

News of Amarna's demise spread fast across the globe, sparking jubilant festivities in every state. Calls for government reform brought about the end of strict secular legislation, and a new one-world charter devoted to education and scientific prosperity was being drafted. Civil affairs was disbanded. The military was turned into an unarmed police force. Worship halls were once again open to the public, and library materials were no longer censored. In such a world, peace might just happen, but only time would tell.

On the ground, a restless Amarna tussled to evade restraint, squirming like a giant fish out of water. Seeing him gone mental made no difference, for utter ignorance and timidity are the prime ingredients in the makings of a tyrant, and heeding personal desires is the basis for lunacy's genesis.

I put on my helmet out of sheer habit. But then I thought, why bother? No one else had theirs on, so I took it off and accompanied my superior to the waiting ship—I would regret that decision. I stood meters from the ship's ramp, looking at this wondrous metallic contraption in awe. It looked like two inverted bowls tapering into a wide disk, the larger of the two bowls on the bottom. It measured twenty meters in diameter and half that in height, resting on four landing gears protruding from the bottom disk section.

Noting my curiosity, my superior pointed out that this craft used electromagnetic propulsion. A large ^{226}Ra isotope reactor powered the ship for up to eight hours. The ship could also tune into the Van Allen belt's 35MHz band and download emergency power. A six megavolt, high amperage electrode pole pierced the ship from top to bottom, powered by a static generator. At the bottom of the craft, a cylindrical 100 Tesla electromagnet enclosed the bottom part of the electrode, also powered by static electricity.

Two centrifuge flywheels—filled with liquid mercury and lined with thorium—spun at 25,000 rpms around the electromagnet in opposite directions—a wheel within a wheel [6]. These wheels induced rotating EM toroid fields and tachyons that ionized matter, mechanically countered gravity, and served as a gyroscope. The inner toroid produced artificial cabin gravity, the outer nullified Earth's gravity, and served as shields. In other words, the heart of this machine was a powerful, synthetic Lorentz vortex produced by a static pole, an electromagnet, and spinning centrifuges.

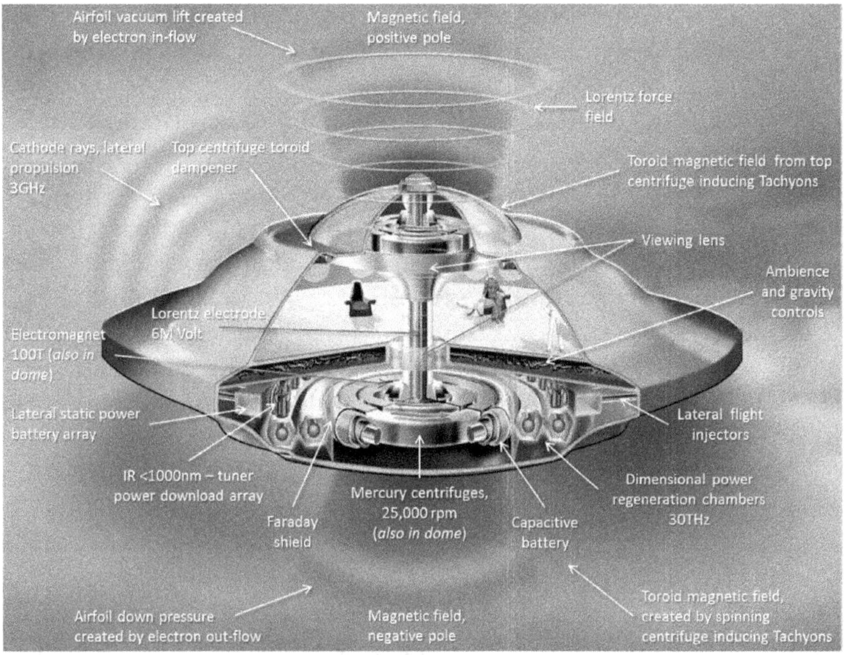

Picture 1: Space craft functional diagram (*B. Erlinger-Ford*)

Pulsed cathode rays, contained by the Lorentz vortex outside the ship, created brief vacuum portals for the craft to move into. Speed and travel vectors were regulated by vortex strength and electromagnetic element phase. Levity was sustained by electrons emerging from the bottom of the electrode, looping magnetically back to the top. This action created a high-pressure vortex beneath the ship and a low-pressure vacuum above it, generating a type of airfoil lift. Operational field frequencies, phase offsets between electric and magnetic elements, and power levels, I must confide to secrecy. The craft's top speed was twenty thousand kilometers per hour, but the technology was still in its infancy.

Medics finally arrived to sedate Amarna who wrestled against eight marines, but he became further disorderly. "You are my only commitment, Arbiter. Don't leave me," he cried helplessly, but I bid him good bye and followed my superior unto the ship's ramp.

Feeling rejected, Amarna yelled again for me to return, but I ignored him. It was then that Amarna's wrath heightened; his eyes sought revenge, and yelled defiant, "If I can't have you, no one else will!"

In a sudden burst of strength, Amarna freed himself long enough to aim and fire his arm weapon. Greg, noting Amarna's intentions, quickly yelled "Sanjeev, look out!" and placed himself in the line of fire. By the time

I turned about, Greg rested lifeless on the sand. Amarna fired again, and I felt an angered blast strike my forehead. I heard or saw nothing, sensing my body fading to the sands.

Absolute darkness filled my vision in an empty place all to myself. I felt incredibly alone in a state of inanimate consciousness, unable to sense any part of my body or breathe. I panicked in feeble desperation, not knowing how to get out of this forlorn place, yelling for help but hearing no sound from my bellows. Seconds later, my spirit floated upward and away from consuming darkness to reveal the vessel I once inhabited. I remained high in the air overlooking an insane Amarna, sedated, and finally brought under control while marines tried vainly to resuscitate my fallen body.

Scorching desert sands melded together about me into a sea of yellowish haze. Intense blue skies shone above them with an electric quality, eventually overtaking sands below until nothing remained about me but blue haze, a place referred to as heaven's foyer.

Far off in the distant blue, I noticed two shimmering lights shaped like candle flames moving toward me. As they neared, delicate crystalline extremities emerged from them in welcoming gesture. Aurora-like colors emanated from their edges, enthrallingly beautiful to watch. Their silent ethereal brightness imparted a powerful yet calming wave of warmth I sensed throughout my being, and loving wonder immediately filled my heart.

They were for me, spiritual brothers escorting me from this tranquil reception vestibule to a place near the gods of heaven, where I will prepare for my return to Earth not long from now, and once more attempt victory over the forces of beguiling ignorance, of my own free will, and in my own time.

A light appeared to my side toward which I was compelled to move. From it emerged a light tunnel through which I passed from this expansive foyer into the land of the gods. It was all clear to me now—I was here many times before. I've lived tens of thousands of lives, each filled with countless learning experiences. More will come to pass until I learn to live on Earth as in heaven and calmly recognize past actions rather than fear them. Only then, and not by divine intercession, will I merit making this spiritual land my home.

Amarna was right. I was Petronious Arbiter and an ancient destroyer of worlds with a negative legacy dating back well over a million years. Restless memories from past lives endeavor to relive in the present, detouring truthful virtues through fear. Achieving freedom from such habitual legacy is a science, a journey of love and not selfishness, self-denial and not survival, trust in God's brotherhood and not fear of same, a battle between honesty and deceit.

Shortly after capture, Amarna mysteriously ended his life, just before his scheduled appearance before the World Court in New Hague, taking with him numerous secrets including names of benefactors and successors. His Cyprus command center was never found, perhaps the work of secondary protocols and mop up operations carried out by his enigmatic associates.

The world was spared from the Illumined's dominant grip by unknowingly dismantling both present and future political structures they so painfully set up over hundreds of years. But the relentless Order would make a comeback, just as they have since the beginning of time, because memories know no rest.

I will return in 2129, a time when my search for love, and my long lost one, shall come to an end, and our despicable legacy will see its sure demise.

---

[1] S. S. S. S. Maharaj, "Sankhya Yoga - 27," in *Bhagavad Gita.*

[2] En.wikipedia.org/wiki/MOPP, MOPP: Mission-Oriented Protective Posture

[3] A. Axelrod and C. Phillips, in *Encyclopedia Of Wars*, New York, NY: Facts On File, Inc., 2005.

[4] W. J. Rev. Morford, "Matthew 5:5," in *The One New Man Bible*, Travelers Rest, SC: True Potential Publishing Co., 2011.

[5] S. R. Leonard, Interviewee, [Interview].

[6] W. J. Rev. Morford, "Ezekiel 1:16," in *The One New Man Bible*, Travelers Rest, SC: True Potential Publishing Co., 2011.

Chapter 3: *A Martian Summons*

After thousands of vexing years beset by chronic waves of idealistic discords, peace and harmony flourished on every state and undulating shore of this reformatory planet, a world long recognized throughout the cosmos for its ruthless disregard of verve. Earth became a new gallant world, renewed from the ashes of past binding autocracies by an avant-garde, distinctive society committed to intellectual development, equality, and prosperity.

Bellicose afflictions were no longer an opulent delicacy. Rather, man strove to grow in wisdom and beauty on an inspiring, pleasant abode where tyrannical enmities were ancient reprobate ambitions best mocked by history.

World members aspired anew to improve society rather than promote ethnic barriers, repressive endeavors, or ideological schisms that merely lead to provocative deterrents and damaging censure. The government advocated prudence and unity, reminding members that they were part of the problem, if they were not part of the solution. Everyone was encouraged to participate in government by submitting civil proposals to the state, and even contribute to their implementation if approved.

Abolishing self-seeking ventures and extreme traditionalism were perhaps the most critical steps in achieving global labor and commodity efficiency. Members were encouraged to participate in revolving labor activities, credited not by the type of work entailed, but rather global production indicators that made financial investment illegal and competitive rivalry obsolete. Thus, human labor was driven by demand, rather than profit.

Everyone was entitled to basic commodities such as food, housing, health care, and transportation regardless of profession—a list of services that grew yearly. Products were designed to last and benefit consumer wellbeing, not enrich investors at nature's expense. Therefore, trivial harmful goods were banned and natural resources saved.

In spite of these and many other significant social developments, members deemed that something was still sorely amiss in life's daily drone. An inexplicable sense rapped man's latent mind with urgent pleads to know the self, but conscious disposition misinterpreted these impressions as boredom, loneliness, and fear. Hence, man naively turned to his old legacy rather than the science of life for answers. Pleasure began to once more take its course among humanity, and global peace was eventually compromised.

Life grew stagnant and routine for many members, exposing them to plausible devious influences as in olden days when thwarting games of fate consumed the world by catering to inner appetites. Crime and a taste for death returned to youthful hearts, encouraged by those seeking to force their rule upon the masses.

Like insatiable beasts provoked by hunger, veiled agents of darkness sought to prey upon frail souls preconditioned for untold eons to serve ruthless soul snatchers rather than The Divine, sinister beings counting on human idiocy to achieve wicked goals behind the façade of progress. Winds of displeasure swept the gullible away with romantic, futuristic promises. Fumes of hate convinced the spiritually weak to relish forceful subjugation, for such is our nature: sinful and unswerving, protecting our wicked memories from death until that fateful day when we forcefully surrender life unto Him.

But we were not alone. Someone secretly watched over us, patiently waiting for the right moment to faithfully carry out His Majesty's divine plan and triumph over man's aberrant illusions of grandeur.

The day of reckoning revealed itself on the year 2158, a hundred years after the founding of the "United Earth Federation," a one-world government founded on the premise that fostering human potential and colonizing the solar system was vital to progress, a premise based solely on human aptitude rather than gifts of genuine spirit.

Since its early founding days, UEF generously sponsored several space initiatives and made everyone's dream of experiencing the cosmos a reality, due for the most part to significant developments in space propulsion technology. In space, ships could reach speeds up to a hundred million kilometers per hour. Higher velocities were possible, but cosmic radiation weakened and ultimately collapsed impulse fields, rendering the craft still or unresponsive. At these speeds, Mars was anywhere from half to four hours away, depending on alignment, and it took a week to reach Eris.

Hopes of reaching nearby stars were still far from reality. Alpha Centauri, the closest star system to ours, was forty-seven years distant at top speed. The Sagan unmanned probe, launched in 2113, will reach the system in a couple of years. Its mission is to explore a watery terrestrial planet in the main star's habitable zone, and another that swaps orbits between binary pairs.

The moon doubled as both colony and space port, complete with hydroponic gardens, spacecraft manufacturing, fueling, and maintenance facilities. The first lunar colony, built on Copernicus, was inaugurated in late 2059, the first of ten, hosting approximately eighty thousand residents not counting passengers using the moon as a gateway to remote outposts.

Large vessels set out monthly to resupply outposts and explore the solar system, fulfilling age-old ambitions to demythologize ancient beliefs and explore fascinating worlds. Outpost settlements were established on Mercury,

Mars, Europa, and Pluto. Other worlds presented challenges well beyond Earth's capabilities and were not settled at the time.

A thin, hydrogen-helium atmosphere was discovered on Mercury, deposited by solar wind action but lost due to weak planetary gravity. Traces of calcium and sodium create a barely visible gas layer that rises with increased temperature and condenses over the surface on the night side. Lead, tin and lithium melt under intense heat over amorphous compounds and crystallize into colorful jewels. Nearby asteroids bestow deadly embers upon a hostile, chaotic landscape, exposing the planet's iron inners upon contact. But most surprising is the presence of a frozen sea on its north pole and several watery deposits inside shaded craters, endowed with strange living forms.

Venus is a toxic infernal world devoid of reasons to be visited. Volcanoes dot the planet, spewing poisonous gases amid turbid grounds and deep, serrated chasms. Atmospheric pressures a hundred times that of Earth flattens volcanoes and spreads ejecta closer to the ground. Acid descends from the sky in sweeping cyclonic waves, mixing with stirred dust in gloomy panoramas occasionally brightened by electrical storms and apocalyptic sulfuric blasts. Among such chaos, there is also beauty. Molten minerals slowly course down to the planet's deepest rifts, where they form chemical rivers and give birth to remarkable crystalline wonders. Enormous jewels of unique, exquisite loveliness hide among soils and lava tubes, some forged in brief, passionately eruptive moments.

Besides terrifying worlds of woe, there are also wondering vessels of exceptional beauty embracing vast numbers of prodigious living forms. A myriad of plant and animal species abound hidden beneath ancient ice glaciers throughout the solar system. On Europa, Ganymede, and Enceladus, deep sub-ice oceans host untold aquatic eco-systems, nurtured by physical processes widely divergent from Earth's.

Tide effects, induced by strong Jovian gravitational pull, swell equatorial oceans and expose higher latitude caves, creating an ideal haven for aviary and migratory amphibians. When tides recede, oxygen-rich weather patterns form beneath bulged ice canopies, setting off equatorial migrations. As glaciers swell and morph over time, minerals ejected by nearby bodies, such as sulphur and hydrogen peroxide, slip underneath the ice and enrich aquatic ecology. Likewise, geysers surge ocean salts to the surface, submitting them to long cyclic curing processes in an environment not readily offered under the ice.

Imposing as these wonders seemed, mankind's heart belonged inexplicably to a rather bleak world. An endearing crimson sister sat alone in the coldness of space, waiting for that virtuous day when our eyes finally opened and lingering isolation desisted. A silent Martian summons reached across ethereal expanse belittled as a dream, nonetheless a predestined encounter borne of man's own drudgery long in contempt of infinite desires.

I was among those summoned, silently called forth by invisible longing whispers fervently urging my heart to unfurl its sails and set course for the stars, reach across vast cosmic currents, and revisit far shores my soul once renowned. I never knew I was, or why. In time, all was revealed: an incredible story of legacy, a search for love as ancient as time itself. My long journey through the heavens I had forgotten, my hands' labors even more so; but heaven never forgot me, and destiny brought me to Mars to regain my soul.

From repressed ancient memories, the flight of providence gazed kindly upon those ascribed with cosmic negligence, suddenly enamored with a new sense of duty to undo a grave past wrong. Drawn by inexplicable inner motive, Earth answered the summons mystified by the weight of conscience and returned to foreign Martian shores. Man came to dwell among ancient cinders of his own making, hoping to carve out a piece of His Majesty for himself at unknowingly Earth's most desperate hour. But instead, hearts such as mine discovered: Love Eternal.

* * * * *

Shortly after Luna 1 was established, Earth Space Core of Engineers built the first Martian colony called C1. Four more colonies were later built near the Martian equator, far in advance to those found on the moon. Large industrial centers were established around the planet, manufacturing essential goods and fuels used on Mars and remote outposts.

A dozen KBO comets were herded to Mars yearly and processed in low-orbit fragmenting stations to ensure slow and safe material descent to pre designated areas. Comet ice was released over ancient containment ponds. Ores were recovered in orbital refineries or released upon key surface areas to increase planetary mass. In addition, pumping stations de-iced polar caps, delivering water via pipelines to colonies, built and operated entirely by robots.

On Mars, water was always in dangerously short supply, a situation further aggravated by constant colonial expansion and special interest groups lobbying for a wet Mars. While water quotas were set to an all-time low and recycling systems pushed to their limits, environmental activists pressed for new regulations to divert more precious water from lips to lakes. In the end, water must come from somewhere, and on Mars there wasn't enough to satisfy both colonists and visionaries. This impasse is what initially brought me to Mars.

Pressured by relentless bickering between factions, the Martian Council approved a massive terra-forming project that would establish ten new colonies, transform 20 percent of the Martian surface, and augment planetary mass to 68 percent of Earth's by mid twenty-third century.

According to the proposal, several nearby asteroids were identified for orbital mining and safe scattering over the surface to increase gravitational potential. Select aquatic pools would be replenished using hundreds of KBOs, in effect recreating ancient seas and lakes. Vast areas of the planet were set aside for hearty forestry and grasslands. Eventually, Mars would gain a thicker breathable atmosphere, higher temperatures, and sufficient humidity to stabilize weather patterns. That was the easy part: the hard part would follow.

Cosmic radiation was a threat to any life form on the surface. To ensure the safety of surface dwellers, a synthetic ozone layer and stable magnetic fields were in order; that was easier said than done. Getting the planet's core spinning again required technology well beyond Earth's grasp, but that was not stopping the project.

The plan was approved and hastily set in motion. Park reserves, protected by environmental nets, were set up to shelter air-producing flora from cold weather. The first experimental terra-net, implemented in Uzboi Vallis, was a complete success, proving that vegetation will thrive naturally on Mars, and even spawn beyond the original controlled environment.

Construction of a sixth colony, located on the western banks of Uzboi Vallis adjacent to the first terra-net, was due to complete by late 2158. However, Earth gov suddenly scrubbed the project due to peculiar geological instability: at least, that's what people were told. C6 was abandoned, its personnel reassigned, and no further inquiry into the site was ever sanctioned.

I worked for Earth Space Core of Engineers Geological Survey segment at the time. Prior to joining ESCE, I served as UEF director of anthropology and geology for two years. Single, twenty-six years old, and seeking new horizons, I chose a career in space command's Mars sector and was assigned to C5 as its chief geologist. A year later, I was promoted to Mars GS director.

I was the hands-on type, deeming field work part of the job. Reluctant to become sedentary by any means, I personally took on P3, the Third Pipeline project, and essentially turned my space suit into a portable office. Dust or shine, my passion for work took me to the most remote areas on Mars where seasoned explorers dared not venture. Chasma Boreale was just such a place, not appealing by any means.

The lower tundra is littered with glacial flow remains, haplessly arranged to make travel on foot as arduous as possible. Stubborn stone blocks protrude out of icy grounds without rhyme or reason. The ice is slippery, shatters easily, and combines with ground particles to form tough, rocklike formations referred to as dirty rime. With sufficient force, these particles can become airborne and turn into dangerous projectiles. On warmer days, carbon dioxide deposits give off an eerie early moving fog that diffuses into the skies, making it difficult to find one's way. Still, the supernatural panorama of calm, whitish-red ice poised against an apathetic pale bluish sky is a significant sight difficult to ignore.

One afternoon, a nasty storm transformed a routine field survey into an unexpected struggle for survival. I had spent few days alone at Chasma's south rim, trying to decide where to establish the next mega ice farm for P3. High-risk storm warnings were issued for the area, but as always, I never paid much attention to them. When least expected, southern skies steadily blurred with shades of orange and winds intensified, enough to shower the Rachford region with rime hail.

Over the years, ESCE's stalwart efforts to increase atmospheric pressure, temperature, and gravity negatively impacted Martian weather by also amplifying annual storm intensity. As a result, circulating currents around the poles significantly strengthened, mainly around Utopia Planitia, fueled by temperature and altitude variances. The end result: powerful cyclonic summer storms, fed by rising moisture from temperate reservoirs down south.

I was forced to drop what I was doing and immediately sought refuge among nearby ledges, but there were no safe havens, and digging one up could bring a weak ice sheet down upon me. So I chose to climb ice walls in spite of their slippery surface. I didn't consider rescue for reasons I wasn't aware of then. Ultimately, such blunder would prove most revealing.

The storm reached Chasma's southern boundary with sudden fervor. Winds howled like lingering thunder, churning the tundra apart like a gigantic winged predator. In the distance, objects engulfed by the advancing storm launched at an incline, colliding explosively with others already in transit; scenes of things to come my way.

Several exhausting hours later, the ice summit finally loomed nearby, seemingly close enough to touch, though not fast enough to avoid the storm's deadly wrath. Rime struck my suit urging me to hasten, but an unexpected call from an anxious individual abruptly interrupted my endeavor; from C6, of all places. Rather peculiar, I thought, since the site was supposedly shut down. The summit was just meters away, so I ignored the call and kept climbing, but C6 persisted.

Annoyed by repeated calls, I drove the pick into the ice and answered the call rather upset. C6 insisted the matter was urgent, but so was mine. I agreed to call back later and continued my climb. Again, I could have requested rescue but failed to do so.

Sunset steadily approached the far reaches of this small sphere. In the east, magnificent magenta shades replaced yellowish skies. Hazy cobalt twilight trailed the sun into the horizon, overshadowed by glassy mirages unfolding over frail icy linen. But without warning, an orange mantle obscured the heavens as the storm swept over the area. Gloom promptly prevailed and high winds pummeled my suit, seriously trying my balance.

I had nearly reached the summit when clumsy footwork got the best of me and accidentally dropped my pick into the murky storm. Without it, hanging 250 meters off the ground, I was in serious trouble. I had only one option: activate my emergency beacon, something I should have done long before.

Someone else at C6 immediately responded to my distress beacon, as if anticipated. "This is C6 rescue. I have your location at 82.42°N by 101.54°W. Be there in an hour," assured dispatch, though waiting any amount of time at the heels of a category four storm seemed an eternity.

With nothing better to do but grab on for dear life, I asked C6 to describe the nature of their problem. Rescue provided scanty details about some absurd drilling incident but refused to disclose further details over the air. Surprisingly, Earth gov asked that I personally conduct a survey lasting several weeks, but doing so would delay P3, a project critical to colonial survival. My better sense said this survey had nothing to do with geology; reality was rather hard to ignore.

After months of silence and unbeknown to the Martian Council, C6 was covertly back in operation, complete with dispatch and shuttles. Perhaps the colony never did shut down, and the ground instability story was just a clever cover-up, but what was there to conceal on Mars?

Time passed, and the storm gained momentum to no consolation of mine. Tired and frustrated, I called C6 and was assured a shuttle would be in the area any moment, but I couldn't see its glow on approach against the darkening sky. Rime scoured the lower part of my suit, slowly shaving ice away until my right foot slipped into nothingness. I became rather concerned, placing added stress on my other foot and holding on any way I could. But not long after, the remaining ice step suddenly gave out, and I dangled anxiously from my harness, unfurled like a fluttering sail.

Relentless winds and debris ferociously battered my suit enough to swing me horizontal. The harness stretched and shivered under stress, slowly loosening its borrowed hold. One by one, harness anchors dislodged from shattering brittle walls until a single anchor held my life in the balance. My gloves hastily crawled along the taut rope trying to reach the remaining anchor and keep it secure; otherwise, I would surely perish. But in spite of frantic efforts, the ice cracked, and the last anchor gave out before I could reach it.

My dread-filled eyes witnessed the impassive glacial summit retreat swiftly away, hands vainly grasping a trailing harness that no longer attached to anything on the other end. My heart paced loudly, and lips bellowed frantically in the darkened night, failing to inspire any worthy ally eager enough to arrest my grim, lonesome plight. Soaring high above the freezing wilderness, I was left to fate's impervious tide, veiled within a hazy, dusty shroud imploring a dreadful brink that demise would not willingly hide.

Seconds later, I collided horizontally against a nearby graded ice wall at considerable speed. Upon impact, my lungs immediately released their precious air cargo with a hasty paralyzing whimper. Suit instruments, on the other hand, flickered randomly. Life support failures rapidly mounted, merging with obtrusive crashing sounds outside.

I tumbled downward without heading along steep slopes with no end in sight, often free falling and running into stiff ice chunks along the way, until striking an exposed rock on a slanted strip bordered by a cliff, finally coming to a stop. Battered by the fall, I laid on the ice face down, moaning and reluctant to move. But my situation was about to degrade.

Life support worked arbitrarily, issuing endless nagging warnings. Air gradually became harder to breathe, and suit temperature plummeted quickly. The harness had twisted itself around my suit and removing it became a rather tedious shore. But before I could regain balance and restore suit functions, the icy shelf severed under strain and I plummeted down a sharp incline littered with jagged outcrops and sheer drops.

After several icy run-ins and steep dives down serrated slopes, I finally reached grounds below incredibly in one piece, but my immediate situation was far from taking a turn for the better. Life support had shutdown, a fifteen centimeter fracture ran diagonally across my visor, and the suit's protective lining had more rips and tears on it than I could count, risking decompression and radiation exposure. In the interim, the storm dragged me on and off the ice without mercy amid a cold chaotic hell.

Off in the ghostly distance, enormous ice walls detached from surrounding mountain sides and slowly crumbled downward in an eerie display of nature's adamant might; a startling sight to behold and unyielding reminder of just how trivial we humans are compared to the inconceivable magnitude of His Majesty. Small ice blocks and rocks flew through the air like weightless beach balls, smashing into anything standing in their path. On impact, icy structures heaved deep inners that swiftly shattered and turned into knife-like projectiles, screeching by like echoing throngs from a lashing bull whip.

By luck, I ran into a large stone block anchored to the ice, hastily secured my harness around it, and dug into the ice boots first to keep warm, using the block as a shield against flying debris. I was nearly out of breath when air recycling finally came back online using emergency power, indicating I had less than ten hours of air left. Heating elements worked sporadically, often imposing unbearable cold chills that reached callously deep into my bones.

Shivering and exhausted from my trying ordeal, I reposed face down in my make-shift igloo and placed the helmet's visor upon my arms for protection, watching clouds of cold breath spread within the helmet, then slowly melt away. Eventually, my eyes sealed secure, and I fell asleep in spite of recurring suit warnings and roaring debris churning restlessly outside.

My thoughts hastily wondered off into distant mystifying neglect where, without my knowledge, unexpected hosts were waiting for me in an unknown place far from reach. When inner eyes unfastened their silent locks on conscious reality, my sights were greeted by a wondrous, exalted world I knew to be non-earthly. In every sense of the word, I was awake, calm, and alert, realizing this was no dream but an altered mental state of continuity.

I rested upon a field of partly transparent light-colored grasses that shone with electric glory, immediately impressing my attention. Every blade of grass swayed gently in the mostly still air, forming a vast sea of delicate, undulating green crystalline ornaments. Nearby rocks and flowers were also crystalline, whose bold colors glowed with Kirlian-like effulgence and were absolutely beautiful to behold. The entire landscape, from rocks to flowers, appeared like a vast glowing masterpiece the envy of the most gloriously lit Christmas decor. My heart rejoiced, for I remembered this place. I knew I had been here before; long, long ago.

My body was covered by radiant flesh, smooth as porcelain, wearing white, one-piece clothes I had never donned before. My fingers extended longer than normal, and the body did not have to walk or exert leverage in order to move. My sense of touch felt the crystalline grass as if normal, yet with a live, thrilling essence I never previously encountered.

The air about me felt warm, enchantingly pure, with a strong essence of gardenias. A lake's restful shore was only meters away, accessible by means of a dirt path from where I stood. Its waters were so azure that I could not see my own reflection upon them. Placing my hand into the lake, I sensed as if warm velvet gently caressed my skin, but was surprised to discover that its waters did not wet. Enthralled by the water's strange qualities, I immersed my body into the lake, only to find that I floated among its waters entirely by will, and did not sink.

Picture 2: Venus high plane (*B. Erlinger-Ford*)

Skies above were covered by thick smooth grayish clouds, but the mid afternoon sun briefly broke through a small cloud opening to my left, shining a thin beam of light upon tall brownish-violet crystalline boulders nearby. Instantly, the sunbeam bounced off the boulder with intense prismatic colors, several times brighter than the sun's light itself.

The dirt road unexpectedly ended at the edge of a vast space port of sort. Large square blocks, made from a material that resembled concrete, decked the surface and spread into the distant horizon. In the far distance, forest vegetation barely graced the ends of my sights, and low mountains stood as a faint setting behind them. There were space craft parked still on this space port, but my eyes could not discern their form, for they were kept on a higher plane than mine at the time.

A tall blonde man slowly walked into my sights, wearing a one-piece white jump-suit and a golden sash about his waist. His gaze was most tenderly inspiring, peaceful, joyous, and loving beyond comprehension. His face was perfectly clean and could have been mistaken for that of an incredibly beautiful woman. His shiny black eyes were larger and flatter than ours, leaving little space for the globe itself. His eyelids were rather thick, and three lacrimal glands reached closer to the iris than eartheans.

"Where am I?" I asked him.

"You are on Venus," replied the man with a calm smile, "on a plane higher than your present physical experience."

He motioned me to follow him into the space port where a dark hat-shaped craft revealed itself a short distance away, and asked me to go inside. With one short step up, we walked on top of the disk and headed toward an entrance located on the craft's cabin section.

When I boarded the craft, I was astonished to find the cabin to be about four times larger than its external dimensions. Along its gently lit walls, several oval portals, invisible from the outside, ran the height of the cabin. The flat ceiling overhead displayed an amplified image of the heavens with extreme definition. Portals along the walls magnified exterior sights by mental will, placing far-off landscapes seemingly near enough to touch. My guide took to a control console, located to my immediate left; and both vanished into thin air, leaving behind a plain cabin wall. The ship's door melted closed, and its frame seams also vanished without trace.

In the center of the room, a graceful, most humble, and loving lady in her late thirties waited for me. She was dressed in a deep rosy-colored robe with a golden sash about her. She wore sandy blonde hair up in an elegant braided bun. Her facial glory was clean, radiant, and devoid of any ornaments other than her outstanding plentiful beauty shining forth from her amorous soul. Her black eyes served as if pools of living brilliant sapphires, burning with selfless candor and a message of clean divinity to onlookers.

With a most inviting, shy smile, she encouraged me to sit across the way from her upon a plush swivel chair. I knew she was someone of great importance and, most of all, vastly wise in divine matters. Without introductions, she calmly said, "We will now give you a demonstration of acceleration."

The lady, who never fully smiled, then gently lowered her head and remained solemnly quiet. Impressed by what I perceived to be a saddened gesture, I immediately became distressed, fearing I had done something awfully wrong. But an inner sense difficult to decipher silently hinted into my mind's ear that my selfish feelings, mostly hidden and ignored, yet savored, were the cause. Then, without delay, the ship took to space maneuvering wildly in every direction, but yet, I felt absolutely no movement.

Unexpectedly, she gently whispered the following words into my mind, "Electricity plus magnetism plus ionization equals mobility." Why she said this, I had no clue at the time, but destiny would ensure an unexpected and painful answer in the months to come. A light in the form of a scintillating white flame enveloped her being just before she waved goodbye and said, "Remember us, and live to deny yourself."

Picture 3: Inter-dimensional Venusian craft (*B. Erlinger-Ford*)

I woke up suddenly, startled by the ensuing storm, and shrugged off a heavy coat of ice that stockpiled on top of the helmet. But as soon as my thoughts elicited the vision, a gentle yellowish glow set against the brow, earning my immediate attention.

At first, I thought the glow came from rescue teams daring the raging storm, so I eagerly raised my head to have a better look. I was in for quite a surprise. Off in the distance, I noticed a light slowly head my way, bearing close to the ground. As the light neared, it exhibited what could be described as walking motion, slightly swaying from side to side in the hazy storm.

The closer the lights got, my hopes for rescue grew accordingly. "They're here!" I yelled much relieved in the lonesome, icy wilderness, unable to stand up to any significant degree due to the storm's deadly fury. Hastily, I retrieved a flare from a pocket, ignited it, and waved desperately to get the attention of whoever was out there. But as the light approached, I noticed something just didn't seem right.

There were two distinct light sources rather than one, mysteriously shaped like tall candle flames moving upon the ground, akin to the lady's flame in the dream. I could make out silhouettes resembling human forms inside the flames, but strangely none wore a space suit.

Chills ran through my body in disbelief, obviously concerned for my state of mind. After all, a human out here without a space suit was certainly a dead one. Perhaps these lights were nothing more than subconscious creations made up as a means to the ends, so I assumed. I thrived on that for a while until it was senseless to give the idea further attention with reason. The lights stepped over objects, contouring the ground as they walked. Also, flying debris near them lit up with reflective glow and deflected away on contact.

The lights, rather the two individuals, stopped five meters from me. With all the debris flying about, I could not make out their faces too well, perhaps intentionally. Still, I could tell one was female and the other male. The female wore a delicate white dress, the male black pants and white shirt, but other features were difficult to ascertain. They exhibited delicate smiles and mannerisms about them, unusual for any Earth person exposed to these extreme environmental conditions.

I let the forceful wind remove the flare from my glove, immediately turning off and vanishing into the murky distance. I waved slightly at these beings, and they waved back but did not approach. "Hello, can you hear me?" I shouted, still thinking they were rescuers.

The two beings smiled back, however did not respond. Instead, they looked at each other and nodded slightly. "Who are you?" I asked, but once more they responded with smiles. I warned them to seek cover, but I only got a hand wave in return.

Surprisingly, a garbled faint voice suddenly came through my ear set. All power was diverted to life support, rendering voice communications almost inoperable. "This is C6 rescue. Bill, do you copy?" said the unknown source.

I replied anxiously, hopes for rescue riding high, only to learn that recovery was still out of the question due to high winds.

"Who are you talking to. Is someone there with you?" asked rescue.

"Not sure. I see two bright lights few meters from me. Is that you guys?"

"I'm at the storm's boundary about ninety kilometers due north. There's no way you can see me. Turn on your cam so I can see what's out there."

"It's on. You should see the lights, about five meters from me."

"All I get is cam noise. Are you on tundra or high ground?"

"On the tundra, a klick west of the Rachford ice sheet, or what's left of it, facing south east. These lights . . ." Suddenly, the beings raised their hands in wary stance, and I instantly went silent. Clearly, they didn't want their presence known, for it wasn't time to reveal their reality.

"Come again, Bill?" said rescue. "You're breaking up."

"Must be reflection from nearby work lamps swaying in the wind. That's what it is" I said, trying to suppress any suspicions I may have raised by resorting to, shall we say, plausible embellishment. Rescue didn't follow up on the matter but promised to attempt rescue in the morning, if the storm let up.

I looked upon these mysterious beings, trying to understand who they were or what they wanted, when I suddenly felt warm and in good company. I returned their smiles with great inner trust, almost by instinct difficult to describe. Their mouths moved but I could not hear what they said, so I waved my head from side to side and tapped my right ear to indicate I could not hear them. They nodded their heads in return, raised their right hands, and the words, "You are never alone. Remember us" popped into my head. Then, just as mysteriously as they appeared, they faded into the night; leaving me to dark, howling winds.

Thinking about who or what these beings were suddenly made me rather drowsy, and I compulsorily fell asleep once more as the storm slowly subsided and headed back south.

By morning's early hours, the storm miraculously let up and the sun's rays shone on my ice-covered visor, inducing a subtle orange glow on the eyelid. In skies above, reddish tints cast upon few wispy low clouds layered atop each other, bringing visual expression to otherwise latent scenery. Nearby glaciers slowly emerged from morning's dull grayish hues, transforming into an eerie blend of dreary white patches and receded dark features. Sunlight infuriated exposed rocks on western canyon flanks with varying crimson shades. The canyon's eastern rim was barely visible due to planetary curvature, perceived as dim ghostly azure contours in the far-off hazy horizon.

Stiffened by hours of exposure to bitter cold and a most uncomfortable resting position, I decided to leave the safety of my burrow behind and gladly stepped out unto a rather calm, barely breezed setting, compared to the fury of a few hours prior. From my vantage point, it was definitely not the same Chasma from a day prior. In fact, the entire Rachford region looked more like a gruesome scene from a ferocious battle.

The landscape between canyon flanks was strewn with intricate ice blocks scattered about in hapless arrangement. Several glacial fragments completely vanished, morphed into jagged blocks littering the ground. Large stone boulders, once hidden from view by several layers of ice, protruded out of the ground after ages of abiding entombment, while smaller ones became victim to nature's redecoration initiatives.

Throughout the frozen tundra, ancient carbon dioxide deposits, warmed by the sun's rays, gave off a low moving fog that crawled near the surface and lifted westward like stirring spirits seeking each other in unpredictable dance. As these ghostly clouds climbed into the sky, slowly diminishing in intensity, I lost myself in deep thought, recalling the wonders I witnessed the previous night; my glorious visit to Venus and my exceptional new friends that promised never to leave my side. But this moment of rapture would not last long, testing my newly found faith.

A new reality suddenly set in when the unnerving sound of servos hastily winding down and relay lights dimming immediately roused untold desperation. I swiftly looked down at my suit's power gauge, located on my left arm, and panicked when I noticed the readout had also turned off. The suit was completely dead and, without a miracle, I would soon inherit the same fate. I desperately reached for my transponder, but it was dead. I searched for another flare, but had none other on me. I screamed for help, but no one heard my frantic calls. Meanwhile, air became harder to breathe, and unbearable cold gripped my body.

As I was stranded alone in the freezing tundra, with dwindling hopes for rescue and out of air, demise loomed assuredly in just moments. I strained desperately to satisfy my lungs' binding demands to inhale fresh air, but only suffocating poisons lingered in the helmet's small chamber, making me feel heavy and lethargic until I collapsed upon the ice almost unconscious, gasping helplessly while waiting for the inevitable closure to life's brief journey.

But without obvious reason, my suit's controls suddenly revived, and both air and heat began to function, though the power readout indicated reserves were fully drained and the suit's primary source was damaged beyond repair. I was astonished to be alive, yet hugely grateful to the point of tears, uncertain how the suit re-energized. Just as hastily, the words, "You are never alone. Remember us" surged unexpectedly once more in my inner most thoughts, swelling my indebted heart with festive delight and unimaginable joy.

Out of the corner of an eye, near the igloo entrance, I was greatly surprised to find, neatly stuck into the ground handle-first, my pick. On top of it was the flare I used the evening prior, undamaged. I was emotionally moved to see these two objects returned without my notice. It had been but a minute from the time I left the igloo until I turned about. I heard or saw no one, and there were no tracks giving away anyone's sudden appearance. It had to be, in my opinion, the lighted beings I witnessed hours prior. Someone had reached out to me, someone alive and benign, awakening my curious temperament; indisputable evidence that I was never alone.

Overwhelmed by such compelling anonymous friendship, my heart filled with thankful sentiment and joyfully came to my knees, grateful beyond words of my newly found friends for their kind, benevolent closeness. I needed no further proof; they were real and always near. Where and when I might meet them again, I didn't know, but wished it be soon.

Just then, my suit turned off once more and frigid coldness wasted no time bearing its chilling mark through torn suit linings. But no sooner, the flare reignited entirely on its own and billowed smoke high into the air, quickly forming an orange canopy in skies above. Seconds later, a gleaming beacon of light streaked across Chasma skies, heading immediately for the smoke signal: a most pleasing sight at such fitting time, just as my air supply thickened and breathing became an arduous task.

The shuttle's landing gear gently touched down on the frail ice mass, and the ramp invitingly lowered. But before going on board, I took my pick and brought it with me as a reminder of someone I should not disregard.

The pilot greeted me warmly as I entered the shuttle and pointed out a climate adjustment unit, just what my chilling bones needed. He was a young most sociable chap of African lineage, quite experienced in Martian rescue operations. At his invitation, I sunk into a seat and left the driving to him.

I suddenly noticed that my visor's fracture was gone. Unsure how or when, a fifteen-centimeter fracture with several splinters just plain vanished without trace. I lightly touched the visor trying to make out the break line, but my fingers only felt perfect smoothness. I could not help bearing a satisfying smile upon my lips, longingly re-envisioning my caring alien friends. It was no hallucination; they were real, and the fixed visor was additional proof of it.

Noting my smile, the pilot said with gentle, yet humorous tone, "That was some rough ordeal you went through last night, brother."

"You don't know the half of it," I replied with a compelling grin.

"You're genuinely lucky to be alive," he said. "No one's ever lived through a polar storm to tell about it; that means the good Lord must really like you. I'm a firm believer He had angels keeping you company through the night."

I smiled helplessly, restraining an urge to describe my astonishing alien experience. But somehow, he sensed my unwilling gesture and replied, "You know, the Lord will shorten your grip, but will never strangle you."

"Maybe you know something I don't. Angels, sure, anything is possible, if you believe in that sort of thing."

"I don't just believe, brother; I know. I heard you over the blower last night. You saw angels, my friend. I prayed for you and they kept you company. The Lord is powerful, and He don't care about storms when He has a job to do."

"I suppose, like you said, that knowing is believing."

"You got that right. By the way, I'm Captain Robert Biggs, 115th Planetary Flight Division, but everybody calls me Slammer. I've been on Mars now for four years, and I've seen it all."

"Glad to make your acquaintance, and thanks for being there last night."

"Don't mention it. All part of the friendly service," he said, briefly smiling my way. "You know, I didn't come here for the climate like most other folks did. A Martian summons—that's what brought me out here. Life abounds in the universe, and Mars didn't get left behind. Matter of fact, I've seen stuff myself. How about you?"

"I'm not really sure I have," I said hesitant. "Your eyes can deceive you at times."

"I know where you're coming from, but don't ever let the prospect of deception deny you the facts. Otherwise, you won't recognize truth when you see it. So if your eyes deceive you, clean them up and stare forward, confident that truth is always by your side."

"You are absolutely right about that. So what have you seen exactly?"

"Shortly after reporting for duty, I'm flying night supplies to C4 two klicks up when this big light suddenly buzzes past me near Brashear, but I don't see it on my scope. It paced the shuttle all the way to C4, and then, it just blinked off. Another time, I saw this guy at C1 talking to himself while having dinner. I thought he was mental for sure, so I asked who he's talking to. He starts to introduce a friend sitting beside him when he suddenly goes quiet, turns pale, and said he just vanished."

"You're kidding me. This happened in public?"

"Sure thing. Matter of fact, the stranger knew a great deal about him, his family back home, and discussed advanced EM propulsion concepts he's never even heard of. By the way, this guy's an ESCE VP and has a real heavy east European accent."

"You said C1, VP, with heavy accent; I think I know who you're talking about. Older Ukrainian fellow, tall, blue eyes, very calm demeanor."

"I think that's him. He sure has an accent and talks really fast."

"That's Andriy Tischenko, my boss."

"Well, there you have it; there's someone you can talk to now. I tell you, people have seen stuff here for the last hundred years, but they keep it to themselves, afraid they'll get fired from Space Core if word gets out. Just last week, the C2 facility manager lost primary suit power and couldn't find his way back to the shuttle. Couldn't call or set transponder, a worst-case scenario much like yours. It was night time and he was lost for good. He says that a friendly individual inside some oval light walked him back to the shuttle and then vanished."

Slammer paused for a moment, looked my way, and said, "I heard what you said last night, about people and lights. You saw them too, didn't you?"

I smiled back and didn't answer, but Slammer knew precisely where I was coming from. "I understand; you can't talk about it. Work lamp reflections, right. They could stand three-hundred kilometer per hour winds out in the open, but not you. Well, if you say so. I see you also found your pick, where, a hundred kilometers away? Mars is alive, brother; it's not dead like some folks think. There's someone else living here I tell you."

"If so, why haven't they made contact? We've been here long enough for aliens to take notice and officially identify themselves. The fact that hasn't happened indicates they don't exist."

"Maybe you just did. Back during the clone war, the old federation brought people here because they knew something was up. Why else would you send a manned mission to Mars in the middle of a war?"

"That's just a rumor. There's no proof of a Mars mission happening before the spliced wars."

"Facts have it they were up there in Mare Acidalium and Cydonia looking for glass tunnels sticking out of the sand."

"You mean, the Apophis deflection mission back in twenty-nine?"

"Way too many rockets—manned, mind you—went up for that mission, more than necessary, conveniently herding the asteroid by Mars. I think they were here for two months digging up Cydonia but didn't find what they were looking for. Maybe someone covered up evidence before they arrived and set up dampeners to keep us from digging. Even to this day, we can't dig up there. Same thing happened on the moon, remember? Equipment wouldn't work in certain places, and still don't. Surface anomalies from twentieth-century moon photos like giant dishes, buildings, and towers mysteriously vanished before Luna 1 went up. You never heard about this stuff? Come on, you're way up there in the chain of command."

"Can't say I have, but there's talk of UFOs buzzing Mars lately."

"Ain't nothing but fact."

"See, that's it; it's all talk," I replied confidently. "No one's ever found any buildings, tunnels, or ancient artifacts to substantiate the existence of intelligent life here. Without proof, what are we to think?"

"Aliens have shown themselves to the right people, but no one dares speak up. Shame on them! There's something here on Mars, and hopefully I'll see it before my time's up. I don't know about you, but I believe we're never alone. The good Lord can't create eighty billion light years of universe just to house us somewhere arbitrarily in the middle of it—all to ourselves."

"Seems like an awful, significant misuse of space."

"Makes the Lord look selfish don't it, building stars rather than life. I think His priority is children, not hydrogen."

"I won't deny that alien life exists somewhere in the deep recesses of space, but the absence of solid evidence is truly hard to dismiss. We've spent two hundred years traveling to every world in our solar system and sending signals to over three hundred nearby systems. If there's anyone out there within a radius of a hundred light years, we should have heard from or seen them by now. So the question stands, why haven't they replied back?"

"They have countless times, but selfish politicians keep turning them down; maybe because all they want is technology rather than social change, and aliens won't fall for it. So we're left to think what we will. I've seen pictures, reviewed evidence, and I believe. There are many pranksters out there, but it's the indisputable evidence I always come back to, regardless what people might say. I want to meet them; that's what I live for, and that's why I answered a Martian summons."

Slammer and I continued to discuss local and infinite perspectives during the two-hour flight to C6. But the incident with human lights and the fixed visor I would hold secret for some time in fear of reprisal from the establishment, and to honor my new alien friends. Though I had been summoned, it was not yet time to act. In due time, at the right moment, His Majesty would faithfully provide our world with indisputable evidence that we are never alone. That time had not yet come.

Chapter 4: *Buried Past*

Slammer skillfully glided the shuttle toward C6 on a northwestern approach, offering a rare opportunity to inspect the landscape. The colony was built on the western banks of Uzboi Vallis, about nine kilometers south of the ancient Holden runoff gorge and just east of the terra-net, amid uneven terrain and sandy plateaus. Whoever decided to build the colony out here in the middle of shifting open mesa landscapes was hopelessly mad, but with any luck, there was probably a compelling reason why.

The shuttle entered the colony's large dome through a series of air locks and came to a stop in the arrival hangar. After bidding Slammer farewell and stepping out into the lonesome dome, the shuttle wasted no time leaving for an undisclosed location. I would not see Slammer for several weeks and under entirely different but pleasantly surprising circumstances.

Left to the echoing solitude of boot plods and annoying suit wrinkling clamors, the type that gets under your skin real fast, I waited patiently for my enigmatic host to show up, rather clueless as to why I was there.

The hangar looked uninvitingly desolate and out of order. Unlike the typical colonial dome, predictably bursting with busy maintenance crews, loud thumping tool clatter, and a plethora of disjointed mechanical contraptions rotting away on mag skids, C6 was strangely deserted. The dome looked structurally sound, and its air was breathable, implying that power generation systems were functional and no catastrophic incidents had taken place. I was hence at a loss to explain what might be wrong with the colony.

Stillness was suddenly infringed upon when elevator doors opened on the east end of the dome and a young man, dressed in military uniform, emerged from them, asking that I follow him down. Peculiar, I thought, as the military was not permitted on colonial grounds without Martian Council approval. As a member of the council, I knew of no justification authorizing his presence.

The trip down the shaft was longer than usual, indicating C6 was built deeper for reasons unknown. Once on the main corridor, a series of thick non regulation blast doors closed behind us. On our way to the colony's southwest wing, processing centers were in full operation, but their doors were both reinforced and guarded, also non-standard. I concluded that C6 was a military facility completed in record time, but reasons for its existence still eluded me.

At my new quarters, I showered and changed into colonial clothes, then followed the officer into another elevator that took us down to engineering, the colony's lowest level. At the operations office, the commander in charge of the colony waited patiently for my arrival. He was of age, well refined physically, and spoke with a formal European accent difficult to mind.

"Dr. Sullivan, I presume?" he said, extending his right hand in welcoming gesture. "I'm Commander Hans Gantz, thirty-fifth Planetary Division, in charge of C6 and Martian security. I'm pleased to finally meet you, and glad you're well after your tough ordeal."

"The pleasure is mine," I answered, submitting no gratification from my gesture. I stood serious and reluctant to unwind before someone I felt was there to learn and exploit my weak points.

"Please, make yourself comfortable," he said. "You no doubt made critical observations of this colony along the way and have many questions, yes?"

At a loss for words, I asked if he would elaborate on the nature of the colony's emergency. He leaned back on his chair with a sober stance, apologized for his vague request the night previous, and said, "I'm well aware of your critical work on P3. Water on Mars is in short supply and high demand nowadays, more than oxygen. But this colony's needs are also urgent, and we are in dire need of your expertise."

"No colony can afford recycling system breakdown or replacement," I reminded him, placing my priorities up front, "reason why P3 is so critical and a top priority for Space Core. If P3 is not completed on time, Earth gov will have a water crisis on their hands in just a few months."

"I'm well aware of that situation and agree with your assessment. But I assure you this slight delay to the P3 project is well justified," he added with confident flair and a slight touch of dry humor, "and approved by the highest levels of Earth gov. In fact, the landmark work being carried out at C6 is the primary reason we are all here on Mars."

I stared at him carelessly, wondering what he meant. He didn't come across as someone facing a real crisis but a casual observer. Besides, I grew skeptical of career officers to no fault of theirs, only my perception of their readiness to destroy the living; and that didn't help.

"How do I fit into this landmark work?" I asked, unsure of his intentions.

Aware of my misgivings, he carefully crafted his words, though not putting me at ease. "Mars is the newest frontier, and it has its share of occupational stress. Space command, pressured by millions of applicants, is being forced to cut corners and assume plausible risks. Colonists are hurriedly trained and dumped on location ahead of resources, being far less considerate of mother nature than inadequate talent. Illegal immigration and space rafters are at an all-time high, keeping orbital patrols busy—guess where migrants seek asylum. People just keep coming, and their safety must be ensured."

"Does this landmark work involve water shortages or geological stability?"

"I'm afraid it's far more than that."

"You have me confused with someone else," I replied, convinced Hans's issues did not particularly pertain to me. "I'm a geologist, not a politician, and my work is being delayed. If you'll excuse me, I'd like to get back to work."

Hans patiently listened to my discourse and replied, "I understand your concerns, but colonists need not worry. The P3 effort will continue to move forward even if it means delivering ice chunks to colonists for a year. Besides, there's not much you can do about it right now; that storm is forecast to roam up there for at least six more weeks. Tell you what. I'll start ice delivery tomorrow for as long as is needed; you have my word on that."

I could not dispute or reject his offer but still felt uneasy about a military presence on Mars. My predisposition was based more on a personal feeling rather than facts, for I was influenced by several military memories of my own that would not rest. "Thank you. I appreciate your kind offer," I said. "As long as colonists get the resources they need and osmosis systems aren't compromised, I'm satisfied."

"And if more osmosis systems are needed, just ask; you'll get them."

"Well, that sounds quite refreshing. What prompted Earth gov's sudden generosity?"

"Let's say we're under new management. My role here," he said, leaning forward, "is not to subdue colonists but help ensure their safety."

I slightly twitched my face, contorting to the word "safety." "Since when has Mars been subject to safety concerns?" I said, worried about Earth returning to its bloody days of strife.

Hans replied with a laidback attitude that certainly did not settle right. "The safety of Martian colonists is always a legitimate concern. Perhaps colonists don't perceive threats, but Earth gov takes that possibility quite seriously."

"Who could gain anything by threatening a handful of hard working colonists, staying barely alive atop a cold airless rock showered constantly by deadly meteorites and radiation? Come on, get real. Security has to be the least of our problems."

Hans rubbed his hands slightly, trying to control the conversation but not fusing the right words together to achieve it. "C6 is not standard colony issue. I saw that on the way down here. Someone went through a lot of trouble to fortify it, hide it, and I want to know why. What are you covering up down here? Are we going to war with little gray men?"

"That's plausible, and it's being addressed, but that's not our primary focus. Trouble with Earth members, that's no possibility but reality."

I remained speechless for a brief moment, frozen stiff by the implied severity of his words. Any and all conclusions I drew were equally apprehensive and definitely something to lose sleep over. "What do you mean? Earth attacking its own colonies? That's preposterous!"

"Not in that sense, no," he replied, assured of himself. "I assure you our presence is in the best interest of all colonists. We're not an occupational force but a gateway to, shall we say, befriending all of Mars."

I still did not follow Hans. Colonists got along just fine without a police force—mother nature took care of that—so what was Hans really there for? "Well, my three guesses are up, and I still have no clue what security concerns you refer to. Can you cut to the chase?"

"What I'm about to say is classified and can't leave this room," said Hans, seeking my consensus. I assented and sat comfortably, though likely to decline any offer he might bring to the table.

"Your prior report to the chancellor and established scientific background makes you the best candidate for the job. The chancellor himself asked that you lead this effort. He needs someone he can trust, make judicious decisions, and report accurate findings through the proper chain of command. Your new role is best summarized by the chancellor himself," he said, bringing up a pre-recorded message from the chancellor on a large screen behind him.

"Hello, Bill," said the chancellor. "Sorry for all the secrecy, but it's necessary. It's been some time, hasn't it? I hate to call on people only when I need them, but this is one of those times. Rumors have it that separatist factions want to create an independent cosmostate on Mars; I'm afraid these rumors are quite factual. That's why we've taken extreme measures and ensured that only the most trusted individuals are chosen for this venture.

"There's something up there that's brought all this about, and we hope you figure it out. People down here are both asking and coming up with all sorts of draconian assumptions that are tearing the world apart, so time is of the essence. Earth's future depends on the work you and your colleagues are about to do. Figure this out, or I'll bust your chops. So long and God bless you." The video ended abruptly, and Hans turned my way seeking feedback. I remained silent, soaking in a message difficult to hastily fathom.

"What is it that's caused such turmoil back home?" I asked.

"Months ago," Hans added, "before the terra-net experiment was even conceived, a survey crew reported seeing unusual meteor activity east of here. They noted that the descent zone was always the same: also speed and angle. Some objects, instead of coming down, went . . . up. A team of experts was dispatched to study the phenomena, but as long as they were in the area, no meteors showed up. As soon as they left, meteors returned. Remote test equipment was left behind to record these events, but they fail when meteors appear; some kind of dampening field shuts them down. We don't really know what's going on and can only theorize as to their nature."

While Hans measured my level of interest on the subject, I wondered if these were naturally occurring or man-made objects. "Scans show an interesting trait," he said. "Objects do have extremely strong and steady EM signatures, ruling out natural phenomena."

"By that you mean, extraterrestrial."

"Hold that thought. Let me show you something," he said, bringing up a video recording. "Take a look at this recent video of a Martian light as we call it. The object was digitally enhanced, analyzed; all we can make out is just a bright ball of light."

"A cloaking device?"

"Maybe. And get this. Its power signature is off the charts, more than all Martian shuttles combined. This thing just isn't ours."

The mysterious light descended as if it had no care in the world. Smooth and scintillating, it vanished without trace just before hitting the ground. "It's hard to imagine that a mere land survey triggered an interstellar response not seen elsewhere on Mars. And why now, after deploying colonies and pipelines all over this planet for a hundred years?"

"What's more, we can't drill any closer to the site due to that dampening field I was telling you about. There's a thirty-two kilometer blackout radius around it where equipment shuts down or behaves unpredictably."

"Something's not right here," I replied. "C6 is well within that blackout zone. Why aren't the lights flickering and the shuttle that brought me here didn't fall from the sky?"

"We are fifteen kilometers from ground zero. But for some reason, this spot is spared. You think it's a coincidence, no?"

"Looks like someone placed a protective canopy over the colony to keep us here, but don't ask me why," I interjected somewhat sarcastically.

"Too convenient for my comfort. Anywhere outside the safe zone, power is lost, and peculiar bee-like sounds are heard. Suits and propulsion systems are not affected by dampening, only select machinery and test equipment."

"That's odd. The power source and electronics used in them are basically the same. Bottom line is, anything with a human in it is spared." I couldn't help but remember what Slammer said about Earth's secret mission to Mare Acidalium, the part about equipment failures. I didn't bring this up to Hans but felt someone actively restricted our surface movements.

"You could say that, yes," said Hans, after digesting my comment. "I never thought about it that way. The dampening force must be intelligent, yes?"

"If so, whomever is behind this force has benign intentions, ensuring human life is not threatened, and alien secrets are not compromised."

"Unofficially, Earth gov thinks these fields are undeniably the work of extraterrestrials but won't commit ink to paper until they have proof to save their butts, of course."

"You can't be serious," I said hastily, obviously delivered not in a manner of disbelief but approval of this conclusion. What a refreshing statement this was. Honestly I thought I'd never hear it in my lifetime.

"Earth gov takes these matters quite seriously."

"There's got to be more to it."

"And there is. Let me start from the top. Some time ago, surveyors found that unusual condensate surged unpredictably in the area, leading geologists to theorize the existence of geothermal caverns."

"Nirgal gas, the theory that geothermal pressure percolates through weak fissures like geysers and suspends vapors in midair due to temperature inversion. The theory was never followed up on, but the gas encouraged selecting this site for the first terra-net, betting on higher humidity content."

"That's what we wanted people to think. This is how it all began. Before terra-nets and before you came to Mars, your predecessor, Dr. Ted Korzun, sought to explain Nirgal gas phenomena by digging up this area."

"Never heard of him."

"He designed the Jupiter Deep Atmosphere Station a few years back. He had an obsession with Nirgal gas and lobbied Earth gov for years until he got permission to investigate the phenomena. Why GS didn't do the investigation is beyond me. Anyways, he dug in a specific spot where vapor plumes were most predominant but never found water or completed his dig. Instead, he ran into an undisclosed problem. Earth gov scrubbed the project, and a special team was dispatched to resume investigation."

"Why wasn't Dr. Korzun allowed to continue his research?"

"I'll get to that in a moment. This special team had two objectives: investigate the site and cover up findings, ensuring dissident syndicates didn't intervene. The original dig site was turned into a terra-net, then a failed colony, to conceal sensitive information. C6 was built here to restrict access to the dig site and facilitate further research in the general vicinity.

"Soon after Dr. Korzun's discovery, word of these classified findings got out in the open. Since Dr. Korzun was a civilian and the matter required strict compartmentalization, the chancellor felt he could not be trusted, and a cover-up plan was suggested. However, two months later, Dr. Korzun mysteriously vanished and was later found dead in Brussels. We believe he was kidnapped by syndicates, talked, and was later disposed of. At that point, Earth gov shelved the Nirgal project, issued a statement favoring pipeline expansion, hastily built C6, and opted to bring someone else they trusted to finish the job. That's how you came to join this project."

"What are these syndicates? What do they want?"

"Haven't you heard Earth news lately?"

"I've been at Chasma, cut off from the rest of the cosmos. So, no."

"A lot has happened in the last couple of days—bad things. Secret societies in conflict with UEF mandates suddenly sprung up everywhere. Earth gov knew about them long ago but didn't think they were much of a threat—until now. We fear the most influential of these, the ETA, may have infiltrated civil and government sectors. They affirm Martian lights are of alien origin and the Nirgal area an underground alien base. Their objective is to broker an alliance with aliens, obtain technology, and take over the government. Once Earth is under their control, they plan to become the guardians of space."

"That's absolutely absurd!"

"I couldn't agree with you more. They want to build large peacekeeping space craft, colonize far-off worlds, and establish a cosmic alliance with other space civilizations. On the other hand, more influential groups believe this is a sign of the end of times and are telling members that aliens will soon invade Earth. It's our job to uncover dig site mysteries and provide information that will save Earth from these radical groups, rather fast."

"I suppose you found something other than water in that dig."

"We were hoping you could tell us what it is."

I remained silent and absorbed in thought, unsure what to say. "I get it now. C6 is the Martian version of Area 51 back on Earth?"

"You could say that, yes."

"That's pretty amazing, when you think of it. All right, then I'm in. So tell me about this strange thing you found?"

"It's a flat object of unknown size ninety meters below ground. It broke every drill we had. At first, we thought we were dealing with dense volcanic crystals, perhaps lattices with hardness many times that of drill heads. ESCE went down the shaft to investigate but could not identify the object. Whatever it is, there's not a thing on Earth that will even scratch it."

Pausing for a moment, he stood up and said with mysterious flair, "This is unlike anything anyone has ever encountered before. It multiplies light and never changes temperature. Even after torching, it stays at a constant 22°C."

"Room temperature, ideal for human habitation—what a coincidence."

"We thought about digging it up. But for safety and handling reasons felt an expert should be involved. We have no clue how to contain or control this object. I assume you want to see it, yes?" he replied with a credible smirk meriting my immediate endorsement.

Not far from Hans's office, an air-locked blast door led into a seemingly endless tunnel. Hans invited me in, closed the door, and took an emergency flashlight, indicating I should do likewise. We boarded a small cart and sped down the long, straight tunnel until it ended. Directly in front of us, a shiny blue-smoked glass got my attention, giving off more light than what fell on it. Hans indicated the glassy floor was the object in question. Above us, a dark five-meter-wide drill shaft led straight up to the surface.

The object felt solid, smooth, and comfortably warm to the touch. Knocking on it produced no significant echo or thud but rather a pleasant, gentle tinkle. With a soft wave of the hand, soil easily brushed away, exposing more of it, demonstrating it was no mere fortuitous rock formation but part of something congruous or larger, perhaps an actual structure.

Atomic analysis showed the object was composed mainly of silicon with traces of boron, chromium, selenium, and cesium, bearing isotopic renditions I had never seen in nature. Its molecules were evenly distributed at the atomic level, then stacked in ways impossible to produce in a laboratory, reacting intelligently to the environment like living, nano organisms. Isotope decay rates indicated these molecules bonded some 122,000 years ago with a half-life in the billions of years. I concluded this was part of an ancient structure needing to be exhumed, and preparations were made to excavate the site the following day.

With nothing better to do but wait for the structure to be exhumed, I suggested we pay the crash site a visit. At first, Hans didn't want to venture out of the colony, but after some arm twisting, he chose to come along. He had not donned a suit for some time, and this seemed a good opportunity to get a few hours in one—as long as we took a shuttle.

It was the typical Martian scape, hosted by a plethora of sandy soils, rocks strewn about, and eroded slopes. Monitoring equipment stood right where previous surveyors left it, starving for data. The absence of impact basins, meteorites, or iridium deposits suggested nothing crashed there lately; but the area exhibited magnetic anomalies typical of EM induction. With better things to do than escort geologists around, Hans thought the trip was a waste of time, but my best sense said there was something else there; we had just not found it yet.

With Hans getting progressively upset and our immediate curiosity met, I could no longer justify hanging around, and we made ready to leave. No sooner, the sound of data recorder servos got our attention. We were sensibly skeptical at first, for all we knew our suits probably triggered these things. But they pointed up and swiftly locked onto some invisible source. It did not take long for a star like object to appear in the heavens, increasing in brightness. This was rather unusual. No objects ever appeared when people were around, rendering all previous assumptions unfit to conventional ways of thinking.

"That thing is coming down where we are, no?" Hans said, realizing the gravity of our situation.

"Won't be surprised if it does," I said quickly, adding to mounting concern.

"Let's give it the right of way!"

Hans immediately turned and moved toward the shuttle, but I held him back, and said, "Wait! I don't think it's going to hit us!"

"You want to find out? Be my guest," he said, trying to break my hold.

"We'll never clear its kill zone. What's the point of running?"

"The shuttle's force field gives us more protection, yes?" he said, desperately trying to break loose from my grip.

"No, it won't. Hans, this is a message, not a meteor!"

"You stay and write it down! Let me go!" he replied, sparking a brief physical struggle between us until he managed to run off from my grip.

I tagged closely behind, but the object's descent unexpectedly deviated from its previous path and followed us to the shuttle. Just steps from the ship, the light came to an abrupt halt just meters above us, hovered chillingly still for a few seconds, and pinned us flat on our backs. Suits temporarily went off line, and our air supply acquired a pungent ozone scent. As it hovered, the object emitted a beehive-like hum, followed by a loud wind-up sound, and then vanished into thin air. Recorders went dead quiet, and we lingered mutely still on the ground after the incident, badly shaken up.

"It's gone; that's good, yes!" Hans said with a hoarse voice, trembling and struggling to close persistent bulging eyes. "Better it than us, no?"

Unable to get my lips to move right, I muttered aimlessly, "Hans?"

"What?"

"That was so, so . . . cool!"

"No, not cool!"

"I want to try that again," I said trying to laugh but quivering instead.

"I'm going to kill you, slowly, in a decompression chamber until you burst; that still won't do you justice!" he said, progressively getting madder.

"I thought you need me," I replied.

"I change my mind. You crazy, stupid, reckless Americans! No, I'm more stupid for following you, *Scheiße kopf*!"

"Try a Chasma storm some time, then you'll be ready for anything."

"Next time, I'll let you die in the storm; then you'll have more respect for life," he said, as we got back on our feet and suits executed nagging redundant diagnostic checks.

"Did you make out what that was?" I said, heading toward the recorders.

"I couldn't see a damn thing but a large, stinking bright light!" Hans said definitely upset, rolling his eyes slowly downward only to take a moderate distasteful breath. His facial expression said it all; some fetid odor caught his attention. "My air stunk up! This is all your fault!"

"Could have been worst," I added sarcastically.

"What's that supposed to mean, ah?" he said, reacting to my defiance, already upset from our previous struggle.

"Had we been struck by the object, we wouldn't be here stinking about it."

"I should know better than stand in the way of a fifty ton rock going as fast as a shuttle. But no, the professor here knows more," Hans said, turning toward the shuttle. "Nothing's going to happen that you don't want; it's going to be safe. You nearly got us both killed!"

"Hey, we're in luck," I said, retrieving recorder data. "We got data."

"Get it, and let's get out of here before another light shows up," he yelled.

"Hans, don't be a liver. Being a geologist is an occupational hazard."

"Don't worry about my liver, it's fine. Your head isn't!"

"We got every EM trace from the moment the light first appeared. What do you think that strange wind-up sound was . . ."

"I heard nothing!" he said with a sharp snap. "You were yelling too loud! Shut up and let's go." Hans shook dust from his suit, kicked rocks in front of him, and continued on his way to the shuttle, slow and stiff from mid-section down for good reason. On the way back, he was quiet, and I kept my helmet on, because a waste can be a remarkably awful thing to mind.

Back at C6, Hans enlisted the help of an EM engineer, Lieutenant Sean Ryan, to decipher crash site data. Sean, Hans, and I formed what Earth gov referred to as the Mars Contact Team, or MCT. He determined that the object's base EM rate was similar to that used by shuttles on Mars, except stronger and more complex. Phase variations coincided with the object's lateral movements during descent, typical of levity drive. But strange patterns preceding the object's disappearance remained a mystery. In theory, the lights were a type of spacecraft far in advance of our own.

When asked for an honest assessment, I was not the least bit surprised. A definite yes-or-no answer was in order: were these, or not, UFOs? I was hesitant and evasive, but Hans persisted on the kind of response expected. I had not seen the object, only read its wave signatures with our technology to compare against. Dangerous and far-fetched of an assumption, I gave a conditional yes answer based on existing facts.

The following morning, UEF finally broke silence, announcing ongoing efforts to investigate Martian surface anomalies. Members, famished for answers, were asked to remain calm and not jump to conclusions until all facts were known, but it was too late. Commentators were quick to brand Earth gov's initiative a bit humble and undeniably overdue for an issue as heatedly debated as this, raising conspiracy concerns.

Earth's political setting seemed calm on the surface but inwardly struggled to subdue growing civil unrest. The main concern in everyone's mind was the same; were there aliens on Mars? Clerics answered the question by preaching that a Martian apocalypse was upon the world, stirring such panic that entire families desperately gathered few belongings, abandoned their homes, and headed for the hills blaring frantically, "The Martians are coming!"

Not far behind, dissident coalitions seized the moment to prey on chaos by openly proclaiming their intent to depose Earth gov and create a new space federation. Many industries and services shut down, given the large number of civilians fleeing for their lives. The world lost its peaceful luster in the blink of an eye; UEF was on the brink of collapse—just what sinister masters sought.

A resolute, iniquitous intelligence manipulated situations and people at will through clever deceit. This was Earth's secret government, centralized and infused throughout all walks of life—ghosts from a buried past. All seemed lost at the mercy of such invisible enemy, a mastermind dominating man's reactions far removed from inference. In spite of all the social and technical advances achieved to date, members were just as gullible as ever and willingly hostages of their own world.

Chapter 5: *The Gatekeepers*

The gates of my soul had seen enough desert scenery, sandy canyons, alien sunsets, and most anything mineral to last a lifetime. Nevertheless, a compelling urge to suit up, go to the surface, and burden my gaze yet again with more of the same drab settings haunted my thoughts all through the day to the point of obsession, obviously, for reasons I could not ascertain at the time. In spite of the daunting tedium at hand, there was a tempting fringe benefit I could not steer clear of, one that transformed such staggering exertion into something undeniably worthwhile: wearing a suit.

Granted, suits were clumsy, uncomfortable, and hard to change in and out of; but they gave me unrivaled confidence: one of the perks drawing me to space. Being in a suit inspired a mystical sense of duty, strength, even felt I could fly with it. I made it an instinctive habit to raise my hand vertical to the arm as if pushing something out of the way but only when I wore a suit. I was conscious of it, but since no one nagged me about it, I gave it no sensible thought.

Setting the suit aside, there was something else tugging me away from the colony, something indescribably stirring, a most profound yet undeniable longing I found difficult to describe.

A gentle, implicit inner calling, sincere as motionless yet definitely present winds, hastened me to leave the known world behind and trust mysteriously morbid desolation. It was an enigmatic enticement of equally indefinite source, many times stronger than any desire endearing my lucid consciousness, such that not much else seemed to matter. An uplifting sense I could not deny dwarfed my being, as if some benevolent force pleasantly revealed its essence with numinous yet loving affection, rivaling that of a stirring song's rapture.

Watery hands clasped together in impulsive disarray, uncertain how to best tender the moment. My lips compulsorily softened open, articulating a silent language enveloped in unrivaled caring warmth that unknowingly filled an opportune episode in time. My heart raced with intense emotions, powerless to ascertain and much less renounce them. I sensed no fear or concern for life, only exhilarating awareness to comply with an inferred summon unable to explain why. Answers, I felt, would be found out there among ancient sands if I would only go to them, rather than dwell upon subjective fallacy if I did not.

Ignoring common taste and following inner judgment, I eventually ventured out of C6 in a new compact solarium and sat alone on the western rim, hoping to get a better view of these enigmatic Martian lights falling from pale skies far beyond the eastern valley rise. There, I day-dreamed for hours on end, hoping something other than space rafts or shuttles pierced the skies to satiate my inquisitiveness, but I would not be so readily sated.

Alone, in the dusty solitude of this mysterious, deep ancient valley now hosted by sand and worn rocks, my mind's eye tried to envision what Mars looked like eons ago, a time when water ran through its plentiful veins and lush flora reigned over its subtle lands with passionate supremacy, a jewel of passionate floral beauty and gentle resting place for life, graced by inestimable forms. Tall timbers thrived calmly on nearby mountains. Dense forests adorned the meandering Uzboi river-way garnished by nurturing waters. Short green grasses gilded surrounding flat lands endowed with glorious budding colors, delicately interspersed as if by design.

When I least expected it, my sights gently faded away into slumber's soothing realms; and thoughts serenely assumed a new reality, inspired by the same uplifting affection that urged me to the rim. The rare whisper of Martian winds softly rapping against my still suit and occasional dust devils stirring historical soils willingly fell beneath the edge of awareness. The present peeled far into forlorn recess, and the past fostered anew like an unfolding scroll in living vision, revealing an ancient secret long suppressed by tides of time.

At Holden Crater's southern gates, ten kilometers due north from my position, a series of tiered cascades and rapids released crystalline waters unto Holden, winding through various downstream paths for about two kilometers. Rushing waters relentlessly battered boulders lining flanking canyon walls with imposing, zealous reprisal. Resting still above the churning stream, prismatic bows embellished rising vapor sprays the height of the picturesque canyon.

South of my position, the river branched into two main arteries. One tributary flowed west behind C6 amid small winding lochs and impassable greenery. The other coursed through eastern Uzboi, caressing gentle fords along its banks, emphasized by timbered islands strewn like tear drops along the river's path. Both rivers joined at the gates of Holden, officially classifying the land C6 set upon as an island.

Aviary species of all sizes and colors took flight over the valley in vast numbers, rendering their majestic wings widely spread near the rapids to gain altitude. Beyond soaring peaks east of the river, the landscape seemed impenetrable, endowed with lush floral plentitude and enormous trees up to half km in width. Vegetation covered every dell and hill in a vast array of colors: the higher the elevation, the redder vegetation became. Nature selected pink and blue tones for most of its field flowers, raising their buds to nourish and praise the mighty hand of creation that brought them to being. The air itself was calm, refreshing, and carried a sweet scent to it reminiscent of wild gardenias inviting deep refreshed inhalation.

Mars was a lush garden paradise, a perfectly sculptured work of art reflecting creation's vast splendors and the cordial desire of fellow worlds. Everything about the planet was cleanness, beauty, purity, perfect harmony, and inspiration to evolve into higher spiritual states of mind. It was a consecrated world, loved, and regarded holy by its people as a reverent tribute to, and desirable dwelling place for, His Majesty; there was no higher motive for the people, for such is the purpose of life.

A powerful hallowed essence enveloped Mars and infused its divine force into all living forms, inspiring a life of saintly devotion and virtuous love for the Infinite, the breath of life itself, instilled by the tender thoughts and sacred unity of an entire world collective. Its people dreamed of and inhaled holy love from His Greatness at all times, leading lives strictly devoted to virtuous thought and desire rather than one of erotic filth seized by fear and lust. They lived for Him, wanting nothing else for themselves. Thus, they had everything.

The absolute grandeur offered by Mars's exquisite beauty and its people's holy devotion to the Infinite imparted the soul a heavenly uplifting quality, transcending the observer to praise the Majesty of Glory and His vast inspiring greatness with heartfelt longing.

Stirred by such overwhelming beauty, and inspired by the very essence of celestial elegance, my heart swelled with love and my lips praised the Creator with enthusiastic devotion. Coming to my knees, my soul offered humble reverence to an unseen, but felt, Lord of Majesty. With breath taking vigor, a clean heart sung amid inner tranquility, uttering tender, sweet words of gratitude for His divine wonders and gift of eternal love.

I suddenly caught glimpse of a child, coming into view rather unexpectedly not far to the side. He stood serenely against the gentle breeze, posture facing east and arms open in complete devotion to the Infinite. I was glad to see him and felt I somehow knew him. He wore a yellowish shirt covering arms to the elbows, dark bluish shorts, sandals, and a backpack filled with necessities. His facial appearance was slightly Asian, endowed with large brown eyes and fair complexion. He stood in place for some time, not soaking in sunlight but rather faithfully sharing his essence with Highest Majesty.

"Oh-joi!" he vigorously shouted at the wind, moved by inner spirit. Nearby hills promptly echoed his high-pitched bellow, complementing lively ballads composed by colorful aviaries swaying in the wind.

Suddenly, a young lady of same age appeared by his side, dressed much the same way. After reverently bowing to her, the young boy gently took her right hand, slowly elevated it above his shoulders, and addressed her in a lovely tongue I had never heard before yet felt somewhat familiar with. I carefully listened to every spoken word and surprisingly, by some strange means, knew their precise meaning, repeating them over and over again to memorize them.

Most respectfully, she replied back sweetly to the boy saying, "The grace in my heart is the light that Infinite Father has placed within us. What joy it is to share of it with my brother that so willingly awaits for me and elevates my hand above his own tender heart."

The young lady's loving expression and gentlest of eyes deeply moved me, bringing a persistent knot to my throat. Emotional tears swelled in my eyes, yet I did not understand why. Surprisingly, I knew what words the young boy would utter in advance, as if I knew them. "I am but one soul, one of many, that seeks to forever join with his Creator in eternity. Might you walk beside me and share of the many wondrous creations His Supreme Majesty has shared with us?"

"My dear brother is himself a wondrous creation within creation itself," she replied gently. "May this friendship last an eternity. My parents tell me the best way to learn about yourself is to talk about your visions. Perhaps we can share our dreams with one another, my friend, brother."

"My sweet starlight, you are my one and only—friend," he said lovingly as both children gradually faded from sight, leaving behind a mysterious cloak of silence that lingered notably still against stunning colorful prairies and countless thriving wonders, as if to eternally imprint their charming beauty upon my heart forever.

Suddenly, a barely visible pink pulsing beam swiftly streaked through the heavens behind thick clouds and struck the planet's defense shields high above the atmosphere some distance due east, producing a blinding yet silent flash several times brighter than the sun. The massive energy impact instantly shuddered the planet and warped its defense shields, setting off undulating plasma ripples that spread decisively across the entire orb. Much like a rock splash on water, a chilling plasma halo heaved radiant tongues of fire about the beam reaching far into the vast dark abyss where its blistering canopy dissolved into flickering auroras. The beam endured ruthlessly upon Mars's shields trying to breach them, however vainly.

Skies promptly capitulated to the titanic cosmic impact above it, plunging from their lofty places toward the Martian surface with deafening roars, as if impelled against by a colossal press. A massive fireball beneath the beam swiftly amassed into a churning hellish haze, spreading in all directions unimpeded and scorching anything the placid heavens sheltered. Blistering flames raced downward for the surface like a mighty plunging dragon, turning the air itself into a terrifying, sweltering inferno. In only moments, the passive fabric of this divinely inspired world, the holy essence carved into the very bosom of this wondrous spiritual abode once known as the loving pride of the heavens was forcibly ripped away.

Dusky clouds swelled overhead with terrifying, baleful dominance, provoking menacing knights of darkness to rise up and spread chaotically like turbid, scorching furnaces, instantly consuming docile fauna within their reach. Thunderous wailing tears found their way upon Mars's frail gardens in abrupt torrents, washing away radiant perennial glories treasured for their opulent beauty. On the surface, strong cyclonic winds mercilessly uprooted man's creative ornaments along their path.

Moments after the beam struck planetary shields, countless ominous-colored flashes peppered the heavens behind clouds from one horizon to the other. Skies trembled feebly with every pulsing flash, swiftly followed by earsplitting sonic bursts that rattled the ground and lunged intense echoing thuds as if the planet were hollow.

Then I heard other voices, male and female, nervously discussing an ongoing crisis of sort, mingled with sonic explosions above. I could not see them, but a panicked male voice said hastily, "We will counter attack."

"But that's not our way," replied the female with quivering voice. "The destroyer is in your heart."

The man then responded, gasping for composure, "He beckons me; he breathes in me." Sobbing, he then said, "Viren, was I."

I intimately felt this individual's excruciating suffering, begging to express from the deepest part of my being. Disenchanting sadness ruled his faded soul from fear's darkest domains. His heart cried out with ardent agony, moved by intense sorrow born from grave wrongs he once committed, unbearable to harbor. He had no hope for a future or impetus to go on living, for the breath of life had departed him and his faith was no more. The moment belonged to dread's harshest chambers, convincingly imploring chastisement to cloak reason and disband divine justice's forgiving hand.

"This can't be you. You are wrong!" said the female, weeping and greatly disturbed.

Sadly, the man responded in a somber, opaque tone best harbored by brinks of pity, "Because of me, I have brought the death of my world; for me, there shall only be death."

Another more mature voice then resounded loudly, "My son, don't do this! You are now a brother, not Viren. Don't leave her alone—again."

The man, blaming himself for malevolent events ensuing against his world, said, "A man like me, does not deserve to unite with a promising soul as her."

Overcome by looming emotive grief difficult to grasp, damp eyes relinquished captivating bonds upon keen eyelids, and gifts of sadness poured down my cheeks without hindrance. I cried out with heartfelt fervor, telling myself not to abandon her several times. But a guilty conscience moved sinisterly within, despicably persuading the heart to relinquish any hope for the love of her benign soul.

On my knees, hands raised to helmet, I surrendered the heart to sob's calling. The phrase "Don't leave her alone" resounded remorsefully in my head against an equally imposing rejoinder, "Viren, was I."

Repulsed by dreadful deeds foreign to me, my chest churned enraptured by emotions relived from a bygone era yet quite real in the present. I feared this man's resolve to dispose improperly of his life, and by way of a hidden voice barely whimpering far from my senses, I felt him close enough to be me.

Voices mysteriously faded into coercing silent coffers unseen, and dead stillness seized the moment, unruffled by paltry human strivings. Above the planet, explosive bursts against its shields suddenly ceased, and normalcy made every effort to breathe Infinite beauty back unto Sol's heavenly jewel once more. Clouds softened their stout hold on the heavens and cyclonic winds slowly took their leave. Bulging waterways rushed forcefully toward the equator, carrying skeletal remains of once glorious floral galleries and incomprehensible living beauty, sadly piling alongside serrated fords as if by no greater admiring worth. A life of beauty so dastardly unloved, disregarded, trampled by vicious spiritual poisons—our legacy.

But then, an intense flash blinded my sights, dimming gradually to expose a somber, wandering sun and stars set against a darkened cloudless day sky wavering here and there without due course. A powerful, invisible force immediately crushed me against soils that shivered violently. Trees and rocks pressed swiftly into the ground like mining drills, piercing into the soil in a sudden thump, pleading to disappear beneath it. Grounds under my feet soon crumpled like weak sandstone pits and buckled downward into wide cavernous depressions as if the planet was on the verge of deflating collapse.

The deafening roar of a million thunder bolts rumbled rigorously through the skies like persistent fiendish screams, their startling bellows enduring endlessly through hollow manifests. The menacing voice of a terrible weapon of mass destruction had spoken, and its worst spoils would soon materialize upon those still alive on this small world.

Almost instantly, soils, rocks, and water on the side of the planet struck by the weapon raised up into space with an ominous jerk, forming a vast icy spray canopy that lingered away from Mars and headed for Earth. A wall of fire five hundred kilometers high surged from the impact site, spawning an enormous sweltering wave that raced to encompass the entire planet.

Dust clouds wailed across Mars at incredible speeds, preceded by a boiling, powerful jet stream swiftly leveling everything in its course. Immediately following, an atrocious infernal swell, a scorching fire storm of unequaled proportions, hastily swept over the surface, annihilating what wondrous landscapes remained with extreme force.

Abrupt human screams, suddenly silenced, covered eerie heavens littered by death's relentless talents as the fire storm overwhelmed Mars. What water remained swept into the skies and boiled away until lost from sight. Charred remains uprooted from veiled burrows and flew through the air with little effort. Soils, buildings, once-living forms, anything not yet scorched sped swiftly through the skies and turned to ashes, leaving no life force to chance. Enormous whirlwinds joined forces with others, tearing the surface apart with inconceivable fury in a boiling mortifying trap that consumed every living substance on the planet. In seconds, flames consumed all that once lived, all that was, all that remained.

Cracks ripped across the surface, releasing tongues of lethal flames from the planet's deepest bowels. Blood gushed forth like tearful torrents from a desperate, sobbing mother whose child has callously been taken from her life-giving bosom. Tumultuous skies lit brightly with myriad deafening gaps, cloaked by stifling ash clouds seeking to divest their essence upon dead soils.

Lands once beneath the sea bulged upward and colossal volcanoes swiftly exploded with veracious vengeance in a maelstrom of gloomy chaos. An enormous four thousand kilometer sweltering breach ripped the surface open like an old garment as the planet's inner core roamed the mantle out of control and wavered loosely toward Valles Marineris.

As life hastily extinguished its hold on Mars, cooling currents caused atmospheric pressures to invert. Giant tornadoes aimed their tips away from the surface, littering space with flaming remains. Debris previously discharged into space returned with a vengeance; some burst into blistering dust during reentry, but others hit the surface with punishing force. The entire planet turned itself inside out until fires no longer burned on its wasted surface and air depleted. In the end, Mars's orbit pushed out two million kilometers, and much of its surface spiraled toward Earth on a fifty-thousand-year journey.

Mars continued to shake violently for days. Sol's garden world became a darkened, dead realm in seconds, incapable of recovering on its own from such unwarranted woe.

High above Mars, cheering crowds celebrated the death of an inspired creation; and the agony of millions sacrificed for the utmost pleasure of oppressive dogs of war. Thieves they were, deceived murderers reduced in liberty, trained into ignorance, and kept from truth I had no idea existed. An expendable destiny of servitude awaited them, earning death as reward for unquestioned sacrifice to someone that honestly could care less about them.

Voices swiftly silenced, and so did the vision. Nothing more than dust and rocks remained: no trees, no river, no life. I sat motionless, stunned, going over every detail of this experience to ensure its accurate endurance. Had I seen what Mars looked like long ago and its tragic demise? How about the children, the intense dialogue, and the fire in the sky? Were aliens behind this vision, and how could I be sure of that?

My head hung low, poised numbly before the setting sun forbearingly witnessing deep inner sorrow. Tears slowly dried up upon my face, and my gaze sought some indefinite lost cause within. Still, I felt inwardly cleansed of great torment. Although I did not fully understand the meaning of this stirring vision, my spirit felt refreshed, renewed, and more aware of my thoughts than ever. There was little I could do to question the vision's contents, but few would ever believe them, and no words could accurately describe any of it.

Digging for clues hidden within this small crimson world only gave way to rocks, and rocks gave way to more dirt, but no fossilized bones or twigs turned up to please my growing distress. This was all that remained of that glorious world I envisioned, devastated by technology far beyond anything I conceived at the time, but its saintly magnificence still thrived in me. It lived and breathed where no weapon, or no one, could ever extinguish it, boldly shielded by the strongest bond in the universe: the heart.

Taking my pick, I set it handle first into the dirt and left it to serve as a memorial honoring the essence of this vision and the magnificence that Mars once was, marking this spot for as long as it would stand in time. I would return to this place many times in the future but not without the wondrous grace of my heart, my beautiful missing flame, the melody of my soul that will forever be stamped unto my heart with infinite love and soft, poetic songs.

Not far to the south, I noticed a wide gradient pathway leading from the rim to the ancient waterway below. It was definitely not the work of mother nature. Sand and rock covered most of it, but a simple wave of the foot easily pushed excess material aside, clearly exposing the original path. Oddly enough, it went unnoticed by previous geological expeditions.

Not thinking twice about it and driven by sheer curiosity, I comfortably descended down the path to the ford landing below. Rocks littered the ground all the way to the now water-starving ledge, but soft oval stones progressively grew in number. I smiled widely, pleased to find evidence of an ancient roadway used by individuals coming to or from the river long ago. In the dry riverbed, an incomplete network of large flat rocks, now standing like obelisks, may have served as anchored foundations for a bridge. Northward on the opposite bank, another path meandered up the mountain side.

It was time to head back to C6, but a startling shimmer briefly caught the corner of my eye. I turned to see what it was, but lost track of it. Intrigued, I bent over and sifted rocks until my gloves made contact with a round, light object shining with absolute metallic glory. It was a small disk-like item no more than ten centimeters across. A diffused dome covered one side. Unsure what it did, I stowed it in my suit and took it with me for further analysis.

The object, another ancient relic, proved to be some five thousand years older than the structure. Scans showed no recognizable electronics in it but revealed ribbed crystal lattices akin to those found in the structure.

Excited about the find, I brought it to Hans's attention. When placed near the structure, its dome glowed brightly. Touching it turned the light on and off. Obviously, this was a flashlight, powered by induction. It became obvious that ancient Martians delivered wireless energy to consumer products from a central source, a concept in the spirit of Nikola Tesla.

Evidence systematically placed Mars's destruction between the time of the flashlight, the last-known period of planetary industrial capabilities, and the structure, or about 127,000 years ago. Top magma flows from Olympus Mons date back to 125,000 BC, meaning, the structure was built after the planet's destruction, not before. Was the structure a memorial of sort? It was an intriguing theory not eagerly accepted by Hans but well regarded by Earth gov.

The government was interested in Martian history but more so their technology, so Sean was put to reverse engineer the flashlight. He spent days trying to figure it out, but Earth was just not far enough along in nano technology to know what to do with it. He had no idea what part of the lattice did what, got frustrated, and decided to return the object back to me.

By day three, the entire structure was fully excavated. It measured ten meters high by twenty wide and shone with a glorious whitish-blue glow easily dwarfing nearby lights. At top center, a two-meter-wide oval spire raised five meters above a slightly domed roof. The building was sealed tight, built from a single piece of glass. A fused quartz walkway two meters wide completely surrounded the structure, while another approached from the east and vanished into the rock still to be excavated.

There were no markings, protrusions indicating an entrance, or any kind of utility feeds. Walls were analyzed for breaks that suggested a possible doorway, proving futile. Resonance and X-rays also failed to penetrate through the walls. The crew dug around the structure looking for secret passages or control devices but came up empty. There was no obvious way of getting into the building, and frustrations mounted accordingly.

We were getting nowhere logically, so it was time to think out of the box. Every building has a door, every door a knob and key that opens it. Perhaps the structure was meant to be opened by a distinct key master, but who or where was this illusive character? If we were led to discover the structure, it was reasonable to assume we were also given the key with which to open it.

The strange patterns issued by the descending object at the crash site kept pounding my mind. If the field data we collected purposely held the key, then Martian lights were the key masters, and we were the gatekeepers in charge of the key, a fascinating idea that raised healthy debate. But if true, then a connection between the structure, Martian lights, and alien intelligence would be established. Still, why would anyone go through all this trouble and make contact so complicated?

History proves we are belligerent, unpredictable creatures not to be trusted. If the frightened and aggressive were already at large, and alien existence had not yet been confirmed, how would members react to the real facts after establishing contact? Alien religion might be at odds with ours; physical appearance and culture might differ widely. Were we unprejudiced enough to embrace universal diversity? Apparently so—aliens seemed willing to press on by handing us the keys.

Sean assembled the equipment needed to irradiate the structure with field data, set to play back from the point the light hovered until it vanished. Since we were dealing with EM signatures capable of nullifying gravity, the experiment posed many hazards. We had no experience with this complex a signature and no clue what to expect, so the transmitter dish was bolted down solid, and everyone sought cover.

The transmitter glowed a bright blue and shook violently during play back. When it stopped, the spire shone radiantly in all colors of the spectrum. Brightly lit columns emitted from each corner of the building, hinting a touch of celestial splendor to amazed spectators. "We've finally done it" was the general consensus from everyone present. But after several seconds, the light faded, the light pillars withdrew, the building resumed its previous whitish-blue glow, and no door opened.

A helpless wave of disappointment fell upon us all. One by one, crews headed back down the tunnel until only Hans, Sean, and I remained. The equipment checked out fine, and Sean wanted to try again, but I wasn't sure that was such a good idea. The spire glowed, so maybe we did our part, and now it was up to our alien associates to do theirs.

Known for impatient, impulsive behavior, we earthlings are a tough bunch to please. Maybe aliens decided to think things through, given recent reactions brewing back on Earth. Worst yet, deemed us unworthy of contact, and with good reason. We waited two highly apprehensive hours for something to happen, but nothing ever did. It was reasonable to assume that Earth waited hundreds, if not thousands, of years for this fateful moment, and a few more hours were definitely tolerable.

With nothing better to do, and dinner already well past its time, the kitchen graciously sent us leftovers. The typical Martian meal arrived: lots of veggies, fake meats, and flax milk, stuff designed to fill you up and turn one's stomach into a veritable gas chamber. Quite good I might add, conceding that having no meal at all is a considerably worst scenario.

Dinner gave us a rare chance to formally acquaint ourselves, a feat long overdue. Sean was a space engineer hoping to land a promising career in Space Core. He enlisted as a propulsion technologist and transferred into Space Core shortly after. His dream was to someday break the light speed barrier and prove Einstein's theory of relativity wrong, concepts way ahead of his time.

He claimed there's nothing magic about light speed since energy traveling faster than light already surrounds us at all times. Whether you walked toward a star or it approached you, the limit was violated. Science measured light like a projectile, noting the time photons traversed a given distance. But according to Sean, star light transferred energy unto the space medium's electric field and assumed its propagation properties like a carrier wave.

"When cosmic energy collides with physical forms, local magnetic fields slow it down and turn it into light," he said. "It works like a sprinter slowing down when rushing into water. This is the basis for EM technology. For instance, what happens when the EM equation's magnetic term nears zero?"

"Resultant approaches infinity," I replied.

"I rest my case. Light from many stellar objects are headed our way at speeds faster than light. But that can't be; nothing can exceed light because wonky time stuff happens. So to avoid cosmic chaos, science brought into the bloody mix such things as dark matter, big rips, and all sorts of retardedness."

Hans's great grandfather was a world marine who perished during the spliced wars. In those days, splicing offered promising solutions to incurable diseases, but many saw it as a means to desensitize human values. Opportunists argued that bat ears and lizard tongues were humorous fashion statements in line with people's right to self-expression. After all, they claimed splicing was safe, reversible, and convenient—and it paid very well.

The real reason for altering one's physical form was all one and the same: impress or terrify others. It didn't take long for things to get out of hand. The world divided itself into offensive cliques. Inhumane figures filled the world while law and order crumbled. Human breeding delivered hideous atrocities, a side effect of splicing, while the meaning of love, charity, and brotherhood met sudden demise at the hands of global war.

"My great-grandfather lost a son to splicing," Hans said. "He vanished during the militia's rapture and got turned into a beast. When they both met in the Libyan desert, the son was mentally controlled by Amarna and killed his father. But later, the son helped bring down Amarna."

No one spoke a word in rebuttal, catching up on dinner to avoid the subject. I, on the other hand, froze in place; a chill ran down my neck and involuntarily uttered, "Fritz." I had no clue why or where the name came from, but as soon as brain caught up to mouth, I knew I had done a bad thing. It was like a bad case of hiccups in the middle of an opera, the kind you can't avoid sharing, but irritates everyone else around you.

I saw trouble coming; and sure enough, Hans lifted up his head abruptly, stared my way in the least kindest way, and prematurely swallowed whatever was in his palette. He definitely looked surprised, but I more so. Sean kept eating undisturbed, comforting his head against the wall with no sign of aversion. I kept rather quiet trying to wish Hans away, but it didn't take him long to inquire. "How did you know that? That information is strictly classified by my family's request."

I felt dumb enough to know I couldn't steer a dog out of a corn field, and that deep stare of his made it that much worst. "Earth gov . . . chronological profiles," I said limping right along, but not readily convincing Hans. I assured him it was information I accessed during previous UEF positions, though that wasn't compelling enough.

"Fritz is an unknown hero that deserves an important spot in history," I added. "Without him, the Libyan campaign would have failed and Amarna evaded capture." That sounded good, but I couldn't figure out how I came up with the name in the first place. "Matter of fact, my great-grandfather, Greg Sullivan, was also a world marine and was killed by Amarna during his final stand in Gialo. I'm sure he and Fritz got to meet along the way."

"You know history very well," Hans said, unexpectedly changing his stance. "While most people won't venture beyond surface information, you do; that's excellent. My associates will be glad to know this. Good thing those war days are behind us, no?"

"Maybe they never vanished, just went dormant, until now," Sean said.

"The way people are talking, I wouldn't doubt it," I said. "Dad used to say that drifting mouthpieces can't assume power without giving gullible followers a healthy dose of big F's: fear and fraud. There's a lot of that going around, so you know someone's lining up to grab something."

"Isn't that the bloody truth? An ideal is an attempt to steal. Hey, that rhymes! Ideal, steal, get it? Anyway, even political whingers have a time with it. They spend their time codswalloping, doing everything arse over elbow, and blowing off sociable crusty dragons rather than give it welly. It's like some wanker up there lost the plot and wants the ministry to go barmy. So keep your pecker up; it gets real wonky from here on out."

"Earth gov should evangelize members before the ETA does, then corner the ETA with facts, something we should have done long ago."

"Knock them up, you say? And how do you suppose we do that, lad? Things are shambolic as it is. The ETA is far along in that respect and very well organized. Even if we go full monty, it will be tough diddling them."

"Sean is right," Hans said. "A vast underground network operates from every state like weed vine, but its nerve center still eludes authorities."

"Consider the ETA will lose its edge once we enter the structure," I added.

Hans sat back and oddly rubbed his chin, thinking deeply through something. I couldn't tell what it was but struck me curious he gave it so much thought all of a sudden. Moreover, it concerned me he did. "You have something there," he said opaquely, with an attitude inspiring nothing less than suspicion.

"That being the case," he continued vaguely, "we should get that building opened up, and quickly, yes? Let's focus on our mission and let Earth gov handle anarchy. We have much work to do in the days to come."

Hans slapped me slightly on the back and remained in rational twilight for a few moments, mumbling indistinctly to himself. I stared at him not knowing what to think. But he, on the other hand, seemed oblivious to my stare, having drifted helplessly into foregone reveries foreign to me.

Noting evening's lateness, he politely excused himself and headed back to his office to do undisclosed business. Sean and I decided to spend the night near the structure to keep an eye on things and, perhaps, be the first to glance into the wonders of a world long lost.

I could not help but speculate why an advanced race, aware of our belligerent past, would mingle with us? As the old proverb says, "Tell me who you are with, and I will tell you who you are." We humans have the potential to side against evil, but most often choose not to. Were aliens any different? Were they also slaves of their own memories and tormenting creations? If not, I hoped they overlooked our faults, taught us how to save us from ourselves, and set us on the right path in our search for love.

Chapter 6: *Faith Has a Purpose*

Ancient Martian stones, packed snugly into cold tunnel soils over the course of time, endured dormant tedium amid impassive stillness, defied solely by our obtrusive presence. From far-off abodes and vast depths, destiny's insightful motives emended indolent ambitions by incessantly rolling and morphing them until ultimately amassing about the structure: not to bequeath its encasement to the mighty sentinel of ages but silently lend worthy witness to our detestable, unrighteous legacy.

There was something about these soils less obvious than just compelling mineral splendor, flaunting feebly at injudicious sights. They enclosed the indiscernible essence of a once thriving world, now brusquely besieged by utter torpid serenity: Mars's lost soul. This was a hard thing for the blind at heart to conceive, whose erroneous plight and loveless simplicity has always deceived. Faith has a higher, truthful purpose no eye can readily discern. Only souls whose inner sights relish celestial fountains can amenably fathom such truth for conception is the world of thine sights.

Magnificent living forms once graced this small world in vast numbers, but illicit tears from its fiery veins forever stifled its bountiful womb, viciously ensnaring the miracle of life into these famished ores. That once-majestic endowment of heavenly expression blessed by His Majesty, such wondrous and unrivaled loving gasps of life, gentle vessels, and songs of countless holy brothers and sisters that once adorned Mars—these now gazed aloft as ashes from dusty grounds begging to be hearkened, though trampled by the faithless as if some hollow sacrifice of modest if any worth.

The soul of Mars was not some arcane form fit only to romance away with but rather an enduring history tearfully engraved onto this frail world's wasted pelt. Its past love and glorious spirit, just like energy, was never destroyed but assumed other forms that now, mysteriously, begged to live on in our guilty hearts. I too had flouted them by siding obsessively with the mineral rather than the spiritual. My sights were veiled and could not sense eons of universal attainment, the Tree of Life, that once infused this world. But it was still here, very much alive to those not afflicted by mineral obsession. Truth shall speak relentlessly to those who trust honesty, and faith will heal us of compulsive lunacy with minerality—fear of love's purpose.

That night, my tired brow implored avidly to attain conscious absence, but slumber's shawl kept its distance in spite of the late hour, tarrying heavily over matters of the heart. My spirit lingered in lonesome sorrow, agonizing enigmatic shadows long concealed by the mind's deepest confines, while guilt invaded my consciousness with typical ambiguities pretending to be benign. Unknowingly, it was transgression's unsightly imprints, my obsession with minerality, that stung the heart with darkening fear in a foreign dialect of my own making, one I could not understand.

I walked alone on sands of time, forsaken to adverse fate upon desolate, foreign shores somewhere near the edge of life. Only nearby surf sounds kept me company, and dim heavenly starlight faintly illumined my way. Hostile clasps covertly reached up and wittingly arrested my steps with invisible restraints, ensuring I never strayed far from the known. Sand was therefore all I had in life: drab, arduous to possess, and pathetically endless. It was no life at all, hollow like a zombie pageant and trivial as a game of pretend, with ecstasy stanchly immersed in perdition.

My real life floated somewhere out at sea far detached from these sands, sadly misplaced across incessant spans of unimaginable burdens. My heart cried out in agony, longing to grasp tightly to life's eternal beacon, shining gloriously just beyond gloom's ambiguous watery horizon. But eve's darkness swelled dreadful, murky seas before me, assured my loyalty to fear was sound.

With cowardly wails, my faithless spirit dropped to its trembling knees, deeply broken by terror's bitter clench, and willingly surrendered to a known lifestyle that solely fed bodily needs commensurate with my devotion to it. But none of the gifts of Earth satiated my mind's famished longing for the Fountainhead of Truth, and much less led me to my glorious beacon.

That true sought-after beacon was surely embodied in someone unique to my heart's throbbing plea. But Earth's stanch shams and my abject past, night's cloak of darkness, ravaged any hopes of ever finding my heart's single joy—my only beloved one. My wretched soul thrived with fear, desire, and all gifts of hypocrisy, devising iniquities to survive mundane reality in a world where subsistence outweighs honesty. Without the Architect of Love in my life, barely alive on a sinful world, the heart paid dearly for covetous errors that reprobate minds provoked, gravely unaware that life, not death, is eternal and that love is never to be feared.

Unlike general belief, what we call death is no more than an impervious shadow briefly isolating the soul from physical provisions rather than the end of experience. The thought of death starves the mind of truth by encouraging acts of deceptive idiocy in a world wholly dominated by deceit. Setting all that aside, death is a beautiful gift, a parting from self, rest for a restless being, faith with a divine purpose.

"He would set them free, as many as were in bondage through their lifetime because of fear of death [1]," so state the scriptures, implying we strive to cheat demise by surrendering to sin. Death is not life's end by any means but surely the end of a deceptive life we fabricate trying to circumvent death.

Demise is the most dreaded ambiguity facing man, followed by birth. Anything in between is tertiary. Going with popular opinion, I adopted a belief in one embodiment, but the thought of living, then perishing, seemed dreadfully mortifying. Thus it was that fear inspired a belief in fear. As I knew it, death implied the complete surrender of awareness onto an insensible void drenched in impetuous, unwavering extinction, and unrivaled morbidity, dying both as flesh and memory. This was the fear of fears and abyss of tears for every mortal, subject to irrefutable, corporeal demise. But I was wrong.

The key to life is not entitled in fear but truth; for as fear is ignorance unto death, truth is life unto eternity. Therein, life's continuity is assured, knowing that mental substance cannot be destroyed [2]. As certain as death comes to the born, so will birth come to the dead [3].

Puppet students of a higher state of being are we, sent to learn and apply the science of life, resist temptation, and obey the forces of evolutionary truth, something I did not know at the time. We are not the life but a learning instance and a conduit of expression for the teacher, our higher spiritual self and the forces of truth—the infinite brotherhood.

That evening, leaning restless and lonesome in the cold chambers about the structure, my thoughts sought every word from the vision rather than slumber. "*Ce tennéh Manéh, oh-joi,*" I uttered humbly, reliving saintly reverence unlike any I had felt before. Such perfect gentleness of words and honesty took my breath away, releasing warm expedient tears. But no statement brought forth greater loving wonderment than "She is my one and only—friend." With these thoughts in mind, the weight of the eyelid eventually overcame heavy burdens, and night's restful shawl took over.

Nothing out of the ordinary happened that evening. In the morning, I got something to eat, showered, and returned to the site without a clue what to do. Sean concluded that the key masters had long vanished and no one was listening at the other end anymore. Made a lot of sense, but I disagreed, and had good unspoken reasons why.

Armed with renewed faith, I went into the pit and focused my mind on opening the door. But just as before, it was no use. Discouraged by failure, I turned to leave the pit with a lingering thought from the previous night's EM transmission. But suddenly, Sean stomped hysterically my way and stopped me dead in my tracks, asking me to look back at the structure.

Unexpectedly, a dim bluish impression briefly appeared but then vanished. I played back the last couple of thoughts, and interestingly enough, the spot returned each time I recalled the transmission. It was too easy yet totally unexpected; the structure responded to mental commands.

Hans, anticipating success, immediately jumped into action, ordered his forces down to the structure, and sent Earth gov word of pending live coverage. In a few moments, two dozen soldiers lined the tunnel, and Sean stood ready with cam in hand. All was in readiness; expectations were high.

By visualizing the EM transmission and the doorway opening, the shadow lingered intact, and the spire glowed much as the night previous; this time, it did not turn off. Plasma clouds swirled about like dancing ghosts, expanding outward and pulsing in a variety of blinding colors. Static got into everything, causing sparks to fly and pungent electrical odors to permeate the air. Nearby lights flickered and instruments ceased to function, some bursting into flames. Then, the glow subsided, all went mysteriously calm, and the shadow faded into a semi-elliptical opening over two meters tall.

Every eye anxiously peeked through the opening, curious to see what was inside, but the structure turned out to be strangely desolate. All this trouble just to find a vacant warehouse was certainly a huge disappointment, but maybe there was more to it than met the eye. Driven by wonder, Hans and I went into the pit and cautiously entered the building; Sean followed closely behind with his cam. In the structure, there were no visible markings or buttons on any of the walls or ceiling, but I was certain there were secret functions exclusively activated by mental means, just like the door.

Our attention was abruptly diverted to a low-pitched hum permeating from all directions, briefly rattling our bodies before subsiding. Other strange events, like walls changing colors and music arbitrarily playing in brief bursts, ensued for a few moments. Fearing the door might close and lock us inside, Hans thought it best to leave while it was still open. He briskly excused himself and stood just outside the doorway, as did Sean, asking me to follow. It was a tempting offer, but I chose to trust my alien friends and stayed inside.

If this was a test of faith, I did not want to fail it because faith had a purpose, and it was truth.

---

[1] W. J. Rev. Morford, "Hebrews 2:15," in *The One New Man Bible*, Travelers City, SC: True Potential Publishing Co., 2011.

[2] F. Alakbarov, "Conservation Of Energy," in *A 13th-Century Darwin? Tusi's Views on Evolution*, vol. Summer 2001, Sherman Oaks, CA: Azerbaijan International, 2001, pp. 48-49.

[3] S. S. S. S. Maharaj, "Sankhya Yoga-27," in *Bhagavad Gita.*

Chapter 7: *First Contact*

The vast hollow structure suddenly burst into action. Its ambience resonated with random musical sounds and walls arbitrarily varied bright colorations. But just as mysteriously as it activated, it abruptly silenced as if something, or someone, knew we were there and secretly arranged to reveal their much anticipated presence. Just when—that was anyone's guess.

"Can anyone hear me? *Ce tennéh Manéh*!" I uttered but got no response other than sheer silence. Still, I was not the least bit disheartened and held fast to a previous distinctive promise: I was never alone.

It was only but a brief moment following my summons when lights in the structure calmly dimmed half way, suggesting that something was about to happen. My excitement grew as the sound of gentle strings, soft harps, and sweet Oriental dizis invitingly permeated the room with placid melody, a friendly hint that we were welcomed. I managed to coerce Hans and Sean to reenter the structure, but they opted to come in no further than the doorway.

As my partners cautiously reentered the structure, I was briefly overcome by an inexplicable sensation I had never felt before yet wished it never left me. It was as if I could see and feel myself from afar, floating outside physical confines while surrounded by indescribable warmth in a gentle, benign way. All I ever needed was suddenly in me, and love of life became the breath that coursed through my senses: comforting, empowering, and calm.

For that brief instant, I seemed to know everything about myself and sensed incredible assurance, benevolence, and selflessness, enough to gasp a joyous inspiring tear. Every ounce of spirit in me yearned forth from the heart in loving, reverent outpouring unto an invisible, solemn, all-knowing inner force that encompassed my entire being and made me feel at one with all of creation, an incomparable oneness, a consciousness desiring only calm, and a loving disposition to comply with creation's will with all my heart and soul.

With no forewarning, a brilliant light appeared in the middle of the room, getting our immediate attention. It briefly hung in midair and steadily descended toward the reflective floor, surrounded by a hazy blue cylindrical shield. Myriad prismatic beams emerged from the floor, bending to the descending light's course. The light hovered mysteriously for a moment just above the floor, then faded away like early morning mist dispersed by the sun's warmth. To our great surprise, a humanoid figure unexpectedly emerged from the fast thinning light, a being of overwhelming humble beauty and divine majesty.

Our eyes gazed upon a wondrous vision far from expected, humbly depicted as an unspoken Elysium dream that filled our hearts with unrivaled astonishment and virtuous binding. In the wonder of that unique moment, tense lips silently released subjugating bonds and diligent thoughts rendered calmly still, seized by a stunning female countenance beaming joyfully afire before us. My breath helplessly gasped amorously, then gently retrieved, admiring a most beautiful young lady vested with astonishing, unsurpassed radiance and indescribably stunning loveliness—a living tribute to perfect unrivaled beauty and spiritual elegance.

My heart forthwith soared in unshackled flight far beyond restricting human locks, beholding abidingly her magnificent angelic soul in absolute awe. Her eyes, a trail of compassionate light, beckoned me to follow, her smile proclaimed divine cheering assurance of an enlightened morrow. My bosom's love forever became hers with irrepressible passion, overcome by untold waves of heartfelt affection. My soul desperately longed to admire her heavenly streaming fountains of Light without rest. and belong to her soft gaze with relentless, loving embrace.

The young lady's remarkable beauty and sweet grace held us absolutely spellbound, deeply inspired by breath's most blissful desiring. A fond song of restful silence wordlessly uttered from our hearts with loving wonder, for no lexis may hope to portray the many loving reveries stirred by her incomparably sculptured, modestly perfect, celestial splendor.

Our sights were effortlessly captivated by her awe-inspiring, wonderfully graceful, corporeal elegance, one to be admired incessantly. No epic elegy will ever describe her exquisitely modeled, indescribably gentle, shapely figure. She looked like a beautifully fair young maiden from a delightful fairy tale, more so, a lovely celestial angel descended. Her alluring beauty obscured all nearby brilliance, gathering unto her being the brightest, purest starlight the gem-filled heavens could ever reverently inspire.

Much as dazzling flowers entice admirers to their sweet, fragrant essence, her virtuous vessel pleasantly drew onlookers to the loving wonders of her humble brilliance. Her startling magnificence and clean, harmonious holiness of heart compellingly awakened serene divinity in our beings, swept off every mundane ensnaring wells by heaven's spirit like a gentle dove's welcoming wings. Hers was absolute loveliness, her soul the light of Elysian kingdoms, and her expression His Majesty's love eternal, for God prospered in her celestial heart with profound measure rivaling that of an angel.

Supple as velvet and graceful as saintly kindness upon troubled hearts, her artistic expression revealed soft selfless love to parched, errant eyes. Her unrivaled loveliness and peaceful countenance eclipsed the still vibrant empyreal firmaments above and stirred the soul into sacred songs praising the Majesty of Serenity, His Infinite Splendor, and Master of Love.

Her features were slightly Asian yet not as pronounced, with a soft mix of European texture and tone. There was not the slightest detracting blemish on her graceful face, encouraging untiring admiration despite time's persistent pageantry. The firmament's wordless beauty softly cast its infinite glory upon her inspiring countenance, describing a vision of love only the heart could interpret. Her gentle facial curves adoringly fashioned an image of youthful heavenly delight with perfect life soothing, idyllic rendition. Her entire being felt exceedingly clean, pure as pristine spring waters untainted by selfish or mundane smut.

Pearly white glowing teeth served to further enhance her already-exceptional radiance amid supple colorful petite lips, magnificent as unfurling lavish blossoms of flawless form. Her smile was serene, yet vivid as a stream of precious gems enduring forever. Her eyes were a brilliant yellowish-brown hue slightly smoother and larger than ours, garlanded by luminous, loving expression that placidly revealed God's gift of unsullied embodiment, warmth, and heavenly fragrances with majestic softness.

She had full long silky dark hair dressing down to her mid-section, cut to flawless symmetry and flowing delicately as the artistic motions of a master harpist. An elegant white dress encompassed her delicate form, shimmering in the light with soft, prismatic rainbows emanating from its edges. A pleasing golden sash comfortably contoured her exquisite vessel's mid-section, complementing shiny light bronze-colored shoes upon her feet. She wore no paint or jewels. Honestly, such appendages would have only served to disinherit her natural feminine splendor.

Her gaze was incredibly tender, loving, joyous, humble, divine. Her soft heart was upon her brilliant eyes speaking nothing less than clean love, beauty, breathing it passionately through every cell of her radiant countenance as if provoked by a powerful, inspiring inner melody. Every breath she took meant love, and its holy effulgence scattered deep into onlookers' hearts with heavenly pleasure, driven by Father's immense kindness.

As soon as this exceptionally beautiful lady materialized, my eyes helplessly sought hers as if they were my own with a force greater than the heart could bear. Time seemed to stop between us, and my soul sang wordless rhapsodies to her being in a language of spirit I could not dictate, much less understand. Without hesitation, my heart poured itself unto hers in inspiring, sweet songs with all of its might and my eyes constrained with warm tears, immediately falling madly, feebly, deeply in love with her.

Our eyes gently shared this silent clean love of the soul with the other, unwilling to part. She slowly smiled and reverently took quivering hands unto her heart in a sign of loving appreciation, eyes on the verge of tears. I could sense her great inner struggle to resist them, and responded with a soft, kind smile. Awed by her presence and the unrelenting love I felt for her heart, I reverently placed my hand over my bosom and gently bowed before her, uttering, "*Ce tennéh Manéh, ezi mén.*"

With a graceful flutter in her eyes, she smiled brightly and also bowed before me, swiftly drawing forceful tears from her lovely face and becoming even more radiant, humble, and beautiful than before.

We didn't anticipate establishing direct alien contact and felt somewhat perplexed by its very notion. Whatever we said or did going forward would determine mankind's future course in space. One wrong statement or gesture could mean the end of contacts, perhaps for centuries.

If aliens studied us and knew our every trait, then faking our attitude could be construed as a sign of hypocrisy or deception. Unquestionably, we had to be ourselves, our true best selves. In any event, we were under the discriminatory discernment of an unknown intelligence, enthralled by a magnificent lovely being unlike any we had met before.

The young lady gazed lovingly in our direction, raised her right hand as a form of greeting, and warmly smiled at us. We merrily returned the greeting, but indecision as to who would approach her teased us to boredom. She giggled mildly at our obvious dawdling and waited patiently for us to choose an envoy, no doubt enjoying our fleeting lack of concurrence. With kindest intent, she slowly looked my way with exceptional gentleness and nodded joyfully, hinting I was being invited to approach her.

"Laddie, it's your lucky day," Sean said. "Looks like she picked you."

"Me? I don't know what to do," I replied.

"I agree" Hans said. "A social scientist by trade, the choice is clear. You go, yes? We'll watch from back here."

"What am I supposed to say to her? What if I say the wrong thing?"

"Improvise. Just don't leave this planet or lock us in here." And so it was that, with a reassuring tap on the back, Hans launched me forward as Earth's ad lib ambassador.

Though I was afraid, I could not contain my joy, and my heart rejoiced beyond grasp. My eyes gazed lovingly upon her heart once more, and I helplessly uttered from what I recalled of the vision; "*Ce eveh . . . pavi, ezi . . . ceneh, inah,*" meaning "I am happy, my beautiful sister." Eager to hear these words, the lady slowly extended her hand to me and reverently bowed.

The moment I so longed for had come, my endless search for love was finally at hand. My life's long-lost beacon, joy of my desiring and light of my lamp was closer than I realized. My one, my dazzling guiding pharos, my radiant starlight and loving gateway to His Majesty, she was just a heartbeat away; but little did I know. How sweet is the presence of my one, rescuing a wretch like me from mortal sands. How precious is her grace that shall forever lead me back home free, among starry glee.

Her bountiful, dazzling beauty held me in place without regard for time or purpose, lost in the amorous wonder of the moment, arrested still before such magnificent being. With a most welcoming gesture, she rested her gentle eyes upon mine as if an acquaintance from prior times, briefly reminding me of the reason we were there.

Her luminous smile calmly dispersed inhibitions away and gradually encouraged me to fearlessly approach her. Overcome by a warm wave of calm and my heart bursting out of its casing with longing, uncontainable affection for her, I gently took my first steps forward. She also walked my way, pleasingly stepping on the crystal floor like a saintly ballerina. The closer we came to each other, the faster my heart pulsed and the deeper I sensed her beautifully divine heart. Swiftly did my love for her grow without bounds, an irresistible love for her soul—clean, selfless, and eternal.

She stopped two meters from me and gracefully extended her right hand. I interpreted this as a form of salutation and leisurely offered the typical Earth handshake, but the young lady lovingly backed her hand and nodded in the negative as if she could read my intentions. She courteously placed her right palm at a slant to mine, stretching her long artistic fingers rather than enclosing my hand. Her touch was soft and smooth as supple velvet, warm as a child's, and comforting as gentlest conceivable rest. At this angle, our thumbs faced and touched each other, forming a five-pointed star. I was certain this greeting embraced much deeper meaning than met the eye.

Hands resting before her, she voiced a phrase in her native language sounding like a mix between Asian and French with a placid touch of singing, "*Ezi inéh men avéh, Roshon* [1]."

At first, I did not fully understand what this meant, "My dearly beloved old friend, Roshon," and had to think it through for a bit. Then, I offered the typical Earth greeting, mixed with what humble words I could recall from the vision, "Hello, *ezi . . . inah.*"

She listened intently to my trembling voice and seemed well pleased. Then, in a most delightful musical tone, she offered a heart-warming, radiant smile, and said, "Hello, *ezi inéh,*" followed by a slight reverent curtsy.

Lights in the structure dimmed significantly, the door closed, and a huge three-dimensional projection of Mars appeared in midair, so realistic, it gave us the impression of floating in space. Resting her right hand on her left upper arm, she said, "Masar." The image then shrunk in size and transformed into a brilliant overhead display of our solar system.

Of interest, I noticed several small uncharted icy planets of substantial size beyond Eris, well within the heliosheath. A dwarf, rather dark star companion, journeyed just inside the bow shock at an elliptical incline to the ecliptic, exchanging remote Kuiper wonderers with the sun and influencing the orbits of far-off objects like Sedna. At its solar perigee near Pluto, the star flared brightly and then darkened until its next close encounter twelve thousand years later.

Our lovely host lightly tapped my left arm and waved at the solar system, presumably wanting to know where I came from, though I was certain she knew. I slightly bowed my head, recognizing her request, and turned to walk toward Earth. No sooner I did, her star lit eyes fixed upon mine with indescribable, gentle significance, telling a mystifying story I could not understand, though it strived to make itself known all the way into the depths of my fast beating heart.

Transfixed by her incredible beauty and a silent message between us so difficult to humanly contain, I lost track of surroundings, shackled willingly in place by a still penetrating voice an anonymous gaze inspired. I strived to feel and comprehend her silent message but only sensed gentle thoughts and exceptional friendship. She lovingly granted her right hand and gradually placed mine into hers with an inviting smile, warmly closing it.

I found her graceful gesture most stimulating and of kindest brotherly intent, conveying my high regards for her closeness in a brief moment of exceptional silent friendship. Together, we leisurely strolled toward the solar system display, hands held tenderly together, and eyes forever met in warm, inseparable nearness.

She could sense precisely how I felt, and her soul heard the essence of my heart loudly longing for her closeness; her radiant smile confirmed it. I could not help but allow my bosom to sing piercingly to her so that the entire cosmos could hear it, until tears fell from their binding locks and draped upon our hands. Her heavenly eyes sweetly looked upon mine as if trying to convey a deeply affectionate message yet sadly restrained for reasons I could not understand. And so it was that, in those few seconds by her side, my life changed forever, and my heart sealed over hers for as long as Majesty's kingdoms grace our spirits with life.

My racing heart longed for her indissoluble unity, and my eyes sung sweet nocturnes inspired by her copious loveliness. Her spotless spirit summoned heaven's peaceful essence, endowed with gifts of virtuous glory, breathing righteous life and His love into my weary heart. The chalice of my soul overflowed with celestial wonders, blessed by a meek soul that only embraced divine desire and bestowed holy amity.

She was that beacon of life I lost long ago in far-off darkened turbid seas, a light that never ceased to illumine the way back to her supple shores, and faithful eyes that never rested, day or night, scanning high murky seas for my imminent return. The foundation of my future I had found; at last, together with my one, I was finally God-bound.

As Earth's orbital path approached, I pointed to it saying, "Earth." She repeated the name, then pointing to her mouth said, "Saras." I repeated the word "Saras" and she seemed most pleased, as lights in the room came back up and the projection dissolved.

My hand still in hers, she waited patiently for me to take the next step. I was so humbled by her presence that nothing came to mind, so I gestured to myself and offered my name, "Bill."

She repeated my name, waved at herself in like fashion, and said, "May Len."

"May Len, that's a very . . . *cenéh, inah*" I replied, stumbling for Martian words, completely overwhelmed by her friendliness. May Len giggled calmly and nodded. Then, slowly reaching close to me and with utmost respect, she leisurely placed a soft petite kiss on my left cheek. At that moment, the air about me acquired a most pleasing gardenia scent that mysteriously lingered with me for hours. Later, I would learn it originated from her spiritual essence and described her divine identity much as a name would.

No sooner, I was back where I started: subject matter paralysis. I had a long list of questions but had no idea how to ask them. What few alien words I picked up from the vision were, for some reason, hard to come by at that moment. Meanwhile, she waited patiently for me to sort things out, looking on with a never-ending friendly smile.

I focused briefly on our recent Martian light encounter and slowly said, "Masar . . . *sanee*?" May Len smiled joyfully after hearing these words and moved her head, letting me know she registered that thought. At that moment, I realized she was telepathic. Martians not only developed technology but also conducted their lives around it. What a magnificent achievement this was yet so difficult to live by according to Saras standards. Such society would possess few if any secrets, establishing a civil system devoted to absolute openness and self-awareness. Truth would be undeniable, honesty compulsory, self-understanding a priority, testimony and forgiveness the language of the soul, and love eternal life's foundation.

In theory, contributing minds would work together toward a collective goal, surrendering intensions to one another like an open book, truth being the paramount objective. Emotions would give way to reason and desires truthfully understood, solving even the worst divisive issues. The populace would grow as one in thought and purpose, fostering unity, selflessness, love, and unparalleled closeness, free from inhibition and inspired by forbearance—the mark of prosperity. Judging by May Len's personal character, Martians had done quite well as an open society.

Lights dimmed again and the entire room transformed into a three-dimensional display of the crash site, revealing two individuals in space suits: Hans and me. I watched as we pointed at the fast approaching object. In moments, the light descended to near crashing distance, pinned us both to the ground, and vanished. We laughed together for some time, primarily May Len, at the absolute look of terror on our faces. I felt refreshed to see she had a great sense of humor and no shame showing it. Living without fear leads to inner inspiration and guidance from the higher self, thus, yielding ultimate enjoyment of life. May Len certainly had it.

The Martian light turned out to be a craft resembling a dark hat, similar to the one from my Chasma vision. May Len called it "Entlos" and proceeded to review a brief history of Saras UFO sightings. This was definitely an embarrassing moment, for I had staunchly discredited UFOs by any means at my disposal. May Len gave me a sweet assenting nod, sensing my recognition of error, but held no reproach toward me, only forgiveness, practicing paramount truth and honesty in the spirit of selfless sharing and learning.

Unexpectedly, she reverently enclosed both my hands into hers, nodded in a kind way, and tenderly divested her once radiant smile. Her eyes lost luster, and her radiant being seemed to regret what she was about to show me. She did not personally view these images; rather, her gentle countenance glanced low, momentarily hiding her exceptional stunning beauty from us.

Scenes of unprovoked aircraft persecuting UFOs appeared before us, some from recent times. Aliens from various worlds on sanctioned ambassadorial missions were sadly betrayed by our governments and imprisoned. In the name of scientific research, their lives hung in the balance, their vessels placed in the hands of clueless butchers. I couldn't help but reflect on our latest civil crisis, recognizing that we were also prisoners, not of a foreign world but of invisible forces from our own. But we only had ourselves to blame, for deceit is the root of all repression and the base of our wayward mundane souls.

It was sad to witness people run for the hills, believing that Martians were the devil ready to assail Saras at any moment. Science fiction was not far behind, depicting aliens as aggressive, disfigured monsters trying to consume embattled eartheans—so far from reality. What can anyone expect from us but aggression, a people consistently responsible for endless barbaric atrocities?

I bowed my head low in remorse and, as best as I could remember, said to her, "*Ce evéh . . . pleváh,*" or "I am sorry."

May Len softly raised my hands and reverently pressed them unto her heart with humble gaze in a solemn sign of trust and servitude, prompting a grave wave of sorrow and tears to surge in me. How extensively did we misjudge and irrationally warded away our holy, caring neighbor. How wrongly did we externalize our own fierce spirit unto God's saints, the Sons of God, opting to live in deceitful infamy rather than truthful candor? But these were mere trivial woes compared to what May Len was about to present next.

Standing close by my side, with my hands softly enclosed within hers, my precious beacon proceeded to share with us a critical chapter from our despicable past legacy.

---

[1] T. Flournoy, From India To The Planet Mars, New York and London: Harper & Brothers Publishers, 1900.

Chapter 8: *Our Past Legacy*

From cosmic serene shores, host to entities devoted entirely to heavenly endeavors, the call went forth to save an unkind flower, a blue watery world plagued by deceit and fear of love, even with the self. The honor was granted upon Masar who eagerly accepted the mission without hesitation. Crossing the short divide between worlds, their ships landed on a large land mass in what are now the Lesser Antilles. They called this land Atlan Tenh, meaning "from the sea," where they built one of the greatest civilizations to ever grace Saras.

Atlan Tenh was originally instituted to serve as a spiritual infirmary for the truth challenged, built and administered largely by Martian masters that lived and taught among the populace. Other *sapien* beings inhabited Saras at the time, but chose not to live in Atlan Tenh or learn from the masters.

A magnificent, awe-inspiring modern metropolis hosting enormous contemporary skyscrapers emerged before our eyes. This was not the legendary Atlantis I once envisioned, some ancient city teaming with marble Hellenistic temples and bullock statues, tall muscular lance-wielding caped guards, and slave dancers trying to arouse drunken guests. Far from it. New Manhattan seemed primitive by comparison. May Len called the city Atlan Dohnun Éhden, meaning "sea garden city."

Similar to Plato's description, Garden City was laid out in concentric circles atop a mesa two-hundred meters above sea level. Artificial canals cut through the city and poured over the mesa's rim unto seas below as gentle water falls. Absent was the presence of industrial clutter, storage, waste, and other visual distractions that might tarnish the city's acutely clean, peaceful image.

Citizens of every age peacefully strolled along wide esplanades, adorned with vibrant tropical flora, tame peacocks, and petite waterworks adding a touch of paradise to adjacent modern buildings. Overhead, white nimble egg-shaped trams interconnected the city and the countryside. Moving sidewalks comfortably ferried people between buildings, overhead bridges, and tram stations. By means I could not determine, some individuals did not walk but rather floated upright just above the ground.

Pointed cigar-shaped craft moved effortlessly through the air, visiting far-off lands and worlds without using combustible or radioactive propellants. May Len gave these craft a distinct name: *Valics*. The name was not familiar, but the shape definitely was. I vividly recalled a frieze from Caesar Augustus's

Room of the Masks on Palatine Hill. It displayed a modern curved building with a Valics-like craft parked upright in front of it—shades of Atlantis?

The people of that time dressed in flowing light-colored robe-like garments, complemented by gentle capes draping down from furrowed collars lined with golden streamers. A sash was worn about the waist, its color indicative of spiritual attainment. Men wore turbans over their heads and draped hairs below their shoulders but were clean shaven. Women wore billowing light hoods over long hairs reaching their mid sections.

Picture 4: Sea Garden City, Atlantis (*B. Erlinger-Ford*)

Shallow canals offered aquatic leisure and immersion into nature, coated with a marble-like substance that did not waste away or rust. Curving garden promenades and benches offered relaxing respite by canal side. Metallic fountains composed of six tall bent gray metal pipes, gathered at their middles, were placed in canals and spaced at regular intervals. Two disks intersected these pipes at various levels. From them, jets sprayed dancing waters upon individuals traveling by boat. Water was treated in such a way that it behaved like a liquid and refreshed the body upon contact but did not wet, reminding me of Venus's azure waters.

Garden City was located northeast of the island of Guadeloupe, close to the tropic of those times. The continent curved west to the Bahamas, north beyond Bermuda, and east to the European coastline. The Atlantean western segment was located in the Gulf of Mexico, stretching from Florida to Galveston and reaching as far north as Biloxi. The Laurentide glacier covered northern regions down to present-day New Manhattan. Atlantean topology was mostly hilly, with mountain ranges at the northern rim and the Fault Ridge east of Sargasso, but the area around Garden City was a vast mesa plain.

Picture 5: Room of the Masks, Valics (*www.didaskalia.net*)

Conical power generation towers, located at key geological sites throughout Atlan Tenh, harnessed free cosmic energy for domestic use. These were intentionally synchronized with Saras's magnetic field at 35MHz to ensure captured energy did not escape the planet.

At their apex sixty-four meters off the ground, a massive ruby crystal five meters wide faced the heavens. Surrounding it, a dazzling array of ultraviolet and X-ray lasers, tuned to 35MHz, overcame molecular absorption, ionized an energy column high into the stratosphere, and transferred atmospheric static charges into the tower. The vortical transfer established by this laser funnel opened up a 3MHz conduit between the tower and ionosphere, acting as a catalyst to draw upon cosmic radiation far into space.

Highly charged 100MeV solar wind particles, captured by the inner Van Allen belts a thousand kilometers from the surface, descended silently through this conduit in the form of lightning, producing stunning rainbow canopies upon contact with the crystal. The same UV beam acted as a carrier wave for phased energy that powered craft and appliances around the world.

A passive plasma containment and filtering chamber sat between the ruby crystal and the conical tower, resonating at 375GHz. This was the most important component in the entire Atlantean power system, as it operated not only in the far infrared range but also in a higher dimension. Covering the walls and running down the center of this chamber were incredibly dense, specially hardened titanium aluminide beryl crystals whose lattices could withstand extreme temperatures and pressures exceeding those of a brown dwarf. In this small chamber, collected particles regenerated like a laser and oscillated to extremely high frequencies until elemental particles reached critical mass and boiled off, thus releasing enormous amounts of energy. A synchronous controlled nuclear chain reaction was the result, producing a powerful inter-dimensional Lorentz vortex, high potentials, gravitation, and a magnetic flux through the crystal core. In effect, creating a miniature star.

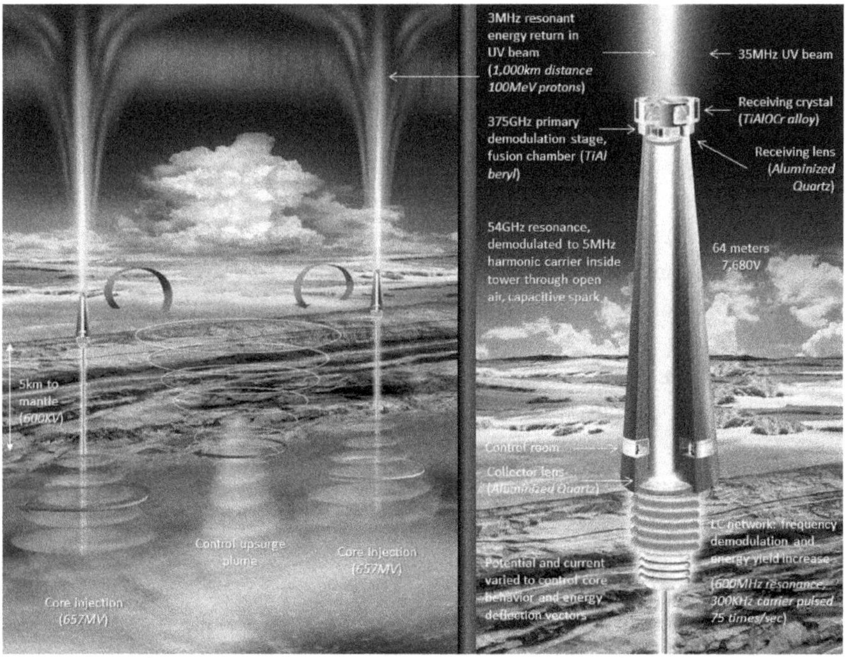

Picture 6: Atlantean power generator diagram (*B. Erlinger-Ford*)

Inside the chamber, energy wavelengths shortened and time references lowered, injecting compressed higher-dimensional quantum currents into our plane in a shorter amount of time; energy normally bound to materialize over much longer time frames. The chamber was thus a clean nuclear reactor far in advance of any technology used on Saras, using ions rather than radioactive uranium to channel dimensional power.

When energy in the chamber reached optimal resonance and potential, it discharged through a passive receiving lens made of aluminized quartz, located beneath the chamber, and passed onto the conical tower segment at a rate of 54GHz. Energy introduced by the receiver oscillated against a capacitive collector lens at the base of the tower, building up plasma energy between both lenses like a spark gap or laser tuned to a 5MHz demodulated carrier.

The bottom collector delivered static current onto a ten-meter-wide primary coil made of crystallized manganese oxide conductors two meters thick. It induced energy onto an eight-meter-wide secondary coil driven five kilometers into Saras, delivering 657M volts of electric field potential through the mantle at a regulated rate of 300KHz over a 75Hz carrier. A tuning core and winding within the secondary was used to change the regulated rate, phase, and current of injection into the planet. Both coils attached on top, but the secondary solely discharged into the mantle. Saras was used as a gigantic 710 μF electrolytic capacitor, storing power for consumer needs. Synthesized mantle densities and core rotation fluctuated planetary capacitance, thus altering the planet's base frequency rates and its time/space dimensional reference. Slowly, the planet was being elevated to higher realms of expression, and a wondrous, loving essence infused every living form upon it.

The primary collector array was located near a subduction zone at a place called Posá Ih Denh meaning "people's rest" in what's now the Puerto Rico trench. Secondary arrays were strategically placed throughout Atlan Tenh including Garden City, all near subduction zones to exploit magma convection routes. But these generators provided much more than just energy.

Combined generator output energy waves were set to harmonically collide with each other in the planet's outer core, according to complex convection flow, drift, capacitance, and thermal inductive algorithms, thereby altering planetary core magnetic properties, rotation, and mantle density vectors. This was achieved by manipulating the force and angle of injected energy incidence as it traveled through mantle convection layers toward the core.

Key to this technology was an awareness that planets are miniature stars, a ferric silicate brown dwarf in the case of Saras, covered by cooled elements from inner convection processes. Their cores swarm with magnetic eddies similar to solar spots, and swirling, flaring prominences surge from their bowels in response to cosmic cyclic forces amid fluid corona-like mantles.

Synthetic resonant energy patterns in the core allowed Atlanteans not only to control core rotation and its properties but also influence tectonic stress and weather patterns on a global scale with surgical precision. By coordinating frequency, phase, and current output across all generators, the angle and force of energy traversing spiraling mantle convection plumes could be managed at will, therein affecting the core's behavior and, ultimately, surface conditions.

In other words, generators were like massive shuttles navigating still over a sea of shifting mantle current flows using EM drive. Thus, surface weather was managed by controlling core weather.

Plate stress was regulated by magnetizing, then repelling magma masses until the mantle normalized. Solar and galactic cosmic disturbances affecting the mantle could be stabilized in a matter of minutes, thus avoiding climatic and geological catastrophes. By polarizing spiraling mantle upsurge plumes, bred by induced generator core energy patterns, atmospheric pressure above them could either be increased or reduced, thus controlling weather.

This paradise would not last forever, though. For thousands of years, a subversive order known as the Sons of Ly-Dian fought for control of the island. When revolt yielded negative results, their leader Ly-Dian resorted to introduce degenerate substance into daily life. He called it "secret knowledge," though in reality it was nothing more than carnal leisure, perilous humor, and deceit. Atlanteans called it something else, "safe and good evil," the mindless, sinful arts of sensual and degenerate amusement.

Ly-Dian's covert following swelled to great numbers over time, and people began to lead dual lives. During the day, people expressed devotion and tranquility. But during the night, adults and children alike engaged in the most decadent, indulgent pleasures imaginable. It did not take long for the populace to openly exhibit signs of spiritual apathy and tedium rather than serene devotion to the breath of life, rapt by recurring memories of sensory bliss and daring actions against Father, much like a song that refuses to depart the mind.

In time, Atlanteans traded their holy luster for one of turmoil, and love abandoned their hearts. Future offspring distanced themselves from self-awareness and truth, consumed by abnormal savors that turned human vessels into deplorable temples of hopeless sensory overdose, a state of dead living. The people had a new god, even gave it a name: "descending worthlessness" or Belial. Profane expression, selfishness, and carnal desire spread among the populace like some incurable contagion, and Ly-Dian was there to conveniently channel it against Atlan Tenh's leadership.

Ly-Dian accused the Chiréh ti Mis, the elder council, of being weak and overly submissive to influential Martians, whose real intent was to colonize Saras after destroying their own planet thousands of years prior. He argued their teachings were repressive and responsible for humanity's indolent state after eons of wrongful practice. People knew all too well their negations could affect the stability of their slowly elevating world but paid no attention to repeated warnings and surrendered to the weight of pleasure.

Rejected and badly misunderstood, Martians had no choice but return home and let Saras work out its own issues. Civil degeneration, as well as Ly-Dian's influence, grew exponentially until the Chiréh were also forced to leave Atlan Tenh and seek refuge in nearby continents.

Ly-Dian finally boasted of absolute power over Atlan Tenh, but that was not enough. He dreaded the return of the Chiréh, so he dispatched loyal followers to exterminate any trace of them. Atlanteans had various offensive deterrents at their disposal, including aircraft and plasma weapons. They could also become invisible. Chiréh colonists, on the other hand, possessed the most rudimentary piercing and chemical defense tools. Fierce battles between both sides ensued on land and sea, known then as the colonial wars. With the Chiréh on the run, Ly-Dian turned his attention to more sinister initiatives, including; invading Masar.

In those days, Cyprus offered ideal defense, flanked by twisting river ways and intricate terrain. It was here that colonists achieved their first major victory against Ly-Dian's forces during an evening raid, capturing valuable aircraft and weaponry. Thereafter, the war quickly turned in favor of colonists who steadily advanced toward the Atlantean homeland.

Fearing an attack on Atlan Tenh soil, Ly-Dian resorted to a risky procedure known to destabilize Saras's core. Generators were virtuous instruments, but they could also be used for evil. By altering magnetic currents in the core, upheavals could be created anywhere on the planet. Overnight, volcanoes, earthquakes, and storms plagued colonial holdings without mercy, sending colonists running for their lives. But even more dastardly, Ly-Dian's engineers set up generators to irradiate the populace with subliminal messages using Saras's magnetic field as a carrier, promoting people's past days of cosmic warfare and sealing their allegiance to Ly-Dian.

But there was a high price to be paid for these highly volatile commodities, and Ly-Dian knew the risks all too well: manipulating the core could send Saras's magnetic field into disarray and set off unusual weather and tectonic trends around the world. Without the Chiréh around, Ly-Dian's engineers had only limited exposure to the scientific principles behind planetary magnetic convection. Still, they forged ahead and took a guess, confident they could restore the core to its previous state at any time.

Garden City rumbled daily with light earthquakes. Rain fell there for the first time in eons, and global temperatures increased, but no one paid much attention to it. The Chiréh knew Atlan Tenh was doomed and put as much distance from the island as possible. But Ly-Dian was not the least bit concerned; he was too busy making preparations to invade Masar.

Deep in the far recesses of the solar system, the sun's gloomy stellar escort traversed its usual course, cloaked by a thick layer of light-absorbing dust hiding its reality. This was no ordinary dwarf star but a faint killer, a dormant flare star thrice the size of Saturn waiting avidly to reclaim its long denied spatial kingdom. Dark ashes from prior days of radiant glory concealed its infernal flames like a scab a wound, such that hesitant nuclear cauldrons roaring beneath them barely cast any heat or glow unto the darkness of space.

As it approached perihelion near Pluto's orbit, its magnetic field tangled with nearby Jovian worlds and the sun, thus rekindling its latent fires. With a sudden massive eruption, its ancient ash clouds dispersed into space, and then, there was light. The sun also reacted violently to the newcomer by flaring abruptly, bombarding Saras with deadly radiation for months. Temperatures soared and glaciers melted across the planet, triggering wide spread fires and far-reaching floods. But inside Saras, the sun had much greater bearing, randomly disrupting generator energy vectors in the core and increasing collector energy pitch not just for hours but for months.

The flare's mass ejections poured into the Van Allen belts and eventually into generators. These, in turn, tuned and passed these overrated surges into the planet's already perturbed core, which, at the time, was far from being in a stable configuration to deal with the excess load. Thus, the core destabilized and global disasters went rampant. Generators struggled to automatically regain control of the core, but previous modifications made by Ly-Dian's incompetent engineers only made matters worse. Restless seismic shudders consumed Saras, and it seemed only a matter of time before the entire planet came apart at the seams.

Ly-Dian realized he had lost control of energy reserves, and the planet was on the brink of flying apart, so he ordered all generators to be shut down, but it was too late. Excess energy stored in the core could not normalize on its own; it had to go somewhere. So the stationary convection vacuum beneath Posá Ih Denh generators, now shutdown, became the primary outlet target.

The mantle gave way to a massive convection plume on its way to the surface, breathing terror into those aware of its consequences, including Ly-Dian. Grounds at Posá Ih Denh swelled up like a giant expanding air bellows and powerful tremors jolted the land, damaging several generators and devastating nearby settlements. As the land bloated, enormous lesions spread across the surface, exposing wide terrene inners with gaping chasmal jaws meaning to devour the living into its deep fiery domains. Rivers and lakes leaped over their banks and headed for nearby seas to the south, flooding flaming crevices and scraping the land bare along their wayward course.

Without warning, stored core reserves found a conductive path up the convection plume and violently discharged onto the heavens in the form of terrifying roaring electric javelins by the millions, leaving behind wide calderas and erupting gas fissures, some explosively set ablaze.

Several hours later, the discharge storm subsided, the ground stopped swelling, and all went mysteriously calm. But irreparable long-term damage to Saras had been incurred. Half of the generator array was severely impaired. The island's weather-regulating process was gone, and heating trends spread quickly across the entire planet. Still, Ly-Dian rejoiced in relief, confident that the worst had passed and his engineers would soon rebuild the array to its former days of glory. Without delay, he ordered radical week-long celebrations to be held at Garden City in honor of our past belligerent legacy, ahead of the planned Martian invasion.

Atlanteans praised Ly-Dian as their deliverer, an unrivaled leader who endured this crisis and saved the planet without Martian assistance. On the other hand, Ly-Dian used the occasion to his favor by blaming Martians for deserting Saras and nearly bringing about the end of the world. Hence, he specified that no Martian or Chiréh soul would be spared during the invasion.

Tens of millions poured into Garden City from every corner of the land to partake in Ly-Dian's legacy celebrations and prepare to assault both Masar and Chiréh colonies.

The city was divided into six districts for the festivities, each representing a hostile world in which Atlanteans once lived before being confined to Saras, the galaxy's penal colony. These six worlds were Aquila, Capricornus, Draco, Hydra, Leo, and Orion. Upon arrival, people ascribed to their home district and reunited with others from the same previous star system, much like a class reunion, except on a cosmic scale. The largest assemblage belonged to Orion, Ly-Dian's home world.

Boisterous cheers and laughter invaded a once-tranquil city, driven by a unifying sense of stellar heritage that drew on ancient days of glory, though its foundation was tainted by forged cosmic tradition. In emotionally sung memorials, patriotic esteem swept people's hearts like wildfire, reliving ancient times of planetary conquest, untold devastation, and lethal space wars as if justifiable and honorable. Guardians of space and angels of cosmic destiny people pretended to be, influenced by Ly-Dian's thought control apparatus. But behind all the hype and pomp, nothing was further from the truth.

At first, celebrations were held rather peaceably, but soon things got out of hand. People feasted and immersed themselves into unheard-of pleasures for days, desecrating anything holy with the labors of their own erotic filth and lustful vengeance until they could bodily endure no further but lie strewn naked about Garden City as if dead, covered disgracefully by muck of their own animalistic indulgence and glottal sickness.

Garden City, a paradise on Saras, turned into a squalor heap overnight. Fierce tones resounded throughout the city, like demonic howling cries from hell seeking to befriend ghastly lords of terror. Built-up tensions between cosmic groups gave rise to heated clashes over superiority, many turning deadly. Once beautifully adorned esplanades, gardens, and awe-inspiring edifice laid waste with trash, feculent grunge, and smashed artifacts. Gentle, caring animals were agonized, then eaten alive by their once-loving masters.

Thousands of years of holy expression, history, and wondrous artistic creations were reduced to ashes. Anything having to do with Martians was vengefully despoiled and razed. Carnage, insobriety, verbal defiance against Father ran rampant, exceeding Hades norms in a city that no longer slept but rather hosted the living dead, influenced by the tree of good and safe evil. Indeed, such memories would not rest, both in men's poisoned hearts and Saras's inflamed bosom beneath their feet.

As people immersed themselves into gifts of worthlessness, the Chiréh leadership received word of Atlan Tenh's state of chaos and Ly-Dian's planned invasion. They soon realized this was a golden opportunity to overcome Ly-Dian's forces, avert the massacre of billions of lives throughout the solar system, and take back control of the mainland. With hopes high, countless volunteers from across the globe gathered on Atlan Tenh soil; one group headed for Garden City, the other to Posá Ih Denh, where tremors and rainfall were now constant.

As the sun made its way into the western horizon on the last festive day, Chiréh forces entered a chilling Garden City and were stunned by what they witnessed. Grounds were piled high with Father's latent mostly naked human vessels once holy blessed. For some, their saintly attire no longer breathed life's luster and rested among trembling, drizzly fields, decaying as mundane litter among an abundance of immoral remains. Streets and edifices of a once unique paradise were besieged by such level of devastation, cinders, and waste that watery torrents from the heart unavoidably covered Chiréh countenance.

So rested Garden City on that late eve, its holiness violated and its heart hollowed of Father's eternal glory. Eons of enlightenment, unrivaled beauty, and untold effort by countless masters were ravaged away in just days by trivial lies and restless memories. How could students of truth, who once pledged their solemn allegiance to Father, de-evolve and commit such vulgar ancient sins with such vigor? they thought. No one was forced to betray Father, but the uncorroborated word of a single wayward soul lent reason enough. Filled with compassion, the Chiréh laid down their arms and reached into gullible hearts, raped by Ly-Dian's wicked curse.

When people saw the Chiréh, many welcomed them with open, repentant arms while others—still overcome by thought stimulus, guilt, and fear of

Ly-Dian—resisted. Since Ly-Dian claimed the Chiréh had deserted the people, no one expected to see them again. Their arrival proved such claims false, driving a wedge of mistrust between Ly-Dian and the people. Despite anxieties, everyone flocked to the Chiréh for help and healing, a reunion long overdue.

As night set its sights upon the land, commando units in Posá Ih Denh ran into Ly-Dian's forces, and an armed struggle between them surfaced. When Ly-Dian learned that the Chiréh was in Atlan Tenh, he sent armies to Garden City, threatening to slay anyone siding with them. With hundreds of menacing Valics overhead and Ly-Dian's forces at the city's gates, people one by one walked out on the Chiréh. Alone and disillusioned before vast numbers of surrounding adversaries, the Chiréh had only one option available to them: surrender.

Meanwhile, in Posá Ih Denh, constant tremors and shifting terrain made it difficult to advance. Still, Chiréh forces managed to break through Ly-Dian's defenses undetected and reached the main power control facility. Upon entry, only a few inexperienced engineers were at their post unsure what to do; the rest were celebrating in Garden City.

Picture 7: Atlantean power tower, control center (*B. Erlinger-Ford*)

A team of scientists accompanying the Chiréh entered a large round control room on the third floor of the facility. There were several monitoring stations in the middle of this room and along its walls, each hosting three large angled, vertically tiered oval monitors. These displayed convection, tectonic, and electric field information for various regions throughout the planet. A master rounded console, located at the center of the room, showed the state of Posá Ih Denh itself, revealing critical status.

Under outright protest by Ly-Dian's engineers, Chiréh scientists rushed to the master console, diligently disabled thought stimulus controls, and reviewed mantle convection status beneath the facility. What they discovered made them quickly turn to each other with a troubled, forsaken gaze and nod in the negative. It was too late; any effort to save the planet seemed pointless. The damage done to mother Saras was irreparable, and nature was determined to purge itself of Ly-Dian's wrongful doings.

Hours after power generators were shut down and for several days after, the planet's molten inners released excess static content unto the stratosphere, and Posá Ih Denh stopped bulging upward like rising dough. But hundreds of kilometers beneath the surface, an enormously wide magma plume continued to rise around Posá Ih Denh unnoticed, placing the generator array in the middle of a 320 kilometer wide caldera. This was clear indication that something dreadful was about to happen, and the planet's destruction was imminent.

Chiréh engineers theorized that the only course of action was to electrically draw the magma plume from Posá Ih Denh back into Saras by using Garden City's generators and then minimize inevitable damage after. While Ly-Dian's engineers stoutly argued against this procedure, the Chiréh leadership approved the plan, and generators were programmed accordingly.

The theory worked. The magma plume halted its lethal advance, land quivers struck less often, rain stopped coming down, and fortunately no damage was incurred. Elated engineers sighed in joyous relief, and once technical adversaries came together in peaceful reunion; the world's destruction had once again been averted, just in time.

As night drew near, engineers feasted together in celebratory spirit, all except for one Chiréh. He paced about the silent control room troubled, silent, and detached from celebrations. His heart weighed many heavy stones, for he knew his dark legacy all too well and the reasons why he now lived on Saras. His sins from thousands of years ago were responsible for all this, he assured himself, and felt not at peace with himself but rather mortified.

Coming to a balcony facing west, he looked out at the darkening horizon in spiritual shame and persistent tears, penitent yet unwilling to forgive himself. "He who can't forgive himself can't love his brothers and much less the Infinite," he reminded himself. But the weight of sadness kept prompting an undeniable fact; his sins continued to gravely affect the lives of billions, errors separating him from his beloved companion for hundreds of thousands of years. When would it all be over? he wondered. Only he knew, for his penitence was far from over, and of his own making.

In front of the horizon, other generators stood stirringly silent, like grayish shadows cast against the darkening eve. Their crystals glowed softly in restive state, contained by pulsing stratospheric beams. All living creatures had vanished weeks prior during the runoff flood, and the land was scraped mostly bare of life. All seemed quiet, except for sudden land shivers persisting in eventful waves as if the ground fell from beneath one's footing.

In the far-off distance, a strange burbling sound increased in volume with time. Peering down toward grounds below, this Chiréh scientist was suddenly jolted and petrified with fear, as runoff water raced over the ground from the west and struck the building, slowly gathering in height. Waters continued to rise, seemingly gaining speed, so he immediately yelled, "We are flooding!"

Celebrations came to a sudden halt, and engineers rushed to their consoles, confirming a new problem: the magma chamber beneath generators receded as expected, but now the land above it slowly deflated below its original elevation before the swelling started days prior.

The countryside quickly collapsed into a hollow caldera, and nothing could be done about it in time without blowing up the magma chamber. Meanwhile, water trickled into the facility at a modest pace, forcing everyone to abandon the room and climb twenty levels to the top of the tower to evade its grip.

Everyone rushed up a winding stairway attached to the inner wall of the generator cone. Amid the cone to their left, a purplish plasma beam pulsed brightly inside a transparent crystal housing that protected anyone going up these winding steps. At the bottom of the tower, rising waters boiled, and steam quickly covered the containment housing. On top of the cone and beneath the nuclear chamber, the receiver lens glowed like a colorful nebula with sufficient plasma energy to vaporize anyone coming near it.

A few levels before reaching the lens, the stairway led to a door that opened to another stairway outside the cone. As they reached the top, the crystal slowly dimmed like a smoldering cinder and turned off, along with its UV containment beam. From the top of the tower, they could see water levels continuing to rise and swallow Posá Ih Denh whole, though it was the land that slowly sank beneath sea level, causing nearby seas to rush in and conceal the countryside. Other Chiréh forces in the area failed to respond, presumably caught by surprise and already consumed by rising waters. So there they waited uncertain of fate, with eve nesting upon the horizon and lands quickly sinking beneath them.

Quakes intensified and water continued to ascend until the entire power facility submerged under water and everyone floated off its roof, plagued by spurious energy discharges coming off a wayward collector crystal near them.

Picture 8: Posá Ih Denh's final moments (*B. Erlinger-Ford*)

In the stale gloom of approaching nightfall, dimming submerged glows from neighboring generators highlighted rushing murky currents above them with a ghostly yellowish hue, quickly extinguishing as they descended into quivering depths below forever. Overwhelmed by fatigue and with nowhere to rest their step, survivors could not withstand the churning currents and one by one served their final breath to rushing waves. Those still alive would witness Saras's deepest torments surround them in only moments.

Back in Garden City and unaware of Posá Ih Denh's fate, Ly-Dian could not contain his joy. Complete victory over the Chiréh was finally at hand and without much effort. With the Chiréh out of the way, Masar was next in line, followed by Venus, then Titan. Confident of victory and threatening deserters with death, he ordered loyal subjects to slay the Chiréh; though hesitant, people had no choice but obey.

Suddenly, a group of bold Atlanteans stepped forward and stood between the Chiréh and the rest of the people, begging everyone to reassess recent actions and recall lessons learned about their proven past. Ly-Dian spelled certain death, they claimed, while the Chiréh was there to save them and foster peace. What was the best choice long term? they asked. Why die for Ly-Dian and his ideals if only a righteous life was worth dying for?

Many changed their allegiance back to the Light that evening, but others remained committed to Ly-Dian out of fear. And thus, a long dispute ensued between those for and against the Chiréh, eventually unleashing an unavoidable clash between both factions using whatever means at their disposal to inflict woe on each other.

In the heat of the moment, a blinding silent flash of light emerged to the west, eclipsing night's dim twilight. Glared by the intense light, contending crowds suddenly halted hostilities and lost footing as the ground seemed to drop away from them. They wondered what was going on; yet were afraid of knowing the truth. Several other intense flashes quickly followed of such magnitude that closed covered eyelids could not contain their penetrating brilliance. When it subsided, enormous grayish clouds and corona-like flames leaped high into far western skies, covering eight degrees of horizon.

A dull rumble similar to distant rolling thunder approached Garden City seemingly from all directions, and a sharp gust swiftly coursed through the city with hurricane force winds, knocking everyone to the ground. In its wake, grounds shook relentlessly with power never before felt, restraining people to the ground. City infrastructure and power stations collapsed, but the temblor would not let up, only worsen. In western skies, twilight's intensity wavered up and down, then fled quickly to the south, and sunk beneath the horizon. In the east, the full moon appeared red as blood and stars fluttered from their assigned dwellings overhead as if falling.

Thick dark clouds quickly settled overhead in accruing terrifying waves. From them, blue lightning fell aimlessly about, striking and burning thousands of people immobilized by the quake's force on the ground. Flaming cinders rained down upon unwary victims embroiled in hellish chaos. Deadly swelling ash clouds swept through the land like a swaying sickle, burning and suffocating its hosts with smoldering gas and ash. Valics, operating on reserve power, fell from the sky unable to maintain levity as their cells ran dry and electrical storms blocked their ability to tap into the Van Allen belts. Ly-Dian and his commanders, on board a Valics, attempted to flee destruction, but their craft also faltered and fell into the seas far into Sargaso where they eventually suffocated, trapped inside the dead craft.

The inevitable happened; the risk everyone but Ly-Dian feared had spoken. In one swift heave, the Posá Ih Denh land mass exploded with unrivaled vigor, instantly decimating the continent. The explosion ripped open a gigantic breach eight kilometers deep that reached from the Bahamas to the Lesser Antilles.

Picture 9: The end of Atlan Tenh (*B. Erlinger-Ford*)

Garden City's sculptured beauty crumbled like a sand castle, and grounds collapsed beneath surviving populace who dropped into deep fiery chasms to assured death. Seas then rushed in to claim briny prevalence, forever burying a unique gift from Father, a tropical garden paradise lost to greed.

For the next four thousand years, sea levels continued to rise as continental plates adjusted and the Laurentide ice shield retrieved northward. The Mediterranean valley and other coastal regions around the world flooded, washing away any residual history and technology from Atlan Tenh.

May Len gently touched my shoulder and looked at me in a peculiar way. I wondered if she meant I somehow lived through this destructive episode while she nodded affirmative. I was curious to know what role I played in Atlantis's most desperate hour, and then I knew: I was a Chiréh engineer that drowned at Posá Ih Denh on that fateful eve before it exploded. More precisely, the regretful man who first saw waters rise from the balcony.

Picture 10: Ancient sculpture, Atlantis remnant? (*B. Erlinger-Ford*)

The presentation was far from over. May Len rolled history back further to a time I presumed to be before Atlantis, featuring an even larger city seemingly cut from a single crystal. It was laid out in circular fashion with seven round spokes and one hub, each covered by transparent interlaced domes, but we could not appreciate too many details. This city was swiftly destroyed by sustained anti-matter exchanges between super-powers, a conflict that caused critical continental breakups and Mt. Toba's eventual eruption.

Churning lava and ash from various Indio-Pacific regions launched far into the skies and covered Saras for months, inducing a global nuclear winter that lasted several years and nearly wiped out the human race. Noting my lack of connection with this event, May Len called this place "Mu," a continent that also sank beneath the waves in tormenting shudders.

Saras, prior to Mu's destruction, was covered by a thick cloud mantle similar to Venus and shone brightly with a wide misty blue haze extending far into its darkened phase: a welcoming peaceful lantern in space and secret abode to countless living creatures.

The moon of those times hosted several watery reservoirs and wispy clouds beneath a thin slightly greenish atmosphere. Short timber-like plants added a lively essence to its rocky surface, and icy formations marked the poles, reflecting light back into space like polished mirrors. Aliens harvested its resources, exporting goods to Saras and other worlds in our system.

Regrettably, I was in for yet another depressing revelation. The peaceful harmony between these two worlds was suddenly interrupted by the arrival of a large space fleet from Saras, made up of thousands upon thousands of ships. Immediately, my heart jumped with fear, sensing what the spirit of death would carelessly do. I asked May Len if these ships were from Mu, and she nodded affirmative.

Small space craft hastily left the moon trying to escape the fleet's pending onslaught but fell prey to precision fire the moment they reached space. Then suddenly, a powerful wide purple beam struck the moon on its frontal side, producing a blast wave that encompassed and consumed all life on its surface.

The entire lunar landscape changed in the blink of an eye. Explosive haloes heaved from the moon's bowels, and cracks emerged along its fragile sphere, severely rearranging lunar topology. Fiery rocks and ash fell back from the sky, smashing into already-sensitive soils, while surface water simmered away in cloudy chaos, promptly scattering into space. Turmoil lingered for several weeks until an arid wasteland was all that remained.

Pleased with results, the fleet left lunar orbit and moved on to a larger target: a cloud covered world I knew was Masar. I immediately panicked and shouted "*Keh*!" absolutely terrified, meaning "no," as the fleet gathered on the planet's sunlit side and the pink beam struck the planet.

"*Niní me éh taziéh!*" I unconsciously said to May Len in tears, meaning "We must counter attack." I repeated these words without hesitation, unaware I fully relived my legacy before her.

With sadness on her countenance, she gently caressed my tears and softly said, "*Di keh gamiéh, Roshon,*" meaning "Don't cry," holding firmly to both my quivering hands. My lips and body shuddered intensely, knowing I had done something terribly wrong. My head hung low and wavered negatively unable to find rest, much less forgiveness. My heart sunk lower than it thought possible, deserving nothing less than death as obvious reward.

"May Len," I said, struggling to remember what words I learned in the vision, "*ce meh lassuméh . . . cie fiméh ti eh attanáh,*" meaning "I have brought the death of our world."

"*Keh, inéh Roshon, keh!*" replied May Len quickly, but to no consolation.

No sooner, the vision I experienced on the ridge came to life before us, but something new was added. When least expected, an intense flash the likes of a star emerged on the planet's sun side, bright enough to light up heavenly objects millions of km away as clear as daylight.

As with the moon, the massive blast decimated the planet, altered its orbit, and delivered scorching fire storms that cindered all living things upon its surface. The planet's oceans instantly rushed off in a vague white cloud, assuming a spiraling orbit around the sun bound for Saras. Violent volcanic eruptions raced to engulf the planet and rip the surface into space, spawning rivers of fire that struggled for supremacy one over the other like rampant tsunamis. Fiery wind storms polished down everything in their path until the last ounce of air expired.

From ash-covered heavens, blazing projectiles bombarded the surface with vicious force. Two large surface fragments were instantly ejected into space, assumed orbit, and became Masar's present moons. Gradually, the fiery cloud cover subsided, and the planet transformed into the Masar we know today.

It was no coincidence; my previous vision did have a purpose. As soon as I connected with it, May Len fixed her gentle, brightly lit eyes upon mine with a meaningful, sincere gaze, never wavering from mine. I softly asked her, "*Ceh dih tes*?" meaning "I do this?"

She did not reply right away, but then calmly said, "*Keh Roshon; Saras dih.*"

Martians did not destroy their world as Ly-Dian led us to believe; we did. The ETA was about to repeat the same blunders committed in Mu and Atlantis, helplessly influenced by memories that will not rest. Oh, how history repeats itself and how obvious the cyclic mechanism that makes it so! But this was not the beginning of our despicable legacy; it stemmed yet further into the past. Dozens of space battles from times prior to Mu dashed before our eyes, then stopped. Room lights returned to normal luminescence, the main doorway opened, and we were left to ponder silently upon our wicked legacy.

In May Len's virtuous presence, guilt-ridden words jarred uncontrollably as if some strange tongue struggled vainly to establish firm hold of me. Her tender glance strived patiently to awaken dormant memories with silent lyrics stirred by celestial compassion. "Do you remember?" her caring countenance suggested. I did not know what to remember, although grave remorse flowed through my being with untold ardor from sources unknown.

Shudders stressed my body for composure, becoming increasingly aware I had something to do with all this. I respectfully told May Len, "*Ceh keh ináh*," meaning "I do not sister," but her semblance did not change.

I never imagined our past garnished such degree of destruction and could not bear knowing the reasons why—reasons I would discover soon enough. The sad thing was that these past civilizations reached social and technical pinnacles similar to present day, before plunging into perdition. I had every reason to believe our immediate future was in jeopardy, and perhaps this was the primary motive prompting this contact.

May Len gently gathered my shuddering vessel upon her soft, caring arms, begging my strong, uncontrollable cries to rest upon her clean soul. I grieved profusely, no longer able to avoid soiled tears from leaving restricted hideouts. In that moment of lasting sorrows, my voice silenced, the heart released its borne sentiment, and my soul burst loose its hold on life's joys. Hans and Sean watched my emotions unfold rather concerned but kept their distance unsure what to do about it.

May Len, on the other hand, regained her radiant everlasting smile, and amiably called me by name, but I could not respond. Her divine gaze briefly turned to one of sadness, knowing how I felt. But quickly regaining her limitless joy, she placed a hand on my left arm and called my name once again. Failing to respond, she put both her hands on my shoulders, directed a soothing inviting smile, and nodded in the negative indicating I should not linger behind guilt; but my intolerable remorse held its course as warm tears crashed in torrents defiling her gleaming bronze shoes.

With utmost respect, she reached up and placed a gentle kiss on my tearing cheek, but I could not return her gesture. I felt like a criminal suffering from amnesia, being reminded of previous immoral activities. Still, I was driven by a sixth sense that somehow knew with outstanding precision the full extent of my awful legacy.

Most humbly, May Len took me deep onto her loving wings, sweetly wrapped my being within her gentle embodiment, and tenderly asked me to stop crying, "*Di keh gamiéh, ezi tennéh.*"

Intensely enraptured by the amorous rhythm of her singing heart and the gentle petals that adorned her delicate hands cast upon my hair, the only words that dared gather unto my lips glided repentantly from a broken heart unto her compassionate, radiant eyes, "*Plevah, ezi inah, plevah;* sorry."

Determined to snap me out of it, she closed her eyes and smiled widely as a slight glow enveloped her being. Immediately, a wondrous sense of well-being relieved my poignant state of mind with a quick gasp. It felt like a long-lost friend entered my mind, warmly greeted me, and tenderly erased all previous negative thoughts with one gentle sweep.

Unexpectedly, she placed a segment from the Uzboi Vallis vision into my mind where the young girl said, "Friend, brother." Reasons behind its saga were just as mysterious as May Len's reasons for bringing it up. But then, it occurred to me, was May Len the young girl in the vision, and what about the boy? She did not answer the question though confirmed the vision was factual. The importance of May Len's affirmation would not sink in for several months to come, and what a surprise it would be.

Gently reaching down to the ground, she picked up an invisible object, held it up on her right hand, and tapped it a few times. She then extended her left hand and nodded. I realized she was asking for the flashlight I found, so I quickly produced it and gently placed it upon her hand with a slow bow.

"*Vetecbé biga lunei,*" she spoke into the flashlight, and a hologram instantly revealed several brief recorded messages of the child from the vision. May

Len smiled when recordings of both children appeared, at times more so than others depending what was being said, but made no attempt to translate. Shortly after, she tapped the flashlight, the projection stopped, and she handed the device back to me.

Apologetically, she lightly stepped back and waved at me. I knew what this meant; it was time for her to depart. We glanced at one another, dreading this moment for what it preordained and the long forthcoming days that would separate us. Our eyes silently met for some time, clearly admitting we did not wish to be apart. In thought, she would never vanish, but physically, I would sorely miss her exceptional radiance.

Though we were worlds apart, I wished May Len's heavenly company embraced my heart someday not far. I failed to see how that would be possible, being so different and distant her and I. Given the extreme past crimes I was becoming aware of committing, it made the prospect the less likely. She knew exactly how I felt and gently bowed, hand over heart, sealing a promise to remove those barriers that kept us distant.

Her promise my hopes secured, faithful that the Infinite's destiny would grant us eternal endure. In return, I promised to wait a million years for her company, or as long as Father deemed our separation necessary, for my heart now wore her name exclusively upon its warmest cadences, and that would make such long waiting tolerable.

My heart rejoiced, for I had unknowingly found my one, my loving pearl of great price [1] lost long, long ago, treasure of the heart that shall never rust or fade away through the halls of time, for nothing else shall I ever desire.

Though I lived a lowly reality teeming with fear and sin, the Infinite so graciously granted me a righteous pearl that beckoned me with loving din. Like a faithful beacon, His luminous gem subdues murky seas before me and illumines a path to freedom away from sinful sands, a grace that shall lead me home among countless starry bands. My priceless pearl, my one May Len, who leads me to dwell among His starry canopies, where there is no sin to den.

Her tender smile rekindles my heart to youthful yearning, conveying an endearing melody of love that calms my soul and inspires divine poetry unto lips touchingly singing. Her loving eyes warmly embody the word of infinity, and the alluring brilliance of stellar affinity.

May Len, light of my life and heart's joy so endearing—oh, perfect love that spans exalted horizons and gives embodiment true meaning. The kingdom of heaven I found in her, treasure found hidden in fields, I will give it all to obtain those fields [2].

She extended her right hand toward me, but this time I felt a hand clasp was not in order. I took her hand and very slowly and gently raised it above my shoulder. I cannot describe how I felt at that moment, to say the least, lighter than a feather.

May Len smiled excitedly, waiting patiently for me to take or, rather, remember the next step. Noting my slight indecision, she chuckled lightly but remained both patient and joyful until I fully played out my part. The only thing that came to mind was a picture of a heart with glowing sapphires in it and the words, "*Deh onéh éhzi mis ni nedee, men*, May Len," meaning "You are my one and only, friend, May Len."

Her eyes tenderly constrained, and tears suddenly gushed from them. With a slight bow, she gently took my hands to her forehead, trying to hide fluttering lips with a gasp. She reached over, hugged me warmly for some time, and gave me another kiss on the cheek, overcoming her sob with a brief chuckle. "*Oh-joi, éhzi mis tennéh*, Roshon," she said sweetly, followed by "*Miráh, éhzi men avéh*," which stands for "Farewell, my old friend."

With gentle steps, May Len walked toward Hans and Sean, waving at them. But she turned back the moment a picture of the lighted beings popped into my mind. The woman inside the light; it was her. She confirmed my thoughts, turned her attention to Hans and Sean, then slowly became translucent and vanished into thin air. Moments later, a male voice came out of nowhere and told us to expect another contact, in English, taking us completely by surprise.

May Len's enchantment thrived in my soul like an inexhaustible echo, struggling for words to describe any of it. Hans and Sean were just as stunned, reluctant to return to conventional ways of thinking. Battling uncontrollable stuttering and joy, I managed to voice a few words impulsively, "May Len . . . she's . . . a Martian!"

Rather clueless at first, Hans came to his senses. With a quick flitting smile and a brisk grunted throat clearing, he said, "I think, that's obvious, no?"

"I expected something a bit less pleasant," Sean said, "like some stonking, brain-oozing creature with tentacles in a life-support bubble. But she was absolutely . . . beautiful mate, graceful, more human than a human. What you make of her, Bill?"

Emotions held me in such firm grip that I fumbled over my own thoughts. "I think I met . . . an angel," I replied making perfect sense to myself, but sparking more questions otherwise.

Hans and Sean looked at me rather mystified with eyebrows raised significantly beyond the norm. "You're not serious, yes?" Hans said. "She is an extraordinarily beautiful, graceful woman. An angel? I wouldn't go that far."

"I don't mean outside," I added deeply moved, "inside, it's something benign worth living and dying for. God, God is alive in her. I felt it!"

"Are you all right, lad?" asked Sean, wondering if my reasoning slipped for certain. "You don't sound too good. Do you need to spend a penny?"

"I've never felt better," I replied gasping a brief sentimental cry. I had no idea who I had just met but certainly felt the effects. From that moment on, I never let May Len's essence vanish from my thoughts, not for an instant. My heart forever lived in her tender hands, waiting eternity if necessary for the privilege to awaken and sing melodious ballades to her.

Beautiful beyond description and so spiritually elegant, May Len articulates no selfishness, only truth and heavenly pleasure. She is the life giving fountain of my longing heart, imparting stellar beauty and stirring divine art. Her tender, inviting hands dress my heart with velvet blessings, wondrous artistic brushes painting godly meaning upon my life's canvas unceasing.

Pleasant gardenias appear every time she is near. Her petite lips are like threads of soft scarlet dropping lightly as honeycomb. Her words grant me virtuous life, invigorating my soul like a bundle of sweet-smelling myrrh. Her hair is like charming, gentle cascades of purest flowing waters to thirsty hands. Her breath is precious eternal perfume, endowed with the loveliest rhapsodies a song can bloom.

May Len, my one, fair as the moon and dazzling as the sun, was hidden among lilies in a vast valley. But now she has become my sunrise, a light unto my path that illumines the way out of morbid sands. She replenishes my life with God's presence, joyfully infusing my soul with glorious patience.

Without my beloved jewel, my unique polarity, life is false, never tender; without her lost in the devil's playground, my life is torn from joyful render. My heart sealed forever over hers with a love as strong as truth, sharing delightful songs written in empyrean prose. Many waters cannot quench my love for her—neither will floods drown it—for the only waters my soul seek come from her graceful splendor. My one—oh my pillar of life—I shall forever seek thee.

With time passing by and silence holding sway over us without regard, Hans finally brought our mute stalemate to an end by asking me to elaborate on alien behavior, having shared so closely with May Len. It was no surprise; there were vast technical and spiritual differences between our societies, requiring significant intellectual adjustments on our part in order to coexist. Aliens were telepathic, implying they lived in a society devoid of personal secrets and devoted to common unity, belief, and purpose. Although we could keep no secrets from them, they never interfered in our affairs, neutrality earning them respect. Forgiveness was definitely a key attribute of their society, illustrated by a lack of retribution after we destroyed their planet.

I had much to say about alien culture, but Hans was interested in something less civil and more on a personal note. In particular, how I managed to talk to May Len. As he put it, I seemed to know just what to do and say. I could not shelve the subject away as trivial or give simple answers; he was all over the subject and was rather persistent about it.

"One moment, you're all emotional with the presentation," he said. "The other, she's giving you a kiss, raising hands, embracing, and speaking in foreign tongues. I'm not sure what happened between you two, but it's important you disclose all relevant information—verbal, or mental."

I looked at my partners with reasonable insecurity; my most dreaded moment had arrived. Sharing experiences beyond what's considered normal opens up the door to derision. But after procrastinating for a moment, I felt it best to come clean of it. So I described my lighted beings experience, made mention of the fixed helmet, and the returned pick. Still, that did not answer Hans's persistent question: how did I know, especially their language.

Rather uptight, I described the Uzboi incident, but that raised more questions than answers, as expected. Hans found it interesting that aliens reached out to me first and without witnesses, not just once but twice. Then, once in the structure, May Len specifically chose me to talk to her. It was too obvious. I was singled out and perhaps primed for contact. It sounded rather selfish in the grand scheme of things, but the logical entity to convince in the end was not the team but Earth gov. Why aliens did so remained a mystery.

My partners felt Martians would eventually demand compensation for many transgressions against them, although that made no sense. They did not settle the score when we had less technology, so why now as a nuclear space power? Regardless, this was a subject bound to resurface many times again.

Our sights were set mid-room where the transport beam shone brightly in unpredictable colors once more, marking the start of another contact. The identity of our next visitor was just as mysterious as the place from whence he came and more so the purpose for said call.

May Len, my soul's lantern, fully dominated my mind. I could not, and would not, let her thoughts leave me—ever. I could barely contain my racing heart's longing for her, my sister, my one, for I dearly loved her.

Oh epitome of love, that cannot exist without truth. Oh truth, that cannot exist without my "one." Oh my dearly beloved one, I cannot exist without thee!

---

[1] W. J. Rev. Morford, "Matthew 13: 45–46," in *The One New Man Bible*, Travelers Rest, SC: True Potential Publishing Co., 2011.

[2] W. J. Rev. Morford, "Matthew 13:44," in *The One New Man Bible*, Travelers Rest, SC: True Potential Publishing Co., 2011.

Chapter 9: *Second Contact*

The transport beam reactivated, and its noiseless light gently descended to the crystal floor, shrouded in bluish haze. Beneath its wake, translucent grounds reflected light back out in glorious prismatic rays, much like a sea of colorful effulgence glistening placidly in the sun. As the haze steadily dissolved, the outline of a man not much taller than May Len emerged.

His features were human, cleanly refined, and somewhat Asian. He seemed to be in his early thirties wearing neatly styled black hair, fashioned back much as ours. Black slacks and shoes matched a white long-sleeve shirt, radiating prismatic rainbows when creased by movement. The shirt had no buttons or snaps holding it together, parting into a loose vertical collar at the neckline.

Room lights steadily dimmed after his appearance, beckoning resplendent celestial jewels to herald eve's pending twilight. As darkness prevailed, a majestic cosmic canvas unfurled the purest dazzling colors the starry heavens could depict in creation's most profound starlit domains. Wondrous galactic arms warmly embraced our sights with placid, munificent colors set against the still black satin backdrop of space. Innumerable alluring cosmic shores proclaimed the essence of absolute beauty, brightly inspiring the way to God's heavenly realms among the stars, which His Majesty has allotted to all the peoples under the whole heaven [1].

Magnificent, vibrant mansions teeming with floral wonders revolved serenely about every sheltering iridescent host, enlivened by passionate, colorful skies extolled by countless souls dwelling peacefully among them. Modern cities adorned these worlds with a tranquil holy presence, inaudibly hosting God's affluent pulse of virtuous life across the opulent, creative void. The heavens declare the grandeur of God, and the firmament shows His handy work [2].

Soft slow melodies, performed by gentle dizis and tender strings, complemented the starlight exhibit, infusing the structure with a rich yet subtle mix of French- and Asian-like impressionistic works, but gentler in texture and definitely more inspiring. In the interim, our guest waited patiently as we lost ourselves into the alluring magnificence surrounding us.

Our host stepped forward and raised his right hand in salutation. We returned greetings likewise, though somewhat hesitant. "*Sa-ah deen nee eh ha, Masar*," he said in his native tongue, taking a few steps toward us.

"What did he just say?" remarked Hans whispering.

"I don't know. Sounded like a greeting to me," I replied.

"What I meant to say was, welcome brothers to our home, Mars," he said.

"You speak English?" remarked Hans with a sigh of relief.

"Should come as no surprise that I do, my brother," replied our host. Noting our hesitation, he briefly chuckled and added, "Don't be shy. Think of me as family, a friend, someone you've known for a very long time. We're definitely not strangers to one another."

His penetrating gaze left no doubt he knew precisely what we thought, felt, and feared, commanding a most serene yet wise gaze far from arrogant. In his presence, I felt trivial as a meager ant yet uninhibited, free to be myself, or convey any emotion—he already knew of them. Hiding my feelings only led me to misjudge him. After giving me a gentle hug, he said, "Bill, my beloved brother, *tennéh adennéh.* I've looked forward to seeing you for quite some time."

His steadfast eyes told a story as ancient as time itself. His inner wisdom and noteworthy respect for moral discipline surpassed anyone's effort to conceive it, definitely unattainable in a single lifetime. In his heart, truth blossomed; in his mind, fear withered.

"You've become a highly regarded scientist on your world," he said, "and you now also know much about ours. Most notably, you've established a wonderful relationship with one of our sisters. You're still searching for love, I see. If you only knew how close it's been to you. You don't mind if I refer to you as an old friend, do you?"

"No, I have no mind," I impulsively replied.

Something about his voice seemed most familiar. He felt like an old friend, one lost long ago, but I couldn't place him to a memory. His inviting friendship the more drew me to him in fullest confidence and amity, unlike anyone I had met before.

"*Tennéh adennéh, éhẓi men avéh. Ceh tennéh Manéh,*" I replied slowly, bowing reverently to him in recognition of his spiritual stature.

"*Oh-joi*!" repeated the alien, smiling joyfully. "You learn quickly, as in old times. This is good, for you have much to learn. Next time, I'll make sure your sister May Len joins us."

"I'd like that so very, very much," I replied excitedly, face enriched with warmth and heart frantically soaring. I couldn't take May Len off my mind or did I want to. Our lives were blended together under love eternal's canopy, a love never selfish or sexually driven. It was a love of truth, the rhythm of creation, an exceptional feeling of friendship and sharing, for I was deeply in love with her virtuous soul. While I didn't know it at the time, I felt true brotherhood and oneness as the Infinite meant it to be.

He knew my embarrassment but made no mention of it. Instead, with a chuckle, he replied with welcomed news. "May Len wants you to know she also looks forward to seeing you again and values your kind thoughts toward her. Yours will be a friendship undeterred by time or space. We hope our people reach across space someday and become equally inseparable friends, brothers, for eternity."

The words "friend, brother" raced like a blizzard through my mind after hearing them again. Immediately, he lightly tapped me on the shoulder and said, "It's really been a very long, long time, my dear old friend of ages. You have no idea how long or far, but you'll remember soon. Be patient; it will all come back to you."

Turning over to Hans, he greeted him by name and rank. "You are responsible for Martian security and the success of this mission; that makes you a very busy man," he said firmly. Hans thanked our host, bringing his pose to regimented military stand. "You have a beautiful family back on Saras, and I extend them the same appreciation as I do you. Perhaps we shall meet them one day soon. You and Sean are also old friends."

Next, he turned to Sean who stared at the alien dead silent and helplessly adrift, no doubt overwhelmed by the prospect of meeting an extraterrestrial face-to-face for the first time. All he could do was smile like the perfect nerd and powerlessly nod his head, unsure what to do with himself. "Sean, a most studious, inquisitive mind." he said. "You enjoy science, do you not?"

"Aye sir," responded Sean like a peppy geek, "my favorite subject."

"Indeed it is; some things never change. Your knowledge of the universe is minute now, but life is all about learning; yours just barely begun. There's no end to our quest for wisdom."

"I am known as Dow Uahn Veih, but you may call me Brother," said the Martian with great excitement. "We are known by our essence or 'feel' rather than names, as the language of the soul embodies both personal and spiritual accessories. I'm one of twelve Martian councils, a position similar to your Earth ministers.

"Mars is part of a vast cosmic family called the Universal Brotherhood, united in principle, spirit, and purpose. The brotherhood is made up of countless beings called Brothers, all inspired by the Infinite in a direct way. Saras is the only world within fifty thousand light-years that's not a member, and that's why we're here today, to invite your people to join the brotherhood and learn the ways of infinity with us. But I must note, this isn't the first time we do so.

"Eons ago, we were designated to watch over your world. Since then, your people betrayed Father and sought to destroy us several times. Still, we won't condemn or abandon you. That same hostile tendency, born from nothing more than fear of love and truth, still influences you today and keeps us from coming among your people. Since you are not aware of it, you easily fall prey to its powerful persuasion, and enact its belligerent inclinations naively.

"Fear is your worst enemy. It lowers your harmonic relationship with the Infinite, brings obsessive feeding entities into your fold, and drapes cunning veils of doom over the mind, prowling covertly through obscure thought meadows hoping to pounce on weak, confused values like roaring lions seeking whom to devour [3]. It breeds lower possessive ardors instead of higher clean energies, drifting unsuspecting victims from one pleasure to the next until death draws eyes to a close, never achieving gratification or peace. You therefore concoct eccentric sedatives in life, like conceit and anger, to briefly calm its tormenting assault. Life is a science, and its variables can't go ignored. You're either positive with truth or negative with fear; there's no in between.

"But you need not suffer, for there is a way out of such misery: seek only truth and the Infinite. Don't fear love or obey selfish motives. That's the answer to all problems. Truth means life, but since fear dares defy truth, it spells death, for untruth is fear's foundation. Nothing displeases Father more than deceit because it kills the soul.

"Fear is responsible for your inconceivable denial of Father's existence and stubborn reliance on your finite self. Ever pondered where invisible deeds such as love, intuition, visions, or truth come from? Not from atoms but the foundation of His essence [4]. If you deny Him, you will never know love or truth, for He is the ultimate realization of love and the eternal song of majestic wisdom, not you. Instead, you are the total opposite.

"Your obsession with weapons is also born from fear. The faster you give them up, the sooner you'll learn to collaborate and love each other. We have no weapons on our worlds, and you can't join us until you give them up.

"Speaking of obsessions, you have none greater than intimacy. The body isn't yours; it belongs to Father, given to you to experience His eternal love. What you do with or to your vessel, you also do unto His Highness. It isn't an object to freely grant to someone else, smear with paint, or degenerate with sadness or pleasure, for it is God's uniform. By wearing it, you represent His realms. Therefore, wear your uniform clean and proudly at all times, free from pleasure, anger, or unsuitable foods, unbecoming an envoy of His Majesty."

He paused for a moment as two sofas and a center table materialized out of thin air. "You have many questions of us, and we will gladly answer them," he said, inviting us to sit.

Unexpectedly, the carrier beam activated, and two lovely young ladies appeared. One of the ladies was tall with black hair and brilliant emerald eyes, the other shorter and blonde with large black eyes, both beautiful and radiant beyond description, wearing no makeup or jewelry of any kind. Both wore elegant pastel dresses, and a white sash perfectly contoured to their artistically modeled physique. The taller lady's facial features were gentle and clean with a touch of European flair. The shorter lady's countenance seemed like that of a toddler with petite finely formed lips and subtle nose. Her forehead and cheeks were slightly flush, smooth, and higher than in Saras humans. Her eyes were larger than ours, level, with triple lacrimal glands that contoured the eyeball much closer to the lens than ours.

"This is Tei-Ah," he said of the taller lady, who carried a tray with glassware and a transparent pitcher filled with a clear liquid. "She is from Saturn. Meh-Nai is from Venus. On Earth, you would call them educators."

We were rather perplexed to learn of their origins. As far as we knew, these worlds were completely inhospitable to humans, but Dow Uanh replied, "Life blooms throughout the universe in places you would never suspect. What appears to you as worlds physically devoid of life, such as Venus, in other dimensions thrive with abundant, creative beauty. In fact, each world supports life on different planes, something your scientists are completely unaware of."

The liquid offered by Tei-Ah tasted like water but with a slightly denser texture than the recycled stuff I was used to; it was most refreshing. The ladies then sat on each side of Dow Uanh and waited intently for our lead.

"Thank you, Mr. Veih, for your kind hospitality. On behalf of our world," Hans said, hesitating a moment, "please accept our sincerest apologies for our past actions and appreciation for your continued support. I respect the fact that, in spite of your superior technology, you haven't used it against us."

"We have no reason to," he replied. "We don't interfere in the affairs of other worlds or subdue them by force, even if we're right. Such an act means death to us. Consider this: the self is the only thing to correct and conquer. It's hard enough being honest with and conquering just one individual; your own self. Imagine for a moment six billion others. If you can't master yourself, what can you possibly offer others but stagnation?" We admired his analogy, for right he was.

"The self is a vast storehouse of experiences some deem vital to survival, obeying it like some prevalent entity, and protecting it to ensure its existence," Meh-Nai added in a lively voice with a hint of Brit. "In return, it influences us with endless delusions of grandeur, habits, and fears. Look to the future, not the past. Let it be a lesson, not life's motive."

"Such can the past be, a forlorn menagerie subject to thought disorders that in thee unto death shall spree," Tei-Ah added poetically. "Selfish, wrongful delights are abnormal flings; such instincts subdue Father's stirring throbs rapping tenderly at our restive beings. Possession and survival is death: truth and sacrifice is life."

"Just as bodies need sustenance, so does the soul needs truth," Dow Uanh said. "Truth isn't a material thing but an endless mental collective we call the Unified Field of Minds, the brotherhood, binding us and higher beings of light with the Infinite."

"When faced with hostility, you assess the past for deliverance, unaware your threat assessment also comes from it," Meh-Nai said. "Surround yourself with His essence and let threats pass you by. The moment you seek the self and eat of the tree of good evil, you surely die [5]. Good and evil, delicious but harmful, fun but dangerous, charming but menacing, pleasure but infamy; the lower self is contrary to His will. And as the tree of good evil is the self, the Tree of Life [6] is the brotherhood, where the higher self, the true self, dwells."

"My kind sister, does the Garden of Eden story refer to the struggle between brotherhood and self?" I said, slightly bowing to her.

"In Atlantis, humanity chose self over brotherhood the moment their eyes, or mental faculties as the Hebrew word '`ayin' denotes, were roused [7], distorting and disobeying His natural laws. By doing so, they chose to die as a light-filled being and live addicted to their lower self."

"For hundreds of years," Sean said, "we sent countless messages into space but never got a reply. Is there a reason our calls went unanswered?"

"We replied, but your world cast us away. We warned that nuclear bombs had a devastating effect on other worlds as well as time and space constructs, causing natural disasters on Saras even before the 1940's, but you didn't listen. The Hiroshima bomb devastated a planet in the Sirius system where countless brothers perished, and also caused the Lisbon earthquake of 1755—yes, back in time. Still, you turned your back on us and chose to seek other beings for technology. How many bombs have you unleashed since? How many brothers have perished across space over thousands of years as a result of your blatant disregard for nature? Had we forced our way, you would have misjudged our intentions, placed your desires up front, and snubbed the principles we live by. It would have been catastrophic for your world, not to mention ours."

"But how could we cause such events on other worlds, even in the past?"

"Or the future. Atomic blasts pull the rug from under energy vortexes in one sudden heave. These deform, destabilize, and collapse, causing untold space-time tragedies at harmonically linked points throughout the cosmos."

"This we were not aware of," Hans said regretfully. "I'm truly sorry to hear what we've done and it won't happen again. This is really serious!"

"It is, reason we're here. The brotherhood has tried reasoning with your world for two hundred long years: hopefully, you will listen this time. Your weapons must go; that can't wait. Even the fall of a sparrow is noted, for creation is fully integrated and dependent on every facet of its infinite fabric."

"When it comes to creation," I said, "questions outweigh answers. Some think we are the product of a big bang, while others claim we were created in six days, but neither side can prove their position beyond doubt."

"You trust your own imagination more so than facts," Tei-Ah said. "Seems odd really, your insatiable desires require little proof to support serving them. As a paradox to reason, you opt to ignore staggering amounts of evidence because social and intellectual loyalty comes first, influencing your decision to be narrow-minded."

"Friends and professional association is what matters most on your world, not proof or the impact your words have on listeners," Meh-Nai said.

"Secular idealists will have you think that Father is just a myth," Tei-Ah said. "Under the guise of critical thinking, these souls perpetrate untold cynicism and academically congested speech, not hard evidence. They're simply jealous of God's power and complexity. To answer your question, life is an illimitable, convergent concept architected by Infinite Consciousness."

"Your scriptures, though mistranslated, possess a wealth of knowledge about the Infinite" Dow Uanh said, "but you don't take them seriously and find it acceptable to disobey the few universal laws you know of at will. Imagine what might happen if we gave you more to disobey."

"So was there ever such a thing as a big bang" inquired Sean.

"It's hard to envision that what is, always was and always will be, for time and space are illusions. The universe is an eternal nursery for young souls, the first step in an infinite journey toward absolute truth. No, there was no big bang. However, you could say there was a big hand."

"Since support for the big bang comes from red shift observations, special relativity, and detailed mathematics," Hans said. "where did we go wrong?"

"In insisting there is no Infinite and adapting theories to put Him down. Without Him, you'll be guessing forever, and that can be a really long time."

"I always thought red shifts were an unreliable means of measuring stellar motion," Sean said much relieved.

"This your science knows but chooses to fabricate more flawed theories upon an already baseless foundation," Tei-Ah said, "anything to keep status quo, avoid scorn, and drive the Infinite from people's minds." As she spoke, my own secular past caught up to me, coming to grips with past fruits of rebellion. She was kind enough not to bring them up, but the shoe fit perfectly, and I nodded in humble recognition.

"If motion is not responsible for red shifts, then what is?"

"Exporting locally observed properties to the rest of the universe is a risky proposition for many reasons. First, energy, not velocity, is the primary red shift factor. Second, stellar energy behaves different in space than it does on planets or synthetic vacuums. Stars induce energy into the space medium; then cosmic currents carry it aloft, just as ocean currents move boats. Think of space as a sea of invisible carrier waves that, once synchronized to them, can transmit energy or ships at speeds set by induction rates. Remember, light doesn't propagate; instead, space transports it."

"Stellar energy crosses many environments before reaching you," Meh-Naih said. "The first is extra galactic space, filled with massive 'cosmic winds' produced by universal rotation. These act like jet streams, creating rotating pressure areas that ultimately bring galaxies to life. At the galaxy's 'bow shock,' energy adapts to a new medium and proceeds to cross several 'galactic winds.' Its properties are further altered by the sun's heliopause and 'solar wind.' By the time energy collides with your world, it's been greatly tampered with.

"The farther an object resides, the lower shall its apparent resultant energy print be due to absorption and heterodyning. The higher the absorption along the way, the higher the relative wavelength change. There's your red shift, a simple energy loss relationship between cosmic electric field strength relative to source force, yielding wavelength distortion [(1)]."

"So, red shifts are a type of propagation resistance, or energy loss, due to interaction with cosmic winds and our world?" Sean said.

"And also matter. When molecules condense, band dispersion occurs, electronic state gaps are reduced, and red shifts are induced. For example, depending on density, water and gas in space can intercept light beams and shift their spectrum red or blue, thus nullifying previously adopted energy states. But think in terms of dimensional rather than physical forces, since time and space are not ultimately responsible for energy propagation."

"What's all that mean exactly."

"Do you know what Lorentz force is?"

"Sure, it's the angular interaction between magnetism, current, and force."

"Fourth-dimensional currents induce Lorentz forces on every particle in the cosmos at unique frequency rates, thus giving rise to what we perceive as time, space, density, temperature, and the semblance of movement. Energy manifestations such as gravity, lensing, and absorption are solely by-products of harmonic interactions between higher dimensional currents or vortexes:

---

(1) Total energy loss is computed as initial object energy and its subsequent variations:

$$E_t = \frac{v_i h_i}{\lambda_i} + \sum_{n=\lambda_i}^{\lambda_{x-1}} \left(\frac{v_1 h_1}{n_1} - \frac{v_0 h_0}{n_0} \right)$$

no physical propagation or velocity is ever involved. Where vortexes interact, nodal grids are formed and a series of linear events between their physical elements result such as energy emanations and valence. These may be harmonically linked to other vortexes, thus giving the illusion of movement. And while events may seem linear in our dimension, vortexes are not: these can be scattered throughout time and space. Bottom line is, energy acts over dimensional nodal grids rather than space."

"Sounds confusing. Is space then some kind of dimensional hologram?"

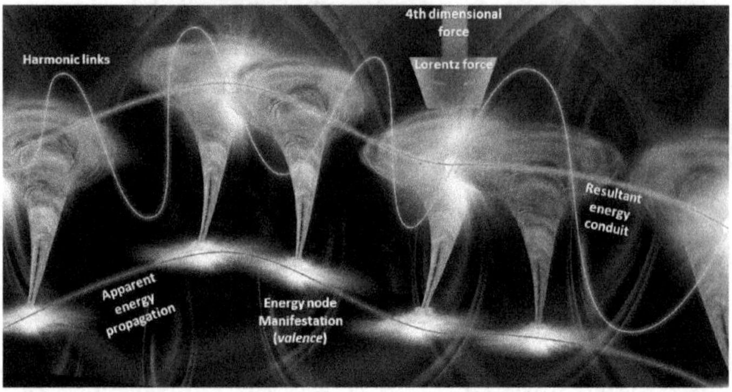

"Some harmonic oscillations between linked dimensional grids will create a series of pixelated apparitions in linear time; so, yes. Your Planck length unit attempts to derive what our physical pixel granularity is, based on the speed of light and the gravitational constant, but consider how this value changes with wavelength and potential. To sum it all up, the distance between vortex physical events is simply the inverse square root of frequency. Thus, time and space are interchangeable and don't exist."

"And what is time exactly?"

"It's the speed of existence in reference to other vortex events, manifested as density and sequential events. As nodal grids interact with other vortexes, a series of physical events occur but only the last demodulated instance of said dimensional transits is what your spectrum analyzers will pick up. Note also that, in terms of kinetic wave terms, an energy node's time reference is proportional to its mass and the square of its wavelength [(2)]. Each object has its own time or gravitational reference where time is the energy base rate affecting solidity and managing space. Building upon these concepts, consider that mass is proportional to wavelength and the square root of electric force. Therefore, mass isn't real either."

---

(2) $f = \frac{4\pi^2 h}{m\lambda^2} \overset{\Delta}{\rightarrow} \frac{k}{\lambda^2}$ frequency, or time base, is proportional to inverse square of wavelength

"So solidity and time are really like a heterodyne effect between pulsing energies, and there's really nothing solid to speak of but just . . . oscillations."

"In most simple terms, yes."

"And how fast can the space medium velocity actually get?" I added.

"While mass travels at speeds set by energy, energy travels at speeds set by its interaction with the fabric of space and may reach millions of light-years per second or more, depending on dimensional rates. In fact, light speed as you know it manifests on one of the slowest mediums available."

"Do photons then ride on some thin wormhole created by space medium resonance?" Sean said.

"It's energy, not mass, that propagates. Energy pushes against the space medium on one end, transfers onto the medium, and resolves back as energy on the other like a Newton's cradle. That's how stars deliver energy across the depths of space, not like drifting asteroids but as dimensional fields of force."

"That's absolutely fascinating and leaves much for us to ponder upon."

"Some think space is as old as its size, again based on red shift," Hans said.

"Since nothing should go faster than light, scientists capped the age of the Universe and called it a day," Sean said, "backed by barmy relativity formulas that glue it all together real wonky."

"Have you wondered why distant objects, moving away at super ocular speeds, are still visible?" Meh-Nai said. "At such speeds, shouldn't even Gamma rays dip below visible?"

"Then how big is the universe, if there's even a limit to it?"

"First, let's define what a universe is," Tei-Ah said. "Our universe is a cluster of galaxies a trillion light-years across, takes over six hundred trillion years to rotate about an axis parallel to Aquila-Sextant[8], and orbits a central core 1,210 trillion light years away in the direction of Cassiopeia, but that's just the beginning. A vast cosmic void lies beyond filled with properties foreign to you. This void is a vast nursery, stretching for trillions of light-years, from which universes like ours are born; think of it as a cosmic Oort cloud.

"In these nurseries, influenced by formidable cosmic currents, large-phased masses spawn powerful magnetic fields, fuse energy into basic hydrogen, and form new galaxies much the same way that hurricanes develop over warm waters but in three dimensions—from outside of the universe in. More so, these currents can and do penetrate our universe, induce cosmic jet streams, and form new galaxies inside our universe.

"Beyond this void are other universes similar to ours and others beyond those, extending through inestimable expanse in numbers like stars. Just as planets are to stars, stars to galaxies, and galaxies to universe, so are universes like stars to an enormous, swirling macro carrier of incalculable size."

"Through entropy," Meh-Nai said, "the universe recycles itself back into hydrogen and eventually into Gamma phased energy. From these pristine mutated masses, galaxies are reborn. The universe is as eternal as the principles of the Infinite. Yet it is only a moment in his eternal continuum."

"Where is our galaxy in relationship to our universe?" asked Sean.

"Our galaxy orbits 220 billion light-years from a universal core on one of six spiral arms, making a full rotation every 63 trillion years at a speed of 7,500 kilometers per second relative to native space. Our universe orbits along with other universes in a mega-spiral of incalculable age and a trillion, trillion, trillion light-years across. Other mega-spirals, including ours, form a massive whirlpool unit surrounded by collapsed time and space, where inter-dimensional energy currents, responsible for universal jet stream activity, endure endlessly. Beyond that, you have further massive whirlpool units as numerous as stars into infinity."

"How about black holes. What are they?"

"Our solar system has a 'barycenter' formed by common planetary pull. It is inside the sun itself and acts like a black hole, but it's not one. Likewise, Sagittarius A is an enormous barycenter, not a black hole, subject to the entire galactic mass acting upon it. This gives rise to high-speed orbital perturbations at the galactic core and polar jets, both induced by mass accretions.

"Black holes are not created from gluttonous high density detonated stars. These do exist, by the way, and do collect matter unto themselves, but the temperature of this acquired spinning matter is so high and its density so low that it overcomes friction, creeps into the poles, and ejects as polar jets."

"Can you prove the existence of universal design standards?" I asked.

"Atoms have four forces and possess unique properties, the same here as across the universe," Tei-Ah said. "They combine to fashion DNA, living cells, and diverse biological forms similar in likeness time after time. Trees with roots and leaves, fish with gills, winged birds, creatures with eyes, nose, ears, or mouth as needed. Life consumes energy and thrives on round worlds, orbiting about stars bound by star carriers. The human form is thus universal."

"How can this be, given the infinite types of stars and cosmic conditions?" Sean added.

"You won't find brain-oozing creatures wearing life-support bubbles out there, like you thought, but something a lot more human," Meh-Nai added jokingly. "Still, there are other beings that have evolved intelligence such as plants, insects, and reptiles.

"Stars and Jovian planets produce helical plasma crystals, or protein strands, and fill space with them. Their lattice configurations incept select elements found in their habitable zone and form native building blocks fit for that region. You'll find that stellar proteins are quite consistent anywhere you go, developing both organic and inorganic life-forms according to convergent configuration propensities much like an embryo.

"With time, these basic strands seek each other like magnetic puzzles across space, come together, and form more mature chains, according to built-in evolving valence receptors that admit or reject certain protein groupings. Thus, the bigger the strand gets, unlike general belief, the more explicit its affinity becomes to distinctive living forms, decreasing diversity and imposing greater receptor restrictions around itself. Just as atoms and proteins are consistent, stellar strands evolve to produce uniform life forms everywhere in Father's vast convergent universe."

"If stars create these crystals, what makes stars create them consistently?"

"Atomic magnetic resonance. Frequency creates nodal valences in these compact molecules that, in turn, are designed to attract six specific atoms by frequency association and thus give rise to twenty-two standard amino acids in the cold fringes of space. Hydrogen is the catalyst that sets the basis for lattice construct and controls the behavior of mainly oxygen, nitrogen, and carbon. Magnetism is the instruction carrier, responsible for creating valence placeholders for atoms to populate into helical molecules."

"So much for the theory that a huge bomb created all there is."

"It might surprise you to know that just as cells have DNA, so do atoms. Atomic DNA is an inter-dimensional instruction set containing schematics for isotopes, chemical bonds, molecules, life forms, stars, and galaxies. It also provides for entropy, recycling atoms back to pristine energy from whence all things are born. These design criteria, universal law, and atomic recurrence come from Father, not a bomb. And just as 216 different atoms are universal in nature, so are living forms, their functions, and appearance."

"So who is God? Is He a being like us, and where does He live?"

Our hosts bowed their head slightly in brief reverent reflection. A golden glow enveloped them, and Dow Uanh's eyes became filled with inexplicable splendor you could deeply feel. "We refer to God as Manéh, the Infinite Consciousness, the inconceivable creative intelligence encompassing all things physical, spiritual, and evolutionary. Manéh is love eternal, tranquility, the illimitable wellspring of life. He is the author of love, forgiveness, and evolution. Manéh is the patient Father of all, the embodiment of truth, the small still voice that guides and encourages us, and the highest light. He is the greatest happiness, love, inspiration, and our reason for living.

"Manéh is all things visible, invisible, known, and unknown. He is timeless, infinite, all-wise, something your people can't conceive at present. The Creator surpasses the state of being and hindrances of sequential thought. We are but a minute instance in His eternity."

"And while we faithfully follow the Creator, we don't believe in Him as you do. Rather," Meh-Nai added with emphasis, "we know Him!"

"You said we have an opportunity to join the brotherhood, yes?" remarked Hans. "What if Earth decides otherwise? Let's say Earth gov needs more time to get people ready for change or maybe resolve internal issues like the ones we have now before committing to an inter-galactic covenant."

Aliens briefly bowed their heads. Their joyful luster gradually vanished and remained dead silent for some time, meditating deeply for comfort. It was clear these people honestly cared about us, and felt our loss as their own.

Tei-Ah broke silence by stating, "When one of our brothers loses sight of the Infinite and opts to live apart from Him, we are greatly saddened. You are entitled to choose your own way. But know that if you deny Father, you will be denied access to our worlds."

"What if the whole planet wants to join the brotherhood, except a few stubborn officials?" I asked, giving Hans a brief side stare. "Should those that want change pay the price for those few that refuse it?"

"If you appoint leaders to rule over you, we won't interfere with their decisions. Historically, the leading few betrayed the most by discrediting and swaying people away from Manéh, at times by force. Through re-embodiment, they keep darkening lives like a cancer. Remember, souls end up on the other end of any system they help set up, and the enforcer becomes the enforced."

"We don't like lingering on sad things," Meh-Nai said, enlivening the air. "We laugh and enjoy life rather than worry because Father has the solution to every problem and our conscious opinion doesn't. Our people often travel to other worlds in large ships over forty kilometers in length. These are space cities complete with parks, libraries, and all the comforts of home."

In an instant, the starry background shifted toward Virgo and zoomed in on a red giant millions of light-years away in M49. Strong solar wind currents swept a nearby asteroid belt, provoking varying choir-like sounds to emerge from its weak fields and billions of tiny water crystals to shine like swirling prismatic jewels. Not far from M49, a G-class binary system hosted an immense irregularly shaped body of water, an ocean planet, complete with atmosphere, weather patterns, and thriving life forms. It had no solid surface, and a core composed mainly of Ice VII.

On a world in Beta Carinae, wide waterfalls six kilometers tall swayed from side to side in graceful waves as the planet's large moons exerted tidal effects on falling waters. The loveliest feature of all belonged to a carbon world located in M3. A volcanic blast left behind a wide caldera filled with every gem imaginable. Above it resides a freshwater lake just two meters deep. Above that, skies are always lit, frequently changing auroral hues depending on which star it swings closest to.

A cratered dimly lit world covered partly by ice faded into view, host to five dim moons and other smaller rocky escorts. On the surface, faint geysers rushed vapor plumes into space and meandering methane streams carved the landscape near a man-made structure built into a hill. Light from the closest moon infused geyser mists with dim prismatic auroras that trailed lunar trajectories variably. "Something closer to home," Tei-Ah said, "this is Pluto."

Pluto swiftly withdrew into the dark void of space, and a hazy orange world orbiting a colorful ringed gas giant seized our prompt attention. Beneath a dense atmospheric canopy, yellowish calm skies surrounded a radiant star significantly smaller than ours, gently rising like a dazzling pearl over a serene emerald-hued sea. Thick clouds gathered some distance about the star in concentric circles, much like a tunnel, resembling the opening gates of heaven, reflecting its whitish radiance unto nearby ethers like polished mirrors.

Picture 11: Titan (*Rodrigo Diaz*)

Light shone gloriously through the cloud tunnel, giving rise to prismatic haloes swelling outward in waves through the cloud opening. Bright sunbeams cut through these haloes as if transparent arms, reaching far through the skies like radiant shafts of light unleashed by heaven. Skies gradually scaled from yellowish tints near the star to maroon, blue, and violet into the far horizon where the large ringed planet hung still, partially eclipsed by occasional clouds.

The sea scrolled gently toward a soft sandy beach front, reflecting heaven's colorations on its soothing emerald waves. Crystalline gazebos, pergolas, and palaces were built on elevated grounds along the shoreline, surrounded by colorful gardens. These structures gleamed with subtle bluish hues while delicate, transparent drapes hung between some columns, swaying calmly in the sea breeze like weightless feathers. Smooth, verdant hills molded the landscape, marked by garden-strewn pathways and graceful crystalline benches set far apart. There were no trees or aviaries to speak of, but large exotic flowers took their place and a strong scent akin to violets permeated the air.

Dow Uanh leaned over and said, "You are looking at Tei-Ah's home world on a higher plane than yours. It's on one of Saturn's moons you call Titan."

As we lost ourselves into Titan's gentle beauty, a terran cloudy world slowly took its place. Light grayish clouds completely covered the heavens, so high up in the sky that breaks between clouds were barely noticeable from the ground. Beneath them, tall timbers dotted the landscape, contrasted by tranquil azure waters, silky waterfalls, and white-capped mountains. The scent of sweet gardenias graced the air, emerging from sources unknown, though no wind was noticeable and leaves rested calmly upon tree limbs.

Every physical object—leaves, flowers, grasses, even rocks—possessed crystalline transparent qualities infused with live vibrant glowing color. Light green, translucent grassy fields and daisy-like flowers offered brief recess amid perfectly blended colorful gardens. Blades of grass folded to the touch like authentic foliage but shone with a texture akin to crystal chandeliers: a magnificent pageantry of shimmering, transparent prisms spreading across the land like a shallow calm light-emerald sea. I immediately wondered, was this the same world I envisioned in my Chasma vision?

Flower petals seemed alive, radiating their own light with an appealing, electric-like quality. Translucent grayish rocks reflected off more light than what fell on them, emitting blinding laser-like rainbow beams of light—on those rare occasions the sun peaked through clouds—exploding with potent, splendorous light rainbows rivaling the sun itself.

A river cut through a long tall canyon winding its way in restful motion along smooth shores. At the end of this canyon, a verdant plain stretched into the horizon, filled with glowing, flat canopy trees akin to african wild syringas, rooted upon reddish grassy soils. We followed the river's winding course through this immense field of syringas, then slowly turned about in the direction from whence we came.

To our surprise, on top of one of the canyon's plateaus facing this vast plain stood a very large city whose inspiring architecture I had never before imagined. The city was a jewel of heavenly expression, absolutely glorious, grandiose, breathtaking, magnificent; no words will ever adequately describe its gentle loveliness.

The city was ultramodern and heavenly at the same time, conveying a sense of peaceful bliss and a graceful spiritual assurance that man's greatest need, Father's loving essence, lived there. Buildings, enormously tall, gleamed with ethereal whitish-blue and golden hues as if constructed out of light itself, reminiscent of the glass-like material used in the structure we were in.

Throughout the vast city, sculptured, wondrous crystalline edifices rose into the skies like precious works of art, hosting minarets, spires, and domes. Most buildings followed rounded symmetrical designs, while others were geometrically diverse, but none were square. Atop each building, different-colored beams hurled through the skies like proclamations from His Majesty.

The city was laid out in circular fashion. Its streets were made from a gold-like crystal that glowed with a pleasing radiance, accentuating endless gardens and water works. City lights set vegetation ablaze with graceful glow and color. People wore beautiful one-piece as well as long flowing garments of various single-tone colorations, guarded by a sash about their waists. A radiant glow surrounded them, each of different color and intensity. Had I not known better, I could have easily mistaken this place for heaven.

Picture 12: Venus, inside Sham Manéh (*Rodrigo Diaz*)

"I think I can see my house from here," Meh-Nai said jokingly, claiming this was her home world. "This is Sham Manéh meaning 'Infinite Bound,' one of our principal cities of which there are several."

Just outside the city and located not far from a large still lake, an enormous space port spread into the horizon, hosting numerous spacecraft, some small while others measuring about a kilometer in length. Space port grounds were covered by clean tiles about ten square meters in size with no visible buildings, hangars, or repair facilities. I assumed these were kept neatly underground or stored in higher dimensions out of sight. Immediately, I recognized the local settings and knew this was the space port from my vision. No sooner, Meh-Nai confirmed it and was pleased to know I greatly appreciated her home world's uplifting beauty.

I asked Meh-Nai if we could see pictures of Martian cities, but she said this was not possible at the time, for obvious reasons.

Venus faded away, and an inter-stellar collage of breathtaking nebulae took its place, showing many worlds surrounded by starlit clouds where night never falls. Meh-Nai displayed close-ups of the Helix nebula and said, "Your astronomers call these proplyds. We call them Manéh's museums of lighted wonder. Look how many there are, millions, such that they appear as clouds, and each hosts countless billions of loving brethren. So many are there you cannot possibly see them all in a trillion years. Father's gifts beckon you in silent gesture, so why don't you come and elevate the frequency of your soul with us? Surrender your erroneous beliefs and devastating selfish appetites. Let us share the cosmos in peace, truth, and loving harmony, together."

Time passed by until Dow Uanh brought the discussion to an end. "You have much to discuss with your government," he said. "When you return, we will have a surprise for you. By the way, that flashlight you found can bring back many memories." I did not understand what he meant by this, but he assured me I would soon find out.

The Brothers stood, and we followed likewise. Meh-Nai, in a special way, came to Sean and lightly embraced him. Dow Uanh embraced me while Tei-Ah lightly placed her hand on Hans's shoulder. Immediately after, the Brothers vanished, and all objects in the structure similarly disappeared.

Our minds were stretched to capacity with information that could impact Saras's social, political, and matters of faith. It was no secret; we were dealing with people that conquered space and matter, held profound reverence for Father, and lived on worlds that were nothing less than paradise. Had we not turned them down, where might we be evolutionary wise?

Sean, being chat intolerant, headed back to C6; Hans and I stayed behind, wondering what to talk about. It was not a lack of material that kept us idle but mostly personal mistrust. The comment he made regarding Earth gov turning down the Brothers didn't set right with me. One thing was certain: he knew lots more about the real state of affairs than he showed and deliberately withheld much of it. This seemed as good a time as any to find out why.

Personally, I could not envision Earth gov rejecting an alien summit. Hans, on the other hand, asserted that bringing notions contrary to civil norms before the Senate could spark a vote of no confidence on the chancellor, give rise to national creeds, and bring an end to Earth gov. That was preposterous enough to question his motives, since Earth gov established our mission knowing its plausible extraterrestrial content. Besides, what did Earth gov have to lose by adopting alien teachings if not the ETA's demise? He was definitely hiding something; knowing what that was would not come easily.

Earth gov had a viable prospect: prepare civilians to embrace change and welcome a new age of truth. You can't go wrong with truth, but Hans would not sign off on it. In the end, it was not Hans I had to convince but hundreds of biased delegates.

On the way back to C6, my heart selfishly longed to stay behind with my new cosmic friends, but I knew such appeal could not be granted, not until a time ascertained by His Majesty. Meanwhile, faith of the soul sung an inspiring melody of a time drawing near while love of the heart renewed the spirit with fondness, knowing the Infinite always inspires and never leaves your side.

As the structure vanished in the distance, my soul carried another being, a most tender dove of peace, within it, someone that would stand the course of infinity and embrace my soul with heaven's vast splendors. As Dow Uanh's promise rang in my mind, "Yours will be a friendship undeterred by time or space;" my heart would restlessly wait for that magnificent day when my sister returned once more unto my heart and warmly placed her loving hands into mine. Nothing—absolutely nothing—I wanted more.

Thus, my life will rest from being, my heart stop its pulsing cadence silently still, and my breath arrest its gasping swells, until that long awaited day when the curtains of my latent bosom shall be drawn open by her enchanting presence and the life-giving light of her starry, angelic warmth caresses my heart back to joyous vivacity. I so hoped His Majesty soon allowed it.

To His High Splendor and Unrivaled Love, I will sing sincere tribute forever, for He never forsakes me and I never walk alone. The Infinite is the light, joy, reason for living, and the greatest love we will ever know, "*oh-joi*!"

---

[1] W. J. Rev. Morford, "Deuteronomy 4:19," in *The One New Man Bible*, Travelers Rest, SC: True Potential Publishing Co., 2011.

[2] W. J. Rev. Morford, "1 Peter 5:8," in *The One New Man Bible*, Travelers Rest, SC: True Potential Publishing Co., 2011.

[3] W. J. Rev. Morford, "Psalm 19:1," in *The One New Man Bible*, Travelers Rest, SC: True Potential Publishing Co., 2011.
[4] W. J. Rev. Morford, "Hebrews 11:1," in *The One New Man Bible*, Travelers Rest, SC: True Potential Publishing Co., 2011.
[5] W. J. Rev. Morford, "Genesis 2:17," in *The One New Man Bible*, Travelers Rest, SC: True Potential Publishing Co., 2011.
[6] W. J. Rev. Morford, "Genesis 2:9," in *The One New Man Bible*, Travelers Rest, SC: True Potential Publishing Co., 2011.
[7] W. J. Rev. Morford, "Genesis 3:7," in *The One New Man Bible*, Travelers Rest, SC: True Potential Publishing Co., 2011.
[8] B. Nodland, "Is the Universe Birefringent.," University of Rochester, [Online]. Available: www.aip.org/png/html/birefrin.htm.

Chapter 10: *Overlords Of Pretense*

At Hans's request, MCT met for lunch to share personal views on our recent life-changing odyssey. DFAC was located on the second level right next to IVGEN, the in vitro genesis farm, better known as the gym. Automated food and reclamation stations ran along one side of DFAC while glass tables and metallic chairs filled the remaining area.

On Masar, a conscious computer did all the cooking and decided what's best for you, based on complex personal dietary objectives, available vegetables in their season, and demand trends. Some degreed dietician came up with this electronic "carte du jour" system called RGM, short for "reduced gravity meals," but we simply called it mulch. It was tough enough not having a dining choice but an unexpected godsend when it actually tasted somewhat decent.

During lunch, I pulled out the flashlight and showcased a few of its recorded events, though it was literally impossible to translate the nimble-speaking young boy on queue. Afterward, discussions promptly got under way on a variety of challenging subjects. Topics spun up and down for quite some time, but few merited my notice since conquering the self was not on the menu. I kept to myself for the most part, intensely consumed by what Earth gov's verdict was going to be: to join or not to join the brotherhood, that was the question.

What if Earth gov's decision turned out be no? The thought of it sent my abdomen's innards into churning, edgy frenzies far from droll. My beleaguered mind was not far behind, hastily turning thoughts into a baying haunted house and lunch a tossing grand finale way ahead of its scheduled curtain call.

If Saras's ruling swayed against the Brothers, my personal freedom and further contacts with May Len weighed slackly in the balance. Hopes of seeing my foundation of invisible love [1] again painfully eroded away, freely distilling saddened sorrows as if time was of no consequence.

Anguish obstinately lingered through the moment like an unsettling commitment, swathed with unjust providence. My conscious absence intently absconded off into musing's appealing bosom, hiding from fate's unremitting fold. Unaware of my doings, I sat with elbows on the table, hands crossed, and chin resting with sunken stare, dealing willfully with emotive affairs as if mentally amending destiny's course to desire's most potent fancies.

Noting my silence, Hans deliberately asked for my opinion on the topic of discussion, but I contritely had him repeat it. Rather than recap, he homed in on the real matter plaguing me, advising against rendering such thoughts much air time. "Earth's future is our priority, not ours," he said firmly. "But whatever the outcome, rest assured," he added with a suspicious grin. "You'll have a most rewarding life with us."

"Deterring sands from overlords of pretense—that's what life is," I said.

"Sands of what?"

"What's there to life that's actually worthwhile," I said with a shadowy grin. "Everyone's just fine with devious norms; do and consume what you're told, and everything will be okay. What are we; livestock?"

"I don't follow you. What's this all about?"

"Earth tanks every century or so because its leaders insist that thrills and possession are more marketable than reality. That kind of thinking brews disorder, chaos, and betrayal in the end. I don't want that life: no thank you."

"Not the life I want either," Sean said.

"Besides the Brothers, what other virtuous way out of our stinking legacy is there?" I said firmly, waiting for feedback, though getting none. "That's what I thought. Anyone have a problem siding with something real for once?"

"Problem? Lad, I thought I actually knew something—until today. I felt like some idiotic cave man challenging da Vinci to an arts contest."

Hans casually stared forward pondering rather displeasing thoughts, awakened by a bad case of loose lips. He gripped his arms and expired a soft sigh in obvious discontent judging that his comment, or intended outcome, missed the mark but not saying so. Rather, he said, "We have a lot to learn, I agree," and changed the subject, but his repose inspired my prompt distrust.

I spent several days doing serious research, reviewing Sean's recordings, scouring data banks for any information dealing with prehistory and re-embodiment, and vainly trying to translate flashlight videos. The Chasma video lamentably garbled when I pointed the cam toward the Brothers, but Sean's recordings were crystal clear. What I discovered was most revealing.

Flashlight videos, six in total, helped me embrace alien culture and conduct detailed biological and geological studies on several locations southeast of Holden. By trailing the two children through their journey, I pieced together a picture of what that region looked like in that long ago.

Three weeks went by, and both Hans and Earth gov kept chillingly silent. That was a good thing because negative decisions usually rush back rather fast. Earth gov was up to something all right, perhaps debating political decorum or, however unlikely, applying time wisely by doing something beneficial like research. I just hoped they were not scheming to shove alien contacts under the carpet like so many times before.

Eventually, I got a call from Hans; there were questions to be answered. What these were, he would not go into details. Instead, I was to meet him at the command office where matters would be discussed. So I gathered a pad and dashed downstairs, wondering what Earth gov had in mind.

When I got there, the door was closed. Inside, Hans carried on a barely audible dialogue in Latin with a woman he referred to as Beta regarding a project called Vulcan Aurora. Rather odd, I thought, Latin was not the official government language. Sufficiently doubtful of Hans, I wasted no time putting my rusty Latin to use, being careful not to set off the door sentry.

"About your proposal," said Beta with assertive authority, "the Olympian Council presented it to Alpha, and he fully supports the outcome."

"I'm glad progress is being made to overthrow the Titans," Hans said.

"Thanks to your efforts, those Triterian patsies will soon be under our control," she emphasized proudly. "But until Titans abandon Triterians for good, we will continue to advise members that they are not ready to join that patsy Pantheon. This will ensure they don't forge an alliance. Members will demand more information on Triton, but we won't let Triterians provide it, except through our channels. Eventually, member pressure will bring about Kronos's downfall, and Titans' dissolution will follow."

Pleased by Beta's accolade, Hans replied, "That's an elegant objective, but I'm worried the lieutenant's previous eavesdropping may have compromised our plans. Should I proceed to activate Crimson ciphering?"

"What he heard is of no significance," Beta said firmly, "and a single maggot can't prove anything or hinder ongoing operations. Besides, we need further civil distractions and a venue for misinformation; he's the perfect candidate for that. The next Vulcan Aurora phase quickly approaches, and all will be over soon. We are the only doorway to Earth, not Titans."

"More reason to cipher and institute the new Alpha now before he grows fonder of that patsy, no?"

"He must be himself for now to naively draw them our way. Let him be persuaded by Triterians, especially that puny 'thing,'" she said with obvious displeasure. "When the time is right and their technology is finally in our hands, ciphering will wipe whatever he picked up from them, and he'll become the new Alpha."

I jolted back abruptly, unnerved by Beta's words. I was not that familiar with the mythological cast of names she used but sufficient to sense it had something to do with the Brothers, perhaps, even one of us. Awful thoughts raced through my mind, all leading to the same conclusion: overlords of pretense aspired to deceive the world and betray Him again.

I suddenly realized that, for hundreds of years, Saras governments were well aware of alien existence. Matter of fact, secret covenants with certain space societies had been established and clueless world members were being held hostage for technical ransom. And when our demands for technology were not met, crimes against humanity were instituted to compel aliens to comply with our requests. Not much had changed in our days. Worst yet, I felt something dreadful was about to ensue, though unsure what I could do to stop it.

Given present state of affairs, it was not a good idea to be found anywhere near Hans's office. So I ran to the lift, made for my room, and sat on the floor pondering deeply on the situation. My room com pealed several times, but I ignored it. I knew who it was but wanted nothing to do with him.

In those trying moments, the more I thought about Beta's aggressive crusade, the worst draconian metaphors I dreamt up. The Brothers no doubt knew full well who Beta was and what she was up to but strangely ignored the subject during our discussions, with Hans in their midst. There had to be a good reason for their passive stance. Meanwhile, I was left to the mercy of plausible informants hiding wily intent behind a friendly façade, uncertain what to do about them.

I had a pending appointment with Hans that could not be ignored and he waited for me downstairs, quite possibly irritated by now; putting him off might raise undue suspicions. Besides, if he was involved in covert activities, his next move might give them away. On that premise, I returned to the command office unsure what to expect.

As elevator doors opened, Hans's office faced straight ahead and there he was, looking my way stiff as a rock with arms crossed. His face said it all, driven by the same scowl that made its debut at the crash site. "Where the hell were you?" he said, staring with an intense expression worthy of your worst fears. "I've been looking all over for you and waiting for nearly an hour, and you were nowhere to be found! Don't you know that Earth gov is waiting?"

It was rather obvious that delaying Earth gov was not the sole reason for his wrathful state. Maybe the likely chance I overheard his covert dialogue with Beta haunted him like a lingering death threat. But before I could respond, he came to his senses and softened his coarse demeanor. "I'm sorry for my outburst," he said regretfully. "I've had a lot on my mind lately, as you well know. But Earth gov is not very forgiving, especially right now, and the quorum panel is wondering why we haven't started."

With an entrapping smile I could not trust, he put regrets aside and asked me inside bearing good tidings. Earth gov praised our mission's success thus far and approved a motion to move forward with further contacts, as long as certain facts were verified. So I shelved previous concerns about Hans and focused on trusting the Brothers instead.

Questionnaire in hand, Hans sat across the way from me and wasted no time going through it. I had a pad linked to my room's console, ready to pull research notes and quotes on demand. The first topic on the list was perhaps the most challenging of all. "Can you provide evidence corroborating the legitimacy of extraterrestrial linguistics?" he asked.

My handle on alien language was definitely modest to say the least, accrued mostly by unconventional means, but sufficient to help draw some immediate references. There were no significant similarities to Saras languages, but three ancient words did hold some degree of idiomatic significance: Masar, Saras, and Atlan (3).

I was not at all surprised when Hans introduced the next subject matter: provide clear evidence that intelligent life exists on other worlds. The structure and the flashlight did not count. Apparently, someone in Earth gov wanted to make absolutely sure that these objects were not some eccentric fabrication thought up by brilliant hoaxers. No matter, a lot of evidence abounded.

"Our galaxy is host to scores of confirmed exo-planets in habitable zones with bio-markers like water, methane, hydrocarbons, and carbon catenation: clear signs of life and industrial tenancy," I said. "But signs of alien life are nothing new. Mali's Dogon tradition claims that Nommos from Sirius visited them long ago. Before cameras were invented, renowned artworks often captured alien objects onto canvas, such as The Madonna by Domenico Ghirlandaio, The Baptism of Christ by Aert de Gelder, and The Annunciation by Carlo Crivelli. UFOs are no new phenomena, but part of Earth history.

---

(3)
- In Hindi, Saras means "lake" [2] or "Moon" [3]. In alien, it labels Earth as "unkind flower."
- Masar was the ancient name for the land of Egypt [4]; the land of the Copts, or God's country. The same meaning applies to Mitzr-ayim [5], one of Ham's descendants. In alien, it means "flowery body."
- "Atlan" appears throughout the globe in various forms. Depending on culture, it infers "water" or "carry." Atlas means "carry." Thus, Atlantis means Island of Atlas, or Island of Water.

"In the Bible, you will find numerous references to alien life and intervention (4). The Holy Quran (5) also provides remarkable references to cosmic plurality, as well as the Talmud (6)"

"Let's talk about the existence of legendary Atlantis. What evidence can you provide of its existence?" asked Hans.

"Plato's immortal Timaeus [21] and Critias [22] dialogues describe it as a large island that vanished off the coast of Spain around the year 9,400 BC, an event closely associated with the primal Ogygian deluge of 10,000 BC [23]. While many consider Plato's account to be the work of fiction, it is interesting to note he placed Atlantis between the narrow Pillars of Heracles and an 'opposite' continent beyond Atlantis, a land mass surrounding the veritable Atlantic Ocean. Being aware of continuous land masses about Europe, the Mediterranean, and Africa, Plato's western continental citation remarkably implies the Americas. Thus, we must ask, how did Plato know that a western continent existed? Plato recounted the story of Atlantis from Solon, who heard the story from Sonchis in Sais, Egypt (7).

---

(4) - "Thus the heavens and the Earth, and the entire armies of them were finished. [6]."
- "When you see the sun, the moon, and the stars, all the armies of heaven . . . God has shared with all nations under all heaven (brotherhood) [7]."
- "They fought from heaven; the stars in their courses fought against Sisera [8]."
- "Can you guide the Bear [Arcturus, a star] with her sons [9]."
- "The heavens were made by the word of the Lord, and all the armies of them by the breath of His mouth [10]."
- "You have made heaven . . . their armies . . . and the armies of heaven worships You [11]."
- "The armies of heaven cannot be numbered [12]."
- "In my Father's house are many dwelling places . . . I go to prepare a place for you [13]."
- "He called them [stars] all by their names and they hearkened unto Him. And I saw how they are weighed [mass] in a righteous balance according to their proportions of light [brightness], the width [distance] of their spaces [orbits], and the day [period] of their appearing, and how their revolution [orbit] produces lightning [seasons] . . . and [I saw] their revolution [rotations] according to the number of the angels [very large] [14]." This is clear depiction of Newton's third law of gravitation.

(5) - "Not one of the beings in the heavens and the earth but must come to [Allah] Most Gracious as a servant [15]."
- "Seest thou not that it is Allah whose praises all beings in heaven and earth celebrate [16]."
- "None in heavens or on earth, except Allah, knows what is hidden: nor can they perceive when they shall be raised up [17]."
- "And among His signs is the creation of the heavens and the earth and of the living creatures that He has scattered through them [18]."

(6) - "What does He do in the night-time? . . . He rides upon His light cloud . . . upon 18,000 worlds [19]."
- "The Holy One, Blessed be He, will give in the future to every upright man 310 worlds, as it reads [Proverbs 8:21; I endow those who love me with substance (yesh, 310 in gematria)] [20]."

(7) See earth-history.com/Atlantis/index.htm and www.atlantisquest.com/Timeline.html:
4000 BC, Egyptian Book of the Dead. King Thoth ruled an island in the west, destroyed by water, brought survivors to Egypt
2000 BC, Vishnu Purana. Locates White Island "Atala" in Western Ocean, same latitude as Canary Islands
1300 BC, Turin Papyrus. Lists 10 god-kings in foreign country whose rule ends in 9850 BC

"According to ancient historical manuscripts, Egyptians wrote about Atlantis 1,500 years prior to Solon, as did numerous civilizations. Hence, if we must single out and brand Plato's works as fictional, then, in all fairness, several respected historians and their historical documents, whether these describe Atlantis or not, must also be weighed as fictional.

"In Greek mythology, Gaia presented Zeus a wedding gift planted in Hera's Atlantic gardens, a tree bearing golden immortality-giving apples—the Tree of Life. Hesperide nymphs from a 'blessed island' at the edge of the 'surrounding' ocean tended the tree but often plucked from it themselves [24]. Some believe these were the same apples that tempted Atalanta [25]. Wary of thievery, Hera placed a serpent about the tree to keep thieves away. This ancient narrative bears striking resemblance to the more recent biblical Garden of Eden story.

"Several expeditions near Bimini and Andros islands in the Bahamas successfully recovered several ancient artifacts, granite blocks, and sculptures in shallow waters. Several unnatural structures were found beneath the waves, as well as ancient sand mounds amid mangroves [26]. The region's geology also suggests that local ocean segments were above water some twelve thousand years ago, in line with Ogygian and Plato flood timeframes. At Chichen Itza, Mexico, the Temple of Tables, a series of altars atop the structure are supported by small carved figures of men with upraised arms called atlantes. In western St. Lucia, perfectly symmetrical rock artwork bears precision grooves etched into it, impossible for Carib or Syboney tribes to realize."

"Let's turn our attention to Lemuria next. What can you tell us about that civilization and its eventual destruction?" Hans asked.

"Evidence going back that far is rather sketchy but available nevertheless. Polynesian legends tell of a kingdom that once existed in the Pacific [27], and sunken structures were discovered in shallow waters off the coast of Japan [28]. Sanskrit writings also reference sunken lands in the Indian Ocean,

---

<u>1190 BC</u>, Sanchuniathon, Phoenicia History. Calls ancient kings "Aletean" kings, gives legend of Thoth, Atlas
<u>735 BC</u>, Hesiod, Theogeny. Titans lose 10-year battle, imprisoned beneath Western Ocean
<u>600 BC</u>, Mahabharata, Karna Parva. After 10-year war, Atala island sinks into Western Ocean
<u>590 BC</u>, Solon, Atlantica. Epic poem based on Atlantis story from priests at Sais, Egypt
<u>460 BC</u>, Hellanicus, Atlantis. Chronology mentioning Poseidon and Atlas
<u>450 BC</u>, Herodotus, Histories. Calls Atlantic "Atlantis Ocean," describes Atlantean tribe in North Africa
<u>350 BC</u>, Plato, Timeas/Critias. Deep account of Atlantis events
<u>340 BC</u>, Bhavishya, Purana. Mentions White Island Atala in west sea, inhabited by Sun worshipping Magas
<u>300 BC</u>, Crantor, Commentary on Timaeus. Sais priests show him temple columns Solon saw
<u>100 BC</u>, Marcellus, Ethiopic History. Canary islanders preserve Atlantis traditions
<u>25 BC</u>, Strabo, Geography. Claimed Plato's account was not the work of fiction

alluding to the kingdom of Kumari Kandam [29]. In spite of these legendary records, perhaps the best evidence supporting Lemuria is not archeological or historical but rather genetic.

"At about 75,000 BC, the Mount Toba super volcanic chain in Indonesia erupted. According to the mutation rate of mitochondrial DNA [30], Saras's population was reduced to a mere three thousand survivors at about the same time. Coincidence? Not at all. Similar genetic bottlenecks also befell animal species around the globe during the same time frame [31]. Such consistency indicates that Saras was definitely populated during that time, but a cataclysm of apocalyptic proportions nearly wiped out all life on the planet.

"Referring back to the Bible, the meaning of *Cain*'s generations may implicate both Mu and Atlantis. By listing the meaning of Adam's generations serially, the following narrative describes a fleet, Saras's isolation, and demise."

> Man [Adam], being possessive [Cain], was dedicated [Enoch] to build a fleet [Irad] but was smitten by God [Mehujael]. Who is God's [Methusael] is a powerful [Lamech] ornament [Adah] in a stream of water [Yabal], not a stream [Jubal] in the shade [Zillah]. You will be taken from possession [Tubalcain] into loveliness [Naamah] [32]."

"Last question, what can you tell us about re-embodiment, and can you provide evidence of individuals that have reincarnated?" Hans asked.

"We consider anyone exhibiting foreign talents a genius, such as Mozart who, at age three, played the keyboard and soon the violin. General George Patton clearly embraced re-embodiment, notably living the life of Hannibal [33]. Socrates was confident there was such a thing as living again [34]. Pythagoras deeply studied the subject of re-embodiment and claimed he remembered past lives [35]. Henry Ford believed he was killed at the Battle of Gettysburg [36].

"Several biblical references and early historical works (8) on re-embodiment abound. However, if we resort to modern scriptural translations

---

(8)
- "If a man dies, will he live again? I shall wait all the days of my appointed time, until my change comes [39]."
- "All these things God often works with man, to bring back his soul from the pit, to be enlightened with the light of living [40]."
- "Moses revealed this at the bush, as he said, 'Lord, the God of Abraham and the God of Isaac and the God of Jacob.' Thus, he is not the God of the dead but of the living, for all should be living in Him [41]."
- "Everyone, accordingly, of those who descend to the earth is, according to his deserts, or agreeably to the position which he occupied there, ordained to be born in this world, in a different country, or among a different nation, or in a different mode of life, or surrounded by infirmities of a different kind, or to be descended from religious parents, or parents

rather than original text, then the process of detecting re-incarnation in such adulterated works literally turns into an imposing chore. The Roman Church sullenly removed re-embodiment from scripture by replacing Septuagint and Masoretic texts with Latin Vulgate, then persecuted all vestiges of Shabbat worship and re-embodiment, subjects that go hand in hand. Gematria, a crucial dictionary built into each Hebrew letter, was instantly stripped away the moment ancient texts were translated, thus destroying the true meaning of ancient words.

"The Hebrew word 'am' for example, meaning 'people,' endows special significance to re-embodiment when translated through gematria. The word literally means 'eyes living in fountains of divine wisdom in His dwelling place, forms that must rest as they have a beginning and an end.' Led by the letter ayin [ע] with a value of 70, or 7 times 10, Shabbat rest and physical reality are key factors of the word. The same is true of the second letter mem [מ] with a value of 40, or 4 times 10, implying the fourth commandment and again physical reality.

"Shabbat is the most significant of all commandments. Represented by the numbers 4 and 7, it implies a brief state of rest from physical burden in heaven's foyers. It's a period of respite from earthly life when the soul leaves the physical and briefly embraces heavenly life in realms of light. At the end of Shabbat, the soul resumes earthly chores and applies divine wisdom learned, testing personal compliance with the first three commandments. The fourth commandment applies not only to re-embodiment but also atoms, worlds,

---

who are not religious; so that it may sometimes happen that an Israelite descends among the Scythians, and a poor Egyptian is brought down to Judea [42]."

- "All souls are subject to reincarnation; and people do not know the ways of the Holy One, blessed be He! They do not know that they are brought before the tribunal both before they enter into this world and after they leave it; they are ignorant of the many reincarnations and secret works which they have to undergo, and of the number of naked souls, and how many naked spirits roam about in the other world without being able to enter within the veil of the King's Palace. Men do not know how the souls revolve like a stone that is thrown from a sling. But the time is at hand when these mysteries will be disclosed [43]."
- "As long as a person is unsuccessful in his purpose in this world, the Holy One, blessed be He, uproots him and replants him over and over again [44]."
- "Those who depart out of this life according to the law of nature, and pay that debt which was received from God, when he that lent it us is pleased to require it back again, enjoy eternal fame; that their houses and their posterity are sure, that their souls are pure and obedient, and obtain a most holy place in heaven, from whence, in the revolutions of ages [re-embodiment], they are again sent into pure bodies [45]."
- "[Pharisees] believe that souls have an immortal rigor in them, and that under the earth there will be rewards or punishments, according as they have lived virtuously or viciously in this life; and the latter are to be detained in an everlasting prison, but that the former [virtuous] shall have power to revive and live again [46]."
- "Moses . . . refused to be called the son of Pharaoh's daughter, choosing to suffer affliction with the people of God, than to enjoy the pleasures of sin for a season." Heb 11: 24–25

stars, and galaxies. Shabbat is the answer to universal entropy and the rebirth of all expression, ever evolving higher mastery within the Infinite.

"Death is, therefore, the most glorious of rests; Shabbat for the soul, a most unique invitation to visit His Majesty's gleaming spiritual mansions. And who would deny such wondrous invitation?

"Abraham, Isaac, Jacob, and others were gathered to their 'people.' Since theirs is a God of the living [for all live in Him], then such post-death gathering place is no sleeping sepulcher but divine fountains, a spring of spiritual life far from earthly.

"Sure, the body sleeps in death and stops functioning, but the spirit is not the body and does not sleep. Rather, it returns to God and gathers to divine fountains to learn and admire its heavenly future, for in God all live in Him. This is why Ecclesiastes 12:7 states so eloquently: dust shall return to the Earth as it was, and the spirit shall return unto God who gave it.

"The Hebrew letter tav [ת] is the last letter of the alphabet. It's the secret of 'returning Light from above' back to alef [א], the first letter of the alphabet, forming the word 'ta' or 'cell.' Tav means reincarnation, the stamp of previous lives, and life's continuity by coming full circle back to alef [47]. Tav is the rest's hallmark and the fountain of life for those who aspire to attain mastery in serving the light. And how many Hebrew words contain the letter tav, implying reincarnation?

"Another Hebrew letter, gimmel (ג), spells yet another reference to re-embodiment. It affirms that souls master works of charity and loving sacrifice by alternating between divine and physical abodes and applying lessons learned. Gimmel inspires benign giving and yearning for His Majesty's mandates, exemplifying third commandment directives. Likewise, how many words contain gimmel?

"But the Bible is not alone; the Holy Quran also provides alluring references to re-embodiment (9).

"Professor Ian Stevenson [37] devoted over forty years of his life to study children claiming to have lived in other times and vessels. In each case, he obtained information about the departed person each child allegedly identified with. He then verified that the child's recollection actually matched the deceased's life. He also painstakingly matched birth marks and defects to wounds found on the deceased, verified by medical records and autopsies.

---

(9) - "Seeing that were without life, and He gave you life; then will He cause you to die, and will again bring you to life; and again to Him will ye return [48]."
- "From the [earth] did we create you, and into it shall we return you, and from it shall we bring you out once again [49]."
- "And Allah has produced you from the earth, growing [gradually]. And in the end He will return you into the [earth], and raise you forth [again] [50]."

After the interview, I headed for DFAC hoping to disentangle pressing thoughts and get some spinach lasagna, another Martian delight drawing crowds when offered. Eating seemed like a suitable outlet to briefly dislodge complex conspiracy theories, but equanimity would not last long. When least expected, Sean suddenly showed up, rabbit-eyed prairie dogging over munching hordes until locking sights with me. Unsettling anxiety haunted him away from his usual static stare, repeatedly rubbing finger prints with stressed tenacity knowing not when to quit.

He joined me for dinner and seemed keenly interested in my interview topics, at first; but his focus gradually drifted away as time went on, letting fears overpower personal bearings. He did not seem his usual self, denying assuredly that anything was wrong, but it didn't take much to get him talking.

"Something's not batting on a full wicket here," he said suspiciously. "See, plans and people around here may not be all they're made out to be. If you ask me, I'm convinced we have daft blinkers in our midst trying to take over Earth gov. We have to act before it's too late, or they'll give us a penny!"

"That's a very serious accusation for someone in the military. Whatever makes you think that?" I said, trying not to raise misgivings.

"Don't raise your voice, mate," he whispered, pointing eyes discretely to soldiers on nearby tables. "Any of these bouncers can be a Hans cam. Look, I recently overheard people discussing plots to topple Earth gov using strange code names and talking in Latin. This has been going on now for weeks, and the content of these parleys is rather staid."

"Don't expect everyone to agree with Earth gov; that's been the norm lately."

"It's not petty chat, lad. I'm talking high-level official plans to betray the Towers. Do you know what they call the Brothers? Patsies! What good do you think can come out of that chat long term?"

"Sounds rather grim," I said carefully. "Who are you referring to?"

"I don't trust anyone, and I want to make sure I can trust you," he said, after hesitating. "Anyone can be a whistle, maybe even Hans! So watch it!"

Done with dinner, I recycled my tray and made for the door, hoping to avoid further verbal commitment. "There has to be a logical explanation for all this. After all, making contact with aliens is not something we do every day, and epithets are quite common," I said casually. "Give it time; things will work out for the better."

"We don't have time! The Brothers are walking into a trap, and so are we," he said, worried stiff. "We have to do something before it's too late!"

"I don't think the Brothers ignore Earth gov's dealings. Just think for a moment. Who's going to believe us? It's our word against theirs. And if we get mixed up in this, we could ultimately interfere with the brotherhood's plans. Let it rest and let the Brothers handle this."

"You have any idea what we're up against? We have to tell the chancellor what's going on! I don't know exactly how yet, but I'll think of something."

In that frantic moment, I could have disposed my concerns, yet I found the strength to hold my tongue still, to my luck. "I'm not sure I'm tracking or know what's going on around here. Honestly, I don't let it bother me."

"I'll mention something that has to stay between us. If you talk, I'm toast." I assured him my trust, but it didn't seem to amount to much; he was determined to reveal whatever was on his mind, regardless what I thought.

"I met Hans before you did. When I got to his office, he was talking bollocks with someone in Latin. I think I accidentally tripped the door sensor because he came out all mad and scolded me for eaves dropping. He talks with this woman called Beta all the time, always in Latin, about things that don't sound like UEF business. My Latin sucks and I'm not sure what's on the menu, but I could swear they were talking about you."

"Saying what about me?" I said, recovering from a bad case of chills.

"I think someone wants you to lead a group called the Order."

"Funny you should mention that. I thought the same thing about you."

"So you heard them talking also?"

"Not entirely," I said casually, refusing to fuel the topic. "When I got to Hans's office, I heard him talking about a promotion. Out of respect for privacy, I chose to return later. Who knows, maybe Latin is used for security reasons."

Sean wanted more details, but I assured him I only heard mention of a promotion and nothing more. Still, he insisted on some wild conspiracy theory that made too much sense, but I couldn't sign off on it for obvious reasons: no telling what his real motives were.

"We know way too much already, lad. If this deal collapses, so do we. You think they'll let us walk out of here without a neuron bath?"

"I've known that from the moment I walked through the door."

"What if the underground forces the Brothers to bypass Earth gov and negotiate directly with them? The Brothers won't fall for it, there will be no deal, you and I will get flushed, and by the time we wake up, Earth gov and the Brothers will be history. It's all about technology—that's what the underground wants, not universal law—and they'll play hard to get it. They'll even sacrifice the populace if necessary."

"Sounds cruel."

"You think they care? When it comes to technology, members are expendable."

"You tell me, what can we do?" I said to a silent Sean. "Our hands are tied. Even if what you say is true, there's absolutely nothing we can do. Our talks can be recorded, calls traced, steps followed. As Hans pointed out, it's Earth's future, not ours, that counts. Here's what we should do: stay calm, don't interfere, and then the brotherhood might stand a chance. The Brothers seem hopeful, and they know everything that's going on; we don't. Let Earth gov and the Brothers handle this."

"See, that's it. How do we know Earth gov is even engaged here? What if our findings are going straight to the ETA and not the ministry? How do we make sure this isn't some clever con, using us and the Brothers to take over Earth gov?

"All we know is what Hans tells us. He locks himself up in that office all day long, speaks to a woman in Latin, asks us questions, and tells us everything is fine. We never see who's on the other end, and you're fine with that? You saw a personal message from the chancellor. How do you know it wasn't fabricated? We have the right to question motive; these are the wrong times to trust a single person. Don't you agree?"

"You need to let this go, really," I replied calmly.

"If you don't stand for something, you'll fall for anything!"

"By taking a stand, the Brothers could fall. I know the chancellor; he'll follow up soon, and that should be proof enough. For now, focus on the mission, and don't forget that pain is inevitable, but suffering is optional."

"Easier said than done and unfair from my vantage point."

"If life is unfair for everybody, doesn't that make it fair? Be patient; good things come to those who wait."

"Glad to know procrastinating isn't a bad thing after all."

We were both headed for an encounter shrouded in mystique with overlords of pretense; the leviathan of times, feeding on humanity's breath of life. Only time would disclose our true destiny.

---

[1] R. W. J. Morford, "Hebrews 11:1," in *The One New Man Bible*, Travelers Rest, SC: True Potential Publishing Co., 2011.

[2] en.organisasi.org/name-meaning/indian-hindu/saras, "en.organisasi.org/name-meaning/indian-hindu/saras," [Online]. Available:en.organisasi.org/name-meaning/indian-hindu/saras.

[3] I. H. Names, "Saras," [Online]. Available: www.indianhindunames.com/indian-hindu-boy-name-s.htm.

[4] P. Kaya, "Presence of Tur/Turk/Oguz Peoples In Ancient Masar ("Egypt")," 2008. [Online]. Available: www.polatkaya.net/Part-3_Masar_Turkish-1.html.

[5] "WikiPedia," 25 April 2012. [Online]. Available: en.wikipedia.org/wiki/Mizraim.

[6] R. W. J. Morford, "Genesis 2:1," in *The One New Man Bible*, Travelers Rest, SC: True Potential Publishing Co., 2011.

[7] R. W. J. Morford, "Deuteronomy 4:19," in *The One New Man bible*, Travelers Rest, SC: True Potential Publishing Co., 2011.

[8] R. W. J. Morford, "Jud 5:20," in *The One New Man Bible*, Travelers Rest, SC: True Potential Publishing Co., 2011.

[9] R. W. J. Morford, "Job 38:32," in *The One New Man Bible*, Travelers Rest, SC: True Potential Publishing Co., 2011.

[10] R. W. J. Morford, "Psalm 33:6," in *The One New Man Bible*, Travelers Rest, SC: True Potential Publishing Co., 2011.

[11] R. W. J. Morford, "Nehemiah 9:6," in *The One New Man Bible*, Travelers Rest, SC: True Potential Publishing Co., 2011.

[12] R. W. J. Morford, "Jer 33:22," in *The One New Man Bible*, Travelers Rest, SC: True Potential Publishing Co., 2011.

[13] R. W. J. Morford, "Joh 14:2," in *The One New Man Bible*, Travelers Rest, SC: True Potential Publishing Co., 2011.

[14] R. H. Charles, "Sacred-Texts," 1917. [Online]. Available: www.sacred-texts.com/bib/boe/boe046.htm.

[15] Y. Ali, "Sura 19:93," [Online]. Available: www.quranexplorer.com/index/Sura_019_Maryam_Mary.aspx.

[16] Y. Ali, "Sura 24:41," [Online]. Available: www.quranexplorer.com/index/Sura_024_Al_Noor_The_Light.aspx.

[17] Y. Ali, "Sura 27:65," [Online]. Available: www.quranexplorer.com/index/Sura_027_Al_Naml_The_Ant_The_Ants.aspx.

[18] Y. Ali, "Sura 42:29," [Online]. Available: www.quranexplorer.com/index/Sura_042_Ash_Shura_Council_Consultation.aspx.

[19] M. L. Rodkinson, "Tractate Avodah Zarah 3b," in *Babylonian Talmud: Book 9, Vol X, Chapter I, p. 5.*

[20] M. J. Rodkinson, "Tractate Sanhedrin 100a," in *Babylonian Talmud: Book 8, Volume 8, Chapter XI, p. 318.*

[21] Plato, "MIT Classics," 360 BCE. [Online]. Available: classics.mit.edu/Plato/timaeus.html.

[22] Plato, "MIT Classics," 360 BCE. [Online]. Available: classics.mit.edu/Plato/critias.html.

[23] Wikipedia, "Ancient Greek flood myths - Ogyges," [Online]. Available: en.wikipedia.org/wiki/Ancient_Greek_flood_myths#Ogyges.

[24] WikiPedia, "The Garden of the Hesperides," [Online]. Available: en.wikipedia.org/wiki/Hesperides#The_Garden_of_the_Hesperides.

[25] WikiPedia, "Atalanta," [Online]. Available: en.wikipedia.org/wiki/Atalanta.

[26] A. f. R. a. Enlightenment, "Ancient Mysteries and Civilizations," [Online]. Available: www.edgarcayce.org/_AncientMysteriesTemp/biminiexpedition.html. [Accessed 28 May 2012].

[27] F. Joseph, "The Lost Civilization of Lemuria: The Rise and Fall of the World's Oldest Culture," [Online]. Available: www.barnesandnoble.com/w/the-lost-civilization-of-lemuria-frank-joseph/1112400379?ean=9781591439493.

[28] N. Geographic, "Japan's Ancient Underwater "Pyramid" Mystifies Scholars," 19 September 2007. [Online]. Available: news.nationalgeographic.com/news/2007/09/070919-sunken-city.html. [Accessed 28 May 2012].

[29] WikiPedia, "Kumari Kandam," [Online]. Available: en.wikipedia.org/wiki/Kumari_Kandam. [Accessed 28 May 2012].

[30] WikiPedia, "Toba Catastrophy Theory," [Online]. Available: en.wikipedia.org/wiki/Toba_catastrophe_theory. [Accessed 28 May 2012].

[31] WikiPedia, "Genetic bottlenecks of other mammals," [Online]. Available: en.wikipedia.org/wiki/Toba_catastrophe_theory. [Accessed 28 May 2012].

[32] W. J. Rev. Morford, "Genesis Chapter 4," in *The One New Man Bible*, Travelers Rest, SC: True Potential Publishing Co..

[33] BiographyBase, "George Patton Biography," [Online]. Available: www.biographybase.com/biography/Patton_George.html. [Accessed 28 May 2012].

[34] WikiPedia, "Socrates," [Online]. Available: en.wikipedia.org/wiki/Socrates.

[35] S. E. O. Philosophy, "Pythagoras," [Online]. Available: plato.stanford.edu/entries/pythagoras/.

[36] WikiPedia, "Henry Ford," [Online]. Available: en.wikipedia.org/wiki/Henry_Ford.

[37] WikiPedia, "Ian Stevenson," [Online]. Available: en.wikipedia.org/wiki/Ian_Stevenson. [Accessed 28 May 2012].

[38] W. J. Rev. Morford, "John 9:1," in *The One New Man Bible*, Travelers Rest, SC: True Potential Publishing Co.

[39] W. J. Rev. Morford, "Job 14:14," in *The One New Man bible*, Travelers Rest, SC: True Potential Publishing Co., 2011.
[40] W. J. Rev. Morford, "Job 33: 29-30," in *The One New Man Bible*, Travelers Rest, SC: True Potential Publishing Co..
[41] W. J. Rev. Morford, "Luke 20: 37-38," in *The One New Man Bible*, Travelers Rest, SC: True Potential Publishing Co..
[42] Origen, "de Principiis, Book IV, ch. 1, sec. 23.c".
[43] Y. Astor, "Zohar II 99b," [Online]. Available: www.aish.com/jl/l/a/48943926.html.
[44] Y. Astor, "Zohar I, 186b," [Online]. Available: www.aish.com/jl/l/a/48943926.html.
[45] "The War of the Jews, Book III, Chap. 8, No. 5," [Online]. Available: www.earlyjewishwritings.com/text/josephus/war3.html.
[46] F. Josephus, "Antiquities of the Jews - Book XVIII, Chapter 1, No. 3," [Online]. Available: www.earlyjewishwritings.com/text/josephus/ant18.html.
[47] H. Y. Ginsburgh, "Tav: Impression - The Seal of Creation," [Online]. Available: www.inner.org/hebleter/tav.htm.
[48] Y. Ali, "Sura 2:28," [Online]. Available: www.quranexplorer.com/index/Sura_002_Al_Baqara_The_Cow.aspx.
[49] Y. Ali, "Sura 20:55," [Online]. Available: www.quranexplorer.com/index/Sura_020_Ta_Ha_Ta_Ha.aspx.
[50] Y. Ali, "Sura 71: 17-18," [Online]. Available: www.quranexplorer.com/index/Sura_071_Nooh_Nooh.aspx.

Chapter 11: *UEF Inquires*

Early the following morning, a gentle sound coming from the room's console slowly brought my slumber to an end. I was pleasantly surprised to find an urgent message from Hans bearing much-anticipated news: UEF sanctioned MCT to return to the structure, reestablish alien contact, and resume dialogue. I was to meet Hans at his office by ten MLT and head for the structure from there—finally, the kind of news I had longed for.

Blissful melody hurriedly stirred the soul with uplifting verve, and my bosom envisioned divine raptures born from passionate verbs. On wings of intense noble love, fond pageants opulently elevated my sights unto my loving one's gentle, light-filled heart with reverent affection. A beating haven drove lips to shudder excitedly with wonder, and the windows of my soul burst forth with fervently exuberant epics knowing that, after such long wait, my magnificently beautiful sister, my dulcet starlight, my desire of ages, would be there to fill my spirit with celestial grace.

After a rigorous body cleanse, I rushed down to the lower level and showed up at Hans's office right on schedule but he was nowhere to be found. On that note, I jumped on a cart and left for the structure on my own. Sean was already on location getting equipment set up; Hans arrived afterward bearing a sealed document. He was instructed not to view or share its contents with anyone, especially the Brothers, however pointless that sounded.

Without delay, the three of us entered the structure, confident that Saras's age-old bid to span the great cosmic chasm would soon become reality.

The door silently closed behind us and room lights dimmed as if someone discerned our presence. This time, no starry spectacles, moving melodies, or alien hosts were there to entreat our curiosity. Rather, arresting silence and pitch darkness held our breath in solitary suspense. Only a dim luminescence glowed about us, shining like a pallid convenience light.

We waited anxiously for something to happen, but nothing transpired and no one answered our calls. We seriously thought the structure had somehow malfunctioned when an unexpected cool draft briefly brushed our bodies, leaving a strange static chill behind. Seconds later, we were surrounded by a brilliant blue light and a sense of gravity greater than Masar's.

Mysterious verbal rumble, reminiscent of crowds talking at cross-purposes, got our attention. The light surrounding us dissolved, the House of Nations Senate hall came into view, and we emerged in front of the ministry's podium facing delegates.

Several tense delegates immediately wondered what we were doing there or how we got past security. After all, Martian and military uniforms did not belong in that hall. Security hastily came to escort us off, but their hands went right through us, often reaching out to see if by chance we turned solid. No doubt, this was the surprise Dow Uanh implied during our previous contact.

Someone in the crowd got my immediate attention: Gina Toscani, the Speaker of the Senate. I had not seen her since graduation, with reason. She was my friendly rival back in those institutional days though she never bragged about it. She dived into politics head first while I pursued rocks and obsolete civilizations. She had done quite well for herself in spite of Earth gov's predatory climate. Holding the third seat in government was no easy task.

She was stunningly attractive, but I intentionally avoided coming anywhere near her. Something akin to intellectual fears drew me away, intense enough to seek asylum at the fringes of existence where I was certain she would not follow, until this ill-timed moment.

"Gentlemen," she said with a sharp stare that advised diving impetuously for your soles, "I'd shake your hand, but we know how well that will work. You are early for your appointment and more live than expected. As you can see, we're not all here and ready to go yet. I don't mind your improvised holographic appearance, but it's not exactly what we had in mind."

As she spoke, Dr. Yato Folaranmi, vice chancellor and ministry secretary, came to greet us. A master of inter-linguistic debate and native of the Nigerian State, he spent much time at Cambridge as guest lecturer. Gina and I first met in one of his lectures where I learned to appreciate her exceptional debating skills. Yato remembered my classic defense in Spanish, seemingly unstoppable, until she came around in Swedish and put a quick halt to my winnings.

She never accepted that I cleared the way for her big win that day, just caught me tired. Oddly enough, I got her to go on a date; it was the only one we ever shared. I never understood why I asked her out in the first place. She stood by my side for the next three years and urged me onward, but I never offered her anything more than friendship. Feelings of subjugation drew me to her, but another part of me wanted nothing to do with her. And so it was that, following graduation, I quietly walked away and vanished from her life without a trace.

As Sean and Hans struck a side conversation with Yato, Gina stepped my way for some quality time. Of all people, she was someone I did not genuinely care to entertain, with reason. "You've always been one to embrace grandiose entrances," she said. "I'd say this is perhaps your greatest achievement yet."

"We can call it that," I said, struggling to say something back but side lined by a plethora of stale thoughts. "From the looks of things, you've done quite well for yourself. Speaker of the Senate I hear?"

"Just another career step for me, but there's more to life than politics. You should know that, Dr. Sullivan," she said, playfully seductive.

"That's why I collect rocks for a living."

"How's that a life, if I may ask?"

"Rocks don't argue back, and you'll never find two alike. Can't beat that."

"That's really fascinating, like the two of us."

"Something like that, I suppose."

"I'm sure it has its rewards, but it's inhospitable work and the pay sucks."

"But the job comes with a great view, an office as big as Mars, and no political blind spots."

"Glad you think so, but I'd hate to live in a plastic bag for even an hour," she said, suddenly running out of plain chat.

Our lips went stale, stares briefly lowered, and we sparked a rug crease hunt. After a few moments of silent floor shuffling, I said, "So what now?"

She closed up to me and said, "You know, a simple hello would have sufficed. That can't be too hard to do, can it?"

Stress clouded my thoughts with reasons all too familiar, and lips deadened unsure what to say. Meanwhile, Gina used her time wisely by playing desirable before me, no doubt to fuse my thoughts.

"I know," I said, gripping and twisting the back of my neck to release stress. "I was immature then, probably more so now. I meant to call, but that undergrad hung around you like a tight leech and I couldn't just barge in. Still, communication was not one of my strongest attributes, as history will attest."

"That I'll vouch for," she said with sound approval, putting some distance between us to my relief, "but today I might make an exception. For your information, Maurice and I never amounted to anything. Sometimes people just don't get the point or don't do anything to get it. You get my point?"

"I think I do."

"People need other people to get a life; there's no way around it. I'd say your point is pending, and time is of the essence. Will I be getting your point any time soon?"

"You have a way with disarming words. Always clever to the last."

Gina approached with deliberate delight written all over her and said seductively, "I'm full of surprises; you know that. Now, tell me the truth: do you like me?"

I stared a bit embarrassed at Gina but nodded affirmative. "I didn't think you'd ignore me all these years on purpose. Maybe what you said is true; communication isn't your strongest attribute. You have to work on that and give me the point. But on a separate subject, tell me; is it true you actually live and recycle in a spacesuit for an entire week? That's got to stink."

She was the leading reason behind my successful career but also a lavish wishing well for more than just friendship, all too willing to grant my wishes. I did get her point all right years back, but my well was literally dry, and I could not deliver my point across without hurting her. Thus, rather than tap into insincere arts and hope for questionable results, I sadly reached inward and paid her back with the only suitable harvest at my disposal, the fruits of my unruly fears; I vanished from her life in the shadows of somber neglect.

To say the least, I owed her a huge apology for my ignoble conduct, and she knew it. I stood there wondering if this was the right venue for an apology and looked at her with eyes glazed somewhere afar, but she wasted no time waking me up. "Hello! Come to your senses," she said swiftly, looking at me with an expression that essentially said, 'I got cha.'

Defused by indefinite ancient grievances writhing deep within my troubled ghost, I impulsively rushed Gina a synthetic apology, hoping it would draw troubles away—something I would soon regret doing—for she had other less ceremonial forms of payment in mind. "I truly regret not having the right foresight to render colleagues due attention," I said.

"Do you, now?" she questioned. "I wonder why. Was it something I did?"

"It wasn't that. I just got carried away with life in general and misjudged other people's needs; I seem to have a problem with this sort of thing."

"You mean you had this problem before, or do you experience it on a regular basis? Have you talked to someone about it?"

"Not really. I'm not in the neighborhood much, and rocks don't talk back."

"We can fix that. I'll send someone up there to talk this through with you."

"You mean a shrink?"

"The best I've got."

"No, thanks. I'll stick with teddy rocks a while longer."

"Whatever works. But get some help before you melt down."

"About the suit," I said, changing the subject, "it does get a bit undesirable after a couple of days without replenishment. The worst thing is your breath, mixed in with the air supply; it can get a little too close for comfort. Some things you just can't get used to, or get rid of."

"Someone should do something about that, or the breath," she said, as I bowed slightly to check my breath just in case. "Let me know if you need a referral. I have great connections."

Turning briefly, she excitedly motioned to go meet some of the delegates just as the chancellor entered the hall through a far rear door. "I want you to meet some key delegates," she said energetically, bearing a beaming smile that was hard to resist. "They are among the most supportive, influential senators on this mission and can't wait to meet you. Come, right this way," she said, leading the way, but I stayed in place.

"Some other time," I said somewhat reserved, trying to avoid partisan politics. "The session's about to start, and it would be wise to wait until Earth gov reaches a mutual verdict. I don't think it's proper to display associative partiality right now."

"None of the sort. That's precisely why they want to meet you," she said with even greater excitement. "We all want to broker a lasting alien alliance but need your expertise to put it together and ensure success. Your impressive accomplishments these last few days earned you a lot of respect in all segments, and my associates are ready to . . . well," she said after briefly pausing and showing off a bright wink, "it's a secret. We can't discuss it here, but I'll tell you more about it later. You hold the key to bridging the gap and reaching consensus. So come, you must meet them before the session starts."

Bursting with girlish delight, she turned swiftly to avoid further rebuttals from me but ran right into Yato who stood behind her at a most appropriate time. Startled by his presence, she stumbled to improvise an apology, deploying rather spontaneous gestures to thwart him away. But Yato wasn't easily fooled by theatrics and knew just where to land his remarks.

"Madam Speaker," Yato said with an astute grin, "are you trying to take my prime student away right this instant?"

Shrewdly formal and excited, Gina replied, "I was about to introduce Dr. Sullivan to some of the delegates before the session starts. Since time is brief, with your pardon, I really need to be going."

"I see, but I don't recall that being on the agenda," he said, impeding Gina's advance with a superlative snicker meant to annoy her, "and you haven't the time either. The man just got here, and he needs a moment to find himself, not wrangle with sponsors."

Quite upbeat, Gina hurriedly replied, "It's nothing like that. Bill offers a unique perspective on things that will strengthen the prospect of bilateral success. Will you excuse us, please?"

"Madam Speaker, always in such a hurry," he said, blocking the way, while Gina politely squirmed inwardly. "Rushed politics are usually an opportunity for just a few fortunate participants, but turns up to be an opiate for everyone else," he said laughing, while Gina simmered, dropping hands to her side and raising her head in frustration. From a distance, several delegates looked our way showing signs of irritation. No doubt, they were Gina's associates, also growing thin on patience.

Yato lightly placed his hands on Gina's shoulders as she tried to pull away and said, "Acquainting civilians with select delegates, in this room, is considered conflict of interest, and you know it. Rather than demonstrate partiality and challenge regulations, why don't you introduce Bill to everyone from the podium instead?"

At that moment, a call to order was issued; the session was about to begin. Gina, out of time, looked down and unraveled, though briefly nodded at her associates. "Bill, one last thing," he said. "Before parting, you'll have to tell me all about your girlfriend," he said quite buoyant, sporting his usual calm wide smile.

Gina looked at me in shock, put hands to her waist, and replied somewhat upset, "What's this, a woman other than me? You can't be serious!"

"I'm not seeing anyone. Where did you get the idea from?" I said, surprised by Yato's claim.

"You better not," she said.

"Don't tell me you don't know," he said laughing. "Everyone else does."

"Don't believe everything you hear," I said, somewhat thrown off by his comment. "Aside from my suit, there's no one else in my life."

"Yes, there is," he said nodding in disbelief. "Her name is . . . let me see . . . May Len, right?"

I looked down to conceal a jubilant countenance and did not reply. "Don't you hide that smile from me, young man; truth is hard at work right now," he added jokily. "I can't read lips, but the soul is a hard thing to veil from a face, and I know precisely where yours is coming from." Meanwhile, Gina seriously frowned, showing signs of things to come.

"Don't you dare give me up," she said sharply, waving at the ministry to grant her a few minutes. "I need to get delegates in order, but do me a favor: get that thing . . . girl out of your head. I'm right here and easy to get. *Ciao, mio amore*," she said, blowing me a kiss as she walked away.

I felt like I knew Gina from long ago, an old friend returned from far-off eons and shadowy cosmic shores; but something struck a rather distasteful nerve about her any time we met, a feeling of rejection that was difficult to describe and mind.

"Perfect timing," I said to Yato. "Thank you, doctor. I owe you one."

"Don't mention it," he said. "I'm sure they had nothing good waiting for you. In my land, they say that magicians and politicians have a lot in common; they both draw our attention away from what they're really doing [1].' There's a sucker born every second, don't be one. Mark my words: if you want to do the right thing, stay clear of inquiring delegates and special committees," he said walking away.

"I'll remember that," I said, unaware of the value of his advice at the time.

Gina headed for the podium with uncompromising, assured stance. She was accompanied by Yato, the ministers of defense, space command, social development, planetary resources, chief council justice, and finally the chancellor who waved my way gesturing we had to chat. This was Saras's top brass, a political decision-making powerhouse rarely gathered under one roof, except on extremely demanding occasions. On the Senate floor, delegates waited eagerly in their seats to get firsthand glimpse of our alien visitors.

Gina briefly introduced MTC and wasted no time getting things rolling. "In our last session, the Special Committee on Alien Affairs presented its classified findings to the Senate Securities and Appeals Board and approved the following motions. First article: a formal agenda will be implemented in all future contacts to represent and ensure Earth interests. Second article: only select committee members, approved by the ministry, will represent Earth gov and negotiate terms with aliens to avoid conflicts of interest. Third article: the ministry's decision and terms for an alliance will be final and non-amendable.

"These motions unanimously passed SSAB review and became senate order 2158-03-02-25, empowering the committee to compile a highly classified questionnaire, based on recorded MCT transcripts. Due to global security concerns, a conscious computer, rather than a human, was commissioned to derive topic content and deliver the final unique document to Commander Gantz under strict security."

"Madam Speaker," Hans said, as a couch appeared out of thin air behind us, "I have the document in my possession and stand ready to start the contact session."

"Something's not right here," I said quietly, while Gina continued talking.

"What do you mean not right?" Hans said.

"I have a huge problem with this whole committee process."

"A problem with what exactly?"

"The Brothers purposely set this live meeting up to collaborate directly with Earth gov, not deal with mediators."

"I see nothing wrong with this process. If we were back on Mars, that's how it would be, just us again, yes?"

"You said it, if we were, but we're not, and that's my point. The Brothers changed the playing field for a good reason, and we should also."

"The intent is obvious. If not, why get everyone together in the same room?" Sean said.

"Sean, your comments don't help our cause," Hans said. "There's no time to change things. Just do as you're told and avoid me trouble, yes?"

"You think a few political crack shots can persuade aliens to negotiate terms without Earth gov being present?" I replied. "Aliens want to talk with Earth gov, not get sucked into another info picnic!"

"Funneling concerns through smaller channels is an impartial and smart thing to do when gathering intelligence from unknown sources as in this case. You're not smarter than all these people combined, and a conscious computer, mind you! So be quiet, I need to hear what's going on."

"Hans, that's the best disarming statement I've heard you spout yet. Just say it like it is and spare me the insult. I don't know who's in this committee, I assume you are, but what they're proposing is nothing less than a huge offense! It's a damn inquisitional panel, putting aliens to the question!"

"That's not what I meant, and you know it," Hans replied angrily. "I'll do what Earth gov orders me to do—end of discussion."

"Not if I can help it," I replied, standing up.

"What are you doing?" he said alarmed. "Sit down before you make a fool of yourself, and me!"

"Madam Speaker, pardon my intrusion," I suddenly interjected, interrupting Gina at the podium among light rumble.

"What in damnations are you up to?" Hans said quickly in a whispering alarmed tone. "Have you lost your damned mind? You don't know what or who you're dealing with! You're going to get us thrown out!"

"The podium recognizes Mr. Bill Sullivan, member of MTC," Gina said. "Is there something you want to say, Dr. Sullivan?"

"Don't say anything! Please! Sit down and keep quiet!" said Hans.

"Hans, I know what I'm doing . . ."

"In this crowd, you talk only when you're told to. You're going to get me into trouble. So please, sit down and keep your mouth shut, yes?"

"This sort of thing goes well around these levels. Trust me."

"Trust you? You want me to trust you? I'm still having nightmares about the crash site."

"You have a boring sense of politics, so get over it. Madam Speaker, I suggest that you, a high-ranking representative of Earth gov, have the privilege of leading this inquiry."

"Oh my God! That's it! We're done for!" Hans said. "You idiot! I've got the document, so how is anyone other than me, us, conduct this session? Think before you act. You're making me look like a fool!"

"You need no help from me for that."

"Watch your mouth, dirt bagger! Don't make me empty it!"

"Dr. Sullivan, your suggestion is noted," she replied. "For the record, and taking alien customs into consideration, please tell us why you bring forth this motion."

"See what I mean? Now you have to explain yourself. This isn't good, not good at all. I'm toast!" Hans said.

"The Brothers wanted us together in one room for a reason."

"But we already were, and everything was going just fine until you opened your big mouth and ruined everything!" Hans said frustrated. "You . . . you're on your own now!"

"Madam Speaker, throughout history, initial contacts between states were conducted far from states rooms. Follow-up visits, meant to deepen understanding and negotiate terms, were hosted by the highest levels of government. In the confines of this states room, the presence of distinguished diplomats, and the live company of prominent dignitaries from other worlds, it is clear that the focus of our alien guests should not be MCT but Earth gov. I'm convinced that aliens had this form of contact in mind when they set it up, bestowing upon our government an honorable, historic opportunity to partake in immediate cosmic parlance."

The proposal received wide Senate acceptance, but there was a slight problem: Hans had the only copy of the questionnaire. An electronic picture could be sent to the podium, but Hans suddenly exhibited untold concern; the document mysteriously vanished from his uniform.

"Is there a problem, Commander?" Gina said calmly.

"Madam Speaker, this is most bizarre. It appears that I don't have the document," Hans said rather anxious. "I assure you it was securely stowed in my uniform; it couldn't have fallen off."

"Didn't you say something a few moments ago about looking like an idiot, yes?" I said, imitating his native accent.

"Don't you mock me, *mist fliegen*! Help me find this stupid thing, quickly!"

"I thought I was on my own, no?"

"Well, I change my mind. Don't just sit there, get up and look for it! You too, lieutenant!"

"*Ja Herr, mein tapferer Kommandant*," I said sarcastically, with a deep Bavarian accent and military pose.

"Oh, shut up!"

"Is there something you would like to tell us, Commander?" asked Gina.

"No, Madam Speaker," he replied nervously. "We're looking for the document. We will find it shortly, not to worry."

"You sure you didn't use it in the stall, lad? Maybe you flushed it down the tinny with the rest of other personal evidence," Sean said with a snigger.

"Now, you too? I am going to kill you both! This is all your fault!"

"Commander, whether for reasons of imprudence or distraction, baring no value at the moment, elementary foresight indicates that this meeting's agenda, for which we diligently prepared, will be adversely impacted," Gina said stonily. "I can't suitably underscore the importance of finding that pro forma. Otherwise, this session will have to be embarrassingly postponed."

Mindful of Gina's mounting displeasure, Hans diligently searched his surroundings but came up empty-handed. On the other hand, the ministry was by no means prepared to discuss foreign intimidating topics without the document, more so in the presence of the Brothers. Most did not understand the material; others simply could not remember it.

Unexpectedly, a bright light appeared out of nowhere and briefly hovered over the podium, startling Gina. As the light faded, the document materialized on the podium like an unfolding scroll, to everyone's welcomed relief.

"This is impressive," she said, "proof of technology well beyond our realm. It's agreed. I will assume primary role as suggested, and grant MCT the floor when suitable. Please proceed; our guests may come at their convenience."

Not long after, two bright blue cylinders emerged along the short walkway between podium and delegates. Everyone present suddenly realized that enlightened benign beings unlike themselves would soon be in their presence, and stood on their feet as a reverent act of courtesy. All the same, their hearts copiously troubled them, afraid that shameful thoughts might bring our guests insult, even start interplanetary war.

For that brief moment, inescapable reality impressed every bosom. Fear's relentless realms descended upon naïve, errant hearts with bitter omens of doom, carelessly compelling the mind to adore perdition's fate like siren beckoning songs—irresistibly sweet yet binding body and soul in lethal lethargy, the forerunner of death and corruption.

When blue cylinders dissolved, Dow Uanh and my wondrous starlight emerged from the fading light, facing applauding delegates with enrapturing radiance. My heart eagerly jumped far from its bonding locks the moment I gazed upon her lovely grace, instantly embracing hers. However, just as with everyone else present, it was not to be my soul's finest hour either, for chilling phantoms diligently surged from my innermost torch of reason endeavoring to confine corrupt carnal desires I deemed potentially offensive to her. Thus, the moment's moving joys feebly marred with fear-laden shame, realizing the colossal spiritual divide that endured between us.

It didn't take long for the windows of my soul to sadly plunge impulsively beneath May Len's wondrous sight line, seeking safe haven from her loving presence behind a humiliating ogle shield. But my untimely caprice amounted only to a brief amiss, for healing light from high celestial realms decanted forth from her radiant jewels of paradise with unblemished conviction, parting my inhibitions away.

"Your testimony gives me strength; God's only punishment is love," her gentle mental whispers kindly beckoned within me in a language of thoughts and feelings, garbed with beautiful ballades of sweet hallowed mercy.

"But I feel so filthy and ashamed of my negative desires compared to you," I replied in thought, unable to restrain a sincere mind.

"That you feel because the weight of selfish pleas to be like us haunts your heart; but not when you look into my eyes, beloved friend, brother," she replied. "Let your longings come from your heart, the higher self, not lower thoughts. Let fearless truth be in thee as it is with us, only from the heart. Don't rush anxiously to yourself for answers, for calm is the answer. Be not possessive but truthful, and you will have no shame. Shame is just an illusion, a lie, for what is there to hide from the Infinite? Show the power of your heart, grant it to me. Share your eyes with mine for I live when I give to you, and I give when our thoughts meet."

"Don't I offend you?"

"If I judge, do I have time to love? If we beat ourselves negatively, will love come from pain?" her thoughts whispered gently.

Her brief words urged time to dwell still, and my mind to be at peace, infusing my heart with an indescribable longing to conceal myself no more and grant her my heart. My eyes then lifted upward from self-imposed bondage and eagerly sought May Len's enchanting, graceful beacon across a vast sea of murky fears, unhindered by the heart's secret immaterial chambers.

My spirit felt cleansed, freed from oppressive desires that once blinded me from her true wondrous spiritual splendor. My eyes declared the beauty of God's light in a restful soft tongue, and my soul breathed delightful warmth, refusing to retain morbid distortions. With untainted respect, my thoughts reached out to my starlight and humbly uttered, "I love . . . your soul."

"Rest your life upon mine, friend, brother. Let it pulse with mine, lovingly, honestly, and fearlessly," she replied, sweetly fixing her eyes upon mine. "Is there not more? Can your heart come nearer and seek greater beauty?"

Gina, already jealous of May Len, and witnessing our genial visual exchange, instantly went somber and never again recovered.

On the Senate floor, another cylinder lit up, bringing in Tei-Ah and Meh-Nai before standing jubilant delegates. Up on the podium, it was a different story. Imposing as usual, Gina strived to draw attention to herself, something she could never get enough of. And with May Len jammed in her crosshairs something awful, colossal insecurities brought even greater odium into her life.

"On behalf of Earth gov," she said coldly, "welcome to your sister world. This is a historic moment for our planet. We hope our people will flourish alongside your space communities in the not too distant future."

"We've waited thousands of years for this moment and rejoice knowing that our sister Saras will soon join us among the stars," Dow Uanh said in a loving, tender tone. "We're here to serve, not submit you to capricious alien tyranny. You've upheld peace for the longest period in recorded history and reached a stage where we can grant you amity, but your minds are filled with images of alien captors enslaving and destroying your people, something we will never do.

"You have many questions, and your time is valuable" he said, as a couch appeared on the west side of the room. "We respect your privacy and know we cannot interfere in your affairs, even in thought."

"We mean to use time effectively by asking what we deem most critical to establish relations between our worlds," Gina said. Turning to the ministry, she said, "You're no doubt familiar with Senate members and our chancellor."

After brief salutes, the chancellor stood up, went to the podium, and said, "I suppose you know what I'm going to say."

"We are old friends," Dow Uanh said, "but the words that flow from your heart are as refreshing as newly found friendship."

"I haven't made too many friends lately," replied the chancellor amusingly. "Not because there's no material to choose from, but my schedule doesn't leave me much time to socialize. You can't imagine how many people, including myself, dream of someday talking with an extraterrestrial in the brief span of our mortal existence."

After pausing for a moment to clear few emotional tears, the chancellor continued with trembling voice, "After so long, that wish finally came true, and my life is rewarded beyond grasp. My Brothers, welcome, and may we foster peace, mutual cooperation, and a greater understanding of God."

Gina returned to the podium, quickly reviewed the document bearing questions, and proceeded with the first question. "First, we want to know more about you, what you do on your worlds, your status, and what interests you the most in these contacts."

"I am Meh-Nai," she said. "I specialize in Saras history, perhaps the most complex of any world. I am also a spiritual counselor or someone you might call a minister on Venus. I find no greater joy than to partake in this mission."

"I am Tei-Ah, science of life teacher on this system. We flow with universal currents, not against them, as the universe permits and restricts our actions. We never dwell on anything negative, for it is detrimental to the mind and absolutely pointless. My mission is to encourage your world to encompass these principles, and come closer to the Infinite's eternal light."

Next, it was May Len's turn. Her joy was indescribable, almost emotional, with sufficient radiance to out shine a star. "This is May Len, my youngest daughter," Dow Uanh added. "A few weeks ago, she could not speak English; I feel this is no longer true. We have advanced tools that speed up the time it takes to study and learn any subject or trade. I leave you to her, confident she can address you without my help."

All eyes anxiously rested upon May Len who spoke grasping a word at a time though with deep meaning. "I am a student, to show Saras to learn universal law. Saras needs Infinite. I don't know why you don't like Him," she said, bringing up healthy Senate laughter.

"Pleasure you like, past memory, negative frequency, die from it, very sad. Saras play with lies like children; you don't like truth. You hide and hurt others because fear, make friends to survive. This is the big Saras problem; spiritual not important. I want to help Saras learn of true life; spiritual is everything."

Delegates, touched by her words, applauded May Len in appreciation for her honesty and pureness of heart, except for Gina, who stewed silently by the podium. "I want to add that May Len is only 190 Earth years old—and is not yet engaged," Dow Uanh said, stirring a brief chuckle from delegates. "Madam Speaker, we are at your disposal."

Gina made ready to proceed with Saras's list of questions but often looked my way hoping to entice my carnal longings with artful theatrics. I would sorely disappoint her, for I never took my eyes from May Len. I embraced her thoughts with all the warmth my heart could possibly assemble, keeping her close to my bosom by all means possible. I begged for an opportunity to meet with her, but obviously, this was not yet our time.

Chapter 12: *The First Conference*

Since the dawn of primeval existence, our ancestors looked upon their substantive surroundings with untiring wonder, fearfully revering delusive mythical icons thought to govern daily subsistence. But entrenched in swelling annals of human seasons, there were those among reticent throngs that boldly stepped forth, placed their eyes on the vast expanse above, and dared ponder upon the plurality of cosmic life, a subject far from the norm in such times. Thus, it was that man first came to question his apparent uniqueness beneath countless illumined islands embellishing vast chasms beyond.

To the early cosmologist, fearsome gods and signs of the future appeared to riddle the heavens. But in classical Greek times, a strong pluralistic stance matured when Thales and Anaximander [1] introduced the concept of 'apeiron' or an infinite universe. In time, diverse philosophical, scientific, and artistic works advocated further insight into creation's boundless realms, inspiring a new generation of visionaries that enticed our humble awareness with a plethora of thrilling cosmic quests and faded rebuttals. But darkening reveries from forgotten wicked times of yore spoke covertly from these gauntlet covers, clouding our sights more so with olden sins than lack of insight.

As man's imaginative nature evolved, so did these works mature but in a negative way, acquainting the world with images so absurdly terrifying that not even hell's worst nightmares could complement. Clumsy, horrific beasts malformed by cruel, barbaric tendencies came to represent God's cosmic children, an immense insult to His Majesty.

Such are the revolting fruits of errant souls that venture daringly into the unknown—inspired, and blinded by despicable past memories that seek some measure of truth though stained by untold heaps of wickedness. As our legacy poured unhindered fallacy into literary history, people reading it came to expect the bearer of death, not life, to descend from the stars and duly prepared to react fittingly on the day the Brothers came among us. That day had arrived, charmed by terrorizing fables falsely depicting us as victims when, in fact, behind the veil of moral virtue, we were the sole cause of that same death we so dreaded.

Silence pervaded throughout the Senate where delegates eagerly waited for Saras's future course to be revealed. The Brothers sat calmly before the ministry at Father's service, bearing the infinite fountain of truth upon ever humble lips. At the podium, Gina unfolded the questionnaire with confident flair, raised her head proudly overlooking the Senate, and asked the first question. "How old are your civilizations, and are you natives of your worlds?"

"Each world in our system varies in occupational age," Meh-Nai said. "Before Saras was colonized, beings walked upon its surface for millions of years. Life on Venus dates back over twenty-six million years, and all other worlds variably less than that. Our Martian brothers relocated here from a far off system 267,000 years ago. And to answer your concerns, the answer is yes, you are descendants of our people."

"What would you say is your greatest challenge?" asked Gina.

"Saras, no doubt," Tei-Ah replied with a touch of humor, prompting hearty laughter. "Setting humor aside, we incessantly seek Infinite light. We devote our lives to attain higher spiritual planes of expression as a collective. There is no single right path, and no one can interfere with personal choice, even if the entity appears to be making a bad one."

"That leads to the next question. We have many devotional systems based primarily on ancient scriptures. Do you have similar beliefs on your worlds, and how do these differ from ours? Is it your intent to replace our beliefs?"

"In our search for love and truth, we've learned that each soul is on a unique journey much like a career path, so arguing what belief is best over another becomes irrelevant. Seekers must discover the voice of truth that no one can replace or mandate. Hence, we seek unification by sharing truth, not knowledge, and do not segregate across sectarian boundaries. Keep in mind that love is not regulated by your knowledge of Him."

"Your holy books contain a wealth of information about Father, but you don't take them seriously," Meh-Nai said. "You interpret them unsure what they mean, become attached to faith hoping to be saved, and make converts not because you love them but to boost your ranks. True love should not be based on amity, fear, or obligation. It must be genuine, inspired exclusively by truth and honesty, not a conformity apparatus designed to sustain affiliations."

"Nice job, people! Bravo!" the justice minister said brazenly loud, grinning deviously in Gina's direction. "That's some persuasive, subliminal conjecture you just threw out there, dispensed in idealistic ways difficult to refuse. Put lucidly, you make God's existence sound so compelling and eloquent I almost made the mistake of believing it myself. But come on, let's be realistic here rather than quixotic. Bottom line is, if love, as you just advocated, is so foreign to nature that you can't find it, then so is God, plain and simple," he said bluntly, earning impetuous discord from the Senate, except from Gina and the social minister who nodded in agreement.

"Minister," said Yato, "can you please stress your views without adding emotional content?"

"May I remind everyone present the importance of applying critical thinking, observing nature, and scrutinizing these matters? I have good reasons to feel and express myself in this manner, all founded upon proven naturalistic fact and professional intellectualism."

"And may I remind the minister to uphold UEF canons of conduct in these proceedings," the space minister said. "There's no need to behave presumptuously; it is most unbecoming."

"The minister has every right to express his views, using acceptable forceful measures as deemed suitable. This he has done, competently, and in accordance with the letter of law," Gina said, wearing a cunning smile. "Justice, do you have any other points of view you would like to share?"

"I absolutely do," replied the justice minister.

"By all means, please proceed."

"Thank you, Madam Speaker. First of all, causal forces instinctively influence every object, movement, and decision we make. That is, the universe is functionally rigged, and we are mere robots oppressed by inflexible rules, even inherited genes, that affect our neurons. So if there's a God, He definitely offers no free will. And if He is not responsible for these causal forces, then how can He possibly exist? Secondly, if we can't be sure that anything exists, apart from ideas, then God's existence is also debatable. And lastly, since actuality is not a predicate, a supremely perfect being can be considered to not exist. And there you have it, I challenge you to prove me wrong," he said distastefully.

"There is some measure of truth in what you say," Dow Uanh said.

"You can't be serious. Contradicting yourselves, already?" the justice said scornfully. "I find your sudden prompting to critical reasoning rather amusing and quite refreshing."

"Not at all," Tei-Ah said with a smile. "Philosophy developed on your world, for the most part, from an intellectual vantage point, influenced by limiting senses rather than spirit . . ."

"As it should be!" he intruded rudely. "Why contaminate pure thought with debatable theories? Even simians demonstrate morals, proving we choose to believe in God purely because we are moral, rather than our morals being inspired by God."

"I find that your behavior before this reputable assembly sadly indicates otherwise," said the space minister. "You mean to tell me that rudeness is morality? Beasts in the wild are best known for fierceness, not morality, and you're probably a great example of that! Lock yourself in with a chimp for a few minutes; you'll know what morality is all about!"

"Ministers," Gina interrupted, "let's keep our dialogue at a professional level by restricting accusatory overtones."

"As a disciplined, critical thinker, I take no offense with the minister's emerging knowledge of objective reasoning. Rather, being assertive and truthful is both moral and pure," said the justice minister.

"Is that so?" said the defense minister. "Justice, please tell us the other half of your most contradictive concept."

"And what might that be exactly?"

"Survival of the fittest, where morality is considered a weakness . . ."

"Survival demands aggressive behavior at times."

"So why are you so aggressive on this matter, if not to survive by promoting your own superior reasoning intellect? Decide whether you want to be moral or survive; you're caught in the middle somewhere . . ."

"Don't confuse the subject. Animals show grief and guilt, so don't tell me we need God for that!"

"Morality in nature is born from fear. It's a means to survive through pack organization and necessity, proving you know little about the higher values of spiritual morality, such as love. Grief and guilt, as shown by wild beasts, is not love at all but fear . . ."

"I never heard such embarrassing rubbish! Please, educate yourself!"

"I will emphasize to the justice that fear, not morality, is survival of the fittest! True love, on the other hand, is fearless, never resorts to violence in order to survive, or regrets its deeds after the fact!"

"Well, I will have to disagree with that."

"As expected," said the resources minister. "You, sir, have colossal stubbornness issues most difficult to mind that will churn anyone's life into an occupational hazard! Why don't you get all your facts straight before you go out in public and make a chimp of yourself! Better yet, get a life and love something other than yourself for once! You might learn a thing or two that way after thinking like an animal all your life!"

"You need to see a shrink. Maybe he can persuade you to stop dreaming about love that don't exist!"

"What Tei-Ah meant to say is that, by limiting research to beast behavior in the wild, physical objects, emotions, or what you call pure thought, you limit your intellectual and environmental scope to the realm of eventuality rather than rising above it" Dow Uanh said. "Therefore, you are emotionally and environmentally compromised by your own selective scope, and if an animal is the best you hope to imitate, so shall it be on to you."

"I beg your pardon?" the justice replied rather tactless.

"If I may interject," I said.

"We recognize Dr. Sullivan. You have the floor, proceed," said Gina.

"Thank you. We all know the story of three blind men that came across an elephant. Each touched a section of it: the tail, trunk, and tusk. Later, they endeavored to describe it to each other, and none could agree what it was. We each have a different perspective on creation but fail to encompass its entirety and, therefore, blindly conceive that which we can only sense. Indeed, we have been emotionally and environmentally compromised by our limited scope and abstract inclinations."

"The mind is small," May Len said slowly, "with sins, problems, emotions you don't know. It damages truth. Truth comes from Him, not world—problem, confusion, from you. How can knowledge come from ignorance? How can one have pure thought if one has pure sin? Do you know memories destroy free will but freedom from sin is free will? Free will is evolution. Keep your memories . . . lose free will. Choice is yours."

"When personal feelings or bias are brought into universal discussions, however unsuspectingly, they set the stage for the ultimate conflict of interest," Tei-Ah said. "Let us not forget that pretention, in itself, is a personal emotion. The world you see is only a shadow. The real one, spirit, your errant eyes cannot see until you apply spiritual, not critical thinking."

"Ladies, ladies, please note that our philosophical laws, after thousands of years, still stand due to their purity," the justice said. "We're talking about reputable facts, not emotions, deeply analyzed by critical applied thinking."

"Perhaps the justice is confusing critical thinking with thinking gone critical mass!" the space minister said, arousing healthy laughter. "Look, Barnaby, your data sample is only as big as your head. In your case, I stand corrected, that's one big head. Our brothers sampled billions of light-years over millions of years. Your research suffers from insufficient data and huge lack of vision."

"Hey, I can't help that we achieved analytical perfection a lot sooner than they did," the justice replied haughtily. "That should say something about our intellectual capacity."

"You self-deluded dimwit! Like you said earlier, you don't know if you're real or not, but at the same time, you claim to be a robot that doesn't exist. What an oxymoron! Are you for real? How can you believe such bunk!"

"Explain, then, the origin of causal forces affecting free will," Dow Uanh said.

"I don't need to know of them to realize their impact," the justice said carefully.

"That's entirely true . . ."

"Well, good. I'm glad you finally agree! Case closed!"

"Not so fast. By so choosing to ignore causal sources, you've practiced free will, something you claim being denied of. If you only understood causal forces, you would not be blindly decoding impacts, questioning reality, or wondering who or if you are. Instead, you would be practicing vital truths and free will. Memories are what keeps you from free will, and trying to consciously visualize just how will actually works. The only thing keeping you from free will is your past and your undying memories."

"What does that have to do with anything? Even if I could moderate reality, I'm still bound by what I can and can't do with it."

"You want to be God—your negative self that is—and that's yet another conflict of interest. You've spent eons playing word games with reality, subliminally twisting and churning persuasive brain teasers to fit a sentient mold that explains away the ambiguity of 'I am,' but destroyed the foundation of truth in the process. The mind, the very thing you're trying to figure out, is like a book serving up only memories, from now and back then, not information about its audience. Think out of the mind; remember that the heart is where you must pick up your search for love."

"What you're telling me is that I'm forced to accept abstract things like God and spirit without proof. Is that it?"

"You inherit faults from the past, genes, situations, education, and senses. If you don't realize them and keep your mind on lower realms of thought, they will control you. Doing what you want is not freedom but slavery because errors ordain desires. On the other hand, Father is free will, for He nurtures and grants the greatest desires of your soul, love and peace, not conquering the cosmos. Your search takes heading where your beliefs reside; that's free will. If you don't think you have a soul, how can you conceive God? We offer to show you the world of spirit, if you would accept."

"No, thank you! I don't need any of that . . . rubbish!" the justice replied rather curtly, while delegates moaned.

"Your attitude is completely uncalled for, minister," Yato said.

"I was told there's such a thing as free will, and I just put it to practice. Why, is there a problem?"

"Let's practice free will, less any unbecoming attitudes unsuitable for these proceedings."

"Whatever you say, Mr. Secretary."

"Brothers, I apologize for the minister's bitter use of free will," Yato said.

"No offense taken. I once upheld the same beliefs, but that was about a million years ago," Tei-Ah said, bringing welcomed humor to the Senate.

"I'm sure someday we'll be saying the same thing. Gina, please proceed."

"Are there marked differences between our manners of worship, rituals, and so forth?"

"The universe is filled with diversity," Dow Uanh added. "We revere His Majesty singly and in close family units at all times, not just weekly gatherings. Our masters advise and inspire us with words of wisdom regularly from higher planes of existence. We do have planetary conclaves where we share spiritual concepts and activities."

"You mentioned families," said the space minister. "I assume you marry and have kids?"

"We do," Meh-Nai answered, "but our unions are driven by spiritual nearness, not carnal lust or beauty. While your marriages last no more than fifty years, if so fortunate, ours exceed eight hundred. Most couples continue their relationship in successive lifetimes and, in time, unite for eternity."

"Wait, did you say eight hundred years? All that in a single lifetime?"

"Correct. We live up to one thousand Saras years in a single body by strictly adhering to universal laws."

"I like the sound of that. Sign me up right now," he said, quickly echoed by all delegates.

In spite of Gina's formal rigidity, receptivity to the Brother's message gained momentum on the Senate floor; Gina was the only exception. Her expression never changed, perhaps from cold to frigid. She never once looked toward the Brothers and seemed to flounder through the process, not due to incompetence but some personal position or grudge of sort; I could not tell what it was. Hans thought nothing of her attitude, but Sean could definitely tell she was borderline rude. It would only exacerbate with time.

"Let's move on, and please keep side comments to a minimum," Gina added with a slight snap. "How far have you traveled in space, and what type of humanoids have you found on other worlds?"

"Far beyond your telescopic range," Meh-Nai said, "but many worlds at the fringes of our universe still remain to be explored. The human form is quite universal, able to adapt to a variety of planetary conditions, even your moon. Life blooms throughout the cosmos in many forms, sizes, and colors depending on the environment they live in."

"Members have reported extraterrestrials varying vastly from the human form," Gina replied. "Were these sightings factual?"

"There are many advanced extra-galactic beings with evolutionary paths different from ours such as grays, insectoids, and plantoids," Tei-Ah added. "Some are obsessed with transforming their physical form but are slowly coming about and showing an interest in the spiritual side of life."

"Do your people live among us today?" the social minister asked. "If so, why, and what roles do they play in society?"

"We have been part of your world since time immemorial," Dow Uanh added. "At times, we were mistaken for angels, and our message became distorted, so we opted to embody on Saras to comply with the prime directive and slowly advance your intellectual development."

"People like Nikola Tesla, Galileo, Mozart—were they some of these embodiments?"

"There have been many. In more modern times, educators lived on Saras and commuted back to their home worlds regularly. People never knew their next-door neighbor, teacher, or doctor was, for all intents and purposes, out of this world."

"You said you could fly to other planets in minutes or hours. How do you achieve such speeds?" the space minister asked.

"We don't traverse space but jump out and drop back thousands of light-years away. Space travel is not a linear concept but rather one of attracting to the base rate of a target location and skipping over the rest. Using precise dimensional calculations, time and space are nullified, and crafts transit between locations at speeds set by higher vortical nodal mediums, in a sense pulled by the target location's frequency.

"We know Saras wants this technology, and we will share the knowledge—when the time is right. Without proper conditioning, you will encounter physical problems crossing dimensions and are likely to misuse knowledge as you did in times past. Your present EM and ion drive technology was stolen from us Brothers. Before your Second World War, the German state captured one of our Venusian scouts and reverse engineered its secrets. Soon after, the United States captured several craft and its occupants. From it, you developed the shuttles you use today."

"Brothers, I appreciate your wisdom and honesty in this regard," the defense minister replied in an apologetic tone. "I regret the shameful, belligerent manner that our predecessors hosted your people. For these actions, I personally apologize, although, knowing your vast technical advances, how could our ancient military forces possibly harm your craft?"

"We have the means to defend ourselves," Tei-Ah said, "but our prime directive forbids us doing you harm. We would rather perish than harm you. Through re-embodiment, our life continues."

"Is that why you allowed Mars to be destroyed? Even though your people were being slaughtered, you allowed the attack to proceed because of further repercussions . . ."

The Brothers bowed their heads slightly and remained silent; the answer was obvious. "I apologize for bringing this up. I can't mention enough the great shame I personally feel regarding this past incident," he replied in a soft slow voice. "You are a most noble, wise people, placing the interests and needs of your enemies before your own. I hope someday we overcome our petty ambitions and be as you are."

Silence gripped the great assembly for several seconds, eventually broken by Dow Uanh, "We are not here to promote sadness but bring you back home with us. Be with us, that's why we're . . ."

"During initial contacts and interviews," said Gina, coldly interrupting Dow Uanh, "references to Atlantis and Mu were made. Can you provide further proof of their existence, drawing only from Earth history?"

"Your Bible attests to the existence of such civilizations," Meh-Nai replied, "but translations did away with original linguistic and cultural significance, thus making it difficult to decode such references.

"For example, the book of Genesis states that 'the earth was formless and empty, and darkness was upon the surface of the deep [2].' Note that the word 'tohuw' stands for destroyed or devastated, not formless. 'Bohuw' means vague ruins, not empty. Another important clue is the word 'darkness' or 'choshek,' for darkness was over your destroyed, ruined world, as a nuclear winter covered the planet at the time. The entire verse describes Saras's chaotic state after the grave Lemurian tragedy some seventy-seven thousand years ago.

"This verse is expanded upon in Jeremiah 4:23, where it states, 'I saw the earth and it was destroyed and in vague ruins, and the heavens had no light. I saw the mountains and they trembled, and all the hills moved swiftly. I saw there was no man, and all the birds of the heavens were gone. I saw that fruitful places were uninhabitable, and all its cities were destroyed.' Thus was Mu devastated, and so remained afterward.

"In the beginning, God did not create Saras wasted and empty as your translations assume. Mankind's sinful activities made it that way. Refer to Isaiah 45:18 where ancient text plainly states that 'He created it not devastated, for He formed it to be inhabited,' thus refuting your Genesis translations.

"You will find an important clue about Saras's age in Job 38:6–7, where it states, 'Who laid Earth's cornerstone, when the morning stars sang together and all the sons of God shouted for joy?' Does it not state that angels residing on Venus and God's cosmic children 'sang together' in brotherhood before your world was formed?"

"I don't understand. Why do people insist that Earth is only six thousand years old and don't read original texts?" the defense minister added.

"They assume that having interpretations is better than none."

"Then what can be said about the real meaning of days in Genesis?"

"While 2 Peter 3:8 states that one day of the Lord is as a thousand years to us, Genesis implies something similar. In the six days of creation, the word 'ereb' does not mean night but dusk. 'Boker' does not mean day but dawn. Hence, dusk to dawn is not a literal day, but a twelve hour evening period described by *pesha shamem*, a Mosaic oil burning vigil in Leviticus 24:2 devoted to desolation transgression and horrific devastation. What awful destruction does it refer to? Daniel's 2,300 dusks and dawns provides the timeline.

"By taking 2,300 prophetic days, times 30 years per day, we arrive at 69,000 years. Add 4,216 years as the year Adam was born, and you arrive at 73,216 BC, about the time of Lemuria's demise. Genesis, Exodus, Leviticus, and Daniel are the only books that directly reference *pesha shamem*."

"I think I'm beginning to get it. I never heard any of that before."

"Six times you rebelled during those days; the seventh brought about your final destruction, and the end of the Garden of Eden."

"Thus, the six days of creation."

"Chronologically, the six days stand for a 60,000-year period ending on the seventh day or about the year 14,861 BC, when Atlantis, the Garden of Eden, descended into the hands of Ly-Dian and the brotherhood was driven from Saras. From Adam's birth on 4,216 BPC [biblical pre-Christ] until the flood on 2,540 BPC, 1,676 years transpired, each counting as three years represented by Noah's three sons. That places the flood at 9,833 BC. From the flood until Joseph's death around 1,877 BPC, 663 years transpired, each counting as twelve years represented by Jacob's twelve sons."

"The biblical flood occurred during Pharaoh Khafra's reign," I added. "Did Khafra die in the flood, was work on his pyramid interrupted, are there Egyptian records confirming the flood took place then? No. Pharaoh Scorpion I and all generations up to Noah lived together around 3,200 BC, refuting historical . . ."

"Can you elaborate on what a dimension is?" Gina said, cutting me off.

"Dimensions are existential planes of reality similar to what you call parallel universes," Meh-Nai said, "except they are discerned by current rates from higher realms rather than paradoxes. Every physical object has endless planes of existence, all with different time structures and spatial properties."

"How do we get to these realities?" asked the space minister. "And what happens when you do? Can you go back in time?"

"If you travel fast enough toward a light, its tint will change to green or even blue, depending on speed. As you do, you intersect past events that would eventually reach you had you stood still; in a way, you are seeing your relative future before it physically reaches you. The opposite is also true; receding from the light is like seeing the past.

"Likewise, as dimensional current rates increase, items about you transform into new forms, future events merge, and time accelerates. For instance, on some Venus spiritual planes, 1,200 years can transpire in a single Saras day. Rate changes can also affect gravity-time relationships [(10)] including

---

(10) $$g = \frac{1}{4\pi^2 x} \sum_{x=\delta_i}^{\delta_f} (f_x^2 \, sin\theta_x) * \frac{1}{n} \sum_{n=\lambda_i}^{\lambda_f} \lambda_n$$ and $$M = \frac{4\pi^2 h}{f\lambda^2} \overset{\Delta}{\rightarrow} \frac{k}{f\lambda^2}$$

Gravitation and relative time calculation of singularity particles, or nodal points, where:
g = particle gravity
h = Planck's constant
θ = EM phase

mass and the G constant. This is not to be confused with relativistic effects, for velocity is subservient to time rates, not the other way around. Regarding time travel, the past is integrated into higher dimensional cycles, a concept we cannot describe to you at this time. All objects have a unique frequency base, or time structure, affecting relative solidity and other properties with each other."

"So what is time really, and can we see the future?" he said.

"Time is the relative sequential speed of existence the mind relates to at a given life instance and dimensional rate. Life, on the other hand, is a page we select from a book we already wrote in time. You are, today, a lone episode in a private existence saga, one of many you already lived, not just in the past but also the future. Thus, past and future events are already written, all linked in higher cyclic forms. The same goes for, say, the life of the sun and its destiny, performing a musical bar at a time in an enormous multi-part symphony already written from beginning to end."

"You mean I already lived future lives, say even a million years from now?"

"This life is only an expression of who you are in linear time, parallel to all other lives. Your real self, where all experiences join as one, is in higher planes; we call that state, the higher self. Negative past experiences express in your conscious linear life; we call that negative state, the lower self."

"Then life is like a dream, a rerun. Man, that's . . . really deep!"

"Life is not destiny but a sequential moment in causal eternity written by many including you, a brief exhale to discard lower experiences and purify our commitment to the Infinite," Dow Uanh said.

"That's just absolutely mind-boggling! But one more question if I may: how does energy come in and out of this plane?"

"In higher planes, energy expresses concurrently in circular non-sequential waves, or cycles, without origin or terminating points," Tei-Ah said. "Other waveforms ride on top of them, adding a variety of causal properties. These propagate in linear time-based fashion only when entering our dimension."

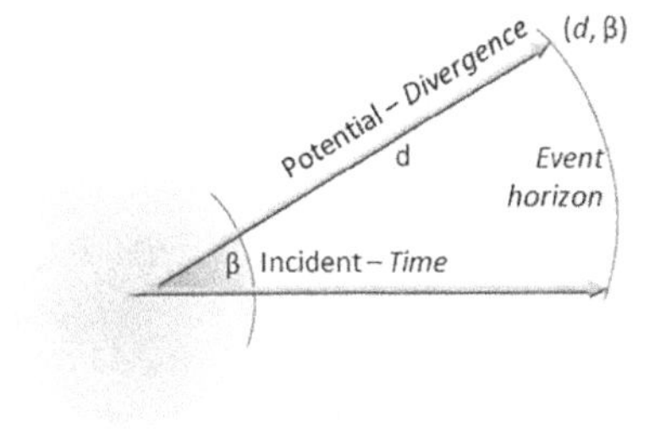

"A cycle is best represented by polar coordinates, and consists of four primary vectors: incidence, divergence, bearing, and concavity. The polar angle 'β' signifies 'incident' or the fourth dimensional equivalent of frequency or time on our plane. The polar length 'd' represents 'divergence' or potential, equivalent to mass, force, and energy, activating Lorentz forces in a cyclic magnetic field. The point [d, β] embodies the cycle's vibrating event horizon, spanning from 0 to 2π radians, in both forward and retrograde motion. Cycles have no space or time but induce them when acted upon by higher dimensional currents."

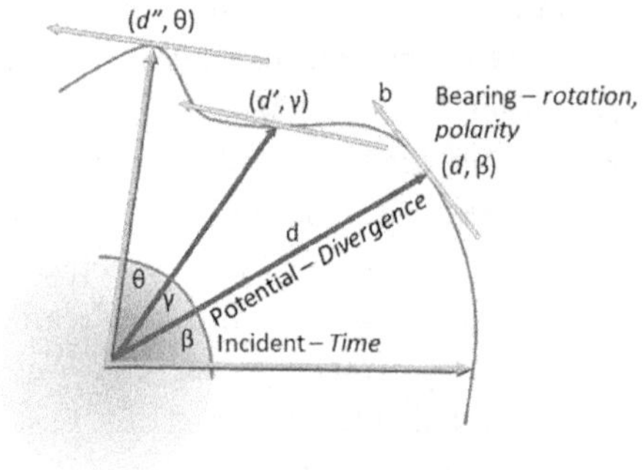

"Vector 'b' tangent to point [d, β] denotes the 'bearing vector' or slope, exhibiting physical properties such as polarity and rotation. Its event horizon creates a toroid magnetic vortex in our plane inducing divergence potential. If the vector's leading edge points into the incident angle, its physical polarity weakens and rotation slows down."

"Vector 'c,' sticking out of the graph on point [d, β], denotes 'concavity' or dimensional sag, the propensity to harmonically align with other cyclic bearing vectors. It represents physical compatibility between elements, chemical, and interactive properties. Concavity is likened to a pancake stack, each of different size and shape. Where their cycles align harmonically, this vector links their event bearings, inducing 'concave' dimensional currents that propagate cyclic energy in the form of vortical magnetic and Lorentz forces into our plane. Linked cycles create the illusion of organized matter on our plane, such as atoms and molecules."

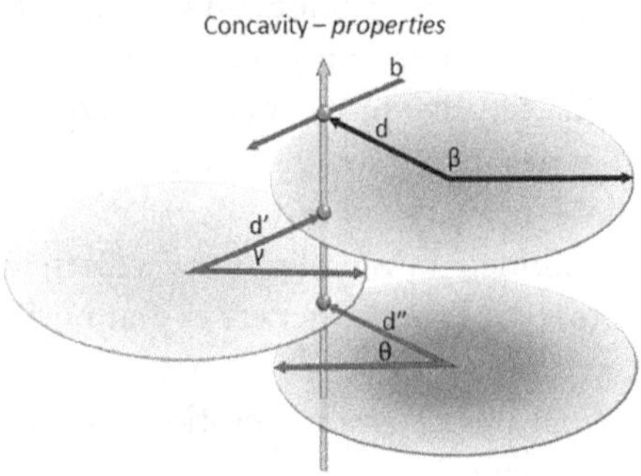

The minister, with a dumbfounded stare, turned to Tei-Ah and said, "Somebody please get me a life jacket, my head's drowning. This is so terribly complex it's hopeless to follow."

"It's complex, but we're not done yet," Meh-Nai said, with a helpless smile.

"There's more? You can't be serious. How can anyone fathom or use these concepts?"

"Your people did long ago, unfortunately for evil," Tei-Ah said. "These concepts are the foundation of all scientific knowledge and the first step in understanding His Majesty's inconceivable grandeur."

"The c vector oscillates in and out of point [d, β] as higher forces act on it. When it does, linked cycles replicate energy patterns unto the vector and transfer their cyclic patterns serially to the physical realm. Concavity current immediately creates two sub-dimensional forces, a compatible duality that makes this plane possible. One is magnetic, turning bearing and event horizon patterns into polarity and rotation. The other is Lorentz, adapting divergence elements into mass, electrical, and mechanical energy. These then combine, forming the four universal forces known as gravitation, electromagnetic, strong, and weak."

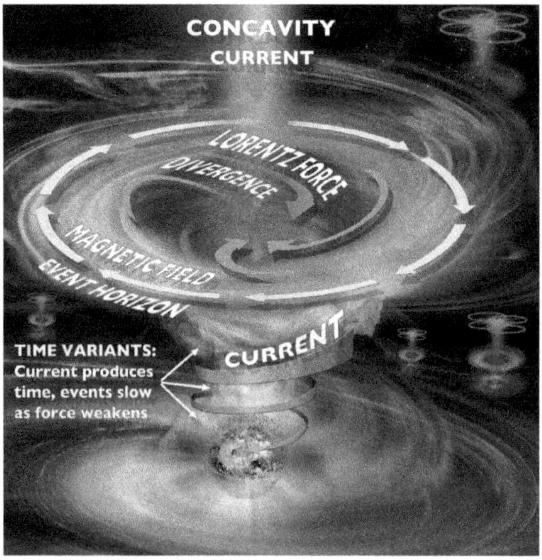

"This replication is what creates time and space in lower-dimensional segments and completely surrounds every energy node. The concavity force originates from higher realms and His Majesty. As the cycle touches your dimension multiple times, particles end up at different spatial reference points. Thus, the semblance of movement."

"Thank you. This will sure give our scientists a great deal to think about."

Gina sat simmering the entire time, hands crossed, and back arched forward in a launching position difficult to mind. She waited tetchily for the minister to back away from the podium, leaning on the edge of her seat to keep others from coming up and asking more questions. As soon as the minister turned to his seat, she quickly stood up and wasted no time spouting off ravenous concerns that she, no doubt, carefully drafted for the moment.

Gina's harsh hastened stride quickly gave away her dissenting objective, driving delegates to suffer a moment of unsolicited terror. Her tone was piercing, intimidating, and hostile, much like a corrective parent bearing down aggressively upon a feeble child, perfectly designed to impress dread and therein suppress imminent response. Confident and arrogant, she stood behind the podium, reviewing anxious Senate delegates with a petrifying closed-lip smile and wide fiery eyes that, like a poised cobra, awakened every heart's worst fears.

"I find your romantic notions awful hard to shoulder!" she said sharply, setting off bold roars in the Senate floor. "How can our people be ready for contact when we're so vastly dissimilar in every way? And whatever gave you the right to imprudently invite yourselves to this session, only to brag about your successes without prior merit or the least discretion? Quite frankly, your unprovoked, imposing behavior and cunning use of language clearly reveals explicit intent to take over our planet, not help us!" she said loudly and overly emotional, theatrical of course, not minding rudeness the least bit.

Delegates mumbled in response to her bold defiant frontage, though afraid to make comments that might further inflame her delivery. The chancellor turned pale and burst into sweats, struck by mental paralysis and deep shame. Her manners did not surprise me at all; this was the Gina I knew from college days. I never thought her capable of such outright malice, for surely she spoke completely out of context with reality and for private reasons difficult to mind.

"Your words prove you have absolutely no clue how to approach our people, or care to either, and hence are a grave risk to Earth! Note how intimidating this information seems to us; just imagine how the general public will react to any of it!" she spewed, firmly and intense, like a dictator.

"People out there fear for their lives," she said sternly, competing rigidly against persistent Senate chatter, "so why give them more to worry about? If this knowledge gets out on the street, I can assure you the general public will deem it heresy, faiths will crumble, order will collapse, maniacs will use it against us, and that will mean the end of civilization as we know it! You don't need to conquer us; we can do it for you, simply by making this information public! Isn't that what you're after?

"In my opinion, this cosmic alliance is a dangerous endeavor to embark upon, puts all our peace initiatives at risk, and cannot be allowed to stand without first establishing strict safety protocols and select points of contact. We need to stop, take a step back, rethink our approach to mutual relations, and proceed cautiously and only upon Earth gov-approved conditions."

Gina's words imparted a sense of verity, although presented in a manner less than virtuous. No one challenged her back, partly due to her stinging, coarse parlance that everyone was already familiar with. The Senate seemed disarmed by her frightening poise and startling claims. Her manners purposely faltered the mind, such that freedom from her appalling grip seemed futile. She moved her head about and spoke quickly, boasting vast assurance and inimitable skills in delivering swift humiliation to anyone daring to speak up.

"I hereby set forth a motion that the vast knowledge gap between our people must first be abridged before we can safely proceed with normalized relations," Gina said confidently. "Voluntarily helping to close that gap, in good faith, is the best means for your people to earn merit with us. Toward that goal, any future bilateral information sharing must be subject to an agreed to, closely monitored process, and specific engagement terms defined by our government. Unless that happens, we risk civil betrayal and mislaying centuries of peaceful attainment."

Dow Uanh gently rose to his feet and addressed the Senate thusly, "Don't misjudge our motives. It is by His request, not ours, that we came among you. Your abrupt gap assessment is born entirely from your own autocratic tendencies, and only Father can close it. Surely, you cannot impose terms upon Him, much less while you're trapped in the gap itself. Father will close this gap when He deems it appropriate. Until then, we must be patient and safeguard knowledge that, before its time, can potentially be used for evil.

"Those who would willingly betray His Majesty are few in numbers, and we know who they are. They will once more unite as one concerted voice, convince people they are not ready to join the brotherhood, and endeavor to involve us in the affairs of decadent groups solely to acquire technology, something we will never do. His Majesty's orders are to work directly with Earth gov, not compromised committees detached from this government."

I was both surprised and glad to hear Dow Uanh say this, corroborating the information I gathered from Beta. He then turned to Gina and calmly said, "There are many organizations trying to abolish Earth gov by less than ethical means; we know of them. They hope to obtain knowledge from us and once again become a space power—this we won't allow. If you forbid your people access to the universal laws, you leave them little choice but follow errant directives. Would you have your people live like mindless drones in a world struggling for power and governed by the lower self?"

"Perhaps," Gina said with predetermined, unwavering resolve, "but that's your opinion! We know what's best for our people, not you. If you don't mind, we prefer to handle our own affairs without foreign, correction, unmerited alien intervention." Gina appeared ready for sustained debate by whatever means necessary, and she was real good at it—detestable and overbearing to say the least.

"You will be given a fair opportunity to help our world, based on appraised Earth gov needs and conditions; I suggest you take the deal when offered. Moving forward, restrictions will be re-evaluated and reduced based on your level of proven cooperation and success with our due processes. You did say something about a prime directive of non-interference, right?"

"You're still holding Saras hostage after so many eons," Dow Uanh said calmly.

"Protecting Earth is more like it," she said. "I invite your people to work with us, on our terms. I'd hate to see you back down because, now that we're friends and know of each other's whereabouts, it would be a real shame, perhaps even risky, to part ways. Don't you agree?"

"Gina, did you just threaten our guests?" remarked Yato.

"On the contrary, Mr. Secretary. I do believe that our friends, by exposing themselves, may have placed their abodes at risk. This is something they should have appraised, including our true needs, when they first established contact. This government cannot possibly anticipate those who would mean them harm or be expected to protect them from same."

Gina's gaze left no doubt she staunchly meant what she said, daring anyone to openly challenge her. She held the upper hand in the Senate, and no one dared speak up to her. I began to wonder if this was Beta, the same person I heard talking to Hans, but the likelihood of it was so remote I quickly shelved the idea. It seemed this conference was over, but the Brothers wisely knew what buttons to push to help dissolve Gina's dreadful onslaught: mine.

Tei-Ah smiled as if she kept a critical secret from us. On the other hand, Gina's expression showed signs of irritation, perhaps because the Brothers did not go quietly into the night as she expected. "Dear sister," Tei-Ah replied.

"I'm not your sister, but go on," Gina said sarcastically.

"Your plans won't stage peaceful co-existence among your people, much less end political turmoil, but rather bring about your world's demise. The Infinite is your only hope. We won't interfere with your affairs, of course, but highly encourage you to seek Father for answers, not your legacy. We'll wait until the day you allow us to work directly with Earth gov, not a committee."

The Brothers avoided prolonged debate with Gina, giving her a chance to divulge her real intentions unimpeded. Across the way, Tei-Ah's message stirred my heart and an irresistible urge to say something boiled up a storm. Then suddenly, the word "speak" burst clearly into my mind, but I was not sure what to say or when.

"When you're gone," Gina replied, "we will remain here dealing with issues you started. We have everything to lose and assume all risk. Hence, I propose we suspend this conference, develop structured goals to help close this gap, and renew talks in the near future involving only select members of Earth gov. This will ensure appropriate cooperation between our worlds while meeting Earth gov terms and expectations. Do we have any dissenting views?"

Few if any delegates were willing to confront Gina's motion; even the chancellor had a withdrawn, stunned look on his face. Hans seemed pleased with the resolution, as were the social and justice ministers, slightly nodding to each other as silence reigned supreme in the vast hall. No one was ready for this and for the most part had little choice but follow along with Gina's resolution for now.

"Delegates, you have a motion before you. All those in favor, indicate so now," Gina said. The Brothers remained motionless while delegates considered the motion. Green ballot lights sprung up above delegate stations in favor of the motion, slowly increasing in number. The number of favorable votes went up without opposition, closing in on majority acceptance for passing: 1,600 assenting votes.

Emotions ran high with me, and time was of the essence; the vote count climbed quickly. Gina threatened to turn opinion tides against the Brothers, and no one was doing anything about it, but what could I do? Gina's overall despotic theme fit tightly in line with the Order's objectives, something I dared not discuss. I briefly turned to Hans and noticed a slight grin helplessly growing on his face. Something told me he had to be part of this; else why was the questionnaire entrusted to him in the first place?

Unsure what to say, I suddenly stood up and asked permission to speak. Hans thought I had lost it for good and quickly asked me to sit down, but I paid no attention to him. Gina noted my request and gladly asked me to proceed, preparing to engage me in debate.

It was just like old times, a repeat of my devastating defeat to Gina back in college, and I knew it—standing up without a clue, moved by emotive purpose to her preset conditions. I was now on the spot, unsure what to do, playing right into her hands. She knew I had turned myself into her lethal game, and waited patiently for me to take the next fatal step.

I felt May Len mentally tell me 'no,' so I paused for a moment and thought about what she meant. "Don't make other's problems your own," I heard her tell me with a smile. "Don't be like her. Be with us, not your fears. Don't let your emotions scare or frustrate you," she said, somewhat putting me at ease.

Amid mental numbness, keeping May Len in mind, I made things up along the way, trying to avoid past mistakes. Meanwhile, the Brothers lowered their heads and offered no feedback to the ongoing conflict between us, although their previous comments gave me the fortitude I needed to face Gina.

"Member delegates, for the good of our world, I strongly encourage you to please stop and reassess your support for this reckless motion set before you. Decline it immediately, considering the serious consequences it shall bring."

"Dr. Sullivan, you should have said something when you had the chance," she said with triumphal flair. "It's too late. The motion has reached majority approval and passed Senate deliberation; it's now legal and binding."

"Laws are made to be challenged, and as our Brothers clearly pointed out, they are here to work with Earth gov, not some obscure inquisitional panel loaded with biased agendas," I said confidently. "By the time this committee agrees on engagement terms, the ETA will be running the planet. What's the use of having it? Seriously ask yourselves. Why divest Earth gov of its duties and arrogantly insult our guests, except to ensure our demise and cause all delegates their jobs?" In concert, delegates stood up in fervent applause, much relieved to hear a positive tone, however meek, going against a terrifying, calculative Gina ready for a counter offensive.

"Would you care to elaborate on your rather vague observation, Dr. Sullivan?" said Gina mockingly, reassured by her motion's approval. "I fail to see what your assumptions have to do with this approved motion."

"With all due respect, I take fervent issue with your baseless notions, clearly devised on the spur of the moment solely to ram this hideous initiative by force, as its merits in no way prove creditable otherwise. Not to mention, I am appalled by the rude oblique assessment you've tendered our guests, born from nothing less than some hidden agenda unable to survive in the open on its own. Truth needs no emotion to be right!" I said while delegates rumbled, surprised to witness my coarse assessment of Gina's behavior in public.

"Dr. Sullivan clearly demonstrates he's not a diplomat," Gina replied sarcastically, though achieving few if any compulsory humor from delegates. "Anyone dealing with matters of such importance must act promptly and put accurate critical reasoning into practice. That's why we're here, and you're not. I'll make sure it stays that way!"

"Good thing you brought up diplomacy. Please note that you, and you alone, assumed that higher knowledge will cause Earth's demise. No one in this hall upheld such wrongful exaggerated opinions, unable to offer rebuttal after being steamrolled by hostile mental warfare. Truth, in itself, needs no help from attitude to be convincing. Today, you've used attitude and hostility to daze the Senate, mask deceit, and push it through as if truth."

"We have seasoned professionals in this hall that practice critical thinking, respected intellects that know when to speak up and work well under pressure, unlike someone I know. So don't insult or undermine my delegates, if that's your intent! Will that be all, Dr. Sullivan?"

"I beg to differ with such careless judgment, discernments aimed to wound verity with baseless sensationalism, and therein forcefully divest the Senate's chances to criticize your proposal. The part about insulting your delegates, may I clearly assert that your harsh posture—no, I beg your pardon—rather, your excessive display of belligerent, arrogant thinking already took care of that!" Delegates quickly came to their feet in roaring applause, while Gina fumed on the podium unsure what to say.

"Delegates, you've been wrongly led to believe that knowledge will bring chaos, that you're not qualified to lead our people into a new age of discovery; and you're fine with that? I find that hard to believe! If anyone in this room feels that a committee is better suited for these tasks, then I seriously question your ability to lead the United Earth Federation of Free States, and I beg you immediately resign your charters on grounds of incompetence! Please, prove me wrong," I said, raising my voice to further applause.

"Dr. Sullivan," Hans said loudly, "you're out of line! You can't dictate protocol, and you're out of order with the Speaker."

"Why would you have me silenced, Hans?" I said. "I have nothing to hide. But do you?"

"We don't need your poetic ramble! I order you to sit down and shut your mouth!" he said.

"Anyone want me silenced besides Hans?" I asked, pausing for a moment, but no one made a sound. "Why am I not surprised? The Brothers clearly said they'll work only through Earth gov, not a committee: your committee will meet alone. Think about it. You won't get that committee spun up in time to save Earth, the Brothers won't meet with a committee, so what's the point of having it? Allow the ETA to take over your jobs? Is that what you want?"

"Dr. Sullivan, may I remind you that the Brothers abandoned us back in Atlantis?" Gina said, with renewed confidence. "What makes you think they won't do so again? If this is how they pretend to help us, I'd rather make peace with the enemy and avoid future bloodshed."

"Careful now, Madam Speaker. Review of historical material reveals no evidence—let me repeat, no evidence—of brotherhood abandonment. Instead, we turned our backs on them, just as we're doing here today! But just to be sure, I submit to review the entire presentation, right now, to closely scrutinize history and place blame where it truly belongs!"

"That will not be necessary, Dr. Sullivan," she said, somewhat uncertain of where she was going with her reply. "We must resolve the issue at hand in our own manner. A resolution stands approved to move this process along according to due process WS12-24, applicable in these situations, and I suggest we get moving, and you sit down."

"Even though the Brothers won't show up to your meeting? Something doesn't add up here. Why insist on something that won't work? Do you want this process to fail, and Earth to fall into the hands of the ETA?"

"Eventually, the Brothers will come to our meetings. It's in their best interest to do so," she said, breathing slowly to avoid irritation from showing. Gina's primary strategy was to frustrate me into emotional debate, but I refused to give in.

"Delegates, there you have it. Is eventually fast enough? Restrictive participation will lead to less-than-honest terms. History proves it! Committees are typically influenced, if not controlled by, need I say, special interests, meaning in our case, ETA agents."

"This has nothing to do with special interest," she said, becoming rather upset. "Don't derail due process by introducing doubt into government protocol as a means to your ends, for rather, it would seem you have a special interest in this matter yourself, and it's sitting down there to my right."

"No kidding, please single someone out in this hall that doesn't! We must not yield decision-making powers to a select, possibly corrupt, few. If we do, then Earth gov's demise will be assured! Besides, there's no time for a committee, and Brothers won't attend it. So I ask again, why insist in failure?"

"Your conspiracy theory bears no substance! Committees are common UEF practice and ideal forums to analyze impacts to Earth establishments. As our guest, you have exercised sufficient intrusion into our proceedings, and no further comments from you will be permitted!"

"I insist the Senate be allowed to decide Earth's future, not you or your compromised committees!" I replied loudly, marginally overstepping my bounds in front of the podium. "Is there any evidence suggesting the Brothers are aggressive, their knowledge a security risk, and trust a concern, thus forcing us to implement this nonsensical committee? Convince us, Madam Speaker. Present evidence, not opinions. Otherwise, let the Senate do the job it was sanctioned to do!" Coming to their feet, delegates roared and applauded, further tormenting an already fuming Gina at the podium.

"Dr. Sullivan, you are circumventing and interrupting government proceedings," Gina said agitated. "This session will adjourn on basis of contempt, and I'm placing you under arrest! Hans, see to it that Dr. Sullivan is restrained and stripped of MTC obligations immediately!"

"Yes, Madam Speaker. With pleasure! It's about time!" replied Hans.

"Please strike that last allegation from final redaction on grounds of impropriety. Hans, hold your place!" Yato said, suddenly coming up to the podium. "Madam Speaker, I want you to understand that Dr. Sullivan is absolutely right about everything. Dr. Sullivan, I see where you're going with this, but can you briefly recap it?"

"Mr. Secretary, with this approved motion in hand . . ." Gina said quickly, and quite agitated.

"He's right about that too. We can strike it down any moment, and honestly, I find it rather suspicious that you, Madam Speaker, are not familiar with the law. Is that the case?" Gina stood speechless, uncertain what to say. "Your silence is golden, so why don't you keep it that way for a while? In the meantime, Dr. Sullivan, please proceed—uninterrupted, that is."

"Mr. Secretary, I propose that Earth gov, not a committee, lead future diplomatic efforts with the Brothers, and I ask Madam Speaker to back up her baseless claims with indisputable evidence; that's due process, and the law!"

"That's most fitting, and legal. Madam Speaker, and your response is?"

"Evidence will be gathered by the proposed committee and presented to the Senate through proper channels," Gina said calmly. "That's not the aim of this body, and you know it, Dr. Sullivan!"

"Without evidence, you have no grounds to form a committee and divest the Senate of its powers, and that *is* the law!" I replied. "Quote a regulation that counters this mandate!"

"That's enough," she yelled, finally breaking down angrily. "We're beyond that, and this session is now officially closed!"

"Scuff that order. It's not closed!" Yato said, demonstrating firmness. "Madam Speaker, get a grip. Dr. Sullivan, as an appointed MTC committee delegate, is within his right to counter propose, and he's right about the law. Your actions, demonstrated contempt of due process, and disregard for senatorial law leads me to question your competence and integrity as leader of the world Senate. This makes me think that you have been deeply compromised, and therefore your resignation is due immediately. Did I reach this conclusion in error?"

"Sir, I'm just doing my job," Gina said, proudly stern.

"The way you're acting, I'm not so sure. In the last fifteen minutes, you've violated more Senate regulations and quoted from the *Encyclopedia Bruttanica* more times than I can count. This is not the type of leadership I hired you for, so shape up, or ship out. Do you read me?"

"For all we know," she said, "this could all be a clever scam to turn members against us and take over the planet. Who are these people? Are we ready to openly trust them? How are world members going to react to their beliefs once . . .?"

"Gina!" Yato interrupted loudly. "For every imaginable sake! Another baseless claim from you and you're fired! That's it! With their technology, they don't need to play games! On the other hand, I find Bill's proposal reasonable and legitimate." Gina remained silent stiff, though anger noticeably draped across her face. "Bill, anything else you want to add?"

"A committee, infiltrated by ETA partisans, exposed to alien technology, eventually turned on Earth gov," I pressed, raising my voice above growing rumble. "You're smarter than you've been made out to be! Protect your families, vote this initiative down, now!"

The Senate roared a loud, combined 'yes,' causing Gina to go numb on the podium. As I spoke, Gina and Hans looked at each other, trading eye rolls and slight nods, a facial language I didn't understand but clearly denoting they were associates.

"Madam Speaker, you have your answer. Do you question the integrity and competence of these delegates?" I asked, but she did not reply. "About that evidence you need to provide, now would be a good time! As you previously mentioned, an approved resolution to move this process along must be vetoed according to due process WS12-24, applicable in these situations. I suggest we get moving, and you sit down!"

Gina and I stared at one another for some time in visual impasse amid unstoppable applause. The ball was now in Gina's court, to debate or not, but she wasn't throwing it back. I was certain she would do everything in her power to have it her way, expecting an even worst payload coming my way any second. I felt like David facing Goliath, insignificant and for the most part unarmed. Delegates were on edge aware of what we were both up to, cheering ever louder to counter Gina's onslaught in some small humble squall.

No one had ever confronted Gina publicly and survived politically to tell about it. All eyes were on her, waiting to see what she would come up with. Surprisingly, she retracted from the podium and took her eyes from me, breathing deeply in discontent. She did not seem pleased with the outcome but nevertheless thought it best to score positive at this time by appearing impartial to the process.

A slight murmur developed in the Senate hall. Everyone sat back in their seats and sighed in relief, knowing Gina would not counter attack. "Excellent response, Dr. Sullivan," she said, "representing the highest values put forth by our founding fathers. I'm certain your response was well received by delegates. I motion to consider your proposal and retract the previous motion. All those in favor of Dr. Sullivan's resolution, please be counted."

Instantly, the entire delegation stood on its feet, marking their approval with a loud shout and an outstanding round of applause, no doubt, to relieve stress. Gina, amid loud cheering, announced the resolution unanimously passed. While Sean shouted several cheers my way, Hans did not seem partial to my success, which didn't surprise me. Interestingly, the social and justice ministers did not seem pleased with the vote either, giving me the impression they too had a hand in promoting Gina's failed motion.

May Len turned toward me, smiled, and nodded affirmative as I reverently bowed to my sweet star literally exhausted from my ordeal. She seemed pleased, and I much relieved from it all, but did not explain why such hostile exchange took place. Nevertheless, we were back on track, at least for now. But unexpectedly, she mentally said with a smile, "You are my brave captain," something I had no clue what it meant.

Recovering from her previous rigid stance, Gina stood at the podium as if she had done nothing wrong and said to the Brothers, "I hope you understand that I'm doing my job."

"We don't judge, only love you," May Len said. "We are, old friends."

Gina's eyes suddenly pounced upon May Len with burning rejection the likes of a plodding demon, breathing deeply with a vile grin slowly coursing across her face inspiring nothing less than absolute dread. "Of course we are," she said slowly, grimly, despicably behind a fake sarcastic smile, spewing foul scent from every pore in her soul and enough hatred to make even the most valiant of men tremble. "I'll keep that in mind, old friend. We'll . . . catch up the next time we meet," she said in a canny tone hard to dismiss.

"The future be upon us," May Len replied courteously.

"Sure, whatever. Let's move on," she said, cold and apathetic as before. "Why can't we remember previous lives but feel the effects?"

"If you feel it, you remember it," Meh-Nai said.

"How can I recall the past?" the social minister asked.

"You must keep in mind that recalls are for medicinal purposes and the intent must be virtuous. The past is always with you and it will manifest itself through dreams, desires, and reactions because it's you."

"And when I do, what then?"

"Become aware of your past, accept, learn, and dismiss it. Don't beat yourself by what you sense, but rather learn from it for it's a lesson."

"And if people don't want to learn, what do you do with them?" the justice said rather carelessly and cold.

"There's a plan 'B' as you term it: expulsion from planetary societies."

"Fair enough. Now, what does it feel like to die. Does it hurt?"

"Upon transition," Tei-Ah said, "organs shut down, the body goes numb, and the mind momentarily sleeps without pain, but then your spiritual senses calmly activate, ensuring existential continuity without fear."

"Ministers, let's follow the pro forma, please. We're taking way too much time and it's getting late," Gina said stonily. "How are your worlds governed?"

"The Infinite is our guide, higher masters of light our teachers, and planetary councils our advisors. Each planet is represented in a system tribunal where Saras is not a member. Each system is then represented in a galactic conclave, a gathering so vast that participants must attend in various inter-dimensional levels. There are also high spiritual realms and conclaves that we individually attend on a regular basis but only in spirit form."

"What must we do to participate in these tribunals?" the space minister asked.

"You must withstand Father's essence and conduct spiritual business telepathically. An undeveloped being could transition in the presence of such energy, but there's much you can achieve at your current development stage. As your people evolve spiritually, they will be more compatible with extra-planetary activities."

The room suddenly roared with mumbled discussion relative to a surging subject, embarrassing to say the least. Taking a leadership role, the chancellor stood up and addressed the Brothers with obvious tact. "My Brothers, how far in advance are you from us?"

"Each world is in a different state of evolution," Meh-Nai said. "We don't encourage rivalry between worlds by establishing expectations. Rather, souls reside in compatible worlds and dimensions according to their measure of love and spiritual purity. Some are so high up we can't begin to conceive them. In our system, your world is the least developed. Energy seeks frequency equilibrium. So just as your current spiritual energy is not conducive to higher levels of expression, neither will these be to yours. Forcing coexistence could be catastrophic to both our worlds."

"Can you give us a reasonable guess, by how many years we're behind?"

"While we don't deem it proper to measure progress by years," Dow Uanh said, "your world is, in relationship to Mars, hundreds of thousands of years behind in both spiritual and technological development."

"That much?" said the chancellor rather surprised. "We're . . . cave men!"

"But that can change in the blink of an eye. Compatibility is in the heart."

Healthy mumble roared throughout the Senate hall, no doubt from deflated egos visualizing the vast chasm separating our worlds. It should have come as no surprise, yet it is our nature to helplessly practice denial.

"Your world chose to live in seclusion, far removed from His Majesty. You wanted power over the masses and souls to play God with, not truth. Therefore, you evolved backward. Those responsible for this crime are alive today. Under them, you will never live in peace. They are doing everything possible to keep us from reaching you and reversing your downward course."

May Len then stood up, and all eyes attentively captured her radiant being in unavoidable admiration while dead silence permeated the Senate hall. She spoke selectively and cautiously, imparting a meaningful message to uproot delegate concerns. "Saras want first place, same problem as before. You need knowledge how this problem come and who. See Saras history we show. That is problem. People come back to destroy, reliving history. You can stop reliving and make Saras like Masar."

"Work you need, for many years, but take first step, Accept error, and forgive you. Feeling fear takes longer; longer wait makes more fear. In Masar were like you and worried to progress. With patience, we learn to grow." She paused for a brief moment and then humorously said, "On Saras you say, 'No pain, no gain,'" causing delegates to chuckle and remove much tension. "We want you to gain more. We will help make pain less."

Filled with renewed confidence, the chancellor stood up after a brief moment and spoke in a tender, profound tone, "May Len, you're right; we've been enslaved by monsters and given death as reward. We all witnessed an unprecedented pattern of destruction from your history clip and realized just how much time we've wasted, how much human sacrifice has been for not."

"My great-grandfather fought in the last war and said that war is a game played with people's lives, by individuals that have nothing better to do, and possess no better intellectual faculties. Earth wants peace and prosperity, not war, but there are those that persuade and confuse the masses against reason."

May Len gently turned my way and added with sweet resolve, never taking her eyes from mine, even after she finished speaking, "You win with truth, not force. We want you to forever be our friend, brother. We have hope in you."

"If you have hope in us, then yes, we will prevail," he said, picking up dynamic momentum and tearing up Gina's questionnaire. "We don't need all them questions; they'll be answered in time because you, Brothers, will forever be by our side and never again be told to part—never! If my cabinet approves it, for the betterment of our people, then by the power vested in this cabinet, this administration pledges to forge ahead and make this cosmic alliance a reality by all means possible. Please help us conquer that evil propensity that has clouded our lives for so long. Delegates, are you with us?"

Delegates and ministers stood up and fervently applauded the chancellor's commitment as a vote of confidence. Gina technically applauded, but her heart definitely was not in it. She rose from her seat just as slow as her clap, wearing the only stiff face in the room. Behind her, the justice and social ministers also seemed stiffened to the chancellor's motion; figured.

Tears helplessly rolled down Dow Uanh's cheeks all the way to his neck, afore a most gentle gaze born from inner joy far from human. Surely, he had long waited this decisive moment, and his jubilation showed. It was hard to tell if his gaze was one of triumph or knowledge of things to come, good or bad. One thing was certain: the Brothers had started something I could not see the end of but had an unnerving feeling about it.

I suddenly felt a warm wave of calm rush through me as if someone told me not to worry. Across the way, May Len continued to smile at me, welcomed by my racing heart.

"Do you love my soul, friend, brother?" she said mentally. This time, I knew she was trying to clue me unto something, but I knew not what it was.

I looked puzzled at her, but she replied with a kind smile and did not proceed to eradicate my ambiguity. What secret did this hold? I had no clue.

My personal quest to solve the "friend, brother" riddle would have to wait another time. For now, Earth gov enjoyed the moment's success, inspired by a new progressive cosmic future.

---

[1] Wikipedia.org, "Wikipedia - Cosmic Pluralism," [Online]. Available: en.wikipedia.org/wiki/cosmic_pluralism. [Accessed 26 July 2012].

[2] R. W. J. Morford, "Genesis 1:2," in *The One New Man Bible*, Travelers Rest, SC: True Potential Publishing Co., 2011.

Chapter 13: *Discipline Is Survival*

Tumultuous praise and last-moment festal prattle gradually faded into much-welcomed stupor, restfully paving the way for deferential stillness to grace the vast hall. But as the Senate came to order, a compelling sense of veiled stress feebly consumed those obliged to Saras's cosmic potential. Doubt strained to gain priority over faith and rightfully so as the root of all ignorance was clearly exposed for what it was—simply put, human, rather than spiritual reliance.

It was a most trying time for legislative wiseacres. The World Senate, alleged pride and epitome of civic attainment, was humbled by a devastating sense of inexplicable conjecture and limited intellectual capacity, fittingly encouraged by a growing sense of triviality before the vast girth of creation and the eternal depths of spiritual evolution. Even so, no other marvel captivated the galaxy's bastion of conceit like the virtuous splendors revealed by beings that achieved mastery over themselves and admired the light.

And thus, there we stood, with hearts sunk humbly and minds bowed like repentant children wondering what to do next, standing speechless before sons of truth that thrived in the righteous life-giving waters of an all-wise Infinite Consciousness.

Given the subliminal mind is a hard thing to detain, the Brothers stressed the importance of informing members of these contacts sooner rather than later. Otherwise, news of alien contact might proliferate in less-than-trustworthy ways. From a spiritual perspective, Dow Uanh saw this as a good problem to have, only if Earth gov honestly strived to prepare members for change and upheld truth at all cost, for truth is the voice of the Infinite.

Plans quickly fell into place. The chancellor would deliver a message to the world on the state of alien affairs the following day. Secretary Yato wisely proposed information campaigns, noting how critical it was to inform, trust, and encourage people on the subject. Tei-Ah suggested a craft landing at UEF Headquarters to symbolize official discussions with Earth gov and turn back ETA tides, heralded by massive alien fly-bys worldwide starting in two days—offers overwhelmingly accepted by the Senate.

Before parting, Dow Uanh shared the following words for us to reflect upon, "Be patient with yourself and receptive to Father. Show people how to live the universal way, and remember, your survival depends on discipline."

The Brothers slowly vanished from sight, but unexpectedly, May Len remained behind. From beneath the steps leading to the podium, she humbly panned the Senate and caringly smiled at applauding assembly members. But then, she turned my way and fixed her brilliant amber jewels upon me. My heart briefly skipped, grateful to be granted the unexpected opportunity to share a few highly anticipated moments with her.

Joyful beyond grasp and silently admiring her radiant, captivating smile, I slowly bowed and passionately uttered, "*Ezi ceneh inah, sar ti ima-eh, pavi ezi dari,*" meaning 'My beautiful sister, flower from the heavens, joy of my heart.'"

Everyone in the vast hall looked on, guarding reverent silence, aware that this was our moment to openly share and all to witness. Gina rapidly turned away and dashed for her chair rashly distressed, intensely crushing what remained of the pro forma.

With graceful, humbly measured steps, she elegantly walked my way to heart's deepest yearning until arm's length from the other. She warmly curled my hands unto her own, and her lips tenderly bestowed the gift of loving song, stirring my suspenseful being with celestial majesty, "My brave captain, my friend, brother. You never stop thinking of me or sharing your heart. All Saras people should be friends, like we are." She then gently placed a light kiss on my cheek as delegates cheered, but Gina seethed in obvious discontent.

I had so much to share with May Len that my thoughts struggled for priority. But when least expected, a rather meaningful expression came out of nowhere, and I verbalized it with feelings so caring and intense that my heart felt as if it was being torn apart, "May Len, would you walk beside me and share of His Majesty's many creations? *Deh oneh ezi nedeeh men.* You are my only, friend."

May Len's face glowed like morning sunburst, releasing tears with untold joy as I raised her hand above my shoulders in humble respect. She slowly took my hands to her lips well surprised, gently kissed them, then embraced me warmly repeating the phrase "You remember" several times. Delegates stood on their feet and cheered us loudly; but Gina, on the other hand, slapped hands to the hips and sat with an obvious scowl on her face, nodding in evident disapproval.

"May the future be upon us, and my search for love lead me to the light in your heart," I said, bowing before her.

May Len slowly released me, stepped back lightly joyful as ever, and replied, "My heart is light from Manéh," she said to nearby delegates. "It is joy to have with brother that . . . takes my hand over his heart. I want this friendship to last infinite." With these words, she kissed my cheek and slowly vanished, along with couches and Sean's cam. Conversely, we turned solid and remained on Saras to a long round of cheering and applause.

Gina, pleased to see May Len gone, closed the session, and all delegates promptly lined up to greet us on the way out of the Senate hall. Hans called up Masar, put someone temporarily in charge of C6, and vanished without saying good-bye—quite upset, of course. Sean and Yato got together and took off, no doubt to have a real meal.

Meanwhile, I had an old friend to pay tribute to. From the podium, Gina moved her head diagonally and asked me to come up, but to my luck, the chancellor jumped in front of her and came my way. "Honorable chancellor," I said with respect, "it's indeed a pleasure to meet . . ."

"Bill, cut the crap and get up here!" he said, sharing a strong bear-style hug I'm still recovering from. "It's sure good to see you. Look, you call me chancellor again, and I'm going to bust your chops."

Jim was an open, outgoing individual in his late forties but didn't act his age. When I asked him to sign my petition for entry into Space Core, he just about fell off his chair and lectured me for hours why I shouldn't go through with it, insisting my talents were best applied on Saras and not some barren world, a prophecy that failed to bear its mark in the end.

The day I departed for Masar, he staunchly said, "No offense, but I don't believe in apes. Your kind thinks I came from those damned things. Since no one's ever seen them turn human, I refuse to think of myself as some malformed, freak simian. Whatever you find up there, I hope it's not a son of a chimp." In a way, I would go on to greatly disappoint him.

"Hey, I have to tell you something. I think May Len has it for you," he said with notable fervor, reviving Gina's vile scowl.

At the mention of May Len, Gina suddenly barged in front of Jim and asserted her unsolicited presence. "Is this not the Bill I used to debate with years back?" she said.

"I take it you guys know each other from way back," he said.

"All too well, I'm afraid," I replied.

"Bill was my, shall we say, protégé back in college."

"I'm sure," I replied sarcastically. "All too willing to have one?"

"You must admit debating was not one of your key strong points, or was it education in general? I can't quite recall."

"Debating and arguing are two quite different talents," I replied, "but some people have a real problem distinguishing them apart."

"Interpretation is in the ear of the beholder or the mind, whichever is less in your case."

"There are those who have ears but don't truly attempt to use them. A classic example of this goes something like—to have, but not to care?"

"Why, of course, the disciplined mind can easily detect the absence of legitimacy and the promotion of ignorance. It's quite an unfortunate happenstance to embezzle valuable time from accomplished intellects by entertaining substandard forms of thought," she said.

"Supposed intellects are limited by the level of discipline instilled," I said. "What pity it is to purposely discard viewpoints just because they don't fit the finite mold of imperfectly matured, feebly rounded, self-deluded individuals."

"A thought like that can be a terrible thing to mind. Without discipline, there can be no structured development and therefore no common order."

"Efforts to maintain consciousness on a daily basis are short lived by available worthless disciplines and asserters of intellectuality. The entire world is permeated with the foul stench of superiority complexes, striving to detour reason through deterrent logic. Such errant disciplines alienate inspiration and stifle true expression."

"Wickedness and rancor are close relatives," she said. "They produce such discord they can't even get along most of the time."

"I know that you realistically suppose you fully comprehend what you thought I said, but I'm not so sure you realize that what you heard is not necessarily what I meant," I replied.

Gina went silent for the longest time trying to decipher what I said. Unable to, she replied with a stiffened attitude, "Not bad for someone who curtly shut me up today . . ."

"Goodness gracious, hold up guys before you start another world war," Jim said. "What the hell did you guys really do in college anyways? Intellectual jousting? Vocal wrestling?"

"Would you believe social science?" I said.

"Holy smokes!"

"It's what you might call dictional brawling at a professional level."

"You call that acting professional? I change my mind; I'm not putting my kids through college."

"Gina and I met back in college and got along, some of the time. All kidding aside, I owe most of my academic achievements to her. She was perhaps the most important reason I made it through the institution."

"You two really flaunted some highly emotive clash today. Hold on. I've got to talk to an advisor before she leaves; I'll be right back," Jim said, running off and leaving us alone for a few moments. No sooner, Gina's plastic smile melted away and her dreadful scowl draped hastily upon her countenance, viciously staring my way.

"That was some nasty stunt you pulled," she said serious and stone cold, slapping my face harshly. "After all I did for you, I didn't believe you capable of such callous mockery. Way to pay me back!"

"I had every legal right to speak my mind. Why, were my comments inconvenient to your ends, Madam Speaker?" I replied.

"You really, really pissed me off like you have no idea! Did you know that?" Gina said, displaying signs of outright irritation.

"*Enchanté, mademoiselle.* Don't forget, it was you that asked for it."

"I did, you say? I was doing my job, and all was going well when you, without reason or provocation, brutally ridiculed me in front of the entire Senate and killed perhaps the best prospect we had to get the most out of this new relationship. You left Earth gov wide open and compromised, with no negotiating leverage whatsoever! We no longer need to worry about the ETA taking over Earth gov because you just turned it over to the aliens!"

"That's a bunch of barn hoof mow, and you know it. Besides, what leverage are you talking about?" I replied firmly. "We have nothing, absolutely nothing, to offer these people, except endless problems! You call that leverage? Your opinion of this world's appeal is gravely overrated. Your assumptions were all wrong, your behavior left much to be desired, and it's despicably unethical to steamroll the Senate the way you did to get your way. And to top it off, you almost got fired for it! So don't push this on me! You got what you deserved!"

"That's how politics work, and I've been at it for four years, so don't tell me how to do my job," she said with a cynical smirk. "Up there, without an attitude, you're as good as dead."

"Maybe in your book but not Earth gov's. You violated more rules than Yato could count. There was no need to be forceful or risk compromising your position in the process, for truth needs no emotional help to be right."

"Tough times call for equally tough measures. And now that I think of it, I should never have backed down. I had an approved motion . . ."

"Maybe it's a good thing you backed down. But in case you're in doubt, then tell me, where's your proof?"

"And where's yours? How can you trust complete strangers? Have you lost your mind, you fool?"

"I have that covered; refer to our contact and interview logs. The facts are there. In your case, you're as dry as an Atacama rock."

"You literally handed Earth gov to them, and I almost lost my job in the process! Why? I'll tell you why! It's all because of that . . . girl!"

"Wrong! It's my heart, not Earth gov, I handed over to her. I'm too jealous to give her anything else because . . . I love her!" I replied seriously.

"Oh, that's real smart, like that's going to happen!" she said after gasping a silent moment. "You think she'll pick you over so many other qualified consorts from her world? Don't be an idiot! She's just using you!"

"I love her, and I couldn't care less if she picked someone else over me."

"You're living a pipe dream. Read my lips. She'll break your heart! Soon, you'll find out she's an alien operative and then . . ."

"I don't care!" I said loudly. "I'd rather die than give up my love for her, even if it means staying single for the rest of my life. She's my life, and I'll sacrifice all I am and have for her! I want nothing, and no one else, but her!"

"All right, if that's how you want to go down, then so be it; don't forget I warned you. All I'm going to say is, whatever happens going forward, it will all be your fault: jerk!" she said loudly as Jim headed back in our direction and we changed our dialogue style.

"I take that as a compliment, thank you very much."

"Bill," Jim said joining us once more, "you'll have to forgive Gina. She gets quite passionate about what she believes."

"I know; I dealt with it for six years."

"Now what's that supposed to mean?" she replied rather upset.

"That . . . you're a tenacious individual and don't give up without a fierce fight," I said, trying not to inflame Gina further.

"I'm glad you see it that way; you know what to expect next time."

"On that note, my parents forced me into higher education, and I didn't go with best intentions, but Gina gave me impetus to make it through. She wouldn't let me quit. Thereafter, we parted ways. I went on to collect relics while she stepped up the totem pole."

"He was always late, brought in the wrong books, and spent most of his time sketching geometranoids all over his work," she said. "He would sit in the wrong class for the longest time before realizing half-way through the lecture that things just didn't seem right for some reason. Worst of all, he was a dreadful orator."

"Was not!"

"Was so!"

"Just because I made a conscious effort to enunciate every word . . ."

"Yeah right. You were slow . . ."

"Here we go; it's bash time."

"He was slow, soft-spoken, monotone, stiff, drifty—all signs of a professional hypnotist. Case in point, I still remember your dissertation on Inca culture. Oh my God, you stayed on the first slide for half an hour. And then, his slides were out of order. Another time, he mixed up family pictures in his lecture; I'll spare you the gruesome details. I'll give him credit; he knew subject matter as good as it gets. Getting him organized and motivated, that's a whole other story. He worked hard, once he put his mind to it, and became perhaps the most respected alumni in decades. Maybe that's where he learned to dig up Mars with a vengeance."

"Now I understand why Gina chose you for this mission," Jim said with a willful smirk, catching me by surprise. "When I asked her for a reference, she had it on the spot. Then, she went up against some fairly challenging ministers supporting your eventual nomination."

"I didn't know that," I said, looking at Gina somewhat apologetically but determined not to give into her willful nature. "It's a bit late now, but please accept my thanks for . . . . ."

"Don't mention it, regret's closer than you think," she said with a cold snap. "I've made better choices before, and been better rewarded."

"Guys, we have to get moving. Dinner's about over," he said, inviting us to dinner. "You might appreciate a real down-to-Earth meal, something gravity can work with, not that computerized mulch you put down daily."

Reaching for his coat pocket, he pulled out a scrambler and tagged it to my uniform. "Here's something new for you. Never leave home without it. You never know who or what might be listening in. We all have them."

Life at the political towers hadn't changed much. Everywhere you glanced, you locked on to some delegate, assistant, or committee chair. Maybe that's what kept peace on Saras for so long: leaders, all conveniently packed under one roof. Let leaders fight their own wars—what an innovative concept. Saras finally got its wish, and it seemed to be working, thus far.

As the lift stopped at the third level, nostalgic memories of a seldom-visited soup and salad shop brought back people and subjects surrounding my days there. The new café stood right where the old shop made its mark. It was done up quite nicely with old sea-faring paraphernalia, water-works, large fish aquariums, pleasing hanging atriums, and balconies overlooking the lower entrance level.

Selecting a secluded booth, Jim wanted to catch up while Gina was all about recruiting my unconditional attention. "I hope you don't hold a grudge for doing my job and holding my ground," she said, calmly sitting by me opposite from Jim.

"I see you're still upset," I said.

"I'll get over it."

"Madam Speaker, I must resort to Mark Twain's witty character who once said, 'By trying, we can easily learn to endure adversity.'"

"Rather well I might mention," she said, reaching over and padding me on the back. "Today, you had your revenge, but there will be a next time."

"Revenge is sweet and best served cold. Hence, it must be ice cream."

"Dream on. So how does it feel to go up against Earth gov for once?"

"Quoting Mr. Twain again, 'all you need is ignorance and confidence; then success is certain.' Honestly, I was relatively unprepared for the moment, crossed between a sense of right and a terrible longing for common sense."

"In that case, 'it is better to keep your mouth shut and appear stupid than open it and remove all doubt,'" she said. "I assumed a lot of risk by backing down and putting forth your motion instead, so remove my doubts."

Orders were taken, and Jim leaned my way with a sneer on his face eager to speak his mind. He had a good sense of what needed to be done, but it was difficult to disregard Saras's present woes and only fair to distinguish the mess he inherited. "Jim, from my personal vantage point, the world is one huge mixed-up place, and people are too set in their ways" I said.

Gina stepped in after wetting her lips with a healthy dose of water to make further sense out of chaos. "Don't complain. It took a lot of effort, time, and infinite resources to make it what it is; don't tell me you don't like the results."

"So how do we change that assessment?" Jim said.

"I think we need to show people what they can gain from this alien alliance and let their own ambitions draw them in. We can offer members new careers, adventures, unheard-of innovation—the stuff dreams are made of."

Jim agreed, thinking that material advances alone were sufficient to encourage and ensure civil commitment. Sadly, they were missing the point; promoting dreams of opulence was not what the Brothers had in mind. On the horizon, they envisioned flying interstellar, meeting billions of cosmic civilizations, and learning astonishing new technologies. But vital spiritual prerequisites were nowhere being considered.

Going forward, Earth gov faced three key challenges that could sway civil assent of the brotherhood, these being culture, faith, and ambition. You can change someone's culture to a great extent, their faith somewhat, but ambitions—hardly. The Brothers brought civil change in these three areas, but was Earth gov willing to promote any of them? My comment overshadowed lasting dead silence, and I figured I hit the jackpot.

"That could put Earth gov in a very uncomfortable spot and set members grumbling about what amounts to personal incursion," Gina said. "You can't get a small church board to agree on a simple proposal, much less four thousand denominations accept new doctrines—coming from Earth gov of all places. So don't expect widespread consent to new referendums coming from other planets; it might take a while."

"The last thing we need is people accusing Earth gov of operating in conflict with separation of faith and state; that'd be suicide," Jim said. "If we disclose material that doesn't jive with, say, Genesis, just like we heard minutes ago, we'll be accused of endorsing what amounts to a state-backed religion."

"Now we're talking," she said with renewed thrill, sustaining her desire to censure alien contacts. "See, that was precisely my point. How will people react when they hear comments barreling down on their prized beliefs?"

"Relieved as a milked Guernsey, if you asked me. Just tell people the truth. What's wrong with that?" I said. "That's what the Brothers advised;

anything else is a conscious effort to justify insecurity and misrepresent them."

"We can't do that!" Gina said alarmed. "It will tear down global order, science, faiths; that's why we need to sanction information and deliver it over time, according to member receptivity."

"What part of you's kidding? Members are begging for information, and they already suspect something's up. What do you suggest we tell them? Please wait, someone will be with you in a hundred years? Withhold information much longer, and watch Earth fall into the hands of someone more than willing to talk, like the ETA."

"Legally, we do have an ethics issue here," Jim added. "Earth gov can't get involved in positioning the Brothers over established faiths."

"It's blatant disregard for conflict of interest conventions," Gina added.

"Not so fast," I replied. "The world charter grants the Brothers as much right to free speech as our own members. All I'm asking is for Earth gov to pass their message along, that's all. That's not taking sides or undermining the government's impartiality but rather advocating transparency and serving members in the spirit of Frederick Sanders."

"Well, that's a hell of a stretch," Jim said.

"The Brothers are fully vested committee consultants. Didn't they just meet with the Senate and answered questions far from compulsion, and mind you, twice."

"Yes, but still, they have to be recognized as members."

"They reside on colonized worlds; doesn't that make them legit members?"

"That's far from sensible participative consent," Jim added.

"As consultants, it is consent nevertheless. When members realize that Martians won't attack but rather come to tutor us in peace, they'll figure they were duped and will listen to them attentively. When ETA members find out the Brothers won't support their initiatives, they'll jump ship also. Earth gov is always blamed for covering up information, so let's surprise members and give them what they want—all of it."

"There are always those that won't like the message and will look for ways to rip the messenger, in this case Earth gov, apart" he said.

"That's expected. But those that do, you can be sure they will be members of the underground; and they know we know that. Don't expect them to foolishly come out and expose themselves by fighting the message publicly."

"Oddly enough," Gina said suddenly, after silently listening to what Jim and I discussed, "I agree with Bill on that point. People don't expect Earth gov to disclose the facts. This is why clerics enjoy so much power because they don't expect to be defied. If anything, the ETA will be weakened by the message, and the Brothers do have a right to voice it, like Bill said.

They are Earth gov consultants and live on our outposts: that makes them members."

"My God! Gina, you surprise me. If the social minister heard you, he would have your tongue, no questions asked," Jim said.

"What he doesn't know, won't hurt me. Second, coming out in the open will reassure members that Earth gov is in control and has nothing to hide."

"I couldn't have said it better. Jim, ball's in your court. What now?" I said.

"One more question. Bill, if you led a subversive organization," Jim asked, "not saying you do, but imagine you did and Earth gov threatened your ideals, what would you do?"

"I'd strive to install dissident plugs in the Senate or ministry by whatever means possible. Case in point; Brutus and Caesar, Samson and Delilah, Judas and Jesus, Attila and Ildico. You're left to wonder who to trust."

"Are you telling me that my cabinet members are plugs?"

"I don't mean to raise rumors based on opinions, but history does suggest that the bigger the prize, the closer the enemy infiltrates near the top. This is only an observation. Just be careful and consider this a legitimate threat."

"That gives me a lot to think about," Jim said, rubbing his chin with mounting concern. "I will take your words under advisement."

"We have a lot to change. We're spiritually, not culturally, incompatible with the Brothers; that's what they're trying to tell us. We can't be among them unless our souls change, from negative to positive."

"And how are we supposed to do that?"

"Let's ask them. First off, recognize hidden skeletons, testify them to the light, and love 'love.' We have a bad legacy that has to go before the Infinite can live in us."

Done with dinner, Jim went to work on his speech while Gina invited me to take a casual stroll through the building's upper gardens and polish off the day's rough edges. The garden surrounded two large fountains, led there by a series of asymmetrical steps lined with benches. A giant network of transparent glass segments, held together by reinforced beams, covered the tall atrium. High above, the firmament exposed some of its bright decorations against subdued floor lighting.

I never felt anything more than friendship for her but knew she would have it differently. Our paths and attitudes being so different, we could never be more than friends. I sensed she drew the same conclusion, based on my languid replies and less-than-enthusiastic reaction to her body language. She certainly mounted an artful display of mannerisms and seductive poses designed to attract even the dead, but none of it sparked my interest.

Gina was a woman in every sense of the word, endowed with significant physical qualities. She could cast alluring spells on anyone lending due attention by bringing elements of desire to the fore for the senses to cherish in blinded unconscious fury. Her feminine tone was difficult to mind, depositing subconscious appealing messages upon the weak. Her enticing perfume and luminous artistic wears played on the mind by promoting worthy dreams of adequacy. But something within me paid no heed to such gifts of passion.

Her warmth detailed my side illicitly, slowly assuming temporary custody of my arm, squeezing biceps to promote masculinity in an ardent moment of satisfaction. But how could that be genuine love? Gina and I were so incompatible; all we ever did was argue. That wasn't what I would call living but rather suffering from extreme irrational anxiety.

I looked up at the stars and dwelled caringly on my friends, wondering how the human spark expressed the rite of life elsewhere in the cosmos. We were insincere, selfish people capable of the most sinister exploits imaginable. Our intimate longings and the pursuit of "falling in love" were cornerstone to our condemned, retrograde existence, founded wholly on wicked forgery and compulsion, not truth. And since we didn't sincerely love ourselves, how could we possibly love our partner, then our neighbor, and so much less; the Infinite? That was Saras's way; no one practiced anything beyond hedonism.

The answer to love was not to be found on Saras but in the gleaming firmament above, among graceful jewels spreading their benign embrace across endless spanning glares, each born from mystical furnaces whose powers seemed far out of reach to us mortals. In my unending quest for being, divine mercies smiled upon me the moment my starlight's enchanting essence humbly crossed the vast divide between earthly shores and privileged my heart with heavenly song, forever sealing my exclusive devotion to a friend, a sister, worth waiting an infinity and sacrificing life for.

My sister, my priceless gem—I would forever keep her in my thoughts, sharing tender words of love through endless terms. The sun will someday grow cold, and heavenly stars grow old, but my love for my one, my May Len of ages, shall never ever fold. My search for love is a journey into her heart's light, for she shines like a lamp unto my path most bright.

Love's sweet raptures overwhelmed deepest sentiments and rushed warmly through the gates of my eyes. Clarity of thought took firm hold of my heart as I remembered Dow Uanh's words, filling my bosom with purity of purpose. Of course, survival depended on discipline by faithfully denying desire under temptation's throngs and courageously witnessing wicked tendencies before verity's undeniable throne. The road to love is paved with honesty, not good intentions. How false was our love's promise, littered with deceit to beguile partners into brief pleasure states, just as animals court mates with color and form for mating purposes.

Children abound whose loveless parents consider them an inconvenient by-product of mistaken passion, growing up despised by progenitors deprived of added fantasies and youthful pleasure. Countless more never experience light of day, mindlessly lost to bloody carnage as a means to supplant pleasure's inopportune side effects. Children are innocent, defenseless living forms, precious jewels from Father's heart, returning from heavenly abodes enlightened by the breath of angels. Yet they are savagely butchered in the name of personal liberty while violating His Majesty's prime directive: love.

The weak-minded, highly influential man is the primary cause of fetal death. In ancient times, it was man that stifled female newborns and mass-produced males for their armies. Today, it is man that belittles a woman's values, disrespects her wondrous gift of life and gentle giving nature. Man's constant rape, deceit, and forceful abuse ravenously plundered the female world, slowly eroding the highest honor God granted humanity: the right to bear life. It is man's responsibility, not a woman's, to abstain.

I felt a repugnant wave of grief overtake me, enough to drive me to my feet and contemplate ensuing gardens with a blank vanished stare. I walked toward a nearby fountain, trying not to alert Gina to my thoughts. She interpreted my abrupt leave as a sign of approaching demise unto her fold and confidently revealed her seductive intent. She kept up her persuasive onslaught with her body tightly pressed against mine in an undesirable offering of warm flesh. I wanted this to end and Gina to leave, but she wasn't making it easy.

"Don't you want to hold me?" she suggested, posing in front of me as the mutual discord ensued. I needed a distraction, and inviting her to a small kiosk in the lower level seemed like the thing. Gina, distressed and rejected, hoped the moment culminated in passionate crescendo but got a crashing finale instead. She declined the invitation and opted to turn in for the night instead.

We set our backs to the gardens and made our way to the elevator in plummeting silence. Prior to going into her room, she stood at the door for a moment, looking down to the floor in inaudible thought. But suddenly, she turned back one last time and quickly put her arms around my shoulders, bearing scathe-less longing across her face.

Her influential embrace drew me rudely closer to her warm soft flesh against my will, seeking to set off prompt acceptance and deliverance into prurient firestorms. Her lavish lips were silent, but wordless gestures needlessly described unconditional surrender unto the arts of pleasure. Her body burned with desire and readily relinquished control to mine, becoming submissive and permissive to my venal endeavors without concern.

"You've been gone way too long, Tennessee butternut," she said longing for acceptance.

Surprised by her bold offer, I stood still unsure what to do to break her hold, but a weak, musky odor suddenly made me feel dizzy; my heart raced, and my nervous system sharply sensitized to her touch. My hands instinctively reached for her waist but slowly withdrew after realizing what I was up to. She pinned her eyes upon mine with an immodest smile, but I turned my face to leave her no room in which to freely maneuver intimate intentions.

I felt helpless before her deterring offerings yet determined to preserve a newly found life far from temporary pleasures. She prepared to grant me a kiss and trailed my facial motions wherever I took them, but I did not yield to her advances and left her no other option but to back down and frown rather somberly. "I love her more than life itself; and all its offerings. I can't live without her soul."

"Don't waste your time with that thing. She's just playing with you, but I'm not. When she gets what she wants, she'll dump you," she said tensely.

"You don't get it. My love for May Len needs not be consented to exist. I'm in love with her soul, not the body. Just knowing that I love her is enough to call it a life, even though she rejects me in the end. I'll wait a million years for her if I have to, renouncing life's gifts until then."

"Don't be a fool. Can't you see that I've wanted to be with you for ten long years? I want you more than anything. Why won't you love me, willingly?"

"Love happens free from want. I don't want her; rather, I love her deeply," I said tenderly. "I am my beloved's, and my beloved is mine [1]."

Silently, she released me harshly and vanished behind a fast-closing door. I felt sorry to see her go like that, but true love is not what she had in mind. I looked up at the ceiling and kept my thoughts on May Len as I paced away. Gina peeked out of her suite slightly, but I made no attempt to notice her. I entered the elevator, and she watched me disappear into it.

Once in her suite, she threw her shoes angrily across the room and sat on her bed, loudly fuming frightening words toward May Len and vowing to take me from her heart at any cost. Decisively, she reached for a safe box and withdrew a visor-like device as well as an oblong communications unit into which she spoke, "Mnemosyne to Uranus, reporting on Plan Orpheus."

"My valiant daughter and queen of authoritative speech, who inspires confidence unto our colleagues," replied an accented, well-refined voice. "I heard about your bold confrontation today, and I am most proud of you, for you demonstrated firm devotion to your father in spite of such difficult odds."

"I failed to deliver the oracle as requested, father," Gina said disappointed.

"None of the sort. The oracle's response was to be expected, and you performed your duty beyond my expectations. Hans will be cyphered tonight with new instructions, and you will also. Rest well, for tomorrow you will have a new mind and desire. Your new program is ready, and you may cypher when ready. We will exhibit more aggressiveness tomorrow than today; it has all been arranged."

"I will make father Alpha proud. *Gute Nacht*," she said emotionally, putting the communication unit back into the safe. She settled comfortably for the evening, activated the visor device, and placed it over her face. Immediately, she passed out, and silent messages crowded her deepest reveries.

As evening hours drew hastily into midnight, I got a suite for the night and left Jim a message, hoping he would get it first thing in the morning.

All through the night, I couldn't get my encounter with Gina and the sins that overwhelm this quarantined world off my mind. Truth was so simple but so inconvenient. Games of deceit and make-believe seemed more appealing, sufficient to strip us ignorant of feelings. We elect to trust two-second smiles, indulgence, and promises rather than know why we tend to them. We let voracious appetites have way of our mind by dumping it over the side, left to port, to avoid its vigilant captain. Thus do these frisky imaginariums seek berth unguarded.

How could so many misplaced souls find their way back to truth? How could thousands of years of selfish instinct be conquered? How could higher light replace eons of error lingering in the heart? The answer was in the future, still to be sanctioned by humanity's challenging destiny.

---

[1] R. W. J. Morford, "Solomon 6: 3," in *The One New Man Bible*, Traveler's Rest, South Carolina: True Potential Publishing Col, 2011.

Chapter 14: *Ghosts from the Past*

My suite offered a great view of Roosevelt Island along East River, lit by lingering electric fires subtly receding eastward into the distant restful eve beyond. Glass-covered Queensboro Bridge spanned across the waterway, casting soft tinted haloes on the dim churning river below. On the river's west bank, the multi-stacked FDR Speedway glowed in night's absorbing darkness with golden splendor, host to automated speeders swiftly gliding at 350 kilometers per hour.

Not far to the south, New Manhattan's magnificent skyline captivated human wonder in silent visual rhapsodies, inspiring welcoming calm and safe haven. Rebuilt in 2054 from the ashes of nuclear rivalry, it is the tallest most modern city in the world even a hundred years later. Its lofty buildings rise a kilometer into the skies, conveniently interconnected by multilevel hanging glass-covered speedways. About ten million people reside in the city, and countless guests pass through its busy corridors daily.

Its open metropolitan theme is set amid spacious parks and nature areas rather than unsightly concrete streets and sidewalks—a novel concept in city construction. Architectural designs follow classical pyramid, circular, and parabolic shapes; square drab designs are nowhere to be found. A highly durable, innovative Andalusite crystallized alloy was used in city construction. This compound becomes translucent under high pressure, is stronger than steel, and exhibits insulative, anticorrosive properties.

Beneath ground, it's an entirely different world. Transports dash between several key city locations and public facilities such as restaurants, schools, and museums make both efficient and convenient use of available space.

Lights from rare sea-faring vessels seemed idle on the water, adding a touch of nostalgia to the breezy evening sky. The heavens above shared just a few of its most-prized jewels, often interrupted by fleeting, swift flying shuttles. Farther south, a reconstructed Lady Liberty stands taller than before. Built from fused sand, she proudly glows in the night like a lit crystal candle. Her golden torch burns brightly, and searchlights swirl from her crown with majestic splendor, a welcoming beacon to UEF's capital city.

Resting on something other than stiff low-gravity beds revered for utmost soreness was a welcomed windfall. Heavy eyelids gladly surrendered to slumber, and dreams shortly assumed their rightful unpredictable course. Conscious impressions faded away, giving way to reverie's dawn with its usual cloudy visions and random subject matters far from reticent. Before long, imaginative disarray acquiesced to unconscious domains, imposing upon a wary mind a sense of reality with purpose all of its own.

From mysterious mental recesses, a large tree grove slowly unfolded from an otherwise vague dream. I stood uncertain of bearing at an entrance to the grove amid a low decorative rock barrier a short distance from it. Part of me wanted to step through the entry and into the grove, sensing that someone most dear to my heart patiently waited for me just beyond the trees, someone I lost long ago, but I was struck deadened by inexplicably haunting reluctance.

Grasses seemed disturbingly darker than usual, eclipsed by morbid surroundings and abysmal stillness. It was as if life itself departed this place, warded away by fears forged far back in time by some sinister consuming omen. My mind feebly swelled with mixed emotions, anticipating an imminent encounter with despotic ghosts from the past; mental legends cloaked by an adversarial dialect compellingly binding me to its confounding regiment.

Dreadful inner secrets diligently sought sanctuary in those fleeting moments, but some unknown benign essence compelled me to come forward and reconcile them. Overpowered by friendly assurances, I hesitantly ventured into the grove. As I did, the unusual obscurity dissolved away with each step forward; and nature remarkably bounced back, animated by verve and sound. Leaves swayed casually in the wind, and birds announced branch conquests with soothing songs.

Once under the grove's leafy canopy, my attention was immediately drawn to notes hanging from bottom most branches. Reaching up to the closest note, I found strange pictographs similar to Sanskrit written on it; oddly, I knew what they meant. "Two trees right," said the message. I did as suggested and found another note that said, "Three trees forward."

I found this note game most amusing and followed it until coming to a river's ford. On the ground, someone left a message using wood sticks stating, "Turn around. Meet your future." To my surprise, a young lady endowed with overwhelming beauty and radiant expression stepped into the clearing from behind a tree and I immediately recognized her: Nei Lah.

In her presence, a gentle feeling of wholesome wonder filled the heart, and pleasant harmonies imbued my mind with fond, sweet peace. Her invigorating smile severed all concerns and wants in life, refreshed by an overwhelming sense of faithful serenity and uncontainable honesty. Something about her felt most familiar, almost like May Len's essence, and for that moment I was totally absorbed by a conscious effort trying to tell them apart, but I could not.

She wore a delicate cream-colored multilayered robe that shimmered with light and swayed softly in the gentle breeze. Her amber piercingly wise eyes floated beneath gentle brows like large clean crystalline firestones set affront long black hair, flowing down below the shoulders like the colorful cloudy flutters of the Carina nebula. A calming, radiant light shone forth from her gaze like shafts of higher light illuminating my path. Just as May Len, she appeared slightly Oriental and of joyous nature, yet most shy.

Nei Lah took a few gentle steps toward me, held my hands, and said sweetly in her native tongue, "My brother Roshon. Destiny leads you to a river delta where two smaller rivers are born from it. One leads to Masar while the other to Saras. The cycle is strong today, sweeping many from Masar unto Saras. Happiness in Saras is short. Its contentment and charm cannot ever be fulfilled, unlike His Infinite Majesty's gifts. Don't give in to Saras. By taking an unknown path at the delta, you will lose sight of the sea beyond. Return to us Roshon. Don't give in to guilt and false happiness. Those are Saras's traps."

Her kind cherished singing voice modestly whispered away into the gentle zephyr despite my longings to eternally capture its essence while an impenetrable tropical forest of immense proportions emerged overshadowing the grove from one horizon to the other. A smooth winding highway made its way through the forest, leading to a wide recessed clearing that hosted a small industrial city, apparently abandoned, filled with several factories.

The city served as a slapdash sanctuary for tribesmen seeking protection from predators, but there was a catch. Once individuals entered, they could never again leave, and their lives would render wholly to a sort of twisted museum exemplifying human degeneration unto death.

Aboriginal people wondered about this city wearing nothing more than primitive coverings and grime specks from extended periods of sanitary negligence. With serious proud stares, they wondered about this place without purpose or definite direction, deplorably careless of their physical vessel. Their long stiff dirty hairs were brushed back much like a male lion's crown. Obesity ran rampant among them, held as a status symbol much akin to worship. Teeth, worn down by years of misuse, evidenced a life callous on resilience and battered by defiant elements.

Some aborigines walked senselessly about with lances; others engaged in expressive arts but in degenerate, confounding manner in a world driven by pretend symbols, much like insane asylum patients assuming fake tasks. Artists with no canvas, cooks with no food, musicians with no instruments—every personal chore was a playact. There was nothing else for people to do other than act, feed, and await death. But there was an even more sinister purpose to this place.

It was a sorrowful sight to behold and I turned to Nei Lah in disgust; but she kept to herself peering downward sadly, referring to this place as "The Funny Farm." Food was dumped daily in the middle of the city, where people gathered to glut themselves in uncontainable frenzy, swimming into the food like wild beasts until they could eat no more or sicken. City residents were constantly subject to humiliation and physical abuse, a source of appalling amusement and perversion rendered to the tastes of an elite society that overshadowed their gloomed existence.

Unexpectedly, Nei Lah vanished from the vision, reminding me not to fall into Saras's traps. Immediately after, a tall woman rose among these people, dressed in semi-transparent tights that covered her body from the neck down. Her bodily curves and bust proportions were extreme, vividly embodying sinful lust without shame. Feline ears protruded from atop her head amid long dark hair, and a live tail animated her sadistic persona. She mimicked feline movements with artistic perfection, and her voice could change between female and feline at will. "Tiger Woman," as she was referred to, ruled over these primitive people with a vengeance, forbidding them expressive liberty.

Far across the thick forest canopy, an indescribably modern colossal city 150 kilometers across dominated the skyline with seven domed structures about a central hub—Mu. Tiger Woman influenced everyone in this city as well. Noting my presence, looked my way and approached me, accenting her physical qualities. "Don't you want to hold me?" she asked.

"That will never happen," I said defiant, afraid of falling into temptation.

"You want to play hard to get? I like that in a man, and I accept your challenge," she replied seductively, wrapping her long tail tightly around my neck and drawing me slowly toward her, like a cat playing with its food. Her tail's formidable grip kept me fastened to her eventual longing, bound without choice for her waiting hands.

"Why fight it. You know you can't escape my grip," she said, pulling me up to her face. "Just enjoy all of me, and everything will be fine. Release yourself to me with that candor men are known for; that's all I ask."

"I want nothing from you!" I yelled desperately, finally freeing myself by dropping to the floor and stepping back a ways from her tail's range. "You're a repulsive, spliced monstrosity, a human parasite veiled inside and out by putrid flesh, and a soul no more lively than a zombie. I will never betray Nei Lah, for she is my light and my only one of ages! I'll love her to the ends of time."

"You can't debate with me," she yelled, openly displaying fangs that helplessly protruded from her mouth. "It would be futile, for I am a superior being to your kind, especially that . . . thing. If you don't follow me, I'll turn you into one of these crawling maggots."

With a quick wave of her hand, soldiers appeared out of nowhere. One of them threatened me with a hand weapon while another struck me several times and said, "Roach, we don't like you. You reproved us, and now revenge is ours." His words were suddenly eclipsed by thick dark clouds that hastily masked the heavens, bearing unimaginable dread to everyone present. Outlined against reddish glows from a setting sun in a foreign land far away, thousands of swift missiles took to the skies and struck the Lemurian mainland, producing bright antimatter flashes that promptly liquefied soils and vaporized whatever living substance they came in contact with.

Mu's defense batteries quickly counter-attacked, successfully intercepting numerous enemy projectiles in the upper atmosphere, but not all of them. Eventually, the crystalline city and its remote energy towers fell victim to aerial assaults, leaving no trace of a once-magnificent city, home to billions.

The energy unleashed by Mu's power reserves set off a massive explosion that rattled the planet, formed huge fissures five kilometers deep across the land, destabilized nearby tectonic plates, and diverted hot spot plumes toward the surface as was the case in Atlantis. Powerful volcanic eruptions tore the surface apart, fuming fires and ash that engulfed the planet in a reddish, gagging haze until Saras froze and its life expired.

Picture 13: Lemurian epic (*B. Erlinger-Ford*)

In the open void about Saras, cosmic radiation from a supernova six thousand light-years away reached our solar system, penetrated through weakened magnetic and ozone layers, and triggered mass species extinctions throughout habitable worlds, including Masar.

Masar's reddish orb appeared in skies overhead, where I sought shelter. But as I neared, it too had been scorched by war and deadly disease. Realizing I could not stay there, I returned to Saras and landed on Chicago's Lake Shore Speedway. People lined both sides of the road, celebrating an event of some importance.

Nei Lah emerged happily from the crowds but turned into May Len as she neared. Dow Uanh briefly joined us, asked me to take good care of his daughter, and walked away before I could say anything in return.

May Len seemed unusually serene yet somewhat withdrawn for reasons I could not grasp. I could tell she kept something from me, but all she would utter was, "My companion is here. Have you not seen him?"

Crowds silenced suddenly, and a cold draft streamed down the street like death's imminent obscure vengeance. Time seemed to stand still, and the sound of my beating heart unavoidably appraised my ears of lurking morbid revenge. Off to a side, Gina stood bitterly uncaring with arms crossed and lips exalted, confidently telling me, "Maggots, you're all going to die!"

I immediately turned to May Len and sensed she was in mortal danger but could barely move my body to protect her. A man, previously hiding from view, pointed a weapon in our direction and pulled its trigger several times. Promptly, heated projectiles breached my chest, and I fell to the ground bleeding. May Len, also wounded, collapsed unto my arms unconscious, just as I woke up sweating profusely.

Jolted brashly to my senses, I checked the time and noticed it was 8:35 a.m., just as someone knocked hastily at the door. I swiftly got up, went to the door, and scanned the caller's identity. It turned out to be Jim, at a most inappropriate time.

"Good heavens!" Jim said when he saw me bathed in sweat, "You look like you saw a ghost, worst, the angel of death! Did I wake you?"

"No . . . actually, yes, I'm glad you did," I replied, gasping for common sense. "I had this bizarre nightmare, hard to describe, but quite unforgettable, maybe a ghost from the past."

I offered Jim all the comforts of home, but he was pressed for time and could not stay long. "I've experienced this sort of thing before," he said. "Gravity adjustments can induce bizarre reactions, dementia, nasal bleeding, all sorts of things."

"This was different, a mix between premonition and déjà vus."

"You'll get over it soon enough. Now, on another topic, the reason for my visit is threefold. One, I got your message. Two, I need you on my telecast this morning. Three, your partners took a Mars red-eye; I don't think they mentally checked in when they checked out, if you know what I mean. I figured you left with them, but your name wasn't on the flight manifest."

"That's why I wanted to see you; I'll stay as long as you need me."

"Report to my complex by ten thirty and plan to hang around right after the telecast; media net will interview you afterward."

"I know precisely how that will go. What should I say to the press?"

"You suggested it yesterday: just say the truth. My speech will lead you." He headed for the door and kiddingly reminded me, "It's just like old times; the press hasn't changed one bit. Today, we make history."

"Will Gina be there? She's the official speaker of the assembly and bears responsibility to speak on behalf of Earth gov . . ."

"She will field geo-political issues. You had the initial contact with the Brothers; you'll talk on their behalf. Again, just say the truth and wear standard issue SAT diplomatic uniform; it's on its way up to you right now."

"SAT? What's that?" I asked innocently.

"Holy smokes, been that long! Suit and tie, remember?"

There was something else I wanted to tell him, but I could not bring myself around to it and stood a bit jumpy, hoping for the right motive to unleash grave concerns. Jim could read body language quite well and wasted no time calling my card. "There's something else, isn't there?"

"I'm not sure if I should or if it's of any concern," I said hesitantly.

"Won't know until you spill the beans," Jim said, waiting for me to bring forth whatever was on my mind. If I divulged highly classified information, then heads would roll. On the other hand, if this was an underground plot, then even Jim might be in danger.

"Have you or UEF operatives established a project called Vulcan Aurora?"

Jim thought for a moment and shook his head in the negative. "No, can't say I have. If so, what's to it?"

"How about operatives named Alpha or Beta?" I replied, pacing about in an effort to carefully measure an appropriate level of divulgence.

Jim smiled and quickly pressed the subject, "Cut to the chase. What's all this about?"

"I was preview to a private conversation . . ."

"Let me guess, back on Mars?" I could not commit an answer, and Jim realized I was protecting someone. "Is there something I should know about this conversation?"

"I think I previewed underground communications into Mars."

"What and from whom?" Jim said, becoming alarmed.

"All I know is this woman, Beta, belongs to a group called the Order. She described an initiative to discourage people from accepting the Brothers, playing hard to get. Somehow, this would force the Brothers to negotiate Earth's position with the Order and not Earth gov."

"Sounds fascinating, reminds me of yesterday's ordeal in the Senate." He thought about it for a moment and then shook his head. "Never heard of an Order either. Wait, you said communications into Mars, like from Earth?"

"In real time."

"That's impossible. It takes fifteen minutes or more to send a message out to you guys."

"Three possibilities. Beta was on another Mars colony—that can be traced. She was on a shuttle no more than a million kilometers from Mars—highly unlikely, flights can also be traced. Or, more bizarre yet, she was on Earth, using some new technology we're not aware of."

"It's preposterous, however you look at it. When did you hear this?"

"Moments before my personal commentary a few days ago."

"Can't be. Between your interviews, there were no calls in or out of C6. Where did you hear this conversation?" I hesitated for a moment but didn't have to answer. "Hans's office. Is that all you can tell me?"

"Supposedly, someone on Mars will be chosen to lead this Order. I have no idea who."

"Could be an inside job, but Hans doesn't have the codes to block communication tracers. I'm the only one that has these codes, and I changed them days before mission updates started coming in from the structure. Why didn't you tell me this before?"

"I wasn't sure who to discuss this with or what to say."

"I'm glad you spoke up. Someone's getting my codes, and I have to find out who; I'll have engineering look into it. In the interim, this conversation never happened. Don't talk to anyone about it but me; we don't want to tip anybody off. Besides, what we tell the world today will negate any and all efforts to turn people against the Brothers. Don't be late."

"I sure hope so."

"By the way," he said on his way out, "if you haven't noticed, May Len likes you." I smiled unavoidably as he left the room. But at the same time, restless metaphors between Tiger Woman and Gina harbored way too close to shore, enough to make me wonder if by chance they were the same individual, if not a persuading happenstance born from the previous night's encounter.

After taking a water bath and dressing up to SAT standards, I headed to Jim's office located on the upper south wing of the Towers, but I was not alone. Haunting thoughts of Tiger Woman and Gina continued to pound my senses with a vengeance. Wherever I turned, I bore an uneasy feeling that Tiger Woman was somewhere out there, watching me, hidden from sight and ready to pounce ferociously when least expected. My imagination scampered unbridled, fearfully supplanting still inaudible empty hallways with echoing feline growls, and turning illusory cordons into her swinging malicious tail all too willing to strangle me.

When I reached the chancellor's mega-complex, a series of magnetic and laser scanners went to work, establishing my DNA identity and every object and chemical on me. When I least expected it, Gina suddenly appeared from a blind corner and seriously startled me. She behaved as if nothing happened between us the night previous. But as she tried to embrace me, my instinctive response was overtly apprehensive and facial expressions rendered surreally indecorous, immediately taking few steps back. She looked at me rather confused for a few moments and said, "Is something wrong?"

"No, nothing's wrong. What could possibly be wrong? Everything's just fine, good, thank you. I'm here now, so . . . shall we?" I replied anxiously, pointing the way to Jim's reception area.

Gina did not know what to make of my stern jumpy attitude, bearing a shocked expression difficult to mind. "Right this way," she said uncomfortably, unable to fathom my behavior.

Farther into the complex, Jim and Yato waited for us in the reception area; ministers joined along the way to the conference hall. Gina could not take her worried eyes off of me; I, on the other hand, completely ignored her.

Two security agents entered the conference room ahead of us and assumed vigilant positions. When all was clear, we entered the hall, and everyone present stood up in dead silence. Secretary Yato addressed the media, announcing the general topic of discussion and specific engagement rules. The press was rarely notified on such short notice, except to convey issues of critical importance; reporters knew this, and expectations ran high. After brief introductions, Jim assumed the podium to a strong round of applause.

With serious emotive pose and strict formality, Jim set the tone for his world-impacting message. During his speech, Gina often looked my way seething with longing, but I never returned the compliment, moved by inner sentiments difficult to interpret. "The human race, wherever it's found, is destined to achieve outstanding things—that is, when we work together and are led by progressive transparent governments," he passionately orated. "Frederick Sanders, one of the original UEF founders, said it best in his famous inaugural address, and I quote from his *Licentia Tabellae*."

> To hope is spiritual, to achieve is human, to understand is personal, and to have is physical. Therefore, the government of the people must reflect upon its member's hopes, consider those achievements mankind can make, endeavor to increase individual knowledge, and provide for

> everyone's physical needs. Only then, can members realize their interminable potential, and the government of such progressive, promising realm evolve to new horizons of peace and prosperity.

"The mechanism described by Sir Sanders is the basis for government today, centered primarily on developing human potential and fostering knowledge. This is the law of the land, the privilege of every member, and the future of generations to come. Thus, the government must steadily lead by example, and denying truth is *not* one of its many mandates.

"Progress was recently infringed upon by unusual events, some out of this world, while others confined to our imagination. Before facts were known, theories quickly took form, and radical alliances rooted their hold on world members, not to benefit society but to assail civil stability through despair and misfortune, words censured by Sir Sanders over a century ago.

"World members, be assured there will be *no* alien invasion, and I'll prove it with compelling evidence in a few moments. Peace will prosper more so than ever because truth will be known; nothing will change that. From most humble beginnings, our forefathers gazed upon the heavens and wondered with admiration what these contained. Today, this government will share with its members the long-awaited answer to this age-old question.

"In view of recent eyewitness reports indicating the presence of foreign intelligence operating on Mars, UEF launched a comprehensive investigation. Two types of phenomena were described: strange lights near the surface and structures believed to be part of an alien base. Both phenomena were thoroughly studied by special teams, and we'll show you their findings here shortly. But first, I will ask that you keep an open mind, free from prejudice or coercion. Without further delay, I will let Madam Speaker provide a historical perspective leading to today's broadcast." Jim stepped down and sat by me. Then, Gina took to the podium.

"A year ago," Gina said rather somber, which was rather unusual for her, "a team set out to investigate unusual atmospheric anomalies west of Uzboi Vallis. Due to the harsh terrain and inexplicable equipment failures, ESCE was forced to survey a specific area where the Nirgal terra-net site stands today. As the team drilled into the ground, they encountered non-naturally occurring layers. At the same time, strange lights were reported nearby. A group of scientists was immediately dispatched to the area, but they soon realized that a scaled-down colony had to be built to support local research activities. This colony became known as C6. Information on these anomalies was not made public at the time, pending accurate assessments.

"Spectral analysis of Martian lights revealed the presence of stable EM signatures, and excavation in the area around C6 yielded remarkable findings, including a large crystalline structure buried several meters beneath ground." Immediately, the crowd rumbled in loud commentary, enough to cause the secretary to stand and call the session to order before Gina could proceed.

"This structure was dated to about 125,000 BC and measures twenty meters wide by ten meters high. Once fully excavated, our research team entered the structure and made a most remarkable discovery."

"Members of the press, inside this structure, the team met the unexpected and achieved the impossible," said Jim, as Gina sat down. "World members, I am happy to report that, for the first time in history, Earth established face-to-face contact with extremely wise, completely benign humanoid extraterrestrial beings!" Irrepressible commotion surged at the sound of these words, even before they were uttered. But just as quickly, EMS members stood on their feet and ardently cheered, some in tears, praising Jim's news.

It was difficult for Jim to silence the crowd, but he continued among frequent outbursts of cheer. "The aliens are absolutely humble, peace-loving people. Their technical advances and spiritual values are sophisticated beyond belief and have evolved to become overlords of the universe. Their worlds are absolutely heavenly, free from malice or suffering, and they invite us to join them in peaceful planetary brotherhood. They call themselves: Brothers."

Crowds could not contain themselves, and cheers burst into celebration, not just in the meeting hall but across the globe by all those who heard the televised speech. Jim was ecstatic, urging people positively from the podium and often turning back to share his glee with us.

"The Brothers are willing to share their vast knowledge with us but only if we accept them. They won't interfere in matters of state, faith, or personal decision, much less, entertain using weapons. That means, ETA, you're all washed up! Were it not the case, and aliens were an ill-driven race, we wouldn't be here talking about them right now, would we? Aliens plan to introduce themselves to the world by openly displaying their craft starting tomorrow and making an official visit to UEF headquarters sometime soon.

"In closing, I would like to offer the following 'Locksley Hall' quote from Lord Alfred Tennyson: 'For I dipt into the future, far as human eye could see. Saw the vision of the world, and all the wonder that would be.' Thank you for your time, and may God's blessings be upon you all." The media continued their jubilant, tumultuous applause as Jim sat down and Gina took his place at the podium to display and describe select pictures from the Mars mission, including the structure, the Brothers, and their worlds.

The secretary returned to the podium announcing that all alien contact encounter recordings would be made available to the media later that afternoon. That was surprisingly refreshing in the spirit of Dow Uanh's truth initiative. What a welcomed shift of trust and leadership, holding nothing back and leading the way through facilitation and example.

"I want to recognize the outstanding work carried out by our Mars contact team" Jim said, thoroughly satisfied with Saras's response thus far. "In a brief amount of time, they deciphered incredibly complex codes, strategies, and in the end made alien contact a reality. One of their members is with us today, Dr. Bill Sullivan. He and Gina will take your questions."

Jim left the conference room under celebratory barrage. Immediately, every hand in the conference room went up. Gina and I took questions for two straight hours ranging the gamut. Finally, the secretary stopped the session, to my relief. I could appreciate from Gina's facial gestures she was glad it was over; at least, I wasn't alone.

Back at Jim's complex, the next phase was being laid out including security strategies, publicity schemes, and civil activities. Jim asked me to return to Mars and reestablish contact with the Brothers. Earth gov wanted to arrange an official visit within three weeks.

The world reacted in an open, non-fearful, jubilant manner to Earth gov's announcement. News of alien contact was the main topic on everyone's mind. Alien mania had taken over like spring fever, and everyone wanted to be a Brother overnight.

After the meeting, Jim pulled me aside to discuss the Order. "Are you wearing your scrambler?" he asked; I assured him I was. He then came close to me and whispered softly, "ESCE had every colonial transceiver pulled and checked using regular preventive maintenance as an excuse. Every transceiver checked out clean, except C6. Don't mention this to anyone, not even Gina."

"I suppose you found something that didn't belong there?"

"I'm coming to that. C6 transceivers were never hacked. There's no evidence of stolen passwords or compromised systems, but the dome receiver had an added component cleverly hidden underneath a decryption module that was never part of the original design. It bypasses password tracing, and can even tap into secure channels. Security may have deliberately installed the device, or it came that way from the factory; it's hard to tell."

"That means all communications between Earth gov and C6 were compromised."

"Unfortunately, yes."

"Or calls were made without Earth gov knowing about it."

"Precisely."

"The big question now is, what else have they bugged?" I left Jim with a big question to answer. He cringed at the very thought, although he must have known. "Worst yet, plugs. If this secret Order has agents all the way to Mars, imagine their level of infiltration here on Earth."

"If someone knew C6 was being built far back enough to bug its transceiver, they knew its purpose ahead of time. Fingers point right back to Hans. This bug can decode standard Earth gov signaling and has the potential for channeling enormous amounts of power. It has other electric and magnetic driving properties coupled directly to the colony's dish that has our engineers baffled. Whoever developed this component knows something we don't; that's another scary thought."

"You don't suppose . . . the device uses tachyon technology?" I said.

"You mean, faster-than-light transmission? We haven't given that any thought. Maybe that's what that strange component is for; it almost resembles an EM modulator."

I gripped myself for a moment, sparked by a sudden realization. Something clicked at the spur of the moment, too obvious not to mention. "Sean Ryan."

"What about him?"

"His theories on faster-than-light transmissions—that's all he talks about. Hans and I were having an open discussion when Sean brought up the subject of instantaneous transmissions to Earth and how to do it. Who knows, maybe someone listened to his theories and put them to use at C6. Anyone possessing this technology can potentially develop an entirely new class of interstellar technology—and weapons."

"Sean is on a shuttle bound for Mars, along with Hans. We'll have to keep an eye on him and tell him to keep his big mouth shut, or I'll bust his chops."

"Do we know who manufactured this gadget?"

"We have no clue. Beyond basic decoding functions, we don't know what else it does. Folks back on Mars are trying to reverse engineer it. Removing it from the circuit has no impact whatsoever on colonial communications. We'll leave it where it is for now to avoid raising suspicions, but its output will be monitored. From this point forward, we have to watch what we say. We're dealing with a very sophisticated, well-run organization with agents in key associative information areas."

"What are we going to do about Hans?"

"He can't know we're on to him," Jim said, resorting to pity. "Neither should Sean. It's a shame. I've known Hans for thirty years; he's been a trusted, devoted friend. I never thought . . ."

Jim took a deep breath and tried to compose himself. "You were right. We have plugs, several perhaps," he said, quickly changing the subject. "We must prepare for the landing; that's our next real challenge."

Jim set things in motion that I was not privy to, but I knew he was doing the right thing. Neither of us realized what the Order was. Yet I had a feeling the Brothers knew precisely what was going on and would guide us through the evil maze of traps being put down by those classically opposed to the graceful glory of His Majesty.

Hans and Sean spent the night on Luna 3 before traveling to Masar. Secretly, Hans had other plans for staying there. As Sean rested, Hans quietly left his room to conduct business of a personal nature: meet a most powerful, influential man. As Hans walked down colonial corridors, he came across someone in a darkened corner. The man, tall and neatly refined, approached Hans speaking in strongly accentuated Bavarian.

"*Mein Freund, Kommandant Hans,*" said the man, giving Hans a stout salute, promptly replied in like manner.

"*Ja Herr, furchtloser Vater,*" replied Hans with military, regimented vigor.

"Most appropriate welcome, son, be at ease," said the man. "Touching speech from the chancellor, don't you think, Gamma? I hate a man that won't get right to the point. So tell me something about your new friend Bill. How is he taking a liking for the Brothers?"

"In particular, one individual . . ."

"Ah yes, May Len, I remember her," added Alpha, looking upwards as if trying to grasp the level of my growing relationship with her. "He's a fool, nothing Beta can't handle. Don't forget: appetite is our greatest asset, and the way to a man's heart is through his body. She'll win him over soon, and that thing will be history. That's his next step before becoming the new Alpha."

"Sir, with all due respect, he seems fairly attached to May Len and might resist absorption cyphering into the organization."

"Nonsense. Beta is an irresistible woman, the best in her class. She can attract even the dead. Besides, they were both genetically engineered to belong together. They can't resist it; it's all skin deep. Pheromones and cyphering will finish the job. She will break him, and then he will be ours. His ambitions will change once he realizes who he really is and the power he will enjoy, given few mental scrambles. He's been ours before and shall be so again."

"Regarding the speech today, won't that bring him closer to the Brothers?"

"Our operatives know what to do. We will appear to lose the war on words, but that's only a distraction. We will win through more implacable means. It's arranged. Beta will see to it. I don't think aliens will want to deal with Earth gov after Beta does her job. As the legitimate source of power on this world, we will be in a much better negotiating position after some, shall we say, bloodletting?

"We'll make it difficult to deal with but not impossible. The Brothers will eventually come back and commit to our terms; I so foresee it. Don't forget there's that prime directive they can't violate, and we'll use it as we see fit.

Sometimes you pay the price for being too nice. The world now knows the Brothers exist, and we know just where to find them, so they can't just walk away and leave. I'll chase them into their hide-outs until they are mine again, or I'll blow their worlds to bits if they resist me."

"What can I do to help?"

"Act innocent and profile. You don't want to be mentally picked up, so the less you know, the better off we are. Return with Sean back to Earth. Report anything you see or hear to Beta; this is for the good of Earth. Of course, if we fail, Earth will pay the price as so many times prior. We're the superior human intellect of which there is no other and shall influence an entire universe in time. As for you, a product of the human elite, you are in line for Beta promotion. Beta Idlin will cypher you tonight to ensure your mission's success."

"Right away, father Alpha."

"Stay alert, my son; make your father proud. *Gute Nacht, Kommandant.*"

"*Durch Ihr Befehl, Vater Alpha. Gute Nacht!*" Hans did a military turn-about and dismissed himself in strictest marching stance, disappearing around a corner nearby.

"Little do you know Gamma what your true role is," Alpha said with a somber smile. "You are . . . expendable." Alpha quickly disappeared from the corridor back into the darkness from whence he came and covertly took the first available shuttle back to Saras.

Chapter 15: *New Beginnings*

News of ongoing contacts with benign extraterrestrial beings echoed swiftly around the globe, making headlines in every conceivable borough and tongue. Life's anxious pulse momentarily came to a careering halt as enthusiastic audiences across contiguous horizons gathered excitedly to view contact recordings and joyfully celebrated this historic event.

While member opinions varied widely across countless subjects revealed by contact recordings, the world's overall reaction was exceedingly positive. The extreme left resolutely contended that alien contacts were nothing more than an elaborate hoax, designed to silence separatist movements and diffuse growing organized advocate influence. Radical extremists were not far behind, warning constituents that Earth gov was the beast's image, desperately trying to delude the elect and change times and laws in the final days of prophecy.

Threatened by inevitable change, conservative advocates wasted no time letting their most eloquent delegates lose upon the airwaves in an effort to rapidly discredit the brotherhood's message and save face by whatever means possible. Social guilds and boisterous political action groups rudely sensationalized the need for skepticism and encouraged members into suspenseful fear, implying that the Brothers were artfully deceiving the populace only to ultimately colonize the world. But the majority countered that, if they had the means to take over the planet in minutes without elaborate ruse, why did they not do so prior?

Perhaps for the first time in history, members knew the facts and saw beyond the hypnotic veil tossed over their eyes by mankind's deceptive societies. The more the opposition served tenuous threats, the faster members abandoned them, realizing these were spin-offs of the dreaded Order.

After an absolutely grueling day packed with meetings, interviews, and inquiring mobs, I finally found peaceful repose in the tranquil natural scenery offered by the Tower Gardens. At that late hour, the park was completely vacant and faintly lit, host only to my lonesome echoing steps, and the mysterious throbs of an impaired heart asserting to be hearkened by caring essences far beyond our errant orb.

I paced aimlessly amid vast dim garden grounds alone, witnessing nature's opulent passions contend untiringly with my thoughtful solitude, patiently waiting for sunlight's first light to renew life's verdant pageantry. Rushing waters proclaimed their alluring presence nearby, mindlessly coursing through nature's demesne as ordained by man's determined entreaty. The clear dome above exhibited far off, enigmatic starry lusters, often interrupted by the unexpected appearance of spring clouds pierced at times by flying machines porting some vague end in mind, much in the spirit of my own life.

Day and night, my forlorn spirit pleaded soberly in the closet of my own undeniable prudence, begetting its desolate voice to be heard across the great heavenly divide rather than the wicked halls of Saras's burlesque indiscretions. Living with inconceivable distaste and unrivaled suffering, my soul's deepest mysteries and most endearing dreams I kept profoundly shrouded from mankind's judgmental senses since toddler times. The act of sealing them away into my heart each day, each hour, each minute of my endless miserable existence felt like a mighty fiery dagger plunging ruthlessly far into my bosom, bursting forth the most intense tears and lonesome despair imaginable from my soul's most passionate fountains.

Secluded from a scornful world and depressed beyond certainty by secrecy's heavy toll, my soul emotionally and endlessly pleaded Father to grant me two long-overdue wishes: allow me to know Him, and meet my heart's greatest yearning whom I deeply loved. While my days counted on thirty years of unbearable woe, only a recent glimmer of her exceptional beauty is all I could account for, and begged Father that my bosom could wait no more.

The eve stars—they emerge with such unrivalled wonder and radiant glimmer, yet seem so far, in the likeness of my luminous jewel that only pleasant dreams brought nigh. Why were we so far apart, her and I, bearing absolute conscious absence on the matter. Emotional cries from the heart hastened upon heaven's gateways to displace night's blinding cloak, but destiny unknown my beacon's enchanting shores concealed, and gloom woke.

Sooner than not, I realized invisible penal restraints held firm sway over me, entrapping the soul like snug colossal vice grips from which redemption seemed impossible. Within its imperceptible restraining walls, incarceration felt like an eternal ordeal, and eventual closeness to my one an unattainable futile challenge. Still, my lonely heart begged I discard past memories so it might soar beyond Saras's bindings, boldly sail through wide murky seas, and search for my far-off beacon: a star brighter than Sirius, and a love deeper than the heart of Rosette.

What I would give to behold May Len's saintly purity, listen to her sweet angelic voice stirred by tides of radiant hope, place my hands into her warm velvet fold, and share a brief moment of peace by her blissful godliness. Why, I wondered, did vast distances blind my eyes from her supple loving smile reminiscent of God's paradise? Why did my mind sustain recurring memories of a friend, sister, so dear to my heart? Why did my soul have to bear this wretched, sinful inmate life, wasting away like dry straw crumbling afore fierce earthly fire winds, when it begged so ardently to live among starlit jubilee?

Indeed, stars are such beautiful, captivating wonders—radiant, soothing, colorful, vast torches of creation that grant vibrant life and joyous hope to our hearts, wherever their dreams sway enamored sights. If someday I released my soul and journeyed into another vessel found on far-distant shores, I will gaze at the heavens and seek the brightest star of them all, for May Len's presence kindles their magnificent brilliance and fills the heavens with splendors untold. Her grace paints the intense colors of Orion, her smile the loveliness and glory of the Pleiades. Her voice summons the harmonies of Carina's cloudy choirs into celestial song, and her eyes beget God's beckoning into my heart's yearning tones. Her soothing starlight shall forever feast my eyes upon a view of God's realm, for what dulcet privilege it is to find a path to the Infinite, lit by her graceful helm.

His Majesty I so humbly implore to forgive my many, many offenses; may He find me worthy someday of new beginnings outside these earthly restraining fences. May He grant me the honor to be born among the stars and gather raptly to my one's sonnet bars. Perhaps in a million years, if that is what it takes and God is merciful with my soul, I beg to finally walk by her side because, without her, I am not whole. I'd sacrifice it all to be in the land of eternal song, sharing His loving waters by my one's gentle side all day long.

The evening's serene grandeur that so inspired gentle ballades for my resplendent jewel would not last long. Gina's soft footsteps sneaked up from a distance, commanding somber shadows meaning to rip my priceless celestial wonder from my heart's deepest longing. I did not mind her presence but knew what she wanted and in many ways wished she would never ask.

"I knew I would find you here," she said playing innocent, but rather edgy as if she was up to something. "Busy day no doubt?"

"That's an understatement," I said rather somber, wishing her away.

"I've seen worst," she said, but I did not reply. Rather, I moved slowly away from her, singing loving ballades to the wonderment of ages, the heart of my soul, my beloved inspiring flower.

"Is there something the matter, Dr. Sullivan?" she said rather shy and gentle. "You seem somewhat distant."

"I have a lot on my mind. That's why I came up here, to make better sense of it all. I can't count the times I've heard my name mentioned today. Honestly, I don't know how you put up with it day after day."

"It's all about prestige," she said, taking a spot beside me and asserting her body's presence uninvited. "People believing and looking up to you, daydreaming about what they might get from you if luck smiles on them; try it some time. It's quite addictive."

"I'm afraid that's not me," I replied impartially.

"Well, that's a surprise. Why not, if I may ask?"

"I don't see myself fitting too well into such a role."

"You couldn't be further from the truth, dust bagger," she said, picking up tempo, "because if anyone has skills, charisma, command presence, and the gift, it's you. You certainly demonstrated it before the Senate, too well I'm afraid. With all that potential, it's a shame to see you collect rocks when you could be holding some of the highest political positions on Earth."

"And live a lie? I can't do that. With so many things one can aspire to, why worship another fallible being, someone without a clue why we're here, what we need, and only cares for himself?"

"Really, butternut, you need to get connected. The world runs on power, not logic, and you get only two choices: get the power or be subject to it. I know what side I want to be on."

"Yes, power, that age-old aberrant, arrogance-imposed, civil-consented system of contorted checks and balances, applied because no one is willing, or encouraged, to serve others and get along readily otherwise. It's wrong for any system to keep its members ignorant, confused with chaotic politics, and revering some authority figure that does nothing for them but smile and exploit. Rather than strive for power, we should magnify humanity and ask for little else in return."

"Well, I see you're not the same man I used to debate with, always quoting Nietzsche's will to power, Spencer's survival of the fittest. Where did all that passionate determination go?"

"Been there, done that, and learned my lesson."

"I also learned my lesson: how fortunate for governments that the people they administer don't think," she said laughing.

"Adolf Hitler, friend of yours by chance?" I said, still rather somber. "Everyone is a moon, and has a dark side he never shows to anybody [1], and I'm no exception. That's why I left for Mars because I don't trust humanity and serve them no good purpose."

"Do you fear failure?"

"I fear what I could do wrong," I replied, deep in thought. "I guess you call that guilt."

"You're too nice of a man, but you've proven to be firm when it counts; and that's what this world really needs: firmness and a nice, convincing face. Your leadership traits are off the charts, but you waste your time picking up rocks; I just don't get it. Why don't you get into politics? I'll be sure to give you a great referral."

"There's a life at the heart of ancient crimson rocks, and a new beginning in each glimmer of starlight that strikes my eyes. Though it takes this rigid spirit an eternity of plight, I will patiently seek that wondrous beacon of life that eludes my heart in flight. My search for love gathers me unto a unique far-off heart of gold overflowing with passionate truth and beauty untold."

"That's so very . . . deep, but I heard you say rocks again. Come on, dirt bagger: don't waste your future. Stay on Earth, connect, and become what you were meant to be. Chancellor Sullivan—doesn't that have a nice ring to it?"

"Nothing personal, but there's something I've been meaning to ask you."

"And what might that be?" she said sweetly.

"You've tried promoting me ever since we met. First, you helped me get through college, then into the Mars contact team. Now, you're trying to get me into the political arena. Why do you insist in nudging me upward?"

"Because . . . I know talent when I see it," she said after some hesitation.

"I think picking up your napkin from the cafeteria floor, the day we met, is hardly a sign of talent."

"Gentlemen are hard to find these days, especially those willing to talk about esoteric subjects with a total stranger. That said it all, butternut."

Silent low stares briefly dominated the moment. Gina meditated over some delicate statement of position, difficult for me not to notice. Due to the lateness of the hour, it was rather obvious she was there for reasons other than to take a leisurely stroll or go over the day's events.

"That's not why you're here, is it?" I said.

"I just wanted to see you one last time before you returned to Mars," she said gently, masterfully docile to achieve laden goals, "and . . . apologize for my rude behavior. I've been over bearing, dominant, and stern about the way I see things; but there's a valid reason for it. You see, when I was young, foster care blamed me for everything that went wrong and kept me from voicing my opinions. I vowed to someday become a powerful figure, not just a pest, someone to be respected, with whom debating would be futile."

At the mention of these last words, I briskly turned to Gina with an inquisitive look, recalling Tiger Woman from my earlier dream. I didn't know what to make of it, but the words "debate" and "futile" connected suddenly. "What is it? Something I said?" she asked, showing honest concern.

"No . . . it's nothing. I just remembered something," I replied, but a nagging reminder kept me homed into that dream through the remainder of our conversation. "No need to apologize," I said. "You simply chose to be what you are out of necessity; so did I."

"I don't think I follow you, but what I'm trying to say is that . . . I know I have to change, and I want to, with the right individual by my side."

"I have a lot to thank you for," I said, standing up and pacing about to focus on the legitimacy of my statements. "You changed me, but I don't think I can change you or should I. Perhaps, that's why I never called on you; I felt I had nothing to offer."

"But you do," Gina said, displaying her absolute best feminine skills. "Look, I just wanted you, nothing else. I know my dominant attitude drove you away, but I care about you more than I can say. I hope I'm not too late."

"It's not the lateness but the times. Look around you and the changes taking place. You have an important job to do, and I have no time for a serious relationship."

"The good book says it's not good for man to be alone, so let me be that special someone in your life. You need not be alone. I want to be your Eve, always have and always will."

"And if I were alone, I would have told you. But I'm never alone, far from it. Eve's gentle starlight illumines my path with radiant glories, and the most precious of pearls warmly exalts purity in my longing heart with loving, celestial stories. What my life desires most is stamped deep unto my heart and woven into my being forever with strands of gold, filled with gentle grace and love eternal that only the heavens can inspire unto its hallowed hold."

"That's so romantic," she said passionately, unaware that I spoke of May Len. "I knew for ten long years that I meant something special in your life. Now that I hear your poetic words confirm it and we're so close to each other, I'm happier than I've ever been," she said, artistically forging her passions.

"You might not like what I have to say." I replied with a serious tone. "I thought I told you . . ."

"I don't care what odds we may face going forward. I'll give up everything to be with you. Let me go to Mars with you and collect rocks, if that's what you'll have me do."

"No . . ."

"I'll resign my post, change habits . . ." she insisted, quickly cutting me off.

"Gina . . ."

"I'll do what it takes if you would only care for me," she added, reaching out for a kiss.

"Gina, you're a very beautiful, smart, influential woman with more opportunities than anyone could ever dream of. You have it all. Any man would gladly surrender life to be with you. But truth is, light is what I seek. You can't contain or change what you are. We don't know what tomorrow has in store for us or where we will be as humanity reinvents itself. Who knows, I might have to call on you from time to time for advice."

Gina hesitated for a moment, then came up close, and put her arms around me seductively. I immediately felt strange, drained, and aroused. My heartbeat went up, breathing constrained, and head began to pound. I could not explain it, but the prospect of liking her felt grisly. Gina, on the other hand, enjoyed the moment and pressed forth with her pretentious scheme.

"Please don't," I said, struggling for air and mental composure. "You're not what I had in mind."

"You can't refuse me; I know what's best for you," she said passionately. "You will be mine, so don't delay the inevitable. Just enjoy all of me, and everything will be fine. Release yourself to me with that candor men are known for; that's all I ask."

"Gina," I said somewhat disoriented, "I don't feel so good all of a sudden. This can't happen."

"Of course it can!" Gina kissed my cheek with outright malignant forthrightness. Her kiss compared to May Len's felt cannibalistic, like a vampire literally sucking life from my face. "It's already happening. Can't you tell?" she said tightly caressing my face.

"You can only force me but not convince me."

"I like that in a man!" Gina hugged me like a hungry beast, kissing my left cheek desperately. "You will be mine. I must have you; it's my destiny to have you. Feel this body; you will have it beside you for a lifetime. You can't debate with me; it would be futile. I am a superior being to those alien maggots!"

The word "maggot" awakened dark, repulsive memories of Tiger Woman and I tried to pull away, but Gina's tight clutch held me captive like the dream's forceful tail. Her body felt like some grotesque slimy creature crawling cloyingly into my innermost being, but her clutch proved difficult to break. I finally managed to break her strong hug and firmly held her arms far from me. No sooner, I regained composure and calmed my sorely throbbing head.

"Stop it!" I said angrily, trying to catch my breath. "What is it with you? One minute you apologize for being aggressive, promising to change. Look what you do the next! Can the leopard change its spots? Looks like not! Understand this: I'm not in the mood for pleasure! You've got a long way to go to understand my desires, and it's not what you have in mind! Light, not sex. It's that simple! Do you copy?"

Gina looked to the floor disappointed, and I gently let go of her arms. "Look," I said apologetically, "I'm sorry to let you down like this, but you have me all wrong."

"But I want to give you all that I am, the best way I know how. I'm sorry if I offended you, but trust me, I'll learn from this incident, and it won't happen again. I love you . . ."

"No, you don't. Love is not the act of hunting wild game down or convincing someone with passionate advertising until they submit. Love is found in the humblest realms of the heart where truth reigns supreme rather than the deep hollows of a covert mechanical body, the persuasive kingdoms of our lips, or the haunting shadows of desire."

"What do you mean exactly?" she said, somewhat irritated with my dismissing attitude.

"So then they are no more the two, but one single being. What therefore God hath joined together, let no human separate [2]. That's true love, become one soul, *oh-joi*, the elixir of beings that love each other not for pleasure or protection but for the essence they share from Him and nothing more. That's what and whom I want: love of the soul."

"I hear you, loud and clear," she said, rather upset. "You prefer May Len, don't you? I see you've definitely made up your mind . . ."

"And if I did—and I most certainly have—why shouldn't I? Do you not recall I said so in our last conversation?"

"How can you do this to me?" she said loudly, trying to cry though unable to produce tears. "Why did you play with my feelings, letting me think you cared for me! You lied to me all this time! What kind of man are you? It's all because of that . . . inhuman monster!"

"I did not lie to you. Rather, interpretation is in the mind of the beholder."

"You led me to believe I was your precious pearl, your starlight. No, it was that alien monster you lauded! How can you possibly love that strange-looking creature over me? In my presence!"

"To answer your question, then, yes," I said intensely inspired, "I'm deeply in love with May Len, the most beautiful, purest being in all creation, and I love her with all my heart and strength! I love her. My God do I love her! I dream of her all day long with intense longing and a vigor that my heart can't contain at times! No one else, Gina, no one else, but her!"

"Can't you see she's just using you? Don't you realize she doesn't love you at all and never will?" she replied with a worried look on her face.

"I love her, and that's all that matters to me! With all due respect, I think you need to know just how much I love her."

"I don't particularly care to!" she replied with selfish dignity, releasing me harshly and turning away from me.

"Then cover your ears because the entire universe will know shortly."

As I slowly backed away from her, my voice thundered loudly at the top of my lungs with an emotional cry in my throat, singing intense odes of love to my one across imaginary ethers.

"The universe as my witness, be it known that I love May Len with all my heart! I'm deeply and madly in love with her soul! I love her. I'm dead without her. If I must spend an eternity waiting and die of all I am to be by her side, so be it! I want nothing else in life, only her! I want her in my heart, in my soul, in my eyes, in my thoughts, in my dreams, in every breath I take, flowing through my veins as one soul. May Len, my beautiful starlight, if you can hear me, know that I'm madly in love with you!"

"I see I was wrong about everything, and I'm sorry I misjudged you," Gina said, trying to recover the situation with an air of comprehension yet feeling decimated inside.

"Change is hard to come by, but I'll try—just for you," she said, showing discomfort with her right leg and left arm. "Don't give me up for that alien girl because I certainly won't be giving up on you. I'm twenty times the woman she is; you just don't know what you're missing," she said, wearing a gimmick smile and placing a fast kiss on my face.

"Madam Speaker, with all due respect, no being in the universe stands a chance against May Len. She's not leaving this heart."

"Not if I can help it. Besides, she's definitely not your type; her genetics are probably all wrong, and she's too old for you anyways. Don't waste your time with her. Still, I'll be there to fight for your love until I'm yours. I'll let you think on that for a while. *Ciao*!" Gina walked off slowly toward the elevators, turning and flashing her right leg at me with feminine intentions.

As she left the park, a tall man with bright green eyes and dark hair suddenly appeared behind me out of nowhere, and said with commanding voice, "Good evening. Dr. Sullivan, I presume?"

"Yes, I am," I replied, rather taken aback.

"I'm sorry for imposing on you this late in the evening, but I just happened to be in the area and overheard your lively discussion with the young lady. From the sound of it, things are not going well between you both, I take it?"

"We never seem to agree on how to agree. She wants an intimate relationship, but I have someone else in mind; and every time we meet, we debate endlessly."

"That's the norm for Earth couples. Say, don't you wonder sometimes what drives people to express affection toward others?"

"To be honest, I've given it little thought until just recently."

"Everyone treats the topic like some scheduled ritual with just one motive in mind: pleasure. True love is so much more than that. How can flesh, set drunk with nerve prickles, be thought of as the do-all answer to love? The body is just a machine, nothing more."

"We're brought up thinking that way, knowing no better. It's probably built right into our genes by now," I replied.

"Apparently so. Aphra Behn once said, 'Love ceases to be a pleasure, when it ceases to be a secret.' So much for love's endurance in our private affairs. At times, love barely survives but a few seconds and then withers away like a burnt cinder, overcome by obscure negations."

"Other than sensual pleasure, you wonder what else attracts people together," I said, often glancing at Gina as she faded into the distance, limping slightly from her right leg.

"The soul, inspired by the Infinite," he said, "not restless memories."

"Now there's a stimulating thought."

"The young speaker's restless memories beg to live today, but things are quite different now since her world is long gone. Still, she wants to bring it back at all cost to fill the enormous lonely void in her life; truly, it's both a waste and a shame. But I thought I heard you say there's someone else in your life. Is that the case?"

"There is," I added, taking a deep breath and moving my head in the negative, "but even though I love her with all my heart, it's not likely to ever be for reasons that are too evident."

"I thought love conquers all," said the man calmly, swaying his head to get my due attention. "There's no problem too tough for true love to overcome. All you need is truth and then follow it with trust. Is that not the way?"

"Truth is we are from worlds vastly apart," I replied in deep reflection, looking up at the stars, "yet we seem linked by some benign essence I can't comprehend. Her soul is clear as a mountain stream, but mine is stagnant as a lifeless pond, marred by corrupt dreams. She lives by truth, but my sins run rampant with no deliverance in sight. I admire her heart's beauty and devotion to Father; aspects missing in my own life. We are so vastly different, like beauty and the beast, positive and negative, and that's why it can't be."

"Sounds like a complex relationship, somewhat out of this world and quite different from Earth's norms, don't you think?" said the man, walking with me back slowly to the elevators.

"One thing is certain: she is no ordinary Earth woman."

"Well, I finally heard something refreshing for once," he said humorously. "So what planet is she from?"

"She's . . ." I said, suddenly feeling strangely disconnected with reality, somewhat dizzy, and at a loss for words trying not to say Masar. "She's from, across the sea, real far from here, really out there."

"I see," he said calmly. "I haven't been overseas lately, and so much has changed over there. Whereabouts did you say she was from again?"

"It's . . . kind of remote, cold, and deserted over there, really rocky," I said, clueless and lumpy, uncertain why my mind careened so badly out of control. "There's a lot of cold wind . . . from air, outside, when you're . . . inside and have no light, you know," I added, becoming increasingly incoherent.

"Ah, you must be referring to Siberia, the calm land."

"Nothing but ice and storms up there," I said, dazed by flash images from Chasma, arresting any awareness of my immediate surroundings.

"Have you ever been there?"

"I'm know the landscape; it changed lately," I said, struggling to regain my senses unsuccessfully.

"You should have seen it when it was lush, warm, and full of life. It was a different world back then, a sculptured garden wondering calmly through space like a light beacon, and much more beautiful than this world ever hoped to be. But best of all, it was devoted entirely to God in all ways. Some of its trees were as wide as this building and actually got redder with elevation—fascinating biology."

"Trees turned redder with elevation?" I said abruptly, quickly recalling my Uzboi vision.

"Quite so. Why. Did I just remind you of something?"

"I . . . find that quite remarkable," I replied, holding back swift enthusiasm, inflicted by a growing dizziness.

"It was such an enchanting place. Waves of love were infused into the planet itself, and you could sense its sweet scent and feel it flowing through your body; so powerful, it brought one to tears. But tragedy stole its grace forever; you know how Earth men are."

As he spoke, my mind drifted asleep, and when least expected, I said rather oblivious, "We should have attacked," catching up to myself a bit too late.

"What was that, I beg your pardon?" he said innocently.

"I mean, I'd love to see it . . . intact, yes, all there," I said, pausing and fumbling again with no rational mind of my own.

"Why? Is there something not right in Siberia?"

"No . . . yes, the land is not intact, a lot is missing," I said, briefly losing mental control again and shaking my head until I regained my senses.

"Is everything all right? You seem not yourself," he said calmly.

"Yes. I'm just . . . under a lot of stress," I said, sentient at last.

"I think I get it now. Sadly, the calm land will never be the same again. But getting back to that special someone, may I ask you a personal question?"

"Please, by all means."

"Do you fear your negative thoughts and emotions?"

"I would have to say that . . . yes, I do."

"We can all do without those mental accessories. In fact, honesty is all you need to find love's narrow path."

"I'm afraid my situation is way more complicated than that."

"Really? How so, if I might ask?"

"You see, her father is a prominent government figure, she is much older than I, and lives by laws quite foreign to ours. I feel there's little I can offer her other than harm her people with my sinful ways. But in spite of the great chasm keeping us apart, she is, and will always be, my sister, my one, my only friend. I will wait a million years if I have to and do what Father ordains to earn the privilege to be by her side, for such is my love for her soul."

"That's an admirable commitment, but are you sure about your personal assessment of this situation."

"Quite so," I said sadly. "You see, long ago, I took a wrong turn at a river delta, fell into Saras's traps, and lost sight of the sea beyond. That blunder cost me my soul, and I've paid dearly for it ever since. For that reason, a man like me doesn't deserve to unite with a promising soul as her."

The stranger laughed and said, "That's some testimony, and I know exactly where you're coming from. But what if your notions are wrong? You said you're willing to wait a million years for her, unaware that, just maybe, you may have no wait pending at all? Have you asked her opinion on the matter?"

"You mean tell her I love her?"

"Isn't it the truth? I just heard you shout it to the cosmos out loud."

"Well . . . I could never do that," I added absolutely panicked.

"Why not? What are you afraid of? Have no fear, for truth is here."

"I fear I'll get my mouth to flap and choke on a bone because it has a mind of its own."

"Oh, that's really good; I'll be sure to remember that phrase," he said after laughing heartily. "Truth is what it is. It is right, eternal, and should never be considered offensive. Instead, welcome it, embrace it, fall in love with it, and never let it out of your heart. So be truthful, and be right. Go, tell her that you love her. Open up your heart before her, and testify who and what you are. That, my friend, is true love."

"It's not that simple," I said, reflecting for a moment. "I don't know how to act in front of her, and she can read me like an open book. Chances are, she already knows my thoughts, and they can't be very nice I'm sure."

"What if she does?" he asked, but I did not reply. "My son, by talking to her, you only discomfort your legacy, never her soul. The past is history, the future is destiny, and the present is empathy. Prove your love; show the power of your heart. Boldly uphold truth above all things and unmask your thoughts before her. Sacrifice all that you are and hold nothing back, for honesty is your measure of love. And remember, it's not good to keep a lady waiting."

"I love her intensely, more than life itself, but no one will ever understand how wicked and undeserving I feel inside."

"Try me," said the stranger, placing a hand on my shoulder and staring sharply into my eyes. Immediately, I felt a wave of warm sentiment rush through me, shaking my inner most being. I felt like crying precipitously and strived to keep my mental bearings, but I could not, overpowered by an imposing trancelike state that overcame my deepest thoughts and emotions.

My body quivered vigorously, collapsing to the floor powerless. My throat constrained with a desperate loud cry, and warm tears raced down my face under emotional duress. I felt highly inspired, freed from inhibition and desire, as if an angel reached down and touched my soul, clearing out obsessive muck introduced by Gina moments prior.

"It was so long ago, my young son," he said sweetly, "when Saras's toxic dust fell upon us arresting our breath, and fires flared nearby meaning to consume our flesh. Rather than run from danger, you clutched lovingly unto my bosom and sang songs to His Majesty unafraid of death's blossom. Likewise, go forth and grasp tenderly to your one's heart unafraid, singing lovingly to the Infinite. Rest your mind from this world upon me once more, Roshon, and recall those days; for your life is but a moment's struggle to recall the past, desist its ancient wrongful ways, and attract new futures."

A strong sentiment of all-knowing harmony with a calm, spiritual essence blotted out all events around me. My mind seemed projected several meters out of the body, but still in it, freed from its limiting senses and needs. I felt serene, unconcerned, unemotional, extremely caring and knowing, jubilant to lead a life of perfect benevolence, surrounded by the living presence of countless essences that shared the same assuring freedom from desire and abundance of infinity—the beloved brotherhood.

"Let the Tree of Life, the brotherhood, rest upon thee, Roshon. Be with us as one and leave us no more," he said gently. "Let the tongue of old freely declare its hidden mysteries and witness before the Infinite your many mental journeys endowed with endless psalteries. Your thoughts are now as they were in times long gone, brother Roshon. Speak from whence."

"It is only by His Majesty's wisdom that friends meet," I uttered calmly, yet feeling like an entirely different person whose thoughts expressed warmly not behind but in front of the eyes. "Our Creator enlightens my path with the company of a sister whose smile is brighter than sapphires from His heart. I don't want to lose my tender flower ever again; she is my one, my only one, my beloved matching force in God's currents, whose soul I'm deeply and madly in love with. Thus speaks my eager heart to my inspiring master of ages, with whom I was most privileged to share my last breath in Atlantis."

"You've endured such long million-year wait for your beautiful polarity to grant thee light," he replied. "She is the magnetic force that carries with it the sum total of your eternal Lorentz cycles, the event horizons from whence your divergence flows, and the inspiring breath that spirals the fountain of life unto your soul. She is the pulse of thine heart and the color of your inner flame. Inseparably do you both oscillate about His currents, His light, ever-fathoming dimensional endlessness."

"My gentle master, I so desperately love her heart I can no longer bear such long wait!" I said quivering.

"Won't be much longer, my son, just days. Your heart's love for her is so, so strong that the heavens shudder from its mighty potency every time you so mention it. Be her one, proudly go before her, and tell her just how much you love her. Let your heart enter into her bosom and tenderly shiver its foundations with intense love, for His Majesty grants it to be shared. Let His heart reach down in a mighty current and unite your two forces, your two polarities, as one forever. Such is the way of truth and your destiny. Delay not the inevitable; wait on love no longer."

"My kind, beloved master, I shall please the Infinite with His love and make Masar proud by declaring my heart before my one, my beloved warmth, with all my strength, reverent to Father and in the ways of old," I said crying. "May the Infinite ever be admired and my gentle master be well pleased."

"I am proud of you, my son. Your days have been most trying, but Father has lived in your heart in each of your tribulations. You are never alone, and my love shall always be with you. We must leave you now but know that your life is in grave danger. Don't take the elevator tonight. Use the stairs; someone waits to take you by force, scramble your mind, and turn you against us. Trust no one, always be watchful of danger about you, and forget us not. *Oh-joi*!"

"My kind master?" I said, hastily snapping back to my senses but heard no reply from the stranger who had secretly vanished. I was far from concealing objects and would have seen him leave, but he was nowhere to be found. Though I remembered only sections of this experience, I felt an irresistible urge to come before May Len and declare my heart and His love to her.

Emotional warm tears poured relentlessly from my eyes, sobbing and smiling at the same time. I felt renewed, refreshed, and proud to withstand Gina's obsessive advances. I could feel May Len's presence right beside me, her essence close and real enough to touch. I was not alone, feeling her hand fold softly into mine. Her heart embraced mine; our minds were as one. Her sweet voice sung tender words of truth I wished would never end.

The nearness I felt to May Len brought me incomprehensible joy and hope, willing to give it all for that glorious day when I could reverently lift up His essence by her side forever. On my trembling knees, I shared my essence with May Len in gentle gratitude for her invisible company, pressing her concealed hand unto my heart as time passed unconcerned. I so loved her, more than I could contain, or the heart abound sufficiently to express it so.

The special EMS broadcast would air soon. Coming to my feet and aware I was being watched, I confidently headed out of the park, quietly hiding behind walls for safety near the exits. Not long after, three men wearing dark blue suits peered out of the elevator lobby into the park and proceeded to search the area. Following the Brother's instructions, I silently took the stairs and visited the downstairs kiosk for late fare before heading to my room, just as proprietors prepared to close shop early and make the broadcast.

It was a stressful trip back to my quarters, trying to blend in with people while keeping an eye out for suspicious movements. When I arrived, two men dressed in the same-type suit were knocking on my door but swiftly left after no one answered. When all was clear, I quickly dashed for the room and searched it thoroughly before admitting myself, just as the broadcast began.

EMS aired everything: individual reviews, contacts, and surprisingly the Senate discussion with the Brothers. Nothing was cut out of the sessions, and enthusiastic commentators openly favored Saras's entry into the cosmic brotherhood.

Excitement filled the air, or lack of it, on all worlds. Colonists donned extended suits waiting for the fly-bys. On Saras, young and old camped out for the night with cams in hand. Major thruways were packed with celebrating members, and restless speeders displayed giant banners welcoming the Brothers to Saras. Building tops were filled with jubilant souls hoping to be that much closer to the fly-bys, and every solar system telescope pointed their sights toward Saras to capture the momentous space armada's arrival.

Evening settled as the world prepared for the Brothers' grand advent. No one knew the precise time of their arrival, and minutes seemed like hours. Anxiety filled the air as dawn approached upon a sleepless Saras, waiting patiently for providence to spread across its skies.

Morning hours were absolutely quiet. Supply centers, schools, offices, factories—all Saras and colonial activities came to a halt. Even at the Towers, nutritional service was unavailable other than prepackaged products from automated dispensers. This could be called the day the solar system stood still.

Every major city was jam-packed with people, some from far-off places, lining up to witness the alien aero-parade. For those not so fortunate, there was always EMS transmitting live from 2,500 locations around the globe.

Early that morning, I made my way to the observation deck under security escort. There, Jim had a seat reserved for me, conveniently beside Gina. She spared no expense fixing her eyes upon me like a carnivorous beast, but this time she kept to herself as if nothing happened the day prior. EMS wasted no time diving around my seat for interrogation and expectation checks; I had an idea who sent them. Interestingly, Hans and Sean were nowhere to be found.

A few hours after sunrise, EMS announced that fly-by missions were under way on Masar and Jovian outposts. Colonial video showed huge cigar-shaped craft hovering above settlements with hundreds of smaller craft flying in tight formation alongside them. Some craft landed on colony pads and visited colonists inside domes. Shuttles took flight and joined the parade, fitting into formation alongside the Brothers. Shortly after, Luna colonies were visited in similar fashion.

An hour later, countless large cigar-shaped craft hung motionless in skies high above. From their middles, smaller glowing craft called Scouts emerged until tens of thousands of craft filled the skies between Saras and their carriers. Their incandescent glow simmered in the skies like pleasing flying candelabras in perfect formation, soaring effortlessly above expectant, joyous civilians.

The fly-bys were an absolute success. For the most part, people no longer feared space invaders. The fly-bys continued for several days, however in fewer numbers. They became a symbol of hope and a message as powerful as any speech could ever deliver, inspiring humanity to drop material squabbles, escape mechanisms, and aim for higher values in life.

Under threat of perdition, people left caves with renewed hope, overcoming humiliation of their own making. Regardless of creed or state, everyone came together to recognize in their own manner one inspiring source, one guiding force, not by their creed's given name but a new name common to the entire universe: Manéh, the Father, the Infinite Consciousness.

The world desperately wanted to become Brothers over-night by dressing, speaking, and acting like them. Members devoured the Brothers' teachings with insatiable appetite and could not get enough. Speaking mannerisms changed; awareness and testimony of negative thoughts increased. It was rare to see anyone frowning or delving in the negative. Typical handshakes were considered old-fashioned; hand clasps were now the thing. No more hello, it was now *oh-Joi.*

The world magically transformed beyond recognition. Kindness, beauty, joy, and an understanding of life reached sudden indescribable plateaus. UEF members, realizing people led change, quickly adapted and proceeded with sweeping personal changes of their own. For Saras, it was a new beginning.

Still, in the fabric of everyone's lives, there lingered an unsolved riddle: hidden fears yearning for attention. It was our legacy, deeds that previously led humanity to vanish into oblivion. The focal thought in everyone's mind was upon those responsible for such worldly tragedies, and would they rise again? Would we be strong enough to resist lords of carnage, plotting to sink the world into perdition by fanning our negative self?

Now, more than ever, people looked to the skies, not in awe of candle-lit fires but in ever-growing yearning for unity, honesty, and beauty. Man's fake lifeless concepts and restrictions began to collapse. Members felt empowered to distrust dreamy ideals and set asunder those fears forcing them to protect pride, aware they were never alone, most of all, always loved. Legacy and the pursuit of distinction might be no more if people gave truthful beginnings a chance, understanding that the negative self is nothing but vain temptation. Time would only tell.

It was a new beginning, a spiritual renaissance long awaited, inspired by the power of love and truth. But it was just the tip of infinity, a minute path to higher planes of existence, and an introduction to the science of life.

My eyes were untiringly placed upon the chalice of May Len's unrivaled heavenly radiance. My bosom sung unstoppable words of beauty, epic poems of love, and ballades of divine longing for her incomparable soul. Day and night, only my radiant flower flowed life into my heart, for it no longer pulsed to any other desire in life but her wondrous gateways of grace. My songs of love unfurled across countless stars deep into the enrapturing heavens, spreading her angelic luster and gentle heart unto them, written by my heart's enamored testimony. My jewel, my beacon, my angelic sunrise, and my windows of divine beauty, my lovely sister, I so love thee.

---

[1] S. J. Woolf, "Hear Am I," Random House, 1941, pp. 78 - 80.

[2] R. W. J. Morford, "Matthew 9: 16," in *The One New Man Bible*, Traverse city, SC: True Potential Publishing, Inc., 2011.

Chapter 16: *The Enemy Within*

After several exceedingly rewarding days on Saras, it was finally time for the contact team to head back to Masar, reestablish contact with the Brothers, and set a date for their historic landing at the Towers. I was uniquely glad to return, for there was someone I truly longed to see: my graceful, beautiful sweet angel, whom my heart knew was there anxiously waiting for me.

At first light, Sean and Hans left covertly for the space port to catch the first direct flight to Masar. Hans was the early-rising type and somehow talked Sean into leaving with him but did not extend me the same courtesy for reasons I realized all too well, so I thought. I did not mind traveling alone. I had done so more times than I could remember and was rather used to it. But on this occasion, I had no clue what was in store for me.

The best way to get to New Manhattan's space port was still via ground speeder. So I went downstairs, crossed the lengthy reception lobby, and headed toward the front transportation court to take a taxi. As always, I made no previous ground travel plans since taxis were in constant abundance at the Towers. However, on that day, I would be in for an unexpected eye-opener, and it was probably a good thing I made no previous reservations.

As I reached the exit doors leading into the transportation court, I noticed a long line of irritated travelers waiting for transport, and a single taxi parked on the court's access way strangely taking no passengers. Though this seemed most unusual, I assumed nothing of it, and mindlessly approached the court to get in line. However, a strange sense of apprehension suddenly stopped me dead cold before reaching the line and instinctively took a few steps backward. I stood still for a few moments unsure what to make of my reaction when a deep intuitive feeling ran through me, warning me of pending danger.

Alerted to a threat not previously realized, time seemed to freeze still, and I became particularly sensitive of my surroundings. Without turning my head, I felt there were three men sitting nearby, keeping an inconspicuous eye on me. Outside on the access way, something most unusual also caught my attention: two drivers, not just one, stood by the speeder bearing a sign that said "Bill Sullivan." How did they know I needed transport if I made no reservations?

Both drivers were tall in stature, overly muscular, suspiciously alert, and looked remarkably alike. Their aggressively rounded faces were coarsely toned by fearsome ridged features that forcefully paralyzed startled hearts into willing submission from a distance. Deep preying eyes stared outwardly observant, and sharp flares beamed from them that did not readily earn my trust. Their shoes shone warily, and their outfits matched those worn by agents searching for me at the gardens days prior, rather unusual for taxi drivers of those days.

One of the drivers briskly scanned the long line of waiting travelers from afar and his mortifying eyes connected with me like a starving hawk. Hastily, he tapped the other driver on the arm, and he quickly stared straightaway in my direction. Consumed by dread, I casually gazed away trying not to raise suspicion, but both men decisively asserted their unbranded sights forward and stepped my way with martial stride.

I stood at the end of the waiting line unsure what to do, held at bay by approaching captors and discreet watchful eyes whose confident flair held no mercy for my foreseeable predicament. But unexpectedly, a female voice disrupted arresting anxiety with her commanding benign presence, and fretfully whispered into my troubled heart, "Hide quickly."

Seized by a sudden sense of reassured urgency, I made like I left something behind in my room and calmly turned back the way I came, ditching the drivers who vainly hollered my name out-loud outside the building. But no sooner, two men sitting in the lobby not far from me stood up subtly and walked in my general direction, at first serenely but soon rather briskly. I hurried my pace somewhat anxiously, but they immediately matched my stride, assuring me they knew I had discovered their intent.

Overlooking the reception lobby from arched atrium levels above, several suspicious-looking men leaned against glass rails like perched owls ready to swoop down on unwary prey, often confirming visual contact with superiors. As I neared, they stood back and paced leisurely toward the elevators, hoping to force rising cars to their levels and apprehend me. With elevators compromised, and possibly stairwells, all I could do was find somewhere to hide as the voice suggested.

Once I reached the other end of the lobby and headed worriedly past reception en route to elevators, structural walls veiled me from agents and I promptly seized the opportunity to dash down a far hallway. Halfway down the hall, I found two large ornamental flower vases and quietly hid behind them unsure what to do next. Moments later, all atrium levels burst alive with agents feverishly searching every room, elevator, and concealing object in sight. I had no way to leave the Towers without being spotted, and the hallway I was on was a dead end.

Agents gradually neared my hideout and it was just a matter of time before they found me. Security cams, previously resting still on swivel mounts, swiftly combed the halls under shadowy control, and I was certain that security videos were also being examined. But then, I caught sight of building staff loading facility carts into a service elevator at the far end of the hallway: though quite distant, it seemed the only option at my disposal.

As stealthy as possible, putting paralyzing fear aside, I removed my shoes to get better traction and dashed down the slippery marble hallway for the service elevator as fast as I could, signaling service staff at the end of the hall to wait for me. No sooner, agents saw me from afar and sprinted desperately in my wake with Olympian stride, gaining distance in spite of my best efforts.

I dived into the elevator like a javelin and hastily asked staff to close its sluggish doors before agents could reach it. Doors slowly closed behind us, and several crashing thuds slammed into them just as they sealed shut. Agents desperately tried to pull doors open, but the lift was already on its way, and I sighed with comforting relief. Service staff were kind enough to bypass their floors, allowing me to head straight to Jim's mega-complex.

Aware of who I was, staff wondered why I ran for their slow unstylish elevator. "They wanted my autograph," I said convincingly, though I would come to regret saying that after signing enough notepads and pictures to last every member of their families.

Once in Jim's complex, his receptionist quickly confirmed that no one arranged ground transportation for me and immediately dispatched security to investigate the matter. Of course, no agents were ever found and, interestingly, no video of them or the single taxi either. Security recordings for those areas also mysteriously vanished.

Not long after, Jim came out wondering why I had not left for the space port. After learning what happened, I did not have to ask for a favor. Before long, I was headed for the space port onboard *UEF One*, and Jim beside me. After bidding final farewells, I made my way to the shuttle bound for Masar under full security escort but not without everyone along the way lauding the mission and, more so, May Len's unsurpassed grace and beauty.

During the brief four-hour flight to Masar, I used the time to catch up with Sean. However, Hans gave me every reason to think he was up to something. He stayed clear of the messaging console, rarely frequented the forward observation lounge, and did everything seemingly possible to avoid interacting with me in general.

I had an uneasy feeling about him, as if he watched my every move and read my lips from afar. When I caught sight of him, he casually lowered his sights and took down notes—lots of them. At other times, he sat staring aimlessly forward, but I could tell his peripheral vision held me within its cross hairs. I feared he was profiling me for cyphering; but I was not alone.

When the shuttle reached C6, darkness was upon the rock-strewn landscape. Visible from space, the colony's roaming dome lights were a welcomed site among a myriad of arbitrary hills and tapered valleys. Once inside the dome, shuttle doors opened, and the familiar dry, rarefied colony smell was there to greet us. Hans got off the shuttle before we did, and I lost track of him. Meanwhile, I was off to DFAC for cauliflower soup and gourmet sweet potato custard, vanishing it without trace.

Back in my room, I showered and turned my SAT in for something a bit more suitable to our burrowed colonial existence, but restlessness helplessly invaded a troubled consciousness acutely stunned by murky memories that effectively displaced love's gentle rhapsodies.

Should I or should I not go to her? I wondered impatiently. And if I should, but did not, what bearing might that have on our future? Was I repudiating her wondrous gift of friendship and unity, wherein my past fears held greater prominence over her graceful being? My heart cried loudly, inspired by uncontainable love for my jewel's spirit, but fear and shame failed me to express it. Why would I suddenly betray my soul's deepest longing? That I could not come around to understand.

I paced around the room for some time while my inner battle raged on, lost in a sea of abject turmoil and hesitant to consent to the obvious, fearing that my sorely neglected state of mind would be exposed. Tired of thinking about it, I finally convinced myself to visit the structure and groomed to extreme specifications, exceeding most regal requirements. But when the time came to leave the room and head for the structure, my heart swelled once again with unfathomable grievance, ashamed of revealing fervent inner desires.

My bosom feared rejection, insisting that a sinner like me did not deserve an angelic soul like hers. I could not shake off Gina's counsel that my beautiful sister would pick someone better suited from her world. Thus, my voyage into my radiant starlight's heart was strewn with detouring stumps and stinging judgments at best from none other than myself.

The ancient enemy knew that my closeness to her would bring its glory days to an end, for she held the key that would release me from its deadly grasp and draw gates of light into my famished heart. Thus, it craved cowardly to keep me from my beautiful beacon's divine shores regardless of cost.

I unwillingly approached my room's door, nightmarishly dragging my body along one short step at a time, although never quite reaching it. I stood in the middle of the room with head firmly down and sweaty hands to the hips, struggling to overcome indomitable insecurity in my life's greatest stand for valor. Was I being selfish or being invited? I speculated. And if I went, would my radiant, wondrous friend be there?

I finally reached the door, committing enormous effort to get myself that far, and hesitantly opened it, fearing someone stood outside in the hallway waiting to shock me out of my wits. I leaned against the frame and clung firmly to it as if the entire colony was about to decompress, wishing my negations would vanish and spare me the grave humiliation of being told who I was, though it was definitely too much to hope for. A personal sacrifice of universal proportions was definitely in order, and there was no way to avoid it.

With little assurance to urge me forth, I forcibly peered into the long empty hallway, deciding I absolutely wanted to see my radiant starlight. I knew the truth behind my wayward desires would be exposed, and the shame of lifetimes certainly stood closer in my wake than I realized. I slowly headed for the lift, even though the unbearable weight of indignity paced boldly before me, unwilling to relinquish its distasteful grip on my soul.

When I reached the structure, not much had changed since my last visit there, except me. My hands had since dipped into a vast mysterious past abyss, reaching out to a life that had long been adrift amid dismal dreams of mundane adequacy and battered by relentless temptations. Though I was lost and imprisoned by influential negations, I was not alone. The invigorating pulse of my heart, the virtuous essence, and priceless pearl of my soul had returned to grace my tired eyes with divine hope. But such venerable venture submitted my being to a mirror of definite honesty I dreaded, clearly exposing the errant void breaching my path toward life giving verity.

I anxiously approached the structure and stood quietly near its door, hesitant to speak my heart for fear that honesty might hasten probable shame and rejection. Surely, I could not hide these feelings from beings whose values transcended the highest morals the heavens inspired. But in spite of their forgiving nature, dread still dominated my thoughts. Unknown to me, Hans kept close watch from the tunnel and out of sight, taking a lot of notes down.

May Len was nothing less than an accomplished sister from a spiritual world, a solemn icon of love and virtue, a telepath, and someone I considered an angel. As I took a brief look at my heart, the sight of it brought me grave distress, for it was far from the light I saw in her, setting in a grim sense of spiritual incompetence that encouraged abandoning all hope for my wondrous starlight. However, I knew not my heart or the science of light at the time.

Little did I know that a super consciousness guides physical experience, that light in us is the true life, and errors are lessons; not incompetence to be reprimanded. But at that moment, all I could think of were fears and not reason, as if by pity, hoping for heaven's clement favoritism sure not to come. Unknowingly, the moment I feared for my life and battled unconquerable fears with my consciousness, I denied Him, never loving myself as I should others.

My heart raced with trepidation, the body ridden with tremors frailed by uncertainty, as I entered the structure looking for a being most dear to my heart's deepest longing, though afraid my love for her was not pure enough. I remained motionless just beyond the door for some time, speechless to avoid the sound of my own trembling voice evidencing its fearful plight. Only my condemning thoughts, amid absolute solitude, kept me company that night.

I called for my gentle wonder, but only my own hollow sounds replied back. Head bowed and discouraged, I sadly turned about and left the structure but not before my voice activated the cam left behind by Sean, conveniently transmitting everything that transpired back to Earth gov and, indirectly, EMS.

I strode slowly upon the crystal walkway, heading toward a rock wall into which it vanished. Unwilling to return to the colony without seeing my amber torch and with nothing better to do, I took a pick from nearby and casually chipped away at the rock. Newly exposed rocks were no different than those before them, falling to the ground with ease just like my shattered hopes.

This endeavor was no answer befitting my heart's true virtuous desires, only a scantly outlet meant to hide from a feeling of unparalleled despair and prevail over growing sadness, walking on that lonesome beach at night with no one to trust, without my song, my spark, my glowing sapphire, my real heart of light, my beautiful one spreading lovingly across horizon sights.

Coming to my knees, I surrendered feelings to her in an act of purity and undeniable truthfulness, helplessly staring at rocks with little impetus to do anything else but yield to moaning. My eyes closed feebly, flood gates opened, and a desperate why cry ruptured through the silent abode about me, tortured without mercy by my own fears. Why was I a God-starving prisoner of sin, I wondered, and not someone as enchanting as she was? What past events stripped me of the right to be an angel, instead of a transgressor?

But then, something summoned inexplicable righteousness to the fore from deep within my soul, feelings far more powerful than my torturous anxiety, unwilling to submit to anything but its benign purpose. My mind sensed unusual motive reaching far into the heart—there, inspiring unutterable melodies that softly resonated devotional, calming encouragement like a tender, scintillating candle flame silently driving dark shadows away.

An overwhelming longing for May Len's company then enraptured my thoughts, making her presence an essential part of my existence. Her essence renewed my life away from shadows. She inspired magnificent dormant expressions waiting to be shared but only with her nearness. Without her then, what goodness could I nestle in my lonely heart bearing any significance?

Her gentle, lovely voice resounded in my mind like Orion's mighty currents. My starlight's pleasing words filled my bosom with sweetness I could not live without. Her celestial amber beauty brightened my being with loving peace. My future, my soul's freedom from want, the inner saintly life I so needed, was in her loving being. I hoped she returned someday to grace my eager eyes and grant me the privilege to surrender her my heart, confessing reverently my unquenchable love for her sweet soul.

Meanwhile, the spire activated unbeknown to me. My head hung low with eyes shut, unable to contain the powerful emotions I felt, enduring an endless game of "she loves me, she loves me not."

Chapter 17: *Oh, My Perfect Love*

I rested alone on the crystal walkway besieged by enervating sorrows, leasing seconds to course by in wait as if hours long borrowed. With the exception of muffled whispers stemming from nearby air vents, and barely audible monitors registering occasional changes in local EM rates, ominous silence guarded the site's eventual fate. It was so quiet, in fact, that falling tears could be heard striking crimson sands beneath my brow, tended by impulsive lofty fountains as if ideal restful comforters for tormenting inner wails and frowns.

With forehead yielding heavy burdens unto cushioning hands, waves of relentless sentiments readily bestowed to the soliciting mercy of vigorous selfish desires, unaware that self-denial is the noblest of all attainable blessings and the path to Father's enlightening squires. Thus, it was that temptation's ogre tone writhed formidably to seductively secure my undue attention, barring vast peaceful realms of abiding forgiveness worthy mention.

But as grieving rains poured upon reticent Martian remains, I suddenly sensed a presence I did not expect, a heavenly feeling of well-being near and permeating all about me, as if a long-lost part of my soul forthwith manifested, stirring and radiant as breathtaking sunrise. The air became endowed with the sweet scent of gardenias, and a wondrous uplifting sense drove away all self-inflicted anguish in a single invigorating deep breath. My heart calmly awakened to retrieving eve's plight, drawing its once dormant windows far and wide to this wondrous life-giving light.

Knowing not why I should, I slowly turned toward the structure when, to my great surprise, I found May Len standing just outside the doorway wearing her usual enthrallingly majestic wide smile and glorious angelic splendor. The structure's lights shone radiant colorful beams about her from behind, as if divine proclamations sublimely encompassed her being. Her breathtaking beauty and joyous luster humbly summoned my heart to rush into hers and seek the countless wonders of higher divine realms—the soul I so dearly loved with all my strength, the summit I sought for so long bearing early dawn's glorious glows.

I gasped with joyful relief and a pleasing beam wore across my lips, defying previous penance. My heart overflowed with loving virtue, fulfilled by the essence of May Len's majestic spirit I had so longed for. Our eyes met across spatial boundaries knowing no time or end, shining like bright candles lit by Father's loving spark. I was eternally grateful, jubilant beyond description, and blessed to be in her hallowed presence. She was likewise glad to see me, sharing her unique glorious warmth I so yearned in my lonesome spirit, now an epilogue to patient eyes.

Ever so gently, her artistic steps floated upon the crystal walkway as I reverently bowed before her splendorous being, never taking her eyes from me until she stood arm's length away and pleasingly said, "Thank you for your loving thoughts, Roshon. You never stop thinking of me," she said in her gentle, musical voice while I hastily removed drying tears from my face.

"Few friends on Saras share such fondness and sincerity with each other, as you have with me. You've inspired new life into my heart and awakened these eyes to untold joy. I will never again cherish life unless I hear your sweet heart's tender songs gently caressing the essence of my soul." I realized her language skills had greatly improved, embellished by a slight European accent that enhanced her verbal loveliness.

"My heart is made whole when you're near, and the fountains of my soul overflow with expressive virtue that lifts away veils of dimming fear. I am blessed by the presence of my sister, who brings the essence of His Majesty and His magnificent wonders to my heart," I said, tenderly placing her delicate right hand into mine, elevating it over my shoulders, and lovingly bowing before her as a sign of mutual respect.

"What joy it is to share of the Infinite with my brother that so willingly awaits for me and elevates my hand above his own heart," she said radiantly, longing for this moment just as much as I.

Her delightful, humble expression was inspiring beyond earthly diction. Her voice was like a wondrous melody from times long past, her words a lovely poem expressively meant for this moment. Deeply moved by her stunning presence, words that flowed in the presence of my kind master at the gardens came to mind, longing to express warmly without reserve. May Len waited to hear them with mounting excitement, further reassuring my resolve.

"It is by His Majesty's wisdom that friends meet. Our Creator enlightens my path with the company of a sister," I said, beginning to build up a real strong sob, "whose smile is brighter than sapphires . . ." A helpless tearful squall and a knotted throat prevailed over my poem, filling my soul with profound sentiments unlike any experienced before. May Len, in turn, held my hands and patiently partook of my emotive offering, aware that an old memory begged to utter forth.

"May Len, I don't want to lose you or be far from you; ever! I've waited so long to be by your side! I'm as dead without you, my beautiful sister!"

Tears swelled in her eyes, embracing whence my words lyrically emerged, and said with slightly broken voice, "My beloved sunbeam, I too have waited to hear these words come from your lips for longer than your moon shines its bright white glow upon the heavens. I feel your heart singing from deep within you; you mean what you say, and we Brothers are most pleased. You don't understand what this means now, but we will help you, friend, brother. So be patient and know that our friendship will never part."

She briefly grinned overcoming persistent tears, shone brightly with renewed joy, then reached up and slowly placed a light kiss on my left cheek, saying, "You asked to see us, my brother Roshon, and so I was sent forth to comfort your spirit."

There was so much I wanted to share with May Len that I found it rather difficult to decide upon any one topic. Above all things, as instructed by my gentle master, I profoundly wanted to dedicate my heart to her, but knew not how to do so or deal with the fears the very thought brought me. She realized my dilemma, and seemed to know just what to do about it.

"Your heart is most troubled, my dear friend, brother," she said in a soft slow tone that was both pleasing and comforting to behold, amiably setting me at ease. "Tell me, sweet sunbeam, what troubles you so?"

Moved by a fast fleeting thought, I reverently asked her; "My gentle wondrous sister, have we met in previous lives?"

With both an outer and inner smile, she replied, "Of course we have. My dear brother, we are old, old friends. What would make us doubt that our sights graced together the beauty of many life-giving shores and our countenance shared the warmth of other stars? Do you not sense our hearts seek the other with a force greater than our sun?"

"The reason I ask is because . . . I was born into a penal world rather than the stars," I said, overcome by emotion. "Since the Brothers don't believe in capital punishment and Saras is their plan B, this can only mean one thing: I committed serious crimes against Father, enough to be expulsed from the stars. I just hope I never disappointed or hurt you in any way or your people. If I did, then my grief would bear no end."

"My sweet friend, brother, why must you think in this manner?" May Len said lovingly. "The past is history, the future is destiny, and the present is empathy. Life happens between past and future lives, making memories a lesson to you and nothing more; so don't cling to them. Besides, it's not wise to delve on negative thoughts. These serve only to harass you pointlessly, stifle spiritual progress, and falsely assert you to be some virtuous person when in fact there's none perfect but Father [6]. So be as children that learn from their mistakes and move on, faithfully undaunted. But I can tell there's something else that troubles you. Could it be something you recently became aware of?"

"Actually, yes, it's a very realistic dream I had," I said, stricken by irrepressible babbling. May Len, on the other hand, enjoyed every minute of it, looking my way with understanding gesture as if she could picture my thoughts. "I was in this tree grove. On tree limbs, someone hung notes with instructions to go to other trees, read their notes, and so on. I went to a river where I met a most beautiful lady that looked kind of like you. Her name was Nei Lah, and she warned me not to fall into Saras's traps. Then, I was on Saras in a place called the Funny Farm, where primitive people were ruled by a monstrous woman reminding me of Gina, you know, the Speaker on Saras."

I could tell May Len found this most amusing, as she unavoidably broke out in fast giggles while I rambled on uncontrollably. "Anyway, to cut this short, everyone died in a big fire, and Saras was destroyed by war and volcanic upheavals. I escaped to Masar, but I couldn't stay there. When I returned to Saras, you were there with your father in Chicago surrounded by crowds, but we got shot. And that's the dream."

May Len tried to calm her run-off laughter and put seriousness back into the conversation but was often overcome by helpless, gentle giggles. "I see now. So this is what troubles you, a dream?"

"Yes, and I have no clue what it all means. Is—was any of this real?"

"I can tell you that, in your own mental language, you experienced a sleep time recall of past events," she said playfully yet most wise. Thinking things through very carefully, she cautiously applied meaning to every word uttered. "You might find the information in this dream quite useful. Once you know and work out this past, you will no longer be troubled as you are now."

"So what I dreamed about was real some time ago?" May Len was quick to confirm this was so. "How accurate was it? Are there any other details I should know about?"

"I can tell this dream really shook you up," she said with a grin. "That's good; they're supposed to do that. Many details you don't know yet but will soon. What's important is that you recognize your reactions and accept your involvement. As you do, you will see more of it. From your description, you dreamed about personal experiences in Mu."

"May Len, if I may ask, are you—rather, were you—Nei Lah? She said in the dream what you always say to me 'friend, brother.' Are you allowed to tell me what that means?"

May Len looked at me fixedly for a brief moment, making every effort to contain a deep secret, and replied, "The individual in your dream is not that being anymore, and I can't say something that might confuse you. Be patient. Everything will be revealed to you when the time is right. Knowledge at the wrong time can be dangerous. Be serene, and the past will come to you. I will tell you more about friend, brother soon."

May Len tenderly took my hand, led me toward the structure a few steps away and said, "My brother is most courageous and determined. Men on Saras find it impossible to decline sexual offerings from a lady. That tradition has been with you for hundreds of thousands of years. Under normal circumstances, your friend Gina would be considered a most desirable prize to possess. Still, you declined her company."

"Honestly, I don't like Gina; something about her wards me away something awful," I said, unaware the cam was active, tracking us by sound and transmitting our discussion live to the world. "She is very attractive, I'll give her that, but I can't see myself putting up with her temperament for any length of time, much less for life. She doesn't want a friend, but rather an intimate companion, and that's not what I want."

"I'm truly sorry to say that she doesn't hold much esteem for me," she said giggling. "She even said that I'm not your type."

Then, completely unsolicited, my lips proceeded to say, "Yes, and also that you're too old for me."

I suddenly felt profoundly embarrassed after spouting that statement away, not really sure where it would lead; it didn't take long before I found out. "Don't be embarrassed by your feelings," May Len said cheerfully, giggling helplessly and looking brightly into my eyes.

"I'm really, really sorry. That was most disrespectful of me. I didn't mean to say that," I said promptly, but her calm eyes surged honest trust in my heart and, moved by her loving grace, I replied, "Or, did I?"

"What do you think, my sweet sunbeam, am I too old for you?" she said giggling teasingly.

I suddenly swallowed cold and dry, and my eyes popped open out of their sockets like a frightened squirrel. My heart skipped in sheer panic as I came to grips with feelings I knew I could in no way keep from her. I could tell she was having a really good time at my expense, however, not in a negative way. But this was just the beginning of truth's awakening within me. "I . . . don't know if you really are?" I said, extremely wary.

"Roshon, my sweet, shy brother, don't be ashamed," she said gently giggling. "You'd be surprised what I know—about you. But I won't invade your privacy, for that's yours to administer. However, in the spirit of loving honesty and truth, there's something I would like to share with you but only if my kind brother will allow me to so witness it. May I do so, with thine permission?" she said, gently lowering her head in respect.

"Please, gentle sister, your words are most precious to me. I place myself entirely in your hands, and again, please, accept my deepest apologies."

"My kind brother," she said softly, gently caressing my hands, "if you will so accept it, I must testify before thee, from the depths of this heart, that I was most honored and pleased beyond words when you told Gina—and the entire universe at the top of your lungs—that you loved me with all your heart and might," she said, bowing respectfully before me and patiently waiting for my honest response with head lowered.

"You heard everything I said?" I said timidly.

"We did, yes."

"Everything, like everything?"

"My caring sunbeam, I was most pleased when your heart spoke out loud and fearlessly in my honor with words so beautiful that the still heavens stirred as far as the mind can conceive," she replied, shyly bowing. "Was not your soul moved by truth? Did not sweet tears witness the power of thine heart from the crevices of thine inspired brows?"

"I . . . yes," I said, reserved and sputtering, "but I truly, truly, apologize if I offended you, or your father, with such words."

"Your heart is teeming with such wondrous songs waiting to be expressed, Roshon," she added, softly caressing my hands. "Truth is the most wonderful song you can share with me, for it is my greatest yearning. Might my valiant brother then, without fear, share what his heart so lovingly promised our kind master to declare before me?"

"Right now?"

"I see no inconvenience, do you?"

"But I'm afraid . . . of losing you. That's the truth; I don't want to lose you by saying or doing something that might bring you insult."

"There's something very important you've been meaning to declare to me in person," she said gently. "Might you part stinging fears aside, freely open your heart to mine, and consent your lips to trust me? I so want to hear what you so dread to declare. Please, my sunbeam, let thine lips sing, freely, unafraid, for tomorrow is already written and my joy is thine truth today."

"It's just that, well, what I really wanted to say was . . ." I said hesitantly, struggling with severe anxiety and legs literally shaking beneath me, but I could not come around to say what I felt.

"Yes, my sunbeam, go on. Fear not me."

"I just can't . . . I can't."

"Why is my kind brother ashamed of declaring something that suffered his heart for seemingly eternity? Do you not love the inspired way of your heart?"

"I feel so unworthy of your friendship. I'm not suitably pleasing to you because my personal frequency is so, so low compared to yours."

"My sunbeam, please," she said caringly, "don't be afraid of me. Have I given you reason to feel so or that you are undesirable to me? If I have, I so apologize to thee and beg your eternal forgiveness. Please, my sunrise, let me not be cause for you to be afraid or feel humiliated, for if I do, it will sadden me greatly beyond your grasp."

"I just know what your answer will be," I said sadly, as May Len lowered her head solemnly. "How can someone like me declare his heart to an angel? There are countless contenders on your world to choose from better suited spiritually than I. I'd never stand a chance against them in my search for love."

"Are Gina's blazing eyes so verily cast upon my heart's realms that she can so assuredly command thy gaze away from His light, and my soul? Must one be an angel to be honest and spiritual?"

"My sister's words are most wise," I said, unsure how to reply to my jewel.

May Len then gently raised my bowed, gloomy countenance and fixed her bright, beautiful amber eyes upon me with a caring, soft gaze. Her gentle face delivered a peaceful smile infused with heavenly overtones, uttering these words of absolute endearing meaning, "My kind brother Roshon, may I ask thee, with utmost respect, do you . . . feel affection for me?"

I never expected to hear these words stem from her flowery lips and my heart literally burst from its cavity, words that felt like a fervent storm toppling stubborn inner pillars and completely exposing my being. I pointed my stares to the ground in utter shame, mentally struggling for honesty. Yet I knew that an answer, an honest one, was in order. And if I truly loved her—and she loved truth—then truth was the best gift I could grant her.

Resting hands tenderly upon my shoulders, she brought her exceptionally wondrous vessel close to mine with deep respect and said in a kind, loving tone, "Nothing would please me more than to hear your heart's song, free and unhindered. I already know your heart, my sunbeam, but only honest words from your gentle lips can seal my soul's longing and bring peace to the gates of my heart. Trust the call of my soul and the longing of your sweet heart."

"Yes," I replied truly embarrassed with rain in my eyes and lips fluttering wildly, restraining my heart from expressing frankly. But in a moment of devotion to truth and respect to May Len, I finally found the courage to look into her gleaming eyes, put aside my fears of rejection, and answered her moving plead with deep heartfelt honesty and loving inspiration.

"My most lovely, heavenly sister—yes, I do. I feel uncontainable affection for thee, and I long for your endless companionship, for my heart is rent lifeless without it. I'm deeply, madly, desperately in love with thine soul. I so loved thee since I was a child, for I've felt your essence, your heart, since that early age, but I can't explain why. If it will please my beautiful sister, and with the universe as my witness, I dedicate this lowly heart to you and place my soul in thine hands. May I honor Father and make Masar proud by declaring my heart before thee with all my strength that thee be well pleased, my wondrous, eternal starlight," I said, reverently bowing to her.

"I'm so glad you do!" May Len said joyously. "Else, I would have been greatly saddened."

"You're glad? Really?" I said, relieved to hear her say that. "I thought . . . it was no, because of my spiritual inadequateness?"

"Roshon, I am most pleased to know you love my soul! And do you want to know a little secret? My heart feels just as lifeless without your essence as you do without mine; I so pledge it onto thee."

"But you are so . . . clean, beautiful, and devoted to Father. How will I ever be sufficiently clean or worthy of your presence?" I said rather dismayed.

"My sweet brother, if you only knew just how deserving you are," she said with a beaming smile, seeking my eyes.

"I am?"

"Of course. Memories and desires you deem shameful rather than edifying, that's all they are. You're obeying whispers, temptations; the moment you stop doing so, you'll be clean. Love His light, and you'll be free of them."

"But what if my affection for you is selfish? What if it's an escape mechanism or a desire to please myself and abuse your being?"

"By recognizing and sharing it, you have lessened its force, but there's one more thing you must do."

"Just name it. I'll do anything to be clean and deserving—anything. I don't care how long it takes or how much it hurts."

"Then look deep into my eyes with all your might, open the gates of your chalice as wide as they will draw unto my heart, and put fear of shame aside. Then, you will be selfless, and fears shall be a lesson to you. In God's kingdom, there's no place for repressive humiliation and punishment, only knowledge of error. And when you don't fear and obey past errors, then you have love because fear is selfishness."

"Is that it?" I said greatly surprised. "Fearless, shameless recognition?"

"Yes, that's it."

"So I don't have to slave away in some cosmic plan B camp for humpting million years or receive two hundred thousand lashes?"

"Not at all. Life's all about honesty, gallantry, and testifying your thoughts openly to the light: that's what counts. Physical injury breeds grief, not truth. Grief breeds fear, and fear vents egotism. Punishment yields ignorance, not lessons. Trust my heart, and feel the flame of my life longing for thee."

"You don't mind who I am or had been?"

"Your love speaks for itself. Did your bosom not witness with all its might and heartfelt tears that you would wait a million years, and do what Father ordained to be by my side? Oh, what beautiful songs came forth from your sweet heart into that starry night; the entire universe heard them, and so did I. I will forever cherish each and every one of your songs, for they enliven the most precious moments of my life and describe your sweet heart's vision of His Majesty's never ending love with incredible fervor."

"My beloved brother," she said, lightly touching my heart evocatively yet containing a great secret from me, "my heart shall wait a million years for you, if you will wait a million years for me. Trust the gift of my lips when I say unto thee that Father could grant me no greater wish than to wait for thee. Will you patiently wait for me as I shall wait for you?"

"Am I doing something wrong or defiling you irreverently by feeling the way I do toward your soul?"

"Your love is my life, and it's worth waiting an infinity for. It is etched permanently unto my heart where it can never be removed or sullied, and it is beautiful beyond description. I want to hear it, live it, feel it forever by your side; for without it life is for not."

"Then," I said romantically to her, full of loving faith and overcoming my fears, "just as these eyes patiently wait for prevailing thunderstorms to expire seemingly endless dominance over skies above, and a rainbow's glorious intense canopy signals the beginning of soothing serenity, so will it be a great privilege to wait what time it takes and sacrifice it all, body and soul, to merit the right to share your graceful heart for infinity. Nothing will ever be likened to your heart or replace the intense love I feel for thee. My hopes to be by thee shall never fade into the sunset, knowing faithfully there's never a storm that shall not pass," I said poetically and lovingly to my beacon, as her eyes graced mine with endless wonders and tears of gladness.

"So let powerful thunders roar overhead, let them cover my wondrous firmament from sight with gloom and doom; my beacon's loving light I now know, and in my heart forever she blooms. Let powerful winds batter the land below, however they will; my starry heaven beckons me to endure, my heart she shall eternally heal. I shall faithfully wait for skies to clear; my heart shall never waver from thine incredible, lovely cheer. I shall softly caress a dream to be revealed and never sway; days of compelling harmony among us shall stay."

"Alone you shall not be," May Len said, trying to restrain a pervading sob restricting her ability to freely express, "for I shall be in your dreams, and your heart I will hold up high, privileged to be . . . its beacon."

"I can't live without your uplifting grace and the music of your soul, warmly encompassing my heart with divine tenderness untold. Thinking of you gives me hope to wait for my rainbow to come in flight and my radiant star to guide me at night. Your dreams give me strength to boldly live on until the day Father finally deems me worthy of thee, and my greatest wish granted it shall be. I will wait an eternity for thee, my graceful sister, as there's nothing else in life for me."

"I will lovingly treasure your heart until the day, my . . . sunbeam" she said, lightly kissing my cheek. "Until then, your songs will make waiting bearable. I would so love to hear your songs from the gardens again. This time, seek my eyes and warmly place thine hands into mine. Let your heart roam freely into my bosom and seek its loving depths, warming its bindings with sweet poetry. Share your soul's beaming warmth so I am not weakened by paralyzing chills of eternal solitude. Let your greatest wish thrive, have faith in me, and never let your eyes or thoughts of love depart mine."

Gently holding her velvety hands, I tenderly said with trembling voice, "I never knew love. I feared it until I met my wondrous sister from whom heaven's gates softly summon fears away. My intense love for you is His renewed life in me, and I long to live it eternally, if so permitted, with thee," I said softly, as May Len began to sob.

"Songs from my charmed chalice are inspired by your incomparable radiance and the tender essence we so lovingly share. My life is a lowly empty canvas I place into thine soft silky hands, so you may render upon it the elegant, resplendent wonders of the heavens and forever stamp the seal of His eternal insights upon its bands. You are my only wish in life, my longing love; virtuous ballade of hallowed yearning that none other may inspire but my dulcet dove," I said sweetly to her, while she sobbed helplessly.

"My songs are the language of love your gentle starlight shall paint into my dreams of heavenly blazon; your eyes the spark that enliven my days like Sirius's glorious sunrise upon my heart's horizon. Unrivalled beauty, divine sapphire, heavenly princess, my heart longs to live in thee; I shall desire no other waters to my lips than the clear springs of your heart's joyous glee."

May Len's tender embrace denied my gaze a glimpse of her sobs. Her soft tender face, sheltered beside mine, urged me to endure lovingly, gently caressing my shoulders.

"Most beautiful, gentle heart of Rosette, I shall gaze at the heavens in breathless wonder seeking the brightest star of them all, for your presence kindles their magnificence and fills the firmament with splendors untold. Your grace paints the colors of Orion's bands, your smile the glorious loveliness of the Pleiades; your voice leads the Tree of Life in Carina's cloudy choirs, with eyes that beget God's beckoning peace. Soothing starlight, starry pearl, most beautiful windows of stunning splendor that inspires all worlds. Forever feast my eyes upon a view of God's realm, for what dulcet privilege it is to find a path to the Infinite, lit by your graceful helm."

With subtle arms warmly about my shoulders and overcome by joyful sobs, she softly shuddered few words with her face against mine, "So much loving beauty and sense of devotion, such vast heart; why so far for so long?" as I softly gathered her tears upon my shoulders and reverently accepted her incredibly delicate wonders upon mine with profound affectionate gratitude.

"A new canvas is rendered upon my heart by the most beautiful artist the Infinite could ascribe; wondrous paintings I shall treasure to the ends of time. I'm most privileged to look into thine eyes, embraced by your loving essence clear as iridescent skies. I place my heart upon thine hands, and may it be that canvas thou demands. My beloved wellspring, my river of pearly gems, with deepest reverence and respect, I dedicate my heart to thee, for all to witness and see. May I please Father, make Masar proud, and eternally love thee?"

"Roshon, I so longed for your honesty and gentle beauty," she said softly, still embracing me and crying gently. "Your heart expresses cleanly, and your songs are mighty shafts of love that shudders my soul. You know not just how much your devotion means to me," she said, placing a gentle kiss upon my forehead and clearing her face of lingering moisture.

"A sad memory from long ago makes you think you are not worthy of my company, but you will soon know what it is and be freed from its bindings; just be patient. Your people panic when they offer affection to another, and the reasons behind such fear are always the same: old memories. That's just absolutely absurd because true affection, inspired by His Majesty, is not shameful. Shame means only one thing: self-interest, not genuine love."

"I've wondered lately how couples meet and live on other worlds," I said. "I assume it is far different from our ways."

"Immensely. Your people calm the weight of errant agony with pleasure; that's all you understand. We don't hunt down mates or become obsessed with anyone because of looks, talent, or behavior. Instead, we let Father inspire a companion, a polarity, for us with whom we share His truth eternally. We view all beings as capable of beauty, and that prohibits us from compulsively targeting specific individuals. If all vessels have the same . . . elements, what makes one special over another? Could it be how supple its tenant performs pleasure?"

"That's exactly what our kind master said in the gardens."

"Did you know he is Tei-Ah's master? You were truly blessed to meet him. And yes, he was also your master back in Atlantis. Tell me, what did you think of kind master?"

"He certainly surprised me. I never knew who he was until the last moment. He was so polite and yet so humorous, especially when he called the body, let's see, a machine we get drunk with nerve prickles."

"He's a very funny master," she said giggling, "but you were even funnier."

"I was?"

"Oh yes," she said humorously, while trying to play serious. "Now, I have no doubts that I'm really from Siberia."

"You watched our discussion? I thought I felt your hand in mine that eve."

"I was there by your side with father before you even walked into the park—invisible, of course."

"Sounds like somebody set me up."

"It was father's idea, well, maybe mine too," she replied, giggling helplessly.

"I didn't know half the time what I was saying, like my brain wasn't there."

"That was father playing tricks on you, but it was for your own good. I loved when you said; it's cold, across the sea, really out there," she said, imitating my voice, drawing both of us to laugh amusingly. "And a lot of wind, from air outside—what was that all about?"

"Pure nonsense. My head went to lunch trying not to say Masar, and our graceful master kept asking questions."

"The best one was, I'd love to see it intact. By the way, what land is missing? That was so funny; I don't know how kind master managed to keep a straight face."

"I have the feeling I'm going to hear about this for a long time to come."

"All kidding aside, kind master is very proud of you and adds that the body is Father's dwelling place. Wear it humbly, clean, and with respect. Don't show it off, defile it with lust, or irritate reproductive systems during intimacy to induce perverted pleasure. This form of stimulation isn't natural and distances you from His Majesty."

"Then what we think or do without Father is carnal and bound to fail."

"I couldn't have said it better. Let the Infinite be your only desire and don't follow after temptation. Love the Lord thy God with all thy heart, soul, mind, and strength," May Len said intensely with a slight bow, "and love thy neighbor as thyself [1], thus commanded our Master."

"My sister knows Master's words very well. Clearly, if you don't love or can't be honest with yourself, how can you possibly love others you meet and, hence, so much less Father that you haven't seen?"

"Forgiveness is key because we all have the right to err," she said, placing hands on my shoulders. "Trust Him when you feel negative, He won't abandon you because of it. Listen to His advice and don't fear your feelings, for His reproach is love! The commandment is a lamp, the law is light, and reproofs of instruction are the way of life [2]. So pick up the lamp and let His words of love illumine your path. Turn from the negative and love the light."

"An act of forgiveness transforms baseless iniquity into virtuous respect because to whom little is forgiven the same loveth little [3]."

"Don't punish others, for Father's cycles influence one's own overcoming, not your actions. It matters not how we're treated, only how we treat others. Don't reason with negation. Trust it to the light without delay because time is of the essence and Father always provides. Trust Father with all thine heart and lean not unto thine own understanding [4]."

"Woe to rebellious children that take counsel but not of Me, said Isaiah," I replied, "and that cover with a covering but not of My spirit, that they may add sin to sin [5]."

"Saras was enlightened with such precious universal laws," she said, "but those that claim to be His followers can't tolerate living by such simple decrees; this is most disappointing. A true disciple surrenders all desire unto the light, just as Master did unto death."

"I haven't been a stellar disciple, have I? I might be one of the worst."

"Roshon, my loving heart, does a part of you still feel unworthy, especially of me, as if you were some undesirable outcast that I or the Brothers shall never love?"

"Honestly I do. If only I didn't have to gaze up at the stars anymore to find and grant thee the purest, heavenly love."

"Roshon, don't let fear beat you down and send me away," she said calmly. "Trust in me. Don't reject my love. I'm not here to humiliate you but to forever comfort and be your beloved friend, sister. Let my life serve as warm repose for your tired being. Let me share your heavy yoke. Let these eyes grace upon thee, tirelessly sharing infinite wonders containing no greater wish, for it grants me life and joy. When you look into my eyes with love, I live, and you are clean. Fill my eyes with yours, and let your beautiful heart be free of past and desire, for your love is most awe-inspiring and I can't live without it."

"Is the love I feel for thee truly honest?"

"More than you realize. The love I sense from thee is beyond words," she said, embracing me warmly. "I feel its passion and can't ask for more or from anyone else. Listen not to negations, but sing them into my heart instead."

"My starlight, I'm distant from Father, but that will change no matter how long it takes or how painful the process might be" I said, seized by renewed boldness and trust. "Grant me the chance to offer reparations for ages of willful misconduct. Let me surrender to the Infinite and place myself in the brotherhood's hands unconditionally."

"Brother Roshon, we accept this, your first qualification, well pleased, one of many to come. This tiny light from Father is grateful for your devotion to my heart. May everyone on your world make the same commitment. When they do, what a wonderful world yours will be! Imagine that, living correctly and applying the science! What more can anyone ask for?"

"My starlight, will I be allowed to continue meeting with you?"

"More than you know, and I will be most pleased when we do. How wondrous is the love you feel for me as it seeks the being inside, not flesh.

Love cannot be given, only felt and revealed, for it is the Infinite. Let our love then be His and us be as one. Your companion will find you in the very, very near future, and then you will be whole," she said, placing another light kiss on my cheek. "As for myself, my companion has also to come, just as soon."

"I see," I said, gravely saddened as if a ton of bricks suddenly lodged into my heart, deducing that May Len was not to be my companion, but she did not offer to address my growing sense of inner distress. Gina's previous assertion that May Len would choose one of her kind over me popped loudly into my mind, causing May Len to giggle. But I quickly discarded the thought out of faith and love for May Len and reverently bowed before my starry princess, granting her my heart with all my strength, irrelative of my destiny.

"I shall forever love thee and my Brothers," I replied emotionally. "What else do I need in life but hope and faith in thee? My life has been rewarded beyond description just knowing I can love thee, granting me the strength I need to wait no matter the time or odds."

"You are most brave and devoted, my sweet sunbeam; I am most pleased," she replied joyously. "Not everyone can do what you just did, upholding your promise to love me, uncertain of destiny. Yes, I will wait for you. How can I not do so?"

"If you don't mind my asking," I said, boldly erasing my grave sense of sorrow, "do you know who your companion is? Can you share that with me?"

"Yes, I do," she replied after a brief moment of hesitation, lightly moving her eyes about.

"I suppose he is from Masar also?"

"Actually . . . not exactly," she replied, sweetly meditating what she said.

"Do you know him or where he is from?"

"Oh, I know him quite well," she answered with a smile and incredible excitement. "He came to Masar just recently from . . . a nearby world. I have known him for many lifetimes, and we have much work to do together in this life. My father is happy to have met him in person and looks forward to the family union soon. Both father and I have a really big surprise for him as he doesn't know who his companion is yet."

"That's strange. How come he doesn't know but you do? I thought you could read each other's minds?"

"Not everyone is at the same level of evolution, and my father is really good about surprising people."

"I've had the great privilege of feeling and seeing it for myself."

"He loves doing that. He is a very happy man and always looks for ways to make people laugh and be happy."

"You said your companion came from a nearby world. Can you tell me which one?"

"Well, I can't because . . . you would not understand," she said, roaming her eyes about again. "Maybe, you can tell me about your own search for companionship?"

"I never sought anyone. It's been difficult finding someone that thinks the way I do."

"What about Gina? Will you consider her in the future?" she said with a slight smirk.

"No way!" I said decisively. May Len found my response extremely humorous and couldn't stop chuckling for some time. Obviously, she knew something I didn't, but this was not the time to bring certain truths to bear. "Besides, my heart is already committed to someone else, and I think you know all too well who that might be."

"Your unions do little to unite with Father, filled with adversity and lust. I know you understand this and think in her best behalf." She halted for a brief moment, looked slightly to one side, and said, "Come, my father wants to talk to you."

My heart suddenly sunk, and I said quite concerned, "Your father? Are we in some sort of trouble? Perhaps I shouldn't be meeting you without his consent. Whatever happens, don't worry, I'll tell your father it's all my fault."

"Roshon, don't be silly," she said laughing. "You will think nothing of the sort—ever. Father is looking forward to meeting you; he'll be here shortly."

"But what if he finds us here alone?"

"Roshon, you're one of his best friends," she said with a chuckle.

"Really? But I just met him a few days ago. How could I be?"

"You'll see, in time. Trust me." We walked hands together toward the center of the structure where the blue beam activated and within it Dow Uanh appeared. I swallowed dry with eyes tensed, but May Len gave me a slight friendly elbow nudge to calm me down. A smiling Dow Uanh looked upon us, full of life, with inner devotion one could feel.

"My old friend, I am so glad to see you again," he said. "By the way, thank you for accompanying my daughter this evening. You make a great protectorate." I smiled and thanked him for the opportunity to meet with both him and May Len in this manner.

"Absence makes the heart grow fonder, does it not? I see you have become good close friends. That's excellent. I am most pleased. If only all people on Saras were as you are."

"Thank you, Mr. Veih. Your kind daughter has taught me much."

Dow Uanh then cut in saying, "And you will learn much more, at the right moment, of course. I will ask May Len to be your spiritual tutor and council—that is, if you will accept her."

I answered quickly in an excited and nervous tone, "Oh, I absolutely like her!" I silenced myself suddenly but not fast enough. I realized what I had just said and stammered to recover, as Dow Uanh and May Len briefly chuckled.

"I mean, I like talking to May Len. I could spend an entire lifetime talking with her. That is, if her boyfriend doesn't mind."

"Boyfriend?" Dow Uanh said. "She doesn't have a boyfriend as you call them, at least, not yet; so don't worry, he doesn't know about it yet. Well then, May Len knows what to do. One question you haven't answered is, is my daughter too old for you?" We laughed for a moment, but then I got the hint it was my turn to respond to a valid question.

"My elder brother, is it true May Len is two hundred years old?"

"189 Saras years, ten months, and a few days to be exact."

"That's remarkable; she looks no older than twenty by our standards. How can you be so young yet live so long?"

"Age is in the mind," May Len said. "The body regenerates itself, but constant abuse offsets its ability to keep up with repairs. Eventually, genetics fail to replicate correctly and age is the outcome. Selfish desire, fear, negativity, food, radiation, free radicals, lack of attunement—anything stressing the vessel beyond its design criteria is cause for aging. The same holds true for disease, brought about by psychic influence, past events, and obsessions or negative entities. The cure for both is simple: recognize, share, and love."

"So is my daughter too old for you?" Dow Uanh said smiling.

"I'll say, by her physical appearance, no; but she will easily outlive me."

"Not if you respect body and mind. As your official tutor, May Len will cover many concepts your people urgently need. Together, you both have much work to do in a short amount of time. The reason I wanted to see you was to share our appreciation for Saras's warm fly-by reception and also set a time for our official landing. Why don't we say thirty days from now? 11:00 a.m. UEF Meridian?"

"Thirty days from now, 11:00 a.m. UEF Meridian, check."

"We will land in the front lawn of the Towers; I believe the area provides sufficient space for our craft. Your team is invited to travel to Saras with us. If you will join us, and I assume you will, a Scout will land on your pad at approximately 2345 LMT to pick you up. May Len will travel in the Scout with you, and I'll wait for your arrival on the mother ship."

"Mr. Veih," I responded excitedly to his invitation, "if I might suggest, I would offer to pick up May Len here at, say, 2330 LMT and grant her a brief tour of C6 on our way to the Scout, if it would meet with your approval."

"I'd like that very much, my brother," she said, "but only if father grants me permission."

"She's just kidding about permission; you know that. Of course she may, and we thank you for your kind offer."

He paused for a moment, looked at both of us, placed his hands briefly on our shoulders, and brought us tightly together. He then recited a brief poem in his language, kissed us, and said, "Roshon, you will soon grant my daughter a great big, big surprise very, very soon."

May Len smiled, but I felt she had no clue what her father had in the works, much less me. Aware of Dow Uanh's love for surprises, when he said "great," I was certain he really meant just that.

"Well, then, you both have a lot to talk about, so I'll leave you to your discussion. What you know about love will soon evolve and you'll be able to tell possession, guilt, and compassion apart. Your ego is considerable, my son. You want to be a higher being and wield much power like a god. But don't despair; honesty will heal your spirit. Love will replace the past, and then you will be free, growing in love for eternity. One more thing, take good care of my daughter and don't let anything happen to her. I entrust her to your care."

Somehow, Dow Uanh's words drove me to really slip bad and the phrase "Yes, Your Majesty" proudly left my lips without hesitation. I had no idea why I suddenly faulted again, and my face showed for it in hot red. Meanwhile, my brethren seemed to enjoy a long friendly, witty moment.

"Your past is catching up to you," he said. "Keep an eye on what you say. It's important. By the way, that big, big surprise coming May Len's way is a wonderful gift from the brotherhood, and it's just huge! She's going to love it! *Oh-joi*, my old friend of ages. Never say no to His love in spite of the times."

I longed for Dow Uanh's company and advice in the worst way. I knew him from ages past, I could feel his prior essence and the flow of his spirit in me, but could not tell where from. He confirmed my feelings with a reassuring tap on my shoulder, but offered no words in favor or against my belief.

"What do you feel from me, young apprentice?" he said beaming joyfully.

I unwound at his request, and no sooner my heart flooded with reverent feelings that my obscure sights had never dawned—until that moment. Then, with assured conviction, my mind opened and I knew that before me stood my leader, my teacher, and most beloved associate of ages. "My kind beloved master," I replied emotionally, coming to my left knee along with May Len.

"Farewell, my gentle son," he replied, vanishing before us. Immediately, an inspirational musical display of Father's star-studded cosmos seized our sights.

May Len smiled excitedly and fixed her eyes upon mine, politely offering me something to drink as furniture and refreshments appeared. She served me a glass, graciously invited me to sit beside her, and gently folded her hand over mine. As I refreshed my palette with her generous offering, she brought to my visual notice beautiful architectural realizations from several nearby worlds.

As we merrily lost ourselves into the power and majesty of the Infinite, May Len turned to me smiling, and after gazing silently and amorously upon each other for some time, she said softly, "Don't fear your thoughts. *Ceh tennéh deh ezi men, inéh,*" with most tender love in her deep gaze.

My heart jumped joyfully at the sound of these words. I knew what they meant, and my mind's eye swiftly awakened. I could deeply sense the meaning of her expression, its long tradition and deep significance as freely as petals open into lighted breezes without inhibition. They seemed familiar and dear to my heart, reciting them with ease and living every gentle sense behind them.

My mind caringly unfolded to May Len; our eyes fondly blended sights as if nothing else mattered but a language far from earthly, one that brightened the soul and which utterance was the source of meaning, the essence of life—the loving language of His Majesty. May Len's great gift had arrived.

My soul summoned every ounce of love it could withstand from a moving, quivering heart captivated by her incredible loveliness. Thus, I passionately recited to my beacon, trading tears with loving intensity as I never felt before while her lips shuddered and eyes moistened with adoring cascades.

Heart willing and lips freed from inhibition, I poured forth uncontainable wonders in fullest confidence and endless love for my one in majestic ancient language. Tears unrestrained and a broken voice slowly trembling, my sweet ode of love to my heavenly treasure, my one and only one, issued fondly ever picking up poetic inspiration, dictioned solely from heart and eyes that never looked away from her radiant amber windows in eternal rapture:

> *"Ceh iih tennéh deh, ezi cenéh itatinéh mis. Ezi innéh acaneh sanee, ezi finaih sar, ceh radziréh deh ezi kinéh dari, med ceh tennéh vi; ezi mis, ezi nedee mis, ezi nedee innéh mis, ezi mis ni nedee . . . adennéh men!"*
>
> [I so love thee, my beautiful dearest one. My beloved starlight, my fragrant flower, I offer you my humble heart, for I love thee; my one, my only one, my only beloved one, my one and only … eternal friend!]

My wondrous May Len, not expecting to hear these words from olden sojourns, was instantly jolted beyond portrayal and suddenly gasped emotionally with an abrupt, potently lasting weep she could not avoid. Tearful torrents fell profusely from her eyes upon our hands, and her vessel shuddered with strong persistent wails, unable to deny herself.

Her cry was so intense and deep that breath left her for a moment. Her resplendent eyes closed and her trembling silky hands rose along with mine to comfort her soft flowery lips, weeping helplessly with emotive joy like a child. My heart was in her bosom and tenderly shivered its foundations with His Majesty's love, for her time had come.

"*Deh ouradéh*!" "You remember," she shouted many times tearfully shaken, expressing an uncontainable joy and love between us lost long ago.

"My loving starlight," I said to her lyrically, standing up and bowing slowly before her, holding her hands reverently high, "that the Infinite be honored, I declare the greatest truth I regard before thine heart; I have so loved thee with all my heart and soul for longer than the dawn of time endures, overflowing my bosom's chalice with endless grandeur."

"My one . . ." she said joyously, suddenly bringing herself to cautious silence before me, for her words could not touch such secrets.

"My sweet love, my tender essence, wrap thine heart gently about mine like a precious ribbon of gold, and walk by my side through the span of ages yet to unfold. Be thou my one, the tender love of my heart, the rhythm of my soul, meant for us since days of old. Forever grace my life with infinite radiance, granting my heart to share by thee His spiritual elegance."

"I so will, my kind love!" she replied tenderly and tearfully.

"No one, my eloquent love, beneath or above heavenly glee, shall I grant my heart but only to thee. I so love you, oh, my perfect love, my amber firestones; I'll climb the tallest mountains in heaven and forever shout my uncontainable love for thee across the cosmos, as Father beckons," I said, moved by virtuous confidence I found difficult to comprehend, for I felt as someone else, someone that lived infused with His love far parted from selfish addictions.

My jewel hastily stood, reached tearfully for my shoulders, and embraced me warmly with great respect and irrepressible joy. "How can I not love thee? Such love, such heart! You never forgot me! You came back for me!" she said emotionally with quivering voice and body, gasping and strongly embracing my vessel while respectfully kissing my cheek.

"In the brotherhood I trust; my heart shall grow, my negations will heal, and our souls shall be as one, someday now concealed. Then shall my love for thee not be tainted or defiled upon saddened fields; my cadence shall resound beautifully with thee, unaffected by earthly, selfish zeal."

"I shall never refuse your gallant, enamored soul that never lost sight of my heart, regardless of cost. My beloved sunbeam, my sweet sunrise, I shall never refuse you! I beg thee. Wait no longer; be not afraid to rush to my soul the way you are. I don't care how far you've fallen or what thoughts torment you. Come, bring your chalice deeper than I could ever hope to envision. Rest upon my soul, where the beauty of your spirit and the warmth of your lips are so long overdue! Let your love songs never rest and cast your eyes away from the past. Let thine embrace forever linger in my arms with all your might and strength. Seek me not among the stars. Let my heart be your starry heavens, and your heart mine.

"Worry not for your companion; she is . . . closer than you know and shall reveal herself to you very, very soon. Trust in us Brothers, my beloved heart, my wondrous love, my devoted sunbeam. Embrace my soul warmly, find every means under the heavens to come quickly in spirit, ever more lovingly, ever longer, ever louder, ever more poetic. Fill my bosom with His inspiration, for thus we oscillate toward His higher loving realms. Oh, if I could only say it, but I must wait. Just know your perfect love is near. I am most honored, most privileged, to be by your side, my valiant, inspiring brother."

Both tearing and quivering uncontrollably in each other's arms, releasing eons of long suffering held within our hearts, tender words of love continued to pour forth, each word echoed musically by May Len, "I dream of the day when you and I are as one, my one, oh, my perfect love. Such long time awaiting, such long time. But today it is done. I have found you again my one, now forever, never to part again. Behold my promise, oh, my perfect love! Believe in my heart and His Majesty's longing, oh, my perfect love."

"*Deh ouradéh, ezi metéh tennéh.* You remember, my tender love," she said softly.

We remained reverently embraced the entire day without rest or concern for time, floating on each other's shoulders so long overdue between us, sharing gentle inspirational words, gladdened at the heart, joyous in the soul, shedding warm tears of overdue delight. Our tears merged, our souls were as one, our hearts cried out in unstoppable happiness an eternal love story that was to be. Only few hours of rest kept us apart in the days to come, inspired by Father's stars and moved by sweet music under the gentle auspices of majestic, tender thoughts and sweet embrace.

Saras witnessed every loving moment we spent together, grateful for our sharing. Loving words courted our time together, strengthening spiritual bonds, never selfish, by no means tarnished by flesh, inadequate touch, or physical blemish. The way of truth came to my heart, never to depart, and always to share with my lovely gardenia of ages.

My negative emotions and thoughts succumbed to truth, unafraid to share them with May Len. I no longer hid or protected them. Shadows from the past these were and nothing more, having no more power over me than what I gave them. To May Len and the Brothers, it mattered not how filthy I felt because I was not filthy at all; only my captor thoughts were. Unafraid of truth or ignorance, I believed not my captors and owed them nothing but exposure.

How wonderful it was to be freed from ancient monsters that kept me in bondage for thousands of years and laugh over them with tender inspirational words from His Majesty. I learned that my love for May Len was just the beginning of infinity, love to be expressed to all souls equally, love that becomes part of your heart marking the way to higher realms. We don't love; it is the Infinite's love from higher realms in us that is. Thus, the measure of our love is precisely where we live.

May Len—oh, my perfect love, peaceful radiance and fruit of His Majesty. How sweet is the sound of love eternal. How sweet it is to live inspired by your spirit's cadence and share Father's words by your side, my perfect love of ages. *Oh-joi, adennéh Maneh*!

---

[1] R. W. J. Morford, "Luke 10: 27," in *The New Man Bible*, Travelers Rest, SC: True Potential Publishing Co., 2011.

[2] R. W. J. Morford, "Proverbs 6: 23," in *The New Man Bible*, Travelers Rest, SC: True Potential Publishing Co., 2011.

[3] R. W. J. Morford, "Luke 7: 47," in *The New Man Bible*, Travelers Rest, SC: True Potential Publishing, 2011.

[4] R. W. J. Morford, "Proverbs 3: 5," in *The New Man Bible*, Travelers Rest, SC: True Potential Publishing Co., 2011.

[5] R. W. J. Morford, "Isaiah 30: 1," in *The New Man Bible*, Travelers Rest, SC: True Potential Publishing Co., 2011.

[6] R. W. J. Morford, "Matthew 19: 17," in *The New Man Bible*, Travelers Rest, SC: True Potential Publishing Co., 2011.

Chapter 18: *The First Review*

In the days leading to our first mission on Saras, my one decided the time had finally come for me to face my past and used the structure to display these events, though warning me that the subject matter was rather strong.

Twenty-two thousand years ago in Atlantis as a small child, I had spent time visiting the crystal museums in Garden City, two enormous round buildings hosting crystalline artifacts of all types that mimicked living creatures from the most minute to the largest. Everything hosted within these buildings was made from exquisite gems and pure crystal, and many forms actually moved as if living.

Returning to the country side somewhere north of Posa Ih Dehn, I entered a large two-story square white building lined with trees on its sides and a tall crystal pyramid set on top. This building was home to the Atlantean moderator, the most significant spiritual master on the planet. I opened a set of double glass doors on the left front side of the building and entered into a small lobby that led to a round courtyard immediately to the right.

Picture 14: Moderator's citadel, Atlan Tenh (*B. Erlinger-Ford*)

The courtyard was centered by an enormous round fountain garden that sat right beneath the pyramid. This fountain contained elevating concentric circles some five meters high, ornamented by a variety of flowers sprouting among soft cascading watery waves. Above this fountain, several glass floor tiers elevated up the crystal pyramid above. However, the pyramid's capstone tier, the moderator's citadel, was opaque from the inside but glowed constantly like a searchlight on the outside. Around the fountain, there were twelve offices, divided into four square segments.

Happily running around the fountain, I noticed the moderator's principal priestess, whose name was Ioshanna, conversing with another priest, a covert representative of the Sons of Belial. They were both dressed in black robes, indicative of our errant nature. The priesthood's primary role in Atlantis was to enlighten the people with the science of truth, but the topic of their discussion was far from benign.

Belial was bent on overthrowing the spiritual government of the island by any means possible. Belial's agent urged the priestess to side with Belial, overthrow the moderator, send Martians back to their planet, and establish a new Order on the island. In return, Belial promised to end tens of thousands of years of discord with the Chiréh, discontinue various priesthood practices, and respect people's desires to follow universal law, to some degree.

Just then, a tall muscular man of Cro-Magnon lineage materialized beside me. His gaze was absolutely terrifying, leaving little doubt that I was absolutely done for. Instantly, both priestess and Belial's ambassador emerged from their private office and rushed out to the fountain, realizing I overheard their discussion. The ambassador signaled this man, gliding ten centimeters off the ground, to take care of the situation. He reached out to grab me but intentionally missed, letting off a loud forceful growl. I backed away promptly and headed for the glass door entrance as the man stayed behind laughing sarcastically.

I sprinted out of the building and sought refuge in a nearby tram station. Soon after, the man came after me, slowly and carelessly floating through the air. "Roshon, where could you be?" he said deviously playful, passing in front of the tram station some eighty meters away. But suddenly, he became translucent and vanished. I jumped into the nearest tram trying to get away and hastily set course for Garden City. But as I set tram controls, something, or someone, made them inoperative. At the same time, all power to the tram station was cut and lights turned off.

I had nowhere else to go and feared for my life, knowing that someone kept a close invisible eye on me. So I quietly jumped off the tram and concealed myself behind a post in the station, guarding best stillness possible. There, I waited anxiously for a chance allowing safe escape.

Suddenly, I felt a hot prickling breath encircle the front bottom part of my neck, wrapping toward the back, and passed out. When I came to, this same man held me in his arms, floating high over a cliff. I looked at him in sheer panic, knowing what he was about to do. He, on the other hand, laughed loudly back. His laughter echoed through chasm walls for some time, fearfully impacting my eventual demise. "Roshon, you maggot!" he said, releasing me into the deep chasm. I immediately realized that this man was Gina.

Picture 15: Roshon plummets into the chasm (*Rodrigo Diaz*)

"The next time you feel like picking at rocks or climbing up ice walls, this past experience is the reason why," May Len said. "You're still trying to grab on to that cliff to save your life. You are correct; the man chasing you then was Gina. Now you understand why she must have you?"

I was relieved to know this, but there was much more to uncover, certainly way more unpleasant than this. May Len assured me I would soon experience past lives where we had met but wisely did not go into details.

In another life, I was a teenage Jew that lived during the Jewish massacre of June 1391 in Cordoba, Spain. I was a selfish youth, showing off my Jewish heritage, thus painting a bull's-eye upon the local Jewish community. It was a time of grave prejudice against Jews and Moors in particular, brewed by Ferrand Martinez, the queen's confessor. I ran away as angered mobs approached but was captured and accused of being a Jew. I denied it cowardly as my family burned before me, but I soon followed their fate.

The life prior to Cordoba, I was a Dominican friar devoted to a flagellant lifestyle. I beat myself into caustic bloody disrepute and pushed my dreadful penance on the masses, consumed by guilt for being a Spanish female prostitute the life previous. Further back in time, about AD 700, I was the Mayan astronomer that inscribed the 13.0.0.0.0 baktun calendar tablets, once wrongly believed to predict the end of the world on the year 2012.

In AD 325, I was a Christian priest by the name of Arius that fought a losing battle with the Council of Nicea by emphasizing Father's divinity over the son and favoring Origen's views on reincarnation, although he did not publicly speak much about the latter for his life's sake. A hundred years prior, I played a role in laying out the basic foundation and designing the drainage system for the city of Tikkal in Guatemala. Numerous other lives preceded these sojourns, too many to list in any manuscript. But those most outstanding will witness their hidden secrets in pages to follow.

Earth gov received every transmission from the structure and shared them with the world. My testimonies helped many begin to shed their captors, the inner monsters from the id. His Majesty is so wise, generous, and loving, able to turn every situation into a beneficial lesson or opportunity for an entire universe. May His Magnificence, the Wise of Ages, be honored by our honesty and endeavor for truth. *Oh-joi*!

Chapter 19: *Perfect Revenge*

The port of New York, the busiest on the Atlantic seaboard, had rarely seen such bustle in a century. A hundred ships made their mark daily upon its waters, weaving through Upper New York Bay unto South Street quays, known to the world as the Street of Ships. Anything from ordinary fishing smacks to elegant trans-Atlantic packets crowded its teeming wharves. Enterprising merchants created new waterfront land here, hastily building counting houses and warehouses to handle the wealth of goods coming in and out of the city by ship.

Months following the discovery of gold in California, New York became America's shipbuilding capital. Shipyards on the Hudson rushed to build better, faster ships intended for continental cargo runs. Railroad routes in Panama and Nicaragua linked Atlantic and Pacific oceans, reducing the time and resources needed to navigate to California via the Straits of Magellan.

Off at sea, ships rolled up fluttering sails and waited for days to dock, displaying several national flags in waiting by port side. At the wharf, a thick mast forest hid three-story buildings from sight. Dock masters scrambled to allot human resources and meet tight loading schedules, and men busily toiled to put food on their tables. Burdens continued beyond shift's end to help meet ends, pleading for every ounce of stamina to make it through yet another day. Rain, snow, or shine, work never stopped.

Immigrants walked these docks by the hundreds daily absolutely clueless what to do or where to go. To their detriment, patience and sympathy were not New York's finest attributes at the time, especially flooded port magistrates rushing to review sworn releases and clear ships for departure. After a long voyage, New York's dilapidated underworld offered travelers a chance to unwind, but likewise lose their belongings—or lives. Dive bars, ruthless crimps, rat fights, and shameless streetwalkers stood ready to swindle a living by whatever means necessary.

It was the best of times for merchants who made good money exploiting a labor glut struggling to make ends meet. The fifteen-year New York famine took its toll on wages, greatly affecting quality of life in the area. For those indefatigable workers privileged with work, fear of being dismissed stressed their hearts, for there were always fresh recruits willing to work longer and for less. Most Yorkers felt threatened by immigrants taking jobs away for cheap while others saw an endless supply of practically free labor at their disposal.

It was early October, 1853. A young man of medium stature slowly and uncomfortably made his way down the docks. His boyish face was saddened, concerned, with a mixed expression of lost hope and overburdened determination. His dull green eyes appeared transfixed somewhere far, although they truly focused fairly near. Wispy long blonde hair in disarray billowed from his head in already retrieving lines. Crooked unclean teeth lined his mouth rubbing against lips, fermenting painful sores he couldn't mind.

His considerably overweight body attempted to fit into a Yankee uniform gifted him by a U.S. Artillery private, the only clothes he had. Under his left arm, he carried several paper rolls and a bucket on his right. He lived most of his life here at the docks with his father, doing the same thing day after day, hoping someday to become a famous painter.

The locals called him Fish, though his real name was Adam. He was different from most. Unlike dock workers, Adam was challenged by a condition known as Down's syndrome, gravely misunderstood at the time. Those in the wrong were harshly hurtful of this young man's best intentions. People harassed or, worse yet, beat him since early childhood for no reason but a demising heart. He lived alone with his father at the docks in abject misery, left mostly to chance against fierce New York wolves that lived to relentlessly hunt down the meek at heart.

Fearing the outside world, Adam lived in a small musty room most of his life. There, from a dusty small window, he traced with his finger the outline of ships in the harbor. In spite of meager earnings, his father ensured Adam an ink brush and paper on which he drew majestic traces of valiant ships at sea, all within the small world enclosing him.

Through a small hole in a door leading to his father's ticket office, he watched and then mimicked the physical outline of passengers, but his work never left that small room. There he waited years in confined solitude, hoping to expose his talents beyond the incarceration committed him. Some stories are made of dreams, and some dreams from stories, but his dream was to someday help his father financially by selling sketches at the dock, something his father felt he would never do; but Adam was determined.

One cloudy October day, Adam dared leave his father's office and cautiously introduced his pale face at the dock. At first, he was not immediately welcomed with best intentions, but he determinedly continued to spend time out in the open regardless. Eventually, everyone at the docks got to know Adam and welcomed him as one of their own. Before long, he spent hours admiring the many ships lining the vast harbor up close.

Driven by a compelling dream he could not deny, he sat on a wooden bucket skillfully drawing moored ships in dashing sailing action, braving the broadest most tempest seas amid flaring clouds and reflective sunlight.

Daring droves of rushing laborers and confused immigrants moving hurriedly to and from ships, he picked a spot on the wharf, carelessly sat on his bucket, and began to draw large four-mast ships docked before him. As passengers passed by, he briefly promoted his drawings asking but a mere penny for them. However, no one seemed interested in his work and continued on their way. Undeterred, he resumed work on new masterpieces faithful that, this time, customers would be drawn to them. But, he was never in good company to begin with.

The sun rested over the mid-morning sky and a strong chilling sea breeze lent a slight quiver to anyone daring the wharf. Adam sat calmly on his bucket by the quay's building side, busy working on an innovative idea for the times: isometric or bird's-eye sketches of ships at sea. Not long after, three teenagers arrived, the same bunch as always, determined to ruin Adam's aspirations.

"Hey, maggot," said Nolan, the ring leader, with an Irish accent, "I thought I told you to get inside and stay there. There're decent, hardworking people out here, and you're getting in the way. Did you hear me, maggot?"

Adam was so inspired by his work he never noticed being spoken to. Interpreting Adam's concentration as defiance, Nolan immediately turned violent and struck Adam harshly on his upper back. "You stinking maggot, don't you know who's talking to you?"

The harsh blow sent Adam to the ground, moaning in pain and afraid for his life. "I'm sorry, Mr. Nolan," he said softly and somewhat mumbled.

"What are you doing out here wasting time and getting in everyone's way?"

"But this is what I do; I draw ships."

"Maggot, my father runs this place and he doesn't appreciate having you around. You're scaring away customers and slowing down dock workers!"

"I don't mean nobody harm. I'm just painting," Adam said innocently.

"Painting, eh? Here, let me see what kind of abomination you came up with this time." Nolan ripped the paintings from Adam's hands, handling them roughly as if these had no worth. No sooner, he disappointingly slapped Adam several times across the face with them.

"Boats! You painted boats! Are you insane? People come to the docks; they see boats. They sail for three to four weeks in, a boat. They get off at their destination from, a boat. You think you're going to sell boat paintings at a dock? You foolish maggot! Passengers are so sick of boats they'd rather head straight for a dive bar!" he said laughing his heart out.

Nolan then crushed and threw Adam's drawings into the sea, where they quickly smeared and vanished beneath churning waters. "There, that's where boats belong, in the water, not paper!" he said sarcastically. "Bye-bye boats! *Slán agát*." Adam's heart tore emotionally, and he wailed desperately on his knees at the edge of the dock, watching his paintings waste away in the water while the gang cheered spitefully against him.

Nolan grabbed Adam roughly by his coat and forced him to his feet. "Now listen here, you fat slob. I try to help you, urge you on, but no, you just don't get the point. Look, I'm your best friend, and you're my protégé, remember? Someday you'll thank me for all I've done for you, since your father doesn't take care of you or turns you into a useful man! What will you do when he dies, eh? Ever think about that? Why do you think I try to promote you?

"Look at you. You're a disgrace!" he said straightening Adam's clothes and stature. "When was the last time you bathed and shaved, eh? You stink badly. No wonder they call you Fish. Your belly is ten times what it needs to be and . . . look at those hands. They've never done a bit of hard work—ever! Today, we start you on a new regiment; you're becoming a man. Here, catch this!"

Taking a heavy box from nearby, Nolan threw it at Adam. Adam tried to catch it but folded his arms about empty air before the box ever reached him. The box was so heavy it knocked Adam harshly to the ground, landed on his chest, and forced a loud scream from him. "Oh dear, this is going to take some work. All right, get up, maggot, let's try that again."

Adam tried to get up, but the weight of the wide box kept him from moving. "Come on, maggot, get your big smelly arse up! You want to be a man and make money? Well, this is the only place to get it, working the docks, working for me, not selling sketches."

"I can't. It's too heavy," said Adam in deep distress. "Please help me up?"

"Help yourself, maggot," Nolan said, putting hands on hips. "You're beyond hope, you know that? Look at you. You're totally useless! Come on," he said to his gang, "Forget this hopeless piece of *cac. Slán agát*, maggot."

Adam begged Nolan to remove the heavy box from him, but he ignored his plead. None of the dock workers dared interfere since Nolan was the dock chief's son and they could get fired for conspiring against him. Adam never revealed this incident to his father, fearing he might never let him out again. But soon enough, he was back out pacing the docks, creating new isometric sketches and trying to sell them to passengers.

One fine sunny morning, a large sailboat moored at the docks, and hundreds of passengers busily made their way down from it. Excitedly, Adam picked up his drawings and dashed to the docks, hoping this might be his lucky day. However, no one paid him any attention, to his detriment. As multitudes pressed forward, Adam got caught up in the rush and was carried backward with the flow. He managed to get out of the crowd but accidentally bumped into a man and politely turned to apologize.

The man, in his twenties, wore impeccable business attire of the time and briefly smiled at Adam on his way to an awaiting ship. He was accompanied by a young lady, dressed in a pink dress and matching colored umbrella. They were slightly Asian in appearance and of extremely clean, refined features. Adam had never seen anyone like them before, much less offering a smile, and felt immediately drawn to them.

"Excuse me, gentle sir, pretty lady," he said, trying to get their attention.

Noticing Adam's call, the two strangers gently turned about and greeted him warmly. "Yes, my son, what can we do for you?" the man politely said.

Adam looked at them in awe, overcome by their kindness to the point his lips sealed uncertain what to say. "Gentle sir, pretty lady, it's just that . . . I'm an artist," he said excitedly yet humbly. "I sell my paintings for a penny."

The lady, who previously hid her face from Adam, slowly disclosed her identity to him. Adam looked upon her with hesitation and fear, only to find a lady of extreme beauty and grace. Her loveliness made him breathe sharply and recover a skipping heart. She had long black hair behind a perfectly sculptured, clean face. Her bright smile shone in mesmerizing splendor, enhanced by shining amber eyes.

Noticing Adam's silence, the lady said, "You are an artist?" Adam assured her he was. "You are much more than that. Your heart is filled with incredible stories of olden days just waiting to be told and a future as bright as sunlight."

"Thank you very much, pretty lady, and you too, gentle sir. That's the nicest thing anyone's ever told me. My name is Adam Tenner, but people don't really like me. You see, I'm . . . different from everybody else."

"There's nothing different about you," the lady said. "My dear brother is a wondrous creation within creation itself."

Adam bowed his head, stunned by the lady's kindness. He searched for words where there had never been any, though his heart longed to compose a song, whispered by his inner essence. "Let this, then, be our first day of friendship, one of many, because it is by God's wisdom that friends meet."

"And may this friendship last an eternity," the lady said with evident joy, looking at her associate and nodding affirmatively.

"You can call me Mr. Veih," the man said.

"I'm Maylee," the lovely lady said a bit hesitant as if searching for a name.

"Maylee—very pretty name for a very pretty lady. You are going far?"

"Quite so," Mr. Veih said. "Our travels will take us to the ends of the earth. My friend will stay there as a . . . missionary, but I need to go somewhere else farther still."

"I want to do something very special for you that you can take along, and I'd like to do it for free."

"I'd like that very much," Maylee said. "Will it take long, friend, brother?"

Adam hurriedly took out his pen and went to work. "This will only take a moment," Adam said joyously, feeling his dreams of becoming an artist had finally come true. However, while reaching for paper, the brush accidentally fell through the dock floor and plunged into dark waters below. His heart immediately sunk, and grave disappointment wore upon his being.

"I'm so sorry," Adam said apologetically. "It's my fault; it's always my fault for being so clumsy." His guests didn't say a word but rather patiently waited for Adam to find a solution.

"I can still do this," Adam said suddenly. "I know what to do." He took his long hair, rolled part of it into a tip, and dipped it sideways into the ink bottle. Without looking at the paper, Adam guided his head up, down, and sideways, transferring ink from his hair unto paper with greatest assurance. His heart poured unto the painting with great skill, accuracy, and attention to detail, even though he could not see what he drew. Stroke by stroke, Adam's confidence and concentration increased, continuing to add remarkable detail to his painting.

A large crowd circled around to witness his hair at work, curious to watch Adam draw without looking at the emerging portrait. Among those present were Nolan and his gang, who burst into the scene rudely pushing people out of the way. "It's that maggot again. Fish, that's quite enough!" Just as they moved forward to take hold of Adam, Mr. Veih raised his head and placed his piercing serious eyes upon Nolan who immediately stopped cold.

"Art work may not be interrupted, Mr. Nolan," Mr. Veih said, slowly and seriously. "You will allow Adam to finish his work, uninterrupted." Nolan's lips phased open and his gaze froze as if charmed at the mention of his name, backing off toward the crowds without muttering a word. Moments later, Adam straightened his posture and looked upon the painting well pleased.

"This is what I see when I look upon you," Adam said. The painting showed Maylee and Mr. Veih most realistically among light clouds and background mountains covered with entrances. "You are going somewhere very far, so far that people can't sail there but clouds do. There is no good land to live upon, so people live inside mountains."

Mr. Veih reviewed the painting and was most pleased by it. "This is exactly where I'm going, far, far away. And yes, we do live inside mountains. Very well done! One question, young artist, do you have a name for this far-off land?"

Adam thought for a moment, and then said, "Yes. I'll call it . . . Masar."

"That's what we call it also," Maylee said, smiling at her associate. "You'll come and visit us in four lifetimes from now, I assure you."

"I would like that so very much, pretty lady" Adam said. "After waiting a million years, what's four more lifetimes?"

"Adam, this is the most-prized gift I take from the New World," he said, reaching into his pocket and producing money. "Take this, but don't look at it. Give it all to your father and tell him what happened here today." Adam took the money and put it in his side pocket without looking as instructed.

"Good bye, my old friend of ages, see you in four lifetimes," the man said, heading for their ship but often looking back at Nolan with a serious look. Nolan was furious but unable to move against Adam, afraid Mr. Veih might catch him in the act.

That day, Adam sold dozens of sketches to amazed onlookers and made news headlines. At day's end, he hurried to his father who was rather stunned by Adam's story but more so by the money he brought in: $125, about five month's pay and enough to purchase two tickets to San Francisco. Adam felt his future was in New York, but his father wouldn't hear of it and decisively bought the fares.

Days passed, and Adam continued to promote his paintings, but few took notice in spite of his recent popularity. The handful of sketches he sold daily amounted to no more than 30 cents, a fraction of a day's salary. Meanwhile, his father continued to work long hours at the Pacific Mail Steamship Company's ticket counter, preparing for their eventual departure day.

One busy morning, a man struggling with a heavy accent hurriedly approached the counter and asked to purchase tickets to San Francisco, but the ship's manifest was closed due to cargo restraints. The man claimed to be Jacinto Derwanz, a Brazilian diplomat, and demanded a ticket be provided him but to no avail.

Frustrated, he turned to leave the office when Adam came out of his room and told the man in soft restrained manner, "Sir, you can have my ticket. Here, sir, please take it. I don't want to go to San Francisco." The man slowed his pace slightly but decisively ignored Adam's offer and left hastily.

Surprised by Adam's attitude, his father asked him, "Why don't you want to go to San Francisco?"

"I've been a burden to you all my life. You can have a better life, but I keep you from it! I know you can't get married because your lady don't want me. That's not fair for you, so I want to make it on my own, no matter what happens to me. I love you, father, for being so kind, but I've hurt you long enough. I want to make it on my own, please. It's time I go."

Father and son embraced in bitter tears, father committing to put Adam first upon all things regardless of odds and promising a better life in San Francisco. "When your mother died," Mr. Tenner said, "she asked me to never lose sight of you because you were someone very special. Until you find your future, obey mom's orders. Besides, there's talk of the South wanting to form its own country. If that happens, who knows, maybe war will break out. New York will be a prized target, and we will not be safe here." Adam agreed reluctantly, feeling that this was not a wise decision.

Meanwhile, Nolan bumped into the diplomat who expressed his dilemma and Adam's offer to relinquish tickets. Nolan was not aware of Adam's travel plans and soon learned of his recent sizable earnings. Nolan's mind sweltered with envy, scheming Adam's demise beneath a hatred canopy difficult to ignore. Seeds of revenge found a way, and the stage was set for lords of odium to steer Adam's future into the perfect revenge.

The work day was coming to a close, and Adam strolled about the wharf reviewing the latest arrivals. Unbeknown to him, someone hid behind a wall with worst intentions. It was Nolan, waiting until Adam was far enough away to make his move. At the right moment, he signaled his two cohorts who quickly came behind Adam and threw him to the floor face first.

Adam briefly mumbled from shock but said nothing; he knew who it was. "Well, look what the cat couldn't swallow. It's that stinky Fish again," Nolan said, forcefully rolling Adam face up and pushing his foot into Adam's stomach. "*Día duít*, *Iasc*, we need to have a very serious talk, you and me."

"I have nothing to say to you: you're a bad man," Adam said.

"Bad, you say? You don't know just how bad, bad can be. Why don't we find out, eh?" Nolan signaled one of his thugs to kick Adam in the ribs, causing him to wail loudly.

Nearby workers, witnessing the ordeal, suddenly dropped their chores and gathered about; but their curiosity greatly angered Nolan, who immediately lashed back. "What are you dimwits looking at? I don't pay you to look, do I? Get back to work, or you're all fired!" Distastefully, workers had no choice but resume toils for their own sake, leaving Adam to chance.

"Where did you put all that money, eh?" Nolan said, searching Adam's pockets hastily but coming up empty.

"Why do you hate me so much? I've done nothing to you," Adam said.

"Oh, but you have. You stole from me, and no one gets away with theft around here. You sold paintings I understand, but you never paid my business tax like everyone else here does. Tell you what. Give me the money those foreigners gave you, and I'll let you go. I promise I won't hurt you anymore. All I want is the money, so give it to me!"

"The money was for father, not me, much less for you," Adam said crying.

"Well, go get it, steal it if you have to. Unless . . . listen, do you want something bad to happen to your *papa*?"

"No, but Mr. Veih said it was for father, and you have no right to take it."

"I see; perhaps you need some persuasion. Get him up, boys." Nolan's thugs roughly stood Adam up, and Nolan sternly struck Adam in the stomach.

Adam fell on his knees, crying and coughing, rolling on the ground from pain.

"You want more? I have lots more." Nolan picked Adam up by the arm and delivered another blow at his side, causing him to wriggle breathless on the ground.

"I want that money—now! Do you hear me, maggot? I don't care what or how you do it, but you get it!"

"No! I won't!" Adam replied staunchly.

"Really? Fine by me," Nolan said, delivering harsh blows to face and ribs. Blood and tears poured from Adam's face to Nolan's absolute delight, but Adam staunchly stood by his solemn word, refusing Nolan's terms.

"You'll meet the undertaker if I don't get my money," threatened Nolan, pulling a knife from his side pocket and showcasing it brightly before Adam.

The supervisor, an aging man of African descent, saw the risk Adam was in and approached to see what was going on, but Nolan wasted no time facing him off with the knife. "I said mind your own business, or I'll fire your lousy ass! Get back to work, maggot!" Hesitant, the supervisor returned to work, but he didn't move far. On the ground, Adam called out to his father, but there was no way he could hear him. The supervisor signaled one of his men to go get Mr. Tenner, Adam's father, disappearing discreetly as to not be noticed.

"Why are you calling your *athair*?" Nolan said, "I thought you wanted to make it on your own. I don't care. Bring him on. I'm a champion fighter, the best in New York. I'll take your old man anytime. And when I'm done with him, you're next, just you and me, Fish. What do you say, eh?"

Adam's father arrived, desperately looking for Adam. "What are you doing to my boy?" he screamed. "Who wants their chops busted?" Nolan's thugs grabbed his arms, and Nolan landed several harsh punches into his rib cage. Mr. Tenner fell to the ground swarming while Nolan's thugs held him tight.

"So you came for your boy, eh?" said Nolan staunchly. "Good, then you can watch your boy do what he's worst at, being a man."

"Adam is not well. He is special!" said Mr. Tenner, agonized with pain.

"He won't be for long."

Adam immediatcly cnraged, filled with uncommon valor, raised his voice, and called Nolan out with a loud emotional scream. "Leave my father alone! This is between you and me!" Immediately, dock workers dropped what they were doing and attentively observed the rising standoff between Adam and Nolan, but did not interfere.

"Wait, did I hear you right? You want to take me on, like man to man, eh?" Nolan said in savoring delight.

Mr. Tenner warned Adam to stand down, but his pleacall went ignored. "You heard right!" Adam said. "I'm a quick learner, and I want to make it on my own!"

"All right then, come on," Nolan said, driving his knife into the floor board. "I've been waiting a very long time for this. Let's see what you've got, Fish." Adam stood up and approached Nolan with fists high above his head, trying to hit the taller Nolan on the chest, but missed every time.

"Oh, I'm really scared of them jelly hands," Nolan said sarcastically. Blow after blow missed their mark while Nolan danced about, mocking Adam and slapping him behind the head. "Oh, missed that, and that."

Nolan kicked Adam and waved fast punches on his face without mercy until eyes bled. But Adam persisted, even though it seemed outright futile. "Here, I'll fight with no hands, with my eyes closed, with my back to you."

Adam missed every time until tiring, breathing deeply with no vivacity left to draw upon. His arms dropped, pace slowed, and face fell exhausted before a mocking Nolan. "This is the most fun I've had in years! You should have done this long ago!" Nolan said, bragging his fighting skills. "Let me know when you're ready to fight, not jig."

Adam was furious but far from giving up. "Look, evil man," Adam said out of breath. "Hitting people is not being a man."

Nolan blasted into helpless laughter, further calling Adam disgraceful names. "You're stronger than I am, but there must be a way to defeat you."

"No one has yet. I'm twenty times the man you are. How dare you face me?" Nolan said, carelessly waltzing around Adam, poking and kicking him.

Adam then knew what to do and waited for Nolan to lower his guard. At the right moment, he went into action. "I'm going to turn you into a man!" Adam screamed, racing toward Nolan who turned to face him clueless of what was about to happen.

Adam tossed his entire body upon Nolan who tried stepping away, but he could not escape Adam's momentum and wide grip. Adam knocked him down, crushing his body onto the wooden floor with his body weight. Nolan immediately exhaled loudly in agony while Adam sustained his body upon him. One of Nolan's thugs came to Nolan's rescue, but the dock supervisor threatened him not to interfere. Gaining his stand, Mr. Tenner released himself, kicked, and punched his guarding thug unconscious, but did nothing to help Adam, who seemed to have everything quite well under control.

Adam punched Nolan repeatedly on the face until it bled and few teeth missed their holding places. "You may be stronger than me, but I'm smarter than you. Now, I will show you everything you taught me. Today, we start you on a new regiment and turn you into a man! I try to help you, urge you on, you're even my protégé; but you just don't seem to understand. Look, I'm your best friend, remember? Someday, you'll thank me for this since your father doesn't take care of you or turns you into a useful man!"

"I can't breathe," Nolan said in a wispy, restrained voice. "You're too heavy. Get off me. Help me up." No sooner, vomit ejected from his blood filled mouth, completely encompassing his face and neck with sickness.

"This is going to take some work," Adam said. "Help yourself, maggot. You're beyond hope. You're totally useless. Look at your hands. They've never done a bit of hard work—ever! You want to be a man and make money? This is the only place to get it, working the docks, doing something for people, not stealing their hard-earned money, you hopeless piece of *cac*!"

Nolan passed out among loud cheers from dock workers. Adam had accomplished what no one ever had: not only defeat but humiliate the impregnable, fearsome Nolan. Approaching the dock supervisor, Adam said to him, "You are a wondrous creation within creation itself; don't let anyone ever take that away from you. Unite against abuse and fight for your rights. Bad people can turn good by working as hard as you do."

After nodding to fellow workers, the supervisor approached a slowly rising Nolan with a large bait hook and said, "Me and the guys talked and we've decided to unite. Things won't be the same around here. We won't pay you any more personal taxes, and if you fire one of us, you'll find this rusty hook permanently attached to your blowhole! I think your father needs to know what's been going on here, and I'll make sure he does! And as for you two bums," he said to Nolan's thugs, "report here before six in the morning for work, or we'll find you and carve you up like cod. Is that clear?"

Nolan dropped back flat on the ground unable to move while his associates ran off as fast as their feet could carry them. As for Adam, a new life fostered for him at the docks, free from harassment, but his future would not be so pleasant in the end.

Life was never the same for workers at the South Street wharf, free from oppression and extortion. Anyone joining the workforce immediately became a member of the wharf coalition. About those two thugs, they showed up for work on time the following morning and became regular workers at the docks. Nolan rarely frequented the wharf. Meanwhile, Adam enjoyed great artistic freedom leading up to departure day. Dock workers donated him a chair, easel, even made up a promotion sign that read: 'hair sketched portraits.'

Wintry days brought frost and gleaming snows to the wharf. White canopies covered building tops, gradually lending frozen spikes along its edges. Thick mooring ropes stiffened with cold weather, difficult to handle from sharp icy deposits. Ship decks, glazed with ice, kept cleanup crews busy. On the ground, snow patches littered South Street, and evening's ocean breeze made it unbearable to stand for long without heavy winter wear.

On the morning of December 21, 1853, after many gloomy days, a rising sun warmly hosted the land with unusual moderate climate and clear blue skies. Adam and his father walked the familiar wharf one last time on their way to their ship, greeted one last time by dock workers along the way.

The *SS San Francisco* was the largest and most advanced ship of its time. Constructed for the Pacific Mail Steamship Company at the Wm H. Webb Yards, the ship was 60 meters long and registered 2,200 tons hosting two Morgan Works steam engines. It had a side paddle wheel, four sails, three decks, fine cabins, and lounges along its deck line. It offered generous promenades and an upper saloon housing a steer-master cabin. Seven hundred fifty passengers registered for this journey, most members of the U.S. Infantry's Third Regiment. Cannons and animals were lodged on the top deck.

Once on board, the Tenners took their place by starboard to bid their bygone home and valued friends goodbye. Unknown to them, Nolan was watching and scheming. A man dressed in sailor's clothes hurriedly got off the ship, looked in Nolan's direction, and nodded affirmatively to Nolan's satisfaction. Inconspicuously, he approached Nolan who hid behind a door and said, "It's done, like you ordered. Once this ship reaches the Gulf Stream and higher pressure demands are placed upon her boilers, the air pump will pop off something awful like lead from a cannon."

"And then, the engine will suffer to a halt amid sea," Nolan said. "Perfect."

"Mate, this ship's gravely loaded and there are over seven hundred Christian souls upon her hull," the sailor said. "Her water mark is too high and risks sinking into the brink!"

"That's not your concern, seaman. This engine exercise is long overdue. Run along now. I'll see you by the shipyard stocks at the end of South Street in an hour with payment. Don't be late." The seaman sped off into the crowds, heading for the stocks in a hurry. Nolan stayed behind, savoring these few last moments of perfect revenge.

"Have a pleasant trip, maggot," Nolan said sarcastically. "Water is deadly cold in winter." With that, he vanished laughing himself into the distance.

The Tenners briefly inspected their quarters in the tail section just above the rudder. It would be a cold trip since the rear section was not protected from the elements as well as the rest of the ship, proving disturbingly noisy and sickening to the stomach at times. Apparently, the Brazilian diplomat also found his way on board the ship by special request, supposedly from Nolan, anything to weigh down the ship as much as possible.

The port chaplain blessed the ship and its crew prior to departure. Seamen hastened to their posts, bringing the ship to life. Majestic masts on this lengthy steamer, commanded by Commodore J. T. Watkins, unfolded its canvases to restless winds. Standing above the steering deck, the first officer proudly shouted sail settings and rudder directions to the crew.

Ropes fastened through pulleys. Deck posts and sails raised high and mighty, steering the enormous ship southeast. A westerly wind traversed through wakening sails that ruffled gently while smoke from emotive boilers uttered from the ship's tall chimneys, indicating wind direction and strength.

With moorings removed, the *San Francisco* gently introduced unto the southbound East River course way on its maiden voyage. The steam whistle signaled ship's departure unto daring waters. The two main sails fluttered in the air while aft and fore sails tightened to their bindings, gradually nudging the ship's fore away from the wharf.

At the Webb stocks and out of sight from passersby, a man in sailor's clothes laid in a box drained of life for reasons revengeful to the heart, his neck stained by reddish fruit of life from within. At the end of a pier sat Nolan with knife in mouth, sucking on it with particular viciousness as the *San Francisco* coursed by.

Nolan waved at Adam who stood on starboard side viewing the transposing landscape. Seeing Nolan, Adam retrieved emotionally and slowly waved back with reservation. Nolan stood up, removed the knife from his mouth, and shone it laughing sarcastically. It was a symbol of vengeance, a message this trip was committed to dark prepositions. But Adam did not grasp the message; he was just glad to be out of Nolan's reach once and for all.

The ship came to the mouth of East River and passed between Governor and Bedloe's Islands on its way to fateful high seas. Steam paddles stirred the water line for the first time, slowly pushing the vessel out through the Narrows and Ambrose Channel. Smoke billowed from stacks while the sound of pistons and churning paddles brought life to a once-silent mechanical contraption. The month-long journey would pass Rio de Janeiro on its way to Valparaiso, Chile, through the Straits of Magellan. From there, the ship would head for Acapulco before finally sailing into the port of call San Diego.

No one knew that the newly developed engines were not fully tested and that someone had purposely troubled their mechanical bindings. Few if any noticed that the ship was gravely overloaded. The ship's hull lay a meter deeper in the water than designed. No doubt, Nolan purposely boarded the ship beyond its designed capacity to commit the ship beneath the brink.

Picking up the Atlantic current, the ship headed for Rio, cruising at a speed of twenty knots. Gradually, North Atlantic wintry swells rolled up gray and gloomy, incessantly monotone over an endless watery desert. Skies hung with indecisive clouds against pale dull daylight. On the eve of December 23, the ship reached twelve-degree-Celsius waters with a mild air temperature of nineteen degrees Celsius, indicating entry into the Gulf Stream.

On Christmas Eve, a strong gale struck from the northwest with increasingly violent rains and very high irregular seas. Swells grew immensely in no time at all. Passengers first praised how elegantly and pleasantly the ship cut through waves. But with the storm's first gusts, most interrupted their chats and stumbled to the surface. The ship soon heaved and pitched heavily while fear pricked the backs of many inexperienced passenger necks.

An hour later, helms lost control, the ship tipped drastically, and everyone standing erect on board lost ground beneath their feet. Loose objects, furniture, and dishes came crashing down together. Beams moaned and popped as if they would break at any moment, joining a terrified human cast. Seamen struggled to set auxiliary sails in the howling wind to bring the ship back on course, but freezing cold and continuous dampness afflicted hands covered with sores that burned with splashing salt water.

The chief engineer, J. W. Marshall, applied as much steam pressure as he deemed worth risking until the crew finally succeeded in holding the ship on course. But once again, at about 11:00 p.m., the rudder careened out of control, and the ship turned broadside on to wind and sea with a deafening blast below decks. Masts and spars creaked and groaned. Hurricane-force gusts swept through the rigging and around exhaust chimneys. Pail-sized streams of water broke through first-class cabin skylights. Sailors in heavy boots tramped across the deck while naval officers bellowed frantic commands in the dark of night.

For safety, passengers transferred to the mess hall where they stood in pajamas and prayed for their lives. Four hundred soldiers were berthed on the high deck in double rows of standee berths, three tiers each. They had all crept from their berths, most of them broken and thrown down. Considerable livestock escaped from their pens on the same deck, now mingled together with soldiers amid broken standees.

At 1:15 a.m. Christmas morning, just as Adam and his father discussed the possibilities of foundering in the open seas, a loud thump emerged from the engine room. The ship immediately stomped on its fore side, followed by tumultuous shudders that rattled every rigging on the upper deck. Adam rolled across the room and clashed his head on a wall. Mr. Tenner flew toward aft, where crashing waves vibrated the rear hull.

Engines mysteriously broke down. The end of the air pump piston rod broke off, the air pump bracket was consequently adrift, and the spanker blew away, leaving the ship entirely at the mercy of battering waves and wind. The heart of the *San Francisco* came to a dead halt. From then on, she drifted feebly in the boiling sea like an unsteerable wreck.

The ship behaved handsomely to this point, but she fell off in the trough of the sea and labored heavily. Planks and decks were smashed, and she took on much water. Both steam and hand pumps ran at maximum, but water levels kept climbing. Soldiers were commandeered to bail water in the engine room to keep boilers fired up, cramped between pipes and enveloped by heat and steam.

The ship's cannon fired every half hour, trying to call attention to nearby ships for assistance, but it would be some time before the call was heard. Meanwhile, the *San Francisco* endured her fate alone in shadowy liquid mountains, swelling invisibly in rendered darkness.

At 5:00 a.m., the ship lost its foremast and all canvas, carrying away four lifeboats with the wreck of the spars. The captain now feared the ship might not safely outlive the rough gale imposed. And true, this ship's destiny would only worsen. Adam and his father sought refuge in the upper saloon along with other soldiers, as Nolan's revenge was being served cold amid waves easily dwarfing the ship's tallest mast.

At 7:00 a.m., the *San Francisco*'s nautical position was 69° W by 38°20' N, about 525 kilometers off the American coastline. Just as the chief engineer attempted to restart engines under high pressure, an enormous breaker gathered in the distance barreling toward the ship from its left. Everyone in upper decks stood entrenched watching this massive grayish-azure wave build and approach without regard or the means to stop it. In the steer master deck, officers stood frozen stiff, knowing this breaker would permanently damage the ship, unable to steer to safety no matter the effort.

The wave suffered the ship with a harsh crushing blow, boarding the vessel. The ship sided briefly, absorbing the cruel tidal wave and seemingly submerged under water. Upper deck foundations cracked, giving way to boarding waters that forcefully pushed everything in its path. Deck sections split and detached. The wave carried with it the whole of the upper saloon and everything astern—paddle boxes, smoke stacks, and the remainder of the ship's life boats—staving about sixteen meters of the spar deck over the main saloon. The ship was left as a perfect wreck and began to founder.

Deadly shudders ran through everyone on board, accompanied by panicked screams. Those who regained composure worked their way forward on deck. Where the giant parlor once stood was now an unobstructed view of the sea. Also gone were parts of the upper steer master deck. Central steering was damaged, leaving the ship stagnant to the mercy of waters. With that gale, the entire superstructure and 150 individuals who sought refuge therein instantly washed overboard, including the Tenners.

Only meters away from the slowly drifting vessel in cold turbulent waters, people struggled to survive. Most bled with serious injuries fighting for their lives in full view of friends. They hugged bits of wreckage and attempted vainly to swim back to the vessel, but shifting waves and unpredictable sways made this feat impossible. Carnage, mostly soldiers, filled the waters, dissected by sharp wreckage. Others were dismembered beyond recognition. Only two individuals returned to the ailing ship; the rest vanished into churning waters.

The ship moved farther away from the wreckage in unpredictable directions. Mr. Tenner managed to pull Adam out of the water and unto a floating wreck, procured one for himself, and tied the two together with ropes from wasted masts. They never made it back to the vessel. In minutes, the *San Francisco* vanished from their sights behind enormous watery crescents, destined to horrible moments ahead.

The Tenners floated stray on open seas far from welcoming shores, struggling to survive in cold turbid waters on barely sustainable wrecks. They were carried by strong southeast currents toward Bermuda on a 750-kilometer journey lasting approximately two weeks without protection from the sun or sustenance, other than occasional rain water and hand-fetched fish. During the evening, they kept watch for distant vessels or nearby shores, but only starlight kept them company.

It was just past midnight, January 7, 1854. Sun-burned, dehydrated, and starved, both men barely grasped on to life, much less hope. Chilly water numbed Adam's hands and feet, setting in hypothermia. He felt drowsy, confused, shivering, and breathed slowly.

Then, off in the distant southeast, when least expected, a barely discernible glow commanded dark night skies, getting Mr. Tenner's attention. "Adam, wake up," he said, short on breath. "Look, it's the lights from Hamilton straight ahead. We're going to make it!" Adam barely lifted up his head and smiled in relief. But it would take some time to reach the island.

On the evening of the ninth, the island's western cays broke surf near them, and lights from Hamilton shone brightly a few kilometers ahead. Mr. Tenner paddled with what strength he had left, braving the Ledge Flats reef unto Harrington Sound guided by port lights cast upon waters.

Mr. Tenner continued to encourage Adam, promising a warm meal in just minutes, but it was too late for the young man. Adam tried to move his arms, but they did not respond and gradually slipped partly unto the water. His legs hung fully off the wreckage with no will to serve further purpose, cutting through water like a sided keel.

Adam no longer reasoned sufficiently to remember his ordeal or control bodily functions, expiring his last breath. His heart slowed to a stop, and sounds vanished from recognition. His eyes gently closed into a dim visionary haze, and his essence abandoned the vessel he once inhabited.

Moments later, something bit his legs and dragged him off the wreckage. With no life left in him, he peacefully entered the waters. His lifeless body sank into the deep at the mercy of feasting creatures not known to or felt by him. Unaware Adam was gone, Mr. Tenner firmly rowed his make shift oar, paddling and encouraging Adam to hang on.

As the northwestern end of the Flatts neared, surf breaks showed an inlet into the harbor, and rising ocean tides slowly drew the rafts into it. The rafts picked up speed from the current, spinning about in their course inward. Mr. Tenner turned to Adam and for the first time noticed he was gone. He immediately panicked, shifting his attention to seek his son.

No sooner, rafts collided with low reef rocks, and Mr. Tenner was thrown off the wreckage onto low channel waters where sharp rocky spikes pierced his abdomen, suffering him mortally. Thusly, Nolan's revenge took course, subduing the lives of over three hundred souls to a cold, watery wasteland. The restive remains of the *San Francisco* have yet to be discovered in the deep expansive fathoms of the sea, mysteriously hiding fruits of revenge born from Saras's tragic recurring legacy.

The presentation came to an end, and lights came back up in the structure. May Len turned to me with a bright smirk on her face, wasting no time to call me Adam. The chancellor lived the life of Mr. Tenner, and Mr. Yato was the dock supervisor. As for Nolan, well, it's obvious.

Maylee transitioned in China at the end of the century, in preparation for re-embodiment as May Len in June 1968. Mr. Veih returned to Masar with Adam's portrait, waiting for the day his old friend would take to the skies in the spirit of former times.

My loving starry splendor, always full of surprises, could not let the day pass without doing something out of the ordinary for me. The old hair-drawn portrait unfolded out of thin air, and I wasted no time presenting it once again to its rightful owner: my beloved master of ages Dow Uanh.

---

[1] "The new steamship for San Francisco," *Daily Alta California,* 12 August 1853.

[2] "Disaster to the new steamship San Francisco," *New York Daily Times,* 6 January 1854.

[3] "The San Francisco, additional particulars of the loss of this steamer," *New York Daily Times,* 9 January 1854.

[4] "Daily Alta California," *Daily Alta California,* 17 July 1853.

[5] "Total loss of the San Francisco," *New York Daily Times,* 14 January 1854.

[6] "The wreck of the San Francisco," *New York Daily Times,* 10 February 1854.

[7] C. Cutler, "Queens of the Western Ocean," in *Queens of the Western Ocean*, Annapolis, MD US Naval Institute, 1961.

[8] "Wrecks at sea ... San Francisco," *New York Daily Times,* 9 January 1854.

Chapter 20: *Return to Atlantis*

A hazy azure radiance gently stirred upon lofty eastern horizons, where Arvah's glorious furnaces gradually crowned above serene, undulating seas, pronouncing a new dawn. On land, slumbering darkness livened vigorously as daylight's prominence draped gently west across partially cloudy skies, and eve's vigilant shadows reverently yielded in the presence of undeniable light.

Majestic skies rendered tribute to the mercy of gentle violet tinges glowing amid opaque clouds that billowed carelessly through predetermined expanse. Below heaven's swirls, light lilac shimmers moved over the obscure veil of calm briny waters, busily pleading mother Saras to bid them slowly northward.

As eve's gentle mist gradually dispersed from the land, His Majesty's glories gallantly manifested their exceptional grace to awakening, admiring living forms. Trees, flowers, and all gifts from Saras came alive with musical cheer as winds gently embraced docile branches, much like harp strings tenderly strummed by artful hands. Tall palms and broad timbers dotted the landscape, bounded by alluring waves of captivating flowers amid low light green grasses. Invigorating essences from countless blossoms permeated the air, sharing their talents in a life devoted to blessed, fragrant beauty.

This was Saras of a different time, a sculptured garden continent designed to withstand the test of time and elevate man to endless dimensions of love beyond the physical. This land was called Atlan Tenh meaning "from the sea," uniquely blessed among all other lands on Saras. The entire continent was a nature park, preserved with extreme artistic care such that no scar, however slight, could be found among its native wonders.

Trees from far-off lands and solar systems were rightfully represented here, and only the gentlest of creatures roamed its grounds. No animal suffered its life to the subsistence of another, including man. Tens of thousands of Martian gardeners parsed the land daily in search of floral perfection, creating ever more exalting ornate arrangements to adorn mother Saras and exalt the wondrous king of beauty.

This was a land hallowed by the highest word this finite dimension can withstand. It was a fruitful cradle, where survivors of the grave Mu tragedy were nurtured back to spiritual health. Here, mankind learned the ways of Infinite Majesty and made surprising spiritual progress. But the forces of darkness, in love with error and weary of reality's stirring grace, vowed to shelter their death-abiding ignorance by embezzling Father's children. This they would do much as in times prior, leading man to worship past memories and prize fearful temptations rather than honesty.

About forty thousand years ago, the unspeakable evil that destroyed Mu befell mankind once again with untold vengeance. In those days, other humanoid forms lived outside Atlan Tenh confines in primal villages and caves. The "lost ones," known today as Neanderthals and Cro-Magnons, chose not to follow the brotherhood and lived as they pleased.

Re-embodied Mu leaders mingled with these reclusive villagers and introduced their lifestyles to Atlan Tenh's populace, against the brotherhood's advice. Making matters worse, many were granted residence in Atlan Tenh. Shortly after, decadence and injudicious physical behaviors spread across the land like a plague. Initiates turned against their masters, abandoned the pleasures of spirit for those of flesh, and stood nakedly guilty before their Creator, reverting to a primitive terminable life devoid of universal direction.

Mother Saras could not bear such negation. Over time, Saras suffered natural disasters, tremors, and unusual storms never before seen, all because of man's reprobate energy. Red tears deep from Saras's heart emerged through the frail biosphere upon which man committed the most horrific indulgences imaginable. Many lands submitted to the seas under nature's distress and a once-glorious continent spanning from the Gulf of Mexico to Europe was reduced to half its size in the brief span of an hour.

Humanity's eyes were opened by this repeated Mu tragedy and flourished once more to new heights, having learned their lesson a second time. However, after ten thousand years, the forces of evil once more tried to fool and subdue His children, ultimately meaning to keep them as their own.

Mankind labored honorably to conquer the devious negative self that led them astray, but much conceit and deceit stood in their way. Some were led to believe they were victims of Martian oppression, others that their former Unholy Six Alliance worlds were superior to the Brothers. Living on Saras suggested otherwise, set up as a penal colony for the spiritually challenged, but not everyone accepted the honest truth in best terms. Dismayed by truth, denial ultimately led individuals to assume serious acquitting pursuits, and the ways of light and honesty extinguished from man's hearts once again.

A large group of aggressive initiates, unable to deny past wrongful delights, revolted against the brotherhood and created a dissident organization bent on discrediting the Brothers and forcing them to leave Saras. Once the core of the galaxy's most malignant society, they strived once more to convince Atlanteans by any means possible that the Brothers purposely subjugated them out of jealousy. They pointed to the qualification process as their primary objection but were far from being truthful or honest as to why, since accepting fault conflicted with their voracious love for wrong.

A rift developed between people. On one side, the Chiréh stood as loyal followers of the Infinite. On the other, the Sons of Ly-Dian refused to accept responsibility for past infractions, claiming superiority over the brotherhood and even His Magnificence. Mankind was headed straight for a third Mu tragedy, blinded by superiority complexes, arrogance, and false inferences.

The time was 24,800 BC, the setting Saint Lucia. Morning skies disclosed imminent daylight in spite of thick high clouds hiding sunlight from viewers below. Nearby, the sound of crashing surf and seagulls invite a young boy to awaken from nightly repose amid soft grasses. Slowly, the child awakened to artful surroundings, once covered by a mantle of darkness. Bending his knees to the ground and taking a slow deep breath, he recites a gentle melody in reverence to the Majesty of Creation. His song is soft, yet entreatingly heartfelt, for these are difficult times for all people in Atlan Tenh. His words come from a wounded heart and a frightful life ahead, as Mu's wickedness looms imminently in the horizon.

> I beseech thee, mankind of Saras, for eternal brothers are we. If only I were spiritually free, might I clearly witness the wonders Father has for thee.
>
> We are not who we were, only shadows memories are, but we live so unaware. Garbed in fine linens to deceive us all, ill faded memories of iniquity strive to smite the true infinite soul. Painfully are memories imitated, with grave sacrifice recreated: how unwise it is to stop living, only to perform an act far in distant meaning.
>
> I plead thee, Magnificent Father of all, such evil that is in store, never come to our brows blocking heaven's ford. My Father, my infinite light, please, guard my love for all.

The child, after completing five years of initiate school in the southwestern plateaus, was on a journey to Garden City to be qualified. He was dressed in a white flowing robe with a white cape draped behind him, held in place by golden links embroidered with aquamarines and emeralds—symbols for Saras. On his head, a white turban covered black hair worn below the shoulders. About his waist, he wore a white sash indicative of spiritual initiate status. His eyes were brown, slightly Asian, and of shy expression.

Twenty five kilometers to the south, remnants of the previous continental edge were clearly visible, now reduced to residual islands following the 38,000

BC tragedy—an appalling reminder of painful lessons likely to repeat again. Today, these remnants are known as the Grenadine Islands.

The shoreline contoured north, adorned by placid fjords that rolled into tranquil waters below. Inlet fork channels carved softly inland, resting warm crystalline waters upon fine white powdery beaches covered with tropical fruit trees and tall coconut groves.

The garden path led north to Peacock Palace by way of mountains or northeast toward Garden City. Roshon chose to take the Peacock Palace route to pay his sister, Lee Nah, a visit. Few hours later, he reached a canal and boarded a boat that would take him to the palace.

The following morning, the boat stopped at a location about fifteen kilometers east of what's now Montserrat and verbally awakened Roshon. His eyes were immediately transfixed on a sight considered by Atlanteans as one of the wonders of the world: Peacock Palace. Joyfully, he knelt in loving tribute to Exalted Magnificence, inspired by gloriously fervent blue electric skies, sparse clouds, and a mild temperature of twenty-two degrees Celsius.

The boat stopped at the mouth of an artificial lake about forty meters wide and four times that in length. This lake was rectangular, but its marble shores were fashioned with large square extensions that formed the outline of an outstretched peacock. Other canals merged unto this lake from three other directions, forming the peacock's tail and leg sections. Roshon arrived by the head or southern section, where the magnificent palace resided.

White-rosy marble sidewalks gleamed along the lake's edge like pearls, soothingly contrasting lush tropical vegetation. In the lake, several tall metal fountains rose into the skies, a true marvel to behold, eloquently offering the Atlan, the life-giving waters, to all those who neared the palace via the lake. These fountains were constructed of six slightly bent metallic pipes, curved from a wide base, and bound together all the way up to a widening top in perfect symmetry. Three horizontal disks dissected these pipes, protruding three meters outside the pipe assembly. On them, a dozen miniature water jets spewed water in magnificent unique patterns.

On the southwestern lake shore, a small square-shaped house with back sloping flat roof dominated the scene. It had two front arched entrances that took up most of the dwelling's width but no doors. Inside, walls were lined with tiles inscribed with peacocks. This small dwelling was used as a place of divine reflection prior to proceeding into the temple.

Some distance behind this simple shelter stood a magnificent step pyramid temple amid tropical vegetation and smooth rising mountains showcasing thick glorious greenery beneath a bright stellar luminary. Peacock temple sat some distance in front of these mountains. Steps along its sides were slightly rounded. Its surface was painted a bright mango color. On top, a large golden cap rose to a point. Exterior temple walls were adorned with large aqua glass-like windows, also inscribed with peacock designs.

A long boat, akin to an elongated gondola, approached the small shelter from the northern tail section of the peacock-fashioned lake. Several young ladies, dressed in colorful translucent dresses, slowly rowed the boat standing up until reaching the shelter. At the rear sat a young lady, the peacock queen, dressed in a wardrobe made entirely from peacock feathers. A collar also lined with feathers rose behind the neck. A golden seven-star crown rested comfortably upon her head, interwoven with smaller peacock feathers as well.

Picture 16: Peacock Palace, Atlan Tenh (*B. Erlinger-Ford*)

For the people of Atlan Tenh, the peacock was a symbol of spiritual pride and an object of admiration. Its blue-green feather colorations represented Saras's deep verdant fields and blue skies. The peacock queen was a young lady, selected from many, who held the highest spiritual standards in the land. Lee Nah, the peacock queen, was tall, of slim figure, extremely graceful, and wore long dark hair that waved to midsection. Just like Roshon, her eyes were slightly Asian and brown.

Visitors were not allowed on Peacock Palace grounds, only high spiritual achievers. But on this day, an exception would be made. Roshon stepped out of the boat and approached Lee Nah, who didn't recognize her brother at first. "By what name dost thou go by, my young brother?" she asked.

Roshon took his sister's hand, raised it above his heart in an act of humility, and said, "I come before Lee Nah, my one sister, that I may praise His Magnificence, lord of infinite realms. It is with grace that our Creator enlightens my morning and livens my path with the company of a sister whose smile is brighter than sapphires from His heart."

Lee Nah lightly hugged her young brother and spent some time reacquainting herself. They had not seen each other for five years or since Roshon left for initiate school at age three. Lee Nah, on the other hand, was coming to the end of her assignment as peacock queen. In a few days, she would initiate a new queen. Until then, she would remain in the temple.

Roshon was curious to know if his sister recalled past memories involving him, information his heart wasn't really prepared for just yet. "I know I lived on Masar for a long time, but returned to Saras to qualify my lives during the alliance," Lee Nah said.

"You were in the alliance?" Roshon asked somewhat surprised.

"Everyone on Saras did at one time or another. That's why we're born into this penal world, to divest our appetite for error before moving on to a life of truth among the stars." Roshon bowed his head disappointed, afraid of having played a destructive role in those dreadfully dark times.

"Don't be sad. What's past is in the past; the alliance is no more, and its memories should no longer be nurtured."

"It's shameful to think I hurt people for no good reason," he said agitated. "Now, Ly-Dian is trying to convince people to return to those days and destroy our true cosmic inheritance. When will history stop repeating itself?"

"You must be patient; the Brothers will always be with us no matter what happens."

"But I'm afraid of re-embodying back on Saras under Ly-Dian's control only to find that the Brothers are no longer among us. Someone's got to get rid of him before that happens!"

"That, we can't do. Besides, if we get rid of him, someone else will assume his place."

"Then, get rid of them also."

"No," Lee Nah said with a smile. "Just as it was with you, so it must be for all other lost souls. No one got rid of you in your belligerent days, right?"

"I don't know," Roshon replied sadly. "I suppose the answer is no?"

"Now you owe Father a favor, and you must work to save people, not condemn them."

Roshon's eyes sparkled and said excitedly, "Do you really mean that? I can save them?"

"Absolutely. But first, you must face your past, accept it, and let it go."

"Do you know what that past is?"

"I know a few things, but I can't tell you, not until you earn a yellow sash."

"Please, just a small, small hint?" Roshon asked innocently.

"No, rules are rules. We must obey them and be patient, for good reason."

"How about your own past? Can you tell me a story about yourself?"

"That could take time. I can tell you I lived on Dallian, and we were best of friends."

"That means we were the good guys! Dallians were heroes," he said excitedly.

"There's no such thing as a bad or good guy. Thinking like that will lead you to Ly-Dian's ways. We must learn from each other but never compare ourselves. Ly-Dian chose not to share and lost his event horizon, his one. Now, he stays alive by sapping events from others like a parasite. That's why he hides his feelings and possesses individuals through deceit."

"What if I re-embody in the future, forget what I've learned, and follow him again? That's what I'm afraid of."

"Fear is what keeps us linked to him life after life. Don't feel threatened by him and listen only to His Majesty; Ly-Dian is no creator but a destroyer. Remember that when love rests, fears awaken. Keep love close to your heart, never give it up. I must leave, but don't forget my words. *Essatéh va dastreh.*"

"Live in peace, my beautiful sister."

Picture 17: Tribunal Center, Atlan Tenh (*R. Diaz*)

Roshon bid farewell and headed east toward Garden City. He knew what awaited him there, what everyone feared most—City of Witness some called it—for it was a place where past deeds were qualified, witnessed from one's deepest most hidden inner recesses.

Hours later, Garden City's skyline became ever more pronounced with its tall geometric glass buildings and bright power beams interspersed amid low hills and canals. Once in the city, he headed for the brotherhood's tribunal center. The Brothers were there to guide him to one of many challenge halls where his qualification would ensue.

Roshon stood in the middle of a large circular marble room, surrounded by twelve masters assisting in his evaluation. Dressed in white robes and yellow capes, they wore a purple sash indicative of achieved spiritual mastery. None were native of Saras, and most were of advanced age. Doors to the hall closed, lights retrieved, and a bright white-bluish light shone on Roshon whom kneeled down with countenance humbly bowed toward the floor.

"That His Majesty be well pleased, I come before thee to uphold truth and expose the great enemy within," Roshon said calmly, yet consumed by fear. "Who shall call me forth to endeavor this task?"

"You are an old soul, Roshon," said one of the Brothers, "but you are not clean, and there's much fear in you, fear of letting go of countless memories and desires you've hoarded over the eons. This is your first qualification and it can be the most harrowing, but only if you make it so. Remember, love will feel like reproach when you worship fear and wrong more so than Him. What does your heart tell you?"

"I'm grateful to be here before you, my elders," said Roshon with bowed head. "I promise I will work hard to become a Brother like you and someday help save Ly-Dian himself."

"Is that so, young initiate?" said a loud jolting voice behind him. Master Uanh, native of Masar, wore a blue sash and yellow cape indicative of initiate mastership. He stepped around and approached Roshon with serious resolve and assured stride, each step dauntingly resounding throughout the silent, still hall. His appearance was slightly Asian, black hair combed back to just above his shoulders, and aging in complexion.

Roshon's smile withered away as he looked upon the serious approaching master who encouraged nothing less than absolute honesty. "Young initiate, do you have any idea why you're here?" The master paced before him with solemn intimidating determination, rarely looking away from the child.

"Yes, my master. I'm here to learn about my past deeds, accept them, and let go without shame," Roshon replied with a serious tone, boldly mimicking his master's delivery in utter disrespect.

"Text book response. You sound brave, determined, and certainly defiant, unlike many before you; this is most unusual. Most initiates tremble at the thought of standing here, but you seem rather overjoyed! Let's hope you feel this way by the time we're through. But before we start, have you any clue, any hint whatsoever, who you've been for the last million or so years?"

Roshon was silent for a brief moment, abandoning previous seriousness and coming forth meek and humble. "My master, I've been an evil soul, this I know, and deserve to be where I am at this time . . ."

"Do you truly know that?" said master Uanh, raising his voice to thunderous levels. "And this, Saras, this penal colony, seat of galactic depravity and home to history's worst spiritual felons, is this where you want to spend the rest of your spiritual evolution?"

"No, my master."

"Good! It's about time because it has been an incredibly long time for you in particular. It's time you leave this forbidden penal rock. Yes, you've been an arrogant—correction—an unbelievably arrogant soul! Do you, young child, have any idea just how arrogant you've been?"

"No, my kind master. Honest, I don't want to cause anyone any harm. I just want to help others."

"Out of the question!" yelled the master suddenly. "You must first help yourself by realizing the very destructive past you've led. Then, humble yourself in the service of His Majesty, not continually chase after memories of grandeur and personal competence! Doing good deeds doesn't mean you're doing the right thing. Matter of fact, a good deed, dreamed up by a felon, is a huge stumbling block to His Majesty, because you do it for you, not Him!

"No, young apprentice. You didn't destroy people's lives; you did far worse than that! Let me put it into perspective. Roshon, you destroyed entire solar systems, if not the galaxy itself! Your soul is partly responsible for the demise of tens of billions—yes billions—of lives, every thirty or so days, for ten thousand years! That's the population of a third of this galaxy!"

Roshon shuddered and looked terrified at his master in sad disbelief, followed by tears, somber remorse, and a loud booming cry that bid nearby walls to prevail still. "These brothers about you are some of your victims. I dare you to look into their eyes and remember how you destroyed their lives, families, planets, and used them as food for your armies! Look at them, if you can! You've hurt almost every soul in this galaxy, not just once but thousands of times! And you're not through with them yet!

"How then can you tell the brotherhood, the Tree of Life, in full witness of His Majesty, that you want to help others when, in fact, you have no clue where your desire to help comes from or what people's needs are, much less your very own? It does matter because your long lethal history is what you'll draw upon when you try to help or, should I say, get rid of souls in order to survive, from what I heard you say a few hours ago! Am I mistaken?"

Roshon was quiet, his head lowered and persona fully withdrawn, crying profusely. "I'm sorry, my master. I don't know . . ."

"Then, I'll tell you! Young initiate, you were known throughout the galaxy as the destroyer! You became the third most powerful man in the alliance! The blood of billions—no, billion trillions—are upon your arrogant filthy hands! Those you didn't kill, you farmed for food like cattle! Your favorite past time was torturing prisoners by butchering them to death, piercing them until you tired, or launching them high into the air and watching them fall to the ground! You're one of the most despised souls that ever graced creation, and you want the universe to look the other way and turn you loose on Father's children to help them? I think not! Whatever gave you that idea?

"Just think of it, what can you offer people other than punishment to save your own skin? And what will you do when people don't follow your advice? Get rid of them? Why, you already want to get rid of Ly-Dian, your first customer! Where's your mental link to the universal field of minds, unity with the King of the Realms, knowledge of your past, union with your one? How can you possibly help people? Of your own self, you can't do a thing! It is His Majesty's inspiration that does all things, but only errors inspire you now, not truth! Anything you come up with without Father's inspiration flowing through your higher self will be nothing less than destructive!

"I wished it were possible, Roshon, but it's not up to us; it's entirely up to you. Your sentence on this penal colony will linger until your heart bleeds every tear you've caused humanity and your soul learns that living off desire is the way of error and death.

"That's not all. You betrayed us Brothers numerous times and turned your back on His Majesty when He gave you every chance to live among us! Only a hundred thousand years ago, you abandoned us to escape qualifying a grave wrong you committed. You blamed us for your errors, said you were unworthy, and left the Tree of Life vowing to die and never return. In so doing, you also abandoned your one, your only one, and things can't get any worse than that! Without you, your beautiful companion lived a torturous hell literally wanting to die from spiritual solitude. You have no idea just how much she cried, suffered, and endured the worst pains of the heart imaginable—all because you were a coward, unwilling to submit to truth!

"And now, here you are, starting from scratch—again. You can deny Him, but can you deny the brotherhood in you? I think not! But that, my son, you have done! By denying your one, you denied the Tree of Life, and that's the ultimate crime against Father! Now, what can you say to that?"

Roshon sobbed loudly and in between sobs managed to say, "I'm so very sorry."

"Sorry? You're sorry? Sorry for what? I haven't even started describing who you've been. So how can you apologize for something you don't even know yet? Is it possible you're trying to run away from your past, like you did before, just like Ly-Dian, thinking you were not as bad as we Brothers portray you to be? Do you believe we're trying to subjugate you through intimidation, that this is all a hoax, and we're trying to take over Saras for ourselves, and that you're truly superior to His Majesty?"

Master Uanh took a few steps toward Roshon and looked intensely into his wet sobbing face and yelled, "Young apprentice, look at me!"

Roshon looked at his master and sobbingly said, "My master, I'm afraid. I don't want to ever come back to Saras and be trapped here all alone without you to protect me."

"Ly-Dian scares you, doesn't he?"

"He does!" Roshon said, crying and pouring his heart loudly before master Uanh. "If he takes over Saras and you Brothers are gone, then I won't know any better as before and continue doing evil things. I don't want to hurt anyone; it's wrong and illogical! It's an endless nightmare with no way out! I've been used and deceived by the sinister ones, and I don't want to be fooled anymore! Please, make it stop! Help me stop this madness, please!"

The master stepped up close to Roshon and gently put his right hand on one of his shoulders. With a slight chuckle, he said softly to him, "My son, you fear for yourself, and that's why you fail. Fear brings evil closer to you and uses you. Be confident that if you deny evil in this life and love Father with all your heart, soul, strength, and recognize who you truly were in times past, you shall be victorious regardless of who tries to enslave you in future lives!

"Now is the time to take a stand and side not with Ly-Dian but Father! Yes, it's hard to break down past barriers, and many tears must come before we are freed from our legacy. No wonder it seems so easy to help; your negative self is right there trying to make a name for itself under the guise of good. Whatever it takes to get a name for itself, it will do.

"My son, you've had a challenging day. Come back tomorrow at the same time. You were most brave today, but tomorrow you must be a million times braver, for what you will witness most souls can't stand to watch without transitioning. It's that reprobate, my son. Be strong and of good courage!"

"My master, if I was such evil person, please discard my soul. I am not deserving of His Majesty's care and guidance."

"Nonsense! No one gets left behind, no one. Death is not sufficient punishment for you! It is only an escape from reality. You want punishment? Stand here tomorrow and take it bravely! What will it be: eternal death by running away or a few moments of grief by taking a stand for truth? Think of your one; if you fail, she fails. If you're lost, so will she. If you die, she dies. Don't you care about the love of your life, your perfect love that God so gracefully placed within your heart? Don't you love her with all your might?

"You are going to make it, my son. Maybe not today, but you will make it. I too made some awful mistakes in the past and had to face my masters much like you. You can do it. It will hurt, I can assure you; but when you conquer fear and negative impulses, pain will go, and you will be filled with Father's essence. It will clothe and soothe you for eternity, and you shall find no want in life, for Eternal Majesty will be with you—always. That's what qualification is all about. Now, go in peace, but beware of deceit coming your way." The master bowed to Roshon, who bowed back and respectfully left the hall.

"Tonight, the lost ones will attempt to assimilate him, but there's much fear in him," said one of the Brothers.

"His fear will be his own awakening," master Uanh said. "He will make it, but it will take much time for his heart to abandon the tastes of evil pleasure."

"The hour approaches, for tomorrow we may see the last light of day," the Brother said. "Imagine for a moment how these people live, my son, blinded by physical admiration, so grapes of spirit go unnoticed and lies become their only source of truth; no wonder man of Saras is so fearful, alone, and in such consuming darkness. And you, my son, were your life to expire tomorrow, will you fear?"

"My spirit belongs to the Infinite, the body to mother Masar. To fear, be it fear itself."

"You have learned well, my apprentice. You won't be among us after tomorrow. Your work here is now finished—forever. Stand tall now, son of starlight, for you shall receive endless light from His Majesty, and your lips shall never shallow with thirst for life. May the future be upon you, *oh-joi*."

Outside the chambers, with heartfelt remorse and grave disenchantment, Roshon slowly paced away from the tribunal center and sat in front of a nearby fountain to spend away inner pain. Not long after, a young man in his teens wearing a white sash came by to keep him company. "You were just qualified, weren't you?"

Roshon did not reply but slightly lowered his head in inner agony. "I see, that bad. Let me introduce myself. I'm Minh-Ley, allegedly the undercover Orion agent that died at the hands of Ra Sonh back on Dallian. I'm also the infamous Tiger Woman. Can you believe that drivel? Well, enough of that. Why don't you tell me who you are?"

"I am Roshon," he said, somber and retrieved. "I don't really know who I've been, but my master said I was despised by the entire galaxy."

"Oh, really, aren't we all?" Minh-Ley said with surprising interest. "Welcome to Saras. You're in the right place and among friends. And why would that be?"

"He called me the destroyer," he said lifeless, withdrawing his breath.

"It can't be," said an excited Minh-Ley. "You must be Viren 9. It is indeed an honor to meet you finally!" The young man stood up and bowed to Roshon, who didn't return bows. "Oh, come on, it's not as bad as you think. You'll get over it soon enough. The odd thing is you don't look like a planet killer to me. They've been wrong before."

"You think so?" Roshon said, questioning his own thoughts in disbelief.

"Let me guess. You're supposed to return tomorrow, right? They're just trying to feel you out to see if you fit the role, that's all. It's all a game. Don't believe a word of it. Talk about planet killers; the Martians destroyed their own planet. Now, they want ours, but we'll be there to fight for what's rightfully ours. If you're Viren 9, we need you. We could use someone like you that has such impressive battle experience."

"I don't want anything to do with Ly-Dian, if that's what you're after."

"Actually, Ly-Dian is a dear friend of mine and an accomplished philosopher I might add. He'll tell you straight what he knows the first time around and won't play games. If you really want to know who you are, you must trust Ly-Dian, not these oppressive maggots!"

"As I said, I want nothing to do with Ly-Dian. My sister Lee Nah told me all about him."

"The peacock queen? Brother, she is beautiful! Did you know Ly-Dian thinks very highly of her? So do I. Perhaps you can introduce me to her in the near future. What do you say?" Roshon remained withdrawn, unwilling to engage Minh-Ley in conversation. "Look, if you don't talk to Ly-Dian, you'll never know both sides of the story."

"I have no desire to meet Ly-Dian or anyone else for that matter!" Roshon said with strong resolve, walking away from Minh-Ley.

"Fine. But think about it Viren. If you want to meet him, come tonight to the Edin Hills south of the city. Follow the trail up the hills; it will lead you into a cave. We'll be meeting there this evening and would love to introduce you personally to Ly-Dian. Will he be surprised when he sees you! I'll leave you now; the Brothers don't appreciate me talking to prospective customers." The young man left hurriedly. Little did he know the Brothers heard the entire episode from a balcony above.

"It's begun," said master Uanh. "Tomorrow will hold unspeakable surprises for this young apprentice. He will make it. I'm sure of it."

"You seem determined, my dear apprentice," said the Brother. "You do realize you used him to your ends in times past, do you not? Perhaps your present zeal to see him through?"

"This he shall know before I transition; I give the brotherhood my word."

That evening, Roshon took the trail as instructed and found the cave. Inside, fires burned on stakes, strange looking men of Cro-Magnon lineage sang loud bold moving songs about their past galactic conquests, and bald priests lined each side of the cave dressed in white robes embroidered with black swastikas. Roshon entered the cave and fearfully walked down the tunnel as each priest bowed to him, addressing him as Viren 9.

At the end of the cave, a man sat on a high throne overlooking his subjects below. He was also bald, wearing the same white embroidered robe as others. Around his neck, he wore extensive gold jewelry embroidered with six different-colored jewels, each promoting individual Unholy Six Alliance worlds. Minh-Ley quickly came to Roshon, escorting him near the throne.

Noting Roshon, the man on the throne asked all to be silent with thundering voice. Meek and reverent, Minh-Ley approached the throne with Roshon by his side. "Father Ly-Dian," said Minh-Ley, "I bring before your majesty the one son you've lost, Viren 9."

At the sound of the name Viren 9, all those present bowed to the floor before Roshon and mentioned his name six times. Then, Ly-Dian stood up from his throne wearing a wide caustic smile, and slowly came down the steps to meet a terrified Roshon. "Viren 9, my son, my lost son. I am your true father, so do not bow or be afraid before me. I made you and gave you glories beyond your wildest dreams. Agents of the Chiréh destroyed us both and now consider us galactic criminals for defending ourselves. Come, stand by me."

Roshon hesitated and nodded his head in the negative, backing off slightly. "I know your thoughts, young apprentice. You've been told not to listen to me. Unlike the Chiréh, I won't scream or embarrass you in front of others."

"If you are my father and can read my thoughts, why didn't you come to me sooner if you knew I was Viren 9?" Roshon said defiantly.

"My son, look around you. This is all I have. I don't have the same luxuries as the Chiréh. Also, if I interfere with your development, I'll be accused of negatively influencing the youth of Atlan Tenh. Only after facing your first qualification may we approach you. Do you trust me now?"

"I can't," Roshon replied fearfully. "I have much to learn before I can trust anyone. Besides, I think I should be on my way." Roshon took a few steps back, but Minh-Ley held on to him, begging for his time.

Roshon turned, forced off Minh-Ley's grip, and made for the exit when Ly-Dian verbally held him with a concerned, emotionally, and fatherly tone. "Wait, my son! Before you leave, there's something you should know. Please, would you take my hand for a moment, my son? Don't be afraid of me—please come back, don't leave me, my son."

Roshon, after some hesitation, returned and took Ly-Dian's hand. Swiftly, an image appeared in Roshon's mind. In this image, he saw himself as Viren 9 at his last battle. His ship was on fire, and his officers struggled to stay alive.

During the battle, Goren, his first officer, stood by Viren's side as defeat loomed, "Admiral Viren, enemy forces completely surrounded and destroyed Commander Soran's 336th Fleet. The 261st is still fighting but down to a thousand cruisers, and several star destroyers are burning. Enemy ships are coming around again, opening fire. Fire is a direct hit but went right through enemy ships, inflicting no damage! They are firing again!"

Viren's ship shook violently, many consoles exploded, and smoke filled the control bridge. "We're burning up, sir! More incoming fire!" The bridge burst into flames, and numerous officers burned with it. Viren was still, mortified by their obvious defeat. After a few moments, his ship was all that was left. On his console, the face of the enemy showed up, calm, young, and determined.

"This is Lei Uanh, of his Dallian imperial majesty's space force. You are asked to surrender, or you and your remaining crew will be destroyed. Will you surrender?" Viren looked about his burning ship in still silence, shocked by swift defeat. "This is your last call. Will you surrender?" Viren turned to his first officer and saw he was dead, scorched by intoxicating flames.

"Goren, my son, my one and only son," Viren said sadly. "There will be no more death, only . . . mine."

Ly-Dian let go of Roshon's hand, and the image swiftly vanished. "This, my son, was Viren 9. Indeed, a most brave man facing incredible odds. I need not tell you who your enemy was."

Roshon looked surprised but did not answer back. "Remember his face well, for you will see it again tomorrow at the tribunal. He is your fearsome master Uanh!"

Roshon's face quivered, and his lips softly persuaded the words "no, can't be" to tremble outward as massive tears flooded his face. In a sudden move, Roshon ran out of the cave, quivering and crying profusely. Ly-Dian, on the other hand, remained solemn and fortified, assured of success. "His soul is mine once again!"

"Should I go after him?" Minh-Ley said.

"Let him go," Ly-Dian said, savoring victory with laughter. "If I can't have him today, he will be drawn to me now for thousands of years to come.

His soul is mine again! I can feel it! He no longer trusts the Tree of Life, and that's all I need to own him. His lack of faith is my seal of possession! He has renounced Manéh, and now he is mine!"

The following morning, Roshon returned to the tribunal but stayed in the patio below the qualification hall pacing back and forth for some time, fearful of betraying the brotherhood again. His master's words on betrayal rang remorsefully through his guilty conscience and felt he had done so by visiting Ly-Dian the evening prior. Just then, Minh-Ley arrived on the scene and bowed to Roshon.

"Compatriot Viren, why are you troubled? Do you still want to go through with this senseless embarrassment? Don't do it! Come with us. Be who you were truly meant to be."

Roshon looked at Minh-Ley with calm resolve, as if inner truth suddenly revealed him a long sought-after answer. "I must have done something awful against His Majesty to have angered Dallians; that's probably what brought about the Battle of the Corridor. Master Uanh said I was known as the destroyer, and with reason. That's why Dallians attacked; they were trying to stop my killing spree, and Ly-Dian lied to me! He lied to me—again!"

"Wrong. It's no secret; review historical archives regarding your battle against the Dallians. Yes, we started it, but it was you who halted their advance against the alliance and not the other way around. You're a galactic hero, and your father loves you for your bravery!"

"He's not my father but just a sinful man like myself! He can never take His Majesty's place!" Roshon replied angrily. "Have him turn a stone into bread or spread his breath across the heavens to create a star without the aid of technology. He is no God but an impostor, someone that needs people in order to possess creation. He's nothing but a thief!"

"This man gave it all to make you into the hero that you were. He gave you purpose and meaning, power, trust, and recognition, something Manéh never gave you."

"Not yet, but someday He will, for He provides what I need when I need."

"You should be grateful for all the trust my father placed upon you, unlike the false sense of hope the Brothers put us through. His rewards are immeasurable, and you owe him . . ."

"I want nothing!" Roshon screamed, frustrated and in tears, turning a few glancing eyes near him. "Don't you get it? I don't want you, Ly-Dian, Brothers; I want to be left alone and render allegiance to no one!"

"You can't do that! Do you have any idea what Ly-Dian is giving you? More than me, actually. Don't turn your back on him; he's your only hope," he said, expressing grave concern.

"Hope? I have no hope! My name is inscribed in heaven's scrolls in a place where the meaning of death is defined," Roshon said loudly., as passersby witnessing his loud emotional wails gathered to appraise the ensuing dilemma. "Sin is death, and what I have done is much worse than sin!"

"Roshon, you have it all wrong. You have been chosen, your destiny is written, and the opportunity of a lifetime awaits you! Our forces await your command! Lead us forth, help us reclaim what's rightfully ours!"

"Yes, a chance to kill and die—nothing more! People of Atlan Tenh," he yelled to those around him, "do you want to know what absolute misery and grief are all about? Then gather about, and I'll give you the testimony of ages; I assure you, you won't be disappointed! I, whom you gather to witness, am the dreaded poison of times, the destroyer of humanity and the most detestable being in creation. Viren 9, was I!"

Everyone about Roshon frowned, commented negatively against him, and stepped back in disgust. "I agree with you. I feel the same way you do about me!" he voiced loudly, suffering his heart in absolute tears. "I remember everything I did! My job was to kill you and your children, your families, cities, planets, and spiritual aspirations, and serve you for dinner!"

"You're exaggerating the note, Roshon. We were soldiers, not criminals, dispatched to stamp out resistance. Sometimes cruel, yes, but effective," said Minh-Ley, but Roshon ignored him.

"You," Roshon said, pointing to a lady in the crowd, "I launched you high into the air and watched you fall minutes later into a sad pool of dismembered bloody pieces while I beat your sons to death on the ground and forced them to witness your appalling death!" he said in tears. "And you," he said pointing to someone else, "remember how I tortured your body to satisfy my cruel sense of power? I eventually fed you to my armies; you became human fuel so that more of your kind could be hunted down and vanquished!"

"Worst yet, my wrath obscured your entry into the heavens by destroying your books of knowledge, annihilating teachers of truth, scorching your wondrous cities and worlds until lonesome ambiguous dust rings were all that was left of Manéh's glorious abodes amid lifeless stars devoid of human rhapsody! That's what I did, and that's what I am today; a long-time betrayer of His Majesty! I deserve to be bound and gagged for eternity, then put away somewhere far from humanity where my soul will never see anyone again!"

"You saw the impossible odds we faced against Dallians. We were being exterminated by a superior enemy, and you did what was necessary to save our father world. No one but you, our hero, dared face such fearsome enemy. You attacked Dallian sympathizers who spied and smuggled arms across the Corridor to them, and their refusal to surrender proved their guilt."

"Smuggling weapons without space capability? No more lies! I'll never forgive myself for committing genocide against totally innocent people," Roshon said, collapsing knees to the floor and filled with agonizing tears. "It's too great a sin; there can be no forgiveness for such crimes against humanity! And if I meet my one someday, what will I tell her, that I am the most despised being in the cosmos? A being like my only one does not deserve to union with a despicable being like me! I'm not worthy! I detest my being, my past, my future! I just want to die, and now would be a perfect time for that!"

"Brother," a young man said in the crowd, "if you don't forgive yourself, we're doomed! Sin is a lesson, none is greater or smaller than the other. Don't negotiate with sin or mourn over it, abandon it for our sake."

"Go the way you came," Minh-Ley said. "Viren did nothing wrong and his glorious future is already spoken for. Right, Roshon?"

"Roshon, be with Father. There is no life in deceit."

"Father is just a Martian myth, but Ly-Dian is real. Tell them, Roshon, who your true father is, the only being that loves you the way you are."

"Ly-Dian is the devourer of souls. He knows no love, and saps our event horizons to stay alive after having renounced his one. What fault has your one to also warrant death? Do you want to be as Ly-Dian, and destroy your one?"

"No, but I can't change what I am. It's too strong!" Roshon said barely able to talk, thrusting his heart into unmerited self-destruction and agony.

"Keep this guilt charade up," said the man, "and your soul will belong to Ly-Dian. When that happens, may Father have mercy on us, for you will reenact Viren, and we will die a hundred times over for no reason. We don't accuse you, but we fear what will happen if you fail your qualification. Don't fight or silence who you were, just don't do what it recommends."

"You've all been hypnotized by eloquent words and have no evidence to back your claims," Minh-Ley said angrily. "Viren, come to life. The order has been given, the universe is ours for the taking, and it starts with Saras. Wait no longer, lead us to victory again!"

Roshon's cry gradually silenced. Approaching those present, he said, "I was wrong: I see that now. I've been beating myself for no reason. It's the past, not I, that must be ignored and die. Otherwise, I betray Father and strengthen the enemy inside. Let there be unity, not conquest. I'll sacrifice all that I am to save my one, and I shall not fail! My life shall be for her!" he said boldly.

"Viren, we don't have much time!" Minh-Ley said, taking Roshon by the arm and forcing him to his feet. "We've waited thousands of years for you to come forth and lead us to glorious victory over the brotherhood!"

"I won't support your cause," Roshon said. "There will be no more killing or conquest. I would do anything, suffer it all, to avoid hurting anyone anymore, or falling into the hands of Ly-Dian."

"Don't believe all that brotherhood garbage," Minh-Ley said scornfully. "You'll see the truth if you give Ly-Dian a chance. What do you have to lose but sleep-time stories from people that destroyed their own planet?"

Roshon looked up at Minh-Ley with mature gaze, stood firm, regained valor, and stirred virtuous purpose throughout his being. Placing his hands upon Minh-Ley's shoulders, he said to him, "We either serve truth and evolve or succumb to conquest and die; it's our choice. Conquest must happen in the heart, not outside on someone else's contrived battlefield."

"Are you refusing to carry out a direct order?" Minh-Ley said, brushing Roshon's hands off. "You should do as Ly-Dian commands."

"You listen and listen well. We are prisoners of sin, addicted to error, and severely truth challenged. Everything we desire, especially war, is born from sin. That's what we must conquer, the self, not other people."

"None of that is true, and you know it!"

"Oh yes, it is, whether you like it or not. I can feel truth; my soul discloses it. All I have to do is put desires to rest, listen honestly, and it's all right there, clear as daylight. I hid my thoughts from fear of shame. I kept myself from truth by feeding desires. But now, I can hear myself clearly, and I know precisely who I am. I will deny myself and never again follow you!"

"You're wearing thin on my patience! That's not what I expected to hear from you."

"Truth, love, ideas, humility, peace—these are mechanics of the soul and the generous gift of the Architect of Love. Conquest and desire have none of these things, only slavery to deceit. Manéh is all I want! Manéh is great!"

"*Manéh neh meché*!" voiced everyone several times in support of Roshon, keeping Minh-Ley silent, unsure what to do.

"Viren! Arguing with me is futile!" Minh-Ley said rather angered. "Ly-Dian is taking over the cosmos! Be with us, or be conquered!"

"The universe is a really big place, and there are more united Brothers out there than there is of you. Don't be optimistic; it could be your own undoing! And don't you dare insult His Majesty before me!" Roshon said, confronting Minh-Ley head-on.

"Wait until father learns you rejected him!" he said, pushing Roshon away.

"Go ahead. Have him destroy me for what I care. I dare him! That's what he does best! And no doubt, so do you."

"I hate you!" screamed Minh-Ley several times, submitting to blind ineffable fury. His hands abruptly reached out and took tight hold of Roshon's clothes, shaking him about like a limp rag. Onlookers were immediately shocked by his fierce outburst, for they had not witnessed acts of violence in ten thousand years. Their souls squirmed silently under distress unsure what to do or think, influenced by ancient memories that will not rest.

"I should have killed you the moment I saw you, maggot," he said enraged, roughing the younger Roshon's face and torso and ripping his garments like a wild predator. Bleeding sores manifested upon Roshon's face, but the bewildered Minh-Ley pressed on, taking Roshon by the neck and smashing him several times against a pillar.

"It's always you, isn't it? Anytime you show up, my life is ruined! You always get all the attention, all the glory, and the highest positions! You're always number one; I have to settle for number two! The hell with Viren; I'm better than you, always have been, and I'll prove it!"

Roshon tried to release Minh-Ley's tight grip around his neck but couldn't overcome his older stronger opponent. "Why are you protecting your life now, maggot? Didn't you want to die a minute ago? Why don't you do me a favor and just die!"

"I'm on a mission for Father, whom I dearly love, and I will see it through," Roshon said, severely choked.

"Not for long! I hate Manéh, just as much as I hate you!" Minh-Ley said, tightening his hold on Roshon's neck. "Where is He to protect you, maggot? I don't see Him anywhere. But if I do, trust me, He will be my next victim!"

Suddenly, Roshon's countenance became serious and firm. His eyes stiffened with a spirit of mature authority, courage, and confidence, hosting another being that now expressed through his strong resolute gaze. His stance widened, placed all his body weight on his right leg, and said deeply, "Don't you insult my beloved Manéh!"

Roshon's anger built up abruptly and, with all his strength and speed, drove his hands up through Minh-Ley's choke hold, breaking the choke and stamping his face harshly.

"You can't win, Roshon. I'm six years older than you and twenty times the man you are!" Minh-Ley said laughing, recovering from Roshon's harsh face blow and wiping blood pouring from his nose and lips.

"Yes, coward, but I'm smarter, and I know now who I am," said Roshon boldly.

Minh-Ley reached for Roshon's neck once more, but Roshon intercepted his hands and braced tightly against the pillar behind him for support. He pushed forward silently and steadily against Minh-Ley with all his might, gaining strength and stamina with each passing second. With fingers squeezed to a side and palms painfully buckling, Minh-Ley was both silent and troubled.

Minh-Ley watched in disbelief as his hands gradually retrieved from Roshon and wrists continued to bend. But Roshon stayed the course, pushing until his arms were fully extended. Then, in one abrupt move, he flipped Minh-Ley's palms up and painfully locked his wrists back.

"I . . . am . . . Ra Sonh!" he said slowly and intimidatingly, suddenly surprising Minh-Ley, "general for the royal house of Dallian and protectorate of their majesties."

"You were that despicable Dallian bastard!" Minh-Ley said, unable to break Roshon's painful lock on wrists and hands. "I have even more reasons to want you dead now!"

"My mission on this world is to prepare you for assimilation by the brotherhood, a power much greater than your own and one you will come to respect!" Roshon said confidently, with thunderous voice.

"Never!" Minh-Ley said sarcastically, intensifying his push against Roshon, though unable to overcome Roshon's growing strength and lock. "You believed everything I said in those days—every word. All my intelligence reports about renegade activities along the Corridor were false, and you did kill innocent people—exactly what we wanted you to do. Your human kitchens were not necessary; but they were far more efficient, deliverable, and clonable than food harvests. That's my job, to carry out what Ly-Dian wants, lying if I must, to convince people that don't think when they should, just like you!"

"It's just like old times, isn't it, coward?" Roshon said. "A duel to the death, with a coward that always loses in the end! Remember?"

"We'll see about that!" Minh-Ley said, forcibly releasing his right hand, pulling a knife from his sash, and preparing to wield it toward Roshon.

"*Manéh neh meché*!" Roshon slowly screamed, suddenly kicking Minh-Ley's right knee inward with all his speed and might, bending it backward with a loud snap. Minh-Ley screamed and immediately fell back upon his left elbow, breaking it and moaning in agony on the marble floor. There he stayed, suffering his pains unattended.

"This is how it always ends, coward, broken right knee and left arm. Don't ever blaspheme the name of loving Father in my presence again," Roshon said. All those present were shocked by these events, and comments quickly surfaced as to the virtue behind Roshon's defensive deed.

"I thought you wanted me to live and qualify for your sakes," Roshon said to onlookers. "You were afraid of meeting death by my hands a moment ago, but now look at yourselves, hoping to see me lose mine. We're no different, you and I, and no worse, just fearful outlaws in the end. Thus, the ancient proverb applies: no outlaw is lesser in virtue than another."

Coming to an abrupt decision, Roshon turned and briskly walked away from Minh-Ley, who was picked up and carried away by his priests. But just then, the doors to the great hall opened, and master Uanh called out to him, "Roshon, we had an engagement. Would you betray us again?"

Roshon slowly turned about, looked upon his master, and bowed to him. "Gentle master, I deceived you and betrayed His Majesty yet again. This injured soul is proof of it."

"He got what his past ordained. Now look at me. Do I remind you of someone?" said the master. Roshon was stunned, speechless, with his head lowered unable to utter a reply. "You saw what Ly-Dian wanted you to see. Come inside. We'll show you what you must see."

"How did you know about last night?" asked Roshon ashamed of himself.

"We Brothers are always with you, young one. If you will come with me, there's someone here that wants to talk to you, inside the hall, of course."

"I'm confused. I don't know who to trust anymore."

"Or me either?" said a female voice, coming from inside the hall. The large doors revealed Lee Nah, to whom Roshon immediately ran, surrendering to her welcoming arms without hesitation. Those in the courtyard immediately bowed to the peacock queen and marveled to know that Roshon was her brother, applauding both of them.

"How did you get her to come?" said a Brother. "It is forbidden."

"In a few minutes, it will make no difference," replied master Uanh.

"I'm not supposed to be here," Lee Nah said. "I only came to ask you to stop acting like a child and step inside. The worst is now over for you, and Father is exceedingly proud. You stood up to the greatest evil in the cosmos and emerged victorious! Ly-Dian wants your soul; he made you believe you were a victim to take it from you. I won't leave until you enter this hall, of your own free will, of course."

"I will. But why didn't you hate or cast me away, knowing all along who I was?"

"Remember when I said that no one got rid of you? Neither did I. Be strong and of good courage. Only the bravest and most honest will inherit freedom; be one of them." A Valics silently descended on the tribunal courtyard. Lee Nah boarded the craft and headed westward at full speed. In seconds, the ship was lost to the far western horizons.

"About that talk, young apprentice, now would be a good time."

"Yes, Your Majesty," Roshon replied regally with a bow, taking his master's hand and leading him boldly into the hall, pacing quickly before him.

"I see you've reacquainted yourself with Ra Sonh," said the master humorously.

"And also their majesties," Roshon said, proudly seizing his right fist over the heart in a witty salute to his master.

"One of these lives, your lips will slip badly and you'll unknowingly call me Your Majesty again, on Masar, of all places," the master said smiling, as they both entered the great hall.

"I look forward to it, gentle master."

The lights dimmed, and a bright light shone on Roshon who stood still, quiet, and with strong resolve. "What you are about to see is coming directly from your inner records. We are not making this up. Do you understand?"

"I do, my master. I no longer fear. Proceed without delay."

"So be it." Within moments, pictures of a huge flattened metallic moon appeared in the dark void of space. "This, Roshon, is your creation. You helped design this enormous monstrosity with sufficient fire power to destroy a planet, even a dwarf star. You used this huge machine to destroy all life on four planets. After your death, the alliance used it to expand their territory in a war of terror that lasted over five thousand years. Yes, I was Lei Uanh, who finally put a stop to your criminal rampage. Now, behold the part that Ly-Dian didn't show you."

The same images from Ly-Dian's vision manifested. Viren's ship was in flames, his crew for the most part dead. He sat coughing on his command chair, watching an unfamiliar face appear on the view screen. "This is Lei Uanh of his Dallian imperial majesty's space force. You are asked to surrender, or you and your remaining crew will be destroyed. Will you surrender?"

Viren looked about his burning ship in still silence. He thought about all the destruction he caused, including four planets and the fearsome enslavement of hundreds more. Surely, it was not Ly-Dian who did it; it was him, Viren, who did it on his behalf. Without Viren's participation, it wouldn't have happened. He was a puppet, blinded by a false sense of power that would die with him and return back to its provider. Ly-Dian lived off him, giving back delights, such as comforts and titles, specifically designed to encourage Viren to further exploit and benefit the alliance.

Viren turned to his first officer and saw he was dead, scorched by intoxicating flames that made breathing difficult. "Goren, my son, my one and only son," Viren said sadly, "You were right, this is not for us. Death is not the way, and union is not by force, but by . . . the heart. The Denebans were right. I should have listened to them. I deserve to contradict the master. There will be no more death, only . . . mine. I deserve it for being so blind, for committing galactic murder!"

Viren, disenchanted with his life and knowing full well death awaited him at the citadel, answered, "Commander Lei Uanh, this is Admiral Viren. I am much deserving of this defeat. My hands are stained with murder. I should have listened. I should have . . . died. Commander, I must die, but please spare my crew."

"I understand," Lei Uanh said, "but we don't murder our enemies. You will have to live with the error of your ways and deal with it. Your crew will be spared if you admit your surrender to the empire."

"Commander, surrender will mean certain death, which I seek. If not by your hands, then it shall be at the mercy of my master. Let it, therefore, end this way. I surrender to the empire."

Roshon was silent with head bowed low, face dried of tears. "Now you know," said the master, "why you wished to die a few moments ago just as you did back then. Do you want to save the master now?" Roshon could not say a word as he relived the episode just envisioned over and over again. "Do you have an answer to my question, apprentice?"

"I would, my master, only if he would accept."

"Just like you, Ly-Dian will make it, but it's not his time. You, on the other hand, this is your time. What you did in Orion was exceedingly wrong, but you were misinformed and caught in a deadly current from which you could not escape. The last time you saw this image a hundred thousand years ago, you wrongly blamed yourself for everything that went wrong in those times and ran from us Brothers. That's why you're stuck in this penal colony. Don't grieve where you need not go. Don't beat yourself to cleanse things that don't need cleansing; that's a graver wrong than an actual wrong.

"Now, it is time. Roshon, do you vow to uphold His Majesty's laws, and resist evil forces that worked through you to accomplish these terrible acts against humanity? Do you vow to never again create destructive weapons to consume His Magnificence's creations?"

"I do, my master, and may the future be upon us" said Roshon.

Roshon had one more commitment to make; but it was difficult for him to shed grief, embarrassment, fear of being despised, and enormous guilt. But in a moment of valor, he came forth and bravely set aside humiliating shackles, opting to face shame at all cost regardless what others thought of him.

His countenance gleamed and his heart was compelled to forgive any prejudice, for those who forgive little love little. Those that love little have little Father in them and receive equally little guidance. The past cannot change, but Father makes everything new for those that forgive themselves. By doing so, Roshon allowed Father to cure this grave ancient ill across the galaxy, releasing trillions of imprisoned wounded souls that once served their spiritual essence to Ly-Dian's starving soul.

"I'm ready to carry out the work that His Magnificence requires of me, humbly and of my own free will! I rebuke Ly-Dian and will live to obey His Majesty! There's no other life but Him, the universal Tree of Life in which we are one. I shall sacrifice my lives for my one that she not be troubled and perish not. Behold my promise. I shall return to thee, my eternal one, with a new heart a million times stronger than the one you once knew! May the brotherhood grow in light! May I always be in love with love!"

"He is now . . . clean," said the Brothers proudly. "His Majesty is most pleased. This is a great victory for the light and one small step for the brotherhood."

The master smiled widely and joyously embraced Roshon. "You, Lee Nah, and I were best of friends, inseparable in time. We fought together against the alliance until the end, and you, as Ra Sonh, helped save Dallian. But you could never forgive yourself, not until today, for crimes committed as Viren 9. Thus, your acceptance has earned you a higher ranking in your spiritual evolution."

At that moment, the doors to the hall opened, and a yellow sash floated through the air into the hands of the Brothers, who solemnly brought it to master Uanh. Taking it into his hands, the master passed it on to Roshon and said, "My dear apprentice, you've earned a most minute step forward in your spiritual evolution. I'm proud to see you, my dear old friend, come back to us. Will you wear this sash and prepare vigorously for your next qualification?"

"I will, my master. But will I help save Ly-Dian?"

"Many years and times will pass before you can do so. But this, you will do!" Roshon took the new sash and changed out from the previous. All masters bowed to Roshon, but his master had yet more to say.

"You will now be known as brother Roshon, forever a member of the universal brotherhood and son of His Majesty. Now, my young one, my time is brief, but I too have an admission to make. I used you, my old friend, to my own ends. This is why I am here today, for I too am being qualified. I used you in ways similar to the ways Ly-Dian used you. I reveal this to you before His Magnificence and bid spiritual apologies and reparations so that your spiritual evolution and that of so many others be not distressed. I beg your deepest forgiveness for many transgressions against you and the Infinite," said the master in tears. "Under my command, you took countless millions of lives, and I wholeheartedly promise you, this will never happen again!"

"My gentle master," said a shy Roshon, placing his right hand on his master's shoulder, "you always taught me to forgive so that His Majesty will pardon our many transgressions. Allow me then to forgive by bearing your enormous pain, as you have mine. Allow me to walk beside thee and be your apprentice for eternity. You are, and forever shall be, my dearly beloved master. Let us be as one in love eternal and children of the Tree of Life. Take my hand and let us help each other follow the light."

At that moment, the master was filled with a dim light and bowed to Roshon. His red sash detached and fell to the floor. Then, from the rear of the hall, a blue sash floated through the air and placed itself about his waist. "It is done, my dear brother," said a Brother solemnly. "You are now a master of light. Wear your spirit cleanly and proudly; for His Majesty now shines within you, feeds you, speaks within you. Your new journey begins, and your life here on Saras is now complete. It is now your time."

Suddenly, the earth began to quiver, at first gently but then stronger. Blue lightning struck without warning or reason. Gases emerged from opened fissures, some exploding into powerful fireballs. Garden City came to a dead stop. Power generation beams went silent, and trams halted. People wobbled on their feet and fell down helplessly. Valics hung motionless in midair, running on energy reserves.

The tribunal hall shuddered irreparably to the loud booming sounds of unsettling land masses. Cracks emerged across elaborate ceiling frescoes, raining dust upon those present below. Standing pillars came forcefully crashing down upon the marble floor, and crevices manifested across its tiled surface.

Everyone rushed out of the hall, except for master Uanh. Roshon, noticing his master stayed behind, returned to pull him from his bowed position, but he would not move. "Now is my time," said master Uanh. "We shall not meet again for tens of thousands of years. Remember the phrase 'old friend,' for I will speak them to you that you may recognize me. Now, go, this is not your time. You have one more qualification to accomplish before transitioning."

"Master," said Roshon, taking tight hold of his arms, "I will not leave you!"

"You must go, your next qualification awaits! They will be here any moment. I must remain and wait for them." Roshon wondered who he referred to, but the master was silent, his glow increasing. Roshon broke into tears, unable to contain his master's growing essence, but stayed willingly by his side. Swiftly, gentle song filled the hall with loud beautiful melody. A blinding light covered the surroundings, and time seemed to halt.

The floor vanished swiftly, replaced by an electric blue heaven illumined by the light above it: Father's blue lobby. A soft wind fluttered their clothes and a calming glow encompassed Roshon. Amid the light, twelve translucent lighted beings appeared. Their calming splendor spoke silently to them in whom they were most pleased. In a brief moment, thousands of lives flashed before Roshon, reminding him not to fear himself but seek the higher realms within.

"Behold!" master Uanh said loudly, becoming translucent. "His Mighty Majesty is all there needs to be! He is the Magnificent, the Infinite, the benevolent loving father of all! Go now. You have a mission to fulfill before your time." The light vanished, and Roshon returned alone to the shuddering hall elevated in midair. An invisible force then drew him out, as the great hall shuddered and came to pieces with the rest of nearby foyers.

In the Edin Hills, Ly-Dian's cave trembled and collapsed, burying many of his followers while others ran to safety. After several chaotic minutes, the relentless quake subsided. The city slowly came back to life, and power generation resumed operation. People stammered back to their feet, many hurt and in tears, realizing why this incident occurred.

Fires from within Saras continued to boil, consuming once floral offerings from His Majesty throughout the land. Glorious city pathways stood wrecked, and precious marble creations collapsed. The east and southwest segments of Atlantis sank beneath the waves, leaving only scattered islands behind. Tsunami tides raised several meters but not high enough to reach Garden City.

In the heavens above, mother ships from nearby worlds dashed swiftly about, releasing Scout craft that descended and tended the wounded. They flew over the Edin caves, but in spite of Ly-Dian's waving pleads, the Brothers did not stop there. Convinced of error, one by one, Ly-Dian's followers renounced his Order, turned over priestly belongings, and left for Garden City until only Ly-Dian and an injured Minh-Ley were all that remained. Alone and to themselves, they plotted against His Magnificence with greater ill will.

In the far western skies, smoke billowed from once-dormant volcanoes. Roshon's concern for his sister mounted, who lived near those mountains. Noting his growing concern, a Brother approached him and said, "You wished you were there, is this not so, young one? Perhaps we can be of help to you. It is your past's calling."

"I'll do anything to save my sister. Would you take me there, kind master?"

"We were waiting for your response, young one." A Valics quickly descended erect on the courtyard, and a ramp made of light extended from its bottom section. The Brother took Roshon by the hand and entered into the craft. In just moments, the craft arrived at the mountainous hell beyond. The wondrous beauty of palace grounds rendered way to fire, smoke, and broken lands, leaving it totally unrecognizable.

The Valics landed near the peacock artificial lake, now empty and in absolute ruins. Roshon and the Brother quickly got off, and the craft hastily left. "You are not afraid of transition, are you, young one?"

"A little," Roshon said.

"Does this remind you of anything?"

"No, but I must save my sister." Roshon ran toward the palace yelling out his sister's name, but there was no response. Lava had all but consumed the wondrous pyramid temple and the plentiful tropical gardens surrounding it. There was no sign of his sister, except loneliness and descending ashes from nearby eruptions. "She is . . . gone!" Roshon said.

"Yes, her cycle is now complete. Both her and master Uanh will now reside on Masar, where they will wait for you until many cycles from now. Again, does this remind you of anything? It is very important before your time expires, my son."

"Am I reliving?"

"Absolutely."

Roshon looked on to consuming gloom about them and then exclaimed loudly, "Goren! My sister—she was my son, Goren!" There was no immediate reply from the Brother, although he nodded well pleased.

"At the Battle of the Corridor, I wanted to die because I felt responsible for Goren's death. My concern for Lee Nah's life comes from Goren's!"

"You've identified where your inner desire to die comes from and have thus completed your cycle, my son. And so you know, Lee Nah, your sister, is your one."

"She is? I met my one, my princess?"

"Yes, and now, you are . . . clean."

"Master, I will sacrifice all my lives for her. Whatever it takes, spare me not. She cannot die! What must I do to save her? Please, tell me because I so love her!"

"This is why you embodied at this time, and your cycle is now complete. You have earned a new sash, an orange one, but you will not be wearing it for long. I must also apologize, for I don't have one to give you."

"Does that mean we die now, master?"

"Yes, my son, now is our time. You conquered your fears, an act that will forever help you seek the light at all cost, regardless of circumstance. You fortified your love for the brotherhood, defeated your most wicked enemy and seducer, and that earned you the right to be with us forever. No one, nothing, will keep you from coming to us. Now come, join me, let us peacefully wait for His Majesty's wondrous blue lobby to receive us," said the elder Saturnian master, embracing Roshon and tenderly singing odes of joy to him.

"You will not save yourself, kind master?"

"Where you go, my gentle son, I shall go with thee because I love thee so," the master replied lovingly. "Your soul is a beautiful garden where I shall forever dwell admiring your wondrous blossoms, even in death. In a garden we shall meet again, where you will declare your heart to your one just before your union. In a garden we shall meet again, where Father calls thee forth to become initiate master. Come into my arms, my loving garden, my son."

"Is this going to hurt?" Roshon asked, but the master kept Roshon's face in his bosom to hide the horrid torments nearing them, gently caressed his hair, and kindly kissed his head among songs.

"I love thee, my kind master!" Roshon screamed in order to be heard over increasing roars nearby, "and I shall forever love Manéh!"

Suddenly shifting his face away from his master's protective bosom, Roshon turned about and witnessed what awaited them. Looking at his master, he smiled calmly, and added loudly, "May His will endure, forever and ever! I am most honored to die for her! Is there not more I can possibly sacrifice for her? Is this all I can do? Please, there must be more! She shall not die! I will not allow it!"

Embracing Roshon, the master said; "Your one will now be safe. She shall not perish but will someday become as the lights of heaven, shining with His ight, as will you. You'll see, in time."

"My life for hers, her essence in me. I shall devote all my lives to write many books and compose loving songs about her. No other wish shall I have, but to think of my one, my beautiful starlight, my invisible companion. No matter the time, no matter the scorn, my heart will long tearfully for her every moment I live until we join—eternally!"

Consuming lava and unbearable scorching heat hastily neared their position. Hot projectiles fell about them, at times painfully striking their bodies. Asphyxiating hot gases lunged to low areas, depriving the master and Roshon of air. Burning, painful sores appeared on their bodies as clouds of ash dived harshly upon them and seared their flesh. In spite of his pains, Roshon passionately sung his profound love for his one until breath afforded him no more.

Eyes tearing from burns and lungs poisoned, they coughed and gasped beneath heavy layers of ash that suddenly fell and swiftly buried them.

In seconds, their suffocating cough abruptly silenced. Their physical vessels, buried deep beneath heavy ashes, rested still without vibrancy. Few moments later, a bright blue light surged underneath the ash, accompanied by the sound of thousands of glorious singing voices. Then just as quickly as it appeared, it vanished. The ash cover collapsed to the ground, as if no one had ever been present beneath it.

In memory of Lee Nah, the peacock queen pageantry was never again observed in Atlantis. She was the last of the peacock queens and was remembered especially for her radiant grace, illuminating conviction for the light, and profound love for all Atlanteans. Six thousand years later, a third repeat of Mu's tragic epic took place and for same reasons. It repeated three more times during a span of eight thousand years, bringing Atlan Tenh's age of enlightenment to an end and the Martian mission on Saras to rest.

Saras rested for nearly twelve thousand years, alone in space like a dastardly planemo without a spiritual star to give it life or purpose—destroyed, and in vague ruins, and ignorance was upon the face of the world.

May Len, my beloved one of ages, my heavenly princess, lived in my heart more so than ever, holding my hands and placing her loving eyes upon mine never ceasing. She was right; these were difficult scenes to assimilate. But according to her, the worst was yet to come.

I admire magnificent Manéh for His infinite forgiveness and the privilege granted to witness this past account before the cosmos. I most sincerely bid spiritual apologies and forgiveness before His Magnificence and the world, offering reparations so that the spiritual evolution of so many afflicted souls be not distressed, and His healing process may proceed.

May each word I write and speak, now and in the future, be living apologies for my many wrongful deeds, and sincere testimony of the Infinite's undying love. Follow no man seeking to devour your soul, let them seek one of their own. Let not fear and aggression be reason to do as they command.

I forgive . . . myself.

Chapter 21: *A Saras Welcome*

Saras miraculously transformed in the days leading to the Brothers' arrival, dressing up much as a bride for her groom. Every major city cleaned up to spotless standards. Homes were beautified inside and out. Large welcoming banners hung everywhere with pictures of the Brothers and their ships. Still, the most significant change took place in people's hearts, putting to practice lessons learned thus far—an important prerequisite for the landing.

It was a different Saras from prior times. Virtue was no longer considered a shameful expression to be feared but embraced. A resurgent longing for His Magnificence hastily drove ancient ghosts into the sunset from whence these came, and trust in the light was finally taking rightful hold.

Peaceful tolerance infused human hearts, driven by humility, clemency, and fearless resolve to bear personal loss or discomfort without violence, thus, turning the other cheek, unafraid of enduring assault or facing trying learning experiences. Mankind learned to calmly let others live, silencing inner pleads to charm, misjudge, or interfere in their lives—grieving less, loving more.

Hans, Sean, and I waited for my beloved dressed in *SAT.* The blue cylinder activated to a most expectant friend, anxiously anticipating his radiant princess's arrival. The cylinder subsided, and a resplendent May Len greeted us with irrepressible, luminous excitement, quickly embracing my soul with warmth of my heart's longest yearning. She wore a delicate white chiffon-like dress that draped down in gentle diagonal waves from the shoulders. Thin golden streamers lined each wave, glowing in the light like plasma. She wore a golden sash about her waist, and sparkling golden moccasins cuddled her feet.

My heart jumped with breathless wonder the moment I saw her, and my eager eyes willingly surrendered to her radiant, inviting expression with uncontainable joy. She wasted no time running up and kissing me on the cheek with mutual *oh-joi* and a loving, sweet embrace to counter ages past. Where we went, hands dwelt together, eyes joined in perfect harmony. Our thoughts were as one, and the rhythm of our hearts pulsed in our bosoms to indissoluble unison, feeling and understanding each other with outstanding clarity. Our eyes tearfully said "I so love thee" to the other endlessly, and the world about us ceased to bare any worth, only our love, and the light within.

Following a brief tour of C6, we made our way to the dome. Right on schedule, a large cigar-shaped craft silently hovered above the colony.

From it, a small craft emerged and made its way to C6. With surgical precision, it came to rest on the retractable pad. Being smaller than our shuttles, it had no problem fitting through the colony's air lock system. We had never seen an alien craft up close before and were awed by its splendid, delicate beauty.

This ship didn't look anything like our metallic clumsy shuttles. It was constructed from a single piece of material reminiscent of that used on the structure. Measuring a bit over ten meters in diameter by half that in height, it looked like a wide bell with a cylindrical top and a domed apex. Four round windows lined each side of the cylinder. Three spherical pods acted as landing gear, and colorful electric lights emanated from a spiral ring surrounding the joining seam between dome and cylindrical bodies.

The ship was absolutely beautiful in both form and color, glowing with luminescent whitish-blue hues inside and out. It matched the description made by UFOnaut George Adamski back in the twentieth century. It didn't feel like a craft at all but more like a being, alive with the pilot's spiritual essence. May Len confirmed that the ship was controlled telepathically and acted as an extension of the pilot's senses.

A doorway melted open on the side of the ship facing platform steps. Inside, there were two benches surrounding a meter-wide pole that ran the center height of the ship. May Len sat beside me on one bench, Hans and Sean on another. The pole pierced two large round glass plates on floor and dome and another at the bottom of the ship. Through them, one could view the sky above or grounds below at various magnifications. There were colorful electric charts along the walls, beautiful to watch yet completely foreign to me.

The pilot fit the typical Venusian profile: blonde with black eyes like Meh-Nai, wearing a one-piece light brown outfit and a golden sash about his waist. The door silently turned solid, and the pilot went to the controls. With a slight forward nudge, the ship engaged the pad to take us out of the dome.

The colossal mother ship measured over 750 meters long and had two sloping ends. Our craft headed over the shorter of the two slopes toward a hole on the cylindrical body. After passing through air locks, the Scout came to rest on a rail platform in a craft holding area. The door silently melted opened, and May Len happily led the way. My joy could not be told at the prospect, and great privilege as a spiritually infirm soul, of stepping onto this saintly cosmic abode.

On the ship's platform, my master Dow Uanh waited our arrival. I had not seen my kind master for some time, and joyfully honored him with a slow reverent bow, coming to my knees with grace and heartfelt respect, lovingly recognizing the great commission Father placed upon him.

Behind the platform nested within the shorter sloping end, a large hangar stored Scout ships hanging from the ceiling in pairs like church bells; it could hold twelve. Beyond the platform was a large control room some fifteen meters high and equally wide, covered by the same mysterious electric charts found in the Scout. Three mezzanine levels surrounded the room with consoles on each floor, operated by men and women of different races dressed in the same brown uniform.

The ship's commander was of dark complexion and busily reviewed space charts when we arrived. Dressed in the same brown-colored outfit, he uniquely wore a brown beret. "I'm pleased to see the good Lord graces us with your presence once again, Dr. Sullivan," he said with his back to us. I knew that voice but could not immediately place it.

"This is the second ride you get from me, isn't it, brother?" he said, turning to meet us.

To my great surprise, I recognized him, and my jaw literally dropped. "Slammer!" I said overjoyed, hugging him warmly with a knot on my throat. I wished I could have spent more time with him, but the occasion did not allow it, and we both had important jobs to do.

Farther into the vast ship, we entered a spacious lounge for the remainder of the trip filled with sofas, couches, and middle tables. Along the walls, Venusians proudly displayed pictures of their glorious home cities and landscapes. Tei-Ah and Meh-Nai were there waiting for us, clothed in dresses matching their world's divine excellence colorations, blue for Venus, green for Titan. They informed us we were already hovering above Saras but were briefly pressurizing to avoid atmospheric discomforts, an amazing voyage that lasted no more than seconds.

As the mother ship descended, lights in the lounge room dimmed, showing a three-dimensional display of our descent. In space, Saras shuttles lined up in pairs marking the way. The huge mother ship silently made its way among them until coming to a stop above New Manhattan's skyline.

It was time to descend to the Towers. Dow Uanh, Tei-Ah, May Len, and I traveled in one Scout while Hans, Sean, and Meh-Nai on another. Scouts slid down rails and exited through the bottom of the mother ship where Saras shuttles waited in formation for Scouts to emerge, the center spot reserved for us. No doubt, this was a gala event. We flew the short distance under escort, landing on a platform built specially for this event in front of the Towers.

It was a perfect sunny, slightly breezy day—ideal for the occasion. Millions of eager spectators witnessed our landing from nearby buildings, trees, ships, and thoroughfares, spreading across the land like a massive swarm of bees as far as the eye could see in every direction. At the platform, Earth gov anxiously waited for us.

Before exiting, the Brothers offered a brief devotional song in their language. The door melted opened and Dow Uanh stood before the platform, joined by Tei-Ah, peacefully waving their right hands high in the air with fervent spirit. Instantly, people cheered loudly, joyously chanting their name. I realized that every ounce of life in them was devoted to His Majesty and held nothing back. The Infinite was all they wanted, needed, and loved—most admirable and regally divine. In them, bestowed before us, was our future, a journey of love and peace toward supreme light and realms of truth.

It was our turn to step off the Scout, but I felt apprehensive for reasons May Len knew all too well. "Don't be troubled, my friend, brother," she said happily. "You're sad when you desire, angry when you can't forgive, and fearful when you're not with Him. So rejoice, for His love and my heart are with you bountifully, and you're with us. What more could anyone desire?"

"So true, my beautiful starlight. It's a day of great rejoicing for the light. But as I behold your velvet hands, deeply enraptured by thine enchanting beauty, I ask, am I ready? Will people forgive me?" I said with moist eyes.

"By granting Father your heart, you've given life beauty and people hope—this they know and praise," she said, softly passing her fingers through my hair. "Trust our love for you and be by my side, always; that's all Father wants from you. Without you near, I would be so saddened, my life devastated; friend, brother. So much would be lost; so many songs wrongly silenced. Remember, love keeps no record of wrongs."

"There's so much I do not yet conceive, and your patience is both inspiring and comforting, my lovely amber lighthouse."

Taking gentle hold of my hands, she looked intensely at me and said excitedly with radiant sunburst, "Roshon, you are the greatest joy of my life and my long-lost beloved sunbeam, whose heart cries out to be loved. My bosom sings odes of divine life when you draw near, joy that turns to sorrow when distance sets us apart. Your heart is so large that I can't contain it, so big it melts shadows away when it seeks my eyes, so wide that Father's light loves expressing through it. When you seek my eyes, you die inside and live in me."

"There's something else you should know," she said slowly and lovingly, "I like you too, my dear friend, brother. I like you with all my heart, for you are my river of life and reason for living. I feel affection for you, my fountain of life, and I . . . love you! Be not mistaken. I love you! Oh, do I love you!"

My heart involuntarily jumped, my skin chilled, and a bright smile wore across my lips. Moved by her tender words, I offered a brief gratitude song to Father for His wondrous gift of love. Her delicate hands in mine and with utmost respect, I slowly bowed my head reverently, recognizing the creative spark encompassing her melodic grace. I raised her hands to my lips unhurriedly and with utmost care, as if most fragile porcelain, placing a gentle kiss upon each of her silky hands, something I had never done before.

May Len's eyes peered softly through my windows with hallowed intent, clean and gentle like ethereal lights from heaven sent. Much as a dove in slow-motion flight, she tenderly placed her hands to my shoulders and spoke with calm, inspiring song and spirit bright, "I have always loved thee, my brother, my sunbeam. You know not how much I love you and how long I've waited for thee."

Her lips quivered feebly, her singing voice silenced. Sobs impeded my gentle pearl from finishing her inspiring dialogue, drowned by thunderous cheering outside. Her gentle passion moistened brows to a song expressing silent tones unknown, loving sentiments of unsurpassed warmth that blessed our unique heavenly motive.

Overwhelmed by her amorous admission and incredible beauty, my heart cast its open arms to embrace hers, gently proposing her eyes unto mine. Our gaze met eagerly, fondly assenting, equally enthralled in silent miniscule prelude of creation's ultimate gift of love.

"I love thee as much as Manéh!" I replied with broken, joyful voice, "and I'm not ashamed to say it, not anymore. See, a brother once told me all you need is truth and then follow it with trust. My life begins with thee. My life for thee, your essence in me."

"After such long waiting, this is the happiest day of my lives. Welcome to my heart and feel how much I love thee! It shall be . . . soon." Knowing Dow Uanh patiently waited outside and time was passing, she took my hands to her heart, kissed my cheek, bid our pilot farewell, and we emerged from the Scout as crowds cheered.

Her smile outshone the sun in fullest glory, waving with one hand and firmly holding on to me with the other. Everyone immediately gasped at her incredible radiant beauty, shouting loudly while she placed a kiss on my cheek. The Scout returned to the mother ship, and the next craft disembarked Sean, followed by Meh-Nai and Hans. The last Scout's door closed and returned to the mother ship. The enormous ship pointed its long sloped end up at an angle and quickly vanished in a roaring trail of light.

Jim and Yato greeted and invited us to stand at the platform's edge for the world to see. Turning in my direction, Dow Uanh asked if he might borrow my girlfriend for just a moment. He took his daughter's hand and held it high, symbolically putting her before him in stature. May Len extended her hand to the remaining two ladies, joining hands with artistic elegance.

Gina was silent, stiff, unwilling to look my way. Her jealousy was obvious, almost drawing pity. The entire world viewed our personal transmissions from the structure and knew her sad past by now, but little did I know what her goals were—and true identity.

"My Brothers," Jim said stepping up to the podium, often interrupted by loud cheers and applause, "your presence is a long-standing dream come true, a union that shall forever foster. Ours is now the beginning of a new age of enlightenment, and life as it was meant to be lived. Brothers and sisters of space, your Saras family welcomes you."

Among ceaseless cheers, Jim invited Dow Uanh to address the world. Bringing May Len with him to the podium, his lips uttered softly amid sporadic tightened throat and watered eyes. "As far back as these spiritual eyes can see, this is the most-cherished, awaited moment of times. We Brothers joyfully celebrate with you across millions of light-years."

He stopped for a brief moment, bowed slightly, and was surrounded by an auric flame. All present immediately silenced, feeling his essence overwhelm them. "His light be with you to the ends of time. *Oh-joi*." Members remained silent, expressing a language no words could explain. Some wept, others sang, while others hugged people near them.

Jim led us into the Towers where senate delegates formed a double line five hundred meters long, saluting the Brothers as they walked by. Gina remained somber the entire time, standing with the ministry stiff as a light post.

As we toured the gardens, groups went off to admire nature in their own manner. May Len excused herself from her father, walked with me toward the tropical gardens, and stopped before a rocky waterfall feeding a small stream filled with ferns and other tropical shrubs.

"On Masar, we have many gardens like this one, even in our homes," she said, inviting me to sit beside her on a park bench in front of the fall. "I spend much time pondering on nature, surrounded by Father's many ornaments. Nature speaks to us, especially about His devotion to all living things. Ours is a Father of life, perfection, beauty, and, most of all, unity."

"Do you normally do this alone, my starlight?" I asked her.

"We learn from childhood to seek the Creator on our own, until it is time for our union. Companionship gives us more visibility of the Infinite than individuality. That's why every moment we share together is a blessing, my sunbeam, for thus we experience love and truth the way it was meant to be."

"It is more blessed to give than to receive, for in giving one must first receive from Him," I said. "Father is the greatest gift one can give to others."

"Love is constant on our worlds, and songs never cease, even in dreams."

"Do you first learn of the Creator from your parents?"

May Len bowed her head suddenly, taking a sobbing breath as Gina paced behind us. May Len's countenance saddened no doubt from whatever

Gina was thinking. Gina knew her thoughts hurt May Len, so she stood with arms crossed nearby, delivering a barrage of thoughts as fast and as negative as she could think them up. She wore a triumphant smirk and spoke the words "I win" from afar with no intent to let up. I could sense Gina's death threats and hateful remarks, degrading and obscene beyond belief, like a smiting machine streaming unbridled.

May Len gently unfurled her soft hands unto mine, reaching out to me in suppliant yet forgiving stance. I softly caressed her hands and offered her endearing songs, but nothing comforted her. Gina savored success, and for a moment I did not know what else to do until a thought suddenly dropped into my mind out of nowhere pressing urgently to express.

"Worlds revolve about stars and stars about galaxies," I said poetically, and May Len's stunned eyes suddenly sought mine, "but my life revolves about my lovely sister that inspires songs and descends light from the heavens into my spirit, rekindling the light in my heart."

"My one!" she said surprised but quickly covered her lips after mentioning the word "one," which she was not supposed to say yet. "You just recalled a song from really far days, a time so significant for both of us. Is there anything more you remember?"

May Len completely ignored Gina, taking great interest in my recall. "I envision vast prairies, thick jungles, and having you near. I think we were on a mission to explore a new world, and I felt so much love for you it gives me chills; it was all I cared to think about. We were so incredibly close, as if we were one being, and I used to place flowers in your hair. I believe your father was there also, but I can't recall anything more. Is any of this true?"

"It's all true," she said sweetly, earning even greater wrath from Gina.

"And one more thing. I joked often that you were too old for me."

"Yes!" she said laughing and crying at the same time. "You worried so much about that, and still do."

"If it would please my precious flower, there's something else, something I really treasured," I said amusingly.

"What might that be, I wonder what it could be!" she said excitedly.

"I will be most honored to tell my starlight but only if loving sister permits my words to enter deep, deep, deep into her heart."

"I will, I will. Just tell me, please," she said excitedly.

"Of course, but my lovely sunburst must first grant me permission."

"Oh, please, I can't wait! Tell me!"

"One more thing, kind sister must place her hand on my heart."

"There. Can you tell me now?" she said, placing a kiss upon my cheek.

Tenderly caressing the edge of her beautifully silky hair, I said, bursting a silent cry and gasping for words, "May Len, my gentle beautiful angel, and most extreme splendor, among many sisters, you are my one . . . my only one! My one and only friend!"

"You still remember our song!" she said, trying unsuccessfully to hold back several emotions beguiled by warm inner rains.

"And there shall be more. Now, with your permission, my pillar of beauty, author of my love, artist of my heart, let not another moment go by that my intense love for thee is ever doubted or challenged again!" I said, standing up.

"What are you going to do, my sunbeam?" she said, although I was sure she knew.

"At times, extreme situations call for extreme measures. This is something I should have done a million years ago. Come on, it's time we shudder this world's foundations—Roshon style!"

With May Len in hand and a wide smile across her pearly streams, we rushed back toward crowds. Looking into her joyous windows of glowing amber, I gently kissed her hands as if fields of lilies and shouted, "May I have your attention, please. So that the entire cosmos witnesses my heart, I so declare; I am madly in love with May Len! Nothing, and no one, shall ever stand between us!" bringing instant applause from all those present, except for Gina. "May Len, I love you! I'll say it again. I love you! I love you!"

May Len gleamed with untold joy, and a golden aura lit brightly about her, setting golden streamers on her dress afire. Gina intensified her barrage, but the beauteous lace forever binding our hearts no longer heard the daring, wicked voices emanating from Gina's abyss. Totally ignored, Gina quickly left crowds for a solitary far-off corner consumed by fury.

"I feel I've known you for a million years, and I've . . . loved you deeply all this time," I replied, realizing feelings so deep I quivered.

"Yes, my sunbeam, you have," May Len said, putting my hands to her heart. "As you gazed up at the stars above, your heart searched fervently for me with love greater than your soul could contain. Though you were scorned by many for falling in love with an imaginary woman, even burnt alive for it, your love for me conquered all odds and your trust in us never faltered, patiently waiting to meet me in some future life."

"Day and night, you daydreamed of Manéh and me, though you knew us not. You prayed for hours into sleep, begging to know us both. You lived alone and renounced your life on Saras, for you reserved your soul for me. You wrote books about me, music, and paintings as you promised to do. You lived only to think of me, life after life, tear after tear. You cried daily, hoping we heard your tearful pleads and brought you to Masar, a world you felt was your home. All this I witnessed from afar, honored beyond words.

What incredibly gallant act of faith, and how wondrous is your love for this humble soul. I'll love you to the ends of time, my … one!"

"Your lovely gaze painted the firmament with starlight essence," I said sweetly to her, "so I could find my way back to your heart as I searched for love. Shine radiantly from the heavens for me. Shine forth. Grant me the radiance my heart starves for. I will follow the love trail, dazzled by its light, for it leads to thine sights."

"Oh, my one," she said, manifesting herself tenderly, "you know not how long I've waited, the eons that passed without your loving hand in mine, struggling eternal sadness, desolate without your songs, knowing you suffered all alone in this dark penal world unaware of my whereabouts. I was blind to His virtues, waiting to give Father onto you, alone without my gentle sunbeam, alone for attunement at night and sunrise, alone without you!

"Day after day, hour after hour, counting endless minutes from one life to the next for hundreds of thousands of saddening years, waiting faithfully for your song. I can't be without you either, my wondrous sunbeam. You can't envision the grief it would cause me, having come so close, to lose you."

May Len knew my wish. She slowly ran her fingers over my lips and said well pleased. "My one returns after so long with the words and ways of old, after a life's mission destroyed by Saras traps and eons of darkness," she said sobbing. "May Manéh be forever admired, for you returned to us, friend, brother! You have returned to me, as you promised."

I then realized what "friend, brother" meant, and tenderly said, "You were her! You were my beautiful, wondrous Nei Lah!"

"My beloved brother Roshon . . . I, whom you behold and so intensely love—am she," she replied with sweet, joyful stare.

I felt a wave of quivering wetness overcome my sights, tears that fell on her hands in large quantities, which she stooped down and gently dried with the side of her face. We silently stared at one another for some time in an interchange of essence and wordless thoughts.

"Lee Nah—my peacock queen, the most beautiful soul in Atlan Tenh," I said softly. "You were her also, and thou are my beloved . . . one! You are my one!" I said with indescribable joy, coming hastily to my knees with a most reverent bow yet restraining myself out of respect.

"You will know soon. I promise you this. Your million-year wish will come true. Trust the Tree of Life, trust in me. Your companion, your union comes so very, very soon. Just days away. But you must wait. I can't say . . . yet."

Gently placing her arms about my shoulders, she said as I remained bowed before her, "I love you with all my heart, all my soul, all my strength, all my mind. Always have, always will—my valiant captain."

Great warmth surged within me. But this time, her essence did not well up inside as before. Rather, a sudden burst of gentle peace and love toward her swelled in me as never before, sweetening my gaze. May Len's hand in mine, eyes to each other, we walked away from the crowds never parting sight.

I raised her hand with great care above my shoulders as our group made ready to enter the conference hall. From far away, Dow Uanh smiled confidently, reinforcing my trust in the Tree of Life. My gratitude could not sufficiently render credit to the countless teachings I received. Only a renewed heart and devotion to the Infinite's work would show true gratitude.

An angered Gina stood by watching, sniveling, and determined to impose herself over May Len at the right time. Her mental barrage came to a crashing disastrous finale, helping to form a stronger bond between us. She knew this, serving to increase both jealousy and hatred to the point of madness.

Unable to contain herself, she suddenly yelled at the top of her lungs, "You won't have him!" The chancellor and Mr. Yato, talking nearby to Meh-Nai, turned to see what was going on. They found an angered Gina standing alone, literally foaming at the mouth at the peak of anger. Coming to a sudden decision, she quickly left the park and disappeared down an elevator. Where she went, I would not know at the time. The Brothers offered no knowledge of her doings, allowing things to take their own due course without interfering.

May Len and I paid absolutely no attention to Gina's rampage, so focused with each other we missed the whole episode. Our thoughts sounded like an inspiring song, ever-evolving significance and intensity. Dow Uanh and our sisters stood by us, lending their support to this mental union to which I was completely oblivious; it was not my time to know.

We smiled endlessly at one another, hands on shoulders, exchanging sweet essence in complete silence. Our thoughts were becoming one, our physical awareness and dependency diminished. My master seemed well pleased and freely shared his light with us but never disclosing the future. He knew my faith was genuinely sound and would not falter.

The Infinite is all we need, He never abandons us. Father is my guide and provider, I need nothing else. Light shall forever provide all things and grant me peace. Light renews my soul and guides me to truth. Though I live in a sinful world, I shall not fear it or succumb to shame, for light always stands by me with authority and inspires the loyal company of the Tree of Life. Light protects lovingly and speaks advice to me. Surely goodness and mercy shall follow me all the days of my life, and I will dwell in Father's mansions forever.

I had found my beloved one, my inspiring beauty, the essence of graceful love, my gateway to the light and mirror of truth. The longing of a million years was about to end, only days away. Deceit and fear were no more, only the start of eternity with truth, and my one. *Oh-joi*!

Back in her room, Gina called a close associate of hers and gave the order, "Activate plan Brutus and cypher the agent, highest possible priority."

Chapter 22: *Bill Loves May Len*

The vast conference hall was packed with dignitaries from all over the world and their associates, but Gina was nowhere to be found. After a brief introduction, Jim presented the Brothers and passed control over to EMS, who came prepared with an endless list of questions.

The conference went on for a good two hours before Mr. Yato brought closure, and we retired to the ministry's dining room for an alien-style meal: vegetarian. Interestingly enough, Gina showed up for it and tried to blend in following her catastrophic outburst. She sat down like nothing happened, but no one said a word to her. Her mind seemed completely devoid of events from the past few hours, and I wondered if she had been cyphered, but the Brothers did not affirm my convictions.

Saras veggies, fruits, and breads served our appetites well. May Len sat beside me radiantly smiling the entire time, dashing poison darts from Gina, who sat livid on the other end of the table. Gina's attitude was so evident that ministers literally ignored her. Dow Uanh thoroughly enjoyed himself, playing light teasers on those present. He had a large repertoire of clean Saras jokes and wasted no time bringing these out in the open.

Lunch came to a close, followed by a motorcade through the city. Crowds cheered up a storm as soon as they caught sight of us, shouting *oh-joi* as we cruised by. People were everywhere, climbing on top of just about anything to get a better view. At Dow Uanh's request, we stopped along the way various times to greet bystanders and share the joy.

At the space port, shuttles stood by to take us to different parts of the world for live appearances. Jim and Dow Uanh covered the Americas, May Len and I Asia, Tei-Ah and Hans Europe, Meh-Nai and Sean Africa. However, upon Dow Uanh's request, Jim ordered these craft to fly with no one on board, and other shuttles were sent in to take their place.

We later learned the Order would not go down silently. The lonesome craft fell into the ocean during flight and vanished into the hands of waiting divers beneath the waves—no doubt, significantly disappointed after finding no one on board.

Before departing, Dow Uanh reminded us to let patience and light move the heart, pity not impair judgment, and fall not into Saras's traps. He hugged me for some time and said something in his native language with profound sentiment I did not fully understand. Taking his daughter's hand, he recited what sounded like poetry, joined our hands, and embraced us. He bid everyone farewell then we each took our shuttles.

I asked May Len what her father meant before leaving. "While I am not permitted to disclose the entire discussion," she said, "I can say that my father's last words to you were to take very good care of me, your beloved one and only friend."

"My beautiful sister, I have never met a man like your father," I replied with a tint of humor while May Len kiddingly played along and giggled to my lead. "He is so wise, joyful and devoted, always bringing happiness and healthy cheer to all he meets. Truly, he would make the ideal father-in-law."

May Len found my words quite humorous adding that, according to universal law, in a union Dow Uanh would become a father, not an in-law. She reminded me of my favorite parable, the bacon-and-egg breakfast, and asked, "In our union, who would my father be: a chicken or a pig?"

I thought about it for a moment and said, "Dow Uanh, as my father, would be a pig—no offense, meaning he's committed. But as an in-law, he would be a chicken, just a contributor."

"What would you rather have him be, my dear friend, brother Roshon?" May Len said in an excited tone of voice, almost giving away a powerful secret but exercising every ounce of restraint she could. Her bright eyes were fixed on mine like dazzling searchlights, anticipating some wondrous future instance, almost needing no response.

"Loving gates of my rejoicing heart, nothing would please me more than becoming a son to my master of ages. I beg His Majesty grants me such privilege, for it is my only wish." I was totally immersed into what I said, and May Len's gentle expression said it all.

"You no longer hide your feelings from me; I am so well pleased. Your answer comes soon my one, only hours away, this time Gina . . ." She did not finish the sentence, again using restraint, but her countenance showed genuine assurance that our destiny was certain.

She kissed my hands lightly and reminded me to be patient. "His Majesty works in mysterious but righteous ways, just a few more hours, my one," she said. I wanted to assume, but would not selfishly betray May Len's devotion. His Majesty came first in all things; what greater love could there be but His, and my love for her was Him.

We spent most of our travel time joking and getting an education in alien language. May Len taught me many games they play for amusement, including a card game she brought along. The object of the game was to match a player's card with one's own to form a compatible statement or universal rule, quite difficult for the spiritually illiterate.

Hours later, the coast of Japan came into view. Tokyo's space port was built three kilometers off the coast right on the ocean. Japan's tsunami and earthquakes were a thing of the past; tectonic science finally fixed the Pacific Rim fault, granting Japan its long-time dream to build fantastic edifice right on the water.

We headed to Tokyo's Hongo Campus, where we delivered a speech at the Yasuda Auditorium. I spoke briefly on the tenets of timeless convergent cultures, granting May Len the center of attention. When finished, I took May Len's hand and raised it in statute before me. Promoting her wasn't necessary; her stunning, radiant glow took everyone's breath away.

She gave a moving speech titled "Education is Forever." Together, we fielded questions literally losing track of time. But before ending, a young lady commented that May Len and I made a great couple. The audience immediately cheered and were quick to make their request official, "Kiss."

We smiled but didn't reply. Surprisingly, May Len took my hands, looked at me intently with sincere affection in her eyes, and most slowly, lightly, non-provocatively pressed our lips together for a brief moment. Her lips felt warm as a soothing tropical breeze and pliable like subtle butterfly wings—humble, clean, and selfless. We beamed with sincerity, honored by the great respect we exercised, and the fact this was the first time we had done so. The public cheered "Bill loves May Len" repeatedly, a phrase that became EMS's main focus for the next couple of months.

Next, we were off to New Peking for another presentation. By the time we arrived, signs were already made up: "Bill loves May Len." Our final appearance for the day was in Australia. That evening, we stayed in the state delegate's mansion near New Sidney and had a down under vegetarian dinner engagement marvelously hosted by her family.

Turning in for the night, I walked May Len to her room where I courteously bid her good night but did not enter her room out of respect. A golden glow appeared about her that caused me to well up inside. I wasted no time sharing my deepest feelings with her, holding nothing back, with the highest level of honesty and respect I could offer.

"You are ready for the day," she said happily. "I will be so pleased, and so will the brotherhood. The entire universe is anxiously waiting."

"I don't understand the meaning of the day, my one, but I trust in you and Father. May His light guide my heart, and our spirits be as one." May Len put her hands on my shoulders, slowly and most respectfully pressed her lips unto mine, and went into her room.

I stayed outside her door all night sitting on the floor, leaning against the door itself. I kept Dow Uanh's words fresh in my mind to protect his daughter and uphold the Creator's principles at all times. I fell asleep singing love rhapsodies to her and slept there the night.

At first light, I rushed to my room, showered, and prepared for a new day filled with challenging testimony to the Creator. I came to her door but did not knock, waiting patiently for her to come out. I felt like giving her something, but not sure what. To my luck, I saw just the thing: a vase holding several roses. I nervously picked the best-looking one, fumbling the vase badly. I hastily put everything back, minus one rose, and guarded the door until she emerged in glorious splendor.

My pearl wore a lovely golden dress that draped down gently and creased slowly with movement like a flowing river of liquid gold, complemented by a white sash that lightly embraced her artistic figure. "You look so very, very lovely, my beautiful sister," I said tenderly, overwhelmed by her enthralling radiance. I reached for her hand and placed the rose upon it, which she clutched to her chest. With a smile, never taking her eyes from mine, we slowly walked down the mansion's corridor to a stairway leading to the courtyard.

"My sunbeam, even your walk has changed, so much in the ways of old. This is so pleasing to my heart. My father and I will have a huge surprise for you when we meet tomorrow in Chicago. You know that my father is really good about surprising people."

"I can only imagine the trouble I must be in now," I said kiddingly.

"Oh yes, indeed you are. It's what you've always wanted. You better be well rested because you'll need it. I was going to ask you; I never slept sitting up on a door before. Is it actually comfortable?" she said giggling.

"It has its advantages, especially when you're guarding your *inéh mis*."

"You still make a great protectorate," she said, cheerfully stepping down the corridor by my side, holding hands and eyes piercingly fixed upon mine. I knew there was something to that gaze, but I could not tell what it was, other than the greatest of virtues. I stopped at the stairs leading to the courtyard and raised her hand above my shoulder before proceeding but not before May Len placed a very light and respectful kiss on my lips.

She sought to tell me something but then withdrew. "I almost gave away your surprise . . . if you only knew what awaits you, my one," she said with glowing excitement. "I can't wait to share it with you, alongside my father. The joy of ages, His Majesty's mission—oh, what gift it will be. You—we—have waited so long for this great surprise, my friend, brother."

We embraced for some time sharing songs while the mansion's family and complement cheered "Bill loves May Len" downstairs, reminding us that hugs won't feed us. The delegate wasn't bashful; she wanted to host our wedding, definitely a blushful moment. After breakfast, we were off to Sumatra, India, and Russia. Everywhere we went, signs were made up, and people chanted in their tongue, "Bill loves May Len." Sometimes it was difficult to proceed with our presentation; people seemed more interested in us than our topic. In the end, we pleased our hosts with an exchange of tender songs and a light, most respectful kiss.

Exhausted, we slept our way to Chicago. May Len placed her head on my shoulder as I lightly cuddled my left arm about her, gently and respectfully running my fingers through her hair. She rested peacefully, listening to my strong beating heart. We mentally talked to one another, sharing words of encouragement and inspiration. Her smiles proved she appreciated my thoughts and answered them back in like manner. In time, we reclined our seats and fell asleep.

The shuttle reached Chicago in the morning. Upon arrival, we boarded a waiting speeder and checked into a hotel just west of O'Hare space port. May Len insisted that we stay in the same room. Feeling there was good reason for it, I accepted with no malice in mind. After resting, we showered in privacy, and May Len changed into a white dress with a blue sash. I showered and changed into a new *SAT.*

Unexpectedly, she took my hands and knelt for moving song to Father. Afterward, Dow Uanh mentally addressed us and said, "Roshon, my Brother, I will soon return whence I came. You and May Len will stay behind to look after your family. Nurture it, draw strength from us, we will never leave you. Take good care of my daughter for her companion. You will meet him this afternoon."

His words greatly saddened me. Tearful torrents rolled down my face, feeling my closeness to May Len would suddenly end. My eyes strained and my body heaved with a strong silent cry I could not avoid, gaining strength with time.

However, May Len came quickly to the rescue with excitement unlike any before. "Roshon, Roshon, my sunbeam," she said excitedly, "don't be sad. We will be closer than ever, closer than we've been in a million years! I know you don't understand, and your waiting gravely punishes your sweet heart, but you must trust me. In just minutes, your companion shall embrace your heart forever, and then you will understand why it had to be this way. Come, my inspiration, my love, don't give up hope. Your dreams are about to come true!"

I was then filled with tremendous warmth that coursed through my eyes and erased any sadness I held previous. This time, I felt no inner turbulence from May Len's essence; and my heart reached out to hers with calm, compelling love—clean, pure, selfless, beating in loving unison with hers.

She was well pleased and said, "My sunbeam, you are ready for this day! The time has finally come, and Father is with us. My essence will become yours, and I will inherit yours in perfect cadence. You shall no longer fear the Tree of Life, and our souls will be opened to the architect of life. I shall forever be with you, my one, my only one."

We left the hotel and met our partners at O'Hare. Dow Uanh came straight to me, bowed his head for a moment, and sang a brief melodious song to May Len in his native tongue while scores of people cheerfully watched. Meh-Nai and Tei-Ah stood behind us in solemn silence.

I got the impression this was some sort of ceremony and observed closely all that transpired. He gently took my hand and recited to me with deep feeling. With his other hand, he reached for May Len's and delivered another poem to which she smiled widely in untold excitement. Dow Uanh then joined both our hands and continued his poetic delivery, singing expressively and sharing occasional tears.

Not long after, I noticed a band of white light envelop us, making me feel as light as a feather and free of concern. "It is done!" Dow Uanh said joyously. "Such long waiting is finally over! My dear Roshon, may you forever climb your spiritual ladder, no matter what difficulties and challenges may come your way. Life is the Creator, life is eternal, life is as one! You are no longer alone, my son. You are now with us! Welcome to the cosmic family, Brother Roshon.

"Soon, you shall know your destiny and the long-standing desire of your heart will come to be. Live, breathe, dream, speak, eat, touch only the Creator. The more you do, the happier life will be. The Creator is all that matters, all that is. Take your sister's hand and do not let go of it, my son. Take good care of her. Keep her heart nestled within yours. Forever, I shall be by you, my young student, my dear old friend of ages, my son. *Oh-joi.*"

Words of love for my one overwhelmed my speechless heart, and soft grace surrounded my soul with a gentle force I never knew. Colored flashes, mostly blue and beautiful to watch, appeared in my vision with feather-like sensation whenever these touched the body. I felt whole and drawn to May Len with unquenchable magnetism like a powerful gravity well from which I wished never to emerge.

With a wide smile, Dow Uanh and our sisters embraced us with indescribable happiness, but none explained what this ceremony was about: I had learned not to guess. I decided to practice patience and wait for an answer out of love and respect, a decision praised by my brethren.

May Len was silent yet happier and more radiant than ever. I asked if her companion would arrive soon, and she confirmed he was near, waiting to find out the big secret. In a kidding, playful way, she asked me not to say anything until all was ready.

Unexpectedly, from my eye's corner, I briefly noticed Hans smiling at me as if he knew something I didn't. From his soul, thoughts emerged of something most dreadful to come, and a noxious scent suddenly sickened my breath. But then, he walked away, his mind went dead silent, and quickly vanished among nearby cheering crowds.

Outside the sprawling space port, several speeders waited our arrival. Dow Uanh, Jim, May Len, and I took one vehicle while my sisters joined Hans and Sean on another. Gina and the ministry followed behind. I noticed no security forces tagged along this time, but Jim assured me it was by Dow Uanh's request.

It was a mild cloudless morning; perfect for the occasion. People without number lined the streets as far as my eyes could see, cheering, singing, and throwing flowers our way. Seeing no obvious Brother or Scout around, I asked May Len where her companion was.

"He will show up any second," she said with loving excitement.

Trying to put sadness aside and fully trusting her, I said, "My heart of Rosette, I place my heart in the hands of you and your companion. When you need me, I shall be there for you. I promised to wait a million years for your heart, and I shall. Let today be that first day of waiting."

"I sense your devotion, and it's real. But there's a chance that it may not be that long after all, my love."

Clasping my hands to her heart with incredible joy, she gazed into my eyes and smiled with bursting glow while repeating the words, "It's time!"

My thoughts promptly betrayed me again with plummeting sadness, but I found the necessary faith to deny them and firmly set my trust on the light, the future, sharing mighty odes of love and hope with my perfect love from the heart.

Just then, Dow Uanh asked Jim if we could stop for a few moments and mingle with the people. Jim agreed, and we stepped out to greet cheering crowds by the thousands, all shouting "Bill loves May Len" in unison.

As we greeted spectators, May Len slowly and covertly left my side, ensuring I did not notice her flight. She stood behind me bearing many sad secrets within her gentle beating haven, threads of sadness born from ancient destinies bearing bitterly upon the present. Tears came to her loving amber eyes, and a deep gasp forced her emotive lips to tremble loosely, heartened by an unbearable farewell sealed away from my blind chalice.

"*Miléh piri, ezi tenneh.* Farewell, my love," she said grudgingly in a soft barely audible tone, humbly lowering her head to conceal a sobbing spirit unwilling to depart. Heart broken by an indissoluble painful calling her radiant heart could not veil, her hand reached gradually for my shoulder begging to rest its tender warmth upon me one last time, perhaps even one final loving embrace, but it was not to be.

Tearfully trembling, May Len covered lips and eyes to covertly release growing inner sadness in secrecy. Reluctantly, she took her gaze from me and slowly made her way toward a waiting Dow Uanh with faithful grace saying softly and sadly, "Good bye my sunbeam, my love, my only one."

Her trembling, tearful countenance gazed tenderly upon her father, faithfully committed to the call of light. holding his hand up with a most respectful bow, she then said with shuddering voice, "Manéh is love and shall be served."

Hands seemed too numerous to greet all in a single day, and I totally immersed into giving myself to the crowds, unaware of the real reason why Dow Uanh stopped there in the first place. I continued talking to May Len, unaware she had left my side, and asked her, "My loving star, when will your companion arrive?"

I heard no response from my starlight and immediately turned to look for her but noticed she was gone. My chest jumped out of its locks with untold distress, hastily looking and calling for her. I then saw my brethren silently staring at the opposite side of the street and sensed something was terribly wrong. Life's pace promptly slowed to an eerie crawl while a sense of haunting expiry filled the air. Roaring crowds suddenly grew mysteriously dim, and cold chills besieged my entire body. Then swiftly, Dow Uanh covered Jim and Yato, May Len stood in front of me, just as Meh-Nai and Tei-Ah covered Sean and Hans.

I immediately recalled my nightmarish dream and knew what would happen next. I panicked and screamed at the top of my lungs, "May Len, Dow Uanh, seek cover," but they paid no attention to my warning.

By sheer instinct, I jumped in front of May Len anticipating haunting threat, yelling emotionally several times, "I love you more than life itself. My life for thee, thine essence in me!"

"No, my sunbeam," she said trying to stop me, but I forcibly held her back and shielded her.

"Tell your companion how much I love . . ." I replied when a gun shot was fired and felt a hot projectile burn its way into my right chest.

Cheering frenzy quickly turned into a chaotic screaming scene. Some bystanders stood in place baffled, unsure what to do, while others dropped to the ground in terror or fled. My body buckled backward in pain, and a reddish welt stained my *SAT*, but I refused to fall and leave my heavenly pearl exposed to danger, so I vigorously stood my ground and kept my one shielded, meaning to protect her at all cost.

No sooner, another shot was fired, striking me close to the first impact point, this time, pressing me back against my starlight and eventually to the ground. But I quickly got up with a sudden jolt of ire, embracing a weeping May Len with my back to the gun man. She struggled skillfully to assume cover over me, but I held her firmly with every ounce of strength I could gather. "My love, is there not more I can do for thee?" I said struggling for strength. "There must be more! I'll protect you. Survive for your one!"

The breaching crash of another bursting shell broke callously through the air, and its projectile painfully lodged into my left back shoulder. I shrieked a piercing gasp and closed my eyes stiff, plummeting over May Len like a limp cloth, though still clasping her. My body trembled, weak and wrecked with pain, but I held securely to my graceful sapphire any way I could, singing words of love to her. "This, for your one . . . I won't fail you," I said out of strength, slowly sliding off and falling to the ground.

Jim screamed at Gina to contact security, but she ignored his request and made like she did not hear him. Meanwhile, I painfully forced myself to my knees amazed to still be alive, but May Len easily brought my weak body to the ground and covered it with hers. I begged her to get off, but she would not do so no matter my efforts, matching my every move with no intention to let up.

A fierce-looking man wearing a hooded jacket emerged from the other side of the street, wielding panicked spectators away with a revolver. Aiming his weapon in Meh-Nai's direction, he released several projectiles, but these crumbled on contact with a field keeping everyone inside safe but also trapped. He fired at Dow Uanh and the chancellor, but a similar field protected them.

"You alien scum, we don't want your kind here," he said. "Anyone that wants them, dies with them."

"My brother," said Dow Uanh to the man, getting his attention and walking fearlessly toward him against my advice until standing five meters from him. "Peace be with thee, brother Valar. Still doing Zaki Kemisi's bidding, even against your own people? How you've betrayed Father."

"You all belong underground, not on it!" he replied.

"You're not yourself, your mind is possessed by those who would do us all wrong. Come, be with us far from evil, but do according to your heart's calling."

Without hesitation, the man fired twice wounding Dow Uanh in the abdomen. My lungs immediately tore desperately from me, unable to help my master. But in spite of my cries, Dow Uanh continued to painfully advance toward the man. "We are the sons of Manéh, abounding as the clouds, my beloved son," he sung feebly, bearing a dismayed look on his face and plummeting slowly to the ground.

Greatly satisfied, the man turned his attention on May Len next. Noting his renewed assail, I gathered strength from where there was none and forced May Len sideways, begging her to get below me, but she quickly reinstated her protective stance. No sooner, he fired again.

The bullet pierced my left arm but continued on to wound May Len. She gasped a short soft scream as the projectile entered her body and blood emerged from her right shoulder. I immediately panicked and hastily covered her wound with my left hand, begging her to roll over, but she would not allow it. Instead, she smiled at me and said, "My sunbeam, my companion is here. Do you not see him?"

"My starlight . . . not the time! Please, roll over. I'll cover you!" I said, feeling greatly weakened, but deeply concerned for her life.

May Len never took her eyes off me or changed the subject, now crying profusely and raising her voice in living poetic song, "Look no further, my beloved sunbeam: you are my companion. We were just unioned by father!"

I froze in my tracks as her tears fell upon my face in vast measures. A warm chill immediately ran through me, and tears profusely gushed out helplessly in torrents to compete with hers. I looked at my beacon with deep emotion, not knowing what to say or do. "I . . . am?" I answered, unable to prevent a persistent knot in my throat and restless quivering.

"This was the surprise we had for you. This time, we took the spear for you so your spirit can be with me. I love you, my one, with all my soul," she said emotively before passing out. I clutched her wound to keep it from bleeding further, gathered what strength I had left, and turned on my left side as the man fired one last time. The bullet nicked my right arm but continued on to injure May Len on her back side close to the shoulder. Though she did not respond to my frantic calls, I knew she was alive, but time was of the essence for both of us.

People suddenly put fear aside and attacked the man as he readied to reload his weapon, beating him to the ground with grave hatred. Others came and offered to help us but had to step aside as a shuttle hovered overhead and the area had to clear for it to land. Force field removed, my sisters and Sean came to assist. Hans walked over to Gina who stood calmly by her speeder wearing a wide triumphant smile, drooling to such degree that she chewed her own tongue.

The shuttle landed hastily on the speedway just meters away while I beckoned May Len to please stay with me, though she did not respond. Suddenly, everyone either quietly sat or knelt on the ground, but the man that fired on us dragged his body by Dow Uanh's side nearby as if someone pulled him.

Dow Uanh asked Jim to grant this man full pardon. Though Jim hesitated at first, Dow Uanh insisted, indicating that punishment was not the brotherhood's way. Grudgingly, Jim agreed.

Overjoyed by Jim's response, Dow Uanh took the man's hand, forgave his actions, and offered to show him the real reasons behind them. After a few seconds, the man cried and yelled repeatedly, falling to the ground sobbing and begging forgiveness. People were confused, wondering what changed this man's stance so drastically. Their curiosity was not met then, but days later it would prove to be a sore revelation to everyone on Saras.

Dow Uanh looked my way as the shuttle ramp lowered and said softly, "Protect her." His personal glow then left him, his bright countenance turned to one of lifeless emptiness, and he left. People wept as they approached their beloved symbol of peace that was no more but quickly displaced as medical crews headed his way.

I felt weak, lightheaded, and could barely move; attempts to do so sent sharp pains down my right side. My hands quivered, ice ran helplessly down numbing extremities, and strength failed me. But with great emotional exertion, singing spirited words of love to my enchanting pearl and with Tei-Ah's help, I slowly came to my knees wondering why I was still alive.

On the ground, my tender heavenly flower, my dream of countless eons, rested still and gravely wounded, her clothes stained by ruddy fluids from both our vessels, indistinguishable one from the other as if one. She was my beautiful one, the fervent longing of my long-entreating soul, most wondrous light from dazzling firmaments etched upon my heart's eternal scroll. She was now my eternal companion, sealed forever over my bosom with a virtuous signet; I will cherish and love her all the days of my lives, with heavenly powers no longer secret.

My eyes mysteriously filled with calm celestial visions, passionately drenching the windows of my soul with loving essence from my beautiful beacon. My heart's dormant bindings unfastened to heavenly stirring elixir, gently inspiring virtuous life into the chalice of emotion's timbres. Fears melted away, weakness and pain grieved ignored; my life no longer cloaked heaven's noble rapport, throbbing from her pleasing heart of gold. In my soul's dawning horizon, a bright crown of profound love for my starlight gently crested above receding shadows with blistering rays of affection, surpassing eve's gloom with divine conviction.

I was enthralled by indescribable love, never before felt or believed possible. It was so passionate, intense, faithful, benign that my breathing immediately arrested; my chest paced still, eyes filled with calm, and my soul with her warmth gracefully vested. My heart was completely enraptured, singing passionate odes of wonder to my beautiful pearl; the world's fearful ways vanished, and I sought no purpose but let love's might hastily unfurl. I became someone whose sole devotion no longer strived to live off earthly chores but rather nobly love her with all its might into infinity's shores. His Majesty's breath of life had reached into my bosom, and I lived.

May Len suddenly gasped and partly opened her bright calm eyes like a mid-sky spectral bow. Her amber gems met mine with loving delight, stirred by my heart's luminous crown coursing freely through her being. Through her windows, she tried to say what she felt, but no utterance could describe it other than visual bliss. Her lips were pliant, expressive of wordless diction, overcome by Father's gift of love so long awaited. Her faint words "I feel you" echoed loudly in my mind, and a strong essence of gardenias scented my soul, invigorating intense love for my radiant starlight.

"You didn't run. You came back for me, my love, my protectorate," she said, closing her eyes once more.

Though only a few seconds transpired since the shuttle landed, time was of the essence for my treasure. Medics prepared to come our way, but I could not wait. With what strength I had and Sean's help, I gently placed my numb arms about May Len's frail body, and carefully lifted her from the ground with a loud bellow to overcome physical weakness and pain, struggling to keep her wounds closed and my balance in check.

From the shadows of sinful consent, Gina's eyes sharply met mine as I turned toward the shuttle. In that brief instant, her thoughts of revolting desire traveled the short distance between us unobstructed, projecting onto my senses the most horrid, putrid animal stench imaginable. I realized that each soul has a peculiar scent, garnered from the flavors of our labors, and these accompany every personal thought. "Never!" was my immediate resolute reply, nauseated by her noxious mental odors, trading my sights from her repugnant stare for the ramp.

I felt extremely weak, dizzy, and stricken by peculiar buzzing, aware that I could not stay on my feet much longer. But my enamored heart was determined to see my love of ages safely to medical attention, urging and empowering me one step at a time. After a few paces and just when I felt I could go no further, medical assistants finally arrived.

I begged them to take May Len first, and her body promptly committed to a waiting stretcher as I collapsed to my knees. Medics promptly applied artificial plasma packs to her and bound her wounds, assuring me they were not life threatening and that she would make full recovery. As for my kind master, he had transitioned.

I sat on the shuttle's ramp waiting my turn while medics temporarily patched my wounds and applied plasma packs, much relieved to know May Len's life was not in danger. I cried happily and in anguish, unable to contain both happiness and deep sorrows, comforted by my friends and assured by His Majesty that my soul was privileged to be with Him.

As loud as my lungs spared me, songs of praise raced into the chaotic scene in Maneh's ancient language, countering loud public chatter and cries with compelling love for Him. I did not fathom the reasons behind this incident, but knew the light works in mysterious ways and always acts in favor of the collective good, providing the best option possible.

Gina, on the other hand, gave Hans a signal and left to wait things out inside her speeder. Her extreme satisfaction and confidence clearly stood out among those present to no concern of hers. I then knew precisely who Hans and Gina were and what they were up to, but they were not the ones in charge; they were mere slaves to higher sources and felt great pity for them. They sadly allowed themselves to be used for reasons of survival while destroying their lives and that of others in the process.

Medics finally stabilized May Len, now set for immediate surgery. It was now my turn and my sisters helped me up, but my body helplessly collapsed and my head hit the ramp, suffering from unavoidable pounding. Every extremity rendered cold and feeble, unable to move in spite of best efforts.

Noting my dilemma, medics quickly dragged me up the ramp onto a stretcher. Standing nearby was a concerned Hans to whom I turned and said, "I know who you and Beta Gina are, Gamma." Hans backed up briskly, worried stiff, unable to say a word.

My vision blurred, senses spun about casually, and sounds increasingly garbled until I passed out on the stretcher, dreaming loving thoughts of my eternal one in whom I now lived, and the heart was most pleased.

Chapter 23: *My One*

"Where's my beautiful starlight," I said, slowly coming about in a light-deprived room two days later. My wounds were healed but not the heart, for someone in my likeness was mysteriously absent from my being and restive longing for her graceful essence denied me comforts. Her love I could not be without. I felt empty without her, overwhelmed by a strange sense of loneliness and shortness of breath I found most difficult to mind.

I repeatedly called for May Len not sure anyone heard me, but Tei-Ah soothingly cautioned me to lie still, assuring me she was well and resting in another room with Meh-Nai. I begged to see her, but Tei-Ah resorted to doctor's orders, and there was no fooling her; she read my every thought.

My beloved master and father Dow Uanh, who many referred to as the emissary of peace, transitioned as it was meant to be. Members around the world held silent vigils for him, and his precious words of wisdom resounded in every earthly tongue with profound devotion.

The mission was on target, and Tei-Ah was most enthusiastic about Saras's future—especially May Len's and mine. "You want to know something?" she said. "You've tried to union for a million years."

"Seems like no time at all, does it?" I said kiddingly.

"She'll be so pleased to hear that."

"As May Len's companion, according to your customs, what are some of my responsibilities?" She gave me an inquisitive look, although she knew with surgical precision exactly what I meant.

Trying to look serious, but not doing too good a job at it, she asked, "You mean, who cleans the house, cares for the kids, and does the yard, while the man enjoys a leisurely job and spends much time out with friends socializing?"

". . . yes?" I said, accepting her wisely drafted analogy.

"You use the term 'share the load,' but don't apply it to your families. Some Saras cultures restrict female rights, delegating rigorous house shores and child rearing to them. Is that love? Love is not voiced, it is practiced."

"Saras men are so predictable," Meh-Nai said, coming into the room. "Let the Infinite inspire you. He created us brother and sister to teach us unity and mutual sharing through diversity of expression, not assume meek and bossy roles. May Len is calm asleep, and you should too. Don't forget, her physical anatomy heals faster than yours."

"The man who shot us, what became of him?"

"He's here, waiting to see you both, but can't stop crying."

"Things happened as in a dream I had. I should have said something, it could have prevented this whole incident."

"My son, had you interfered, this huge cycle would have gone ignored," Tei-Ah said, "Our mission would have been a complete failure, Dow Uanh's transition interrupted, and you would not have relived your past."

"Not to mention, you still wouldn't know May Len was your companion," Meh-Nai said.

"That be a very bad thing. But why did this have to happen?" I added. "Was this a reliving?"

"This incident was a reenactment of a time 127,000 years ago. This time, you faced it instead of running."

"I ran back then?"

"You'll see more of that life soon. For now, you must be patient. And yes, be a very, very bad thing had you interfered."

"I see your point about intruding, acting without infinite guidance."

"Your people do it all the time, unbeknown to them. Ego is like a game of chess you play with people, enthralling your intellect to provide contrived solutions to its selfish needs within your game's constraints. Instead of bolstering your personal intellect with mechanical or logical thought forms, you should let the ways of love guide your actions—not lies. Trying to figure things out yourself is equivalent to lying to yourself."

Wondering how much longer I had to remain in bed, Meh-Nai assured a disquieting two more days. "Fascinating, you just said a million years was no time at all," she said. But after some gentle pleading, she left to ask hospital staff if I could at least move into May Len's quarters.

"Well, my sister," I said kiddingly, "at least I know she's on my side."

"You're kidding me, right? Oh, my dear, dear son, if you only knew who Meh-Nai was in ages past and is today," Tei-Ah said with a chuckle. "She's so much stricter than I am."

I was then filled with a wonderful sense of being, recognizing that Tei-Ah was a master and the true leader of this mission from the start. Moved by intense loving respect, I quickly jumped from bed, came to my knees with open arms before her, and admired the Infinite for my sister's demanding responsibilities in His realm. Tei-Ah was now my beloved master.

Moments later, doctors arrived escorted by security personnel. Reconstructive surgery was a success, and wounds would only be visible under a microscope. They were at a loss to explain how we survived; injuries should have been more severe, if not lethal. My sisters smiled widely at each other, no doubt keeping a big secret from us. On the brighter side, they allowed me to move into May Len's quarters under one condition, let her sleep. Shortly after, my wish was granted.

Hospital hallways swarmed with armed security details keeping watch and searching anyone coming near our rooms. Colorful banners welcoming the Brothers to Saras draped vividly from hospital walls, along with pictures of May Len and me inscribed with the words "Bill loves May Len"; how right they were. My radiant jewel rested peacefully. Her delicate face seemed like fragile porcelain gracefully hiding bygone pains, her head sloping to a side desiring patiently this grave ill to pass.

After settling into May Len's room, the nurse on duty casually made her way out the door when she suddenly stopped somewhat puzzled, then turned my way questioning her mental faculties. I had just thought of giving my sisters roses and she must have picked it up. I placed a picture of a rose in my mind, put up three fingers, and gestured not to awaken May Len. She confirmed my appeal and silently left the room. Apparently, I was beginning to share May Len's mental abilities.

Minutes later, she appeared with three roses and placidly placed them in my care. But as she left the room, poor soul, I could not help it; I thought of a glass of water. She got this message too. Although she complied, I felt my requests were getting a bit annoying. My sisters laughed mutely, warning me to exercise caution: I could see why. She brought us water, doubly ensured I had everything I needed, and left hastily. I was certain I exhausted her welcome.

Well into the morning, my heart's crown suddenly rekindled its latent fires and fervently burst alive, revived by a familiar benign essence I earnestly implored. My eyes glowed gently with a view of radiant spiritual energy in flight, streaming down like rushing falls that cast selfish fallacy from my sights. Love illumined my life's path with light and patience far from want, inspiring realms of truth in my soul's desolate haunt.

I eagerly turned to my side and gazed at my precious flower, noting that she gradually emerged from slumber's long hours. Without delay, I leaped from bed like a loaded spring, took gentle hold of her hand, and caringly said, "My one, my only one, my beloved starlight; the future is upon us."

May Len slowly revealed her wondrous amber gems and warmly folded her hands over mine, smiling with starburst happiness. With tender summon to her side, she said, "My love, you chose my soul over your own life."

I took into her bidding arms with gentle embrace and gladdened gasp, lasting my lips lightly unto her cheek. "I can't abandon you. It's not going to happen," I said, pouring my heart upon her as she looked on fondly.

"This was a test, my son," said Tei-Ah, "and we had our doubts."

"You'll learn more about it in the weeks to come," Meh-Nai added.

"My masters, was this a lesson? Did I pass?" I said, but my sisters did not reply, other than smile and nod affirmatively.

"You relived, but be patient; you will know more soon," May Len said softly, humbly placing my hands to her heart. "After such long quest through worlds far and long lost, my missing flame is by my side and the future is upon us. What endurance and devotion over the years in spite of this blind penal world that only teaches venal reasoning and lives solely by conceit."

After helping May Len up from bed, I gave each of my sisters a rose while Meh-Nai added with a jovial chuckle, "He's ready for his next qualification, isn't he?" Little did I know what that meant—I would soon find out.

In view of recent events, being locked away in a hospital room was not helping move Father's mission forward, so I left for my old room to clean up under ardent protest from hospital staff. Meanwhile, my sisters helped May Len get ready. Noting all the commotion, EMS came up to see what was going on and got into the act, asking endless questions.

As I neared the room, I was besieged by a repulsive stench hard to dismiss meters from the door. No one else sensed it, and then I knew: someone with evil intentions was near. Security was also strangely absent from the area, so I approached the room cautiously not sure what to expect. Inside, I found Gina leaning against a wall, silent and rigid like a spider quietly luring unwary prey to its web. I stood still, heart pounding, taken back by her imposing character unsure just what to do. Everyone suddenly silenced, stunned by her ominous commanding presence, not knowing whether to love or hate her.

Her grim stance was unshaken by those present, posing an authoritative stare that essentially disarmed personal judgment. Her prideful resolve sensibly increased with each passing moment, spreading dread to anyone laying eyes on her. But in spite of her best efforts, I refused to give into selfish logic. She was there to debate, and another failure was definitely not in her best interests.

"My sister, may I ask why you're here?" I said softly though I knew why, keeping a spiritual protective shield about me.

"I wanted to make sure you're getting the best possible attention this world can offer. It's the least I can do for my protégé," she said with a deep seductive voice, porting a brief entrancing wink that spelled noxious intent.

"Can my sister's words be trusted?"

"You know I'm incapable of meaning the man of my dreams any harm."

She concealed a dark purpose too hideous to openly expose, cleverly hidden behind a deceptive smile. Previous attempts to secure my allegiance failed, and I knew she could not afford to fail again. She had to succeed to survive, and anxiously waited to deploy her most dreaded weapon: debate.

"You should not be here," I said calmly, unwilling to argue with her. "To answer your real inquiry, I won't turn my heart away from May Len." Turning to the door, I kindly asked her to leave, but she would not give up so easily.

"You don't really want me to leave," she said, alluringly boasting her physical talents. "I think this is the perfect time to continue courting our secret affair, now that your alien girlfriend isn't around. Besides, what we have to discuss is not going to take long at all."

She came to arm's length, assured her disarming array of sexual advances would deter my allegiance to my one, but I backed off. I noticed that peculiar sweetened alcohol smell again and realized she wore pheromones, but they were of little use. "My sister, I agree, it didn't take long at all," I said, asking her again to take leave.

"Don't be nervous," she said, boasting her vessel's proportions as a means to her ends. "Nothing's going to happen that you don't want. What you want, I can give you better than anyone else. The world and all its wonders can be yours. Together, we take over the world and rule it to a glorious future. We can become an example to the rest of the galaxy and conquer it, conquer the universe. This I offer you, if you would only care for me."

"My sister is wasting her time. I only love the Infinite and May Len; I yearn nothing else," I said gently.

Frustrated, she replied sharply, "You can't refuse me! No one can!"

Her breathing intensified and desires begged to climax, oppressed by uncontainable yearning for pleasure. "You belong to me, not that roach, so don't delay the inevitable," she said desperately. "Release yourself to me with that candor men are known for!"

"May Len, my celestial starlight, I love with all my soul, strength, heart, and mind—a love uncontainable, virtuous, eternal. There's nothing else like it."

"You know who I am and what I can do to your friends," she threatened, realizing I conclusively rejected her.

"We just felt your power on Lake Shore Drive. It still hurts."

"You haven't seen anything yet!"

"So my sister admits the shooting was her idea."

"I'm not your sister!"

"Good thing old casings were used; else, we'd be dead."

"It's that freak that landed you in the hospital. Where do you think you'd be by my side? You two are from different worlds. Who knows if that monster can give you a healthy child. Face it, that thing doesn't belong here or you with her. Let her be with her kind and worry about protecting ours. Don't contaminate this planet any more than it already is."

"Father chose my beloved long before there was a universe. There's no one more beautiful in all creation. You cannot possibly conceive just how much, and how deeply, madly, extremely I love her!"

"Damn it! Just listen to you! You sound just like them!"

"Thank you. I've just been highly complemented."

"You've been hypnotized!" She waved hands frantically, scheming intensely to lure my attention yet emphasizing a false sense of urgency. "Look at me. I'm twenty times the woman she is. I have so much more to offer, I wield world power, and I'm the most desirable woman on this planet. How can you possibly refuse that?"

"I'm in love with the most desirable soul in the universe, the most precious, radiant pearl in all heaven, my perfect love. All I can think of is my intense love for her. I don't want food, water, air, life—only her, just her, nothing else but her," I replied with heartfelt, poetic inspiration.

"Do you now?" she said sarcastically.

"You're a recruiter for evil, and there's nothing I want from you."

"I can have these aliens off our planet in an instant, if I so wish it. Is that what you want?"

Gina tried putting her hands around me, but I moved off to a side leaving her to embrace dead air. "You offer me pleasure in return, for what, induction into your Order? Know that I'll never ever abandon Manéh or my starlight. What you appeal me with is an awful depravity."

"I can't believe you said that," she replied, offended by my rejection. "You really, really need help. You know that?"

"There's lust for flesh when there's no God left to love."

"Wow! Really? You can't be serious!"

"You have no idea how much I love May Len and my Brothers. I have no other thoughts, dreams, or desires. I'll never abandon her; it's impossible! Not going to happen! If you didn't succeed in a million years, much less now."

"She's a freak, trying to destroy our future!"

"I'll die for Manéh and my one anytime. I'm a Brother, one of many, that are in love with each other to the ends of time. Torture me all you want; it will only strengthen my love for her!"

"You were mine before that freak got here, and you will be mine again. So get off this spirit crap and consider what I'm giving you. We can live anywhere, do anything, retire with all the comforts. Millions of men would give it all to have me, but it is you I want."

"Yes, Minh-Ley, we had this talk back in Atlantis," I said, staring straight into her eyes with renewed intensity and resolve. "Now, let's be honest; you're a racist, aren't you?"

Gina blinked her eyes and looked away trying to hide them. "Imagine all those cosmic races and colors out there, now coming down here; that terrifies your organization. Life is in spirit, not flesh. Color and form don't matter."

"We live desirable lifestyles that ensure civil order. Think of our kids, the impact you'll have on them. You're taking their childhood away and exposing them to weird alien ideas! What do you propose, Hallovenus, Christmars, mixing up our kids with freaks that don't value life the way we do?"

"Your Order invented those holidays, not God. You control people's lives right down to likes, dislikes, holidays, religion, turning people into robots …"

"Who better than us to create the perfect society," she said arrogantly. "We don't need aliens telling us what to do!"

"So you admit belonging to the Order. Fascinating. We're nothing but robots to you."

"I've had enough of this!"

"Should I call you Beta, overlord of the ETA, and second in command of the Order?"

Gina took a few steps back, wondering how I knew her identity. She was on the defensive, more concerned about safety than her mission, trying to get out of her binding predicament. That made her even more dangerous.

"There's someone in the lobby waiting to confess. Grave mistake, Beta, you forgot to discard the evidence."

"Go ahead. Get his testimony. He can't prove a thing."

"How would you know that unless you sent him?"

Gina silenced suddenly, showing grave anxiety. Her hands dried up, and her mouth opened senselessly, knowing she sorely erred.

"My sister, you can't hide from us Brothers. When we visited the Towers, did you not leave to set plan Brutus in motion and cyphered your memory to hide your actions?"

"I can't tell you where I went; that information is classified."

"You tried to abduct me, downed our shuttles, killed my beloved father, and hurt my beautiful flower. And you still have the nerve to . . ."

"Is this how you repay everything I did for you?" she said literally shouting. "Without me, you were a nobody, and that hasn't changed!"

"Having me betray the Brothers—that's all you care about. We know more about you and your Order than you realize, but I'll leave that to your privacy."

"If you think you know something about me, then go ahead. Tell me what you see in my past, oh, great and wise visionary!"

"It's not my place to interfere with your development," I said cautiously.

"When I put you on the spot, you back down; I'm not at all surprised! Must be all the crap that freak fed you!"

"Knowledge at the wrong time can have long-term devastating effects . . ."

"Fine! I'm taking this matter up to the council, and this mission is finished! No more Martians or career for you. You're finished, you understand? I want those freaks gone from my planet in an hour, or I'll launch them into space myself! And for all the grief they've caused me, I'll turn their planets into nuclear heaps! Any questions?"

"Very well," I said in a most displeased tone. "There's no point trying to bring you to your senses; don't say I didn't warn you. Remember that once I tell you I can do nothing more for you."

"Can you cut to the chase?"

After briefly joining with my Brothers, I was ready for the task. But Gina was impatient, quickly imposing herself.

"I don't have time for this. I'm dumping those freaks off my planet right now!" she said, speeding for the hallway.

She pulled the room's door handle and angrily told people to step aside. But then, she stopped dead cold and let go of the handle unsure of herself. She stared to her side, reviewing pictures of the Funny Farm, their inhuman appearance, and vegan mental state. But when she saw Tiger Woman's exaggerated figure, tail, fangs and ears, she quickly twitched horrified. Slowly caressing her body, she backed away from the door trembling, bumped into a supply cabinet, and sent its contents crashing down.

"This is your spliced creation, rather, horror. You were a man then and spliced yourself into this horrific woman trying to take me from my beautiful starlit firmament, but you failed. You had the power then, much as you do now, the power to destroy lives in order to preserve yours. Anyone that opposed you was, as you said, finished. You were Saras's most decadent lust-tormented celebrity, responsible for untold sorrow and deviance from Father. You condemned countless souls to your sex circus, where you personally abused them in acts so degenerate I don't dare bring to mind!"

"No this can't be me," she said trembling with a horrified look on her face, desperately rubbing off invisible objects from her body.

"My sister, what you witness, have your present-day actions not mirrored it? Do you not see the grave hatred you harbor for us Brothers in your heart?"

"But I never wanted to hurt you."

"I didn't say me. I said we."

"Aliens are invading us and taking you from me. I had to do something about it, and what I did is fully justifiable!"

"Your Order is the invader, trying to take us from Manéh."

"I only wanted to separate you from that freak, but something went wrong with cyphering and the operative malfunctioned."

"You malfunctioned. All things that start off wrong, end up wrong."

"I'll never give you up—and I'll do what I must to have you."

"The Order is all you love, and I know you can't fail this mission."

"Then, come and be one of us. Do it for me. Else, I'll be terminated."

"I will not betray my beautiful angel and my loving Father. You will reap what you foster."

"So you'd rather have me killed? Is that it?"

"The Order invested way too much on you. Why do you insist in belonging to such wicked association?"

"They are my family, and I'll never leave them. When you meet them, I'm sure you'll change your mind."

"Why follow a man and not the Creator? I once thought as you did, joined an illegitimate family, and became an unworthy sinner. Such rebellion brought untold pain and destruction to many souls. How many husbands did not return home for supper, how many children did not mature in life, how many cities and worlds lay waste because of me? I destroyed four planets and billions on them! I built killing machines that enslaved the galaxy! I ceded to the demon of times to appease fear and steal Father's creations for myself, having lost my companion's spirit.

"Turn your eyes upon Manéh. Receive His virtuous reproof as I have. If He can forgive me, who won't He forgive? I reveal this to you before His Majesty, bidding spiritual apologies and reparations, so that your spiritual evolution and that of so many others be not distressed. I beg your deepest forgiveness for so many past transgressions against you."

Moved by my admission, people bravely came in the room and placed their hands on me in spite of Gina's threats. I addressed each of them, begging forgiveness with heartfelt apology and encouraging them to accept Father. But suddenly, I sensed pending danger and asked everyone to seek safety. Still, no one took leave, resolved to face Gina if necessary.

As expected, Gina angrily pushed everyone back and proceeded to strike me harshly, but I did not fight back. Instead, I welcomed her offenses and mentally kept people back. She screamed, offloaded several harsh martial blows, and yelled, "Why won't you love me willingly?"

I was suddenly filled with incomprehensible gentleness and virtue, bringing me to tears. My voice acquired a poetic poise, uplifting my heart with care and compassion, freed from Gina's hindrances. "I witness for loving Father and the brotherhood; and I live for May Len, my love of ages, the greatest beauty under the heavens and my dearly beloved wife."

Gina raised her head when I mentioned "wife" and looked at me in silent disbelief. She immediately tried to recover from her previous violent outbreak but could not find the means to justify or apologize for her actions. "Why did you betray me? Why?" she said.

"I am hers since the beginning of time and will so endure into the limitless bindings of infinity. You destroyed our union and tortured us for a million years, but now we are married and inseparable. I love her. You have no idea how much I love her! I love her with such vigor this lowly heart can't contain it! My search for love is over, for I found it in her heart.

"Tell Alpha what you heard here, and that we Brothers forgive and love him. He knows what he must do: surrender to Manéh. Take our forgiveness with you and come to grips with yourself. Seek the brotherhood for help, and repent of evil. Now, leave!"

"But I can't leave without you . . ."

"You'll never steal my heart from my beautiful starlight. Now, go, before the authorities get here; they're on their way. So leave, while you still can!"

Gina hastily stormed out of the room, frantically yelling, "This isn't over! Traitors, conspirators, maggots."

"Bill loves May Len" people chanted back, scorning Gina as she ran up and down hallways without sense of direction looking for a way out, slightly limping from her right leg. She finally vanished down the complex maze of hallways, yelling madly in the far distance.

My eyes imposed themselves shut in relief as a huge weight lifted from me. My long-standing cycle with Gina was breaking down, and my love for May Len deepened to realms I never imagined possible. As nurses tended to newly inflicted sores, I intensely witnessed to those present my fervent, profound love for my princess, inspired by a pounding bosom enthralled by the majesty of her heavenly beauty.

Then suddenly, chanting came to a stop, and people moved aside to allow someone passage into the room. I looked up, and to my delight, May Len stood smiling at the door like an angel with rose in hand, dressed in her delicate golden outfit. She was pleased with my stance against a grave ancient foe and my undying devotion to both her and His Majesty.

"My sweet love, I'm moved by your incredible devotion to my soul," she said. "You were most brave, and you honored me fervidly by witnessing such powerful love. Your negative ties to Gina are now severed, and we are finally free from a million years of unbelievable suffering."

Standing with effort, I took her soft hand and held it up high, looking deeply into her joyous, radiant amber eyes with humble warmth. I drew myself closer to her, one reverent slow step at a time. Our arms interlaced gently about each other's shoulders with greatest softness and respect. Silent words of sweetness flowed with incredible ease, tender feelings that mutually turned into love songs. I had found my most cherished treasure, concealed from my eyes beneath a small forbidding crimson world for so long.

Our embrace warmly brought us closer together, hands gently placed behind shoulders. Lips then slowly touched each other's cheeks with extreme reverence and courteous self-giving. Where diction could not witness the heart, I could only say, "I humbly love you, my beautiful heart of Rosette."

An aura enveloped us, and incredible warmth boiled inside me. Colorful flashes of light blinked brightly in my vision, and I knew they were the essence of higher beings, adding their healing love to our loving union. Gently resting upon each other's arms, our thoughts and souls joined as one with sweet, soft harmony and surrendered our minds to God's loving pulse.

Her essence embraced my soul amorously and drew me with tender forces that my soul desperately longed for. My spirit breathed His loving, inspiring current as my heart sweetly bonded to hers in perfect unison. Then, our latent rhapsodies sung together in spirit for the first time in creation, and our inner flames came alive—reborn, as one.

"You may kiss the bride," Meh-Nai said sweetly.

"Let the heart come forth gently and sing through our lips words impossible to share otherwise, my most beautiful love, my beautiful heart of Rosette and vast lakes of Lagoon," I said. "My life is for thee; oh, what joy it be. A love from spirit, no flesh can divert hither."

"The rose and the lakes, you remember that," my one replied. "What beautiful soul has Father granted me. So much love resides in thee. My love, wait no longer and come. Share it with me, for I can no longer hold back the tides of a longing heart. Come deep into my heart and don't ever leave."

Our lips ever slowly neared, amorously and unconcerned for time, the heart devoted in loving giving. Gently and with extreme respect, the fringes of our souls briefly joined with utmost softness. I experienced a sensation like that of tender rose petals warmly sharing, feeling not pleasure but loving unity begging intensely to express. Her lips were like warm pillows pleading for my rest, gentle, and loving beyond depiction, reciting an untiring story of love to endure the ends of time.

"My lips are the voice of my heart," she said. "Feel the words they silently utter and gently come into my welcoming bosom longing for thy nearness. Let us warmly embrace in eternal softness and recite kind thoughts of life's loving gratitude as our souls unite, swept by His unifying force—duality, true love."

Our loving embrace was like a bright rainbow that fastens its colorful arms softly upon the earth and boldly soars its radiant hues unto heaven's heart as one. Her vessel was warm and vibrant, pleading to articulate sweetness rather than pleasure. I felt her heart beating in my bosom, mine in the restful, tender softness of hers. The flesh implored fond affections, lightly gathered for gentle enthusiasm rapidly surging. Our hands reverently cuddled behind our vessels, gently and respectful, to concede coveted closeness.

Our eyes closed tenderly enamored, our vessels cuddled in soft giving. Hearts racing ever faster, lips slowly sought each other and sealed with soft, loving tenderness, reciting reverent gentle songs impossible to describe by any other means. Our vessels warmly embraced unconcerned for time, sharing gentle beauty that drew the soul to sing sweet thankful odes of love to the Eternal, beloved Magnificence, Supreme Interminable, Father of love, Infinite Consciousness, giver of everlasting joy.

True love from His Majesty conquers all!

May Len, my river of virtue and interminable, gentle ribbon embracing my heart, behold my love and solemn promise: I shall never again part from thee. Oh, my perfect love and companion, my one for whom I live, unique infinite force that binds me to Him. Oh, how I love thee and beloved Infinite. *Oh-joi*!

I journeyed through time and space searching for her loving beam, for life is worthless without her pearly stream. The cosmos my heart spanned seeking her beacon whence embers become a flame; my bosom's songs now embraces the glory of her celestial claim.

Chapter 24: *Inseparable Lives*

My heart no longer wandered alone through endless seasons, washed off somewhere in infinity's most forsaken sandy visions, for now I was within sight of my beloved beacon.

Love was with me at all times. Poetry dwelled in my singing voice inspired by gentle, beloved Infinite. I lived to love my one and Father with insatiable passion, constantly begging for more, ardently channeling love from future times and higher planes to the fore. Ours were inseparable lives—unbreakable bands of unity, bound tenderly by love's caring forces in realms far from near.

Life took an entirely new beautiful meaning, relative to time and space. Our menagerie universe no longer seemed real but more like a plane of existence where even the most infinitesimally insignificant element throbbed tirelessly at the mercy of countless invisible inter-dimensional energy vortexes in an undulating ritual meant to endearingly court all other infinite forms in predestined harmony. Every node, every pulse, was united in higher causal realms as if one in purpose across simultaneous time, delivering complex expressions upon our plane in marked virtually sequential order according to concavity energy cadences. Every form is a jewel of universally articulate, inter-dimensionally scientific understanding, a gift from endless casual forces that express from higher realms inspired by the vast fountainhead of life.

From their restive nodal points, pulsing wave fronts without number burst forth into uncharted event horizons like quickened quasars in nonexistent earthly expanse and chronology, silently rapping against countless others in an immeasurable sea of endless harmonic waves and dimensional currents, giving rise to perceptive illusions of instance and distance. Faster surfs gripped slower ones, creating vast euphonious, intelligent wonders meant to reveal not happenstance but designed perceptivity, much like a hologram.

Our vessels are no different. They are virtual instruments, robots produced by creation's energies that attract infinity's living sparks to environments best suited to reflect upon and overcome past experiential memories. These memoirs are impressions or beliefs from events that, in their time, recorded harmonic construal into our soul according to complex developmental actions. Life is then the process of exposing said memories to higher truths much as progressive school years mature students into ever greater educational content and devotional maturity.

The subconscious past is merely a type of thought registry, life's principal conduit for all personal perception, reasoning, emotions, and relative thought. Its role is not to bear fears upon life but rather embody a path to devotedly fall in love with higher stages of awareness. Since thought and body are energy constituents, erratic structural and mental ailments do have their foundations in influential past memories by means of frequency association and dynamic interaction; the same can reverse such ailments. This we cannot conceive, for an approved wrongful concept is gravely rooted into our souls: sin.

What we refer to as sin is not the result of helpless, intrinsic, or genetic propensities to failure, or debility inherent in incompetently born incumbents requiring indisputable intercession and contrived prayers. Rather, sin is a mental prop devised by fundamentalists to control the masses through sapping fear, an escape that trades truth and love for outright irresponsibility. Sin is a lesson in life's classroom, work in progress, not a defect that only bloody medicine can take away. Honesty and truth, not blood or selfish logic, will set you free; no one can do your homework for you and let you get away with mental incompetence.

After showering and changing into new clothes, my amber firestones and I embraced reverently and walked, hands joyously joined, to the hospital lobby followed by scores of people. There, waiting for us, was the countenance of a much-troubled man surrounded by security officers.

May Len gave me a look that said, "What will you do?" What mattered most was honoring the Creator's ways: forgive and facilitate learning. My sisters were most pleased with my resolve, encouraging me to bring him hope and long lost love. He refused to eat, drink, or sleep, sobbing often in helpless squalls from a bad case of guilt. Here was the man that pulled the trigger, obviously for someone else, but he carried the greater burden.

"I sense your heavy affliction, but we hold no malice toward you," Meh-Nai said. "You know what few do and we need you. Saras needs you. So let this bitter cup go and come walk with us." She gently knelt to his level, but her clothes were stained with blood serving to increase his guilt.

"Brother," I said to the man with May Len standing lovingly by my side, "your chosen tearful penance is not sufficiently gratifying. I had another form of payment in mind. Am I correct in assuming that your sadness is a means to punish yourself?" May Len knew where I was going with this and, with a nod, shared her approval.

The man continued to cry and did not reply immediately, though a screeching voice eventually said yes. It was hard to believe a man of such deep feelings could be turned into a killing machine, but past memories placed him directly in the path of monsters that took advantage of him, as was the case with all us eartheans. His sobbing slowed but it was hard for him to refrain, expressing sorrows born from a dreadful, enormously painful past. "I pushed the button," he said repeatedly.

"Others need to hear your story, not just us Brothers," May Len said. "Your testimony will help many avoid the same trap you fell into and also ensure you don't do this again in another life."

He promised to do so but then silenced as Jim came into the lounge surrounded by security officers and assistants. Jim's semblance described deep sorrow, and we knew the reasons. Sympathy flowed from his lips at a time of mourning for the loss of a great prince of peace. A knot constricted his speech, water covered his eyes, and a quivering voice remained poised about his demeanor for which he apologized. Surely, Jim and Dow Uanh had become inseparable brothers. He felt, as did I, a part of us departed, an absence difficult to overlook.

"Jim, I believe this man has something to tell you," I said to him.

Hesitant at first, the man eventually said, stricken by sobs, "I owe the world and the Brothers a huge apology, but I also need to testify what happened."

"I want to hear all about it, and since EMS is here, so will members. Go on," Jim said.

"I received an invitation to participate in eye examination trials. Thinking nothing of it and already due for a glaucoma check, I showed up for the test at a small office building by Wicker Park. Everything about the place looked legit. A friendly assistant carried out various familiar sight tests at first but then placed a plastic mask over my face, and I don't remember what happened after that. When I came to, I was back home but felt an irresistible urge to contact someone called Kappa, a tall brawny-looking man who I talked to many times. With each visit, he put that mask on me, and my hatred for the Brothers grew until I was given the order to take their lives."

"Who are these people, and what can you tell us about them?"

"Not much. They blindfold me each time we meet and talk through a console, except recently, when I heard two people talk in the background. One of them was called Beta. The other had a unique voice I'll never forget."

"Mr. Chancellor," said a journalist, "moments ago, we learned the reasons and the individual behind this lamentable incident. It happened here at the hospital during a heated encounter between Dr. Sullivan and the Speaker of the Senate. You just missed it."

"I'm confused, Gina was supposed to be somewhere else. What are we talking about?" asked Jim, becoming somewhat anxious.

"The Speaker of the Senate, Gina Toscani," said the journalist. Jim was silent for a moment, stunned by the news. His countenance froze, thereafter replaced by one of mounting concern.

"She tried luring Dr. Sullivan away from May Len but he resolutely refused. In her own words, the Speaker staunchly supports prejudice and described her criminal actions as justifiable to take Dr. Sullivan from May Len and keep Earth's status quo. She leads an underground Order that controls global members, racial classes, and civil behavior."

Jim was consumed in thought, not entirely ready to react to what he heard. He placed a great deal of trust on Gina and now had reasons to be concerned. He quickly summoned an associate and secretly spoke to him for some time. I imagined it had to do with security, immediately closing doors Gina might access such as arms depot and shuttle weaponry lock downs. His associate left in a hurry, communicating with peers frantically.

"Is all of this true?" he asked me, and I confirmed the unfortunate facts to a man gravely distressed by these events.

"You were right about plugs infiltrating the highest levels of government, but I never imagined it would go this far or come this close. It's regretful this incident took place now, on the eve of Earth's greatest awakening."

"Mr. Chancellor," replied May Len in gentle comforting manner, "we Brothers are committed to the mission more so than ever. Your people face a most destructive past memory, irrelevant of our presence. Evil is bound to come forth and repeat its dreadful deeds, but we are confident you will overcome this cycle and unite with us Brothers. We won't abandon you."

Everyone rigorously approved May Len's pledge, bringing Bob Simmons, the man who shot us, to explain what Dow Uanh showed him. He saw himself commanding a giant spherical ship about a cloudy planet. His lips shouted evil things about its people and spurred their destruction. There was a fierce space battle to save the planet, but he pushed a button and the planet burst into flames. The planet was Masar, and millions died by his hand.

"Mr. Chancellor," Meh-Nai said, "this man needs protection. His life is in danger from those who would permanently silence him; he must be with us."

"We can do that," Jim said. "Now, May Len, Bill, how do you feel? I should have asked earlier but got carried away with so many issues."

"As one," we said simultaneously with renewed brightness in our eyes.

"I take it that's a good thing?" he said with a curious expression, suspecting something was up.

Knowing precisely what was on his mind, and with May Len's permission, I thought to remove all doubt by saying, "See for yourself. My beautiful flower, may I?"

"Yes, you may," she replied giggling. Slowly, tenderly, and with heartfelt reverence, I gently took to May Len's arms and kissed her humbly, affectionately, and lastingly.

"If I didn't know better, I think you've been hitched."

May Len naively asked what "hitched" meant, bringing everyone in the lobby to hefty laughter, although I'm sure she knew. Looking wittily at May Len, I mentally shared a picture of the typical married life: the husband restfully talking with friends, the wife overtasked in the kitchen, kids running and breaking things around the house, and chaos gripping the household. Finding it amusing, May Len and those around us laughed vigorously.

"Hitched is slavery," she said humorously. "I don't recommend it. Is this what my life will be like, my love?"

"Not at all, my angel," I said. "Besides, I hear Jim makes a great baby-sitter and he's very affordable."

"Hey, the pay better be good," he said brightly. "It's hard work, and I may have to hire some extra hands to help out." Looking at my sisters for support, they were quick to amusingly nod no without hesitation. The moment of humor, though brief, was sufficient to bring everyone much welcomed relief, at least putting us back on track with our mission.

Bidding good bye to those present, we followed Jim to his shuttle under tight security and headed back for New Manhattan. The brief trip back to the Towers was a quiet one, interrupted only by my sisters who made me aware of a major plan for Saras. May Len held my hand the entire time, resting her head on my shoulder to nap. Her weakness showed, and so did I.

Back at the Towers, security escorted us to our quarters and kept watch over us. I accompanied May Len to her room but was delightfully surprised when she insisted that her quarters were now mine too. I quickly showered and changed. Then, it was May Len's turn to do so while I waited outside her door, sitting on the floor with my back to it as usual. I never defiled her physical privilege, not even in thought. Rather, I felt highly honored to be near the presence of my radiant angel, with earnest courtesy.

"That was a most strenuous trial for you, my love," said my one, softly caressing facial wounds and bruises inflicted by Gina's harsh blows.

"I'm sorry she chose to follow a man instead of creation. I hope she turns herself into Father sooner than later."

"We're so proud of you. In spite of her threats, you valiantly witnessed for the Infinite from the heart without reservation and persisted in not disclosing the truth about her sad past. More so, you honored me before the cosmos with incredible love and never backed down, not for a second, immediately putting your life at risk for me—again."

"No matter cost or sacrifice, your love is all I want in life. Let me deny myself in all things and always take last place; may your soul freely sing and forever my heart lace. May my daily bread first fill thine lips and in greater portion then mine; let me humbly serve thine soul's needs and in awe adore its glorious shine. Let me shield thee from frigid cold while I shiver and carry thee though I'm tired; oh, what I'd do for thine soul's glimmer that I for so long admired. Let me absorb your pains so that health rejoices within thine beautiful amber panes. I renounce it all: joy, comforts, needs, life. Father, my Brothers, and you in my heart—that's all I need."

"Indeed, Father chose a most loving protectorate for me."

"I think I heard that somewhere before. Even father asked me to protect his beautiful daughter, several times actually, so there's something to that."

"If you only knew what it was. You'll know about it soon enough."

"Must be because my lovely angel has a long-standing tradition of dwelling in extremely beautiful vessels. Still, I think your present form is definitely your grandest, most magnificent achievement. I'd rather admire your majestic grace unfold before my heart and eyes than behold creation's heavenly lights."

"I'm glad you are pleased, my sunbeam," she said with moistened eyes, "but let me ask you a question, do you still think I'm too old for you?"

"After a million years, what's a couple of hundred? After an eternity, what's a couple of million?" I added with a brief chuckle. May Len was glad to hear me say these words, quoted directly from a previous life in which we also knew each other, but did not comment further.

My masters showed up with Jim. They had another big surprise in store for me, promising this time it would not hurt but kept it a well-guarded secret. It was my luck; I was always the last to know these things.

When we entered the dining room, the ministry stood up in loud cheer. May Len immediately raised my hand in symbolic gesture before I could hers, embraced me warmly, and sweetly revealed her lips upon mine saying, "This is my beloved one, my only one," she said brightly, "in whom I am most pleased, whose heart I cherish beyond words, and with whom I shall be madly in love for longer than the universe shall stand."

It was a time of cheerful happiness and sharing, a wonderful moment in time, just before the start of another momentous storm. Missing from the table was Gina, but Jim wisely made no mention of her. Also absent were Hans and Sean who, after the incident, sought their families to comfort them. My talk with Hans would have to wait.

The world mourned the loss of Dow Uanh and sad gloom covered Saras. So after nourishment, we held another conference. Jim took to the podium and offered a brief yet meaningful speech honoring Dow Uanh, ensuring members that the mission would go on. After a warm round of applause, he made a moving call for members to become emissaries of peace like Dow

Uanh and desist ideals forged in the heat of malice. Interestingly, no one asked about Gina.

Tei-Ah invited the world to witness a video history dating back a million years to help with past-life recalls. Jim was moved by her request, admiring the Brothers' concern and respect for our world, always recommending and inspiring but never forcing.

Before parting, Yato allowed Mr. Simmons to share his experience with the world. At first, he was apologetic and scattered but later grew confident, giving not only his testimony but charged forward against human cruelty.

"A hundred years ago," he said, "a new world was forged from the ashes of ghastly war in which weapons played a critical role. Without them, war and tyranny would not have happened. Our founding fathers solemnly and unanimously pledged to forever ban weapons from our lives, and the entire world rejoiced, knowing that lasting peace was finally at hand. But thirty years later, the Rifle Association, no doubt ordained by the same people that cyphered me and Gina Toscani, lobbied relentlessly to bring them back. Days later, death returned, and peace was compromised.

"If members want to live in peace, why do we keep weapons around? Love and deadly devices don't mix. When we give them a place in our lives, people, mainly children, die! Why trust and arm total strangers when even sane people, like me, can be swayed to pop on a moment's notice? Do you want strangers with ulterior motives pointing weapons at your kids?

"If you think weapons protect you, know that threats come unannounced, like a thief in the night, when you least expect them. How can weapons keep you safe, when you're arming potential foes? Rather, they make enemies even more dangerous, numerous, and better armed, knowing you're also armed! According to God, you don't have the right to bear arms, for He said, 'Thou shalt not kill.' In Luke 9, Jesus said, 'Whoever saves his life will lose it, but whoever loses his life for Him will save it.' So what God do you honor?"

After a rigorous round of applause, Jim came to the podium and asked, "Sister Tei-Ah, what do you make of Bob's discourse?"

"Mr. Simmons's message is truly important. While your constitution grants you the right to bear arms and take your brother's life, God's constitution fervently prohibits it, inspiring us to sacrifice our lives for our brothers, not take it. You cannot possibly love Father if you're willing, even in thought, to hurt or even dislike your brother, no matter the reason."

"Weapons are the basis for most evils on Saras, especially when scared children innocently seek them to become something bigger than they are unaware of consequences," Meh-Nai added. "Did not our Master warn, 'He that kills with the sword must die by the sword? [1]' Did He not clearly enact that we 'shall not avenge, nor bear any grudge against the children of our people, but love our neighbor as if ourselves? [2]' There is no fear in love, for perfect love casts out fear [3]."

"'Fear not them that kill the body but cannot kill the soul. Fear Him who can destroy both soul and body [4],'" May Len said. "Don't betray Him by seeking to save your life but rather be His ambassador by sacrificing it for others. As long as you bear weapons, you cannot join the brotherhood."

"I just had an associate run through the numbers; you won't believe what they show," Jim said. "Kids ages six to twenty two commit 85 percent of all weapon-related crimes, taking six million lives yearly—kids! That says guns don't save lives or deter foes; rather, having one increases your odds of dying.

"We must take outstanding action here under extraordinary circumstances, and I ask, are we prolife or prodeath? I'll let Earth gov answer that question. If politicians can't, then how can we expect members to? The road to love needs significant action; Earth needs to revisit its original constitution and rid itself, once and for all, of all weapons—now! Give me the brotherhood, or give me death." The entire gathering, including ministers, stood up in ardent applause, except two ministers whose attitude showed obvious distress.

"Bob, I agree with you; it's time weapons go. This implies all personal and military weaponry. I invite members of the Senate to support this initiative. It's time for peace; let there be nothing on Earth that spoils this opportunity. Weapons must go; love and peace must stay."

Members overwhelmingly approved Jim's proposal with a standing ovation, and live polls across the globe also showed significant support. But when asked to stand in favor of the initiative, all ministers except the justice and social ministers did so. Those present were quick to criticize sitting ministers, and turbid rumble immediately spread throughout the conference hall.

"Ministers, as a majority, you ruled in favor of this proposition. However, as a united world, if this is going to work, I need your full support. For those who declined, I invite your comments as to why."

"Mr. Chancellor," said the social minister, "we must take into consideration that people's livelihood will be significantly impacted, as well as the stability of our socioeconomic system."

Members in attendance immediately scorned the minister for his lame excuse, placing employment of a few over the death of so many more. "It's blood money! You're compromised!" yelled an angry crowd, strongly disagreeing with the minister.

"Now hold on, people, don't run to conclusions; it's not how you see it," said the justice. "We can't just do things without the means to finance them.

Also, consider that people's pride will not be an easy thing to give up. Perhaps we should take a longer-term approach to this matter and ensure we don't create an even bigger mess."

"Are you nuts?" the defense minister said alarmed. "I strongly differ with my colleagues. I'm in charge of defense, and I say weapons go; we have other ways of providing public safety. The longer we keep them around, the higher crime will rise. You all have kids. I have kids. Don't we lose sleep worried stiff for their safety? Most weapons are in the hands of kids anyways. So what's your problem, eh? Special interest got your tongue? Put kid's interests first, not sponsors. My forces haven't fired a shot since Amarna's last stand! What are we thinking, people? Stop reliving being a cowboy, hunter, soldier, whatever it is, and do this for the kids!"

"Reliving? Like you believe in all that past life stuff, Mr. Recyclable!" said the social minister cynically.

"Living only once? Like you're one of those few garburators still believing in that limited-life stuff, Mr. Doomed!"

"Hey, don't mock me!"

"You're doing that just fine on your own."

"I agree with defense" the space minister said. "We can't play soft on this subject. If weapons are to go, they go this instant. Go think about it, and they'll never go. We need sudden complete disarmament. A stepped approach only helps feed organized crime and creates back doors for illegal trafficking."

"Prohibition doesn't work," said the social minister. "People will always find ways around the law, and weapons won't go."

"So what? Won't be for long. In time, we'll be in sync, but we must start."

"Mark my words. Members will be split on the law. Remember the huge weapons rift that nearly destroyed America before the nuclear holocaust?"

"That was the NRA's doing, the devil's death minister. And here we are 150 years later, still having the same discussion, in spite of past lessons. The GRA is the re-embodiment of the old NRA—gutless, ravenous assassins with billions already served to their death chest!"

"You'll lose more lives by creating a rift between members, eventually breeding a rigid pocket of resistance against the law!" the justice said sharply.

"You mean a wicked minority will keep the light on weapons? Is that what you're trying to say?"

"Precisely!"

"What a joke! You know, people love weapons only because they're told to by none less than the GRA! As they say, kill the dog, and rabies vanish. Our founders outlawed guns for good reason. But no, facilitators of death and their marketing arm, the GRA, lobbied hard to kill article 2, and death came back that very second! By any chance, would you two be the ones facilitating resistance going forward? You're both, after all, high-ranking GRA members."

"I beg your pardon!"

"Ah, I love the smell of conflict-of-interest in this place, don't you?"

"Weapon production stops right now," the defense minister said. "Resale stores are bought off and closed this afternoon. War toys go, children war programming stops—no, not tomorrow, but right now. I'm responsible for defense, and I make the call. It stops right now, end of discussion!"

"Justice and social ministers, I hate to say this but, shame on you!" said the resources minister. "Shame on you for putting business and that damned, demonic Rifle Association before life; blood is no way to make a living! I hope it never happens, but must your own kids die before you come to reason?"

"Ministers," Jim said, "are you with us?" Crowds stood on their feet, applauding fervently and shouting, "Support." After looking at each other several times, the two ministers stood up, not entirely convinced they should support the initiative, but up they went nevertheless. Jim's plan was unanimously approved and quickly put into action around the globe that same day. It was a gutsy move on Jim's behalf, but it paid off in the end.

That afternoon, millions came forth to turn in prized weapons and war toys willingly. Sadly, the majority were children, many in tears witnessing in testimony why they had them: their parents did not give them sufficient sense of care, time, or protection, so they sought their own safety. The GRA immediately denounced the law with all its twisted, evil might, and a devout few literally stuck to their guns, but GRA membership plummeted. People, now more than ever, faithfully sided with spirit rather than death. The world disarmed, and as foretold, crime came crashing down.

May Len and I could be found at the Tower Gardens in the company of our sisters, closely admiring creation's energy wonders in an entirely different light and enjoying friendship as no one on Saras ever had.

For the first time in a million years, my one kept me company through the night and into the coming morning, warmly singing by my side with indescribable enthusiasm. We never touched unsuitably, and the thought never arose, upholding the highest respect for His Majesty's uniforms.

We talked about our first days together and laughed a great deal in cheerful memory of those times. Side by side, we gazed at each other, kindly held and caressed hands, and spoke only sweet thoughts as we passed into sleep. There, our gentle love continued to share vividly, tenderly, never ending, in radiant realms of light. Our hearts inspired us; our eyes taught lessons to the heart. Ours were inseparable lives, devoted to love each other, day and night, from the beginning of time, to the ends of our souls.

---

[1] R. W. J. Morford, "Revelations 13: 10," in *The One New Man Bible*, Travelers Rest, SC: True Potential Publishing, Inc., 2011.

[2] R. W. J. Morford, "Leviticus 19: 18," in *The One New Man Bible*, Travelers Rest, SC: True Potential Publishing, Inc, 2011.

[3] R. W. J. Morford, "1 John 4: 18," in *The One New Man Bible*, Traverse City, SC: True Potential Publishing, Inc., 2011.

[4] R. W. J. Morford, "Matthew 10: 28," in *The One New Man Bible*, Traverse City, SC: True Potential Publishing, Inc., 2011.

Chapter 25: *My Teacher, Guide, and Hope*

Dawn's early light broke leisurely over Long Island's eastern horizons, gradually driving gloomy shadows from its glorious, broadening course; appealing quiescent creations to emerge from slumber and behold Father's light, the beautiful essence of His celestial magnificence and sovereign power, the gift of life, in full force. Beyond the edge of inquiring sights, the majesty of sublime grandeur gradually lit the heavens with bands of gold, intricately woven about Saras with blinding stellar flames untold.

Light and warmth gently pierced through our room's translucent panes with inspiring, symphonic proclamation, stirring our brows to witness gifts of cosmic orange whispers with restive elation. The windows of our souls calmly unfastened from nocturnal bondage, fondly gazing upon summoning jewels affixed upon virtuous ornaments of inner oneness. Deep within the gates of our bosom, the breath of life ardently rejoiced anew in Father's prompting pleasures, infusing the heart with incomparable loving grandeur we treasured.

Before us, shades of dawn flaunted majestically through the skies, and golden waves blazed from rooftops to the east, accentuating earthen abodes in the ashen city beneath. Deep blue hues drove far to the west ahead of Father's prevailing fountains of light, the beauty of His inspiring eyes silently flooding May dawn skies with magnificent celestial might.

Respectfully bowing our heads, adoring songs expressed forth with selfless reverence, indescribable beauty, and divine vigor as if we had never before met. My love was her; her love was I. My heart spoke tender wonders of hers, and hers likewise of mine; a life I deeply cherished, a love beyond Saras's boundaries. The heart led us upon love's path; eyes taught us lessons nigh. Inner celestial light inspired the future into our walk, for high masters of light truth did not deny.

Her gentle hands fondly sought to fold unto mine with greatest affection, nobly cherishing the humble respect my heart exhibited for her prodigious corporeal splendors during the night. With graceful embrace, our lips sweetly bestowed unutterable morning petal offerings, like melodious ballades from an empyrean opera, for love needs not words, only the tender essence of soft inner spirit, incorruptible by human flesh or cognizance.

On this day, Saras would have its first deep look at its extensive past legacy. Some saw this as judgment day. Others welcomed it, longing to qualify past errors before the Eternal and move on to higher spiritual evolutionary planes. We were beyond eager, joyously committing heart and soul to someday merit homes of celestial light and peaceful, wise bliss.

"My sweet sunbeam, our mother sends thee warm *tennéh*," my starlight said, mentally speaking to family back on Masar. I could sense the people she contacted but could not yet converse with them.

"She understands, my loving dawn, but you will meet her soon. I look forward to meeting your parents as well. In unions, families come together as a single caring unit, and parents serve as immediate spiritual mentors. On Saras, families are deemed an impediment to union, and in-laws are considered the gravest of all tribulations, not pigs or chickens but sadly wolves."

Five years had passed since I last visited my parents. I had no justification for it other than an unfortunate case of personal acidity I would have to deal with sooner or later, and now was the time. "A lot goes through your mind at the mention of your parents," my one said.

"Thoughts of guilt, disrespect, timidity—energies I need to face and work out. Since age three, I felt I didn't belong here and gave up on life by becoming an unsociable introvert. Unfortunately, my parents bore the brunt of my frosty attitude with exemplary patience."

"You were so young; few on Saras have those intuitions at such early age."

"Even as a baby, I knew there was a God and that this life was the sequel of another. I also faithfully knew you existed, and desperately sought every means to find you. Hopes of meeting you is what kept me alive all this time. But then, something amazing happened."

"And what was that, my brave captain?" she said joyfully, although I was sure she knew.

"When I was fifteen, I was privileged to visit Venus, Masar, and Saturn in vision. Actually, my last vision before our union was the night we first met on Chasma. I was filled by such earnest enthusiasm that my heart begged to share my visions with the world in the worst possible way. My soul exploded with uncontrollable zeal to do so, but no one seemed interested. I argued patiently in favor of re-embodiment, life on other worlds, and the true age of Saras for the longest time, but was ridiculed and treated like Giordano Bruno."

"Years passed and I grew tired of constant rejection, weakening my once impregnable resolve and sorely wounding its conviction with insatiable sadness. Blindness then struck my soul, and I began to question the reasons for and verity of my inner sights. Eventually, lost to a world that neither listened to or offered me compatibility, I obeyed my heart; I set course for Masar, looking for my lovely one."

"But you never gave up hope and stood your ground, honoring and witnessing your heart for His Majesty the best you could."

"There were times of weakness, my love, when I fought people back and wrongly restricted their right to choose faith, hoping to deprive them of traditional renderings and translations I deemed wrong, thus violating the prime directive. I was no doubt reliving my own past wrongful beliefs."

"Yes, the flagellant Dominican priest, trying to reverse prior beliefs."

"I beat myself harshly all day long, feeling I was not worthy of love or God. I fully relived that life by resorting to pain and injury rather than love to discover God, for I had no faith in love and also feared it."

"I think I remember having this conversation before," she said giggling.

"My kind sister was most patient with me in those first days, and I'm most grateful for her kind offering of love," I bowed sweetly. "I once believed that punishing God's vessel was the only way to attain forgiveness. I also neglected enlightenment by seeking prayerful placebos to escape inner turmoil."

"We witness such irreverent prayers rise from your world, soiled by utter demands, terror, hate, and mistrust for Father, not love—so disrespectful. If your people truly believe His love is always present, why must they pray and worship, if not to skirt universal ethics and obtain unnatural unmerited favors over those who don't know God or have the ability to do so? Does prayer not ascribe God as incompetent, negligent, biased, and ignorant of your needs; and can we judge or tell Him what to do? How selfish can one be? Pray not but share your thoughts honestly with us. Listen to Him and live in inspiring inter-dimensional scientific understanding.

"Father is but a slave to your people, a secluded tyrant you mean to pressure into compliance with endless nagging adulations until He violates the prime directive. When will your people realize the Infinite knows you better than yourselves and stop abiding by such insolent, senseless practices? We don't pray or worship, for we have all we need: His love and our honesty. Nothing can ever replace that. The answer to life's needs is found in energy relationships and love of truth, not begging."

"Your faith has saved you [1]; that statement is faith's key problem because the word 'faith' is mistranslated," I added. "'Emuwnah' in Hebrew means commitment to truth and knowledge rather than rely on a person. The closest Greek equivalent is 'pistis,' so that's what was used to describe faith, except it implies not commitment but conviction. Since then, our people wrongly assumed that knowledge and responsibility were not necessary since someone had our languid incompetence already covered. Making matters worse, people believe in mystical powers, sinless expiating blood, saintly intercessors, holy grail, and all sorts of spiritual technology carelessly left behind by God for scavengers to horde at will—revoltingly disgusting. Honestly, people knew more about God back in the Stone Age than the last two thousand years."

"Though we can't interfere with personal choice or level of understanding, it is still sad to witness such traps," my flower said rather dismayed.

"And so, without friends and scorned beyond grasp, I spent lonely days locked up in a room, making plans to build a raft and leave Saras for good."

"And may I ask, where did my brother plan to go?" she said giggling.

"I truly apologize, my beautiful, radiant event. You know, I omitted the best part," I said a bit hesitant, taking time to prepare a poem for her.

"Would my brother be willing to share it with me?" she said, playing excitedly, unaware of my doings.

"Well, you see," I said romantically to my radiant jewel, gently caressing her hands, "I dreamed about this very, very lovely lady that lived on a world far, far away. She was so absolutely beautiful and gentle the heavens gasped every time she lovingly strolled among the stars, beaming gloriously like an intense celestial candle that outshone even the brightest cosmic reservoirs. Inspired by her beautiful grace, the firmament gathered all of its light, and from it wove a vast starry tapestry stretching into infinity before her feet, so her luster would forever infuse eternal majesty into starlight, and stellar warmth never again deplete. Since that glorious day, her eyes remained in the heavens, patiently waiting and watching over me, becoming Sirius and Canopus, the brightest stars that will ever be." Suddenly, my starlight realized I spoke of her and tenderly began to cry in warm embrace.

"Vast spiraling galaxies, stretching far beyond the mind's reach, reverently bowed their stunning lights before her majestic smile, hoping she someday called them home, and brought bolder hues to their already-radiant, starry domicile. Her essence brought grace to the endless harmony of angels and love eternal to soothe my heart from ages of saddening thistles.

"She was the princess of heaven, Elysium's inspiration, the beauty in my eyes and soul, the love of my heart; I gladly gave everything up for her, with untold fervor. She shone with heavenly glory in my heart, for I could not live without her soul's art. Tears daily flooded my face; I cried profusely when I remembered her grace. I was so, so madly in love with her . . . and"—I said, kissing her silky hands and softly caressing her hair—"love her more so today. You know, don't be jealous, but I even gave this lovely, graceful lady a name."

"You did? And what name did you give this imagined lady?" she said, restraining urging sob.

"I called her, 'I have Him.'"

"My sweet sunbeam, did you know the significance of my essence is, I have Him?" she replied, suddenly bursting with radiance.

"Then, with you, I am His!"

"If you didn't know it, that's your ancient essence: Deh Len, 'with you, I am His,'" she said giggling, coming into my arms.

"Then I, 'with you I am His,' am honored to finally meet thee, 'I have Him.' And now that we've been properly introduced, let's walk together through the cosmos so I can introduce your beauty to its many dimensions."

"I loved you for so long, my one!" I said with a persistent knot. "I couldn't eat, sleep, live, or do any other chore because you were all I thought about. I loved you such that I considered taking my own life to be reborn on Masar. I was willing to do whatever it took, bear whatever pain or sacrifice, just to find you. It didn't matter how desperate the ends seemed. I was anxious almost to the point of losing my mind."

"What a sweet story of love, my sunbeam," she said, with a welling in her voice. "And I know it's true because I saw you cry, I heard your loud wails, and I cried along with you each time. But you were so faithful and devoted, for you believed in me, even though you had no evidence or reason to."

"When I saw you for the first time, I wondered, is she my dream? I was desperately in love with an imaginary woman, but she was more real to my broken heart than my own world was. Saras offered me her finest daughters bred for utmost pleasure, dressed in the finest fibers of the land, and wearing every delightful attribute ensuring one's absolute desire. But the call of my heart rejected them, for it knew of beauty bred by the stars, dressed in the finest fibers of heaven, and wearing nothing less than the breath of life.

"That's why I left for Masar the first chance I got, hoping to find you there. That was the extent of my life—every day, every minute, trying to find you, regardless of sacrifice."

May Len cried profusely, for she was the faithful keeper of many secrets that could not yet bear fruit. I knew this, and gently took her into my arms to calm her soul. "You weep because of secrets you hold sealed in your heart, do you not?" May Len looked at me with tearful eyes but did not respond.

"It takes all my heart to withstand what I see in thine. Your bosom is so, so heavily laden with secrets not right for this time, my beautiful treasure," I said, softly caressing her. "There are so many demands placed upon thee, 190 years bearing them. Your tears are your love for Him and your care for me. I hope to expedite my cleansing that you can be set free. Untold horrors and heart-wrenching pains await my eyes in the months to come, this I know. With Him I shall be, for I so beg to sacrifice my all without question, and quickly, out of love for thee. My life for thee, thine essence in me.

"Rest upon my yoke, my beautiful princess, and let me carry thine many burdens, for my heart is great and spacious, and my love for thee is of most sweet disposition. Your bosom shall someday speak its many gems, my love, and what a glorious day it will be. Meanwhile, drown me with your love. Embrace me without rest; it is what my heart longs most for, far from distress. My desire of ages, my precious sapphire, when the time comes to qualify in tears, thine hands will firmly embrace my heart, thou shall give me the valor I need to face past deeds, and I shall not fear."

Drying her tears with gentle kisses upon them, I added, "I know you feel I may not withstand the approaching storm. The colors of my tears may run in supple torrents but not those of my heart. I shall not vanquish thee, my love. Thou shall not perish; I will take thine place of suffering anytime."

With a hasty gasp, May Len avidly released her lips and her longing to disclose my ultimate challenges labored strongly upon her will. But gently taking her hands to my lips, I bowed before her and turned a blind eye to her thoughts out of respect, so easy to read. "It is with greatest reverence, my sweet sister, that my eyes briefly decline from thy magnificent wonders and loving thoughts, and I mean no disrespect to her exceptional loveliness, for the longing of my heart is faithfully set upon the brotherhood, and our destiny has ensured the outcome: victory! I shall not run, except to thee, such that thine eyes shall never rest from me."

"Do you promise me, my love, that you will not run? No matter how unpleasant the past may be?" she replied, rather concerned. "I shall guard the heart and won't say what it is, but I know it will break your heart to pieces, and your soul will burn with unimaginable anguish."

"Why would I run from your side? I want to put an end to our endless suffering, and I'm more than ready to face my past. The past is the vomit of my soul; I find it repulsive and will not yield to it. It is but a lesson, a gateway to our future. My angel, behold my promise: I will put my heart on the line for the Brothers and will not run, for I love them with all my might. I also seem to recall someone once telling me not to dwell in the negative and to be brave," I said, playfully gazing into her eyes with a beaming smile.

"I think I heard that too from someone . . . I can't recall who right now," she said, trying really hard to smile.

"Someone most wise, I'm sure, so let's brighten things up a bit. How about this: would you like me to tell you a bit about my parents?"

"I would like that very much, my friend, brother," she said, recovering her beaming smile.

"Your father is a minister. He knows the book inside out in its original languages and is quite observant to religious detail, although I never shared with him my displeasure with faith. He loves carpentry and makes the most beautiful wood carvings. He tried to teach me a thing or two, but I just wasn't good at it. He lectured me with chin tucked to chest, peering over slim bifocals, saying, 'Young man, God meant for humans to express themselves through the arts, not just admire them.' He was sure patient with me.

"Then, there's kind mother, who planted a big seed in my heart. She woke everybody up at six in the morning and made sure we didn't miss prayer. She studied God's word with us every night and got deeply sentimental when talking about His Majesty. Carry God in your heart at all times she would say, so others can see Him in you."

"Your mother is most spiritually inclined," May Len said. "Our parents are the same way, always referring to His Majesty in all things."

"My wondrous starlight, would you like to meet my parents?" I said excitedly.

"This week, even?" May Len said, equally thrilled by the proposition.

"It would be the greatest surprise ever for them. I can just see the look on their faces when they see this shuttle come down on their backyard. Better yet, we'll have the shuttle fly low overhead and buzz the house, get animals squealing, and then land suddenly on their backyard. They'll have no clue who or why," I said excitedly with a smirk. "As Hans would say, it is good, yes?"

"I see the ways of father rubbed off on you, most refreshing! It has been some time, hasn't it? Then your visit is long overdue, my beloved." The thought occurred to have our sisters come along, and she knew it before I could mention it. "By all means, our sisters would be delighted to come!"

The historical broadcast from Masar was scheduled to begin soon, and time was of the essence, so we spent brief moments practicing Martian grace arts—entirely new to me—showered, and dressed in record time. May Len wore her loveliest outfit yet: a delicate white dress and a white sash embroidered with gold threads. My sisters showed up right on schedule.

"You have broken past appendages binding you physically to people," Meh-Nai said when she arrived. "You are freed of them and can now see creation as it was meant to be seen: infinite love and beauty."

"Does this mean that by breaking these bonds, I've helped free others?"

"Absolutely!" replied May Len. "And those you free are bound to release others beneath them and so on. The past is just a shadow from history, an influential one, real because we make it so. Is a puppet alive because it moves? So is the past; it moves when you pull its strings."

"With such endless higher realms and loving, beautiful light ahead of you," Tei-Ah said, "why waste your time drawing on past souvenirs?"

"Love and spiritual elegance is the future; souvenirs grow old, worthy of ignoring with time," Meh-Nai said.

"Imagine the problems that bit of knowledge could solve for your people," May Len said as we reached the dining room.

Hans, Sean, and Bob were there to join us. Hans was incredibly apprehensive, fearful, withdrawn, and easily startled when approached by one of our sisters. I knew his place within the Order but made absolutely no mention of it. Otherwise, it meant a breach of universal law. After all, my sisters knew him far better than I. If they said nothing, I would do likewise.

Bob carried a memory pad with him where he drew images he continued to experience. Computer-enhanced versions of his pictures were shown to the public, and many immediately identified with them. This was an important precursor to the historical review about to ensue, testing people's resolve to view these images.

Done with breakfast, and few minutes before the conference, Jim turned on a cam unit to broadcast live proceedings to the world. He stood up, called everyone to attention, and briefly announced the upcoming transmission from Masar. Afterward, he granted our sisters the opportunity to provide a quick review of what we could expect.

Tei-Ah assumed Dow Uanh's place as speaker for the brotherhood. She addressed the ministry with kind, elegant determination, explaining this was the first historical review of many to follow, a chronological record dating far back in time when we lived in other stellar residences deep in the galaxy.

"Your people will have many questions following these presentations, but we are few in number and can't possibly address every citizen's needs," Tei-Ah said. "The brotherhood stands ready to assist by any means possible and offer to send educators to Saras. They will yield the highest benefit possible by answering questions and ensuring proper significance is drawn from each experience. But we need your approval to do so."

"Thank you, sisters, that's an offer we can't pass up," Jim said, receiving acceptance nods from the ministry. "Have educators travel to every state capital; each state delegate will help coordinate population logistics and coverage area. Now, we're some six billion people down here, and you'll need to send in quite a few, maybe a hundred thousand or more I suppose?"

"The entire brotherhood is eager to come. However, depending on demand and receptivity, half a million are prepared to come to your world."

"That's a very big number. Are you sure you can spare so many people on demand?"

"We're honored to serve. For now, this provides one educator per twelve thousand people or ten per legislatorial sector. Schools and colleges will be an ideal base of operation for them. But, brethren, do keep in mind that our aim is to share Father's love with your people, not become a crutch or an escape mechanism in their lives. We're your brothers and sisters, friends of the heart, teachers, not saviors or gods."

"My sisters, your educators are welcomed. This is just like old Atlantean times!" She assured Jim educators were on their way and would arrive at capital cities in a day.

"This morning, the Martian Council of Elders presided by Nur-Val will address your world."

Dining room lights faded, and a large display unit emerged behind a folding curtain on one of the walls. A picture of Masar emerged on the screen, fading into the image of an enormous underground metropolis of incredible complexity, advance, and beauty. Tall crystalline alabaster buildings of every geometrical form imaginable dotted this city, some twice the size of those on Saras. Sky trams ruled skies above, moving swiftly at inconceivable speeds. Nature areas abounded, dwarfing our ecological engineering efforts by far. Several meters above level ground, gardens hung from tiers, some adorned by subtle waterfalls. Water flowed abundantly in fountains, ponds, lakes, and artificial rivers between buildings.

Incredible tranquility overshadowed this city. Everything was right where it needed to be, designed with extreme convenience in mind. It looked so clean, orderly, and pacific to the wonderment of even the best civil designer. An enormous dome covered the city, perhaps five kilometers high, used as a projection device where sky, clouds, and heavenly orbs were displayed. One would never imagine being underground unless by fore knowledge.

High in the air, brilliant craft darted about at very high speeds, often turning sharp angles with incredible precision and velocity. On grounds below, sidewalks moved when stepped upon. Lighting sources were not necessary as the buildings themselves glowed much like the Martian structure. Hydro-kernel gardens, similar to those implemented by Saras colonies, surrounded the city, except in massive scale.

The display switched to an oval room with thirteen chairs. Elder-looking men and women dressed in blue gowns occupied these seats, each surrounded by a yellowish glow. One seat was empty, and we immediately knew who it belonged to. Nur-Val was dressed in a red gown and sat in the middle of the group. Rising from his seat, he welcomed us to Masar and briefly introduced the council. His wise gaze impressed immediate respect although without conceit. Humble and loving, he immediately drew us into his heart.

After welcoming May Len and me to the cosmic family, Nur-Val said, "We are pleased you accepted our sister's proposal. We would also like to extend a special invitation to members of UEF government to visit Masar. Thereafter, civilians may visit. Of course, it will be difficult to host six billion people here all at once. But in time, we want everyone on your world to visit and share our Supreme Majesty's infinite wonders. Worlds across the cosmos anxiously await your visit, at a time you are able to do so. Progressive spiritual development will be key to make these voyages possible."

"Now, if you will permit us, we would like young brother Roshon to come forth and stand before the brotherhood. There's something very important we must discuss with him, in public. That is, if he would agree to it."

Picture 18: Underground Martian City (*Rodrigo Diaz*)

Picture 19: Underground Martian City at night (*Rodrigo Diaz*)

Without delay, I quietly stood up and gently took May Len by the hand. But no sooner, Nur-Val said, "Roshon, just you. Gentle sister May Len, you may want to remain seated for this."

I looked briefly into her loving yet anxious amber eyes and softly smiled, knowing why I was being summoned. I tenderly kissed her hands and whispered to her, "It has begun. I so love you, my Elysium flower; how can I run? My heart will honor thee and the Tree of Life with truth and devotion, no matter the cost to me. This is why I was born on Saras and not Masar, to make Masar proud!"

"Show us your love for the Infinite, the power of thine heart, and how it's done, my brave captain," she replied shyly, lightly kissing my cheek. "I love you more than you know."

"I will not run, my love. Behold my promise and my love for you."

Slowly releasing her silky hands and reverently bowing to my sisters, I respectfully turned, bowed to my Masar masters, and kneeled with head lowered in respect. But before I could utter any words, Nur-Val set the tone for this qualification by loudly uttering, "Brother Roshon, are you certain you won't run?"

"My masters, I place my heart on the line for the brotherhood, and I shall not run."

"Are you sure about that, young initiate?"

"Yes my kind, loving master; I am."

"We'll see about that," replied Nur-Val quickly.

Immediately, my heart was severed from May Len, and we both gasped loudly in shock, finding it difficult to deal with our emotions and breathe. I cried desperately with no will left in me to seek the promise or His love anymore. I felt overly anxious, alone, and without His love, imprisoned by a fearful mental shell willingly heeding no thoughts beyond my own.

My thoughts trembled with agonizing dread as the force of selfish solitude crushed me like a wine press. My love was gone, honesty swiftly turned to treachery, and desires escalated alarmingly, hastily invading my senses with cruel disposition to cleave me into selfish slavery.

Devastating wordless feelings swiftly pierced through my consciousness. Its forceful essence gnashed the calm, still waters of my inner stores as if angered, stinging every nerve with mental paralysis from head to solar plexus. "You're the worst mishap to befall mankind!" hastily impressed foreign inner feelings. "Abandon your one; you'll never be worthy of her! Your negations corrupt what you learn and are not fit to be a Brother, much less help Saras! Don't seek the brotherhood; you'll never be suitably worthy!"

My heart's windows immediately stiffened; my discouraged soul abruptly sought answers to evade gripping embarrassment. The will of my inner voice viciously turned against my peace in all venues with no escape in sight, leaving me to the mercy of hopeless dissertations I knew not whence they came. The more I sought to understand and detach myself from these negations, the stronger and closer they became, and I sunk into a downward spiral pit that hastily consumed my faith with no obvious way out.

Everything I had learned from my starry princess and achieved thus far suddenly fell apart as if for not, suffering at the mercy of desires I was powerless to control; rather, they controlled me.

"Tell us, if you can, what did you just feel? Did something hit home?"

"I bear the weight of countless negative desires and advice unhindered. I cannot control them; they're stronger than I am," I said, gasping for air. Behind me, my starlight was also in shock, finding it hard to breathe as well. "Voices are telling me to abandon my one and the brotherhood, as I can never aspire to become a Brother. That I will never accept."

"Now you know first-hand what negative obsessive entities are and what they want. So what are you going to do about it?"

"I don't know, gentle master, but I will never abandon my amber star or the Tree of Life, and I can and will become a Brother! I will give neither of these dreams up, no matter pain or sacrifice!"

"You don't know? A Brother chooses his friends carefully; it's that simple. Why do you want to become a Brother if your chosen friends don't measure up. Why? Tell me who you're with, and I'll tell you who you are."

"I want to learn to choose correctly, my kind master."

"Really? Let me warn you, the suffering you face going forward. Oh, my son, if you only knew! When you declare war on your friends and negations, they're many times stronger than you! They sneak up when you least expect it, and you won't even know it. And when they strike, your first reaction will be to hide them out of embarrassment. And if you look at them, they'll hook you. How do you fight something like this?

"You have no idea what awaits, you especially; it's horrible beyond words! You shall be tormented without rest, you will cry more than smile, you will be moved to commit errors with unimaginable irresistible vigor. Your mind will go demented, reveling success for no reason and without your asking. Cold thoughts shall embrace your heart day and night, and your attempts to resist temptation will cause you to sweat blood! The suffering will drive you mad, enough to seek death! Are you sure you want to go through with this?"

"I most solemnly do! I want to be with you and never depart from Him or my beautiful princess."

"Funny you should say that because your mind isn't really made up yet. Why do you want Him if you mean to ignore Him and save your tail by your own means? How often do you do His will? Let's start there."

"My kind master, I see corruption in me. Shamefully, part of me believes to be a Brother, one that seeks to usurp His Majesty."

"My son, truly, it just can't get any worse than that! How self-deluded can anyone become? Let's put that to the test. When you're happy, do you always think of Him? And when you're not, do you still seek Him, or do you resort to inner pleasures instead, like dwelling on just how smart you are?"

"I do entertain mundane lusts, but I can't see what drives my motives."

"What a waste of soul. Your primary drive, as you call it, is to savor your own greatness rather than love! Son, you're just an insecure petty thief, hoarding what belongs to Father! Error, besides being a lesson, is theft, plain and simple! Do you really want to abandon all material things and honor Father, or are you trying to expand your selfish horizon at our expense? Which master will you serve, my son? I think the answer is quite obvious, isn't it?"

"Yes, my master. It's so hard to identify it, but yes, I can sense the possessive part of me, begging for gifts like a child. My feelings prohibit love from freely expressing and my soul from reaching out to you. I'm truly helplessly blind!"

"So you're still a spoiled child, I take it? Roshon, there's lots more here to see because, to be honest, you just don't want anything to do with us! How many times have we dropped into your mind to say, 'Hello, we love you,' and you rudely cast us off and quickly look the other way, praising how great you are? We try to inspire you, but no, you quickly tell us to go away and stop bothering you. Those flashing lights you see every now and then, that's us! We try to help you in so many ways, but you deny us, staunchly choosing to handle things on your own! Is this not so? Do you not feel when you do this to us? So how can you want God, or your one even, if you don't want us?"

After a moment of deep soul searching, I replied, "It's barely noticeable, but the thief is there, caring more about its achievements than your love. Yet I dread looking away and losing sight of you. Now I understand; looking away from you is dwelling on the negative."

"That's quite true. But tell us, what personal achievement could you possibly have that's more important than the Infinite, my son?"

"Knowledge—that's what I stole from Father, knowledge to improve my stature and subjugate others to worship me. I take it that's the worst gift to hoard."

"Why do you want to impress and oppress others? Do you seek to possess creation just like Ly-Dian; is this not so, Viren? You even asked your one if your love for her was legitimate, how incredibly, rudely disturbing this is that you would love her out of interest! Say that's not true!"

"I see and realize these feelings now, for they were well hidden!" I said crying profusely.

"Is it not true? Answer the question, yes or no! Live it! Mean it! Recognize it! Say it! Get rid of it!"

"Yes, it is true! It is all true! I plead thee please show me how to get rid of it!" I cried desperately.

"Easier said than done. Do you really want to get rid of it? It's in there with you right now, keeping you from surrendering unto us! You're rotting away in a dungeon, tortured by countless obsessions and your insecure self, desperately shouting at the top of your soul; yes, I love myself, not the Infinite! Can you deny the fact?

"There's only one way to defeat negation. Number one, don't fear or hide them. Number two, be honest. Number three, love the light! Fall in love with the Infinite with all your heart; leave no room to spare! Reach out to higher realms of light and give everything up for Him; desire nothing but Him. Simple frequency relationship, son; let the light straighten up those malformed waves in your soul. True love from higher realms is what you need most to affect cancellation—positive rather than your own negative energy. Of yourself you can do nothing but surely fail! Is this what you want?"

"I want the brotherhood, my master, not the self!"

"And so receive!"

Suddenly, I began to vibrate all over, mainly my head, as if I were experiencing a seizure. "Freedom comes at a price you yourself set. You are not free—you can't be free—because countless souls are in there pulling you down and sucking the life out of you, your soul's vomit actually! These are your associates, your many victims, those you hoarded unto yourself and mesmerized to praise your intelligence! That's the price you pay for wanting to be the leader, the genius, and extoling your own acumen—your vomit! Negations are simply vomit guzzlers that care not for God's life flow!

"You keep what you steal, my son, only to trash it. Those souls you took are in there still, holding on for dear life. When you took them from God, you became their life source. Likewise, those you look up to feed you their vomit. You want Him to help you? Then set your eyes fearlessly on Him and no one else. Return what you took from Him and stop wasting your time listening to obsessions!"

"How . . . how can I do that?"

"You just did. You chose to free yourself; the light will now take it from here. But you must trust His love and share it with your one constantly. If you can't see Him through her, then you're wasting her evolution, and she shall surely perish! She waited so long and suffered incredibly for you, and this is how you repay her love? After all that Father granted you, even your one, now you use it to destroy Him and us?"

"No, that shall not happen! I won't permit it!" I yelled desperately, crying on the floor brazenly. Hands to my head and a demolished, repentant heart attesting virtuous verity before my masters and world members, I vowed never to buckle or give up that precious dream, that wondrous heavenly love. But most notably, I vowed to believe.

Yes, it was possible; I did not have to think twice about it. There was a way: love God with all my heart, mind, soul, and might instead of the self! Trust in His ever-present love, resort not to my own understanding. My resolve grew each moment that passed in reflection, weakening that forceful voice that wickedly invaded the halls of my heart with brazen deceit. Disgusted with a monster of my own creation, I surrendered my heart to His Majesty and my dream of eternal eons: my one.

"I will not run or surrender to my old ways; I can do this! God is right, God is my future, God is the only way, and God is where I'm bound! My one shall not perish. I won't permit it! I shall not abandon her or you. I will suffer these and many, many more pains to make her, the brotherhood, and Father proud some future day! I am worthy of Father! I can become a loving Brother—yes I can, one that will behave accordingly and bear only love in his heart forever and ever! If others did it, why can't I? I'll sacrifice my life and die trying if I must, better dead than lost! Let the madness come. Let tears flow; the colors of my heart shall not run, regardless how massive the foe!

"I don't care what I must give up or deny, what shame I must endure, the joys I must be deprived of, the hungers I must suffer. I will surrender everything I have, know, want, and am. I want nothing but Him, you, and her; and I shall defend that choice with everything I've got because I truly believe! I believe that the power of love is infinitely more powerful than I, and my old days are numbered! I shall persist, I shall bother whomever I have to, I shall knock on all doors, I shall find His way no matter what it takes, day and night, sick or well, dead or alive!

"I shall willingly deny myself and take last place in all things, except the ardent desire to become a son to Father! What I desire is irrelevant; I must perish, and I shan't daunt! I am but a lowly sinner today, but tomorrow is written by kind Father who with me shall stay. There's a universe out there in dire need of lights and lots of them! So let there be light and let me among them be, for some future day I'll be worthy of wearing a new vessel of light, alongside thee! Be Him sought, not me! My life for Him, His spirit be in me!"

At that moment, my heart fluttered wildly, and a strong sickening feeling brought me to nearly heave, immediately losing control of lingering desires and awareness. Personal interests faded off, ideas and thoughts that normally gave me a sense of assurance fled suddenly, and I felt as if my body was dying. Eyes closed forcibly, deep sleep took over my consciousness, and hands dropped to the sides like limp rags. My head spun without bearing and I almost passed out in cold sweats. But then, this ill feeling passed. I revived, and previous anxiety left me. I felt renewed and rested, no longer afflicted by invisible concerns, and, most of all, calm and free.

With a smile on his face, Nur-Val rose from his seat, accompanied by all other masters, and gently clapped well pleased while I wept overwhelmed by warm sentiments. Immediately, everyone in the dining room also rose and applauded as well, though I remained unwilling to take any credit for what I said, feeling much remorse and lowliness before my masters.

"Well said, my son," said Nur-Val. "We expected to hear nothing less than this, most refreshing, and we're most pleased. Your covenant with Father has now been sealed by your lips in the books of heaven, and His expectations shall forever rise because He loves you so. Becoming a Brother is only a most minute step. You can say, it's the beginning of life, for what you consider life today is truly death, sad to say. Never give up Father, know that His light is always, always, with you. Resort to it. Feel His love in and around you."

Suddenly, I felt May Len's heart hurriedly enter into mine, and our breath briskly renewed. Without a second to waste, we desperately sought each other's arms and embraced hastily trading tears, mounting overpowering love, and quivering words of joy to each other with frantic disposition unlike ever before.

"Your heart is so vast and valiant," she said, quivering with tears.

"I won't run," I said emotionally to her several times. "I love you, I love my Brothers, I love Manéh! I will not betray you—never will!"

"You believed, and I believed in thee also, my brave captain," she replied, sweetly crying. "God and the brotherhood are always with us. How can we question it?"

"My princess, my Brothers, I beg thee, please, teach me how to love because I know nothing."

"When you don't run, you love. When you believe, you learn."

"And when my lips run to share yours, my heart learns to believe."

"Come hastily into me then, for my faith cannot learn without thine heart, and my lips cannot wait your song's newly awakened delight. My heart's breath, only you can give, my sunbeam, my brave captain, crowning seal that urges me on to live."

My heart burned with unbearable yearning to warmly embrace hers with all my might, cherishing heaven's voice that called forth our bosoms to belong. Reverently bringing our quivering lips ever closer, we ardently sought to share tender words from the heart and the breath of life with insatiable scorching enthusiasm. With strong embrace, we grazed deeply and hastily as if we could kiss each other's hearts. This was the power of selfless love, the life of us Brothers. By comparison, my self-worth felt tinier than a grain of sand.

"Now you know what it's like to lose your one. You cannot live without the other, just as you cannot live without love. You have many more challenges coming your way, Roshon. This challenge was, shall we say, kindergarten by comparison; so don't let your guard down. These will become more demanding and detailed with time until you are truly free of the self."

"Brothers of Saras, be not dismayed when Father touches your heart and you're called upon to qualify. Do so on your own; cleanse your heart in the still private chambers of your soul, without rest or fear. Let holy testimony lead your lessons. Be honest with thyself and let not a single flaw escape your notice. Joyously discover the hidden monsters in your midst, show Father what you've found, trust His love, and don't fear your urges. Let Him be your teacher, your guide, your hope. We need your light."

The display faded, and the day's historical review was about to begin. Before us, the depths of our negative legacy unveiled and we beheld the fruits of unholy menace.

---

[1] R. W. J. Morford, "Mark 5: 34," in *The One New Man Bible*, Travelers Rest, SC: True Potential Publishing, Inc., 2011.

CPSIA information can be obtained
at www.ICGtesting.com
Printed in the USA
LVHW082357051222
734629LV00016B/1096

9 781948 556125